Malignant
Summer

"Tim Meyer is the kind of author the universe predestined to write an epic coming-of-age novel. The characters in *Malignant Summer* have a story that demanded to be told and Meyer answered that call; what a gift to readers!"
– Sadie Hartmann, Cemetery Dance

"A coming-of-age horror novel as good as any you'll ever read. The final 100 pages will leave you breathless."
– Ronald Malfi, author of *Come with Me* and *Bone White*

"*Malignant Summer* is a classic coming-of-age horror tale reminiscent of McCammon and Simmons, viewed through the lens of the 1990s, with the kind of horror that could only come from Tim Meyer's twisted imagination. Brutal, nostalgic, and full of heart, I couldn't put it down."
– Todd Keisling, Bram Stoker Award-nominated author of *Devil's Creek*

"Sprawling and immersive, *Malignant Summer* is like McCammon's *Boy's Life* or Simmons' *Summer of Night* but for the alternative-metal and grunge generation. A spooky, coming-of-age tale with tremendous heart!"
– Lucas Mangum, two-time Splatterpunk Award-nominated author of *Saint Sadist* and *Pandemonium*

"Meyer's *Malignant Summer* is the new generation's *IT*."
– FanFiAddict.com

"A spellbinding story of epic proportions."
– Well Worth a Read Book Reviews

"An absolute masterpiece! A coming-of-age horror epic that will leave you cathartic, terrified, and nostalgic for adolescence. Meyer's magnum opus!"
– Joshua Marsella, author of *Scratches* and *Severed*

Malignant
Summer

by
Tim Meyer

This one's for those magical endless summers.

"A bloom in its freshest peak won't take long to wither."
— Light This City, *"Terminal Bloom"*

BOY + GIRL

Summer.

Twittering and birdsong filter down from the treetops, and the morning sun cuts through the leaves, throwing a warm shine on the path before you. You ride your bike on the bumpy dirt road, ignoring the butterflies in your stomach, how they flitter recklessly through your guts. You follow the two ahead of you, the boy and the girl, and you don't dare ask *Where are we going?* or *What are we doing out here?* You just don't. It's rude, and you don't want to be rude—these are your friends, after all. Maybe the best friends you have right now, although that could change later—next month, next year, when you get to high school, any time.

When you're eleven, friends feel like they will last forever. It isn't until you're older that you'll realize the naivety of that mindset. The reality that not all of them will stick around. It happens. Friends come and go, but their memories will last forever.

But that's something to worry about later. Much later. Years down the line. You don't concern yourself with the future, not now.

As you pedal along the path, you concentrate on your destination. The one set by the boy and the girl, the friends you won't have for very long.

"Just a little farther!" the girl shouts over her shoulder.

She knows where she's going. Always does. That's her way. A leader, never a follower. The boy is just a follower, always does what the girl says, no matter what. He's an obedient puppy. You think he should walk behind her at all times with his tongue hanging out, ready to catch the poo that falls out of her ass. That makes you giggle. Poo jokes are always funny. Especially now. They might be later too, sometimes, but you don't think about that, *later, the future.* No, you think about the *now*, the *moment*, concentrate on the poo jokes for a bit because the truth is—you don't want to know where you're headed. You are scared to know.

The girl has a taste for danger, an adventurous streak that is unmatched amongst your trio, one you've been warned about by *your* parents. But you don't listen, and they only care so much. They are not the type of parents to tell you what you can and can't do; only the type that suggests what you should and shouldn't do. They let you make wrong decisions on your own.

A lesson learned is a lesson earned, your father would say.

Makes sense to you, but you don't dwell on parental advice, not now. You're almost at the spot, the thing in the woods the girl wants to show you. The thing she found no more than a week ago. The thing she wants to explore. You're nervous and have every right to be.

The boy glances at you over his shoulder, arches his brow. You can tell he's anxious about the situation as well. After all, this is the farthest from home the three of you have ever been without an adult around. For some reason, that type of freedom is accompanied by a barrage of *what-ifs* from your good ol' brain. *What if I get hurt? What if someone else gets hurt? What if there is a monster in the woods?*

The last idea is silly; there aren't any monsters in the woods and you know it. Because monsters aren't real. They don't exist. In dreams, maybe. In nightmares. In the late-night pictures shown on the telly. But not in real life.

Monsters don't exist.

But you can't deny the feeling that you just might meet one, especially should you lower your guard.

"How much farther?" you ask, trying to avoid sounding like a wuss.

"Little more," Girl says, and she's right.

About three minutes later, you arrive at the spot, the clearing in the woods, the ground covered in brush, twigs, and dead leaves. Thickets surround the place, as well as armies of oaks and pines, towering so high they look like their tops stab the sky. That's not the case, but when you're eleven everything looks taller and more massive, an optical illusion beset on young eyes.

You hop off your bike and lower the kickstand to the dirt. Across the clearing is a cave. Its mouth isn't all that wide, looks big enough for someone of your build—*Skinny as a rail*, mother says—to fit through, but a larger person might have trouble squeezing past. An adult, for instance, and you suddenly get the feeling that's the point. Maybe an adult would come out this way, see this crack in the rock, and think nothing of it. They would probably pass by, hardly giving the black slit any mind at all, never once thinking, *Hm, maybe this is something I should explore.* It would never cross the mind of an adult. But a child? A kid looking for the next big summer adventure? Looking for a story to tell their friends at the next sleepover or next year in the school cafeteria? Well, that looks like just the ticket if you're being honest with yourself, and let's face it—you are being honest with yourself, more honest than you've ever been before.

You're frightened but intrigued, a nasty cocktail of emotions for someone your age.

"Come on," Girl says, waving you and Boy over to the mouth. "Come *on.*"

Boy does not protest, doesn't dare dream of it. He wanders toward Girl and the entrance as if he's been bewitched. He almost floats over there.

You, on the other hand, stay where you're at. You don't move. Not yet.

Girl wrinkles her nose at you. "You coming or what?" She's indignant, but you let her act accordingly. A part of you wants to go inside, the other part wants to retreat, hop back on the bike and pedal home.

"I…guess so," you say, but it sounds more like a question than an answer. Your heart hammers away, beating against the walls of your chest. You know nothing good can come of this, but you take that first step, anyway.

You take several.

Boy and Girl are now inside, and you are standing right in front of the crack, the dark split in the rock, peering into the infinite void, that menacing inky surface. Like a toothless smile turned on its side, the cave welcomes you.

Suddenly being outside of it feels worse than the unknown within. And that's because you are alone on the outside; on the inside you won't be.

You step toward the darkness, into it, allowing the mouth to swallow you up. Once inside, Girl lights the place with her flashlight. You see bugs the size of your fist skitter across the walls, seeking shelter wherever the dusty beam doesn't reach. The cave's interior is covered with leafy patches of ivy. The dirt below you is wet, and your feet sink and clap with each step. Girl swings the light around the cave, illuminating what she can. There are some places the light won't travel in here, and the darkness seems to extend interminable distances. You dare not trespass these *long spaces*. You dare not linger here at all. In fact, you think you've seen enough of the darkness and what the cave has to offer.

You turn. You can see the exit, but it looks a lot farther away now. You don't remember walking this far into the dark. Are your eyes deceiving you? Did you come this far? You don't know, can't tell for sure, but your brain feels fuzzy trying to calculate the steps. Math is not your finest subject, never has been, never will be. Logic is the subject you cling to, and you try to use what skills you have to determine what this place is, what it *actually* is, and how you can escape it—because right now, you feel the need to escape.

"I come here sometimes," Girl says. She shines the light on the wall, a part of the rock where no vines or overgrowth has claimed. "To hear her whisper to me."

Your arms grow cold, the tiny bumps hardening on your flesh, your little immature hairs on the rise. "Her?"

The light focuses on that patch of rock, and you see there is a little depiction there, scribbled in what looks like old paint. Not something you can find at a hardware store, mind you, but a paint made from the earth—a mixture of mud, clay, plants, and earthly pigments. Lots of browns and blacks. Faded. Old.

You get a closer look, your curiosity raging. That burning desire for knowledge is so overwhelming you think you might burst. This is all very exciting and equally scary.

A part of you likes it.

A part of you wants to run.

The depiction shows a circle of smaller figures—children, you think—holding hands around a larger figure with long flowing hair—an adult, a mother. A mother and her children, though her children are many.

You think that sounds right.

"She is here," Girl says. "If you listen close enough, you can hear her whispers. Her *dead* whispers."

You turn and Girl is smiling. Boy wears an eager smile too, enjoying every second of this game. You think he's just happy to be in Girl's radiant presence, and you're probably right.

"Listen…" she says, and everything goes still. You wait. And wait. And wait some more, the silence conquering your headspace, becoming larger than the cave itself. "Hear her?"

At first you hear nothing. Then…there *are* whispers. Slight at first. Like thin pieces of paper gently rubbing together.

Then you feel the wind in your hair.

Wait, what wind? There shouldn't be any wind. There is only the dark and the walls that surround you.

You turn back toward the mouth of the cave and realize the exit is farther now, a lot farther than you expected it to be. You hadn't come this far inside. You're sure of it.

You want to run. Toward the exit, that opening. Back to the light where it's safe.

"I want to get out of here," you say, but your words are strangled, hardly words at all. A mumbling of syllables. A puzzling vocalization.

In the frail light, Girl smiles. Her lips, the way they curl, are warm, like the way a mother looks fondly upon her infant, but her gesture is also menacing.

"Mother wants to meet you," Girl says. "She says she does."

You don't want that. Not at all. Your legs begin to work. You start moving backward, toward the exit, your eyes fixed on Girl's smile, those awful lips.

Then you turn.

Run.

No matter how far and fast you think you're going, the exit doesn't come any closer.

And the whispers follow you.

They will always follow you.

THE FINAL CLUE

(a prelude)

1

On the edge of summer, dark folded over Hooperstown, New Jersey, and for some the sun would never rise again.

A tangy ocean scent clung to the air despite the boys being thirty minutes from the shore. It was weird how certain aromas traveled across town on certain days. Sometimes residents could smell the coast, the wet seaweed and the salty spray of crashing breakers carried by a breeze off the Atlantic. Sometimes, if the air current changed direction, they could catch a whiff of the farmlands to the west, fertilizer and animal sweat. It depended which way the wind blew. That night, under the hot mid-June twilight, the gusts off the ocean were strong, thickening the air with salt and a sulfurous scent from the marshlands.

The boys turned down Atlas Street, heading toward the cemetery at the end of Augustus Lane, over in the Cedarborough section of town. The driver, Randall Benoit, kept his speed around thirty, knowing the cops wouldn't pull him over for doing a measly five over. The cops, most locals knew, were pretty lazy in these parts. A study conducted last month revealed that speeding tickets were at an all-time low, down fifteen percent from the previous calendar year.

Yes, Randall thought, *five over would do just fine.*

His passenger, Alphonso Moffit (Alphie, his friends called him), followed the town map with his finger, a flashlight tucked under his chin so he could actually see the thing, the veins of streets and the organs of notable landmarks.

"Six clues," he said, biting his lip, squinting one eye. "How many of these were we supposed to plant again?"

Randall turned onto Bennet Avenue, taking the turn a little too sharply. The tires squealed, a short, shrill sound that lasted a mere second. "Seven. This is the last one."

"Thank you, baby Jesus." He signed the Stations of the Cross, which was weird because Randall never knew his friend to be of the religious type. "Anyway, how the hell did we end up being the Gamemasters this year? I thought the previous winners were supposed to design the Hunt?"

Randall chewed his tongue. He too was curious how he'd been chosen for the task. "Well, RJ started this thing, so he can bend the rules however he wants."

"Bullshit, is what it is."

"Can't argue with that." Randall took the next right, careening his Civic onto Cedarborough Avenue. In the distance, the cemetery loomed, looking like it had been pulled straight out of a Bram Stoker novel. A moving mist shrouded the backdrop, marching laterally like a parade of undefined specters. Tombstones stood like teeth along gums of freshly mowed greens. The gates were gothic by design, towering wrought-iron barriers that were undoubtedly locked, designed to keep out the living until daylight ruled the sky once again. Randall had planned to pull around back, climb the fence where it was the lowest, not to mention out of sight from any police cruisers that could potentially roll on by. The last thing Randall needed was to get arrested for something as foolish as breaking into a cemetery.

The midnight moon was strangely bright, splashing the graveyard in a cool blue glow. Endless rows of headstones and memorial statues stood, all that remained of the dead; masonry and memories—that was how the world knew them now. Randall followed his plan and cruised around back, the part of the road where the moon couldn't reach, the space eaten up by shadows cast by a neighboring stretch of trees.

Once parked, Randall killed the engine. The two of them sat in silence, looking over the map and the list of clues they'd previously placed throughout Hooperstown.

"Are you ready?" asked Randall, placing a trembling hand on the door handle. His forehead was greased with sweat, and not because of the humid night and his Civic's failing air conditioning. His nerves were jacked with excitement, the anticipation of what was to come.

Alphie continued to bury his nose in the map. "I don't know, man." He glanced up, and Randall could sense something was different about him. The way he squinted, like he'd eaten a bad roll of sushi, suggested maybe he was having second thoughts about their midnight escapade. "I have to be honest, this place freaks me out. I mean, fuck—my grandmother is buried in there, dude."

Randall grinned. "You think she'll care?"

"Weak, dude."

"Think she'll rise up out of the grave or something?" A series of high-pitched giggles escaped his lips.

Alphie shook his head. The soft qualities of his features stiffened. "No, idiot. It just...it feels disrespectful."

"Disrespectful?"

"Yeah, you know. Like disrespecting the dead? Come on, dude. You're gonna sit there and tell me that none of this bothers you? Stepping on people's graves and shit? I mean, there are literally hundreds of dead bodies out there. They'll be right under our feet. Tell me that isn't freaky."

Randall turned to the window, surveyed the grave markers, the various headstones perfectly aligned. Despite the morbid nature of the scenery, there was something beautiful about the darkness and the stillness and knowing the dead were eternally sleeping below the soil. This combination soothed him to some degree, eased his nerves like an expertly rolled joint. The excitement of driving across town, setting up clues for his friends to solve the following night, was somehow numbed by being in the cemetery's presence. Then he thought about the potential repercussions of his actions, the legal ones, and his veins flooded with more adrenaline.

"No," he said, shrugging. A cool sensation washed over him like a shower after a long day of work. "No, not at all. It's just a place. No different from any other spot we visited tonight."

"You're full of shit. You just find this creepy stuff cool, you fucking weirdo."

Randall chuckled, then lightly punched his friend on the shoulder. "You're wound too tight, amigo. You need to relax."

"You got any bud? I could totally get baked after this."

"Whoa! It's a school night, muchacho. Never get baked on a school night. That's reserved for weekend festivities and weekend festivities only."

Alphie gave his friend the look—yes, *that* look—and pursed his lips. "Motherfucker, you're high almost every day."

"I'll have you know, I haven't smoked in three days."

Alphie reached out with two fingers and tried pressing them against his friend's neck but was denied with a forceful swat.

"What the hell are you doing?"

"Checking your pulse, butthole. You must be dead or something."

"Eat a scrotum," Randall said, giggling again. "I'm turning over a new leaf. This summer, you're going to see a whole new Randall Benoit."

"I'll believe it when I see it. You got any bud or what? I'm starting to think we should smoke *before* we plant this last clue. Might make me feel easier about…you know…the whole *meddling with the dead*, or whatever we're about to do."

Randall burst into uproarious laughter, cocking back his head and howling at the ceiling. "Meddling with the dead? Holy shit, man. You sure are a superstitious bastard." He pushed his long hair out of his eyes, checked the rearview to ensure the streets were still vacant. They were and he doubted they would see a passing car at this hour, unless it had a light-rack on the roof and the obligatory PROTECT AND SERVE motto printed on its side.

"I can't help it, asshole. My family raised me on this shit. My grandmother's idea of *family night* consisted of a Ouija board and tarot card readings."

"Jesus. No wonder you're wound tighter than a spool of fishing wire." He glanced over at his friend, eyed him with a spreading smirk, and then tapped his leg. "All right, all right, all right." Randall reached for the cupholder underneath the radio deck. He moved the portable CD player he had rigged to work with the cassette deck and placed it on the dashboard. Then he gripped the cupholder and pulled. With some force, a little extra elbow grease, he was able to remove the plastic insert.

"You son of a bitch," Alphie said with delight. "Your secret stash."

A second later, Randall pulled a plastic baggie through the hole. He held it up, showing off the goods, the half-ounce of Purple Haze he'd bought earlier that day. "You really wanna smoke up now? This isn't that dirt you're used to. This stuff is the bomb-dot-com, Bro Pesci."

Alphie scrunched his face together, his features forming a wrinkled mess. "Get out of here with that nonsense. Crack that bag open and let's blaze."

Randall hesitated, studying his partner-in-crime, then slipped his finger between the bag's seal. Once the zipper was broken, the trapped odor filled the entire car, so heavily that Randall almost had to roll down the window.

"That shit stinks," Alphie said. He tittered with joy. "You weren't kidding."

Randall packed his glass pipe, put his lips on the receiving end, and lit up. He took two hits and passed the bowl to his friend, who also sucked in two hits. Two hits were all either of them needed, but they took two more each for good measure.

After, Randall dumped the ashy leftovers out the window and then returned his stash to the cupholder's false bottom, tucked the bowl underneath his seat. He reached into the glove compartment to grab his aerosol cologne and sprayed it, just in case the police did happen to show their ugly mugs. Then he replaced it and looked at his friend.

"You ready now?" Randall asked, unable to stop a brief chortle from escaping his mouth.

Eyes drifting toward the cemetery and the darkness it held from the world, Alphie flashed his friend an enormous smile. "Hell yeah, dude. Hell-fucking-yeah."

2

The ground beneath Alphie's feet shifted. He'd never been quite this stoned before. Sure, he'd smoked his fair share of the ganja. Not as much as Randall Benoit, who, out of their crew, smoked the most, but Alphie was no newcomer. Whatever Randall had shared with him—well, the kid hadn't been lying; it definitely wasn't dirt. An inkling that the weed *had* been laced, injected with some mind-altering substance, flashed through his thoughts.

Could that actually happen? Is that a thing?

It sounded far-fetched, impossible even. But then again, they were less than two years shy of the new millennium and almost anything was possible. Rumor had it their cell phones would soon have widespread, affordable Internet capabilities. If that was the case, then surely someone could genetically alter their marijuana, give it the power of a potent hallucinogen. People had been doing that for years, probably since the sixties. Maybe even before that. People had been lacing drugs with bad stuff since…well, since *drugs*. He was being a dope. Of course, the weed could be laced. It wasn't an unreasonable fear. *Right?*

He thought about asking Randall how he was feeling, if he felt a little *too* high, *too* gone, but he didn't want to seem weird or act like he couldn't handle a measly four hits.

He didn't want Randall to think of him as a *lightweight* or an *amateur*. *Or a pussy.*

So, he kept his mouth shut and tried to keep pace with his friend, hustling through the dark cemetery, looking for the place they had both agreed upon, the place where they would plant the final clue. Then, they would be done. Finished. He could go home and sleep off his high. Wake up tomorrow feeling fresh, ready to attend the last day of his junior year and celebrate the first day of his final high school summer.

But he had to focus. Concentrate. The pot made it impossible. Whatever had been fused with the Purple Haze made his mind race, scatter in a thousand different directions, conjure up a thousand different scenarios at once. Everything from the dead rising from their graves to the entire police force showing up, descending on the graveyard with their flashlights pointed and weapons drawn. Paranoia rained down on him like carrion birds on expired flesh. He was sweating, and even though it was a reasonably warm summer night, there was a nice, refreshing breeze blowing in from the coast, knocking down the humidity. His shirt shouldn't have been soaked. No, there was something wrong with him. With whatever he had smoked. It was a bad drug, and it was starting to turn on him.

"Yo," Alphie said, grabbing his stomach. "Do you feel...weird?"

Randall turned, that goofy smile stretching to the ends of his face. "Yeah, man. *Weird*." He hooted like a happy owl. Then he turned, slowly made his way farther into the cemetery, half disappearing amongst the shadows and the misty summer night.

Another gust of wind whipped across the open area, causing every hair on Alphie's arm to rise. The nerves in his neck swam with anticipation, and the bad thoughts swarmed him. He thought about doubling back, heading to the car and waiting for Randall to finish the job himself. Or shit—he even thought about leaving him behind.

He dug into his pocket and grabbed his Nokia, checked the time and the service bars. The screen was hardly bright enough to see, even in the dark. He squinted, brought the green light on the Nokia's face to his eyes, and saw he only had one service bar, probably not enough to call his parents or the local authorities, if such an action became warranted.

No, he thought. *I can't. Everyone will think I'm an asshole.*

Better than dead, though. Right?

He almost punched 9-1-1. His finger hovered over the 9. Dropping his thumb on the big rubber button, he hesitated.

Do you really want to do this? Your life is over if you call the cops. You know that, right? Your friends will disown you. Never speak to you again. You'll have to wait until college to make new ones. If you even go to college, you pathetic fuck.

Something grabbed his shoulder, squeezed, and Alphie shrieked. He twisted around, tripping over a small grave marker the size of a brick, and fell onto the grassy soil. He almost screamed again, but the noise stuck in his throat.

"Dude," Randall said, giggling and slapping his knee. "What the hell is wrong with you?"

Alphie felt his chest, checking to make sure his heart hadn't exploded. It was still there, beating, but at a pace that almost seemed too fast to be anything less than dangerous. Alphie closed his eyes, curled into the fetal position, and nearly cried.

Randall bent down next to his friend. "Are you okay, man?"

"I think the weed was bad."

Randall couldn't disguise his amusement nor deny his explosion of laughter. "Dude, there was nothing wrong with the weed. You took too much, man. Took too much."

"I only hit it four times."

"Once would have been enough, you silly dildo."

"Jesus," Alphie said, pushing himself back on his feet. "Let's just do this and get the hell out of here. I either want to puke or go to sleep—I can't tell which."

"Sure thing." Randall waved for his friend to follow before skipping off and disappearing behind the inky walls of night. "I found the perfect spot."

Alphie kept his balance, using the headstones for support, surveying every name he gently dragged his fingers across. Not necessarily a believer in the spiritual world—definitely not like the rest of his family—and never one to place stock in a higher power, Alphie found himself apologizing to each and every person whose grave he caressed. Even though his actions were relatively benign, he couldn't help but feel terrible about the whole ordeal.

He looked up and Randall was nowhere to be seen. *Goddammit.*

"Hey, Randall? Man?"

Back here, deep in the cemetery now, an impenetrable darkness towered, forming four walls around him. He glanced over his shoulder and saw nothing but the black, realizing how far away from the car they had traveled. The Civic was no longer visible, not even that stupid spoiler he had helped Randall install last summer when he'd first bought the thing. A small hill topped by grave markers and tall headstones blocked any view of Cedarborough Avenue. The rest belonged to the night.

"Ran—"

A cool chill swept through him, and he knew he was no longer alone. In a blink, a new shadow stood on the small hill, the thin silhouette of a tall woman. Her hair dangled in spidery threads, hanging in all different directions. So much hair. *Too much hair.* It nearly concealed her facial features, and once Alphie set his eyes upon her, once they adjusted to the mix of shadows and pale starlight, he wished her hair had done just that—hid her face from the world. But the darkness cleared, and her eyes were glowing, two golden rings with black centers. Gray flesh coated her entire body, all that was visible outside a white dress, a torn and mud-ravaged rag thinning in most places. Upon her face, black lips writhed as if there were waiting words behind them, none that ever came. There were only whispers, like the scraping of autumn leaves collecting in a gutter. Dark lines, web-like patterns of veins, were bold against her pallid, dead-like flesh. A horizontal red line stained her abdomen, the clothes and the exposed flesh beneath. Alphie, despite every muscle in his body itching to get out of there, found himself unable to avert his eyes, especially from her cold, golden gaze. They blazed like the glow of an early-morning horizon in mid-summer. And Alphie wanted to touch them, burn himself on their majestic spark.

O' beautiful child, come sit beside me, someone whispered, as if the mouth were right next to his ear. The woman's lips hadn't moved, not an inch of her body so much as flinched. Alphie found his body disagreeing with his brain's commands. He wanted to run like hell, get the fuck out of there as quickly as his two legs would carry him, but there was no action behind these instinctual concepts. He was at the mercy of the cemetery, the strange woman who whispered through the shadows.

You can do this, he coached himself. *Just take that first step. One foot in front of the other. Next thing you know you'll—*

"Dude!" Randall called from his left.

Alphie spun, his pulse firing like a Tommy Gun. The strange trance was broken. He'd never been happier to see his friend in all his life. "What?"

Randall held out his arms, narrowing his eyes, inspecting his friend from head to toe. "Are you... Dude, you don't look so hot."

"Do you see..." A trembling finger pointed back toward the hill. Alphie looked and the woman was gone. Only a few lengthy headstones and the expansive dark backdrop remained, leftover swirls of white mist thinning to nothing. "No...it can't..."

"See what?"

"The woman." Alphie choked on whatever words were supposed to come next. He had wanted to use the word "Mother" but that sounded weird. "She looked… I dunno. Messed up. Her eyes were…" Were what? He couldn't explain them without sounding crazy. "Then she whispered to me."

Randall, seemingly unable to rid his face of that goofy smile, arched his brow. "Dude, you are fucking losing it."

"I'm serious!"

Randall grabbed his friend by the shoulders and looked him straight in the eyes. "Calm down. Okay? There is no one out there. We're all alone. Let's plant this last clue, and then we're gone. Come on. I found the perfect spot. You're gonna love it."

Alphie doubted he'd "love it," doubted he'd love anything except the safety of his own room. His bed. The *Baywatch* posters on his wall. The ones of Jenny McCarthy. He'd give anything to be there again. Safe. Away from here.

Randall led him farther back, and with each step, Alphie felt increasingly uncomfortable. Each step away from the car felt a step closer to certain death. The feeling he was being watched intensified, but every time he stole a glance over his shoulder, he saw nothing but more graves. He was being silly, and he knew it. The woman on the hill had been an illusion, a side effect of the weed. Alphie almost laughed as the minutes passed, laughed at how stupid he'd been. How gullible. His mind—it was just fucking with him, punishing him for hitting the bowl more than once. His greed had caused this, not some supernatural entity that stalked the Cedarborough Cemetery.

"Look at this," Randall said, hopping over a headstone with a flat top. Just beyond it, a dome-shaped mausoleum stood almost by itself, off the pathway that guided visitors through the graveyard. The structure looked new, misplaced in this section where a lot of older headstones rested, some of them dating back to the eighteenth century.

This did not help Alphie's case, not in the least. Chills toured his arms and legs. A shiver coiled around his spine like a curious python, slow and searching. Jolts of fear hit him like lightning.

"This place is perfect," Randall told him, that smile never fading.

Alphie wanted to sock him one, punch that stupid grin right off his face and hopefully knock some sense into him as a bonus. Couldn't he tell they were in danger? That each second out here was one less second they had of escaping? No, Randall was clueless.

He didn't see it, Alphie thought. *He didn't see* her.

"Who's going in?" Randall asked.

"In?" Alphie heard his heartbeat in his ear. "What do you mean *in?*"

"Dude, it's a crypt. That's the perfect place to leave the last clue."

"I'm not going in that thing."

"Come on."

"No fucking way. Are you nuts? Haven't you been listening to a thing I've said? There's…there's something not right about this place."

"Dude…"

"No way. I'll head back, man. Wait in the car. Not going anywhere near that fucking thing."

Finally, the smile dropped. Randall placed his hands on his hips and let go of a deep breath. "All right. I'll go. But wait for me. Hell, head back to the car if it makes you feel any better."

"Oh, I will."

"Don't leave. Don't try to walk home or do anything stupid like that. I'll be in and out. Back before you know it, baby."

Randall strolled off the pathway, across the sporadic patches of grass and puddles of mud, and over to the mausoleum tucked under a collection of arched pines. It almost appeared separate from the graveyard altogether, its own attraction into this carnival of the macabre. Alphie thought the dome-shaped structure looked unusually shiny considering its surroundings, like a bright penny sitting atop a mound of dull nickels and dimes, but it still wasn't the craziest thing he'd seen that night. Or *thought* he'd seen. He still wasn't convinced the woman on the hill was a figment of his altered mind.

"It's open!" Randall called, unable to strip the giggle from his voice.

As he watched Randall open the mausoleum door and fade into the dusky darkness behind it, Alphie backed away, toward the path that would lead him to the car. It felt wrong leaving his friend behind, but the darkness was calling. Whispering. Divulging secrets. Things he did not want to hear.

She was in his head now.

She.

Mother.

He turned and ran to the Civic without looking back.

3

"Come on," Alphie said, checking his Nokia. Not only was there only one bar of service, but there was only one bar of battery. "In and out my ass."

He got a good chuckle out of that. His high had leveled off, and ever since the stroll back to the car he'd become less paranoid. That had him convinced the drug was responsible for his sudden shot of fear, more than the things he'd convinced himself had been real. It was all an illusion. Nothing more.

The night had grown suspiciously chilly since he'd reached the car fifteen minutes ago. Randall had the keys, so Alphie had no choice but to sit on the hood of the Civic and wait, something he wasn't sure Randall would be cool with, but *fuck* Randall. If he didn't like it, then he shouldn't have taken his sweet-fucking-time. How long did it take to drop one measly clue, anyway? Seconds? He should have been back by now. Minutes ago.

Humming the new Weezer tune, Alphie checked his phone again. Another two minutes had ticked by, allowing that familiar dread to settle in. That image of the woman on the hill came rushing back to him. Those brilliant orbs of light shining where normal eyes should have been. The veins in her face bulging like black leeches stuffed from bloody feasts. That rip across her midsection, as if she'd been surgically tampered with. The way her clothes were tattered and torn, appearing as if she'd climbed out of the grave.

Or...

Out of the mausoleum.

Alphie went rigid, his back straightening as if a metal rod had been drilled through his core. A sensation that felt like a bucket of cold water being dumped over him quickly washed his nerves. He suddenly sobered up, became alert and ready to react to anything this dark summer night would hurl at him.

Just as his thoughts began to take a turn for the worst again, he saw a shape materialize on the cemetery's border.

It was Randall.

He was hustling out of the dark, reaching for the top of the wrought-iron fence. Moving as if something was after him, Randall scaled the barrier between the living and the dead, and hurled himself over to the top. He hit the ground awkwardly, rolled his ankle, and went right to the ground, tumbling down the short decline. He stopped himself before he hit the curb, nearly smashing his head on the concrete formation.

Pushing himself to his feet, Randall scrambled in the direction of the car.

"Get in!" Randall shouted, his words strained with that familiar panic.

He thumbed at the car's remote and the Civic chirped. The headlights flashed, and Alphie heard the power locks disengage. He ripped open the door and dove inside, slamming it behind him as if something sinister were closely following, seeking access to the Civic and the warm body inside.

Before Alphie could locate his friend, Randall was already in the driver's seat, cranking the engine.

"What is it?" Alphie asked. "Did you see something?"

Randall didn't respond. Didn't do anything save for throw the car in drive. The tires howled as he punched the gas and sped off, leaving the cemetery in the rearview.

"What?" Alphie asked again. "What is it?"

Randall refused to answer. His smile had left him, vanished without a trace, no evidence it had ever been there. The kid was sweating, his spent energy pouring down his face, soaking the collar of his favorite black T-shirt. There was something else Alphie noticed—dark spillage trickled out of his nose, running over his lips.

It looked like ink.

It smelled like chemicals. His mother's cleaning products.

Alphie turned, looking at the grim road behind them. He swore he saw the silhouette of a woman, two rings burning brightly, setting fire to the shadows. He swore he saw two children holding her hands, their eyes filled with the same evil splendor.

PART ONE

The Great Night Hunt

CHAPTER ONE

School's Out

1

The clock on the nightstand showed 6:00 a.m. and Alanis Morissette began to sing about having one hand in her pocket. Still half asleep, Doug Simms reached out, blindly feeling the top of the clock for the snooze button but unable to locate it. Alanis continued the chorus, belting out the lyrics with a ferocity better suited for later in the day. By the time he found the snooze button, he was fully awake and ready to kickstart one last early morning before an entire summer of sleeping in.

It wasn't the worst song to wake to, so he let Alanis rant as he dragged himself out of bed, to the door. He headed down the hallway to the bathroom where he brushed his teeth, hopped in the shower to freshen up and help clear the sleepy residue that clung to the corners of his eyes. When he returned to his room to get dressed, he noticed the framed photograph on his dresser. It was sitting face down, the family portrait from seven years ago hidden from the world. He left the image that way, not feeling bad about it, and went over to the corner of his room to retrieve his JanSport backpack before heading to the kitchen.

Alanis was almost done by the time he got there. Doug wondered what Billboard-topping hit single would come on next—probably something from 98 Degrees or The Backstreet Boys because that seemed to be the only thing pop radio played these days. If he heard Will Smith *Getting' Jiggy Wit It* one more time, he might just quit listening to the radio altogether, stick to his small-but-budding collection of compact discs. The local rock station always came in fuzzy, and pop radio was all that came across clearly, besides the few AM stations. Doug liked his sports news from ESPN's SportsCenter and had zero interest in listening to some old radio minister preach about Jesus. So, pop radio it was, 98.5 THE BUZZ, and Alanis made the morning somewhat tolerable.

When he reached the kitchen, he tossed his backpack on the empty chair next to his father, who was eating a bowl of Captain Crunch and blueberries. Heading straight for the refrigerator, Doug bypassed his old man without acknowledging him. It wasn't because he was mad or their relationship was currently strained; it was because he'd hardly noticed him. Last night's dreams had left a memorable impression on his mind, so he ambled around the kitchen half-stuck between being awake and asleep. Not even the quick, cool shower had scrubbed the images from his mind, those brief flashes of pedaling through the forest, speeding after the boy and the girl, what the latter had discovered in the local woodlands, that terrible void, that split in the rock, that calamitous cavern of no-end.

But that wasn't the only recent event that left him in a fog, unable to concentrate on any one thing. There was also the note a certain someone had left in his locker yesterday. The one that someone had penned "Hey" in bubbly pink letters and scribbled a smiley face beneath it. He knew who had left it for him, the author wasn't a secret. Maddie Rice had been flirting with him all year, practically since their first gym glass together last autumn. A whole school year had passed and their blossoming relationship hadn't progressed past the casual, friendly conversations during lunch, the jokes and quick barbs they traded between classes, and the *looks*. Most noticeably, the way her eyes sparkled when she thought he wasn't looking.

If only I wasn't such a pansy and actually asked her out.

But he'd never do it. He was too scared. Even if there was a high probability of her accepting such an invitation, there was still the possibility she would decline. He found himself stuck on the latter. Rejection was not something Doug Simms wanted to experience. Not now. Not ever, if he was being honest with himself.

"Rough night, kiddo?" asked Gordon Simms. His father looked up from his morning paper and sipped his still-steaming cup of coffee.

"Uh...yeah," Doug answered, peeling the banana he'd taken off the counter. "Something like that."

"I told you not to stay up all night playing PlayStation," Gordon said, almost sing-song-like, a humorless smile clinging to his lips.

Doug knew his father's comment had been a suggestion and not a demand. He wasn't *that* parent, the authoritative type. His dad rarely told him what to do outside of a few simple house rules—*keep your room clean, take the garbage out after dinner, take care of the dishes*. He merely guided him. And he'd grown laxer over the years. Then again, Doug had gotten more responsible, which he supposed was because his father *needed* the help. With no brothers and sisters, with Mom out of the picture, it was just the two of them.

Gordon wasn't an overbearing parent at all, and for that Doug respected him a lot more. He'd seen the way his friend Grady's parents treated him, like he was a prisoner. Grady was always badmouthing them in private. His chief complaint was that they wouldn't let him watch R-rated movies (unless they were edited for television), a factoid Doug and Jesse always teased him about. Gordon didn't mind if Doug watched R-rated movies, provided the subject matter wasn't *too adult* (he still hadn't seen *Showgirls* or any of the *Faces of Death*). He'd also let him listen to music with the black and white "Parental Advisory: Explicit Lyrics" stamped on the cover art.

Last summer, while shopping at Warehouse Music, Dad let him buy Marilyn Manson's *Antichrist Superstar*. It took some convincing, but Doug's mature and articulate argument had brought his pops over to the dark side. The purchase had come with the caveat of "Don't make me regret this." Doug had also picked up Tom Petty and the Heartbreakers' *Greatest Hits* to offset the imbalance. Besides, Doug really enjoyed Petty's music, primarily the folksy twang of his guitars, so it wasn't like the album would go to waste. They were tunes he could rock out to at full volume when his old man was home. And since the purchase, it had been in heavy rotation in his six-disc player's tray, nestled comfortably between Incubus' *S.C.I.E.N.C.E* and Metallica's *Reload*.

"Wasn't the PlayStation," Doug said, stuffing the rest of the banana in his mouth. He'd made quick work of his breakfast and still had time for a corn muffin. "It was…" He didn't want to tell his dad about the dreams, the ones he kept having over and over again, that trip through the woods with the mysterious boy and girl. It was too weird to explain and the images felt too real, as if they had actually happened. Experiencing them periodically over the last year or so (or longer… Wasn't it longer?) was more than enough. He didn't want to relive them during the day too. No, he'd keep the dreams to himself unless they became something more.

What more could they possibly become? he thought. *They're just dreams. Stupid dreams that don't make any sense.*

Dreams. More like nightmares.

Nightmares he didn't want to burden Gordon Simms with. His father had enough on his plate these days. Doug didn't want to add another spoonful, even if it was something as silly and harmless as recurring night terrors.

"Just couldn't sleep. That's all," he finally admitted before biting into that delicious corn muffin.

"Mm-hm." He shot his son a dubious look. "Well, it's the last day of school, so I guess I can't go too hard on you. I remember when I was your age, man. I couldn't wait for summer. Practically killed me, those last few days of class."

Doug attempted a smile.

"Oh," he said, shoveling the rest of the muffin in his mouth. "Forgot to tell you. I'm sleeping over at Jesse's tonight." He swallowed every last bite, the sweet and sticky flavor clinging to his taste buds. "If that's okay with you, of course."

"Oh?"

"Yeah. You know. First day of summer vacation. Horror movie marathon and video games. Will probably eat a lot of pizza, too. And soda. Definitely soda. Orange. It's my favorite, you know." His palms greased with sweat. Heart quickening in his chest, Doug tried to stand completely still in fear his father would take any movement whatsoever as a sign of nervous energy.

He could practically hear his father grilling him now, the way his eyes fixed on him. *Why so nervous, son? What aren't you telling me?*

But, instead of interrogating him about the impromptu change in plans, Gordon only smiled. "All right. As long as Jesse's parents are cool with it."

"Oh, yeah. Totally."

"I'll call them on my lunch break just to make sure."

"Yeah, sure. No problem."

Gordon nodded and then glanced down at the newspaper as if he'd suddenly remembered something of great importance. "Hey, I wanted to ask you," he said, flipping through the pages. "Do you know a Lauren Sullivan? She's your age."

Doug didn't know why, but even though he passed his father's instinctual lie detector test, he still felt his nerves swimming. A sticky, sour feeling swelled in his stomach. "Yeah… I mean, she's in my grade. We've shared a few classes."

"Saw her name in the paper. Says she has cancer. Leukemia. Did you know that?"

No, he didn't know that, and he couldn't remember seeing her either. *Leukemia* was not a term he'd heard thrown around at all, not even murmured between teachers. And news like that usually traveled through the hallways.

Last year, Becca Spritz had been diagnosed with Lyme Disease and the whole town practically freaked about it. Flyers had been sent home complete with information and pictures of the disease-carrying deer ticks and how they differed from other ticks.

But this? Nothing. Not a peep about it.

"No, didn't hear that. But it sounds awful."

Gordon nodded, agreeing. "Yeah. Suppose it's only a matter of time before people start blaming Hooperstown Chemical. That's usually the first reaction when things like this crop up. Back in '82, a plant in Massachusetts was found responsible for letting hazardous materials seep into the town's water supply, making a bunch of people sick. I guess it happens, but we're…" A wan smile fixed his lips. "We're different. We're careful. In the ten years I've been there, we've always done things by the books."

Doug shrugged, hardly concerning himself with that stuff.

"Sorry, kiddo. Didn't mean to be such a downer on the last day of school."

"It's fine. Hope she's okay."

"Me too." Gordon folded the paper sloppily and tossed it aside. "Go on. Get to school. We'll talk about it later if you want."

"Okay."

"If I don't see you, have fun playing PlayStation all night and listening to that Marilyn Mason character—"

"It's Marilyn *Manson,* Dad."

"—and playing with Pogs—"

"Pogs? Dad, I haven't bought Pogs in like three years."

A pleasant chuckle broke free from his father's mouth. "Well, whatever. You know what I mean. Have fun tonight. Don't concern yourself with…" He motioned to the paper. "This stuff. I'm sure the girl will be fine. Keep your mind off it. Enjoy the first night of summer break. You deserve it."

"I do?"

He perked up at this. "Of course. You always get your chores done. Hardly ever have to bother you about keeping your room clean. Mostly As and Bs on your report card. You're, like, the best son a guy could ask for."

Doug's heart vibrated like a plucked string on a guitar. "Wow. Thanks, Dad. You're…like…the best Dad."

Gordon smiled at this. These moments didn't happen too often around these parts, and Doug was actually enjoying the time spent in the kitchen, minus the whole cancer talk. But sometimes it took something bad to realize the good. Doug had a feeling that was what was happening now.

"I know things haven't been particularly easy since your mom and all." His father shifted in his seat, the mood of the room changing once again. Doug checked the clock on the microwave, saw his time was running out. "But I want you to know that I appreciate you and how you've handled the…uh…tough situation."

He shrugged. "It's fine."

"Are you fine?"

Doug shifted his eyes, bouncing between various objects in the room—the dusty light fixture that hung over the kitchen table, the vase on the counter holding a sad collection of sunflowers, the stack of bills that weren't quite overdue but was getting there. "Yeah, I'm great. Are *you* fine?"

"Of course."

He could see his father wasn't, not as great as he could be, not as great as he once was, but what could he do other than help out around the house? There was something missing from his father's eyes, that special shine that made him *him*. Doug couldn't remember the last time he'd seen it there.

Since before her.

Since before what happened.

Mother. Mom.

"Are you?" Doug pressed, knowing he wouldn't get the truth. At least, not the whole truth. Gordon had to be strong for Doug's sake, and he knew that. The man would never want to seem weak or vulnerable in front of his son. But Doug didn't care about that. He just wanted his pops to be happy. "You can talk to me, Dad. You know that, right?"

"Hey, that's my line," he said with a wink and a half-hearted smile. "Your old man is fine, kiddo. Don't worry about me. I'll get on like I always do."

Doug didn't want to tell him that *just getting on* wasn't a life, not much of one, anyway. But what did he know? He was fourteen. Not an adult. Everything was great when you were fourteen. He wasn't a child anymore, but he didn't have the real world pressing down on him yet, making him do too many things he didn't want to do. Maybe that's how it would be later—the older you get, the less living you do, the more you just survive. *Go through the motions.* He'd heard that term before but never truly understood its meaning until now.

"Love you, kid," Gordon said.

"Love you too, Dad."

In the near distance, a big engine roared up their block.

"Shit!" Doug dashed across the kitchen, scooping the strap of his backpack with one arm. "The bus!"

"Better get going," Gordon said, getting up from the table. He was already dressed for work and ready to head out himself. "You coming home before you head over to Jesse's?"

Doug didn't turn around but shouted "Yes!" over his shoulder.

Before his father could ask him anything else, he was out the door, flying across the freshly mowed lawn, down the cracked sidewalk toward the bus stop.

2

Grady Pope always sat in the front seat no matter what, mostly because it was the only one available by the time the bus reached his stop. Sure, he could have claimed a seat three rows down, but then he'd have to sit next to Philip Rowland, the kid known to occasionally pick his nose and eat the discoveries. There was no way he was subjecting himself to that gross nonsense. Abby Allen always sat by herself in a two-seater near the middle, but Grady wasn't parking himself next to a girl, not if he could help it. The rest of the available seats were in the back, claimed by the rougher, meaner kids. The last three rows were like a wasps' nest—you didn't want to get close enough to attract the attention of its inhabitants.

One of the slackers he'd learned to avoid was Jewel Conti, the Undisputed Queen of Bus 469. *Rough around the edges* didn't quite cover this trashy prima donna. No, she was sharp all over, a porcupine in the shape of a fifteen-year-old girl. Grady hated whenever she made an appearance on 469, which, luckily, wasn't often, because she hardly ever showed up for school. Her home-life, from what he'd heard coming out of the rumor mill, was tumultuous, and although rumors were just that and had the tendency to be false or inaccurate, he didn't think that was the case with the Conti clan. The latest noise was that her father had been charged with first-degree murder, convicted, and sentenced to life at the state penitentiary, a tidbit Grady nor his friends could verify. What they *could* confirm was that both of her parents had spent the majority of their adulthood in and out of the county slammer, mostly for drug possession, theft, and petty crimes of varying degrees.

As soon as Grady climbed up the stairs, he saw Jewel stretched out across the backseat, her legs taking up two seats, her butt occupying the third, her face a sheet of emotionless flesh. She was probably thinking of ways to make some poor kid's summer completely miserable. Typically, she'd be cackling along with her douchebag acolytes, Brennan Scruggs and Dakota Chaffin, two weaselly sock puppets cut from the same material. The three of them looked like they were auditioning for a Nirvana biopic, their T-shirts and jeans ripped and faded.

He avoided eye contact and stepped toward his seat, but nearly yelped when he saw two bodies occupying the normally empty space. The Sanders twins, Jake and Johnny, sat there innocently, looking straight ahead, also avoiding eye contact. Grady stared as if they'd committed some atrocious crime and debated whether to kick them out, if that would even fly. The bus driver eyed him in the rearview, a cold, heartless glare that told Grady to *stop dillydallying and pick a goddamn seat already.*

Shuffling down the aisle, he peeked toward the back. The seat next to Phil The Nosepicker was also taken. Grady wondered what alternate universe he'd accidentally stumbled upon. It was the last day of school for Christ's sake—don't most kids cut the last day? Shouldn't the bus be relatively empty?

But no, it seemed like the entire neighborhood was here. Every. Goddamn. One of them.

Grady felt his heart squirm for a beat as he neared the middle of the bus. He kept looking around, trying to locate a reasonably appropriate place to plant his keister, all without catching a glimpse of that very last seat, the one the Devil had claimed. Jewel's eyes were on him now, glaring. Not that he could see them; he wasn't looking. He didn't dare. Listening to her two cronies snicker at some joke the rest of the bus hadn't been privy to, his eyes scanned the nearby rows, trying to find a seat, any old one. Scruggs and Dakota were cackling now, probably plotting their next nefarious doing, which probably included lighting something on fire or pulling someone's underwear so far up their ass crack that they'd be shitting cotton all summer long.

Damn—he couldn't help it. His eyes flashed up, just for a second, to see if she *was* looking at him. The way her mouth formed a cavernous black hole when she spoke was like a portal to Hell opening up, revealing a chasm into some terrible world of perpetual torture and chaos. Grady swore he saw flames raging uncontrollably there, perfect-circle smoke rings emanating from within. She toyed with the cigarette tucked behind her ear, as if making sure it hadn't fallen off during the bumpy commute. Even though she was in the eighth grade, she was a year older than him. Jewel had stayed back once, *twice* if rumors served correctly, and even if that had been the case, she still wasn't old enough to smoke on school grounds. Just flashing a cigarette on the bus was enough for disciplinary action. But it was the last day of school and the bus driver hardly looked like he gave a shit, so odds were nothing would come of it. Jewel ordinarily wore a rugged plaid flannel, but today was much too hot, so she had on a sleeveless undershirt that exposed her homemade tattoos, the kind done with pen ink and a sewing needle. Grady's favorite was the inverted cross on her shoulder. It really summed up the bitch.

Evil witch. Though, today, she didn't look like she was carrying her broomstick. There was something sad about her eyes. They had softened, and Grady didn't know what scared him more—the fact she wasn't looking to destroy the day of some innocent passenger, or that her eyes looked very close to being *human.*

Grady realized he was dragging his feet and drawing a nasty eyeball from the bus driver, so he opted to sit in the next closest seat, which was next to Abby Allen.

A girl.

It was his only option, plus, it was far enough away from Jewel to keep him safe. Besides, being the last stop meant the drive to school was brief—five minutes, if that. He could survive the next few minutes next to Abby Allen, a girl. He could do it.

Can't I?

Good Lord, get a grip, Grades.

He planted himself on the seat cautiously, like sitting on a bed of thorns.

As the bus sped off, Abby stared out the window, a sorrowful glance at the passing houses. In the window's reflection, Grady noticed her eyes, the tears pooling near the surface. She'd either been crying or was about to, maybe both. Her cheeks glistened with a sheen, proof she'd been at it for some time.

She turned, her head pivoting like a creepy, possessed doll that had suddenly been given life.

Grady stiffened the same way he had when Mr. Treadwell had caught him daydreaming in pre-algebra.

"I'm sorry," Abby said, pinching her eyelashes.

"What's to be sorry about?" he asked her, unable to meet her eyes. He couldn't believe how awkward he was at this. His nerves were ablaze with discomfort and the strength in his legs grew absent with each passing second. Also, he suddenly needed to pee. Talking to girls had never seemed like much of a problem, but lately it was a struggle.

"I'm a mess." There was humor in her voice, but Grady could tell she was forcing it. Probably to keep herself from crying, *really* crying, bawling her eyes out. "Nobody wants to sit next to the crying girl."

"Eh, it's not so bad," he said, his attempt at a light joke, hoping to unburden the mood, but she wasn't having it.

"Have you heard about Lauren?"

Grady was slow to look at her, but he *did* look at her. His eyes finally rose to meet hers. All of this anxiety was crazy—Abby was just like any other girl he'd sat next to in class. It was no big deal, so why was he making it one? Why couldn't he corral the flock of butterflies from frolicking in his stomach?

"Lauren?" He had to think about it. There were a handful of *Laurens* at Hooperstown Middle. "Jankins or Sullivan?"

"Sullivan," she said as if this were obvious. In truth, it should have been. He knew Lauren Sullivan and Abby were good friends and were often seen together. But Grady's brain wasn't cooperating—ever since the Sanders twins had stolen his seat, everything else had gone out the window. The cart was off the rails. It was like the whole day was now destined for a series of small disasters.

Just get through today, he told himself. *Tonight is gonna be awesome.*

He hoped it would be. Jesse had said his brother would allow them to participate in the Great Night Hunt, an all-night scavenger hunt he and his friends put together each year. Grady was pumped for it, even more so since his parents were allowing him to sleep over at Jesse's. They never let him sleep over friends' houses, and he had only convinced them this time around because it was the first night of summer vacation (*a celebration!*) and because he'd aced his report card (*straight frickin' As, man!*). With those facts presented and after a solid two days of deliberation, they had finally agreed.

"No," Grady said, shaking his head. "No, I haven't heard anything. What's up?"

Abby's lower lip trembled. "She has… She has cancer."

Grady arched his brow. "Geez. Is it serious?"

She looked at him oddly, her forehead taking on deep wrinkles. "It's cancer. *Yes*, it's serious."

"Oh…well…I mean…that…uh, that really…sucks."

Abby shook her head and returned her eyes to the window, the passing photographic flashes of suburban paradise.

"I'm sorry, Abby. I…I didn't know."

She didn't respond and kept her eyes trained on the outside world.

Stupid, he thought. *Good job, bonehead.*

"Abby, look, if there's anything I can do, just—"

"Got a smoke?"

He was taken aback. He didn't smoke. The smell of it, whenever he caught whiffs from the kids hanging out near the entrance to the mall, made him want to hurl. He wasn't friends with anyone who smoked, and probably wouldn't be if he knew they did. The only kids he knew that did the dirty deed were Jewel and her brat pack. "No. No, I don't smoke."

With a languid nod, she kept her eyes focused on the outside world.

"Anything else I can—"

"Just leave me alone," she said, and that was how they left it.

Two minutes later, the bus driver parked in the designated drop-off lane, pulled the lever that opened the doors, and yelled, "All right, ya worms! Time to get off!" Which was quite normal behavior around these parts.

3

Jesse Di Falco climbed out of his brother's backseat, turned and faced Hooperstown Middle, gave the school one last cursory glance, realizing this was the last time he'd look at the building from this reflective perspective, and then turned back to Jimmy.

"Come on, bro," Jesse pleaded. "It's the last day. Do we really have to go? Can't we go to the mall and blow our allowances at Suncoast?"

Jimmy Di Falco purred. As much as the idea probably interested him, he played the role of the responsible older brother quite well. "Go to school, fool. You're lucky I'm letting you and your puke friends sneak out tonight for the Hunt. Mom and Dad will literally kill me if they find out."

Jesse rolled his eyes, knowing Mom and Dad would do no such thing.

Jimmy draped his arm around his girlfriend, Karen Howard. She smiled and pecked him on the cheek, leaving behind a faint smear of ruby-red lipstick.

"Blech," Jesse said, sticking his forefinger in his mouth.

"Shut up, idiot. Grab your books. Get the hell out of here. We're gonna be late."

"You're probably not even going to school yourselves." Jesse knew how his brother operated, especially when the June weather hit and the temperatures turned from mildly warm to scorching hot. "We both know you two are skipping and going to the beach. That's what all the high school kids who drive do on the last day."

"Only seniors, bro. So maybe next year."

"Ah, horse tits."

"Hey! Do you want me to smack you?"

Jesse snorted.

"Get your books," his brother said, jerking his thumb at the backseat. "I see your weirdo friends are already waiting for you."

Jesse turned and spotted Doug and Grady standing near the line of buses. They each gave their own version of a subtle wave.

"Go," Jimmy said, this time with more venom than Jesse was accustomed to. The Di Falco brothers always got along, even when they were busting each other's *cajones*. Things never got too heated between them, though, sometimes, Jimmy took the roughhousing a bit too far. A headlock too strong and tight, a punch in the arm with too much muscle behind it—but there was never any detrimental intent behind his foolery. Lately, since Jimmy got his license, they had actually become a lot closer, going on trips to the mall together. The movies. The boardwalk. It had been a fun few months, and Jesse was having the time of his life piggybacking off his brother's newfound freedoms. There would come a time, he supposed, when Jimmy would need his space. But in the interim, he would enjoy the ride.

"Go enjoy your last day of middle school," Jimmy said with a wink. "You're gonna miss this place in a few years."

"Pssh, yeah right. This place sucks giant monkey balls."

"Watch your mouth, turd. There's a lady present."

Karen didn't seem to mind the language, in fact, she snickered at "monkey balls."

"All right," Jesse said, snatching his bag off the backseat. He slung the strap over his shoulder and shut the car door. He watched his brother's Thunderbird pull away and speed through the parking lot, toward the exit. Witnessing them drive down Brower Avenue, in the *opposite* direction of the high school and toward the shore instead, Jesse combed his wild dark hair with his fingers.

"Fucking knew it," he whispered, turning and facing the last day of middle school, the last day before the worst summer of his life.

4

"Dude, your brother's girlfriend is so hot," was the first thing that came out of Grady's mouth when Jesse hopped over the curb and onto the walkway leading to Hooperstown Middle. Hundreds of kids were pouring into school now, the buses purging the last remaining stragglers. Principal Fritz was out on the concrete apron, along with several other administrative assistants, ushering inside the clusters of chatty students. Doug knew they only had a few minutes before he came over to break up their own party. "I mean super hot. Mega hot. Like, *how the hell did he pull that off* kinda hot."

Jesse threw three fake uppercuts at his friend's gut. "You know Jimmy. He's always had a way with the ladies." He retracted his fists and fixed the sliding strap of his backpack. "You fuckers ready for tonight?"

"Hell yeah, dude," Doug said. "I've been waiting for this *all* week. Which reminds me, my dad said he was going to double-check with your parents about the sleepover. They're cool, right?"

"Yeah, of course they're cool. Nothing to worry about on that front."

Jesse's parents *were* cool. The cool*est*. They were the parents that always allowed sleepovers, the all-night get-togethers that skimped on adult supervision. They let them stay up until sunup, eat candy and pizza until they felt like they would puke, and watch whatever trashy R-rated video tapes they could discover in the horror section of Video World. Usually the kind that featured voluptuous victims on the front cover, anything known to expose a bare breast or two. For New Year's last year, the Di Falcos even let them sip champagne. Doug wasn't a huge fan of his first alcoholic experience; the premiere drink of choice, the one the adults seemed to idolize and go crazy for, tasted a lot how he imagined cat urine would. But the Di Falcos were cool, all right. So cool they wouldn't even notice if the three of them tagged along with Jimmy and his friends on their annual scavenger hunt.

It did make Doug nervous knowing his father might find out, and if he did, how severe his punishment might be. He'd get grounded for sure, possibly for the entire summer. And, undoubtedly, he'd never be allowed to attend a sleepover at the Di Falcos' ever again.

The stakes were high. But totally worth it.

"Awesome," Doug said, noticing the principal heading their way. "We better scram, guys."

Jesse looked over his shoulder, saw the man approaching, his authoritative stride on full display, and then moved toward the front door. "Ah, man. I hate this guy."

Doug shrugged. "He's not so bad."

The principal breezed past them, but not without dropping a comment. "Move along, gents. I know it's the last day of school, but let's get to class on time."

"What a loser," Jesse said under his breath once Fritz had moved onto bigger, more concentrated clusters of slacker youths. "Heard he runs some church thing during the summers. Like, who goes to church anymore?"

"My parents do," Grady said. And then, hanging his head, he admitted, "And...I do. But not because I want to."

"It's okay, Grades," Jesse told him. "My parents make me go too."

Doug wanted to comment on how his father hadn't been to church in several years, not since Mom, but a shadow filled in his periphery, and he turned to see Maddie Rice approaching. His heart quickly dropped to his knees like an elevator with cut cables. Setting his eyes on her, the sounds of the early-morning chaos faded, and she was all he could focus on. Her smile widened as she caught his gaze.

"Hey, Doug," she said, her smile never moving. Her best friend, Erika Jones, trailed a few steps behind her.

His jaw suddenly felt dislocated, like someone had squarely socked him with a fistful of quarters. A numb, tingly sensation ran along his jawline, curling around his ear and streaking down his neck. "Hey—hi, uh, Maddie. How're—how ya, uh, em, doing?" Talking to her had never been this hard, and he had no idea why it was now, only that the note in his locker from yesterday kept flashing in his mind repeatedly.

She giggled. "Um. I'm fine."

Behind her, Erika covered a smirk with her palm.

"So, how's your last day of school going so far?" Doug asked, realizing how dumb and corny that sounded.

"Um, literally just got here, so…you know. Too early to tell."

"Cool."

"Yeah." She squinted, her smile fading some. "Are you okay?"

"Yeah, fine."

"Are you sure? You look really…sweaty."

He heard Jesse snickering behind him, and he wondered how long he'd have to hear about that one. *Probably years before he lets me forget it.*

"No, I'm great. Never been better." He felt his pores open, the floodgates beneath opening and releasing a year's worth of secluded nervousness. They hadn't talked *all* that much, excluding the occasional conversations before school and during lunch. Those had been normal, casual talks, but now that he knew without a doubt that she had some feelings that were (let's just say) *more than friendly*, he found talking to her harder and more nerve-racking than last month's IOWA assessment.

Get a grip on yourself. This is embarrassing.

This was the first meaningful conversation they'd had all year, and he was *fucking* the whole thing up.

"Really," he said. "I'm fine. Just…you know. Super hot out."

"Right. Well, anyway. I was just wondering what you guys were up to tonight."

The three of them exchanged curious glances.

"Actually, we're hanging out with my brother tonight," Jesse said, proudly nodding. "High school kids, so, you know, that's pretty cool."

Doug stuck him with his elbow, a perfectly placed jab to his ribs. Jesse retaliated with a kick to the side of his leg, a quick blow that had little effect. They kept smiling the way dueling puppets might smile, perfect on the surface but perhaps hiding something beneath that wooden facade. After a brief scuffle, they collected themselves and ceased jerking around.

Maddie twirled her finger. "Are you guys having...having some sort of thing or something?"

"Nope, not a thing," Doug blurted. "So, what's up? What's going on tonight? What's the haps?"

Erika leaned into her friend's shoulder and whispered just loud enough for him to hear. "Did he just ask, 'what's the haps?'" Her amusement did not go unnoticed.

A short huff of laughter escaped Maddie's lips. "Yeah, I think he did."

"Dude," whispered Grady, low enough so the girls wouldn't hear. "What are you doing?"

Doug shook his head. He hadn't the slightest clue where that silly word had come from, where he'd even gotten it from, but he needed to steer this conversation in a more favorable direction fast. He was blowing it. Big time. *Idiot,* he scolded himself. *How could you be this dumb?*

"Sorry," Doug said. "Got a little carried away there. So, tonight..."

"Yeah," Maddie said, tucking her thumbs under her backpack's straps. "My parents are letting me have a little get together. Nothing crazy. Swimming. Barbecue. Movies. Something to celebrate the last day of school. Won't be a ton of people there, but you guys are invited."

Heat pressed against Doug's face and forehead, and for a second he felt as if he were about to burst into flames. "Wow, well, thanks for the invite. I'll see—"

Jesse shouldered his way in front of him. "That's really sweet, Maddie. Thank you for the invite, but we have that thing tonight, so I don't think we'll make it."

Doug wedged his way in front of him. "I mean, we can try to make it."

"Well, no, we can't. We're *busy.* Remember?"

"Yeah, I remember, but…you know…we can *see* if *maybe* we can make it." Doug winked at him, hinting that Jesse should just shut the fuck up and play along.

"Um. No, dude. We have a *thing*."

Doug stomped on his friend's foot.

Grady stepped in, putting a hand on each of their shoulders, guiding them apart. "Guys, we'll talk about this later. Maddie, thank you so much for the invite. We'll do our best to make it. Sincerely, thank you."

Maddie and Erika tried their best to hide their delight.

The first bell rang, and the girls turned for the entrance. Before they could take a step, Brendan Scruggs, Jewel Conti, and Dakota Chaffin waltzed over, their smug faces gleaming in the bright summer morning.

"Well," Scruggs said, hands on his hips, his tongue probing his inner lip as if something salty had clung to the surface. "Look at this collection of shitbags."

"Jesus," Grady said, "not today, Buster."

"It's Scruggs, fucktard. That's what you call me. Call me Buster one more time and I'mma *Buster* your lip."

Buster was the nickname his parents had given him. People had called him that all throughout elementary school. Over the last two years, he'd grown to despise it and threatened to kick the ass of anyone who dared use it.

"What's that, twerp?" Scruggs asked, leaning toward Grady, a hand cupped behind his ear. "Didn't hear that?"

"I…didn't say anything."

"He's looking for a *sorry*," Dakota chimed in. "And boy, you better give him one."

"Sorry," Grady said nonchalantly.

Doug watched Jewel's reaction to this nonsense. She didn't seem like she cared to join in, the exact opposite of the other two. Usually she'd be all over this. Hell, she was sometimes the worst of the three, the harshest, her tongue holding the most venom. Instead, she hung back like a prop that blended into the backdrop of a stage play—there, but not that noticeable unless you were looking.

"Wasn't the sincere apology I was looking for, shitbag," Scruggs said, and Dakota chittered with delight. "Wanna try again?"

Grady shrugged. "Not particularly."

Scruggs dropped his positive attitude and flashed his rows of dirty, already-yellowing teeth. Some had already blackened near the gums. "Apologize."

"He said he was sorry, Buster," Jesse chimed in, unable to help himself. "Now scram."

"Scram?" Scruggs let go of a hideous laugh. It sounded like a snake weaving through a patch of dry leaves. "Scram? Oh, that's a good one, Di Falco? You gonna make me?"

"Maybe."

"I don't see your older bro here to protect you."

Jesse didn't have a smart comeback for that, a rare occurrence these days.

Scruggs moved onto his third victim. "What about you, Simms?"

"We were just leaving, Scruggs," Doug said, taking a step back, heading for the front door. Once they were beyond those doors, they would be safe from the trio's wrath. Nothing bad ever happened *inside* the school—the bully hunting grounds were usually off the premises. The physical torment, anyway. The mental games and verbal exchanges were constant throughout the school day, but Doug and the others clung to the old adage of *sticks and stones will break thy bones*, and never let anything the three boneheads said bother them. "The bell rang, so..."

"Yeah, I heard it." Scruggs's partner in crime sneered from behind him.

To Doug, the three of them looked like live-action reincarnations of the hyenas from *The Lion King*. Even Jewel—currently directing her eyes at the ground—looked like she fit the role. A mangy animal capable of terrible things, wanting to cause a little chaos and needing to feast off the meat of the living.

"Also heard you cunt-muffins talking about a little party." Scruggs surveyed the group, his eyes bouncing between each of them, as if waiting for someone to give up the delicious secret. "Well...where's our invite, fuck-buckets?"

No one spoke. No one dared to. Doug knew this situation was one more smart-ass response away from escalating.

"Huh?" Scruggs asked, moving in Maddie's direction. "Well?"

Doug felt his right foot instinctively lift off the concrete.

Jewel stormed forward, finally breaking her trance. "He's talking to you, brown bear."

Before Maddie could defend herself, Doug said, "Hey, asshole." He wasn't sure exactly whom he was talking to—all of them, he guessed—but Jewel's head whipped around so fast he thought she'd broken her neck. "Yeah," he said, rolling with it, mustering up more confidence as he snagged her attention. "You, asshole. Don't talk to her like that, you fucking racist psychopath."

Jewel just stared at him, a murderous rage clouding her eyes. "My, my, fellas. Check out the balls on Simms here. He's grown some large ones since last time."

"Just leave Maddie alone." Doug said, feeling his heart jackhammer in his chest, his whole body vibrating along with the rhythmic thrum.

The world blurred at the edges, and he wondered if the adrenaline that had flooded his entire body was responsible. Enough rage had built up inside him to turn things physical, but starting a fight was the last thing he wanted. Not on the final day of school. Not with tonight looming. If he were to start something now, there was no way his father would let him out tonight. Plus, even though she was one of the worst people alive, Jewel Conti *was* a girl. He wasn't sure how punching a girl would be received in the eyes of the community. Or, specifically, the school board. His father had always told him to never hit a woman, no matter what the circumstances dictate. That was a lesson he had always remembered. Maybe that was because of his mother, everything she had put his father through. Even on that night, the night of all nights, the very worst night of them all, he had never so much as lifted a fist in her direction.

Doug backed off.

"That's right," Scruggs said in Jewel's place. "This is between Jewel and that black bitch."

Jewel turned back to Maddie. Maddie turned her gaze toward the other clusters of students, as if searching for some authority figure, her eyes filling with water. Doug could tell the racist comment bothered her. He wanted to destroy Jewel for that alone.

Maddie clutched her notebook and books tightly against her chest and shuddered.

Jewel cast her eyes on Doug, her gaze digging into him. "Tell me, Doug…" She sniffed Maddie's hair, imitating a shampoo model in a commercial, rolling her eyes as if the girl's hair smelled like something divine. "I've seen the two of you talking all year. It's pretty obvious you have the hots for each other. So tell me—is it true? Does black pussy taste sweeter than white pussy?"

Doug immediately saw red. A hot bolt surged through him, head to toe. He charged at full-speed, ready to attack. Dakota and Brennan closed in on his path, blocking his access to Jewel. Before he could take them on, get his fists in position to take a swing, he felt two pairs of hands on him, yanking him away.

"Let go!" Doug wrestled with his friends, but it was no use. They removed him from the potential brawl, though it was hardly easy. "Let go of me!"

"Not worth it, man," Jesse whispered in his ear.

Doug begged to differ; it *would* be worth it. The suspension or expulsion that followed, the stern lecture his father would give him, the summer he'd spend confined to his room, missing the first night of summer vacation and giving up the freedoms tonight had to offer—it would all be worth it.

A sly, winner's smile gripped Jewel's face. She licked her lips like one of those hungry cartoon hyenas. "Come on," she said, waving him on. "I've been wanting to smash someone's face in all morning."

The flash of anger may have blinded Doug, but he wasn't so blinded to the fact he'd temporarily ignored his father's message, playing on repeat in his head.

"Okay," Doug said, giving himself up. He raised his hands in the air to prove he wouldn't do anything stupid. "It's okay, I'm fine."

They seemed hesitant to let go of him, but they did so anyway.

"What are you gonna do?" Jewel asked. She ran her fingertips down Maddie's arm in a sensual manner, except it came off creepy and cringeworthy. Doug wanted nothing more than to see Jewel punished for her actions. "This is a fine piece of dark meat you got here, Dougie. It'd be a shame to let it go to waste."

"You're so racist. Why are you like that?"

Jewel flashed another grin, this one reminding him of the Cheshire Cat from *Alice in Wonderland*. Her lips parted, ready to respond with some cheeky remark or insult that didn't answer his question, when a shadow fell over her.

"Why, indeed?" asked Principal Fritz, hands on his hips. Chewing his tongue, his nostrils flared.

The man didn't normally exude such anger (not publicly, anyway). His temper was currently so palpable that Doug could almost hear the man's blood sloshing through his veins, his heart working in tandem with the rampaging storm within.

"Jewel." Fritz said. "My office. Fifteen minutes. Not a second later."

"But—"

"No, I don't want to hear it." He scanned the rest of them with disapproval. "The rest of you get to class. The bell rang three minutes ago."

Doug returned Jewel's smile until her gaze settled on him. Eventually, her eyes gave into his lure, and in that moment he felt righteous.

Principals and teachers never walked in on the right moment. Bullies were never caught in the act. It was always hearsay, he-said-she-said arguments that amounted to not so much as an afternoon in detention. Most of the time, Doug got the sense they ignored situations like this. Turned their backs on them, looked the other way, pretended not to see or hear things. But not today. Today there had been justice. *Thank goodness for small victories*, something Mom used to say. In truth, Doug felt like he'd won the lottery. The overwhelming sense that everything was currently right in the world broke over him like a gnarly wave.

But the feeling was a fake. Basic subterfuge.

Everything was wrong.

In Hooperstown, nothing would be right again. Not for a long, long time.

5

The last day of high school was a weird, almost-haunting experience. RJ Holloran had spent four years here. And even though, in the grand scheme of life, four years wasn't a relatively long time, four years was nearly a quarter of his life so far. As he walked down the halls of Hooperstown

High, passing classrooms he would never set eyes on again, the memories from these places came flooding back to him.

In the corner of the hallway, near the stairwell, he saw himself getting Nikki Boylan's number, which happened two years ago almost to the day. When he skipped past Mr. Granger's history classroom, he saw himself sitting there, wearing his game-day jersey, daydreaming about scoring the winning touchdown later that night. Also, when he looked out the window at the end of the hall, he saw the parking lot, he and his friends ditching school to head to the beach on a beautiful June morning.

Much like that last memory, today was another senior skip day. If he had to estimate, RJ figured half the graduating class was absent. He had been invited, too. Jimmy Di Falco and his girlfriend Karen Howard were headed over the bridge to Seaside Park to meet with friends. As tempting as those plans were, RJ didn't feel like skipping. It was the least stressful day of his high school career. He wanted to savor it like an exotic flavor he'd never taste again. People could say what they want about high school, how it was the worst time of their life, but RJ had loved it. Every goddamn second.

It helped that he hung out with the popular crowd. And so did being the football team captain, always surrounded by friends and having endless support from the faculty. But those weren't the only reasons the last four years had left such an impression on him. It was the people and the *experiences* (many firsts) he would miss the most. Not to mention, he was shipping himself across the country to Cal Berkeley in a few short months. This would be the very last time he'd have to enjoy these simple moments before the real stress began.

College.

Oh, buddy. Just you wait.

He moved down the hall and located his locker. Opening it, he felt a presence nearing him and wondered who it might be. Another someone—someone he didn't talk to or know that well—who wanted to congratulate him on the free ride to Berkeley. Or someone with whom he'd got drunk and smoked a little pot with during that glorious summer between junior and senior year.

But it wasn't just a nameless face, an obscure ancillary character in the movie of his high school career. It was Alphie Moffit.

"Dude, you look like shit," he told Alphie, who indeed looked a little worse for wear. The kid had heavy bags under his eyes, and he was sweaty, sweating way too much considering he was inside an air-conditioned hallway, positioned under a vent that blew out a continuous gust of frosty air. "Did you and that idiot plant the clues last night? I thought I'd hear from you after you finished. Let me guess; you ran up your parents' phone bill texting again? What did I tell you, man? Texting is dumb. And expensive. My parents don't have it included in their plan, so just call me."

Alphie didn't respond. His eyes wandered across the hall as if he were on the lookout for something or someone. As if he didn't want anyone to overhear the following conversation.

"What's wrong?" RJ asked, shutting his locker after completely forgetting why he'd opened it in the first place. Maybe he'd just wanted to smell it one last time, indulge in that collection-of-old-books scent. "You're starting to freak me out with those bug eyes of yours."

"Something is wrong with Randall."

The way he said it was cryptic enough. RJ couldn't fully tell if Alphie was putting him on or if he was serious.

"What do you mean? Is he in trouble? Did he get arrested? Fuck, I knew I shouldn't have put that little stoner in charge of setting up the clues."

"He wasn't arrested," Alphie said, shaking his head. The band of sweat around his forehead glistened beneath the fluorescent lighting above.

"You look...unwell. You sick? Getting a summer cold or something?"

Alphie squinted as if struggling to keep his eyes open. "I'm not feeling that great, no. But Randall. He's worse. So much worse."

"What happened to you two idiots?"

"We went to the cemetery. The one on Cedarborough."

"Jesus, don't tell me! You'll ruin the hunt if you tell me where—"

"Shut up," Alphie grumbled, his lungs crackling, then he coughed a little. "Listen to me. Something happened there."

RJ was stuck on Alphie telling him to shut up but overlooked his disobedience and addressed the second half of his statement. "What happened?"

His head bobbed as he searched around for eavesdroppers. Once he deemed the area safe, he leaned in as far as he could without violating that unspoken code of personal space and whispered, "There was something in the cemetery. Or... some*one*. I'm not really sure."

"What the hell are you talking about, man?"

"The cemetery," he said, practically hissing.

RJ could tell Alphie's patience had been stolen by whatever sickness had assumed control of his body.

"There was something *in there* with us, man," Alphie continued. "It was only a feeling at first, but then...then I *saw* things, man. Things I can't adequately explain. My mind can't make any sense of it."

RJ looked Alphie directly in the eyes, noticing something different about them. The color of his irises was muted, almost gray, but there was something else too. Small flecks of...*gold*. Like the ribbons and streamers hanging from the ceiling, flaunting the school colors. He'd never looked at his friend's eyes long enough to tell what color they *had* been, but now they were a milky gray peppered with gold splinters.

"Try," RJ said, finally.

"There was a shadow...a woman. I saw her. A ghost, maybe. She had these eyes, man. They were..."

Alphie didn't say, but RJ could somehow read his thoughts. *Gold,* he wanted to say. *Definitely gold.*

"She had these things growing out of her..."

RJ laughed, clutching his stomach for effect. "Are you serious, dude? That's the best you can come up with?"

Alphie's face bunched with wrinkles. Before RJ could dismiss him again, Alphie lashed out, grabbing his friend by the collar. Nose to nose, it seemed Alphie no longer cared about trespassing that invisible personal barrier.

"Listen to me, asshole," Alphie spat. His breath reeked of something nasty, sewer water and gutted fish parts perhaps. "I *saw* something out there, and I didn't imagine shit. Randall saw it too, I think. A woman. She was... I don't know what she was, but I don't want to find out."

He let go of RJ's shirt and backed away.

"Jesus, man. What's gotten into you? And have you ever heard of mouthwash? Fuck."

"Don't do it," Alphie said, shaking his head slowly.

"Do what?" RJ was getting pissed. Whatever game Alphie was playing, he didn't want any part of it. This was supposed to be a peaceful last day, filled with nostalgia and pleasant memories. If Alphie intended on shitting all over that idea, he was doing a hell of a job. "Do what?"

"The Hunt."

"Oh, fuck off, man."

"I'm serious. Tonight...that place...the town... I don't think it's safe right now. Might..." He coughed again, and this time he didn't bother covering his mouth. The wheeze in his chest became noticeably louder. "Might never be safe again."

"You're fucking bonkers, dude. You know that?"

Alphie glared at him. RJ wasn't sure whether he would explode with anger or launch into a coughing fit, but whatever the crazy fuck was going to do, it was going to happen soon.

To his surprise, Alphie only smiled. "You're a fool."

"And you're an asshole. Now go home and take a shower. Sleep off whatever you fucking took last night. Tell Randall to rest up too. We're counting on you dickheads to be around later during the Hunt. Remember, each team gets one hint, and since you two fuckholes are the only ones who know the answers to the clues, we're relying on you. Got it?"

Alphie gritted his teeth. "The town. Is. Not. Safe. It belongs to *her* now." His lips stretched. "It belongs to *Mother*."

And then he walked away, stumbling down the hall like a barfly after closing time.

He watched Alphie stagger down the row of lockers and disappear around the corner. RJ shook his head and returned to his locker, opening it again. "Fucking juniors, man," he whispered, still trying to remember what he needed from his locker because there wasn't much left to pick from. Alphie's bizarre appearance and asinine speech really scrambled his thoughts.

As crazy as Alphie had sounded, RJ got the sense he was telling the truth, that maybe he had seen something out there in the cemetery lurking among the shadows.

That maybe whatever it was, it was evil.

The town is not safe.

A shiver coursed through him, and it had nothing to do with the blast of cool air coming from the vents above.

6

Principal Fritz's office smelled moldy, old, and in need of some new furniture and a fresh coat of paint. It reminded Jewel Conti of home.

She'd been planted in front of his desk for ten minutes, swiveling back and forth, waiting for the douche-canoe to enter. She didn't know exactly what he wanted with her, especially today, the last day of the year. Even if he caught a whisper of what she'd said to Maddie Rice, she doubted he'd discipline her. Kids could get away with more on last days.

When he entered with his cup of coffee in hand, he didn't speak a word. He closed the door behind him, strolled over to his desk, placed his mug (#1 PRINCIPAL!) on the desk, then sat down. Leaning back in his plush chair, which probably cost more than what Jewel's mother had in her checking account these last three months combined, Fritz glared at her. The anger those eyes held bled away. All that remained was concern. And interest. They really dug into her, and she got the sense he was trying to access her thoughts through some telepathic means, attempting to rummage around her brain and unlock the secrets within. His penetrating stare made her uncomfortable, so she fidgeted as if sitting atop a bed of worms.

Rubbing her shoulder, the spot where she'd given herself an inverted cross tattoo a year back. Glancing about the room, she surveyed the accolades the dutiful principal kept on display, mostly to show the bad children of Hooperstown Middle that he was a fine principal and man, one built from strong moral fiber.

"I want to help you," he said plainly.

She scoffed. "Yeah right, man. No one wants to help me."

And she wasn't lying. Not even her own parents wanted to help her, let alone a stranger. Hell, some days it was as if the people who had given her life were determined to tear her down. As if they'd gotten off on the idea of seeing their only daughter suffer a miserable life, one as wretched and dismal as their own. Every fight, every thrown object, every insult that could never be taken back because it had crossed so many uncrossable lines—it was like a game to them. A game they had won every goddamn time.

Luckily, her father had gotten himself pinched last year, gotten hit with his third possession charge—six ounces of pot and a brick of cocaine. The "brick," she had overheard, was enough to put pops away for a long time. How long, she didn't exactly know because Ava Conti never told her those things, but she wasn't stupid—she didn't expect to see Carl Conti's face in the crowd come high school graduation.

Graduation. Ha.

The idea was laughable. She had as much of a chance of attending college as the New York Metropolitans had of winning the pennant. Even community college was out of the question. Forget the grades, the barely-passing results and only "passing" because her teachers couldn't bring themselves to spend another year with *her*—there was also the money issue. *Issue* meaning she didn't have any. And the money her parents *were* able to scrounge up (well, just mom now) went directly up their noses, into their lungs, or was shot directly into the crook of their arms.

Yeah, so, college was out.

"Well, *I* want to help you, Jewel. I know the system has failed you. I know you've been taken from your home and placed in foster care more times than you can probably count. I can't imagine what that's been like for you."

It had been perdition for living souls, but she didn't say so. There was no sense revisiting those awful places, the creepy parents the system had temporarily stuck her with when Mom and Dad were in trouble with the law. The countless times she'd been touched inappropriately and mistreated in devious ways, memories she would burn out of her head if such a thing were possible.

Fritz reached into his desk and withdrew a folded piece of paper. When he opened it, Jewel was staring down at a flyer, one she might have recognized from some nondescript Hooperstown street, stapled to a telephone pole. On it, in big black letters, were written the words "CHRISTIAN YOUTH CLUB." There was a giant cross printed beneath them, three squiggles drawn on each side as if to illustrate the insignia was glowing brightly. She imagined if this were a color copy, the cross would be gold, the surrounding light a canary yellow.

"Are you fucking serious, dude?"

Fritz twitched at the cuss word but let it slide. "Yes, I am."

"What the hell is this?"

"It's a youth group where I volunteer every summer. Just a few nights a week. I think it might help you find a different path."

"A different path?" An incredulous bark popped out of her mouth. She couldn't believe the ballbag on this clown. "A different path? Dude, look at me. Do I look like I belong at a *Christian* youth group?"

"No, you look like you belong in a homeless shelter. Or maybe a juvenile detention center."

"Been to both, buddy. What else you got?"

His eyes sharpened on the flyer.

"Nah, I'm good." She handed the flyer back.

He didn't take it.

She stood up. "I don't need this shit—"

"Sit down," he said with commanding authority.

She froze. She didn't know why. It wouldn't have been the first time she got pissed, stood up, and stormed out of his office. But she stayed, and it definitely wasn't the flyer keeping her there. She had the urge to shred it, spit on it, and throw it in Fritz's face. How dare he suggest such an awful thing.

"Sit," he said again, this time presenting his palm in a relaxed, smooth manner.

She debated. Run or stay. A part of her wanted to dive through the window, run away from Hooperstown Middle and never look back. Hell, a part of her wanted to flee Hooperstown altogether, and for good. Take the bus to Atlantic City on a one-way ticket. She didn't know what she'd do once she was there, but judging from what she'd experienced in foster care, she could probably make some bucks as an underaged prostitute. Probably more than some.

The idea nauseated her though, so she lowered herself back into the chair.

"I'm not saying I have all the answers, Jewel." He tapped the flyer with his finger, creating a hollow knock that seemed to reverberate through her. *Hollow,* she thought. *Like me.* "I'm not saying God has them either. The answers are within you. You can choose how to live your life. No one else. Now, I've seen rough kids come through this place—kids a thousand times meaner and nastier and more screwed up than you. I've seen them change. Get better. Start caring about themselves. About other people. Positive thoughts and human interaction do wondrous things for the body and soul. Don't get caught up on the *Jesus* aspect—this place is very different from the traditional Sunday teachings. We worship Him differently. We don't ascribe to everything the Bible says—we use the teachings and scripture as loose guidelines and—"

She was starting to fade a little. The inverted cross on her arm began to burn, a phantom sensation, but it hurt like a real torch flame licking her skin.

"I'm sorry," Fritz said. "I've probably already talked you out of it."

Her eyes fell on the flyer. Beside the name and the cross, a few other informational bits were printed on it. The address of where it was held—a place downtown—and a few selling points on what the program offered—Music! Games! Singing! Fun!

None of those things sounded particularly Christian, especially that last part. *Fun*. Jewel couldn't remember the last time she had some.

"Look, I'm not expecting you to commit to anything. This isn't anything like that. There's no fee or membership service. You come when you want, leave when you want."

She couldn't remove her eyes from *Fun*.

"Ball's in your court, Miss Conti. I hope to see you there."

She gripped the flyer so tightly her fingertips blanched; she had no idea something virtually weightless could feel so heavy.

7

The day had come and gone, and now, sitting in eighth period, watching the clock, Doug Simms could not wait for the bell to ring. The anticipation of summer was almost too much, and he was having trouble keeping still. Mr. Boxberger, his English teacher, sat behind his desk, three freestanding fans pointed in his direction to combat the classroom's shoddy air vents. He reclined as far back as his publicly funded chair would allow, hands behind his head, a smug smile printed on his face. Doug clearly wasn't the only one counting down the seconds.

"I've never looked forward to summer more than this year," Boxberger said, his face glowing as he scanned the faces looking back at him. Apparently, he'd gotten a new job in another state and this was his last day at Hooperstown Middle. The move had been public knowledge for quite some time, and Boxberger had coasted through the fourth marking period, his lesson plans relying on movies instead of teaching the kids the marvels of classic literature. "I'm not going to miss a single one of you. Not a *single* one."

"What about me, Box-booger?" Jesse asked, his left hand shooting into the air.

"Oh, *especially* you, Di Falco. God, if I could strangle one of you and get away with it, it'd *definitely* be you."

Sporadic giggles circled the classroom, though most of them knew the testy educator probably wasn't kidding. He really would strangle Jesse if given the chance.

Jesse strained his face, expressing uncertainty. "I don't know, Box-booger, I don't think you're allowed to talk to students like that, threatening them and all. What would Principal Fritz think?"

Boxberger cocked back his head and howled with laughter. "Kid, come on. What are they gonna do? Fire me? I'm outta here after today. They can't do a damn thing."

The bell rang and the students bolted from their seats, the cacophony of their chairs grinding against the faux-marbled floor almost deafening. Before Doug and his friends could follow the rest of the bustling herd, Boxberger launched himself from his seat and stepped in front of his own desk, throwing down his arm like one of those parking garage gates, culling them from the pack. Doug watched the last of the students merge with the hallway traffic, confused as to why he wasn't among them.

"You three," Boxberger said, his smile lingering as he demonstrated the most authoritative tone he'd exhibited all year. "Wait just a second."

"Jesus, Box-booger," Jesse said, slumping his shoulders. "You're really holding us up here. Whaddya want?"

"I just…" He took a reflective glance at the chalkboard, the words HAVE A GREAT SUMMER inscribed in perfect cursive.

Doug didn't think he'd written it—the handwriting was too perfect. The notes scrawled on his graded term papers had been written much sloppier. Next, their teacher's eyes wandered to the overstuffed boxes of classroom items, the goofy knick-knacks he had used to decorate the room, the ones that carried his own quirky touch. Doug noticed the bouquet of white flowers that had stood on the edge of the man's desk for the past few weeks. There were also historic paintings and old leather-bound books, posters with various inspirational quotes written on them that were hardly inspiring to the minds of young teenagers. Doug noticed an oil painting called "The Founding of Hooperstown" which had been done by a local artist, detailing the meeting between Henry Hooper, his band of followers, and the local natives who had lived in huts deep in the land's surrounding forest. Boxberger had been a self-proclaimed history buff and lover of local lore. In fact, the new job was a gig teaching history, his dream job before coming to Hooperstown Middle. English, he had grumbled many times, was not his first love, but it was the only job available when he had applied for the transfer nearly three years ago.

"I know the four of us have been through a lot over the last two years," Boxberger said "Not many students have the same teacher all throughout middle school, and things became quite chippy at times—not proud of it, but it is what it is. And even though most of the things that transpired weren't really my fault—"

"Dude, you tried to bang my mom at the seventh-grade dance," Grady reminded him.

Doug bit his lip to keep from laughing. Jesse buried his grin in his shoulder.

But it was true. Boxberger had hit on her, reciting a sleazy pick-up line that wouldn't work on a cheap hooker (Grady's father's words). She had grabbed another parent chaperon—Mr. Stevenson, Billy Stevenson's father—and hung out by him for the remainder of the night. Mr. Stevenson had done right by her, made sure Boxberger didn't overstep his boundaries. The whole thing was weird, especially since Boxberger was married, but no one made a big deal of it. Except Mr. Pope. When he found out about Boxberger and his attempt to sweep his wife off her feet, he had wanted to march down to the school under broad daylight and beat the holy-living-hell out Boxberger in front of the entire faculty. But, thankfully, Mrs. Pope had put a pin in that idea. He also wanted to file a complaint with the school board, but Doug wasn't sure if that actually happened. Boxberger had retained his job, so he suspected the grievance never went further than the Pope household.

"Yes, well, we've gone over this—the whole thing's hearsay. Rumors and nothing more, all right? You have no proof of that, you have *no* proof—" He was getting agitated, all sorts of worked up, pink flowers of embarrassment blooming on his cheeks. His eyes widened as if he'd suddenly realized something important. "Look, I wanted to apologize to you little shits, okay? I wanted to make amends for the things I may have said over the years—"

"You told Jesse he looked like a fuck-weasel," Doug said.

Boxberger seemed to bounce the insult back and forth in his head, as if the comment may have some credence, something he shouldn't be apologizing for. "Well, let's be fair—he's awfully weaselly-looking."

"Oh yeah?" Jesse said, turning toward him and pounding his fists on the desk. "Well, you look like a toad fucked a salamander and gave birth to a goat, you fu—!"

Grady and Doug immediately jumped in, hooking their arms around Jesse's, peeling him away from making a bad decision that could potentially carry over to next year. Doug clapped his hand over his friend's mouth (wouldn't be the first time, certainly wouldn't be the last) before he could finish that insult or say anything else.

Boxberger, who had resigned to folding his arms like an entertained onlooker of some big event, backed himself into the corner, the area between his desk and the wall. He raised his fists as if he was ready to throw down. Then he took a deep breath and dropped his fleshy, bony hammers. Adjusting his tie, he cleared his throat and fixed his glasses. "In honor of our final day, the last time we will ever see each other..." His eyes slimmed, subtly hinting at the *possibility* of them meeting again, somewhere down the line, somewhere in life. Because life can be funny like that. "And starting anew, I will let all of what just happened go."

Grady shook his head. "You're the worst, man."

"I'm..." He shook his head. "No, I'm not the worst."

Doug nodded toward the exit, the hallway of screaming, excited children eager to begin the greatest summer of their lives. "Let's go, guys. We have stuff to do before tonight."

"I'm not the worst," Boxberger called after them, as if trying to convince himself as well as the kids. "I'm a good teacher!" His words now lacked confidence. "I'm...I'm a good person."

His words barely registered as they reached the door, crossed the threshold, headed out into the hallway, well on their way to the most interesting and terrifying night of their young lives.

CHAPTER TWO

All Hunts Have Rules

1

The basement was more crowded than Doug had expected. Even though the space between the cinderblock walls ran the length of the living room above, the amount of people gathered there was overwhelming, giving him a slight bout of claustrophobia.

As he and his two best friends descended the staircase, Doug felt as if maybe coming here had been a mistake, that the three of them didn't belong. Not only that, but the night had presented itself with alternative plans, arguably better choices, and he knew—deep down—he should be there instead.

You don't belong here, he told himself, looking around the surprisingly well-lit, unfinished cellar, surveying the faces of over twenty high school kids. They were all chatting and laughing, and more importantly, they weren't paying attention to their new guests. Doug fought off the notion to head back upstairs and walk home, with or without his two best friends.

Not home, he reminded himself. *To Maddie's.*

Her party didn't start until eight, and it was only six-thirty. If he hustled, he could head home, change, and jog over there in under two hours.

Do it, he thought. *Screw the Hunt. It'll probably suck anyways.*

He didn't actually believe that. In fact, he knew the game would be rad, a night he'd never forget, mostly because Jesse had spent the last few weeks talking it up, telling them about the outrageous things that had happened in years past. Tales of mystery and fun, stories of getting chased by uppity shop owners, getting run out of certain forbidden areas by the local police. Things that made his pulse quicken just thinking about them.

Doug put Maddie's party in the far corner of his mind and concentrated on the activity he had committed to. The Hunt was starting off like it always had, the way Doug understood it. The night kicked off with a meeting in RJ's basement, a brief assembly where the orchestrator went over the rules, the dos and don'ts, divided everybody into teams, and of course, delivered the first clue. In the center of the basement rested a couch where three seniors sat, waiting for RJ to fire up the meeting. Doug figured his crew were the last ones to arrive.

Jesse's brother hopped down the last two steps, Karen following closely behind. Jesse and Grady were right behind them. Doug played the part of the caboose and was last to plant his feet on the concrete slab.

RJ strolled over with his arms open, ready to wrap Jimmy in a bear hug.

"What's up, bro?" RJ greeted him, squeezing his friend as if they hadn't seen each other in weeks. "You brought the kids." Something short of a jester's grin touched his lips. Doug got the sense their presence had been previously approved, which settled his nerves a fair bit. "Good stuff, good stuff." He faced Jesse, mussing up his hair as if he were a kindergartner. "You ready to help your big bro lose this year?"

"Pssh," Jesse said, waving off RJ's friendly trash talk. "We're gonna wipe the floor with you buttholes."

"Ooooh, I can see you've inherited the Di Falco family mouth."

Jesse opened his mouth to say something else, probably just as smart as his other comment, probably to tell RJ where he could put *his* mouth, but Doug kicked the back of his leg to shut him up.

"All right," RJ said, turning to the crowd. "Listen up! We're all here now! Let's get this party started!"

The entire group brought their conversations to a murmur, their voices petering out as they turned their attention to the front wall where a giant dry-erase board stood. The board was sectioned into quadrants, each quarter representing a different color—blue, red, yellow, purple. Below them were the names of each participating guest. Doug noticed the yellow team had Jimmy and Karen's names scribbled beneath it, and beneath theirs was written THE KIDS.

Great, Doug thought. *They didn't even bother to write our names. Do they even know our names?*

Doug figured they probably did not. *The Kids* clearly weren't important enough, an afterthought at best. And, honestly, that didn't bother him much. His thoughts had left the room altogether, floated away from the basement, its occupants, and the giant white board, and had migrated back to Maddie's party, his destination of choice. There was no denying it. Every time he tried to think of something else, Maddie's face appeared in his mind, the hand-written note she'd left in his locker dangling in front of him, the smell of her fruity fragrances wafting across his nostrils. A lungful of those citrusy, floral scents. He'd practically zoned out completely, as if he were dreaming on his toes.

"Yo," Jesse said, snapping his fingers inches from Doug's nose. "You still here?"

Doug blinked several times as his reverie fell apart, crumbling before him, giving way to the basement. "What?"

Grady shoved a finger in his face. "What are you thinking about? Quick. Spill it. Better not be what I think it is."

"Nothing."

A series of wrinkles rippled across Jesse's forehead. "Bullshit."

Grady's finger wiggled in accusatory circles. "You're thinking of her, aren't you?"

"What?" Doug closed his eyes and shook his head rapidly. "No. No way." He avoided their hard gazes as he turned his attention back to RJ and the rules of the Hunt.

"All right," RJ announced. "First order of business, we need team names."

"Good," Jesse whispered to his friends. "Because I'd hate to be team yellow."

Grady asked, "What's wrong with yellow?"

"It's the color of pee, dude."

"Oh, well, yeah—there's that."

"Shut up," Doug told them, concentrating on RJ and his agenda. Maybe if he bought into the night, sold himself on the fun they'd have, the once in a lifetime experience they'd gain from this all-night escapade, then maybe he could push Maddie's party out of his mind. For good this time. There would be other parties, other get-togethers where he and Maddie would meet. Other opportunities to tell her about his feelings. The summer of their fourteenth year was long and offered much in the way of new experiences. It would not disappoint; he was sure of it. If he played his cards right, this might be the summer of romantic affairs.

Tonight, though—tonight was about the Hunt, an opportunity that might never happen again. He doubted he and his friends would carry on the tradition when it came time to run things. And sure, yeah, there was always next year when Jimmy was a senior, when he could possibly take the helm, but tonight was the first night of summer before entering high school. There was something special in the air, an electric spark that seemed to entwine them, something he felt as deep in his bones.

Maddie Rice and her awesome parties would have to wait.

"All right, Sanderson," RJ said, pointing to one of the guys on the couch. "Team name, go."

Sanderson blurted out, "Sandy's Psychos."

Next to the word BLUE, RJ scribbled *Sandy's Psychos*. "Sticking with last year's name. All right. Boring, but all right. Becca, yours?"

A skinny girl wearing a winter beanie despite the hot air outside said, "Becca's Bitches, bitches!"

The entire room got a laugh out of that one.

Even RJ chuckled as he recorded the team name. "*Very* original. Okay." Once finished, he pointed the marker at Jimmy. "Jimmy. Name. Go."

Jimmy looked to the kids, his brother in particular. No one offered a suggestion, so Jimmy turned back to RJ and said, "Team Watchmen."

Some heads nodded in approval, maybe in recognition of the pop culture reference but probably not. Others didn't react at all. Cleary it wasn't the most popular name, but Doug appreciated it.

RJ jotted down the name next to YELLOW. "Nice. Creepy. I like it. Undoubtedly some weird nerd thing I don't understand, but I'll allow it."

It wasn't all that creepy, at least that wasn't the intention. Doug knew *The Watchmen,* Alan Moore's popular comic book, was Jesse's personal favorite. Jimmy's too. They had each burned through the graphic novel a dozen times and bonded over them. Comic books in general were a mutual hobby, but that story in particular struck a chord with the Di Falco brothers. Doug had read it last summer—upon Jesse's persistent recommendation— and thought it was pretty good but nothing to rave about. It certainly wasn't *Uncanny X-Men.*

PURPLE was the last team to choose their name. Their leader, a burly boy harboring clusters of acne on both cheeks he tried to hide beneath the scruff of a young man's beard, elected The Purple People Eaters as their name. No doubt a throwback to the infamous defensive line of the '70s Minnesota Vikings. The boy, Richie Gorva, had started at left end for Hooperstown High since he'd been a freshman, so the football reference made sense. The girls on the team didn't seem too fond of the name and, apparently, had no say in the matter.

RJ recorded the name and turned back to the group. "Perfect. Now that *that* is taken care of, let's go over the ground rules. Real basic, guys and girls. You will each receive one clue. That clue will lead you onto the next clue and so on until the Hunt is over. There are a total of seven clues. The team to solve the last clue first wins the Hunt. You will all be allowed to call in and get *one* hint. Just one, so use it wisely." He tapped the board, the spot where he'd written a telephone number. "This is Alphie Moffit's cell. He'll be on standby the entire night. He was feeling a little under the weather earlier, but I'm sure he's fine now."

Someone asked, "Are you sure? I didn't see him in school today."

RJ paused, nodded slowly. "Yeah, he's fine. He'll be there when you need him. He wouldn't let us down. Anyway, I saw him in school today, and he gave me the first clue." RJ slapped four index cards down on the coffee table. He spread them out across the glass top. "One for each of you."

Jimmy leaned over and grabbed one for Team Watchmen. The other team leaders snatched their respective cards and retreated to their corners of the basement.

Doug tried to steal a glance at the first clue, but Jimmy held it in a way only he and Karen could see it. Once they were done looking it over, he gave the card to Jesse, who shared it with the rest of the squad.

THE NEXT CLUE IS IN YOUR <u>POCKET</u>.
NUMBER 8.

In your pocket? Doug wondered. He knew the answer was simple, as the clues for these things rarely required much in the way of smarts save for a basic knowledge of the town's geographical layout. *Pocket, pocket, pocket.* Why had that word been underlined?

The answer was there, he thought, but where exactly he couldn't put his finger on.

"Now that you have your clues," RJ said, raising his hands as if they were green flags over a stock car race. His arms slashed through the air and he shouted, "Go!"

The teams scattered in all different directions, gathering the items they'd put down upon their arrival—coffee cups, purses, cigarettes. Jimmy, Karen, and the kids hadn't left anything, and they were the closest to the stairs, which meant they had a head start.

Doug rushed up the stairs, Team Watchmen on his heels, the rest of the pack crowding the bottom of the stairwell. By the time he reached the Hollorans' front door, Doug had forgotten all about Maddie Rice and her awesome party.

"The Corner Pocket!" Grady practically screamed, diving into the back of Jimmy's Thunderbird.

As soon as the kids piled into the convertible, Jimmy stepped on the gas and sped off down the street, toward the shade-struck horizon. The final traces of daylight filtered in through the tree-crowded vista, splashing the street with lavender spills. The transition between day and night had dropped the temperature by almost ten degrees, a noticeable and generous amount on what had been a mid-June scorcher.

"Grades, my man," Jimmy said, handing Karen a map of Hooperstown, "you are correct."

Karen had taken the passenger seat and claimed the role of navigator. She stashed the folded square in the glovebox; it was there if they needed it. Grady had the whole town memorized, every backstreet and major highway filed away in his brain like the personal documents on his father's computer.

"Is that the pool hall next to the strip joint on Route 9?" asked Jesse.

"Yep," Karen said, popping a smoke in her mouth and lighting up. Ghostly tendrils were whisked away by the whipping winds as the car crested the speed limit. "We used to go there all the time. Right, Jimmy?"

Jimmy nodded, smirking. "The pool hall, not the strip joint. Used to be one of the finer hangouts in Hooperstown. The old owner bought another space in Red River and sold The Corner Pocket to some dick stain who let the place go to complete shit. Still, a nice place to plant the second clue. Doubt the rest will be that easy to figure out."

Grady was proud of himself for figuring out the clue before Jesse and Doug. It seemed Jimmy and Karen knew almost immediately after it was handed to them, which meant the other teams had probably figured it out too. Jimmy was right; that had been an uncontested layup of a riddle. The race to the second clue would be an important one, one that could help determine the outcome of the Hunt, and it stood to reason they would arrive first since they had been the first ones out of the basement. Grady felt good about their odds. As long as they didn't botch the next few clues, they had a good shot at winning this thing.

He looked over at Doug, saw his friend staring at the passing houses and trees, seemingly lost in thought. The kid's face was a blanket of expressionless flesh, showing no clues of the cognitive art taking place between his ears. But Grady knew Doug wanted to be at Maddie's, and hell, part of Grady wished his friend had gone there instead. Especially seeing him now, the conflict all but etched on his face. That wasn't to say he didn't want to spend time with his best friend in what would undoubtedly become a spectacular all-nighter, but because he wanted to see Doug happy. And Maddie Rice made Doug Simms happy. Almost *too* happy.

This is it, Grady said to himself. *This is the downfall of our friendships. Girlfriends.*

He didn't think that was true, not exactly, but the notion wasn't all that far-fetched. He could easily envision a future where Doug bailed on their plans to go hang out with Maddie at the mall or take her to the movies. Their time together would (at the very least) get sliced in half. He wanted his friend to be happy, sure, but there was also a selfish half of him that wished—hoped?—Maddie wasn't all that into him.

Grady ran his hand through his hair, fixing what the topless convertible and the wild winds had disturbed, extricating himself from his thoughts, which wasn't a difficult task because Jimmy had turned on the radio and was now blasting DMX's "Ruff Ryders' Anthem" about as loud as the sound system could handle. The boxed speakers in the trunk vibrated the back seats, and when they buzzed, Grady's entire body felt like it had been hit with an electric jolt, his spine going somewhat numb each time the 808s hit. Still, the rapper's growling and threatening lyrics was not enough to drown his current thought. He was now stuck on the concern that if his parents were to somehow find out about the Hunt and this all-night extravaganza, then he'd be grounded for life. Forget summer; he'd never be allowed out of the house again. He could picture (almost with perfect clarity) his father shaking a finger in his face, centimeters away from his nose. The disappointment he'd express in so many words. The insults. The blame that would be placed upon him, blame for things Grady had no control over; their parents' financial situation, their somewhat rocky marriage. His father's job was a soul-sucking nine-to-fiver that—over the years—had turned into a nine-to-niner. *Both* of his parents' daily drinking habits bordered on alcoholism. All of these lovely things would surface during his scolding, he was sure of it, mostly because that was how things went down in the Pope household. It could never be about just one thing. A simple argument always sparked a major meltdown, and it was all about Grady. *Grady did this* and *Grady did that,* even if none of it was actually true. And that was because he had no siblings to help absorb some of the blame. Nope, Grady had to shoulder it all.

He pushed these thoughts away, telling himself tonight was a miracle and not to waste it by dwelling on such worries. To let the personal issues slide for just one night. Tonight was about fun, fun experienced with his two best buds in the entire world. Tonight deserved to be savored. For that matter, the whole summer demanded excitement, a festive approach and nothing less. There'd be plenty of time to worry about the real world later. Like in high school or some time beyond it—college, maybe, if Grady lived that long. A morbid thought, sure, but sometimes Grady dreamed that one of his parents would lose it one day, *snap* as they say, take the shotgun his father kept locked in the basement and do all three of them in at once, a double-murder-suicide that would grace the covers of every newspaper across the state. He'd dreamed about this often, ending up on the news, picturing the DO NOT CROSS tape that would surround his parents' property. It was a haunting image, a disgusting notion he knew he shouldn't have conjured in the first place, but brains could be weird sometimes. Grady's was no exception. He often wandered into borderline ludicrous dream-lands, the entire scenario a dark fantasy because things like that didn't happen in neat places like Hooperstown, yet there was a persistent presence that continued to drive these dreams. It was hard work tempering their appearances, keeping them submerged in the inky darkness that crowded his mind.

As Grady forced his overactive imagination to relax, Jimmy pulled into the parking lot of The Corner Pocket. Jimmy was hopping over the driver's side door while simultaneously putting the T-bird in park. He was halfway to the establishment's front door before Grady thought about unbuckling his seatbelt. Jesse and Doug were climbing out of the back, giggling about something Grady hadn't heard due to his unsettling, roaming thoughts.

He followed them into The Corner Pocket and saw the check-in line had been held up. The pool hall itself was old-looking, in desperate need of renovations, and smelled like dead cigarettes and abused leather. The atmosphere was hazy at best, mostly due to the amount of tobacco being smoked, a puffer at almost every table. Some were hitting cigarettes while others sucked on the wet ends of big brown cigars, but the smoke rose together and formed a formidable cloud that blanketed the crumbling, water-stained acoustic ceiling tiles. A guy at the table near the entrance was smoking a black cigarette that smelled like Grady's mother's spice rack. It wasn't the most pleasant of scents, but it wasn't as disgusting as plain tobacco smoke either. Grady didn't care for any of it, and he wondered how long it would take to uncover the next clue. He hoped he wouldn't come down with lung cancer before they found it. The thought of contracting some deadly disease brought back the memory from earlier, on the bus, the somber expression on Abby Allen's face and how he'd failed to comfort the sad girl. He wondered what Lauren Sullivan was doing at this exact moment. She was probably wishing she hadn't come down with cancer, sure. But was she also crying about how the majority of her last summer before high school would be spent in a hospital bed, engaged in a fight for her life?

Grady wondered if it would not only be her last summer before high school, but her last summer *period*. He hated himself for thinking that, but it was the truth. He knew one thing about the Big C—cancer meant death. A disease that grows, filling your entire body with rot.

A chill funneled through him, and he knew it wasn't from the cool air pouring down from the ceiling registers.

The place was pretty packed, mostly with older men who looked like they belonged to biker gangs. There were a few younger folks, some of whom appeared to be in their mid-twenties. A few middle-aged dudes and ladies, all laughing at unheard jokes, taking turns stroking the pool cue, sinking shots and missing them, smiling and frowning depending on the outcome of their play. Absolutely no kids, he noticed. No one under the age of eighteen.

Jimmy approached the guy behind the counter, a crusty-looking fellow, his unshaven face displaying whiskers of varying gray. He folded his arms and puffed away on his cigarette, blowing plumes of white smoke into the already-hazy atmosphere.

"So, my friends planted the next clue, you see," Jimmy said, dragging his finger across the wooden counter, as if he needed the man to visualize how the game worked, as if words weren't enough. As if the proprietor couldn't understand the simple concept of scavenger hunts. "And it's here, somewhere in the pool hall. We're here to find it, man."

The man didn't look puzzled. Quite the opposite; he simply seemed to not give a shit. "Let me get this straight…" He took two quick puffs before completing the thought. "You want to come in here, play your little scavenger hunt game, and not pay for a goddamn table?"

Jimmy prepared a response, but before he could unleash it, Karen stepped forward, leaning with her chest over the counter. Grady wasn't convinced she was trying to bribe the guy with a cleavage shot, but he wasn't *un*convinced either. "Listen, sir. We just want to find the next clue and be on our way. No trouble really. We'll be out of your hair before you can say 'pumpkin pie.' Mm'Kay?"

While Karen tried sweet-talking the curmudgeonly proprietor, using a seductive Marilyn Monroe-tone almost lyrical to Grady's ears, Jimmy craned his head and shot his brother a look. A subtle nod and sideways eye roll in the direction of the sprawling pool hall. Grady knew exactly what he was thinking. Jesse and his friends were to explore the area, locate the next clue, and get the hell out of there before things at the counter escalated.

Jesse slipped behind his brother while turning to Grady and Doug. "You guys go," he whispered. "Follow my lead." He turned back, wedged his way in front of Jimmy, and placed his arms on the counter. "Excuse me, Daddy Warbucks. But where's the pisser in this dirt-hole?"

"Dirt-hole?" the guy asked, lifting his brow. "Why, you little pissant shit. How dare you insult me in my own establishment."

"Well, I wouldn't have to if you cleaned the joint for once." Jesse dabbed the counter with his finger. "Look at this sticky mess! Did someone spank one out while waiting for their order of nachos? Huh? You running a spank bank or a pool hall, bro?"

Jesse continued to run his mouth while Grady and Doug slipped out of sight, down the stairs that led to the seemingly endless rows of pool tables. Once they were hidden behind a half-wall and a cluster of players, they rushed down the main aisle.

"What are we looking for, exactly?" Doug asked, whipping his head back and forth. He put his nose in the crook of his arm as a roaming cloud of smoke entered their space.

"Number eight," Grady said, the statement sounding more like he'd asked it. "That's what the clue said." He looked back toward the counter and saw Jesse amping up his antics, tossing his hands in the air and grabbing hold of his hair as if he were outraged by the particular situation. The owner had some backup now, two burly gentlemen whose biceps were bigger than the three fourteen-year-olds' arms combined. Not one of them looked amused by his performance, and it was only a matter of seconds before they discovered what was happening, before they sniffed out the ruse. "We have to hurry."

"Table eight?"

Grady shrugged. "It's an option. But which one is table eight? They aren't labeled."

They glanced around the setup, trying to pinpoint the way the tables had been arranged, trying to decipher which table had been dubbed the eighth. Logically speaking, the table closest to the stairs was probably *numero uno,* and the one to the right of it was number two. So on and so forth, down the line. If that was the case, then the eighth table would have been the last one in the second row, as there were four tables per row. Of course *numero ocho* was occupied by a crew of gentlemen who looked like they rode nothing but Harleys, drank nothing but cheap beer, and did nothing else but beat up innocent civilians for the sheer fun of it.

Shit, Grady thought, a pang of hopelessness carving up his chest. *This is going to be a problem.*

The boys looked to each other, their solemn expressions not doing a lick of good in the confidence department. Grady deferred to Doug, who usually kept his cool in tight situations. They didn't think of each other this way, had never spoken about the dynamic of their trio, but Grady always got the sense that if there *were* a leader between them, it was Doug. Not that that was a *thing.* Because it wasn't. But when Grady mused about their friendship model, Doug was the one they looked to for guidance.

"You do the talking," Grady said.

"Me?" Doug shook his head. "What the hell do I even say? All of those dudes look like they could double for The Undertaker."

"I don't know. Make it up. You're good like that."

"Damn it." Doug breathed through his nose, deeply. "Okay. Search the pockets and under the table."

Grady nodded and watched his friend take that first hesitant step toward table eight. Once there, standing in front of the group of bikers, Doug waved, an innocent gesture that couldn't possibly be misinterpreted as anything but amiable. There were four men and two women, all six of them tatted from their fingertips to their faces. Two of the men had facial tattoos, obligatory teardrops under their left eyes.

"Hi!" Doug said with nervous enthusiasm. "My friend and I are playing a game with some friends. It's a...a scavenger hunt, and we...uh... We believe the next clue is somewhere at your table."

As Doug rambled and stuttered his way through the introduction, Grady circled the table, keeping a fair distance from the players in case one of them lashed out with a butterfly knife and stuck his belly. He didn't think that would *actually* happen, but he sure imagined it. Carefully peeking into the pockets, he avoided eye contact with the crew of wildlings. For some reason the women's rough appearances frightened him more. They looked dangerous, feral almost. Hungry, like little boys were the perfect snack. The way the Witch ogled Hansel and Gretel. The men just looked amused. But not the women. He got the eerie sense they wanted to hurt something.

The pockets proved empty and as Grady finished scoping out the last one, Doug said, "So you see? It's just a stupid game. Perhaps you've seen something at your table? A clue, maybe? Anything strange at all? A piece of paper with some confusing message on it?"

The players only stared at him. None of them blinked.

"Geez. Tough crowd."

Grady got on his knees and crawled under the table. He checked the table's belly and found copious clusters of hardened chewing gum representing every color of the rainbow, but no clues. No paper, no nothing. Just a slab of wood, a gummy graveyard. He rose up, disappointment clinging to his face.

"Anything?" Doug asked.

Grady shook his head as he shuffled over to his friend's side.

"Well," Doug said, waving to the table of bikers. "Thank you for not killing us."

A smattering of snickers rounded the circle. Even the women cracked smiles, letting go of their crusty personas. Grady suddenly felt better about the whole thing, his heart slowing, but only just a tad.

"What do we know?" Doug asked, turning away from table eight. At the front counter, things had escalated. The shop keep's security squad had ambled around the counter and were now crowded around Jesse, Jimmy, and Karen. The boss was saying something, shoving a finger in their faces and signaling to the front door. Grady assumed Team Watchmen was getting tossed.

"Shit," Grady murmured.

"We need to hurry."

Grady searched the room, surveying the posters on the walls. There were leftover Marlboro ads from the eighties hanging in frames, the giant cartoon cowboy lighting up and looking elated to breathe in that dangerous fog. On a separate poster, a cool camel rocked a pair of hip sunglasses as he puffed away, stoked about the prospects of catching some awful, irreversible disease. A photo of James Dean had been printed out, blown up, framed, and hung on the far wall, centered perfectly. Various other photos and posters decorated the nondescript walls. An official movie poster for *Pulp Fiction,* the one with Uma Thurman lying on her stomach, smoking a cigarette behind a resting firearm, was pinned to the wall to their right. Grady hadn't seen the movie yet (one of the *many* titles eternally banned at the Pope residence), but Doug and Jesse had raved about it on more than one occasion. Seeing the poster made him a bit jealous of his friends and their parental situations, but all of that dissipated the moment he laid eyes on the poster to the right of Uma—the one with a giant eight-ball on it.

"There!"

Doug followed Grady's finger to the poster. His eyes expanded, his smile broadening. "Yes!"

They sprinted across the pool hall, no longer caring about keeping their mission covert. Grady heard someone yell "HEY!" from the front counter, but he didn't glance back. In seconds they reached the poster and were removing it from the wall.

"What the hell?" bellowed the shopkeeper, but they ignored him.

"Hurry, man," Grady said, helping Doug lift the poster off its hangers. They set the frame down on its face. Attached to the backside, four pieces of paper had been taped. They each had a team color written on it, though the words were barely legible. Doug reached for the one marked YELLOW.

Before he saw his friend's fingers grace the next clue, a forceful hand slammed down on Grady's shoulder and ripped him away from the scene.

The men—the pool hall's makeshift security team—ushered the five of them through the door and issued them a stern warning. They shouted things, reiterating their scavenger hunt was not welcome here, that they should send word to any other "little shitheads" planning to trespass. Doug was pretty sure one bouncer referred to Jesse as a "mouthy little trash bag," which made Jesse, Jimmy, and Karen burst into gut-holding guffaws.

Once the bouncers and the owner retreated back into their sanctuary, Team Watchmen gathered around Jimmy's convertible. After the humor from the scenario faded, they were left with mere disappointment.

"Well, that went about as well as I thought it would," Jimmy said, scratching the back of his head.

Karen kissed him on the cheek and wrapped her arms around him. "We tried. Fucker couldn't give us two extra seconds."

Doug was the only one continuing to smile, bouncing on his heels with certain glee. "You guys." He held up the small square of paper with YELLOW scrawled across it in Alphie Moffit's appalling handwriting.

Jimmy's face broke into a wide grin. "Simms, you son of a bitch!"

Jesse lunged forth, wrapping his arms around his friend and squeezing him as if he'd just come home from war. "You got it!"

Grady patted him on the back. Karen laughed merrily as she removed another smoke from her pack.

They were back in business.

"Open it," Jimmy said, cracking his knuckles.

Doug slid his finger underneath the clear tape, broke the seal, and unfolded the square until it became a single sheet of loose-leaf paper.

WIDE. SCREEN. SILVER.

9.

A12.

Doug looked to his friends, somewhat disappointed in the reveal. This clue was even easier to solve than the first. Doug was starting to think Alphie Moffit and Randall Benoit had phoned in the whole thing. It was like they weren't even trying.

"The theater?" Grady asked.

"Yeah," Jimmy said. "There's only one in Hooperstown, and it's in the Star Point Plaza."

"What are we waiting for?" Jesse asked, beaming. He was the first one to plant himself in the convertible's backseat. "Onward!"

Doug hopped in next to him as the others took their seats. Just as they pulled out of the parking lot, a small convoy of the other contestants were descending on the pool hall, the other teams finally catching up. But they were much too late. Doug knew the pool hall, the proprietor and his crew of miscreants, would only set them back. He suspected the owner had probably thrown away the remaining clues, too. If that ended up being the case, the other teams were royally screwed. They had a sizable lead, and Doug was feeling pretty good about their odds. He checked his wristwatch and realized Maddie Rice's party had started fifteen minutes ago. Just as thoughts of Maddie resurfaced, her smiling face, the way she pulled back her dark hair in a frizzy bun, Doug noticed a shadow across the street, facing him, ambling into pools of light provided by the arching street lamps overhead.

It's Alphie Moffit, he thought, not sure at first. *Isn't it?*

But as the shadow meandered along the sidewalk, rocking back and forth like a novice sailor trying desperately to gain control of his sea legs, and entered the well-lit area, Doug recognized him with clarity. Then, Alphie stumbled back into the shadows like a blindfolded drunk. In the moment it took for the T-bird to pass him, Doug caught a glimpse of his face. His pallor was off, akin to the moon of that particular night. Two dark lines ran down his face from his eyes. Upon closer inspection, he noticed the two inky streams met at his chin and ran off, oily blooms staining his shirt near the collar. Drips and drops speckled his shirt as if a sloppy painter had used it as a drop cloth.

It took a minute for the scene to register with Doug's brain. He thought it was weird—*damn* weird—but after they had passed him, the Thunderbird streaking off toward the dark of night and the much-anticipated clues ahead, Doug shook his head, wondering if it had even really been Alphie.

Maybe it was just his imagination and his excitement teaming up to play tricks on him.

Yes, it was probably that.

Probably.

Most likely.

He didn't think of it again until later. Much later, when everything went to hell.

CHAPTER THREE

At The Movies

1

Can't Hardly Wait was an exceptional movie, but Jewel had already snuck in to see it last week. In her current mood, she was looking for something much darker, a flick sans sweet messages of hope and feel-good vibes. Something action-y, something with a lot of blood spatter. Maybe a severed head or two. And *guns*. God, yes, lots of guns and bullets and killing. She wanted to see people (or monsters) slaughtered across the screen in the most creative ways imaginable, and she wanted it right now.

This was partly because of Fritz's chat, his lecture, but also because of home and how miserable her mother had been the second she walked through the front door. She had come home from school and plopped herself down on the couch, ready to immerse herself in an afternoon of Jerry Springer and Maury Povich while snacking on pretzels and cola, after-school traditions that were not to be missed unless she had detention. Her mother had other plans though, stumbling into the living room on wobbly knees, hooting and hollering, her voice several decibels louder than required.

Jewel had asked her—politely, of course—to crank down her personal volume so the neighbors above (and to the left and right, for that matter) wouldn't hear every single filthy word that fell out of her mouth. That only antagonized her mother. Jewel could smell the whiskey on her breath from several feet away.

Ava jabbed her finger in Jewel's general direction, as if angrily pressing the numbers on an invisible telephone pad, she called her daughter a "filthy cunt" several times and asked her how many cocks she had sucked on her way home from school. Jewel had told her she'd lost count after the first hundred, a comment that earned an empty beer bottle chucked at her head. She wasn't sure if her mother's aim was good or just lucky (the latter, she later surmised), because the bottle had sailed gracefully through the air and caught her face above her right eyebrow hard enough to split the skin. The small gash hadn't required stitches, but the blood had flowed freely and longer than an average scrape. Her mother hadn't shown a lick of remorse. In fact, the bitch had carried on and on about how much she'd earned it— practically asked for it. How Jewel deserved so much more.

After Jewel got the bleeding to stop, she snuck out of the apartment via the bathroom window, strolled down the street, and headed directly for the movies, stopping at Dakota's on the way to see if he wanted in on the fun. He wasn't home though, so she'd decided not to veer too far off her path and head to Brennan's. His parents were decent folks, so they were probably taking him out for ice cream or to the arcade or whatever normal people did with their kids whom they loved and cherished and enjoyed spending time with.

Fuck the Scruggses, she thought as she ambled up Star Point 10's concrete stairway. Brennan might have been cool to hang out with, but his life was too normal in comparison. She couldn't exactly relate. Dakota's home was more on par with hers. Though his parents weren't drug fiends or abusive pricks, they were abusive in other ways. The controlling type, always trying to ratchet the kid down, suffocating him by enrolling him in every after-school program imaginable. This tactic had only caused Dakota to rebel. Now, the only after-school activity he participated in was detention and collecting cigarettes from the high school kids who were willing to sell to a minor.

Parents, she thought, hovering near the garbage at the far end of the theater's foyer. *Fuck 'em all, every last one of them.*

When she determined no one was looking, she dug through the trash, blindly searching for a discarded ticket stub, anything she could use to get past the ticket-taker perched on the barstool, blocking access to the long hall of theaters. She rooted around, pushing large soda cups and half-empty bags of popcorn for a good thirty seconds before locating something useful, her fingers gently sweeping the surface of that hard paper square. She pulled out a single stub and saw it was for *Can't Hardly Wait.* If worse came to worse, she actually wouldn't mind seeing the film again. *Blood and guts* was still her preferred choice, but she'd settle on some Jennifer Love Hewitt and Ethan Embry if forced.

She made for the ticket-taker, bypassing the snack stand, not even glancing at the outrageous prices listed on the colorful plastic billboard. She had no money for a single thing, not even the smallest scoop of popcorn. She flashed the ticket-taker her already-torn ticket for an earlier showing, and the employee didn't even think twice about checking the time and date. Instead, he waved her on with a big grin on his face. She flashed him a smile back, but only because the trick had worked, and she was proud of her unscrupulous tactics.

Learned from the best, she thought, recalling the many times her parents had pulled the same exact scam. The Contis had never, *ever* paid for a movie, not in their entire life.

After taking her time strutting down the hallway, passing on the *The X-Files* movie and another rewatch of *Can't Hardly Wait,* she came across a theater showing a film titled, *A Perfect Murder,* which looked ideal because it literally had the word *Murder* in the title. Exactly the type of movie she was in the mood for. Since there were no horror flicks out—the summer was a terrible time for horror cinema—this would have to do.

She entered and took a seat, pleased to see she had only missed the first twenty minutes. That didn't seem like a big deal since the plot was fairly straightforward—the hot blonde wife was cheating on her older husband. So, of course the older husband had concocted a pretty elaborate plan to have her killed.

After the film was over, she left. The story had been somewhat satisfying but short on the violence she so desperately craved. Since she couldn't satisfy her need for a little faux bloodshed at Star Point Plaza, she decided to take the long walk across town to Video World. Then realized she only had about fifty cents in her pocket. A VHS rental was double that for a one-night.

Shit, she thought, stuffing her hands in her pockets, walking down the handicap ramp that led toward the plaza's parking lot. With only two quarters, there wasn't much to do in Hooperstown. She supposed she could hang out at the mall, lounge around those familiar public spaces with the other degenerate losers who had neglectful parents. Linger around the entrances and smoke cigarettes until the mall cops chased her away. That was always fun.

No telling what local dirt and gossip she would get there. Maybe if she was lucky, she'd happen upon a fight. Or maybe she'd be even luckier and find *herself* in one. It'd been a good while since she scrapped with anyone. Tonight seemed like a good night to cut her knuckles on someone's teeth.

Just when she made the decision to head to the mall in search of sinful delights, Jewel spotted two shadows heading toward a small wooded area. The area, she knew, was the entryway to a sprawling, massive forest, one that covered well over three square miles of land and stretched into the neighboring county. Not exactly the true Pinelands of South Jersey, but close enough the Jersey Devil could practically call it a second home.

Why were two people heading toward it, at this hour, under the dim twinkle of starlight, by themselves?

Upon closer observation, she saw the shadows holding hands. *"Curious and curiouser,"* she whispered to herself, quoting Alice from her favorite childhood movie.

The two shadows were laughing, squeals of glee that echoed in the night's silence. The long-haired shadow leaned into the short-haired shadow and kissed him. *Him.* She could tell the shadow was a *him.* The other a *her.* Two lovers, drifting off into the wooded area, perhaps to share another kiss, a forbidden one—otherwise, why the secrecy, right? And maybe, just maybe, a little something more. Maybe something that involved nakedness, the *no-*

pants dance as her father had once dubbed it, well before his last stint in the slammer.

Curious, indeed.

Jewel found herself floating toward the two shadows, feeling a magnetic draw to them. Their jovial laughs attracted her like a moth to an open flame. She followed the couple toward the woods.

And then into the woods.

In the moonlight that cut through the tall pines, they disappeared into the shadows. Jewel Conti followed them down into the dark, curiosity ruling over her every step.

2

Doug climbed out of Jimmy's Thunderbird and followed his group up the stairs of Star Point 10. They ambled up to the ticket booth, asked what movie was playing in theater 9, and how far into the showing the film was.

"*The X-Files* movie," the girl in the box office said. "Just went in. Wanna buy a ticket?"

Jesse did the talking. "My friend here lost his wallet in there and just wanted to check to see if it fell between the seats."

Doug nodded, playing along.

"Oh," the employee said, as if losing a wallet was on par with catching the flu. *You poor thing,* those eyes said. She reached down by her knees. "Here, take this flashlight." She placed a compact flashlight underneath the glass barrier between them. It barely worked when he turned it on, the bulb or batteries needing replacement. "The previews are ending and the house lights might be down. Just bring it back when you're done."

"Sure thing," Doug said, shaking the flashlight, watching the bulb flicker.

Jesse walked with him to the ticket-taker station while the rest of the gang hung back, waiting for them to return. Doug watched Grady drift toward the *House of the Dead* arcade game, pop a dollar in quarters into the slot, and pick up the ruby-red shotgun. A little jealous he wouldn't have time to get in a game, Doug turned to Jesse.

"We're making good time," Doug said as they approached the booth.

"Yeah, I think everyone else is screwed on that last clue. That pool hall guy was *piiiiissed*."

"You were amazing, by the way."

Jesse covered his cheeks as if he were hiding a blush. "Oh, why thank you, my good man. All in a day's work."

"Almost lost it when you asked him if someone jizzed on the counter."

"You missed me calling him a chicken-fucker."

Doug snorted, then straightened out his expression when the ticket-taker asked for their tickets. Jesse briefly explained the situation, and Doug waved the flashlight and pointed over his shoulder to where the girl continued to feed the hungry line of moviegoers their tickets. The ticket-taker let them through without a hassle.

They jogged across the lobby toward the hallway that contained theaters six through ten. When they reached theater nine, the doors were already shut, the film already in progress. Like the counter girl feared, the house lights had come down and the theater was pretty dark. Luckily, the early scene on display was bright enough for them to see what they were doing.

Doug had seen the movie already, last week in fact, and knew the bright tone wouldn't stay that way for very long. He headed toward the front row which was mostly unoccupied. He didn't want to inconvenience anyone for a stupid clue. That would have been Jesse's job, anyway.

The kid would ask anyone anything, which was often one of his finest contributions to their little trio. Sometimes it was funny, sometimes not. Sometimes it got him in trouble. Like the time he asked Mrs. Fender, their seventh-grade social studies teacher, if she was "on the rag." That had earned him a trip to the principal's office and three days detention. Not to mention his parents had grounded him for a week. Jesse had learned from that experience, though. Another one of his finer traits; he rarely fucked up the same thing twice.

Doug found seat A12, bent down, and turned on the flashlight. There was a couple sitting a few seats down that shot them an odd glance, arching their brows as they tried to figure out exactly what was happening. Jesse cleared the air, told them about the missing wallet, and that they could get back to sticking their hands down each other's pants in no time at all. They seemed amused by his comments, which was rare. Jesse was—quite frequently—the only one amused by his comments.

"Perverts," he said, shaking his head and turning back to Doug. "Find it?"

Doug shone the light under the seat, saw nothing but the hard-plastic bottom. "Not yet. It said A12, right?"

Jesse double-checked the clue underneath the glow of the light. "Yeah."

"Okay." Doug stuck his hand between seat A12 and A13. He felt something, paper squares taped to the side. "Shit, I got it!"

"Sweet!"

He left the other three pieces of paper behind and shoved the clue in his pocket. "Let's go."

Jesse waved to the audience and thanked them for their hospitality. "You're all great people, and I like each and every one of you!"

Someone yelled, "Get out of here, asshole!"

As they raced to the exit, Jesse laughed. So did Doug.

So far, the night had been great to them. But it wouldn't stay that way for very long.

Dark clouds gathered over the town, bringing with them more than the average storm, a deluge of despair in perpetuity.

3

Jewel wondered how many ticks were crawling along her flesh, looking for the softest spot to burrow in. She could almost feel them digging at the surface, craving the blood in her veins like little insect vampires. Brushing off every crawly sensation, she followed the two stumbling romantics, thinking they were either drunk on booze or drunk on their own affection. She assumed the latter but couldn't be sure. They were young, maybe her age, but that didn't mean they couldn't have broken into their parents' secret stash. Jewel knew a few things about pilfering from the parental supply.

The lovebirds continued to giggle and smooch each other, getting grabbier with each embrace. Their wandering hands explored every clothed contour of their bodies, and it was only a matter of time before things reached the next level.

Moonlight dropped white puddles of pale luster on the path before her. This gave Jewel just enough light to see, even though the woods were dark and cloaked in sliding shadows. Visibility only granted her a view of a few trees that flanked the path, but beyond that was perpetual darkness, a black wall of nothingness that hid away nature's finest contributions. Frogs croaked their nightly tunes while the bush crickets sung along to their own beat, an incessant chirping chorus that promised to repeat as long as the sky stayed sunless. An owl hooted. Tree branches swayed above her, the influence of summer zephyrs rustling their leaves. Best of all, there were no sounds of tires squealing against blacktop, no horns honking at careless drivers, no rumblings of anything mechanical in the presence of the trees. There was just the calm, soothing sounds of twilight. Jewel felt safe and comfortable here, even though she was in the lair of ticks and enveloped by the immersive dark.

The two romantics continued to play, their kisses growing more passionate, the seconds between breaks stretching. Their hands were getting more exploratory, trespassing parts of the body Jewel knew to be forbidden. The two shadows strolled farther down the path until they came to a small ravine that dissected the woods. The trickling of the brook became louder as Jewel followed them, and the efforts of the frogs' collective croaking doubled.

Jewel hung back, waiting to see where this would go. In the bright spread of moonlight, she could see their faces now and recognized them at once. They were high school kids, Rudy Parnell and Lisa Welch. *Sophomores.* She only knew this because she had been in their third-grade class. Jewel didn't know if the two were long-time lovers or if this was a new fling, but she hadn't seen either of them in years, so both possibilities were on the table.

Rudy kissed Lisa on her open mouth, his tongue visible and glistening in the moonglow. Jewel thought that was gross, the way his tongue washed over hers. She'd seen much worse at the movies, but she couldn't imagine anyone kissing *her* like that, jamming their tongue past hers as if they meant to fill her throat. If someone ever tried, they might receive a hard knee to their ballbag.

Rudy removed his shirt in one swift motion. This was escalating fast. She felt an exhilarating rush, this voyeur business pretty satisfying. She was a little ashamed to admit such a thing, but—well, this was cool, kinda neat, a real thrill.

Better than the movie, she mused.

Rudy unbuttoned Lisa's blouse, revealing the stark white of her bra. He kissed her exposed neck, and she moaned, reaching for his belt buckle. This was going to happen.

Shit is going down.

The no-pants dance.

"Wait," Lisa said in a breath, her eyes shooting open, wide and watery. She grabbed his hand, which had migrated to her southern parts, and gently removed it. "Do you hear that?"

Rudy pretended like he'd heard nothing and kissed the smattering of freckles across her chest. His wet lips meeting flesh echoed throughout the night, rivaling nature's serene sounds. Three seconds later Lisa was shoving his head away from her.

"I'm serious!" she said in a panicked, yet hushed voice.

Jewel tuned her ear to the forest but couldn't pick up on anything threatening. Nothing growled, nothing howled. There were no sounds of marching feet stampeding through the wild brush. It was like it had been; a calm and peaceful night amongst the gentle chords of a flourishing ecosystem. Perfect almost. Invigorating and refreshing. Jewel felt more alive tonight than she had in weeks, months. Maybe her entire life.

"I don't hear shit," Rudy said, killing the moment, and—in all likelihood—any chance of steering the ship back on the path to Friskytown. "Come on. Let's do this. Tonight. It'll be special."

Lisa glanced around the woods, her eyes soft and jittery as they fell on the trees, the path, and eventually the starry sky. "No..." she said, as if the night and everything that had happened was one major disappointment. "No, we can't."

"What are you talking about?" Rudy's tone had grown fiery hot.

Jewel recognized it at once, that heated inflection. It usually meant things were gonna get a whole lot worse from here on out. There might be yelling, screaming, and maybe…just maybe…*violence*. Yes, that voice often led to thrown objects and bloody lips, scars of varying depths, emotional and physical.

"We planned this," he said. "This was supposed to be *our night*."

"I knowwwww," she said, almost pleading with him. "But it feels…wrong. Doesn't it? Plus… I heard something." Her eyes wandered the dark. "Something out there."

Rudy shook his head. He'd clearly had enough. "You didn't hear anything."

"Why are you being such a dick?"

"I'm not being a dick. It's just…this was supposed to happen. Tonight. Here." He pointed to the ground just beyond where Jewel could see. "I even came out here earlier and laid a towel. So you wouldn't get dirty."

She pivoted back and forth as if expecting some monster to come bursting through the trees. "I just… I don't think my first time should be in the woods."

Rudy huffed. "Whatever." He snatched his shirt off the ground, shook out the dirt and clingy wood chips, and threw it over his head. "God forbid it's not a five-star hotel. Fucking princess."

"Fuck you, Rudy," she spat, pushing him. "Yeah, because I really want to *do* you now."

Rudy rolled his eyes, grabbed his stomach, and chuckled in her face.

Jewel wanted to march over there and uppercut him in the gonads, but she refrained and kept hidden in the shadows the pines provided.

"You really need to lighten up. You're always wound so ti—"

A shadow emerged from the trees on the other side of the ravine. It was a pale figure, wearing a ripped T-shirt and jeans sliced open in several places. The kid—no older than seventeen—had long curly hair, dark as the backdrop the woods presented. It looked like he'd crawled through a patch of thorn bushes, his clothing reduced to mere rags.

"*Help me!*" the kid shouted, his voice hoarse, as if he'd spent the whole night at a concert screaming the lyrics of his favorite band. "*Help me, for fuck's sake!*"

"Holy fuck!" screamed Rudy. He took off in the opposite direction, not even waiting for the kid to explain himself.

Lisa sprinted after him, screaming bloody murder, a shrill outburst that pierced the air and silenced the forest's wildlife.

They streaked past Jewel, but not before she locked eyes with Lisa, who screamed even louder when she saw her. The girl lost her balance for a spell, but quickly found her footing. She sped off, trying to catch up with her lover, Rudy, who had abandoned her without hesitation.

Jewel wanted to say something to let Lisa know she was scared too, that she was of no threat to them, but she hadn't a clue how to make them realize she wasn't *in* on whatever the long-haired kid was up to. In a split second none of it mattered, anyway. They disappeared into the distant darkness, the ever-black horizon in the center of the path, as if Satan himself had emerged from the depths of Hell, riding after them on a massive horned steed.

The long-haired kid had made his way across the ravine, climbed up the muddy bank, and was heading toward Jewel. The kid looked familiar, another face from Hooperstown High. Older than Rudy and Lisa, though. Jewel couldn't recall his name, but she'd seen him hanging around Jesse Di Falco's older brother, Jimmy. The kid looked terrible, his skin taking on the same pallor as the near-full moon. And there were things growing on his face, dark knots the size of a baby's fist. They looked like...like...

Roots?

She couldn't be sure, but that's what the growth reminded her of. A tuber from some underground plant protruding from the kid's cheeks. Black spidery veins marred his face and arms, along with several scarlet scratches, probably from sharp branches and the thorny extensions the forest had thrown along his path.

As he gained his footing and stumbled down the manmade walk, Jewel could see a dark substance dripping from his lips. He wiped his mouth with his forearm and then bent over, as if he were about to be sick. Sure enough, a tar-black stream exploded from his mouth, showering the pathway in a steamy pile of thick liquid. The smell was overpowering even with the kid being thirty feet away. The awful malodor reminded Jewel of the small closet where her mother kept the cleaning products, mainly the bleach and toilet bowl cleaner.

"*Help me,*" the kid said again. "*God, please. What did she do to me?*"

Just then, the kid looked up from his soupy expulsion. His eyes were different and hardly human. Golden circles with a black center glowed in the darkness, iridescent globes that dimmed and grew bright from one instant to the next. Just like the nighttime critters her mother was really good at catching in the act of digging through the trash on the front porch of their apartment.

Not human, was the phrase that flashed through her mind.

Jewel didn't know what she saw in those eyes, but she didn't like it. It struck a bolt of fear through her, the terror melting her insides. She felt as if she couldn't move her feet. Once the kid's eyes (*was* it his eyes or someone else's?) locked onto her, she knew she had to run.

Her paralysis broke, and her sneakers sought a grip on the muddy terrain. Slipping on the wet earth, she went right down and found herself on her belly faster than she could blink. Soggy footsteps sounded from behind, motivating her to push herself up. Without looking back, she took off down the stretch of path, the summer crickets' shrill cries filling the night like emergency sirens. Part of her wanted to look back, see the deathly stare of those eyes again, those impossibly human circles of solid gold, but she couldn't bring herself to stretch her neck in that direction. Fear nipped at her heels the entire way out of the woods.

Once she reached the shallow hill where she'd first stepped foot on the path and could see the lights of the cinema brightening up the entire shopping complex, she dropped to her knees, out of breath, utterly winded from the track sprint. In that fragile moment, she wished she'd actually participated in gym class instead of keeping off to the side with the other nonathletic types. A second later she was on her feet, brushing off the dirt that clung to her jeans. She was safe. In that secure instant, she took the opportunity to face the darkness of the woods one last time, knowing damn well what lurked there.

Something…evil.

That was the only word to describe it, seemingly unaware of the nature of its own existence. The kid had asked for help, but Jewel had known that was a trap. The same way a sicko child predator would invite some unsuspecting kiddo to check out the candy in the back of his nondescript van.

She didn't dwell on it, *him,* the sick kid with roots growing out of his face. Whatever he was. Whatever he'd become.

Not human.

She waited to see the golden rings of its eyes, but as the seconds passed, she realized she would see no such thing. A part of her thought she had imagined the whole sequence. And why not? It was too weird and terrifying to have taken place in reality. Surely it was a trick of the dark, the magic of night and her insecurities, her warped imagination at work.

But then what about the lovers? They had seen it too. They had run from it. They had screamed.

Rotating toward the parking lot, turning her back to the dark woods and the terrors within, she surveyed the car-packed area for any signs of the two lovers. She saw no one walking along the pathway, the sidewalks, or the lot itself.

Before she could take one step toward the sidewalk, she heard rustling in the leaves behind her. Then, a whisper, a gentle voice, innocent and pleading: *"Help me...she...did...something... The dreams... God, the dreams... She... SHEEEEE..."*

Jewel screamed, fear flooding her every nerve.

Then she ran for the multiplex, ignoring the ever-growing presence of the swelling darkness behind her.

4

From the parking lot, Grady watched Jewel Conti sprint up the handicapped ramp and duck into the movie theater lobby, darting between two people who were engaged in friendly conversation, forcing them apart. He thought it was weird, seeing her run like that, like someone was chasing her, her eyebrows bent and her open mouth catching gulps of wind.

She was terrified.

He shrugged off the whole thing and quickly buried the odd occurrence in the back of his mind, filing it between what he'd eaten for breakfast that morning and what he might eat for breakfast tomorrow.

He turned to his teammates who were gathered around the next clue, analyzing the words scribbled on what looked like a folded napkin.

207 + 504

"Are they serious?" Jesse asked. "This is the dumbest fucking clue I've ever seen."

Grady didn't need a second glance to piece the puzzle together. The two numbers equaled seven-hundred and eleven, and there was a 7-Eleven located on Beaverson Avenue. Jesse was right; it *was* the dumbest clue they had gotten so far. The sloppiness of the riddles left a sour taste in Grady's mouth. This game wasn't as challenging as it had been built up to be.

"RJ is gonna be pissed," Jimmy said, his lips writhing as if he'd unexpectedly bitten into a lemon. "I should call him, see how far behind they are. I wonder how they made out at the pool hall."

He reached into his pocket to retrieve his Nokia flip-phone. Opening it, he punched the digits and pressed the button with a little green phone. "Yo, it's me." He leaned over and held the phone away from his ear so everyone could listen in.

"*Where the fuck are you guys?*" RJ asked.

"We just scooped up the third clue."

"*The third! You rat bastards.*"

"Where are you and the others?"

"*Dude, you wouldn't believe what happened at the pool hall. I don't know what you assholes did, but the owner went nuts. Fucker freaked out on us, threatened to kick us out. When we didn't leave, he literally called the cops. What a fucking bucket of dicks, man.*"

"That sucks," Jimmy said, stifling a laugh or two. "So where are you guys now? Place is probably gonna close soon."

"*Yeah, it's going to close in ten minutes.*" RJ blew static into the phone. "*Fuck, man. It's not looking good for us.*"

"I guess that's an easy win for us."

"*I guess so. The rest of us will be locked out.*"

"You could always use your one hint. Call up Alphie and have him give you the next clue."

"*Is that even allowed? In the history of the Hunt, this has never happened before, I swear to God.*"

Jimmy shrugged. "I guess it's allowed. It's a hint."

"Well, Tom called Alphie earlier and the fuckhole wouldn't pick up, so I have a feeling we're getting nothing as far as hints are concerned. Goddammit. Why does that guy have to be such a prick?"

"Fuck him, man."

"Yeah. Anyway, let me go, man. The others are getting restless. Let me know how you guys make out with the other clues."

"These clues are trash by the way. Alphie and Randall didn't put a minute of effort into them. I'd say a second-grader came up with these clues, but that would be insulting a second-grader's intelligence."

"Stoner fucks. I'll deal with them. I'll kick Benoit square in the nuts the next time I see him. And I'll probably bang Moffit's sister again."

"All right, dude. We're heading to the next clue."

"And where is that exactly?"

Jimmy laughed. "Heh, nice try, douche." He hung up, slipped the phone in his pocket, and then turned to the rest of the group, raising his hands victoriously. "Looks like we got this one in the bag."

Giving his brother a fist bump, Jimmy's smile widened, eating the lower half of his face.

Jesse cranked his arm like he was pulling down the lever of a slot machine. He let out a loud "Yeah, baby!" in his best Dick Vitale voice.

"All right," Jimmy said, "calm down. The night's not over yet. Still got several clues left, and any one of them could throw us off track. You heard RJ. Alphie isn't picking up his phone, so we're on our own. Think you guys can handle that?"

"Dude," Jesse said, his face wrinkling with confident charm, "these clues kinda suck ass. I could have done a better job setting this thing up."

"I wouldn't go that far," Doug said, snickering. "You once answered 'Who was the 16th President of the United States of America' with 'The 16th President of the United States of America.'"

"Was I wrong though?"

Doug pushed him, barely moving him off his feet. Jimmy shook his head and called his brother a "dumbass," and then hopped back into the T-bird's driver's seat.

As they pulled away, Doug and Jesse argued over who was smarter and who could have done a better job orchestrating the Hunt. Grady saw a figure standing near the patch of woods that bordered the parking lot. It looked a lot like Randall Benoit. In fact, Grady swore it *was* him. The long ratty hair, the black T-shirt displaying Metallica's *Master of Puppets* album cover. He opened his mouth to tell the others that Randall was right there, looking quite unhealthy, to tell Jimmy to drive over and find out what the hell he was doing, but something changed in the kid's eyes that made Grady think twice. Two golden rings glimmered in the dark. They glowed like ancient riches, burning brightly against the nighttime backdrop. Randall's mouth opened, his face twisting with internal torment, his jaw hanging open unnaturally long. The darkness gave way to a cone of light beaming down from a streetlight, and Grady could see the kid's clothes were ripped and torn, and so was his visible flesh.

What the hell?

Before Jimmy left the parking lot and sped back onto the main drag that intersected the heart of Hooperstown, Grady saw a slithering darkness creep up on Randall, slipping through the shadows and wrapping its fluid-like extensions around him, hugging his body. The shapes rolled and writhed, bending nimbly through moonlit patches of shrubs and evergreens, stretching, rising above the dim territory and scaling the starlit sky.

Grady turned from the disturbing sequence, doubting his eyes had just shown him a glimpse of reality. His breath caught in his throat, as did his words.

When he looked back, none of what he'd seen was there.

Just the entrance to the woods.

It had been an illusion.

Right?

The fresh night smelled faintly of window cleaner.

CHAPTER FOUR

Party Girl

1

Abby Allen wasn't *feeling it*. The party, the movies, the Rice's generous hospitality—everything about tonight. None of it felt right. Honestly, nothing had felt *right* after she'd gotten the news that her best friend since the first grade, Lauren Sullivan, had been diagnosed with cancer.

Cancer?

She could hardly believe it. Never had she heard of someone her age getting sick like that. Cancer was for old people, people who smoked a hundred cigarettes a day and survived solely on a steady diet of processed meats and diet sodas. Not for healthy girls and boys who played soccer and basketball, always ate their helpings of vegetables and never so much as entertained the thought of sucking on a dirty tobacco stick. Lauren Sullivan had been the embodiment of a young healthy person, and she deserved none of this.

Unbelievable.

It was, truly, and the whole town had been on edge since the news broke. Every parent had silently muttered the phrase "Thank God it wasn't us," and deep down they wondered if Lauren was an isolated incident or if there was more to come.

When Abby's father first heard the news via the morning paper, he put the publication down and stared at his coffee as if the black drink within had been the one to feed him the terrible news. As if the bleak ordeal had happened to Abby herself and not some random friend of hers. When she asked him what was going on, why he looked so morose, he'd told her nothing and claimed he was "just thinking."

He'd lied to her, of course, and she couldn't exactly blame her old man for doing so. But after he'd discussed the issue with her mother, the two of them decided breaking the news themselves was better than her learning through the social network of the intermediate school hallways. They told her Lauren had been diagnosed with leukemia, and though the cancer had been discovered relatively early, there were no promises she would beat it. The good doctors didn't project any probabilities, percentages of survival. Even though the initial diagnosis trended in a positive direction, Abby couldn't shake the doom-laden feeling that had settled in the base of her stomach. Something about the whole situation felt off, wrong, like there was something else happening, much worse than the story she'd been told. As if her parents didn't know everything. Or were hiding it from her. An important piece of information that just might break apart her soul.

The truth.

Now, sitting in Maddie Rice's basement, watching *I Know What You Did Last Summer* on DVD, an overwhelming sadness swarmed her, a feeling she couldn't shake, a twisting sensation that slithered through her guts, a storm of terror no amount of Freddie Prinze Jr. could weaken. Not even Mr. Rice's drool-worthy collection of DVDs, a towering stack that put her own collection to shame, could shake her from the terrible thoughts. The realization that her greatest friend could possibly die hit her like an unsuspecting slide tackle. She pictured herself standing over Lauren's casket, looking down at her dead little face, crying and praying and wishing it wasn't so.

"You okay?" Maddie asked her, the words wiping away the dreams like glass cleaner would a window smudge. "You look…somewhere else."

In the blue glow of the television, Maddie flashed her a smile, a cheery one that almost brought Abby out of her sullen mood. Abby tried to reciprocate, showed her teeth, the ghost of a smile that had long since died.

She returned her gaze to the television, to Freddie and Jennifer, and told her, "I'm fine. Everything's fine."

"Are you sure? We can talk."

Abby tried to smile again, thinking she could pull it off this time, but also knowing it would come across like a reaction to a shallow paper cut rather than a display of radiating positivity. "Actually, I think I'm gonna grab some fresh air."

Abby forced herself off the couch, the room tilting as she rose. There was no alcohol at this party, so the cause of the spinning room wasn't that. Abby thought her ill-timed thoughts, the nasty images of her dead friend lying in a mahogany tomb were to blame. And they probably were. She felt sick just thinking about losing her BFF and worse for dwelling on these dreary images.

"I'll go with you," Maddie said, jumping off the couch, keeping the overly friendly act on full display.

Abby didn't find it as annoying as she might have, had she not been feeling so lowly, but the flowery positivity sure wasn't helping. "No, I think I'd like to be alone."

"Oh." Maddie lost her smile at once, her face forming waves of wrinkles. "Are you sure?"

"Yeah."

"Okay…let me at least walk you upstairs."

Abby didn't decline that invitation, but she didn't welcome it either. She headed to the stairs and Maddie followed, the Rice's family poodle, Bishop, tailing the girls to the top step and beyond.

Once they reached the top, Abby opened the door that led into the kitchen. Mr. and Mrs. Rice were behind the island, laughing and taking sips from their wine glasses, which had been filled almost to the brim with a deep burgundy color. Abby found the taste of wine disgusting (she'd stolen some from her mother's stash exactly once and vowed *never again*) and just looking at the glasses made her a little queasy.

"Hey honey," Maddie's mother said, her face all smiles.

"What's up, baby?" asked Mr. Rice as he set down his glass. He was careful not to let the drink spill on the thick slab of stone.

"Nothing," said Maddie. "Abby isn't feeling well. She needs some fresh air."

"I'm okay," Abby clarified. "I just need a quick breather."

"Okay," Mrs. Rice said, perky as ever. "You gonna go with her, Mads?"

"Actually," Abby said, sounding sorry, "I was hoping to be alone."

Neither parent responded, not at first.

"Of course, hon," Mrs. Rice finally said, her smile mostly gone now.

Bishop the poodle had made his way over to the front door. He scratched at the moulding and let out a little bark that didn't sound so little.

"Bishop needs to go out," Mr. Rice said. "Would you mind taking him with you, Abby?"

Abby looked over at Bishop, who looked back at her with the saddest puppy eyes she'd ever seen. Only a monster could deny that smooch-able face, and to be honest, it would be nice to have *someone* accompany her. Someone who couldn't ask questions or judge how she felt. Someone who'd listen and say nothing back.

"Sure thing," she said, and then made for the front door. Bishop danced with eager anticipation, his nails clacking on the hardwood floor. Abby grabbed the leash off the hook next to the door, bent down on one knee, and latched the spring hook to the pup's collar.

Maddie opened the door for her friend, still looking sorry, as if she had been the one to ruin her night. "Are you sure I can't come with you? I feel crappy seeing you like this."

"Don't," she said, offering yet another feeble smile. "It's just been...tough lately."

Maddie nodded like she understood, and Abby thought that was pretty funny because Maddie Rice had no clue. She lived in a great neighborhood with perfect parents, had not a single care in the *fucking* world. Everyone liked Maddie Rice, *everyone*. Most *loved* her. Worshipped her like a princess, or better yet—a god. She had only lived in Hooperstown for a year and she was already becoming one of the most popular kids in her class. The sun had always shone on Maddie Rice, and that simply wasn't the case with other kids. Other kids had problems. Real-life problems that dragged a person down, lowered them to the dirt, made them feel worthless and beneath everything. Problems that manifested into fears, the universal terror that they would never escape this den of misery the world has laid out before them.

Lauren was there. Inside the den. Misery pressing down on her.

As Abby walked down the front steps, leading Bishop onto the grass to do his business, she felt guilty for being there. She should have been at the hospital by her best friend's side, helping her, aiding her in the fight for her life. Reading to her, watching terrible, cheesy sitcoms. Just being a pair of ears that would listen, a mouth that would tell her the things she needed to hear—*everything will be all right, I promise*—whenever she needed to hear it.

That's where I should be right now, she thought as Bishop hoisted his leg and unloaded on an unsuspecting rose bush. When he was finished, he happily sauntered over to her, anxiously awaiting their next move.

Abby led him to the end of the driveway, then asked, "Where do you want to go, boy?"

Both directions looked oddly dark, the streetlights providing just enough visibility to make her way down the sidewalk without tripping over any potential cracked concrete, uplifted by a thick, gnarly tree root. The dark night was less than welcoming, and her head space was far from clear. She still held thoughts of cancer and dead friends and other worrisome teenage struggles. The night may have been intimidating, its never-ending aspect leading the charge, but at least she was out of the basement, away from friends that were nowhere near the quality of Lauren.

She picked the sidewalk to her right, passing the white vinyl fence that separated the Rice's yard from their neighbor's. Bishop yipped with excitement, happy to explore somewhere other than the same four corners of that boring property. Abby wondered what was going through the dog's head in that moment, what he thought of the dark and if he was scared of such things. She didn't think dogs had any reason to fear the dark, not the way children did.

I'm not a child. I'm fourteen for Christ's sake. Officially a high schooler now. Start acting like it, wimp.

Even in nice places such as this, the Promising Pines section of Hooperstown, the dark registered as a potential threat. She didn't know the statistics or if what she'd been told was accurate, but Promising Pines was the nicest, cleanest, and most crime-free area in the whole county. The whole state of New Jersey, if talk was to be believed. So yeah, the dark was scary, but the area's strong reputation settled any uncertainties she had about a moonlit stroll.

She turned the corner and took Baker Avenue to Dodgson Street. She caught a whiff of a strange smell, something that reminded her of her mother's incense candles, spicy and simultaneously sweet. She hustled past colonials and ranches, ignoring the many gardens and front-lawn decorations the people of the neighborhood took immense pride in, the well-manicured bushes trimmed to perfection that flanked some driveways, and instead she concentrated on the dark and what could possibly be hiding there.

Stop being stupid, she thought, and nearly jumped out of her pants when something scraped along the sidewalk behind her. Even Bishop hopped off his feet, turned, and let out a less-than-intimidating bark, which sounded more like a mouse squeaking its way into the nearest hole in the wall.

She spun around and faced the intruder, whoever they were. She was prepared to run or swat the creeper with closed fists, but the creeper wasn't a creeper at all. Instead of seeing the silhouette of a child predator—the most horrific thing she could currently think of—looming in the near distance, she spotted the true cause of the noise. A plastic top of a garbage pail had dragged itself along the sidewalk, a forceful gust of air driving it toward her.

She almost laughed, would have had her mood not been what it was.

"Scared us, huh, boy?" she said to Bishop, realizing she sounded like an oblivious child in those Grimm fairy tales she had read all those years ago. The children who had been in denial of their impending fate. If tonight had been like one of those classic tales, there'd be a hairy monster with great big teeth waiting for her around the next corner. An old haggard witch brewing a mouth-watering broth, waiting on the final ingredient to arrive—*her*. A child. The delicious main course.

Stop being an idiot. There's no one out there. Not witches, not monsters, not any other dumb-ass thing you can invent.

It's just dark. That's all it is.

But she didn't buy that. Not really.

She realized she'd taken another turn, heading farther west than she had meant to. Towering over a short row of trees, Hooperstown Medical Center revealed itself, the very place where her best friend was currently lying in an uncomfortable bed, eating food the Rice's probably wouldn't serve Bishop. Had she meant to come this way? She didn't think so, but she'd been so lost in thought her subconscious might have steered her this way, the place she truly wanted to be. She didn't know Maddie's house was so close to the hospital, didn't think it was, and wondered how far she had really come.

But here it was. Visible. No less than a five-minute walk to the emergency room's entrance. In the distance she could hear a commotion, could see flashing lights bouncing off the brief stretch of pines that lined the hospital's property.

She eyed the building as if it were the threat. Not knowing how long she'd been stuck there, staring at the hospital and its giant construct, getting lost in hypothetical episodes about her friend and the grim road leading toward her possible recovery, Abby blinked herself back into reality. Bishop barked, a quiet sound that almost seemed to have come from a place of respect. He nudged her ankle with his cold, wet nose. She looked down and saw circles of moonlight reflecting off his black, beady eyes.

"What's the matter, boy?"

Bishop whined and wagged his stump of a tail. Obviously he didn't like standing there in the dark. Abby could sympathize. Despite the oppressive June heat, a chill filled the hollow of her bones. She turned away from the hospital and the distant commotion, spinning toward the walk that led back to the Rice's, gently jerking the leash to let Bishop know her intention.

There was a dark figure standing on the path, partially veiled in the shadow provided by a tall oak that had grown in the grassy strip between the sidewalk and the curb.

Abby yelped, meaning to belt one out and alert the whole neighborhood, but fear had coiled around her vocal cords, strangling her. Bishop could have done much better, but he didn't make a sound.

"*Abby,*" the figure said, slowly stepping toward the oak tree, wrapping its thin arms around the trunk, resting its identity against the bark. The voice was raspy and dry, the speaker in desperate need of a glass of water to clear things up. "*Abby, it's me.*"

In the darkness, white teeth flashed brilliantly.

Abby squinted, her vision trying to cut through the thick shadows. She thought her eyes would have adjusted by now, especially considering the ample presence of streetlights, but here, down this one particular stretch of sidewalk, the lights weren't operating at their full capacity. The one closest had burned out. Several others poured down dim and dusty cones of frail light. Several flickered, threatening to plunge the street into perpetual twilight.

Abby saw just enough of the figure to know who it was. But it couldn't be *her,* could it?

The tiny hairs on her arms grew tall and stiff.

"Lauren?" she asked the darkness, and the darkness purred like a jolly kitten.

"Yes, it's me."

"Wha— What are you doing here?" She cleared her throat and checked over her shoulder, making sure the hospital was still there, close enough to run to.

It was there, just as it had been.

"I came to warn you, Abby." She didn't sound like herself. *"I've come to warn you of bad times."*

"Warn me of what?"

"Of what's to come. Of what's going to happen here."

She shook her head, unable to follow. "Lauren. You're sick. You shouldn't be out here. You should—"

"Do you dream, Abby? Do you? I bet you do. We all dream."

Abby swallowed what felt like a golf ball. She backed away. That voice—God, that voice—hit her ears as if someone was cleaning the inside of her skull with a steel wire brush. Bishop began to growl.

"I dream. I dream all the time. Of a world far away from this one. A world where sickness is absent and everything is perfect."

"Lauren, you're not making any sense."

"Of course, I am. You just haven't been there. Won't you dream with me? I can show you so many things. She can show you so many things."

"She?"

"Mother."

Abby didn't understand what Lauren's mother had to do with whatever she was talking about, but clearly Lauren was messed up on some drugs and the result was this babble.

"Dream with me. Breathe from her flower and she will show you worlds beyond anything you can ever imagine."

"Lauren, you're scaring me."

Bishop squeaked, letting Abby know he seconded that statement.

"Don't be afraid. Not yet. There will be plenty of time to fear later."

"What the hell happened to you?"

"She touched me, Abs. She touched me in my special place."

A sickened feeling cut through her, and Abby wanted to kneel down and toss up the cupcakes Mrs. Rice had made for the party, the three she'd eaten. Somehow, she kept herself from getting sick, though each time Lauren—or the shadow that wore her skin—spoke, the digested contents gathered like storm clouds threatening an otherwise pleasantly sunny afternoon.

"She touched me so deep. My soul, of course. What did you think I was talking about, Abs?"

Abs had no response for this, the act of speaking suddenly a foreign concept.

"Listen to me and listen good." The shadow crawled off the tree, planted its feet on the sidewalk and faced her. Two golden glowing circles replaced the darkness where her eyes had been. Burning bright, the golden spheres twinkled like starshine. Eyes that weren't exactly human, that belonged to some nocturnal beast that roved the shadows in search of food and other basic necessities.

Bishop yapped as Not-Lauren neared.

Not.

Abby was certain she wasn't looking at the dark shadow of her best friend. Like her pops would say, she'd bet the house on it.

"Are you listening, Abs? Tell me I have your attention."

Abby opened her mouth. Her throat seized.

"Good enough, sweet pea, good enough."

The figure claiming to be Lauren moved through the dark like a snake slithering through a brush of dead leaves. She moved like she was dancing, the outline of her shape undulating as if her body *were* boneless, a husk of pliable muscle. The elasticity of her form injected Abby with another dose of instant fear, gooseflesh rising on her already-hardened skin.

"She is coming. Tonight is a special night for The Mother of Dead Dreams. Tonight, she will become something more than...than..." Bone white teeth appeared in the shadows like the Cheshire Cat's smile. *"...than what she is now."*

"I…" Abby's entire body shook, trembled with trepidation. Her legs had lost their feeling, were ready to buckle at any moment. "I don't know what you're talking about."

Not-Lauren's eyes burned like supernovas in a starless galaxy, her smile widening across the expanse of pale flesh. *"You will,"* she said, her words encased in a feral growl. *"All the children in Hooperstown will know her name, for she is Mother. The Mother of Dead Dreams, the Mother of Everything, Mother of All Things That Must Grow in this world and the other."*

"Lauren, stop." Tears leaked down Abby's cheeks, slow rollers that tickled her nearly-numb flesh. "You're sick. You need help." She didn't know why the nonsense things Lauren was spouting frightened her so much. Nothing about it made a lick of sense, contextual clues aside. "Let me get someone. The hospital is right there and…"

She turned, facing the hospital, the distant commotion of the doctors and nurses and ambulances providing a certain amount of relief, a certain comfort knowing she wasn't that far from safety.

But far enough.

"You need…" She turned back to Not-Lauren and the girl was gone, now one with the still shadows and twilight eyes of the stars above. "…Help," she finished for no one, nothing, not a single thing except the darkness and the puppy nestled against her ankle, shaking as if the night brought temperatures below freezing. Even Bishop knew to be scared.

But there was nothing to fear now. The girl was gone.

Vanished.

Was she ever there at all? She lent the moment to answering that question, though, in those precious seconds she couldn't adequately think, form the right responses. In the end, she settled on none of it mattering very much—real or fantasy, she needed to get off these dark streets and back to the Rice's before—

A force knocked Abby off her feet, planting her on the soft grass of a neighboring front lawn. She went down so hard the wind exploded from her lungs in a harsh wheeze. Facing the shadows to see what had plowed into her, she saw Not-Lauren crouched over Bishop, the untamed look in her eyes, those golden hoops burning with intensity, the desire to hurt something.

Bishop's pupils were wide and full of unchecked terror, more human than the eyes of the slithery thing hiding beneath her best friend's skin, the thing that wore the sick girl like a cheap disguise. The puppy squeaked as Not-Lauren wrangled his neck and dug her fingers into its short, curly hair. Without warning, Not-Lauren opened her mouth and bit down on Bishop's throat. A squirt of dark crimson jetted from the fresh wound. Bishop squealed, his eyes bulging so wide Abby thought they might pop from their sockets.

"NO!" screamed Abby, launching herself onto her feet. She went to charge forth, make an attempt to save Bishop, but Not-Lauren glanced up at her, dribbles of blood sluicing down her chin.

"*Mine,*" she rasped, cradling the struggling dog in her arms, keeping the puppy from escaping.

Abby wanted to save Bishop. She wished she had the courage. But the look in Not-Lauren's eyes warned her, told her that if she took one more step and interrupted her meal, then she would pay the ultimate price. That next time Abby's neck would earn the teeth.

Crying, she ignored the sounds of the feast, turned and sped off down the sidewalk and toward the great toothless mouth of the dark.

2

Trudy Sullivan hit the coffee bar one more time, thankful that Hooperstown Medical Center provided a twenty-four-hour café service. Without it, she would have never been able to stay awake for two days straight. Wyatt, her husband, had to work. Otherwise the mounting bills would never get paid, especially the impending hospital tallies. Well, she didn't even want to think about that. Not right now. Not when they were still there in the middle of it, when their daughter was *literally* fighting for her life. Bills should have been the last thing to cross her thoughts, yet they kept slithering to the forefront.

This will leave us devastated, she thought, and not for the first time.

Earlier, she'd thought about selling their home just to pay for it all. They had put most of their savings into the mortgage, so they had equity. Plus, the value of the house had increased over the last decade. They'd see a nice return when the time came to sell, but not if they had to pay off a bunch of debt. Sure, insurance would cover some of the cost for the hospital care, but it wouldn't help *that* much. Wyatt's construction employer didn't have the best benefits, either. It had been good enough for a family who'd rarely gotten sick over the years, and *cancer* hadn't even been a fleeting notion when they signed up for the cheapest plan. They weren't prepared to deal with this. Financially, mentally, physically—the Sullivans were now in for the ultimate test. Trudy, as positive as she'd tried to remain over these last few days, knew the next few months would probably break her.

I can't do this. I can't do this. I just can't.

But she'd have to. Or at least keep up appearances. If not for her or her husband, then for Lauren.

The barista handed her an extra-large light and sweet and then took her two dollars. Trudy eyed the tip jar and passed on the opportunity to drop in the change, a whopping fifty cents. The barista didn't seem to care, and that helped Trudy feel better about her frugal mindset. She headed back to the elevator, stepped inside, and hit the button for the sixth floor. On the ride up, she fought off more dismal thoughts about the struggles ahead, what their daughter's diagnosis would do to them as a family, the stress it might put on her marriage. She imagined Wyatt and her would fight over things they wouldn't normally get scrappy about. Closing her eyes, she told herself it would be okay because the cancer wasn't strong enough to beat their Lauren. That the doctors knew what they were doing, and this disaster would pass over like a lightning storm on a warm summer night—here one minute, gone the next, and easily forgotten come the following morning.

She stepped off the elevator and strolled down the ward, searching for her daughter's room. Hopefully Lauren had fallen asleep; the poor girl had been so scared that rest didn't come easy. Sleeping was even harder. Lauren had so many questions that were impossible to answer this early on, too: *How long do I have? Will I have a summer vacation? Can I see my friends? Who's gonna take care of Peter when I'm gone?*

That last question haunted Trudy. *When I'm gone.* She had told her daughter to never say such a thing, that she would be home to feed Peter—the family rabbit—soon enough.

Very soon.

But if she didn't make it, Trudy would donate the rabbit to some other kid who was still alive, still able to care for another life.

Stop that, Trudy scolded herself. *Stop thinking like that. If she's not allowed to think like that, then neither are you. She's going to make it through this.*

We all are.

Trudy located the room and shuffled inside.

Upon entering, her eyes falling to the bed, a needle-like numbness shocked her entire body. The lack of strength caused her fingers to loosen on the coffee. The Styrofoam cup dropped to the floor and busted apart when it hit the linoleum tile. Hot coffee shot everywhere, some splashing against her exposed legs. The scathing burn barely registered on her nerves. She was too busy staring at her daughter's hospital bed, fighting off the cold shivers that attacked her spine.

The bed was empty.

She backed out of the room, her eyes instantly filling with tears. *Where did they take her? Is she...*

Did she die?

It couldn't be true. It didn't work like that. One did not just die right out of the gate. There was a fight to be had.

We had time.

That's what the doctors told them. Weeks. Months. Hell, it could be years. It was too early to tell how aggressively the cells would advance, which was good because *early* meant *there is still a chance.*

This was supposed to be a ten-round brawl, not a first-round knockout.

She turned and practically flung herself at the nurses' station, which was located just outside the room. Her legs gave out when she reached the counter; it felt like standing on rubber crutches. Her head swam in a daze. The room spun a little, went fuzzy, the lights dimming as she went. She found it hard to concentrate, hard to swallow. When she reached the station, she leaned her chest on the counter for support.

"Mrs. Sullivan?" asked the nurse behind the counter. She seemed awfully concerned (probably because Trudy looked as if she'd just experienced the projection of some spectral image) and popped up immediately, ready to react to whatever her patient's mother was about to reveal.

Trudy had trouble with the words, her jaw unable to cooperate. "Where?"

"Where what?"

"Did you move her?" Trudy knew her voice sounded frail, broken. It was an effort just to separate her lips.

The nurse's forehead wrinkled with utter confusion. "We didn't move her anywhere, sweetheart."

"She's...*gone.*"

The nurse quickly made her way around the counter with a jog in her step. Trudy followed her to the doorway, fear controlling her every move.

When they reached the doorway, the nurse turned, a friendly smile sticking to her features.

"What?" Trudy asked, hating the nurse for acting this way. So knowledgeable. So all-mighty. She wanted to grip the woman's neck and strangle her. "What the hell are you smiling about?"

The nurse stepped aside, allowing Trudy a view into the room.

The bed wasn't empty anymore. Lauren was resting there, her back propped against the raised support. She looked sickly, pale, not the chipper little girl she had sent off to school each and every morning. No, Lauren looked tired, defeated, on the verge of certain death.

"You must have walked into the wrong room, Mrs. Sullivan."

Trudy looked down at the floor. The coffee was there, a big brown puddle, proof she had been in the *right* room. She pointed to the mess as if that was the only explanation needed.

"Oh geez," the nurse said, backing away. "I'll get maintenance to mop that up right away."

Before Trudy could prove her point, the nurse was heading to make the necessary calls.

Trudy was too tired, too confused to track her down and explain that her daughter *had been* temporarily missing. Instead, she floated across the room in a haze of worry and exhaustion, as if in a dream, and knelt at her daughter's bedside.

A languid smile wormed its way across Lauren's face.

Trudy combed her daughter's hair with her fingers, raking back loose strands. "Where did you go, pumpkin?"

Her smile stretched. "I was dreaming, Mom. I didn't go anywhere."

The certainty in her daughter's voice made her wonder, thinking maybe she had strolled into the wrong room after all.

But the coffee…

Later, when she tucked Lauren in for the night, before pressing her lips against the cool skin of her forehead, she noticed smears of dirt on her bare feet. Not knowing how to test her theory any other way, she brought her nose to Lauren's feet. Inhaled.

The pungent fragrance of damp earth was still fresh.

CHAPTER FIVE

Long Live The Legends of Greenwood Village

1

After the 7-Eleven clue, which led them to the McDonald's on Payton Way, the game had steered them toward the town's limits, the Greenwood Village section of their beloved town. The last clue had been another doozy; Alphie had scribbled, in crayon, the color green next to a childish depiction of several houses clustered around each other. *Greenwood Village* had fallen out of Team Watchmen's mouths almost simultaneously. Jimmy had rolled his eyes (not for the first time that night) and let out a grunt of frustration over the simplicity of Benoit and Moffit's clues. Usually, Jimmy had reiterated, the game would take all night, that it was normal for the sun to be creeping over the horizon as they uncovered the final clue. It was almost one in the morning and they had one more clue left to solve—and if it was anything like the others, it wouldn't take long to decode that one either.

Greenwood Village was the oldest section of Hooperstown, said to have been the landing site of Henry Hooper, the man who infamously arranged the town's first settlement. If history was to be believed, he had led a small crew of explorers up from Jamestown, found a habitable piece of land just off what would eventually become the Jersey shore. Some of the original structures, the houses flaunting colonial architecture, still remained, giving the entire section an eerie vibe, as if it were an old haunted place. Doug's father had taken him to Williamsburg, Virginia shortly after his mother had left them, and on the way to Busch Gardens, Gordon showed him around the downtown colonial sections, took him on tours around the town's most popular stops. Greenwood Village reminded Doug a lot of that excursion. The aged buildings were not so very well preserved; the whitewashed coatings had peeled and blistered, revealing the dead-gray slot-board siding beneath. The roofs wore dents, looking as if they could cave in at any moment. Upkeep on the lawns had not been maintained; weeds and unruly vegetation had scaled the wrap-around porches, vines curling up the downspouts of every corner of every house. Small trees had sprung up from the dirt that filled the gutters, some almost as tall as the grass on the front lawns.

Doug thought the entire area looked apocalyptic.

But it wasn't all like that. There was a small section of Greenwood Village that had been recently renovated within the last ten years. The small community was on the outskirts of town, near the woods that separated Hooperstown from the neighboring county. This was the Greenwood Village Alphie and Randall had wanted them to explore, and they knew this because in the corner of the clue, they had drawn a little tennis ball, so poorly that Team Watchmen argued about what it actually was.

"It's a basketball," Jesse had told them.

"Bullshit on that," Grady had said, swiping the clue from him. "It's a tennis ball, man."

"Tennis balls and basketballs look exactly the same, asshat. It's just a matter of size and color, and these turds failed to clue us in on both."

"Guys," Doug had said, wedging his way between them, a move he found himself doing a lot of lately. "Greenwood Village doesn't have a basketball court. They only have tennis courts."

"See," Grady had said, flexing his brow. "Told you."

Jesse snarled, but his friends knew there wasn't a speck of anger behind it. In a few minutes, the topic would be forgotten, and they'd be arguing about something else—like who was going to win the belt at Summer Slam in two months.

Now, in the back of Jimmy's T-bird, the wind brushing his hair every which way, Doug wondered what Maddie was doing at this very moment. If the kids at her party were still awake, eating candy and drinking soda and watching R-rated movies. In retrospect, the party would have been the better option, but Doug had known that the moment he'd been invited. He hoped the decision to let his friends sway him into the Hunt wouldn't haunt him forever. He prayed he wouldn't find out that Maddie had made out with someone else during a game of spin-the-bottle. He wasn't sure he'd forgive himself if that happened.

Jimmy took another turn. Cruising down a side street, every house looked like a replica of the one before it, the only visible difference being the choice in paint color. Doug turned to Grady, who had been awfully quiet since leaving Star Point 10. He had chipped in his two cents on the following clues, of course, but that was all. Not normally a quiet kid, the silence on his end was somewhat disconcerting. But it wasn't just the silence. It was the look that had fallen over him like a widow's veil, the slumped shoulders that rested against the cushy leather seats.

"You all right?" Doug asked. When Grady didn't answer, didn't even turn his head in acknowledgment, Doug gently nudged him in the ribs.

"What? Yeah, fine. Just…" The streets of Greenwood Village stole his focus. "Just thinking."

"About what?"

He shook his head, clearly not wanting to answer that. Whatever was eating him was doing so with sharp teeth.

"Come on, dude." Doug snapped his fingers, vying for his attention. So far, Greenwood Village was ahead by a considerable margin. "Talk to me."

"It's gonna sound stupid."

Jesse turned to them, finally participating in their conversation. "What's going on? What are you two wiener-whackers talking about?"

Grady let go of a deep breath. "I saw something back at the theater," he said, finally, keeping his voice low enough so Jimmy and Karen wouldn't overhear. The music—Korn's latest—was blaring loud enough to where anything short of screaming wouldn't be heard. Jonathan Davis's incessant, inarticulate growls ruled the airwaves. "I thought I saw…"

"What?"

"Well, first I saw Jewel Conti."

Jesse stuck out his tongue, pretended to barf. "That fucking psycho? Jesus, thank Christ she didn't see us."

"She was running. Sprinting, actually."

Doug giggled. "That's a first. I've never seen her do anything remotely active, unless you count kicking the shit out of the six-graders. Even when she dresses for gym, she just stands there."

"It was weird," Grady said, almost getting lost in the memory. "She looked…*scared.*"

"Jewel Conti?" Jesse asked. "You sure it was her?"

Grady nodded. "It was her. I'd recognize her anywhere." He shook his head, as if the memory was snatching him away again. "Then I saw something in the woods. Well, not somet*hing*. Some*one.*"

Doug's heart thudded. He recalled seeing Alphie Moffit on the side of the road, how odd he'd acted, and what Doug thought had been blood leaking from his eyes. He had settled on the scene being the cause and effect of his overactive imagination, even settled on the notion it hadn't been Alphie at all; that it had been someone who looked like him. After all, he didn't really know Alphie, had only met him in passing a few times, and he supposed it could have been someone else.

But Doug recognized the tremble in Grady's voice, understood he was shaken by what he'd seen, like Doug had been while staring at the high school kid who'd wept tears of wet crimson.

"It looked like Randall Benoit," Grady said, sounding unsure of himself. "And his eyes were…"

"Was he crying blood?" asked Doug.

His two friends shifted their concentration on him, hitting him with confused, questioning glares.

Grady's brow curled like a garter snake. "What? No… No, he wasn't."

"Oh."

"Where the hell did that come from?" asked Jesse, half-concerned, half-entertained.

Doug shook his head. "Nowhere. I mean, I *thought* I saw Alphie earlier, on the side of the road. He looked like he'd been crying, and the tears were dark. I dunno. The lighting wasn't good. I guess it could have been someone else, and maybe it wasn't blood."

Grady and Jesse raised their brows and exchanged glances.

Doug sighed, pardoning their reactions. "You were saying…"

"I… I thought Randall's eyes were…" Grady seemed to struggle with finding the right word. "Glowing?"

"Glowing?" asked Jesse. He recoiled as if the word had teeth. "Glowing?"

"Glowing," Grady confirmed with a shrug, as if to say, *that's the best I can do*. "There was something wrong about him. About…*everything*. About the way he exited the woods. And then Jewel? It was like he'd done something to her. Or tried to. I just didn't like any of it. That's all."

Jesse swiped at the air between him as if karate chopping the situation. "Let's not worry about that stuff. Let's just finish the Hunt. I'm sure there's a logical explanation for everything you two jerk-weasels saw."

Jimmy turned to them, twisting his entire body to face the backseat. "What are you weirdos talking about back there?"

The three of them shrugged, as if the cohesive response had been rehearsed.

"We're almost there," Jimmy told them, and then cranked up the tunes even louder. It was almost impossible to hear each other now.

Doug leaned into them. "There's something wrong with tonight. You don't feel it?"

Jesse shook his head. "You're just disappointed because you're missing your girlfriend's party."

"She's not my girlfriend!"

"Well, not yet!"

"We don't even know each other. We haven't even hung out yet!"

"Doug's right," Grady said, still sounding *off*. Whatever the truth was, whatever he'd seen, it had spooked him. "There is something weird about tonight. It feels…*wrong*."

Jesse continued to roll his eyes. "Dudes. You guys are bumming me out right now."

"You didn't see it," Grady snapped. "If you saw it…"

Doug opened his mouth before Jesse could. "I believe you, Grady. Whatever it was, we'll find out. But Jesse's right. Let's just finish the game. One more clue to solve and we go back to Jesse's."

"Yes," Jesse said, nodding. "We can play Primal Rage until the sun comes up, like old times."

"That game sucks ass," Grady said, unable to crack a smile. "I don't know why you're so in love with it."

"You're on meth if you think that game sucks. It's the greatest fighting game of all time."

"Mortal Kombat II."

"No w—what? You really think that?"

"Yes. I do."

"You just like it because of Reptile and his acid spit. Newsflash, boner breath—that doesn't make it a better game."

Doug clapped his hands together. "Guys, focus."

Both of them turned to Doug. Jesse was grinning like a sideshow clown. Part of Grady seemed like he was still being held hostage by what he'd seen earlier, unable to break free from the horrors that scene had hinted at.

"Focus," Doug repeated as Jimmy pulled up to the tennis courts and killed the engine.

2

Jesse followed his brother up the path leading to the tennis court cage. He glanced over his shoulder at Doug and Grady. The duo had lost some pep in their step, as if they were carrying cinderblocks on each shoulder. The boys had been up for almost twenty-four hours straight, and Jesse blamed the late hour for their lack of enthusiasm, not their strange accounts.

Doug had just lobbied for their attention, telling them to focus on the Hunt, but Jesse knew he was only saying that because he wanted it to end.

Even though Doug had missed out on Maddie's party and there was nothing left of the night except video games and whatever movies were on HBO after-dark, Jesse could tell he was done with tonight. In truth, Jesse had been a little done too. It wasn't as great as Jimmy had talked it up to be.

Actually, it was kind of lame.

Basic, he thought, eyeing the tennis courts, how they sat in the after-midnight shadows.

Basic—yes, but the game had brought his two best friends over for the night, *and* they'd gotten to cruise around Hooperstown in the T-Bird. So, all things considered, the night was not a complete buzzkill. He wished the Hunt was better though, that it had been more of a challenge.

Maybe when I design The Hunt, he thought. *Maybe next year.*

Jimmy stopped when he reached the cage's door. "Shit." He jiggled the padlock that prevented the gate latch from rising. "Locked."

Jesse arched back, looked up. It was only about a fifteen-foot climb. "I can climb it," he announced with no shortage of confidence.

Peering over his friend's shoulder, Doug wrinkled his entire face and said, "You can't climb that, dude."

"Bullshit with a capital B, buddy boy. I'll climb the shit out of this fence."

Of the five of them, Jesse *was* the most athletic. Jimmy never was the fit type, and Karen—she smoked so much she probably couldn't get halfway up without hacking up a lung. Doug and Grady could make the climb no problem, but Jesse was the best choice. "It'll take me two seconds."

"Wanna bet?" Doug dug through his pockets. "Five bucks."

"Five bucks?" Jesse scoffed. "What're you, nuts? You *knoooooooow* I can climb this thing. You really want to piss away five bucks, be my guest, Doug E. Fresh."

"Just don't think you can do it, that's all," Doug told him.

"You're on then."

Jesse turned and ran at the cage. Latching onto the chain-link, he methodically worked his way up with the grace of a house spider. He was halfway up before anyone could blink.

"Careful, little brother," Jimmy said, crossing his arms. "If you fall and break your arm, Mom and Dad will fucking murder me."

Jesse ignored him, doubting his mother and father would chalk up any injury to a bout of bad luck and tell their children to be more mindful going forward. They weren't the kind of parents who handed down strict discipline, even when they should. They gave them a stern talking once in a while, *maybe,* but that was the extent of their approach. Jesse had broken an arm when he was eleven, and it had been no big deal. The pain hadn't been that bad, though, time and pain could be strange like that. The brain has a funny way of flushing those moments of physical agony. It's not until one finds themself deep inside the experience again that they remember how much it hurt.

But Jesse was confident in his ability, knew he wouldn't allow himself to fall, that he could make it over safely. And he did so easily, though it took him longer than two seconds. When his feet were planted court side, he flashed everyone outside the cage two middle fingers. "Better toss me that five bucks, Simms."

Doug placed his hands on his hips, smiling even though he lost. "You'll get it in installments, Di Falco. Five easy payments of go fuck yourself."

Jesse balked at that, then turned to the courts in search of the final clue. "Now, where is this thing? Any ideas, ladies?"

No one offered anything right away, but after a few seconds later Grady grabbed hold of the cage and said, "Check near the nets, maybe?"

"Good idea, Grades."

Jesse made for the nets, examining each one with careful consideration. He came up empty, glanced around the courts, and then looked back to the team, all of whom were waiting with anticipation. Karen crushed the stub of her cigarette under her shoe. Jimmy paced back and forth in front of his Thunderbird. The moon lit up the crew, making them look like the roaming hoard of background dancers in Michael Jackson's *Thriller* video. Jesse chuckled softly when he imagined Karen doing the dance, shaking her shoulders while walking sideways and snapping her fingers.

"Well?" Jimmy asked. "We're waiting, bozo."

Jesse shook his head, held out his arms helplessly. "Nothing here."

"Well, there's gotta be *something.*"

"Check the far side of the cage," Doug said, pointing to the back of the court where the shadows had all but blackened out the moonlight. It was hard to see, but just beyond the chain-link barrier Jesse could see shrouded outlines of bushes and other dense shrubbery.

"Okay," Jesse said, not liking to have to brave the darkness. He'd never been one to fear the dark, but something about the murky projection before him sent a cold jolt through his bones.

There's something wrong tonight...

Jesse pushed Doug's concerns from his mind.

Don't you feel it?

He closed his eyes and walked toward the darkened corner, concentrating on Primal Rage and how he couldn't wait to bust out the old Sega Genesis. When he opened them, the shadows were there to greet him, an ever-black wall that towered skyward. Glancing over his shoulder, he saw his friends shifting their attention to each other, conversations he couldn't hear, ignoring Jesse and his journey into the shadows. He felt isolated and hated it. The dark clung to him like sticky spider webs. He faced what he could make out of the chain-link barrier. Slimming his eyes, he concentrated on what he'd come here for. Sure enough, four white papery ribbons danced in the soft breeze, clinging to the fence via some Scotch tape.

Son of a bitch, Jesse thought, bending down on one knee. All four ribbons were there, undisturbed. Not that he was surprised, but Team Watchmen had gotten to the scene first.

Jesse reached out for a ribbon when the shadows stirred before him. It sounded like an animal rolling through a small mound of brush, tumbling through the mess of leaves and twigs. Jesse recoiled, jumped back as if the dark had teeth. His rear planted on the court, and he heard a wave of snickers and hoarse whispers from behind him. He turned to see four smiles staring back at him. Even Grady, who'd been acting weird as hell since the theater, had found it comical.

"What's the matter, Di Falco?" he heard Doug call out.

"Come on, baby bro!" Jimmy yelled, using his hands around his mouth to project his voice.

Jesse ignored their taunts and pulled himself to his feet. *You're being ridiculous,* he thought. *There is nothing out there. Just the stupid dark.*

But with the dark came the unknown, the endless possibilities it stole away. That was all too real. The unknown was a palpable thing. It had no body, but if he listened close enough, he could hear its heartbeat (*thump-thump*) along with his own. The unknown's dangerous nature was only limited by the imagination of the beholder, and as someone who'd grown up on the R-rated features from Video World, Jesse's imaginative force was quite powerful.

Jesse extended his fingers, tempting the shadows, the terrible possibilities cloaked there.

"*Hi,*" a voice said, playful and sweet.

He nearly caked his underwear. Definitely yelped. His heart skipped several beats and everything inside him turned to mush and numbed.

"Whatthefuck?" he murmured, the diameter of his esophagus feeling like that of a straw. Falling back again, Jesse's elbows scraped against the rough surface of the tennis court, tearing up his skin. The pain was instantly squashed underneath the rush of fear-based adrenaline. Had he really heard that? Had the darkness spoken to him?

The shadows lay still, no sounds save for the winds stroking the trees.

"Jesse?" Doug called out, concern wrangling his voice.

"Did you guys hear that?" Jesse asked them.

"Hear what?"

Nothing. A measure of silence. Finally, air bristled past, breaking up the momentary lull in action.

"Nothing," he confirmed. He sat up once again, brushing off his knees.

This time he didn't hesitate, didn't allow the darkness to hook him. He snatched the ribbon before the voice could speak again, before the unknown could assemble sharp objects and strike. The moment his fingers clamped down on the fabric, he was retreating from the shadows.

He stared at the impossibly dark place, waiting for the unknown to protest his victory. But nothing came of it.

"Let's go!" Jimmy called.

Jesse delayed his return. But the second he spun around, the instant he showed his back to the shrouded corner, the bushes tussled about. What sounded like a young girl giggled—quiet as a paint stroke on a canvas. Jesse had heard it, though, and the abbreviated squeaks were as loud as thunder to him. He turned, expecting to see a deranged child, sick with disease, covered in warts with pus leaking from her eyes and nose. Instead, he saw only the unwavering shadows.

"*She's chosen you, Jesse,*" the shadows whispered, soft as the wind. "*You're not safe here. Not here, not home, not in the Land of Dreams. You will become one of them. One of the chosen children. Your body will die, and your soul will travel the dream-lands, wander endlessly in the fields of forever. You belong to her now, Jesse. So dream your dreams and when she—"*

"Fuck you."

He had had enough of that, turning sharply and sprinting toward the cage. "Shit, shit, shit," he mumbled the whole way there. The climb back over took him even less time, so fast no one on the other side had time to question the reasoning behind his brisk pace.

Once he was over, he bent down and put his hands on his knees, attempting to regulate his breathing and refill his lungs. It wasn't that he was out of shape—far from it; it was the unexpected voice in the shadows that had frightened the air right out of him. Team Watchmen crowded around him, asking if he was all right, why he was acting like the Devil had tossed a pitchfork at his heels. He barely heard them over the pounding in his temples.

"There was...someone...over there," he said between gasps of air.

The four of them looked at the dark corner. Jesse gauged their reactions, but not one of them looked as if they had seen anything. That was because there was nothing to see.

"I swear," he said, gasping. "Someone. A little girl. She was...out there... She said some...really creepy shit."

Jimmy was the first one to lay into him. "Shut up, nerd."

"I swear to God, man."

Karen snorted as she readied her lighter, preparing to light her next smoke. The lighter sparked and she sucked in a lungful, white wisps circling off into the night.

"Stop being an idiot," Jimmy said.

"I'm not, dude."

Jimmy pointed at the dark corner. "If I go over there—"

"Don't!" Jesse raised his hands to stop him, if it came to that. "Let's just go."

Jimmy must've noticed the sheer terror in his brother's face because his finger fell back to his side. "I'm curious now."

"Don't be. It doesn't matter. Let's just go."

"If there is someone being creepy over there, they should get their ass kicked."

"A little girl?" Karen asked.

Jimmy shrugged. "What if it's not a little girl? What if it's some pervert pretending to be a little girl? What if—"

"It doesn't matter," Jesse pleaded. "Let's just go, Jimmy. Please." He handed over the ribbon. "I got the next clue, so let's just leave."

Team Watchmen huddled close together and looked at the clue over Jimmy's shoulder as he unraveled it. Across the ribbon was written:

THE CITY OF THE DEAD
THE CITY OF STONES
WHERE DREAMERS DREAM
IN FIELDS OF BROKEN BONES

"Finally," Jimmy said, sounding impressed. "Some effort."

Jesse barely heard him. The letters on the ribbon all bled together, ran from his vision like wet ink. That dark corner called to him. When his eyes returned to the spot, he thought he saw a shape forming in the shadows—a pale face with oozing warts. Eyes that leaked pus and infectious fluids of decay. Blonde hair that twirled in the wind. A cherubic smile that proudly displayed two rows of dead, gray teeth. Behind the materializing form, long elastic patterns cut through the shadowy backdrop, whipping about like unmanned fire hoses.

He swore he heard some sinister voice cackle, mocking Jesse and his tainted thoughts. But no one else heard a thing. And if they had, no one acted like it. He wasn't going to mention the sounds again. It wasn't worth the ridicule.

"You all right?" Jimmy asked him, bumping his brother with his elbow.

Jesse looked up and saw four faces staring at him, each with traces of worry circling their features.

"Yeah," he said, rubbing his own shoulders as if he were suddenly cold, barely aware of his actions. "Yeah, why?"

"You look like you saw a ghost."

Jesse's eyes cut back to the corner, and there the darkness stood, tall and proud, watching over the strange night and all that it offered.

"No," he said, as if that was that and nothing more.

Karen blew out another breath of smoke. "Let's get out of here, Jim. Place is kinda freakin' me out."

Freakin' YOU out? Jesse thought, a mouthful of laughter ascending his throat. *This place is freakin' me the fuck out!*

He kept those dangerous thoughts to himself.

"Fucking Greenwood Village," Jimmy said, handing Doug the ribbon. "All right. Let's roll. Let's get some snacks while we figure out this final clue."

3

From the Wawa parking lot, Doug looked up at the sky, his eyes glued to the vast collection of stars. The night was at its darkest hour, a little after two. He couldn't remember the last time he stayed up this late. The air had lost its humid quality and was pleasantly breezy. The moon stood like a lighthouse beacon, providing a pale glow to the side of the world that now knew only darkness. That *off* feeling Doug had tuned into—which had slightly faded during the drive over here—was now back at full force, funneling through his body, penetrating every bone, every fiber of his being.

"It could be a thousand different things," Jimmy said with a mouthful of buffalo chicken sandwich. He sipped his latte through a straw. "City of the dead? City of stones? And what's up with the *dreamers dream* bullshit." He closed his eyes and shuddered. "I think Randall and Alphie are just fucking with us in some way. This makes no sense. I wouldn't be surprised if it was a song lyric or something. Fuckers, man."

Grady had finished his six-inch Italian sub and was now pacing back and forth on the strip of grass between the convenience store's property and Route 37, the normally busy highway that was now a desolate stretch of pavement at this late hour. "*City of the Dead* could mean a graveyard."

Jimmy wrinkled his nose and tugged on his lip with his teeth. "You really think so? I mean, I guess it could mean that."

"*City of Stones,*" Karen said, almost dreamlike. She'd opted to spend her Wawa gift card on peanut butter crackers in lieu of a tasty sub sandwich.

She also added on another pack of Marlboro Lights. Already a cigarette into the new pack, she grabbed another one and sparked it up. "Could mean *gravestones.*"

Grady said, "Could make sense. There are three cemeteries in Hooperstown. But which one are they talking about? Two of them are massive. The one on Church Road is like six miles long—well, maybe not that big, but it's big. And Cedarborough Cemetery has like six billion graves. Okay, not that many, but enough to where it would take us the rest of the night to search."

Jimmy glanced down at the clue one last time as if it would reveal some hidden truth in the final moment before they could choose their destination. "I don't get it. Why would they make the first six clues easy as shit, then throw us a massive curveball on the last one? What the hell is wrong with those idiots?"

"Stoner fucks," Karen said, shrugging, as if that were the only possible answer.

"Fucking stoner fucks," Jimmy agreed.

While they were debating what the last clue meant, Doug took it all in. Something about the mention of "dreamers" and "dreams" got him thinking about last night's escapade. The same unusual journey he always had, except it had been some time since he dreamed of the trip through the forest, the adventure in the cave, and the terrifying discoveries that awaited him, the boy and the girl. It had been so long since he'd dreamed it that he thought he was past it. That he'd never experience that adventure again.

I know you dream of them. You do, don't you? You dream of her?

Those echoes left him cold inside.

I won't let anything happen to you, kiddo. I won't let her touch you.

Who? he remembered a little boy asking his mother the moment before she tucked him into bed. *Who, Mommy?*

Who-who? She had giggled at that. *Who? You sound just like an owl, Little Bug.*

Not a kid anymore, Mom.

You'll always be my kiddo, Douglas.

Doug tried to shove the memories aside, but they were resistant. Stout. Unwilling to depart.

(I won't let her touch you)

Who? Mom? Please? Tell me?

He remembered the sigh that had come from her mouth, how it sounded like she was releasing more than just a breath.

Secrets, he thought. She was releasing secrets.

He remembered her leaning over him as if she were attempting to kiss his cheek, wishing him a goodnight and pleasant dreams.

A woman, she had softly spoken, making sure his father did not overhear. He had been in the living room watching the game, cheering on his New York Giants football team. *She comes from the land of dreams. The shadow world. She eats dreams and the dreamers who dream them. At least...that's what they tell me.*

She had spoken these words with a smile that never faltered, showed no signs of wear.

Who tells you? he had asked.

Just the ghosts of this town, kiddo. Just the ghosts. She must have seen a hint of horror on her son's face because she stopped after that. *Now, now. Don't worry about that stuff. Your mother is here to protect you. She won't let anything bad happen to you.*

What about Dad? Will he protect me too?

She had hesitated. *Of course,* she had said, but Doug had gotten the sense she wasn't telling the truth.

Momma will always be there for you.

(she comes from the land of dreams)

(a woman)

(eater of dreams and the dreamers who dream them)

"Doug!" Grady yelled in his face.

Doug blinked several times. When his memories faded and the real world snapped back to life before him, he found all four members of Team Watchmen staring directly at him as if he'd done or said something terrible, something he couldn't take back with an apology. To his knowledge, he'd said no such thing, hadn't uttered a single word, hadn't even moved a muscle. "What? What is it?"

"Dude," Jesse said, his tired voice unsteady. "You, like, went somewhere."

"Went somewhere?" Confused, Doug studied his surroundings. He hadn't budged an inch since wandering into those troubled memories.

"Like, inside your head."

Jimmy added, "We called your name like a hundred times and you were just...frozen."

An over-exaggerated response, Doug was sure of it. But they probably had called his name several times, and he probably had been unresponsive. The memory had stolen him away, taken him elsewhere. The past had never felt so real, like he was actually there, experiencing the moment, the event he'd lived before. He could feel the weight of his comforter pressing down on him, could feel the tickle of his mother's breath against his cheek.

(eater of dreams)

This night was proving to be something else. Maybe not magic, but *something*.

Despite the warmth of summer, Doug shivered. "Sorry, didn't mean to."

"Well," Grady said, letting go of his friend's shoulders, "tell me you went somewhere that gave you the answer to the next clue."

Doug thought about it. "No. I have no idea."

"No hints on the dream shit?" asked Jesse, groggily.

Doug shook his head. "None. But the Cedarborough Cemetery..." His throat felt dry and patchy. "That seems like a good place to start."

"Why?" questioned Jimmy.

Doug shrugged. "I don't know. Feels right."

"We're gonna need more than 'feels right,' Simms," Jimmy said. A condescending chuckle followed. "I mean, we need something we can run with, something we can all get behind. Make sure we're not wasting our time."

For some reason, Doug wanted to say, *Because that's where our dreams will go to die,* but that sounded like sheer nonsense. *Was* sheer nonsense, even though he believed it. Instead, he went with, "Just a feeling, that's all."

Jimmy sighed. "Well, that's great."

It was Grady who came to his defense. "Anybody have a better idea? I mean, if no one can gather anything else from that gibberish," he pointed to the clue in Jimmy's hand, "then maybe we just check out Cedarborough?"

"And if we can't find the next clue," Jesse added, "who cares? Not like anyone else is playing, anyway."

In his head, Jimmy cycled through their options. "Fine. We'll check it out. But we promised we'd finish this thing. See it through to the end."

The three kids, all of whom looked beyond exhausted, their youthful souls defeated, nodded in agreement, although none of them looked like they cared to continue.

The night had won.

"All right," Jimmy said, tossing the sandwich wrapper in the nearby trash can. "Let's roll out."

CHAPTER SIX

It All Goes Down When The Sun Comes Up

1

She tried her best to gently close the front door behind her, but the click of the deadlock plunger snapping into the striker plate sounded like a gunshot in the silence of the crummy apartment. Jewel stayed completely still for a beat, waiting for her mother to swarm her, waiting for the fists of fury to fly unrestrained before she was even greeted with a "Hello, how are you? Where you been, bitch?"

But there was nothing. Not a single footfall on the dirt-smeared carpet or the ruffling of coarse bedsheets. The couch was vacant save for an empty pizza box and several squeeze-crushed beer cans. For a minute she thought she had the apartment all to herself, which would have been nice, but then decided that wasn't too likely. Unless her mother discovered her missing and went out looking for her—but she knew that wasn't the case. Ava Conti would never waste the energy. Even if she had disappeared for days, Mother would just wait at home, stewing in her anger and hate, baking in that perpetual state of misery, but never lifting a finger to do anything about it. Not even a quick five-second phone call to the local police, just to make sure someone hadn't found her daughter dead in a street gutter somewhere. No, if Jewel went missing for good, that would be like an early Christmas for Ava Conti.

Still, despite those sweet thoughts, the silence was welcoming. She knew it couldn't continue, but she hoped it would last 'til sunrise.

Moving away from the door, she tiptoed past the kitchen and down the hall. Her mother's door was ajar, just slightly. As if it were some nightmarish image that conjured unspeakable evils, she avoided looking into the dark crack. She feared she'd see Mother staring directly back at her, her cold, hateful gaze inquiring about the night and everything that had happened.

As if she cares.

Jewel made it past the door and to her room without any interruption. A sigh of relief exploded from her mouth as she slipped inside her bedroom and flipped on the light switch. She couldn't believe it. Even if Mother woke now, Jewel could still lock her door and ride out the storm of insults, death threats, and empty violent promises until either Mother gave up or the upstairs neighbors called the cops.

She closed the door, keeping her eye trained on the dark hallway, expecting to see her mother's shadow emerge. But the crack narrowed and finally closed, and she was free from that particular scenario.

Turning, she almost shrieked when she saw the figure sitting on her bed. *Mother.*

"Where were ya?" she asked groggily.

The woman's eyes were half-shut, huge black circles surrounding the flesh, looking as if she'd taken a good punch several days ago. And who knew? Maybe she had. There were a few crushed beer cans at the foot of her bed and a glass pipe resting next to Mother's leg. Some crystalline shavings surrounded the paraphernalia and a faint, peculiar smell tainted her room.

The subtle stench reminded her of the one time she put a non-microwavable Tupperware bowl in the microwave and nearly lit the damn thing on fire.

"Out," Jewel answered, her throat feeling like a knotted cord.

"Where?" Mother's body swayed to one side, her eyes closing and opening, fluttering back and forth between the two.

"Let me get you into bed, Mama."

The kind offer—kinder than she deserved—jolted her awake. She shook her head like an injured butterfly wing, abandoning whatever dreamworld she had been on the cusp of exploring. "I ashked you a fukin westion, you smartm-thed *cunt*."

Out of breathing room, Jewel felt her back knock against the wall. She thought about running, opening the door and sprinting down the hall. She could reach the apartment's shared driveway before her mother could even stabilize her feet. But she was tired of running. Tired of tonight. Completely bushed. And furthermore, she was scared of the darkness and what it had revealed to her earlier.

She was more terrified of whatever had happened to Randall Benoit than whatever her mother could do or say.

"I went to the movies."

Her mother reacted as if Jewel had expressed some lurid admission. "Bah yeh-sef?"

"Yes. By myself."

"Yeh bish," her mother said, smiling now, her lips teeming with utter disgust. "Oh, yeh bish. Yeh think yeh can do whuheva yeh want, den yeh?"

"No, mother." Sweat dribbled down her brow. The apartment was always an inferno come summertime—mostly because the Contis refused to turn on the air conditioning unit—but tonight, the room was an overworked oven. "No, not at all."

Her mother rose from the bed. Jewel flinched, got ready to run. But she didn't. Something stopped her. Maybe tonight was the night, the night she'd finally stand up for herself, break this cycle of violence and abuse. These nights of blood and tears.

"Yas, yeh do. Yousa bish. Good-for-nothing cunt-rag."

"Mother, don't—"

Like a bolt of lightning, Mother flashed across the room. Her backhand drove across Jewel's cheek with unchecked force. For a second, she thought her mother had broken her jaw. The impact was hard enough to send her staggering into the corner of the room.

"Don't talk back to yo' mother!"

Evidently, the louder Ava Conti screamed, the more coherent she became. It was a remarkable talent, one Jewel might have marveled over if her face didn't feel like it had been fractured in two. "G'dammit," she said, slumping her shoulders, stepping back from Jewel, who was holding her face as if doing so were keeping everything together.

"Look what yeh made me do," Mother said.

Jewel dropped her hands, revealing the red mark that had swollen on her cheek. "You hit me."

"Thas right, bay-bee. Hitcha good." She seemed proud. Righteous. It took everything Jewel had not to retaliate.

"You're a mess," Jewel snapped. "A fucking disaster."

Ava's face turned red. "How. Dare. Y—"

"Shut the fuck up."

Ava launched another attack, but Jewel backed away. Mother stumbled, nearly tripping over her own feet and falling head-first into the wall. She caught herself before doing so and used the wall to support her shaky legs. Jewel felt a rage building inside her that she wanted so very much to unleash.

"Pathetic," Jewel hissed.

She hinted at a smile, which was as good as any punch. The ever-so-slight curl of her lips provoked another spark of fury. Ava came at her daughter again, an awkward, zombie-like stride that was as uncoordinated as her second attack, walking as if her ankles were broken. This time, Jewel saw the swat of her palm coming a whole five seconds before it happened and jumped on her bed. Ava tripped into a shelf holding some of her daughter's possessions, books and stacks of teenager-aimed magazines that all went unread, the periodicals there mostly for the pictures of Jewel's celebrity crushes. In a rush of absolute anger and frustration, Ava used her arm to sweep an entire row of reading materials onto the floor. This thud of thirty or so magazines hitting the carpet undoubtedly woke the next-door neighbors. Which was good, because Jewel figured they'd probably call the cops. The cops would save her. They had to.

Right?

"Shay were yeh ah," Ava said, swaying on her heels. *Stay where you are.*

"No. I'm not gonna let you hit me again."

"Bish," Ava replied, and then burped. Jewel could smell the sharp bite of alcohol from ten feet away. "Yeh listen ta me. *Now*."

Ava came again, swinging her shoulders as if that somehow helped her walk in a straight line. Then her hands started flying through the air, wildly. Jewel saw they weren't open-palm slaps anymore, but fists, balled tight, their only purpose to knock out a few teeth.

Jewel launched herself from the mattress, the springs providing her with more velocity. Leading with her shoulder, she crashed into her mother, catching her in the chin. The bulk of her body impacted her mother's, and the two went sprawling to the floor. Wanting to beat her mother to her feet, she rolled off to one side and leaped to her feet.

Her mother spit up a small squirt of blood. She muttered something that sounded a lot like *you cunt*. Clambering to her feet, Jewel immediately streaked toward the bedroom door, not waiting to see how long it took for her mother to recover. Jewel ripped open the door, was halfway across the threshold and into the hallway, when she heard giggling behind her.

It hardly sounded like Ava Conti.

Skin crawling with invisible insects, Jewel looked over her shoulder and faced her mother. Hopefully this would be the last time until she straightened her shit out.

"*Yeh*," she said like a snake hissing before a lethal strike. "Yeh think yeh can run away. Do betta somewhere else? Fine. Leave. Go. But yeh'll be back." Another giggle escaped her crooked mouth, sounding equally as hideous. "Yeh'll be back. And I'll take care of yeh. Muh..ther will...*always* take care of yeh."

That last line chilled her blood more than anything else that night.

Jewel turned to the shadows that filled the hallway and ran toward a dawn that was beginning to blossom on the dark horizon.

2

About two hours before Jewel Conti confronted her mother in a moment that would undoubtedly forever change her life, Doug Simms gripped the wrought-iron rail of the cemetery gates and climbed. Grady was already standing on the other side—it had taken a Herculean effort from both Doug and Jesse to push him over the spike-tipped top, but they had gotten him over without incident. Once Doug was over, Jesse made his ascent. In the matter of seconds, all three boys were standing on the other side, brushing off the wet grass and dirt that stained their knees.

The three of them turned, faced the thick stretch of fog that blanketed the hills of Cedarborough Cemetery. No one took that first step forward, each of the boys waiting for someone else to take charge, lead them into the mist. Doug collected his breath, his courage.

"Well?" Jesse asked. "What are we waiting for?"

If that was supposed to motivate them, it didn't. The three continued to gaze into the low-hanging fog, envisioning what could possibly await them. Doug couldn't help but think terrible thoughts, that nothing good would come from entering the spooky realm. The night continued to feel haunted, and being here, in this place, at this hour, did nothing to settle his nerves.

"All right," he said, finally, wiping the sweat from his brow. "This is dumb. We're being stupid."

"Agreed," Jesse said, cracking his knuckles. "Let's do this. Let's fuck this graveyard."

"Always so vulgar," Grady said, shaking his head.

"Yep. Can't help it. It's my nature."

"Well, maybe be less like your nature and a little more... I dunno— normal." Grady winced like the edge of an envelope split his skin. "I mean, seriously. How do you *fuck* a graveyard? That makes absolutely no sense."

"You know, not like literally fuck it, but *fuck it*. Like...conquer it. It's an expression."

"It's not an expression. You're just an idiot."

"You're...*you're* an idiot. You're the dumb one. I'm smart." He shook his head. "You're just saying that stuff because you're delegating."

Grady glanced at him as if his head were screwed on backwards. "Delegating? Do you even know that word, what it means?"

"What? Yes." He paused to think about it. "No. Yes. I don't know, man. I'm tired and I can barely keep my fucking eyes open and you're going to nitpick everything I say?"

Doug said, "He definitely doesn't know what it means."

"I know what it means. Just drop it, okay? Come on. Let's get going. Sooner we find this clue, sooner we get out of this creepy-ass place."

"Oh!" Grady said, lightly punching Jesse's arm. "So it's creepy now?"

"Of course it's fucking creepy. Look at it."

"Guys," Doug interrupted. "You're doing it again."

Grady and Jesse clammed up.

"Jesse's right," Doug continued. "Sooner we find the last clue, sooner we can go home." He was the first one to step toward the hill and it felt good to get that initial step out of the way. There was still a fear that the Wolf-Man would come climbing over a headstone, snarling and gnashing its pointy-sharp teeth, but other than that he was relatively at ease, his heart rate climbing back down to its regular rhythm.

"Okay," Grady said. "We're doing this. We're actually doing this. Not freaking out. Nope, not at all."

Jesse chuckled. "Come on, Grades. I'll hold your hand."

"Shut up, butthole."

The rest of the journey up the hill and into the white blanket of fog was quiet, not a word spoken between the three boys. The fog was so thick they could barely see in front of them, but after thirty feet or so, once they planted their shoes in the city of the dead, the city of stones, the fog gave way and allowed them a clear glimpse across the entire cemetery. In the distance Doug could see the bouncing light coming from Jimmy and Karen's flashlight, the narrow beam whipping back and forth, searching for the final clue that would bring this night to a much-needed end. Doug wished they'd hurry up already.

Karen's laughter echoed across the dark, and Doug wondered how much "looking" was actually taking place.

"No hanky-panky!" shouted Jesse.

"Sssshh!" Grady swatted him with the back of his hand. "Are you nuts, dude?"

"What? No one heard us."

"There's literally a neighborhood right across the street! You'll wake people up!"

"Grades, you worry too much, man." Jesse nodded in the proposed direction. "Let's go that way. C'mon."

"Ugh." Grady shook his head. "I knew splitting up was a bad idea." He turned to Doug. "Why did you allow this to happen?"

Doug put up his hands. "Whoa. I was in favor of sticking together. Remember?"

He had been. They both had been. It was Jesse who had lobbied for splitting up, only because Jimmy had suggested it first. As he had rounded up the flashlights in his trunk, Jimmy had told them it was the best plan. *Cover more ground that way,* he had said.

Doug had known it was a bad idea from the start, but Jesse went along with it, unable to refute any idea his brother came up with.

Jesse took the lead and Doug followed, Grady bringing up the rear. They walked along the manmade path, keeping their eyes peeled for any potential leads, anything that would steer them toward victory, an end. Doug tried to concentrate, focus on the task at hand, envision what the last clue might look like and the potential places the game-makers might hide it, but his memories kept getting in the way. Snippets of the past continued to toy with him, particularly of the night his mother had spoken about the mysterious woman, the one hungry for his dreams. Why the clue Randall Benoit and Alphie Moffit had left behind reminded him of that night, he had no idea.

It was the dream from last night, he thought. *The Boy. The Girl. The trip through the woods.*

The cave.

Her place.

The images kept looping through his thoughts, and he was unable to tuck them away in the back of his mind where most dreams go to die.

Pushing the dark imagery from his internal projector proved to be a struggle, and as he passed a series of headstones and marble benches used in memoriam, the war waging within him kicked up a notch. He couldn't fully remember, but he recalled his father talking to someone who'd come knocking on their door one afternoon, someone who had seemed entirely concerned and short on time. His father's voice had been low, just above a whisper, and when he called to his son, told him he'd be right back, that he was just stepping onto the porch for a second, Doug remembered yelling back, "All right, Dad!"

He couldn't have been older than six. He remembered running down the stairs and into the living room, sticking his ear to the outside wall, hoping to hear whatever his dad was about to discuss with their mysterious guest. He'd stolen a peek through the window and saw it was a cop, but not any old cop—it had been Chief Pritchard himself. The big man had seemed concerned, his face sagging with worry, and he spoke in a manner that gravely upset his father. As the chief spoke, Dad had hidden the lower half of his face behind his hand and rocked back and forth on busy feet.

Doug hadn't made out very much of the conversation and now, as he strolled through Cedarborough, he couldn't remember every detail of that afternoon. The past was much like a dream itself, much like the worlds he'd explored while he slept, and only fragments remained clear. Though, he did remember important words like *naked* and *singing* and *Cedarborough*.

Was that why he had suggested Cedarborough? Because of that one conversation he'd eavesdropped on almost a decade ago? The one he couldn't fully recall? He was certain Pritchard had mentioned Cedarborough Cemetery. The words played like fragments of a song lyric only heard once before.

He was talking about Mom, he thought, distinctly remembering the grave expression on his father's face when Pritchard had told him...well, whatever it was he had told him.

Mom was here.

In this place.

Suddenly, the night grew darker. Even though the stars were smashed in a never-ending pattern of cosmic dust, providing the world with natural specks of light, the shadows closed in and around everything.

The dark was here.

And it walked alongside them.

A chill laced Doug's spine.

"What are you thinking about, Dougster?" Jesse asked, seeming to have noticed his best friend's mind had rocketed from Earth once again.

"Just about my mother," Doug replied. "For some reason," he added, shrugging.

"Oh."

Doug hadn't talked about her much around them; it was a subject that wasn't exactly off-limits, but it was awkward for both parties. Any time the subject was approached, the three of them danced around its center and ultimately directed the conversation elsewhere.

"What about her?" Grady asked, and it was the first time he'd ever prodded so brazenly.

"I don't know, actually. It's like… I know it's stupid, but I can't help but feel that she's a part of this somehow."

"A part of what?" Jesse asked.

"The night. The strangeness of it."

The boys kept their lips locked, but the silence wasn't everlasting. Silence between boys rarely could be.

"We've all seen things tonight. Whether we want to admit it or not." That was a shot directed at Jesse, and he gave his friend a knowing glance to punctuate his point.

"I don't know what—"

"Don't pretend like you didn't see something in Greenwood Village. We both saw the look on your face. You were spooked."

Jesse didn't reply, didn't have to. The lines on his face gave him up.

Doug looked over his shoulder at Grady. "You saw Randall Benoit, and I saw Alphie Moffit. Both of them were here. Right?"

Doug stopped walking.

The other two boys traveled a few paces ahead, then stopped when they realized Doug wasn't following them.

"Right?" Doug asked again.

Jesse shrugged. "Yeah, I guess, man."

Grady nodded.

"Guys…why do you think the last clue was so different from the others? I mean, why wasn't it as simple? And why do I feel like my mother being here in the past has some significance to all of this?"

His audience shrugged, not having the slightest clue.

"What are you suggesting?" Jesse asked. The way the moonlight touched his face made the boy look dead, or sick, or both. "I mean, clearly you have some idea or you wouldn't be talking about it."

"That's the thing. I don't."

As if the world wanted to chime in, a harsh wind blew across the cemetery, sounding like warbled static. Doug checked the status of their two teammates, their chaperones for the evening, and noticed they had either slipped into the darkness or beyond a cluster of thick fog.

Probably making out.

Or doing it.

Doug pushed those trashy thoughts under a pile of others.

"No clue?" Grady asked. "Come on, Doug. There has to be something."

"I can't remember. My mother… I don't remember her that well. It's like…it sounds weird, but it's like I've lived two lives. One with her and one without, and the one with her feels less like reality and more like a…"

"Like a dream?" Grady asked.

Doug nodded. "Yeah. Exactly."

"I feel that way sometimes. When I remember things that happened six, seven years ago. It's like none of it was real."

"Guys," Jesse said, his eyes slightly expanding. "Do you think when we're older—like, adults—that we'll look back on these days and think they're just a dream, too?"

Doug shrugged. "Maybe."

Grady shivered. "I don't want to think about getting older, man. Not now."

The wind howled again, and the three boys turned back and faced the stretch of graves as if it were an eldritch creature they had disturbed from a deep, eternal slumber.

"Think, Doug," Jesse urged. "Did your mom say anything about this place?"

Doug tried, but he couldn't bring forth any useful memories. There was the one night she tucked him into bed, the nonsense she had whispered, the time Pritchard had spoken to his father, and there was, of course, the time *they* came for her, the men in white scrubs who'd hauled her off somewhere, a place she never returned from.

Crazy town, people said. Not directly. Not to his face, no. But he'd caught snippets of this information while passing folks on street corners or walking by in the supermarket. He wondered if his father had heard them, too. He was a smart man, very aware of things, so probably. Of course, if he had, he always played it off as though he hadn't. That was either good acting on his part or he truly wasn't aware of the terrible things whispered down the aisles in the A&P. Maybe he didn't know what people were saying about his wife.

Ex-wife.

Were they divorced, though? Like half the parents in Doug's class? Doug didn't know if there was any official paperwork filed or what their legal status was, but he assumed it was a done deal.

It was probably official the night she had tried to kill them.

"I don't remember..." he told his friends.

"Nothing?" Grady asked, pushing his friend further than he ever had before. "Not even from...you know...*that night?*"

He'd been seven, and it was about six months after that night she had whispered those secrets to him. He remembered his dad waking him up, telling him they needed to leave the house. That something had *happened.*

It had been dark.

So impossibly dark.

And cold. It had been winter.

He remembered making it to the hallway when his mother attacked them, screaming like she was in excruciating agony, as if she were being tortured. And maybe she *had* been in pain, maybe she *had* been tortured. Whatever had crawled into her head and made her sick, made her *insane,* had been tearing through her, eating her from the inside out—slowly, methodically, and viciously. He remembered the knife flashing in the darkness, seeing the entire blade disappear inside his father's shoulder.

"No," Doug said. "I can't remember much."

"Like a dream?" Jesse suggested, as if he were currently dreaming himself.

"Yeah, like that."

"Let's keep going," Grady told them, taking the lead. "Maybe we'll find something up ahead. No sense standing here like birds on a wire."

No one argued.

They started back on the path, and the wind sung them the songs of the dead.

Jimmy wanted to get laid. The scavenger hunt had become secondary to that instinctual, teenage need. And where better to get it on than a graveyard? It would be a cool story to share with his friends, a fun tidbit he'd surely remember later in life, a real *hey, remember when you had sex in a graveyard, man?* memory. Of course, it took two to tango, and he knew Karen would need some convincing. He wasn't sure if he could sell her on the dark ambience of their surroundings alone. There needed to be something else besides the thrill of it.

As they casually strolled down the path, laughing and not paying any attention to the three kids they'd left back at the gate, Jimmy grabbed his girlfriend's hand and led her astray, into a heavy patch of fog. On the other side of the earthly vapor he began kissing her neck and reaching around her waist to firmly plant his hands on her buttocks. After a good five seconds of this, she stopped him.

"What are you doing?" She smiled, a twinkle of starlight prominently reflecting off her eyes. Jimmy thought there was something else shimmering there as well, and that it would bring him good fortunes.

"What? I love you. Can't I just love you?"

"Well, I love you too." She eyed him, as if knowing his motives weren't strictly love-based. "But what are you doing?"

He answered by pressing his lips against the softest part of her neck. "Just want you, that's all."

"Here?"

His tongue slithered across her flesh like a slug. "Yes. Here. Now."

Her hand shoved him away, forcefully.

"What?"

"You know what."

He gave her the saddest puppy-dog eyes he could manufacture. "It'll be fun. I'm really horny for you, baby. You've been looking so good tonight."

She bit her lip and toyed with the cigarette behind her ear. "Have you now?"

"Yeah."

"Where would we do it?"

Excited, Jimmy looked around. His eyes fell on a stone bench, a long, six-foot grave marker that had the dead's name and living dates etched into its face. "There," he said, jerking his thumb.

"*Ew* and *no*."

"Come on." He teased her by lifting his shirt, exposing the smoothness of his flat abs. Knowing she couldn't resist. "It'll be hot."

Her tongue was between her teeth, and he could tell she was thinking about it, playing out the scenario in her mind.

"Admit it," he said, dropping to his knees so his mouth was level with her navel. He lifted up her shirt and kissed her stomach. "You want it."

She closed her eyes and did not stop him. Not at first. For a solid thirty seconds, he kissed the smoothness of her stomach. Then he unbuttoned her jeans. Again, she allowed it, put her hand on the back of his head, her fingers swimming through his tangles of hair. He lowered his attention, smooching the treasure her panties covered.

She moaned, a low utterance at first, but once he slipped a hand underneath the fabric of her underwear her sounds grew louder. Jimmy kept working what she called "Magic Fingers." About a minute into his indecent exploration, Karen gasped and backed away, zipping up her jeans. Her eyes shot wide with certain terror.

"What?" Jimmy asked, pushing himself off his knees and wiping his mouth. "What is it?"

She pointed in response.

Jimmy turned and faced the beginnings of the woods, the deep forest that stretched across the Hooperstown border. At first, he didn't see it. But after ten seconds of training his eyes to deal with the dark, the faint shape of something human appeared, like a ghost shrouded in fog.

"Oh, what the hell, man," Jimmy said, almost recognizing the shape. "You better come out of there, you little pervert. Or I'm gonna kick your ass."

He thought it was one of the kids, maybe his brother sneaking a peek. Not that he would blame him. Jesse was getting to that age when he'd start to get curious about sex stuff, and even though he hadn't had *that* talk with him, hadn't divulged all those filthy secrets, Jimmy suspected it was about time. In fact, if his brother was the mystery peeper, Jimmy wouldn't give him a hard time about it. But he still had to play the part for Karen's sake.

"Come on out of there!" he shouted at the shadow that, as he locked eyes onto its vague outline, appeared to be much taller than a fourteen-year-old. As the shape wandered out of the foggy beginnings of the forest, he realized it wasn't Jesse or one of his friends. It was someone else.

SomeTHING, the child's portion of his seventeen-year-old brain thought illogically, believing the intruder wasn't a person but some alien life-form. Realizing how stupid that sounded, Jimmy swallowed his trepidation and stepped toward the approaching figure. It was a move to show the possibly dangerous outsider that he was not afraid, nor would he be intimidated.

"I don't like this, Jimmy," Karen whispered. "We should bolt."

Jimmy disregarded her. Not that he didn't agree, but there was a certain image to uphold here. Not just in front of the girl, but if Jesse and his friends *were* watching, he'd want to make sure they viewed him as someone who wouldn't run from trouble. Especially trouble he could easily defeat, like some drunken asshole.

"Listen cock-knocker," Jimmy said, balling his fists. "If you don't—"

"*Jimmy,*" the shadow croaked.

Jimmy stepped back, the deep, groggy voice hitting him like a punch. "What the—"

From the shadows, Randall Benoit materialized. "*Jimmy, help.*"

He walked like a creature from a late-night horror movie, an old black and white picture. *Creature of the Black Lagoon,* he thought. Randall moved awkwardly, stumbling like his knees were on the verge of failing him. They wobbled with each step he took. Leftover dead leaves that had survived the winds of winter and springtime showers crunched beneath his feet. His feet betrayed him, and he tripped, but the headstone in front of him caught his fall.

"What the hell, Benoit?" Jimmy asked, not knowing what else to say.

He glanced over his shoulder. Karen had backed away, almost all the way back to the path from which they'd come. The fog enveloped her, stealing her away from Jimmy's vision. Turning back to Randall, Jimmy felt his chest twinge as his heart rate rocketed.

"What's wrong with you, man?" he said to Benoit.

"*She's inside me,*" he replied, clutching his chest.

Jimmy could make out his hands; they were dark, covered in some shiny substance. *Motor oil*, he thought. But when the smears he left on the headstone caught the moonlight, he saw the color was red.

Blood.

What the fuck happened to you, man? Jimmy almost asked, but his voice had failed to launch. His extremities ran cold and numb, an odd thing to feel on such a hot summer night.

Randall lifted his gaze as if the stars were speaking to him alone. A patch of moonlight illuminated his face, and Jimmy saw the condition of his skin and nearly shrieked with horror. Boils the size of a child's fist had bloomed across Randall's face, some of them popping and secreting a thick, syrupy discharge. The smell was even worse. Jimmy almost doubled over and lost his Wawa sandwich right there. Randall looked more like a walking corpse than someone on the verge of becoming a high school graduate. He stunk like he'd bathed in roadkill every day since birth.

Jimmy retreated, throwing his forearm across his nose. "Randall— man, what the fuck is happening to you?"

"*She made me sick, Jimmy,*" he said, staring up at the sky and the beauties it held over them. "*The Mother of Dead Dreams, she is here and she is angry and she wants us... She wants all of us... Jimmy, she's going to take us!*"

"Benoit, what the fuck are you talking about?"

In response, a toilet's worth of vomit exploded from Randall's mouth, splashing against the headstone he was leaning on. Dark fluids, a chunky, viscous mixture, crawled down the old stone like molten lava creeping down a volcanic crag.

"Jesus Christ," Jimmy said, turning his head. The stench intensified. If it got any worse, Jimmy thought he might pass out. "Benoit, you need help, dude. Let me get you to a hospital."

"*No... No time.*" He clutched his stomach and vomited again, the splatter soaking his shoes. "*She's coming. For us. For all of us. The Hunt, Jimmy. The Hunt has only just begun.*"

"Benoit—you're not right, dude. You need to—"

"*Shut the fuck up, you insolent fool!*"

Jimmy felt his forehead tighten. That didn't sound like Benoit.

As if conflicted by his own thoughts, Randall crouched down, holding his head, hands over his ears, repeating the phrase, *"Make it stop, make it stop"* over and over again. *"She's in my head. She's making me dream…"*

Jimmy turned and looked behind him; Karen had retreated into the fog. She was gone, leaving him alone. When he turned back to Randall, he was inches away, his mouth wide open. Jimmy saw down his throat, a dark tunnel that seemed to stretch eternally. There was movement there, fluttering like the wings of a baby bird learning to fly. Or…

Eye lids.

As the moment lingered, Jimmy saw it was just as suspected. Eye lids. Twitching. Opening. Then, the brightest gold he'd ever set sights on shimmered in the back of Randall's throat, two rings that shone like lighthouse beacons, though these were not lights of comfort. Bright, blinding, and as numbingly pleasant as they were to look at, these floating orbs harbored not a speck of goodwill. *Chaos* came to mind. Yes, those eyes held eons of chaos. *And death. And rot. And…something else.*

Something foreign.

Something not of this world.

Jimmy couldn't adequately label *what* those eyes were conveying, but everything within them said he wasn't safe here. That he wasn't safe *anywhere.* That no matter where he ran, they would find him, and they would do terrible things to him. Things Randall Benoit was currently experiencing.

Chaos.

Death.

Rot.

Growing anew.

The eyes burned with yellow hatred. The irises moved like storm clouds, almost in psychedelic fashion. For a second, Jimmy wondered if this was the result of some tricky drug. Randall Benoit *had* taken his fair share of mind-altering substances, so maybe his current state was a bad reaction to what he had recently dabbled in.

What drug makes eyes grow in your mouth? Jimmy thought and realized how stupid he was for thinking such a thing. Stuff was growing out of his forehead and on cheeks, dark stems and woody knots. No drug had side effects like this, least none he had ever heard of.

Whatever this was, Jimmy wanted no part of it.

Randall gripped his shoulders, and Jimmy's gaze was freed from the throat eyes.

"*Run,*" he said, "*before she gets inside of you too.*"

The only word Jimmy understood was *run*. He turned and faced the fog, and never looked back.

4

Ten minutes later and the kids still hadn't found the clue. Not a single shred of evidence that the end of the Hunt was near. Doug assumed their game makers would have left something behind, a trail of smaller clues that eventually led to the last—after all, the graveyard was an expansive piece of property. Locating something during the *day* would have been a tremendous challenge. Underneath the darkened skies, however, finding a small piece of paper about the size of a wallet was asking the impossible.

After strolling along a stretch of walkway, with headstones that looked identical to the stretch before it, Doug seriously thought about throwing in the towel. "Guys, maybe we should just quit."

With his legs feeling as if they were carrying an extra fifty pounds, he found even standing there a chore. His shoulders ached. An intense pressure railed against his temples. Every stone bench they had passed looked good enough to sleep on. Grady and Jesse were dragging their feet as well, and he would have been surprised if either of them was still up for the near impossible task.

Jesse was the first one to stop. "Yeah…" he said, dreamlike, looking up at the stars. "You guys ever wonder what's out there? I mean, beyond the sky?"

"I know what's out there," Grady said confidently. "More sky. Duh."

Jesse didn't react; the sky held his attention.

Grady looked to Doug and jerked his finger at Jesse in a *what's-up-with-this-guy* motion. Doug only shrugged, though he knew exactly what was up with him—he was dead tired, just like him.

"No," Jesse said. "Beyond it. Further. Like, what if the sky is just what we can see. And there is more behind it that we can't."

"Um, technology is pretty good nowadays, dude. If there was something beyond it, we'd know by now."

Jesse acted as though he hardly heard him. "No, there's something out there. If you look close enough, you can almost see it." He swayed as if the wind had given him a push. But in that moment, there was no wind. Doug thought it was strange, too, even if Jesse was beyond tired.

Jesse's knees buckled, and Doug rushed forward, yelling out his friend's name. Grady was right on his heels. They were able to catch Jesse before he hit the ground. Doug got his arms underneath Jesse's left arm and Grady hooked his forearms under his right. Slowly, the three of them went to the dirt, where they carefully laid Jesse down so his head wouldn't knock, crack, splinter open on the asphalt path.

Doug saw Jesse's eyes roll up under their lids, the all-white of his eyeballs looking like tiny moons. His body began to convulse, flailing wildly. The jerky movements caught Doug off-guard, forcing him to let go. It was an instinctive move. Grady had done the same. As soon as they noticed Jesse wasn't stopping, they were back to their friend's side, trying to keep his arms and legs still, preventing him from hurting himself. White foam bubbled on his lips, dripped down his cheeks like the fizz of cream soda over the rim of a frosted glass.

"What's happening to him?" Grady said. His face twisted in dismay.

"He's having a seizure." Doug hated the shaky sound of his own voice.

"No shit, but why?"

For that, Doug had no answer. After about fifteen seconds—which felt more like fifteen minutes—Jesse went still, limp in their arms. Doug brushed away the globs of foam with the bottom of his shirt. Once dry, he patted Jesse's cheek, lightly at first, and harder when he got no response.

"Jesse?" he said, his voice stricken with panic. "Jesse, man, come on. Wake up!"

No response. *He's dead,* Doug thought. He was sure of it.

"Jimmy!" Doug shouted over his shoulder. "Jimmy! Karen! Help!"

The graveyard gave no reply.

Something moved behind them. Grady and Doug whipped their attention toward the shadows and the hip-high wall of lingering fog.

"What the fuck was that?" Grady asked, launching himself to his feet. He crouched like a sprinter waiting for the pistol shot.

Doug had seen the shadow move too, but he didn't catch enough to tell what it was. For a second he thought the fog and the moonlight had tricked them, manufactured some optical illusion that fooled their peripheries. But it wasn't just the fast-moving motion that unsettled them. There was something else, a presence of some sort, a physical mass that had been there one second and gone the next.

"I don't know," Doug told him, and turned back to Jesse. The seizure had stopped, and the boy lay still, his eyelids twitching in quick spasms. "Come on, Jess." Doug continued to tap his cheek in hopes the contact would snap him out of it. "Wake up."

Grady hung his head, his spirit clearly defeated. "Is he…"

"No," Doug said sharply. "No, he's sleeping. That's all. Just sleeping…"

Overhead, the sky collected gray clouds. A storm gathered over the boys, threatening to bring rain and thunder and lightning, which Doug thought would not only be fitting, but actually nice and refreshing.

"Sleeping," Grady repeated, placing two fingers on his friend's neck.

He was feeling for a pulse, and Doug wondered if he knew what he was doing. Could it be as easy as George Clooney made it look on *ER*? Either way, Grady didn't seem to find a pulse.

Grady's eyes bulged wide, almost too big for his skull to handle. "I can't…"

He started whimpering, and Doug crawled around Jesse and threw an arm over Grady's shoulder. "He's fine, dude. You just have no idea what you're doing." Doug tapped the part of the neck where *he* thought the carotid artery ran. "It's centered more."

Doug felt Jesse's pulse. It was weak but present.

Grady's fingers replaced Doug's, and his eyes shrunk back to their normal size. "Oh, thank Jesus."

"Don't thank Him yet." Doug pushed himself to his feet.

He rotated and examined the graveyard, which seemed darker than earlier. The night seemed angry with them. Then he realized his flashlight had gone off, and there was only the glow of the moon and the collection of stars to guide them.

"Shit," Doug said, shaking the flashlight. It did nothing.

Next, he smashed the flashlight into the ground, which also did nothing. Either the batteries had died or the tool had. Either way, Doug knew it was screwed.

"Mine still works," Grady said, flicking his on. "Where's Jesse's?" He scanned the immediate area, sweeping the weak beam of light back and forth, but neither of them could locate anything but the dirt and the grass and the stones that marked where the dead live. "Can't find it."

"Don't worry about it. We have one. It'll have to be enough."

As if the universe answered, the lightbulb in Grady's flashlight flickered, died, and came back to life all in a single breath.

The boys looked to each other, as if expecting the other to speak words of encouragement. Instead, they waited for the bulb to inevitably fail, waited for that gathering darkness to come claim their sight. Waited for the impending storm above to rage, to soak them, to make things even more difficult.

"I want to go home," Grady said.

"Me too." Doug got down on one knee, took Jesse's arm and swung it over his shoulder. "Get his other arm. Let's carry him back to the car."

"What about Jimmy and Karen?"

"What about them?"

"Shouldn't we find them?"

"They'll meet us back at the car." Doug glanced down at his watch. Jimmy and Karen were fifteen minutes past their designated return time. "They should be there by now."

Grady silently agreed and took Jesse's other arm. Together, they lifted him off the ground, even though Jesse was taller and weighed more. Jesse's head tilted downward, a foamy-white string of spittle dangling from his lips.

"Which way?" Grady asked, and it was a good question. For one, Doug had no clue. They had gotten themselves turned around, and the lackluster light revealed no familiar graves. The path ahead and behind them looked identical, both dim and haunted.

"I don't think it matters," Doug said. "I'm pretty sure the path loops around. It'll take us back to the main gate no matter what."

"You sure?"

Doug wanted to say, *No, not really, I have no idea,* but decided that wouldn't go over very well. He settled on, "Yeah, man. We'll be fine."

They started down the path they *thought* they had come down and stopped when a shadowy figure took form about thirty feet away, directly ahead.

The boys froze. Jesse suddenly felt a thousand times heavier. Doug's fingers ran numb, and he almost lost his grip.

"What—" Grady managed to squeak out, but the rest of the question died in his throat.

The shadow didn't move. It stood there hunched over and seemed to be waiting for the boys to make their move. Doug couldn't work his limbs; he could hardly breathe. A cold chill sliced through his bones, the frosty sensation trickling through his veins.

When it looked like both parties would stand there forever, the shadow obliged by shuffling toward them. Doug gathered his strength, ignoring the urge to drop Jesse and make a run for it. He glanced over at Grady and, as if his head were transparent and his thoughts could be easily accessed, he saw similar ideas percolating.

"Don't drop him," Doug said, mustering the courage to stay put. "We can't leave him. We stick together, you hear me?" Those words came out sounding a lot like his father, and Doug wondered where that had come from. There wasn't much time to mull it over.

Utter panic gripped Grady's features.

"Grades…"

All in one motion, Grady slipped from Jesse's arm and sprinted off in the opposite direction. He screamed as he ran, his cries tearing through the night's sky. Mother Nature shot off a thunderous boom in reply. Above, the clouds clustered together. The air was damp with the storm's preamble. Droplets sprinkled the path. Doug felt them tickle his arms, his neck.

"*Shit,*" Doug hissed, carefully spinning back to the cemetery's dark guest.

The shadow approached.

Doug's bladder filled, but he managed to keep it from involuntarily releasing. As the figure closed the distance between them, hunching and limping ahead like a mad scientist's faithful servant, Doug recognized him. It was Alphie Moffit, just as he'd seen him earlier. The guy stepped into a pool of moonlight and Doug could see his face with such clarity—it was a mask of dark blood, the blackest blood he'd ever seen. Old blood. Dried and crusty. But it wasn't old, nor was it dry.

Moonlight reflected off the thick streaks like it would the surface of a calm lake. Was the night responsible for this effect? Whatever the case, he was thankful. If he had seen red, he might have puked or fainted or both. Its dark appearance made it look fake, so he was able to maintain his composure. But the worst part of Alphie's face wasn't the blood or its unusual color—it was his eyes, the shiny gold tokens that appeared in their stead. The bright yellow nature was almost hypnotic. Doug had trouble breaking the connection.

"*Where you going, little one?*" Alphie asked. His lips barely moved, his voice seeming to resonate from somewhere deep within his throat. "*Still want to play the game?*"

There was something sinister about the voice. Something that raised the hairs on Doug's arms and neck.

He couldn't reply.

"*Tonight is only the beginning,*" Alphie said in a low, scratchy voice. "*The Mother of Dead Dreams...she is coming. But she needs more energy.*" He lowered his head, his golden eyes burning with bright fury. "*Donate yourself. Give her your life. Let her eat from you. You are the one she wants, little one. She's been keeping an eye on you.*"

Laughter—a low gargle that could pass as such—escaped Alphie's mouth.

Doug backed away, dragging Jesse along. His friend was too heavy to carry by himself.

Alphie kept approaching, closing the gap between the two parties.

Doug couldn't move Jesse away fast enough. He had to make a decision. Run and leave his best friend behind or stay by his side and...

What? he asked himself, though the voice in his head sounded more akin to Alphie's. *What are you going to do?*

Stay? Fight? Defend?

Doug had never been in a fight. Not against someone his own age, not against someone older. Alphie was three years his elder and, probably, had seen a few scraps. Doug didn't stand a chance on a good day. But he couldn't leave Jesse behind. He *couldn't*. He understood why Grady had and, in a way, he didn't blame him. Fear had gotten the best of him, and Grady always let fear dictate his actions. He wasn't surprised; not like he was about himself staying.

Doug was afraid, no question about it. His gut told him to cut and run. Turn around, never look back—no one would blame him.

But one look at his friend and he knew that wasn't an option.

He'd stay for me. Jesse would, absolutely.

Alphie was within striking distance. Gordon Simms had always taught his son to *never* throw the first punch, never hit someone unless they hit you first. Doug figured his old man would make an exception this one time. If he'd been face to face with a bloodied corpse of a teenager who spoke like he was chewing a mouthful of dead leaves, then he'd definitely give Doug the blessing to strike first, ask questions later.

Doug lowered Jesse to the ground and set him down with ease. Next, he balled his fists, preparing to throw down.

Alphie only smiled.

"I'll let you go if you step aside and give him to me." Alphie's bright eyes settled on Jesse's unconscious body.

"No," Doug spat. "Fuck you."

"The Mother of Dead Dreams and Fleeting Shadows needs sustenance, little one. She cannot go on without it." His lips fixed up a snarl, and Alphie growled like a wolf on the prowl for easy prey. *"Give him to me!"*

"NO!" Doug shouted and wound his arm. The strike came with surprising quickness, and Doug's knuckles landed flush on Alphie's chin. The impact drove the dead-looking boy back, sent him staggering into the shadows. The eyes of the creature within burned with intensity, a ferocity that had yet to be unleashed.

In other words, Doug had pissed it off.

"Insolent child!" Alphie shouted. He unloaded a tangent of animalistic snarls. *"I WILL EAT YOU. I WILL RIP YOUR DREAMS APART, PIECE BY PIECE."*

In that moment, Alphie Moffit appeared ten feet tall. His shadow grew, merging with the darkness of that hot summer night. Rain droplets began to fall steadily. Within seconds, the sky opened and dumped torrents on them. Steam rose from the asphalt path, clouding up the distance between Doug and Jesse's opponent.

"I WILL CRUSH YOUR BONES BENEATH MY TEETH. I WILL BREAK YOUR SOUL AND STEAL THE LIGHT OF YOUR EYES."

Alphie's face contorted, his jaw hanging unnaturally low.

Doug dragged Jesse a little farther down the path, realizing he'd set the thing over the edge. Whatever was currently residing within Alphie Moffit, it was coming for Doug.

His best chance was to run. The thought of leaving Jesse behind was stronger than ever.

Alphie surged forth before Doug could make the difficult decision. One effortless shove sent Doug reeling. He stumbled back, skidding across the asphalt on his back. His elbows absorbed the worst of it, the hot friction having rubbed them raw.

Doug quickly recovered, coached himself to a sitting position. His eyes immediately fixed on Jesse and then Alphie. To his horror, the scene had changed. Alphie was no longer standing but crouching over Jesse, holding a fistful of Jesse's collar. A wide, menacing grin flashed across Moffit's features. It was obvious the thing within was enjoying the sport of it all. Maybe Doug's eyes were playing tricks on him, because the skin that made up Alphie's face looked awfully *thin*. It appeared slimy and translucent, and the dead-looking boy's skull was visible beneath.

"NO!" Doug shouted, trying to work his rubbery legs to a standing position. But his efforts were too little too late.

Alphie opened his mouth, and a stream of dark liquid exploded forth, reminding Doug of that spitting dinosaur from *Jurassic Park*. The tar-like substance fanned out, covering almost all of Jesse's face. The rain helped wash it off, almost immediately, but Alphie wasn't done. He vomited again, applying a charcoal-colored coating to the unconscious boy's features.

Doug jumped to his feet, ready to protect his friend. But as Doug started forward, Jesse's eyes shot open, and he began to cough. Some of the dark liquid must have gotten in his lungs because he expelled globs of it with each sharp bark.

"Jesse!" Doug shouted, creeping toward him.

Alphie locked eyes onto Doug and hissed. Opening his mouth, he tilted back his head as if he wanted Doug to see what lay within.

And he saw.

Eyes.

Two of them.

As gold as treasure.

Shining brightly. So bright that the circles were hazy at the edges.

He inspected other things there, things that were long and serpentine, things that slithered through the darkness. It all seemed like a dream, none of it real.

But Jesse was real. He was on the ground, writhing beneath the pressure of Alphie's knee.

Doug collected his breath.

You can do this.

He hunched down.

You can save him.

He charged forth, lowering his shoulder like his favorite football player, Lawrence Taylor. Alphie braced for impact, but Doug hit him just right and sent the kid sprawling onto his back. Doug mounted him immediately and brought forth the dead flashlight he had previously pocketed.

"Enough!" Doug shouted and brought the flashlight down in a blur.

The hard plastic connected with Alphie's nose. The bone fracture could be heard over the falling rain. Freshets of blood burst from his nostrils. Unsatisfied, Doug slammed the makeshift weapon down again, this time hitting Moffit in the forehead. The kid's flesh dented, and Doug was surprised (and disturbed by) how easily it caved in, as if the bones beneath had been made of melty chocolate. The golden rings that made up his eyes remained, though they had faded some. Doug knew he had to put out Moffit's lights or the night would not end.

Oh, it will end, little one. Just not the way you envision. It will end in blood and death and in ways your limited mind could never fathom.

One more time, Doug brought the flashlight down, utilizing every ounce of strength that remained. He drove the blunt end into the center of Alphie's forehead, the hard bone located between the eyes, and the contact extinguished the two golden rims of light. They faded out like a television during a power outage. Alphie's head slumped to the side and he entered the world of dreams.

Doug climbed off of him and faced Jesse, who had gotten to his hands and knees.

"What happened?" Jesse asked groggily.

He spit and made a funny face, like the taste in his mouth was something he never wanted to experience again, not as long as he lived. His teeth were stained like he'd eaten an entire bag of black licorice.

Doug began to cry, shuddering as a wave of emotion funneled through him. "Let's just get out of here, man."

He helped Jesse to his feet. Together, they limped toward the hill, the direction where Doug thought they had already traveled. The direction that would hopefully lead them away from the horrors they had discovered in Cedarborough Cemetery.

Before they got too far, Doug looked over his shoulder. He told himself he shouldn't, but, like most boys his age, it was hard to deny that raging curiosity.

Two figures, dark gray shapes that almost looked human but definitely weren't—maybe would have had their arms and legs not been so abnormally long, lacking the muscular makeup of an ordinary person—had crawled out of the shadows and shimmied over to Alphie Moffit. They crowded over Alphie, seemingly sniffing his flesh. With what noses, Doug couldn't tell— their faces were blank masks of dull flesh, shiny and smooth and inhumanly pallid.

After they'd given Alphie a once over, they dragged him toward the shadows. Second by second, the graveyard's dark gobbled them up.

Doug turned, and, with more motivation and energy than he should have had at this late hour, he set his sights on the cemetery's only exit.

STUFF'S GOTTA GO SOMEPLACE

(an interlude)
2 Weeks Ago

1

A Ford-150 with rust-eaten doors and bald tires that couldn't grip the grit beneath them bounced and coughed to a stop on Bittern Lane, one of the last remaining dirt roads Hooperstown had to offer. The town never bothered to pave it because the road didn't go anyplace worth visiting. It cut through an empty field rife with tall grass and stopped at a dead-end, butting up against a vast stretch of forest scarcely explored these days.

The driver of the Ford, Lenny Howell, cranked the key in the ignition, cursing and angrily muttering to himself while his passenger, Joe Frusco, brayed with heinous fits of laughter.

"Told you to scrap this piece of shit and get another one," Joe said. He knew just which of Lenny Howell's buttons to push. "How many times is this girl gonna die on you before that sinks into your thick skull?"

"Fuck you, Frusco," Lenny said, giving the key one more turn. The way he howled when the engine finally turned over, you'd think he hit the Mega Millions jackpot. He kicked the gas pedal and the motor roared, though it choked and wheezed, not promising them a very safe ride back. "There you go, fucker! Whoo-haaaa!"

"Hmm," said Joe, unimpressed. "Let's see how long before it dies again. I'll take the under. Ten minutes, let's say?"

"Fuck you, Frusco."

"You should put that on a T-shirt, you say it so much."

"Just might do that, fuck-face."

"Boy, you're mighty testy today. Linda giving you grief again?"

Joe knew Lenny never liked to discuss his wife—it was a sore subject, but Joe was also tired of his partner's shit. He'd been crusty the entire drive. The happiest he'd seen him in months was when the goddamn truck started.

"Yeah," Lenny said, returning to his blue self again. He leaned forward, nearly resting his head on the steering wheel. "She's always in my ass crack, y'know?"

"Oh boy. I know. Been married for twenty-five years, buddy. I know it."

"How the fuck do you do it?" Lenny finally put the truck in drive, cut the wheel and hit the gas, then threw it in reverse, parking the tail right up to the edge of the forest.

"Marriage takes work, son." Joe was only pushing fifty, and even though Lenny was less than ten years younger, he still treated him like he was a kid. *His* kid. "You gotta realize that or you're doomed. Ain't always gonna be peaches and ice cream."

"I fuckin' hate peaches."

"Yeah, well. Peaches are smooth. Marriages ain't. Work at it. Be the best man you can be. Be the best father you can be." A sly smile fixed his lips. "And for God's sake, make sure your wife gets everything she asks for." He chuckled but Lenny didn't join him.

The big man continued to stare out the window, the low-hanging sun absorbing his thoughts. "She never lets me go out with friends, y'know. In the beginning, she did. Hell, in the beginning she'd come out with my friends. Do stuff together. Movies, the boardwalk, the bars. But once we had Alyssa and Beckett, well, things kinda fell apart. Suddenly…there was no going out. No more fun. It was all kids, kids, kids."

"Buddy—welcome to the family life."

"Not sure I'm cut for it."

Joe rolled his eyes and nudged Lenny with his elbow. "Such a drama queen, you are."

"I'm serious. Feels like I'm losing my fuckin' mind."

Joe realized he was indeed serious. The man hung his head like an abused puppy. His eyes teemed with sparkles of hopelessness. Joe wondered if the man should be on some sort of suicide watch.

"Okay, look. It can't be *that* bad. Gotta be some good times mixed in there with all the bad. Tell you what—let's make this dump and then go grab a bit at The Ground Round. I'll buy the first round of cold ones. Hell, maybe I'll buy the second round, too. We can talk all about it."

Reluctantly, Lenny agreed. Joe figured the glum son of a bitch might try to bail on the way, cite his wife needing him home as the cause, but Joe would convince him otherwise. He had his tactics, his ways of influence. Free beer and burgers were hard to pass up.

"Okay," Lenny said. "Okay, but what should I tell Linda? She'll be expecting me."

"Tell her you need to stay late. Overtime."

"What will I say when she sees my paycheck?"

Joe shrugged. "I don't know, man. You worry too much. Let's just make the dump and get out of here." He looked out the window, toward the edge of the forest and the surrounding tall grass. There wasn't a house in sight—just a wall of trees and the overgrown grass and a clear blue sky above, the sheet of indigo stretching far beyond where his eyes could take him.

"Okay," Lenny said, abandoning his concerns. "We'll talk after."

"Good."

The two men climbed out of the cab. Joe shut the door and headed for the bed. Placing his foot on the back tire, he hoisted himself up into the bed. Eight unlabeled drums stood upright. Though the tops were sealed, he could still smell the acrid, bleach-like odor that wafted up from each barrel. He winced and pulled his shirt up over his nose. The stuff was nasty and the less he was exposed to it, the better. Next, Joe went for the hand truck, lifting it over the side of the bed and handing it off to Lenny. Then he made his way around the drums and lowered the gate.

"Ready?" Joe asked, inching the closest drum to the edge.

"Ready, fuck-face." Lenny snickered, some of his happiness returning. There wasn't much of a smile, but it was present. Joe was happy his old pal didn't allow himself to sulk in the doldrums for long.

They each took a side and lifted the drum over the edge, and then dropped the heavy barrel onto the ground. Lenny, being lower, steadied the drum and kept it from bouncing all over the place and falling over. He was able to corral the drum filled with dangerous waste with some ease. The steel drum didn't even dent, survived the five-foot drop without so much as a scratch.

"One down, seven to go," Joe told him, as if the man couldn't count.

Lenny lighted a cigarette. "Just shaddup and help me get them all down here, will ya?" He paused for a beat, sucking down a lungful of smoke. Exhaling white plumes, he said, "You know, I wish Walker would come out here and do this shit for once. This little operation of his sure can't be legal."

Joe, looking baffled, shot his partner in crime a dubious look. "Legal? The fuck you mean? Of course this isn't legal. What do you think 'discretionary bonus' means?"

"I know." Lenny dragged his backhand across his sweaty brow. "But…shit. You ever think we shouldn't be dumping this stuff in the woods? So close to the stream?"

Joe waved his hand. "Nah. It's *just* a stream, anyways. Not the river. Stream don't go nowhere. The Red River supplies the water to the surrounding towns and drains into the bay—this stream doesn't do anything. Don't worry about it."

"I just think…sometimes…it feels wrong."

"Well, like I said, you think about things too much."

"Still wish Walker was with us once or twice. Since he's the plant director and all. Feels wrong with him not being here. He ought to be the one getting his hands dirty, least once in a while."

"His hands are fairly dirty, you believe me. But he won't ever come down here to dump this shit. He gets filthy enough sitting in that comfy-ass office all day, the A/C cranked, sitting with his feet up and reading *Hustler*. Probably gets filthier in there than we get out here."

"Filthy rich, maybe." Lenny smoked some more, then tossed his butt aside.

"Better put that son of a bitch out before you burn down the whole town." Joe motioned to the orange nugget that glowed hot despite the brightness of the day.

Lenny squashed the lit cig under his work boot. "How long we been dumping, Joe?"

"Shit, Len. I don't know. Ten. Fifteen years? That old pipeline busted in, what? '85? What of it?"

"I don't know. Been reading things, I guess. About the environment. About what harmful effects pollution can do to the atmosphere, y'know?"

Another dismissive wave. "Gimme a break, Len. Hooperstown Chemical's been disposing their waste out here since the late sixties, whether they were using the pipeline or a good ol' fashion dump; in thirty years, ain't nothing gone wrong yet. What you are reading is just a bunch of tree-huggin' hippy horseshit." He bent down, keeping one hand on top of a drum. "You. Worry. Too damn much. Now let's go. Get this over with. We've got beers to drink, burgers to eat, and waitresses to flirt with."

2

Thirty minutes later, the men had finished escorting the eight drums into the forest, well past the point where anyone would dare look. Peak hunting season wasn't until fall, so there was no risk of a couple of deer hunters stumbling upon their dumpsite. There was always the possibility of some random person wandering into them, a group of kids playing where they shouldn't be, maybe even a homeless drifter looking for a place to camp out for the night. But, as Joe and Lenny surmised earlier, they'd been in this game for a long time and hadn't been caught yet. Besides, it wasn't like *they* would get in trouble. Hooperstown Chemical was ultimately responsible for the hazardous waste they produced, and, specifically, Dylan Walker—the plant manager—would be on the line for any fines and lawsuits that would result from their illegal activity. Nope, Joe and Lenny would be off the hook, at least as far as they were concerned.

Hooperstown Chemical, however, their board of directors, might see things a little differently. Lenny figured if they *were* ever caught dumping, they'd maybe earn a suspension without pay until the two sides could strike a deal. He didn't think they'd get fired, but you never knew in these situations. He supposed, if Walker and Hooperstown Chemical wanted to, they could use him and Joe as scapegoats and say they acted on their own accord, that there was a protocol in place and they had failed to follow it, that the Standard Operating Procedures were ignored. Lenny wouldn't put it past them. He'd seen the shit that went on there, the corners the company cut to make quotas, the desperate things they'd gone and done to fill orders, the unnecessary exposure to certain hazardous elements they'd forced their employees to endure just to turn a profit.

After working for Hooperstown Chemical for the last twenty years, Lenny knew why he heard his lungs crackle from time to time, and it wasn't solely because of the goddamn cigarettes. No, he was destined to have all sorts of health problems. Hell, he expected one of these years, during a routine checkup with Dr. Livingston, to receive some terrible news—a cancer diagnosis or some such shit. And once *that* happened, he would compile all the evidence from the past twenty years and file that lawsuit Linda always talked about.

That place is killing you, Lenny! she'd always screamed at him, as if there were better local options for employment. This coming from the same woman who complained he never made enough. Jobs didn't exactly grow on trees. Besides, the plant paid pretty well. More than well, actually. For a shlep who never went to college and barely passed high school, Lenny Howell made more bank than the average schoolteacher.

Linda would have to deal with whatever future awaited, and Lenny wanted to make sure that future included financial security for her and the kids. He had no problem going after his job if *(when)* he came down with some life-threatening sickness as the result of unsafe working conditions. The company never cared for him, so why should he care for it?

As Lenny tilted the drum over and began to pour the contents into the flowing water, he wondered where all of it would lead. Joe had said the stream led nowhere, that the current just died somewhere up ahead, but he didn't think that was exactly true. He wasn't the sharpest tool in the shed, clearly, having barely passed the twelfth grade and all, but he knew running water always ran *somewhere*—usually to bigger bodies of water. It didn't just stop. That made no sense. Seeing as there were no lakes out here, he figured the stream led to a bigger stream, perhaps the Red River, which he knew led to the bay. Which he knew supplied Hooperstown and some of the surrounding towns with tap water, including the town of Red River itself.

Are people showering in this stuff? Drinking it? he wondered, and certainly not for the first time.

"Ain't harmful, Lenny," Joe said, as if he could read his thoughts. "Not like it's radioactive or anything like that."

"I didn't say anything."

"No, but you were thinking it."

Lenny waved him off. "You don't know shit about what I was thinking."

"I know you, Len. I can read your face like a book."

"You can't read shit."

"Don't be a grump." Joe poured his drum into the stream, and the two men watched the waste stain the clear water a dark and terrible blue.

Lenny pinched his nose, the smell overpowering. The awful chemical odor burned its way up his nostrils, down his throat, and into his lungs. "Ever think we should be wearing masks when we dump?"

Joe shrugged. "Our bodies can handle it. Ain't that bad. It's only harsh inside the plant where the airflow is restricted. Out here, the air is fresh. Helps kill off the harmful stuff."

Lenny wanted to choke him. Joe had covered his mouth with his shirt earlier, yet here he was acting like he was invincible. Like his body could handle anything the plant threw at him. Sure, *now* they were safe. They weren't coughing or getting sick from the day-to-day grind. But what about later? What about in fifteen, twenty years from now when it came time to retire? Would their bodies hold up then? Would they be able to breathe normally? Or would the crackle in his chest worsen over time? Would his lungs still be able to expand and contract after years and years of abuse and negligence?

These were the things that often ate away at Lenny's thoughts, keeping him up all hours of the night.

"Gotta take a shit," Lenny said aloud, not that he meant to.

He finished emptying the current drum into the water, then tossed the empty aside. They always took the empties back to the plant for reuse, under the advisement of Dylan Walker. *Do you know how much those drums cost? A lot. Probably more than your last paycheck.*

"Thanks for sharing," Joe said. "You gonna make me dump the rest myself?"

"I gotta shit," he said, and he did, though he wouldn't dare pop a squat out here. Too many ticks. Too many leafy growths that looked like poison ivy and poison oak for him to take the chance. There was another reason he wanted a break, the *real* reason; he needed to get away from that acrid stench that bit his nostrils and spun his stomach.

Joe dismissed him with a wave. "Go shit. I'll finish up, but that's gonna cost you a beer. Maybe two."

"Deal," he agreed, knowing damn well he had no intention of keeping that agreement. Linda would murder him if he didn't come straight home and help her with the kids, and Lenny had no intention of being murdered today.

He stumbled away from the dumpsite and didn't look back. A cold sweat broke out across his scalp, and despite the warm, early-June temperatures, he began to shiver. A chill swept through him, making him wonder what kind of sickness had hit him so suddenly.

Guilt, he thought. *Years and years of it.*

Shaddup, he told himself, though it sounded a lot like Joe's voice. *You're not doing anything wrong and you know it. You're doing what you've been told to do and nothing more. You have a family to feed, goddammit.*

He walked for some undetermined amount of time, knowing it was longer than it should have been. It had been long enough to forget which direction he had come from. When he finally stopped to examine his surroundings, he worried he wouldn't be able to find his way back to the dumpsite. His best bet was to call out for Joe, hope he heard him. That notion eased his nerves, and he continued to search for a spot to do his business.

Lenny walked a little farther, then tripped.

An odd structure that had been built along the ground was the culprit. It was a dome-shaped extension that ran as far as he could see. Bending down, he already knew what it was, what he would find if he looked a little closer. It was a pipe, but not just any old pipe. This was the drainage pipe that ran from the chemical plant to the bay, the pipe that was supposed to drain the excess waste. The pipe was old, built in the '60s. It had been discovered, over time, that the metal had corroded and cracked in the mid-eighties, and therefore was no longer a viable solution for draining certain materials.

Disposal of hazardous materials was a costly endeavor, one the plant manager—and probably the entire board of directors—didn't want to bog down their bottom line. Plain and simple. In the end, it was all about money. As much as Lenny hated contributing to whatever long-term harm he was contributing to, he understood the importance of bottom lines.

Linda was always so helpful in reminding him.

He followed the pipeline, curiosity getting the best of him. Of all the dumps he'd been on, he'd never seen the infamous pipeline, the one that was miles long and had taken almost five years to build. Production had started in '63 and lasted to the summer of '68. Hooperstown was a lot smaller then, the kind of tight-knit community where everybody knew everybody, and the graduating class was around fifty kids. Now that number was well over a thousand, and there were talks of installing a second high school. The town had grown, and so had the tales of the infamous pipeline. For example, three people had died during its production, each of their stories shrouded in mystery and hearsay.

In one story, Henry Geary had walked off to go relieve himself—much like Lenny had just done—and never came back. His co-workers found his body several days later, hanging from a tree. His throat and wrists had been lashed, most of his blood pooled on the ground surrounding him.

Then there was Vern Sully, the man who'd poked out his own eyes with a screwdriver. Supposedly, it happened in front of a bunch of witnesses, all of whom corroborated the tale. About three hours into the workday, Vern had stood up, muttered some nonsense, took a Phillips-head screwdriver, and drove the metal stem into both eyes. He died in the hospital sometime later, his heart seizing up like an engine without any oil. Between the hours of his crazy ramblings and untimely departure, the man never spoke a word. Not to the nurses and doctors, not to his wife and children. All of which wanted an answer to the very obvious question: Why did a man who never once exhibited any signs of mental illness suddenly go crazy in the middle of the woods and stab out both his eyes? But the damage Vern had done to his brain was irreparable. Even if his heart had survived the trauma, he would have been reduced to a potato.

The last reported death was that of a man named Johnny Wilson. Johnny had been a noted drunkard and, according to many locals, a major asshole to boot. So much so that even his own kids disliked him. Later, his wife—bless her heart—had to force his two sons to attend his funeral. No one had been particularly sad to see Johnny go, but the way he'd gone out— well, no man deserved that sort of punishment. On a hot summer day—June, Lenny believed—Johnny was down in "The Pit," what the men had dubbed the miles-long trench where the pipe would eventually rest. No one had been paying much attention, but he had been acting like his usual self, complaining about this and that, how if he were in charge the job would go more smoothly, how his co-workers and bosses could learn a thing or two from him. Everyone had just ignored him. Suddenly, Johnny screamed, and everyone turned around. The man's face and hands were covered with dark gunk. Not black, exactly, but close enough. He was screaming as if he'd just been set on fire. No one could see where the sticky tar-like substance had come from, but surely it had come from somewhere. The ground, possibly, but no one, not even official investigators, could determine where. Anyway, the stuff was like acid, and it ate right through the asshole's skin, dissolved his epidermis and the muscle beneath as if they were nothing. Soon, the only thing left of Johnny Wilson's face and hands were his bones. He died right then and there, and production on the pipe shut down for three months afterward.

The chemical plant had trouble getting people to work on the pipeline after those incidents. So much so that they had to contract the work with out-of-state companies. It seemed like there was always something happening—someone getting injured or sick. No one ever knew why, and there were all these bizarre reports of the workers seeing strange things, odd shapes and shadows that lived in the woods. Sometimes those construction crews would quit, forcing the chemical company to hire someone new. Eventually, the pipeline got finished. Years later—probably due to shoddy, rushed workmanship—the pipe cracked in several places, depositing puddles of waste throughout the town. In the early eighties there were reports of a dark substance bubbling up from the cracks in the streets, directly above where the pipeline had been laid. Kids had discovered most of these potentially lethal deposits.

Kids.

For a long time, Hooperstown Chemical denied the spills were theirs, but no one really believed that story. The town instructed them to cease all usage of the pipeline, unless, of course, they were willing to shell out the funds to have the thing not only repaired but replaced. The cost would have all but bankrupted the company, so they opted for the alternative—discarding the waste by hand, transporting the materials, hazardous and non-hazardous alike, to the appropriate dumping sites, where they could be disposed of properly, legally and safely. That, of course, never happened. The plant managers—Dylan Walker in particular—resorted to cheaper methods. He and the board members had found a nice cozy spot in the middle of the vast woods that bordered the town and began dumping there. It had saved the company millions.

Millions.

But at the expense of what?

Someone would have to pay. Maybe not with dollar bills and checks that contained many zeroes, but someone would have to pay.

Someone always paid.

Thinking of this particular history lesson, Lenny shuddered.

Mindlessly, he had walked about half a mile, following the pipeline, feeling like the ghosts of those who had died were right there along with him. He'd reached a point where he was sure Joe wouldn't hear him, even if he screamed at the top of his lungs.

Was he about to become another fatality claimed by the infamous Hooperstown pipeline? Normally, he would scoff at the notion, but now that he saw the pipeline with his own two eyes and recalled those fables, he wasn't so sure they were just stories. After all, even the tallest tales were born from a nugget of truth.

The pipe led him to an opening in the woods. The path it ran along narrowed, but here it opened up to a pretty sizable pad, a bed of dirt and leaves, weeds that weren't nearly as high as they ought to be. It was almost like the opening had been maintained over the years, handled with some care. On the opposite end of the opening there was a tall hill. At its base, where a dark, split boulder stood beneath the dirt and mud, was an opening wide enough to walk through if he went in sideways.

A cave, Lenny thought.

The pipe ran directly into it.

"Why would they do that?" he mused aloud.

"Yes, why indeed?" asked a voice from somewhere close. Behind him.

Lenny whipped around, his bowels nearly evacuating. "What the fu—"

He realized it was a woman, one who was younger than him or his wife, but not by much. A few years at most. She was wearing all white, a hooded robe with her blonde hair flowed out from it in tangles.

"What the hell, lady?"

"Sorry," she bubbled, an innocent giggle following her apology. "Did I startle you?"

"Well…" He almost said, *Hell yeah you did!* but backtracked before he could. "Nah. It's okay. I'm okay that is."

"You gave me quite a fright. Wasn't expecting to see anyone else out here."

"Oh, sorry about that, ma'am. I was just looking for a place to…to, um…"

She waited, her lips forming a smile. "To take a shit?"

His eyelids blew open like a door in a storm. "No! I mean, no, not at all. Was just… I was working and needed a break, that's all. Just a break. Some fresh air."

"Ah," she said, her knowing smile stretching even farther now. He could tell she knew he was full of shit, literally and figuratively. "Well, I just came out here to pray."

"Pray?"

"Yes. Do you pray, Lenny?"

Stunned, Lenny couldn't find the right words. Or *any*, for that matter. He stuttered, his brain unable to pick the proper phrases from a sea of drifting letters.

"How did I know your name? Well, let's just say the woods whispered it to me."

"That…that doesn't make any sense, ma'am. Not a lick." A chill rode his spine. He got the sudden urge to run, flee the opening—hell, the entire forest. He'd quit his goddamn job at Hooperstown Chemical if that meant getting away from here.

This didn't feel right. None of it did.

"She can make it make sense," said the lady in white, nodding to the cave behind him.

"She...she can?" Lenny didn't know who she was, but he suddenly wanted to.

"Yes. Go ahead. Have a peek inside. She's waiting for you. For all her children."

He rotated, peering into the dark slit. It seemed to have widened since his first glance. "Are you sure?" He couldn't take his eyes off it. "Is it safe?"

"Oh yes," she said confidently. "No place safer. I guarantee it."

That was enough for him. He shuffled toward the opening. Part of him knew it was wrong, knew the whole damn situation was wrong, but that didn't stop him. As if he was under the influence of some terrible power, some great unknown, he followed the pipeline into the dark. He could feel the magnetic pull of this invisible force, an imperceivable energy that hooked and drew him forward. Staring at the mouth of the cave, which had to be the home of some local animal—a coyote or a bear—and certainly not the abode of some woman. Lenny was besieged by a series of bitter chills. Even though the dark opening filled him with anxious worry, he felt compelled to enter. Feet shuffling, Lenny felt powerless against the draw.

In a blink, he found himself inside. The tunnel was dark, *darker* than dark. It was impossible to see more than a foot in front of him. Even less as he soldiered on, getting farther from the daylight behind him. The omnipotent force that propelled him encouraged him to press on. Each footfall felt like it belonged to someone else. Like he was an outsider in his own body, forced to carry out the mission of another.

Deeper.

Deeper.

He had enough control to look over his shoulder where he saw the light at the end of the tunnel shrink, reduced to the size of a pencil point dot. The farther he went, the less it felt like he'd ever return to the light again.

Is it safe? he had asked the lady. He knew the answer now, the truth.

The darkness continued to grow on him.

From the inside out.

3

When fifteen minutes passed and Lenny hadn't returned, Joe began to worry. He'd already finished dumping the toxins in the stream and corralled the drums into the back of Lenny's truck—all by himself—a fact he wouldn't let the round bastard soon forget. He was waiting by the cab, praying some suburban adventurer didn't fancy himself a ride down one of the last dirt roads in the entire county. Checking his watch one more time, Joe knocked on the side of the truck with his knuckles, as if maybe the man was close enough to hear him abusing his precious, rusted baby.

"C'mon, Lenny. Hurry the hell up!"

He gave him another five minutes, then decided to go in after him.

Joe had never been a hunter or a tracker, someone who liked spending a lot of time in the woods, but he figured following Lenny wouldn't be all that difficult. The man would not have covered his tracks even if he knew how.

Sure enough, he picked up Lenny's trail near the stream, followed it straight into the woods, seeing exactly where he'd planted each step. He kept going until his internal alarm went off.

Did Lenny really come out this far? To take a shit?

The prints in the dirt suggested he had done just that.

Joe continued to follow the path, didn't pause again until he reached the pipe, the metal cylinder that divided the earth. He reflected on it as Lenny had, remembering its infamous history, the deaths it was allegedly responsible for, the list of local legends that had been born from it. He'd heard them all, everything from an ancient pirate curse to vengeful Native American spirits residing over the pipeline, responsible for every single bad thing that happened in Hooperstown. He'd even heard the Jersey Devil used it as a passage from the Pinelands into Hooperstown, creating mischief and terror along the way.

Ridiculous.

Joe cupped his hands around his mouth and shouted, "Hey, Lenny? Where the fuck are you? This is starting to piss me off!"

The trees whispered in response, swaying from a series of western drifts.

Joe decided to see this to the end. He'd go and find his co-worker. *Friend*, if you could call their relationship such. He'd give him an earful and maybe a swift kick in the ass.

The pipeline led him through the brush and, eventually, to the small clearing that harbored the black void in the side of the hill, the split rock. Joe examined the hill, taking note of its height. It would take someone pretty athletic to go around or over it. It had been decades since he'd been in that kind of shape. No way he'd attempt something so rigorous.

Joe followed the boot tracks that had followed the pipeline to the mouth of the cave. He stuck his head inside and caught a foul whiff, a vile stench that suggested death itself lived here.

Lenny?

No, the odor was much too bold. Whatever it was, it had died a long time ago. Days, maybe weeks… Lenny couldn't have wandered inside but fifteen minutes ago.

Joe knew he should pull back. He should walk back the way he came, pray Lenny left the keys in the ignition. If he had, he should drive back toward the center of town, find the nearest 7- Eleven, and use their payphone to dial the authorities.

But he didn't do any of that.

Instead, Joe kept hovering around the mouth of the cavern, hoping Lenny would emerge with a big smirk on his face, one that said, *Gotcha, old-buddy, you son of a bitch, you!*

But that didn't happen. There was only silence from within. Behind him, the trees sprinkled whispers around the forest, waving their arms back and forth like the wave at a professional sporting event. Joe ignored their secrets and returned his attention to the cave, to whatever the darkness inside had hidden from the world.

"Lenny?" he whispered. "You in there, pal?"

No answer, not that he expected one.

"Lenny?" He was getting pissed now, could feel the heat building on his neck. There was no way he could charge into the dark—the dark was scary. Who knew what terrible secrets it kept? None Joe wanted to uncover; he was sure of it. "Len, I'm about to go have that beer and burger all by myself, you hear me? Lenny? Len. LEN—"

Before he could finish screaming his co-worker's name, two gold tokens, shiny and glimmering like pirate treasure, appeared in the darkness. The faint glow lit up a small patch of the dark, reducing a portion of the inky surroundings to pale shadows. In the glow, he could make out the outline of a face. It looked like it belonged to…

A woman?

Joe wasn't sure. He couldn't see. The gold rims were bright, and Joe's vision needed to adjust to the all-encompassing dark of the cavern's entrance. The backdrop of the day, the beams of sunlight slanting through the branches, made it that much harder on his eyes.

"Hello?" he asked the eyes, the faint outline of a face.

There was no answer.

He backed away.

"I don't want any trouble now."

Quit being a pansy, he told himself. *It's just a girl.*

It was just a girl—he could see her shape a little more clearly now—but her face… It wasn't right.

"Just lookin' for my friend," Joe told her. She didn't seem to care what his purpose was. As he took a step back into the light, she took one step toward it. "Don't mean you any harm now."

When he was in the middle of the clearing, she reached the mouth of the cave. Sunlight touched all parts of her body, and he could see she wasn't wearing a single thread of clothing. Under ordinary circumstances Joseph Frusco might have considered himself the luckiest man on Earth. She was young (mid-twenties, maybe), petite, a little dirty but not bad looking. Hell, most men in his shoes might have considered this a dream come true. This was how most of those dirty, late-night movies began. But this wasn't a trashy softcore skin flick. This was real life, though it hardly felt like it. This felt…

Wrong.

"A-are you okay, Miss?" he asked, her expressionless face giving nothing away. He wasn't sure if he was about to be seduced or murdered or both. "I can help you… If you need help, that is. Do you live around here?"

She continued to stalk toward him, each movement and shift in body weight awkward, as if the strength in her knees had been weakened by months of inactivity. Or years. As if she'd forgotten how to walk altogether.

"Ma'am? Please talk to me."

Her eyes dimmed, and they weren't the shiny gold beacons they had been inside the cave. They still glowed, almost like cat eyes when light reflects off them in such a way. Iridescent and strange. The effect made her look even more feral.

Joe tried his best, but he couldn't help his eyes from combing over her naked body. Dirt powdered almost every inch of her skin. Small twigs and earthy crumbs clung to her mane of pubic hair. The longer he stared at the dark brown patch below her navel, the more he noticed *things* crawling through it. Bugs. Insects. Worms.

Ticks.

Now that she was close enough, he could see her entire body was sporadically covered in ticks. Big fat deer ticks, plump from feeding off the woman's lifeblood. They stuck to her neck, arms, and legs, looking like unsightly moles because of how swollen and full they had become. Joe instantly thought of Lyme disease and felt awful for the poor woman.

How long had she been out here?

"Ma'am?" He wiped his face clean of greasy sweat. "Please, for the love of God, let me get you someplace safe. To a hospital. You might be sick—"

"Sick?" she said, her voice low and raspy, a nasally sound that suggested maybe she was sick, indeed. She'd spoken the word like she'd heard it before but didn't understand its meaning. "Sick." Tasting the word for a second time, she sounded more confident.

"Yes, please. Where's Lenny? Was he in there with you? Is he…all right? The two of us, we can—"

Before he could blink, the woman lashed out. She pressed her palms to the side of Joe's head. Even if he had time to react, there was no stopping her. Something about being in her presence; he felt powerless, not in control of his own body. That corrupt energy was guiding him now, and he could do nothing but sit idly by as the next few moments unfolded. In his temples, an electric charge buzzed, sending a shockwave of pain around his dome.

He stared into those shiny golden eyes as they burned brighter than ever. Endless flames moved in circles, whirlpools of dancing fire.

(The smell of wood toasting under the orange glow of the spreading blaze. Men. Garbed in long white shirts, sleeveless jackets thrown over their shoulders to help quell the shivers. Wide-brimmed hats. Bits of food flecking their winter beards. Women. Long cotton gowns, their hair tucked under white coifs. They have gathered around a manmade fire, the logs crackling with angst, the firelight brightening their stunned faces. Fear twisted their expressions in wrinkles and fleshy knots, the shock of witnessing some terrifying discovery.)

His eyes rolled back, disappearing into his skull, reduced to white ovals. He was somewhere else now, at the mercy of whatever the woman wanted to show him.

(The woman stared at the collection of strangers, her eyes glowing and glowing and glowing.)

The world went fuzzy.

(A cage. A prison. A sea of eyes staring at her through the dark. She rubbed her belly, swollen with a promising future, the furthering of her people. She's scared, though. Terrified. The men, they poked and prodded her, called her names, foreign to her. They said things like "earth witch" and "burn her," and although these words held no meaning, she knew they were not words of encouragement, nor words of harmony.)

A hot pain seared his skull, hitting him like an arrow through the head.

(A pyre. The settlers gathered around, prepping her demise and chanting words she could take no solace in.)

Invisible spikes pummeled his entire body, Joe screamed, so loud he thought it would reach the center of town. He hoped to God someone heard him. Anyone.

(Fire. All around her. She burned. There was a shadow through the flames. Bright eyes flecked with gold. A dark smile.)

Anyone. Help, he thought. Dear God, anyone help me. She's going to—
(Burn and burn.)

Every inch of him felt like it was melting, his blood squirting through his veins like molten lava. He wanted it to end. Prayed for it. Prayed—

(There was no stopping the fire. She, though, the eyes, they promised to stop it. Stop it all. Save her, the life inside her. There's a deal on the table. All she had to do is pray, pray and it all ended.)

Death was preferable over this suffering.

(Hours later, the fire burned out. The life inside her was gone. Where it had been was now two flaps of skin folded over an empty womb. Yes, the life was gone but she wasn't. She was still here, alive, barely. Her stomach was flat and ruined. An incredible pain surged through the cavity where the unborn child used to live. She tried to move. Couldn't. Her skin was blackened. Smoke rose from her charred exterior, curling into the air around her like the remnants of a good haunt. The smell of her flesh permeated the forest, and she wondered how far she was from camp.

Eventually, she found she could stand.

Walk.

She does, but not alone. There was something next to her. Someone. Someone with golden eyes and a dark smile.

It followed her. Always.)

She released him, and he fell to the ground. The pain let up, just enough to instill a sense of safeness. He scrambled to his knees, his shoes slipping on the fallen leaves, trying to find a grip. His nerves, confused by what had just happened, hummed with an invisible current. She had done a thing to him, but he had no idea what. Just that he was changed, and not for the better.

"W-what ha-happened?" he asked, unable to ease himself down from the height of his panic. Whatever this was, it seemed far from over.

Two black feet appeared in the dirt in front of him. He could smell their burnt nature, the charcoal scent that suddenly tainted the freshness of the great outdoors. The skin that made up her feet and ankles was scaly and crusty, layers of tar-black that had peeled and begun to flake away. Joe glanced up slowly, taking his time to examine every inch of her now-burnt exterior, and noticed that every naked inch of her was toasted beyond recognition.

In a blink, she had changed skins. There was a crown of white flowers around her head, and he could smell their aroma. The scent traveled up his nose, coating his brain, intoxicating him. He suddenly felt as if this were all a dream.

Maybe it was. Just a dream. Maybe he had fallen asleep back near the truck, and he would wake up at any moment. Yes, that was it. He would wake up and Lenny would be there, patting his cheek, there to usher him back into the real world.

Just a dream, that's all it is, he told himself.

Regardless, Joe yelped when his gaze reached hers.

Two orbs of golden light stared down at him, the blaze within them burning with unparalleled fury. He'd never experienced a hatred this strong, so palpable he could feel her energy coursing through his veins. It made him feel as if the hatred were transferable. Now he could burn at that level of hostility too.

"*You will serve me, peasant,*" she said through charred lips that didn't move. In the visions she couldn't understand their language, the human tongue. But now that she had gotten inside his head, she seemed to understand everything. He could feel her inside, rifling through the drawers of his mind, pulling out whatever information she needed in order to communicate. "*I am your Mother, and you will do my bidding.*"

Joe had no response other than, "Yes, Mother."

"*I am the Devourer of Dead Dreams, and you will do as I command.*"

A dream, he thought again. *Just a dream.* "Yes, Mother."

Movement beyond the Mother, the Whisperer of Dead Dreams, caught his attention. A presence near the cave's entrance, the Mother's lair, stirred in the dark. He didn't have to wait long for the movement to take shape into an actual being. A body. A man. Well, it *had* been a man. Now it was just a shell of its former self, a fraction of the human thing it had been.

Lenny.

He barely looked like himself. In the twenty minutes he'd been missing, he seemed to have lost sixty pounds. His clothes were hanging off him, a drooping, wrinkly mess. His skin had paled, hardly holding any pigment. His arms seemed to have grown longer, his knuckles nearly scraping against the ground as he stumbled out of the darkness and into the light. And his eyes were bleeding. Two red streams dashed down his cheeks. He looked terrified, on the verge of screaming out for help. But his mouth twitched, and no such sound escaped.

Lenny stumbled forward, fell onto his hands and knees. He reached out for help, a desperate extension that went nowhere.

Joe looked back to Mother.

"*I am the Devourer of Dead Dreams, the Whisperer of Moving Shadows.*" Her smile revealed a mouth full of lethal daggers, each tooth whittled to a treacherous point. Even though the clues had been there all along, as if the visions and the strange illusions hadn't been evidence enough, it was then Joe finally realized what he was dealing with.

A monster.

A demon.

The Devourer of Dead Dreams.

The Mother.

He hated everything about her. Yet...there was love. Some sort of admiration for her. An attraction. Despite that dark grin, the uncomfortable nudeness of her body, the bloated ticks clinging to her charred flesh—his stress was alleviated in her presence.

"Feed me your darkest dreams," she said. *"I am weak, but your sleep will give me strength."*

A warm jet shot down Joe's leg. He barely noticed. He was too busy weeping tears of dark crimson. "Yes, Mother," he said, watching her step toward him, mouth open, ready to eat.

PART TWO

The Summer of the Sick
July 5th, 1998 – August 2nd, 1998

CHAPTER SEVEN

New Beginnings

1

Gordon Simms dropped off his son at the Di Falco's around a quarter to nine, fifteen minutes before his shift started at Hooperstown Chemical. Before Doug said his goodbyes, before his dad promised him pizza for dinner, Gordon looked to his son and seemed to notice a difference.

"Doug," he said, facing him.

Doug's hand had been on the door handle, ready to push his way to freedom. The view into the Di Falco's driveway slipped away, and he rotated toward his father. "Yeah, Dad?"

"I was gonna drop by to see Mom after work." Gordon offered a faint smile, but it died before it could gain life. "I know how you feel about it, but…" Sadness gripped his voice, and Doug wondered if his old man would cry. If he was capable of such a thing. He'd never seen a tear fall down Gordon Simms's face, not even in their family's darkest hour, but he supposed there was a first time for everything. "I was wondering if you wanted to tag along."

Doug's fingers slipped off the door handle. The answer to this question—the true answer, not the lie he'd so heavily leaned on—was lodged in his throat. Instead of telling his old man the truth, that he'd never, ever want to visit the woman who used to be his mother, Doug swallowed it. A new excuse was born from the death of honesty, and he opened his mouth to explain why.

"Before you answer," Gordon said, holding up a single finger, "I want you to think about it. I know you haven't seen her in a long time, and I know you don't want to visit *that* place, but I think…" He sighed as if the situation had grown tiresome. "I think it would be good for you. And I think it would be good for her."

"I just don't want to," Doug said, not giving the scenario a second thought. "That place…"

"I know, son." Gordon reached over and gave Doug's shoulder a comforting, fatherly squeeze. "I get it. I do. But I really hope you'll change your mind one day. She misses you, y'know? I know she's not the same person you remember. I know she's…well, she's different now. *Changed.* But she has her moments of clarity."

Doug nodded, and he couldn't fend off the invisible needles sticking the corners of his eyes. "Can I ask you a question?"

"Sure, bud. Anything."

"Why do you continue to visit her? Even after…you know."

"After she tried to murder us?" At that, his father chuckled. *Gallows humor.* Something his old man utilized often, and Doug figured that was just his way of talking about it. "Well, bud, it's pretty simple…I love her."

"But she tried to butcher us."

"Yes, she did. But it wasn't *her*. Not really."

"What do you mean? Of course, it was her."

Dad winced like he'd swallowed a nasty shot of cheap liquor. "No, it wasn't. See, sometimes when people are sick—in the head, I mean—the sickness, the disease, it changes them. It's the sickness that tried to kill us, bud. Not her. Not your mother. You know she'd never do anything to harm you. Or me. She loved us, Doug. She still loves us. I just wish... I just wish you'd give her a chance, that's all."

A shallow sadness filled Doug, infiltrating the back of his jaw and just under his ears. He wanted to cry, but he did his best to conceal his emotions. The tears were coming through and Doug did everything he could to keep them at bay. He thought of other stuff, thought of his friends and the day they had planned. But those thoughts and the fun that awaited kept getting interrupted by images of his mother, the way she used to be before she got sick. Like when she used to tuck him in at night and read him stories, just a single story each and every night, all of them having happy endings and no mentions of the scary spirits that lived in the woods near their house. The proper bedtime stories always ended with a kiss on the forehead and a "I love you, Little Bug" (*Little Bug,* her cutesy nickname for him). Memories of all the goodies she used to bake him, cookies and cakes, and how he'd help her assemble the ingredients and read off the instructions to create their favorite sweet treats. If he concentrated hard and long enough, he could almost smell the sweet, sugary goodness of her baking skills. That soft, tantalizing aroma filled his nostrils, and the overwhelming sense of nostalgia worked its way into his veins, warming his entire body. His soul.

But those fond memories were overshadowed by the night he had almost died. The night she almost killed him. His sadness for those long-lost days was swiftly replaced with anger. Resentment. Total hatred. He wanted to delete her from his mind like an unused computer file. Banish her memories to where the rest of his unwanted dreams now lived.

"You still with me, kiddo?"

"I'll think about it," Doug said, knowing the words were a lie. There wasn't anything to think about. His mother was dead to him and always would be.

"You okay, son?"

His gaze found his father's eyes. There had been concern in his voice and now his eyes matched his worry. "Yeah. Fine, Dad."

A curt nod. "Are you sure? You haven't been yourself lately."

Doug half-smiled, half-grimaced. "Everything's good. Promise."

"Okay. Because you can talk to me if you ever need to. About anything."

"Got it."

"School, girls—"

"Dad."

"Especially girls."

"*Dad.*"

Gordon put up his hands. "All right. Just saying."

"I get it. But I'm good. Everything's good."

"*Allllllll righty then.*" His Ace Ventura impression was terrible, but it still roused a smirk from Doug's face. "Get out. I gotta go to work. The plant has been a wreck lately. Media is all over us, especially with those kids getting sick in the last few weeks. Gotta blame someone, right?"

"I guess."

He nodded at the door. "Go. Have fun. I'll pick you up after I visit your mother in Benton. I'll grab a pizza on the way home."

"Extra mushrooms and sausage?"

"Of course."

"Sweet."

"Get outta here, kid."

Doug opened the door, shut it, turned to the Di Falco's without waving his pops goodbye. Jimmy's car sat in the driveway, looking like it hadn't moved since the last time he'd been here, four days ago. Gordon drove off, honked twice, the horn barely registering in the summer morning silence. He watched his father disappear around the corner before opting to use the driveway instead of taking the shortcut across the front lawn, brushing tears away from his eyes the entire way to the front door.

2

The Di Falco's backyard was pretty big, much larger than any of Doug's other friends. It was deeper than it was wide and contained almost every fun activity a kid his age could ask for. There was an in-ground swimming pool complete with a diving board, a square slab of blacktop that was currently being used as a basketball court. Near the back of the property the Di Falco's had built a swing set with monkey bars and a corkscrew slide. Also, in the oak tree next to the playset, Jesse's father and older brother had built a small treehouse. The kids didn't use it anymore, but it had been such a pain in the ass to assemble that taking it down wasn't exactly a priority.

When Mrs. D. led Doug through the back door, the first thing he smelled was the freshly cut grass, the faint tinge of chlorine hiding somewhere in the background. He spotted Jesse and Grady in the pool (always in the pool), playing water basketball. He arrived just in time to see Jesse slam dunk on Grady's head. The kids laughed. Doug chuckled under his breath.

"Let me know if you guys need anything," Mrs. Di Falco said before closing the door.

"Thanks for letting me spend the day, Mrs. D."

"Of course, Doug. You're always welcome." She smiled and closed the door, and Doug felt that sadness sweeping in again. Mrs. Di Falco was a good mom, the kind he wished he had.

"Dougie-Fresh!" Jesse shouted from the pool. "Get over here, you smelly bastard!"

Doug crossed the backyard, passing the colorful flower garden the Di Falco's had obviously poured a lot of time and energy into. The petals were in full bloom, small explosions of pink and yellow and red scattered across the bed of lively greens. Bees were abuzz, drifting from flower to flower, working their magic across various arrangements. Doug paid them no mind.

Grady launched a basketball from the pool and Doug caught it, slipped off his backpack and took a long-distance shot. The ball bounced off the rim—not his best attempt—and flew into the deep end, a few arm lengths from where Jesse waited for the rebound.

"Get your ass in here," Jesse told him, swimming toward the ball. "We need to finish our game of Twenty-One."

Doug threw down his bag next to one of the lawn chairs and slipped off his sandals. "You sure you don't want to discuss business first?"

The boys froze. Grady's eyes wandered, as if he wanted to bypass this conversation. Jesse pushed wet clumps of hair from his eyes, a dumb look dropping over his face like a window shade.

"Plenty of time for that later," Jesse said, after a brief pause. "It's summer, man. Let's have fun first."

"Okay," Doug agreed, and then took off his shirt.

The game of Twenty-One lasted about twenty minutes. The boys tried to find other things to delay the inevitable, to put off the conversation they needed to have. But there wasn't much else to do, and Doug figured, like himself, the other two couldn't concentrate on anything but what was coming.

They needed to talk.

About what happened that night in the cemetery.

They needed to figure out who this Mother of Dead Dreams was, and what she had in store for the dreaming children of Hooperstown.

3

Upstairs, Jesse led them to his room. They passed Jimmy's room on the way, and Doug wasn't surprised to see the door shut. According to Jesse, his older brother hadn't come out except to eat or use the bathroom. The last few weeks—apparently—had been rough on him.

"Still?" Grady whispered as they crept by.

"He's a mess," Jesse said, waving them past. "I mean, since Karen broke up with him, he's barely even spoken a word. Mom and Dad are a little worried, actually. And you know them—they never worry about shit."

"They gonna throw him in Benton?" Grady joked.

"Dude," Doug said. "Not cool."

"Oh, shit," Grady said, biting his tongue. "Sorry, man. Anyway," he continued, immediately shifting subjects, "why did Karen break up with him?"

"No idea," Jesse said. "But I bet it had something to do with the Hunt. You know, after that night, things got really weird between them," he whispered, keeping his voice as low as possible, the topic clearly forbidden.

Once the boys reached Jesse's room and were inside with the door shut behind them, all outside noise sealed off, Grady unzipped his backpack. He took out a small folder, nearly stuffed beyond capacity with loose-leaf paper and computer printouts.

"You need a Trapper Keeper, Grades," Jesse told him.

"Mine has fucking Power Rangers on it. You think I'm going to bring that shit around?"

"Better than nothing."

Grady shook his head. "All right. I went on WebCrawler and searched for town maps. This is what I came up with."

He collected a few loose pages together and handed them over. Doug was the first one to grab them. Examining them, he nodded.

"This is good stuff." Doug flipped through the various overhead images of Hooperstown. Each page was a different section of town, a hand-drawn map that was surprisingly detailed. The artist had labeled each section. "Great job, dude."

"Thanks!" Grady popped an invisible collar. "My knack for research is finally proving itself worthy."

"You're still a dweeb, dude," Jesse reminded him. "And you suck at pool basketball."

"Well, you suck at Mortal Kombat, assclown. You want to have *that* debate again?"

Jesse puffed out his chest. "I'll kick your ass right now."

"Yeah right."

"No, seriously. Let's go. And why don't you pick someone else besides Reptile? We'll see how good you really are, you button-mashing son of a bitch."

"Button-masher? Button- masher, my ass. I always crush you fair and square, dude." Grady shrugged nonchalantly. "And Reptile is my guy."

"Yeah, he's your guy, all right. I bet you jerk it to—"

"Guys," Doug said, shaking the papers. "Concentrate."

Jesse rolled his eyes. "Yes, boss." He quickly turned back to Grady. "You know, Grades, some kids use search engines to look up pictures of tits and va-jays, and all you do is look up this shit." He took a page from Doug and held it up. "A stupid map."

Doug snatched the paper from his fingertips. "That stupid map is gonna help us save the town, numbnuts."

"Save the town?" Jesse scoffed. "Yeah, okay. Like, what are we, the Ghostbusters or some shit?"

Grady and Doug looked to each other and nodded.

"Yeah," Doug said.

"Yeah, I like the sound of that," Grady added.

"The *Ghostbusters* are awesome."

"Get real," Jesse said.

"Hey," Doug said, handing the papers back to Grady. "I remember saving your ass in the cemetery. Want to talk about that?"

Jesse suddenly went quiet, a bonafide rarity. "Well, I *don't* remember…"

"Do you *reeeeeeally* not remember?" Grady asked him. "Or are you just pretending not to remember?"

"I remember you running away like a little wussy," he snapped back.

"No, you don't," Doug reminded him. "At that point you were out like a light."

"Yeah," Grady added. "Plus, I already apologized for that."

Doug could see it really bothered him, that his cowardice carried over from that night, staining his ego. Over the past few weeks, ever since the Hunt had ended, Grady had apologized to them almost every time they hung out. Especially when they tried to recall the details from that night.

Jesse rolled his eyes, but then walked over to his friend and dropped a hand on his shoulder. "It's okay, Grades." He sounded very unlike himself. "I don't blame you." It was the first time he'd acknowledged Grady's apology.

"You don't?" Grady looked to Doug, seeking his opinion.

Doug shook his head. "No, man. Not at all."

"I didn't want to run, you know. I wanted to…" His words hit a wall. Sniffling, he blotted his eyes, using the collar of his shirt. "I wanted to be strong."

"Dude," Jesse told him, "you are strong. Stronger than you give yourself credit for."

"But I ran…"

"Every kid in your situation would have." Jesse smirked. "Except me. And Doug, obviously. But every other kid…"

A reluctant smile shaped on Grady's lips. "Dick."

"Seriously, though." Jesse wrapped him in a bear hug, squeezed like he meant to break his bones. "I love you, man. You guys are my best friends, and if some weird asshole was gonna puke black stuff all over me, I'm glad it was in front of yous."

Doug jumped on them, and the three of them fell to the floor. For a few minutes, they wrestled with each other, pretending to do the finishing moves of their favorite WWF superstars. Jesse hit Grady with a Stone Cold Stunner and Doug powerslammed Jesse onto his bed. For those few short moments, nothing else mattered. Not the Hunt and what had happened. Not Grady's decision to leave his friends behind, to streak off into the night without any concern for their wellbeing. Not whatever had happened between Jimmy and Karen. Not the terrible things that had come from the fog. Not whatever Alphie Moffit and Randall Benoit had devolved into.

None of it mattered.

But when the moment ended and their eyes settled on the maps, the printouts displaying the town and its defining landmarks, specifically the old pipeline that ran from the chemical plant to the bay, dissecting the town in two, suddenly they didn't *feel* like kids anymore.

"What do we do?" Jesse asked, sitting on the floor, his back against his bed.

"I think we need to talk about the dreams," Doug said, clutching his backpack against his chest.

Grady chewed on his lower lip. "They're getting weirder."

"I keep seeing the woods. That cave…" Doug searched his mind for all the images his nightly escapes showed him, combing over the collection at once. "Where *she* lives."

Jesse nodded. "I've seen her, I think. But I can't see her face."

Grady rubbed his shoulders as if he were cold. To his credit, the air conditioning was overachieving. "In my dreams, she's just this silhouette."

Doug and Jesse exchanged glances.

"How's this possible?" Jesse asked. "How can we all be dreaming of her?"

Doug shrugged. "I don't know. But it's weird. It almost feels like…we were touched by something that night." He waited for the others to chime in, but they were just staring at him, anxiously awaiting his complete thought. "The same thing that touched Alphie and Randall. And it's still trying to touch us. Get inside us."

"I hate this," Grady said. "I wish we never went on that stupid scavenger hunt, dude."

"Don't we all," Jesse added. "At least you didn't pass out and get puked on."

"This is gonna sound weird," Doug said, standing up. "But I almost feel like the thing wants me. Like it's after *me*, specifically."

"You?" Jesse jerked his thumb in Doug's direction, smirking. "What makes this guy so important?"

"I don't know. It's just a feeling."

"Well, we're all in this together," Grady reminded them. "And I'm not running this time."

Doug nodded. "Yeah, I know. Just...I think it has to do with my mother."

The mention of Mrs. Simms cleared their expressions.

"I remember this piece of my past. Before she got really sick and...you know." He made a fist, pretending he was holding a knife and then stabbed the air, making the classic squeaky-knife sounds. When he was sure his message came across loud and clear, he cleared his throat and continued, "She was tucking me into bed like any other night. Usually, she told me bedtime stories. Classics like Hansel and Gretel and The Three Little Pigs, but she would always change the ending, make it totally G-rated. But that night, she was different. She was leaning into me, to kiss me goodnight..." A tear leaked down his cheek. It barely registered on his senses, and he did nothing to wipe it away. "Anyway, she told me something, something that held no meaning until Alphie and Randall left us that last clue."

"What did she say, dude?" asked Grady, who was now nibbling on the tips of his fingers. He'd bitten down so hard that blood had been drawn.

"She mentioned the woman."

"What about her?"

"I can't remember everything. It's hazy, but I'm pretty sure she said something about dreams. Like she comes from the *land of dreams*."

"What?" Jesse asked, confused. "That's...that's the craziest thing I've ever heard. No offense to your moms."

Shrugging, Doug replied, "Yeah, I know." Frustrated, he punched the air. "Fuck. I wish I could remember, but it's all so...*lost*. It feels like it happened so long ago. I had no idea what she was talking about, and I just thought it was weird. Didn't even remember it until we found the last clue. It, like, jogged something loose."

Grady stared at Doug. He instantly hated the way his friend's eyes looked. "What?"

Grady sighed. "You know what you have to do, don't you?"

"What?"

Tilting his head, Grady stared at him and narrowed his eyes. The look practically spoke the message, *Come on, dude. Who you trying to fool?*

"No." Doug shook his head. "No way."

"You have to."

Jesse's eyes widened, as if the answers to the universe's greatest secrets had been unveiled. "Yes, dude. Yes!"

"I'm not doing it, so don't even mention it."

Jesse climbed to his feet. "This makes so much sense!"

"Come on, Doug," Grady said, "What's the big deal?"

"The big deal? Are you seriously going to ask me that?"

"Don't you want to see her?" He raised his brow, waiting for a response. "She's your mother."

"She tried to kill me. She stabbed my dad, dude."

"She was sick, man," Jesse said. "She was delusional. That's not her fault. I mean, it kind of is, but not really."

"Everyone keeps saying that, but I don't think that's true. I think she knew what she was doing."

"That's insane."

Grady shook his head. "Crazy people can't control it, man. Their brains are just wired differently. They're all fucked up on chemicals and shit. Your mom never wanted to hurt you. She just had a really bad episode."

Doug refused to accept that. They hadn't been there; they hadn't seen the feral look in her eyes. They hadn't heard the crazy babble that spilled from her mouth, the tirade of nonsensical phrases she'd shouted at the top of her lungs, practically loud enough for the entire neighborhood to have heard. They hadn't seen her desire to kill, to make him dead.

"You guys don't understand."

Delicately rotating his head, Grady cracked his neck. "I don't think *you* understand. She's probably on all sorts of medicine, you know, to level her out. She'll be just like you remember."

Doug remembered his dad saying she'd been doing better lately. Apparently, she'd been more lucid and her "episodes" were less frequent. She hadn't had one in months, and he thought the medication was really working. But when his old man told him that stuff, he always tuned him out. Doug didn't care how she was doing. Because every time Gordon Simms mentioned his wife and her condition, no matter how positive the spin was, the only thing Doug saw when he closed his eyes was his mother leaning over him, her teeth bared, wild and impossibly sharp like a rabid animal's, the knife held above her head, so tightly in her grasp that every vein in her arm popped.

That was the last memory he had of her. And he couldn't shake it. Nothing would replace it, so there was no use trying.

"I just can't, guys." He hung his head. "I can't look at her again."

Jesse and Grady shared a brief glance, then shrugged.

"Okay, man," Grady said, clearly giving up. "Just saying, if she knows something about this, then we should ask her."

"I know…"

"Maybe you can have your dad ask her," Jesse suggested.

A cool burn shot up Doug's shoulders. He couldn't really tell his pops about this. Could he?

"Or maybe you go there," Grady said, "and just watch from a distance, have your dad do all the legwork."

"I don't know…" Doug lifted his head, directing his teary eyes at the ceiling. "I just don't think I can. Just thinking about being in the same building as her gives me anxiety."

"All right." Jesse threw his arms up in the air. "Where does that leave us?"

Doug collected himself, abandoning the past, his thoughts of his mother. It wasn't easy. His brain struggled for control, the dark half clinging onto the images, not wanting to let go. That night, that one terrible moment that changed Doug Simms's life forever. "Um…we can still locate Alphie Moffit or Randall Benoit."

Grady pinched the bridge of his nose. "The police haven't even found them yet."

"Well, it's worth a shot. We can track down everyone who saw them that night. Retrace our steps from the cemetery."

"Ugh," Jesse said, sticking out his tongue. "We've done all that. Man, the past two weeks we've been running around in circles. It's like the whole night never even happened." Shaking his head, he breathed a deep sigh. "Shit, sometimes it feels like I dreamed the whole thing."

"Me too," Grady said.

Doug nodded. "Yeah, same. But we didn't, and you both know that." He glanced toward the bedroom door. "Has Jimmy said anything?"

"No." Jesse fiddled with the comic book next to him, flipped through the pages of *The Death of Superman*. "No, like I said, he's locked away in his room. Barely comes out. When he does, he's like a fucking zombie, dude. Talking won't help."

"All right." Doug turned to the whiteboard on Jesse's computer desk. "So what do we have? Karen Howard? We still have to talk to her, right?"

Jesse nodded. "She works at The Gap in the mall. We can ride our bikes there later."

"Okay. That's one down."

"What about Jewel Conti?" Grady suggested, perking up.

"Jewel?" Jesse asked, as if the name were an acid spill across his tongue. "Jewel Conti? That psycho?"

"Well, she saw *something*. I'm sure of it."

"I don't know if I want to go messing with her. Odds are, wherever we find her, we'll find Brennan and Dakota, and I don't want to be within breathing distance of those two scumbags. Pretty sure I'll catch chlamydia just from getting within ten feet of them."

"First of all, that's not how chlamydia works, and I'm not surprised that you think it does. And secondly—who cares? Look." Grady stood up. "I know I've been a chickenshit loser in the past, but this is important. If our dreams are any indication, if what we learned on the night of the Hunt is any clue—then something bad *is* coming to Hooperstown. And we may be the only ones who can stop it."

"No shit. And chlamydia is gross, dude. I've seen pictures. On the Internet. And whatever you do, for the love of God, don't web search a 'Blue Waffle.' You'll *literally* puke."

"I'm serious here, man." Grady looked to Doug for backup.

"He's right, Jesse." Doug rapped his knuckles on the whiteboard. "I'm putting Jewel on the list."

Jesse shrugged. "All right. Whatever. Who else we got?"

Doug touched his chin with the plastic end of the dry-erase marker. "We need a historian. Someone familiar with the town's past."

"A historian?"

Grady nodded. "Makes sense."

"How? Since when did Doug become Young Indiana Jones?"

Doug, looking down his nose, said, "We need someone to tell us about the pipe that runs from Hooperstown Chemical."

"What's the pipe got to do with anything?"

"The dreams, dude."

Jesse's eyes seemed to search his memory, as if he needed to recall the dreams to remember exactly what they'd been about. Doug didn't need to; he'd never forget his night terrors. Since the Hunt, the most vivid, lucid dreams he had ever experienced had begun preying on his sleep, often causing him to wake in pools of cool sweat.

"Oh, right," Jesse said, "the dreams."

"Do you even remember them?"

"They're a little fuzzy. Familiar, but also…not."

"Okay, anyway—in the dreams I remember standing near the pipeline. And there is a shadow, which I am assuming is our Mother of Dead Dreams."

"Then what?"

Doug's eyes bounced around the room. "Well, that's it from that segment. Then it cuts to something else." Doug snapped his fingers at Grady. "Grades, what comes next?"

Grady unrolled the piece of paper he had in his hand. Scribbled down were the dream's sequences in chronological order. "Looks like we're inside the plant. Standing on the elevated level looking down at the plant floor. There are vats of chemicals and—"

"Reminds me of *Batman*," Jesse said, snickering. "You think if we were to fall into one of them, we'd turn into the Joker?"

"No, idiot," Doug said. "We'd die."

"Oh."

"Anyway," Grady said, shaking his head. "That's when the tall shadows crawl up the walls."

Doug shivered. He hated that part of the dream. Actually, he loathed the entire chain of events, every single snippet, mostly because of the cold sweats he woke up to, the bedsheets beneath him soaked and impossible to sleep on. The dreams were always the same, varied slightly on some nights, but the message had always been consistent and clear.

She was here and *she* wanted them, all the children of Hooperstown.

"So a historian," Jesse said. "Got it."

"Who though?" Grady asked.

"What about Boxberger?" Doug suggested.

"Box-booger?" Jesse cackled, and the noise—for some reason—hurt Doug's ears. "That asshole? Our *ex*-English teacher?"

"Yeah, but he's a history nerd at heart. Every year he helped organize that dumb Civil War reenactment up in Asbury Park. Plus, remember he had all of those local maps hanging by his desk? The ones of Hooperstown and Red River and Carver's Grove? He has to know *something* about the local history of this place."

"Yeah, but bad news," Grady said, sounding as if his favorite show just got canceled. "Boxberger said he was moving, right? I mean, he seemed like he was packed, ready to go as soon as the bell rung."

"Shit. I forgot about that."

"Good riddance," Jesse said, snickering. "Guy was a total turd."

"He wasn't that bad. He just hated you because you were always disrupting his class."

"It's what I do. It's what I'm good at. Stop trying to limit my potential, Simms."

Doug glowered at him. "Focus, Di Falco."

Jesse tossed the comic book aside, spun on his rear, and sat cross-legged. "I'm ready to learn, teach."

Doug ignored his antics and pressed on. "All right, so we got to track down Randall and Alphie, if possible. See Karen later today at the Gap. Talk to Jewel, even if it earns us a beating and whatever slurs her tiny brain can conjure. And then see if Boxberger—"

"—Booger—"

"—is still around so we can question him about local history. Am I missing anything?"

Jesse and Grady searched each other's eyes and shrugged.

"Okay then. Looks like we got ourselves an itinerary."

4

Jewel stood on the sidewalk of the skinny strip mall located off Route 37, swaying from the lightheadedness that had unexpectedly seized her. A solid twenty feet from the Christian Youth Club's entrance, she couldn't bring herself an inch closer. It was like an invisible barrier had been raised before her, blocking the path toward a new hope, a new beginning, a new life that didn't heavily rely on negative thoughts and emotions, energies she'd harnessed to tear down others, people whom she'd been taught to hate and despise based on various differences.

You start a new life today, she told herself, wanting very much to stop the hate, the negativity she'd been surrounded by since birth.

A few girls her age were laughing as they entered the establishment, conversing about something she couldn't concentrate on because her head, empty as it seemed, was swimming with impure thoughts. Her conscious was rebelling, battling her newfound behavior. She imagined her lifelong buddies, Brennan and Dakota, perched on her shoulders like two devils, sprouting horns and gripping pitchforks, whispering every terrible thing she could do to the place.

Wait 'til the place closes and then spray paint penises all over the brick outside!

Wait 'til the place closes and then smash the windows with rocks!

Wait 'til the place closes and then write 'God is gay' all over the windows!

Shit on their doorstep!

Piss on their doorknob!

She could hear them cackling, which soon devolved into soft echoes. She had taken that first step toward a new *her* and ditched the two heathens earlier. They had wanted to take Brennan's Airsoft gun and do some shooting—mainly at the windows of cars parked in front of any rich person's house. Though, "rich" was a term they used loosely. Anyone who owned a house and a car were "rich" as far as those two knuckleheads were concerned. In actuality, they just wanted to break stuff, destroy anything that honest, hard-working individuals paid good money for. She wasn't down with that, the destruction of personal property, and had told them she didn't feel so hot, that she needed to head home to lie down. They had called her names, of course, had tried to convince her to stay and not be such a "bitch baby," but she stuck to her guns and left them in Dakota's parents' basement, left them with their pack of Marlboro Reds and the bottle of whiskey they had pinched from Dakota's father's secret cabinet.

I can change, she thought, raising her eyes to the youth club's window. Inside, there were clusters of kids, her age and older, hanging out, laughing, engaging in social activities that actually seemed...well, *fun.* Air hockey. Table tennis. Some new game she had never heard of before—Dance Dance Revolution, announced the big bright bubbly letters above the two massive screens. The concept looked intriguing, and the two people playing (dancing) seemed like they were having the time of their lives. The youth center even had one of those basketball arcade games, the kind with two lanes that kept score for each shooter. These were games Jewel wouldn't ordinarily be caught dead playing, but tonight...

Tonight felt different.

The first day of the rest of your life, someone had said, and maybe that was a line she'd heard in a movie. Or maybe it was in a passage she had been forced to read in school. Either way, it resonated with perfect clarity, and she had never been more inspired in all her life.

As she stepped toward the front entrance, she remembered what had truly inspired her, brought her all this way.

Death.

That night, a few weeks ago, she'd seen Randall Benoit creeping in the woods, acting like a goddamn zombie. Those awful images frequently revisited her when she dreamed. No matter what she had done over the last few weeks to forget, experimenting with drugs and alcohol, nothing could rub out those repulsive images.

But the dreams weren't the only thing encouraging her.

Home. Her mother. The fact that Ava had acted more insane over the last two weeks compared to any other two-week span of her entire life. She'd been hitting the booze extra hard. Jewel even found her crack pipe, not that Ava Conti had gone out of her way to hide it. The thing had been left on the dresser, in plain sight, for all to see. A small part of Jewel had wanted to phone child services right then and there, but that would have been more of a punishment for her than her mother. Hell, it was *(probably)* what Ava wanted.

I will not end up like her. Not like that.

That moment had sent her over the edge, motivated her to dig out the card Principal Fritz had given her. CHRISTIAN YOUTH GROUP. She had been surprised she kept it.

With the invisible barrier temporarily erased, she took another step toward the door and then stopped.

This isn't you. Her mother's voice now. Low, raspy like a growl. Judging. Penetrating her focus. A hideous laugh echoed across Jewel's thoughts, bouncing between her ears like a shout down a long, empty hallway. The laugh of a psychotic woman in desperate need of professional help. *This isn't you, child. You are nothing. No one. Never was, never will be. You are dirt, I tell you. DIRT. LIE WITH THE WORMS OF THIS EARTH AND ROT.*

Maybe it wasn't her mother's voice, after all. Maybe a different mother, one that had come to her in the dead of night. A supreme presence that had leaked into her dreams.

She couldn't ignore the weird nightly dreams, either. Maybe they had something to do with her decision, her commitment to turning over a new leaf. Or maybe flying straight was of her own volition, boredom of always being the person everyone hated, despised. The one no one could stand to look at, let alone talk to. Maybe she was tired of being *her*. Her life had become this insipid, wasteful existence, and she refused to live another second in that old skin.

Despite the internal war that raged between her ears—all of that said and out on the table—the dreams were still most troubling. Those warped visions that interrupted her sleep, kept her awake, forcing her to stare at the infinite darkness of her room. Between the disturbing night terrors and the strong possibility that her mother, wrecked on drugs and alcohol, could come barging into her room at any given moment, it was a wonder she managed a wink of sleep each time her head hit the pillow.

Still, she powered through it. Each and every night. Just like always.

Because I'm strong, I'm in control of my life. No one else.

Who are you?

She backed away from the door once more. Who was she kidding? She didn't belong here. No one inside of that building would accept her. Her own mother hadn't, so why would a few strangers? People who knew nothing of her? She didn't dress like them, act like them. She was a fool to think this would work, this personal metamorphosis.

"Jewel?" a surprised voice asked from somewhere close. She hadn't realized the front door had swung open, a body blocking the only way in or out. "You actually showed up." The approval in Principal Fritz's voice was noticeable.

But regardless of his warm welcome, Jewel's eyes found the parking lot, the interest in pretending to be something she wasn't slowly dying within.

"Jewel?" Fritz said again, and she could tell he was concerned, wary of losing her to the influence of those outside forces, those negative charms that beckoned her, called to her, reached out and grabbed hold of her heart. "Come on in."

She hesitated. This scenario felt like a game of tug of war. Her past, everything she'd come to know, her mother and her absent parenting pulling her in one direction. In the opposite way was Principal Fritz, the allure of fun, doing something other than trying to tear down a world she had always thought was out to destroy her.

Fun was winning. She took one step toward the entrance. Then another. She could hear the past shouting at her, screaming her name, calling her a coward and a loser and a fucking stupid bitch. Her mother, Brennan and Dakota, all at once. They spat at her. Their voices became warped, deep, sounding like a gang of mischievous gremlins. Their invisible hands reached for her, their ghostly fingers losing purchase on her soul. She pulled away from them, made it within a few feet of the youth center's entryway.

"Glad you could make it," Fritz said, stepping aside.

The smell hit her first. Scents of lilac and sugary sweet aromas filled her nostrils. Its fragrance was almost overpowering. Stepping inside, she realized what this place was, what it could be.

Home, she thought.

The one she never truly had.

5

After dinner, a couple of hours before the sun crawled down from its tower in the sky, Doug, Grady, and Jesse rode their bikes to the Hooperstown Mall, a fifteen-minute trip from the Di Falco's. They parked their bikes in the rack outside of JCPenney's, secured them together with their trusty rope lock. Grady led the charge inside, removing a pocket-sized notebook and the pen he'd tucked into his jeans.

"How do you think we should approach this?" Grady asked as they made their way through the department store, weaving down the aisles toward the main entrance on their way to center court. "I mean, should we go in together or should Jesse go alone?"

"I feel like Jesse going alone might be the best bet," Doug said, turning to Jess. "You agree?"

Jesse only shrugged. "I have no idea. She might kick me right the hell out if I go in alone. She'll probably think Jimmy sent me. But if it's the three of us…"

Doug knocked the idea around. "All right, it's the three of us then."

Once they were in front of the Gap, they quickly scanned the glass windows that made up the store's exterior, attempting to locate Karen. Doug didn't know if she worked the stockroom, the floor, or the registers, just that she worked there.

Grady took the first step. "Let's just go in and ask for her."

Silently agreeing, the other two followed.

Doug speculated how this was going to play out. He imagined her running like the guilty perp in those cop dramas the second she laid eyes on them, the terrible chain of events that transpired in the cemetery hitting her like a fallen brick. He supposed if that *were* to happen, he couldn't blame her. She probably wanted to forget that night just as much as they did.

But they couldn't forget. They couldn't pretend like it never happened and go on living their lives. No, they *had* to remember. Every single detail as haunting and terrifying as it was—they could never allow themselves to ignore the night of the Hunt.

Because they had a job to do.

An obligation.

To save the town.

It sounded stupid speaking those words aloud. *Save the town.* As if doing so were some ordinary task, an English essay or a science project. But it was true. *Someone* needed to rescue Hooperstown. The place they had been born and raised was in trouble and only a handful of people knew about the evils that lurked in the shadows of their fourteenth summer. Things that bred long dim shapes, clung to dark street corners, a wicked climate that had been trespassing the spaces between spaces for so long, but was now here. In the open. For all the town to see. Perhaps the world, if they weren't careful, if they did nothing to stop it.

Doug recalled the dark sludge that Alphie had barfed into Jesse's mouth. Weeks later and he could still sniff traces of the acidic, vinegary odor. That delicate burn had laid claim to his nostrils and burrowed itself there, revisiting him whenever the memories of that night resurfaced.

Walking into the Gap, they headed straight for customer service. Grady, who seemed to be overcompensating for his previous gaffe of cowardly leaving them behind in the cemetery, led the charge.

"Excuse me," he said, talking to the young girl behind the counter. She had to be in high school, maybe a sophomore or a junior. Doug couldn't tell because he was terrible at judging such things. "Is Karen Howard working today?"

"Yeah," the girl said, chewing her gum. She blew a big pink bubble. "She's outside, smoking. Yous friends of hers?"

The three of them looked to each other. Again, Grady led the brigade. "Yeah. Yeah, we're good friends." He didn't sound convincing, but Bubble Girl didn't appear to care all that much. She seemed more interested in the magazine she was leafing through.

Rolling her eyes, the girl jerked her thumb at the door to the left of the desk. It was marked "Employees Only" but was open, and there was nothing to block anyone from entering.

"She's back there, through the exit. You should see it if you walk straight through."

"We're allowed back there?" Grady clearly had no sense of the phrase *play it cool*. Doug stepped on his toe, harder than he'd meant to. "*Owa*—I mean, of course. Yeah, yeah, that's cool. We'll just...ah, head back there because...you know, we can. Because you said so. Because it's cool."

The girl eyed him suspiciously and then shook her head, unamused. She went back to blowing bubbles the size of her face and flipping through the newest issue of *Cosmopolitan*.

"Are you an idiot?" Jesse asked him when they were out of earshot.

"What? Do you think she was into me?"

"No!" Jesse practically screamed. "She wouldn't be into you if you had a hundred-dollar bill hanging out of your zipper!"

"I'm pretty sure she would be, dude. A hundred dollars is a lot of—"

"Idiot," Jesse said, shaking his head. "You'd make an awful James Bond, by the way."

"Dude, I'd make an amazing James Bond! Do you want to have the whole 'who's better at *Goldeneye*' argument again?"

"Dude, you only beat me because you keep doing that circle attack that's almost impossible to defend and—"

Doug nudged them, an elbow for each of them. "Shut up. Do you guys ever stop arguing about video games?"

Jesse and Grady exchanged glances. "Nope," they replied in unison.

They walked through the forbidden door and into the employee lounge. There was no one back there, and they spotted the EXIT door Bubble Girl had told them about.

"Let's go," Doug said, leading them to the doorway.

Once outside, they spotted Karen immediately. She was next to the dumpster, puffing away on a cigarette. She looked visibly upset, her gaze distant and directed at the ground, as if the asphalt had just finished scolding her. Puffy red eyes rested above glossy cheeks.

"Karen?" Jesse asked, stepping in front of his friends, taking the lead.

She glanced up, their presence not seeming to faze her. Nodding, she said, "Figured you'd be coming by. He send you?"

Jesse shook his head.

"We came because we wanted to know what happened," Grady told her. "You know...*that* night."

She dropped her cigarette on the ground, shredded the leftover tobacco and paper underneath her shoe. Plucking another smoke out of the pack, she sighed, sniffled, then ignited the tip and sucked down a lungful. Exhaling a cloud that nearly shrouded her entire face, she said, "What do you want to know?"

Doug winced as if his next words were shards of glass. "What you saw."

"I don't know what I saw. Not exactly."

"Can you try to explain it? The best you can."

She shot him a sharp glance, her eyes icy and uncertain. "I'm not sure I can. That's the problem."

Jesse sighed, folding his arms across his chest like his favorite wrestler about to cut an intense promo. "We saw you in the cemetery with Jimmy. You guys went off to…do whatever it is you do when you're alone."

She didn't deny this. Instead, she ashed her cancer stick and exhaled a tremendous plume of white smoke.

"Come on, Karen," Jesse pleaded. "Do the best you can. Pretty please with heart disease on top?"

Sighing, she nodded. "Okay. Not that it makes any difference. No one will believe it."

"We will," Grady promised.

"We saw Randall," she said, her eyes looking elsewhere, as if the distance had suddenly projected the images from that night. "He stumbled onto the path. He came from the woods, I think. And he was all…*wrong*."

"Wrong how?"

"Anatomically. He was all…jumbled. If that makes sense."

"It doesn't." Grady waved his pen, prompting for more information. He'd already jotted down several lines, none of which Doug could read. "Please explain."

"His body was…*different*. Like it was changing in some weird way. Like, as if his bones were too big for his skin." She shivered, the memory too much for her. "I had to look away." She glanced down again, became temporarily lost in that night, the horrors it offered. "He kept coming. *Randall*. Though, I got the impression it wasn't…wasn't *him*, per se. His voice was…*off*. He sounded…"

"Dead?" Jesse asked.

She nodded. "Yeah. He was in bad shape. And I… I left. I ran. As fast as I could back to the car." Her cheeks trembled. "On my way back…I saw…" She nearly choked on her words. Her eyes were puddles now. "I saw *her*."

The three kids looked to each other, grave expressions rolling over them.

A chill coiled itself around Doug's shoulders. "Her?"

"Yeah. There was a woman out there. She was covered in filth, dirt and leaves clinging to her. I remember seeing twigs sticking out of her hair. I only remember this because I thought it was kinda funny in a weird way. But I was scared. *Really* scared, and I wanted to run from her, but I couldn't. My feet felt stuck, like the path was a pool of chewing gum. I know that sounds stupid but my shoes wouldn't...lift." She paused as a series of shudders rocked her body.

"It's okay," Grady said. "We saw stuff, too."

She nodded, took a pull off her cigarette, expelled more clouds of smoke. The act seemed to calm her, ease her nerves. She continued to tremble, but it was less noticeable. "She floated toward me. Her feet were off the ground. *Off*. I swear it. I am *not* lying." Her voice jittered.

Doug could tell she was on the verge of losing it. He almost made her stop just to avoid seeing the girl have a complete breakdown.

"She got closer and closer and then she stopped. She said something, but I couldn't make it out. She looked me over, *studied* me, you know—like the way a dog would a stranger. Head cocked to the side. Eyes almost innocent, but you could tell if she didn't like what she saw, she would rip your throat out. I've never been more frightened in all my life."

Her body quivered as tears spilled down her cheeks. Her cigarette fell from her twitching fingers, and she was too shaken to bend over and pick it up. Doug helped her out, kneeled and snatched the cigarette off the asphalt. It felt weird holding it—he had never touched one before. It felt wrong, everything about it, and he was glad when she took it back from him.

"Anyway, she just stood there. She was wearing some gown, a white robe of sorts. It looked... I don't know. I've never been good at history, but maybe...colonial? Something like that. Very simple, lacking style." She rolled her eyes and let out a fake sounding chortle. "Listen to me— I'm actually judging the ghost bitch's wardrobe."

"You think it was a ghost?" Grady asked.

"What else would it be? She wasn't real."

Again, the boys looked at each other.

"Did she…" Jesse stopped. His face folded into a mask of wrinkles, every facial muscle pulling tight. "Did she do anything to you? Touch you?" He swallowed. "Hurt you?"

Karen shook her head. "No, but she removed her gown."

Grady's eyebrows arched. "She what now?"

"She took off her clothes…to show me."

Doug gulped. "Show you what?"

More tears leaked out of Karen's eyes. Slowly, she turned and reached for a notebook sitting atop an overturned milk crate. As she flipped through it, Doug saw it was a sketch pad. Illustrations filled the pages, most of them pretty good, and he remembered Jesse saying something about Karen wanting to be an art major in college. She flipped to the desired page and stared at it, the pad quivering as she grew lost in her own creation. After her eyes had seen enough, she showed them.

The sketch was in pencil but very detailed. It showed a woman floating across the cemetery, her feet inches off the path, just like Karen had said. Her gown was crumpled beneath her. She was completely naked, every inch of her flesh exposed. But that wasn't the shocking part. The part that unnerved Doug—Jesse and Grady too, he assumed—was the slit running from the space between her breasts down to her thicket of pubic hair. The gash was open, wide, and there were things poking out of it—organs, Doug suspected. Something dangled from the opening, something Doug assumed was a tentacle of sorts, maybe an extraterrestrial appendage, like out of John Carpenter's *The Thing*. But when he looked closer, studied the detailed sketch, straining his eyes to get a better perspective, he realized it wasn't a tentacle, the stretching limb of some cephalopod-influenced space creature. No, he'd seen this before, in a very graphic film he'd seen in health class two years ago entitled, *The Miracle of Life*.

An umbilical cord swung out of the gory cavity. Attached to the end of it was nothing, just a raw, bloody root that had once been a connection between the woman and new life.

Karen's body hitched in a series of ugly sobs. "She showed me what *they* took from her."

6

"I'm really proud of you," Fritz said, locking the youth center's front door. "You adapted quickly. If I'm not mistaken, I believe you made a few new friends tonight."

If the sun hadn't collapsed behind the horizon, if the parking lot lights had provided more than a dusky glow, Fritz would have seen Jewel blush.

"It was fun," she said, sounding rejuvenated, very unlike the girl who had been summoned to the principal's office only three weeks prior. "I had a great time."

"Glad to hear it. So, can we expect you back?"

"Of course."

Fritz flashed a genial smile. "It's getting late. Need a ride home?"

"No. I'll walk."

"You sure? It's no trouble at all. It's a long trek to the Huntington Apartments from here."

She smiled, wanting to tell him that a long trek wasn't such a bad thing; that meant less time at home. Less time with Ava Conti. But she kept quiet on the subject, thanked him for his hospitality, and went her own way.

On her journey across the parking lot, she heard footsteps. Her first reaction was to raise her hands, ready to throw a punch at the first face she saw. But the shadows peeled back, revealing a boy who backed away with his hands up in surrender. "Whoa!"

Jewel dropped her fists. "You almost got decked, dude."

"Really sorry," the boy said. "Didn't mean to startle you."

He was cute, had a good head of hair on him. She liked longer hair on boys, which made sense because she loved Nirvana and couldn't stand The Backstreet Boys. Pop music made her gag. He had a gentle face, bright blue eyes that sparkled despite the absence of sufficient light, the dusky cones beaming down from the streetlights doing little for the parking lot.

"It's okay," she said, her heart stammering. She was unsure if his unexpected appearance or his charming good looks was responsible for her heart's behavior, but either way, she did her best to slow the rhythm, taking calculated breaths in through her nose. "I'm fine."

She turned to walk away when he said, "I saw you in there."

"Oh yeah?" she said, stopping. Rotating.

"Yeah. You were pretty good at that dancing game."

"Really?" She knew this was a line, a load of pure rubbish. She had been awful at that game, though everyone watching had been supportive and clapped for her low score, anyway.

"Yeah. I mean, not as good as me—*clearly*—but pretty good. I, for one, was impressed."

She giggled for what felt like the first time in a long while, and it actually hurt her throat. "Jerk."

"Guilty."

They shared a moment of awkward silence, neither knowing where to carry the conversation. She was about to pack it in, wish the kid goodnight, and be on her merry way when he cleared his throat.

"I'm Adam."

"Jewel."

"Yeah, I heard Fritz introduce you." He squinted, leaning against his car, a black Chevy Lumina with a thin red stripe across its middle. "Haven't seen you around school. You new?"

"I'm…I'm only going into high school. Just graduated eighth grade."

"Really?"

She nodded sheepishly. "I was held back. Twice actually."

He made a face, wincing as if he'd unknowingly made his coffee with sour milk. "Oh."

"Yeah," she said, rubbing her neck, producing her best shame-inspired smile. "Not real proud of it. I've…well, to be honest—I've been an asshole."

Adam shrugged, as if he'd expected her to confess this all along. "I figured."

"Screw you, man." A breathy laugh escaped her. "You know, for a Christian, you're kinda mean."

He waved off her accusation. "Not much of a Christian really."

"No? Then what was all that praying and shit?"

"We have to. It's part of the gig. Mainly I just like to come here and hang out. It's a good place to be. Good energy. Plus, it keeps me and my friends out of trouble. As an added bonus, volunteering here looks good on college applications. Fritz said he'd write a letter of recommendation if I helped throughout the summer."

"You'll be a senior next year?"

"That's right."

"Then off to college?"

"Yep. Can't wait. I'm damn bored of this town."

She turned her eyes toward the sky, the thought of leaving Hooperstown once and for all providing an overwhelming sense of euphoria. Her whole body tingled with the prospect of being free from this place. "Oh, man. Lucky you."

"You want out too?"

"In the worst way." Thoughts of skipping town faded. Reality settled back in, crushing her current mood. Images of driving past a sign that read NOW LEAVING NEW JERSEY melted into visions of her mother pulling her down the hallway by a handful of her hair. "But I'll never leave. I'm stuck here."

"Says who?"

Her eyes darted back and forth between the parked cars. "Says everyone."

"*Everyone* doesn't control your future." A knowing grin crept along his face. "You do."

Her heart skipped a note. For that, she had no response. Several times she tried opening her mouth, but it was no use.

"You know I'm right, right?"

She thought about it, then shook her head. "No. It's a nice dream, though."

"I'm serious. You can do whatever you want. *We* can do whatever we want. We're young. Our future hasn't been written yet. We're not pushing fifty, working dead-end jobs, living lives we hate."

"Definitely not the first two, but the last one… Yeah, I'm so there."

"Point is, *Jewel*," he said confidently, pushing himself off the car and walking toward her, "is that we write our own future. It's not dictated for you. It's not predetermined. There's no such thing as fate. We choose where we want our lives to end up. We see it, and we just…go."

The more he spoke, the shittier she felt. All this talk about seizing control of her future, grabbing life by the horns—all of it reeked of bullshit. Smoke up her ass, that's all it was. A preppy kid's reality with Mommy and Daddy's money, sure—but her? She'd never stand a chance. Her broke ass was destined to suffer an eternity. She might as well leave and start hitting her mother's crack pipe now, because *that* was her future. Not college. Not a good, well-paying job. Not a husband who truly loved her, not a trio of kids she could spoil rotten, the bank account to make frivolous spending possible.

No.

She was rotten.

Inside and out. Always was, always would be.

And she was meant to decompose, slowly, day in and day out, until the end of her pathetic existence.

"That's easy to say when you live a good life, have parents that love you." She nodded at the Lumina. "Buy you cars and shit."

He turned, as if he wasn't sure which car she was referencing. "That? Darling, that automobile is a piece of shit."

Now that she had really examined it. The car did have rust stains on the sides. Some of the corrosion had eaten through, leaving gaping holes in the body.

"I got this car for six hundred bucks. Worked at a candy stand in Lea Bay for two summers just to afford the repairs. Taught myself how to do everything, all the mechanical work. Read books...magazines. Did everything myself to save on labor."

"Really?"

"Yep. My parents hate each other. Not divorced, *yet*, but they spend most of their time looking for things to fight about instead of spending time with my siblings and me. So, if you want to talk about someone who hasn't had it too easy..."

"I didn't know. But...they have money, right?"

He shrugged. "My dad is the maintenance guy at Hooperstown Chemical. My mom peddles burgers at the diner down the road. They make do."

"Shit..." Dropping her gaze to the ground, her shoulders slumped in defeat.

He stepped in front of her and lifted her chin with his forefinger. "You. Make. Your own future. I promise." His eyes sparkled like rare gemstones.

She felt a wiggle in her chest.

Then he walked away, heading back to the Lumina. He slipped his key into the slot, popped the lock, and then opened the door. Pausing, he looked over his shoulder. "Need a ride? It's getting dark and— Gosh, I'd hate to see you walk home in it."

"In the dark?"

His shoulders bouncing again, he said, "The dark can be scary."

Her face crumpled. "I'll walk."

"You sure? Might not look like much, buuuuuut…it's cozy." He rapped his knuckles on the roof, as if that proved it.

"I'll pass but thank you."

He nodded, and then snapped his fingers in quick-draw-McGraw-gunslinger-fashion. "Remember—no one lives your life but you."

She swallowed, partially believing that was the truth. Somewhere in the background, her mother barked a rebuttal, but it was drowned out by the sound of Adam's Lumina cranking to life.

She watched him drive out of the parking lot.

The whole way home she planned some other changes in her life, starting with getting out of the damn apartment, permanently.

CHAPTER EIGHT

The Dinner Date

1

The phone rang and Gordon Simms answered the call on the fourth ring, two short of the answering machine. Doug was in the living room watching *Buffy the Vampire Slayer* when the call came through. Normally, he'd ignore phone calls that came in (unless he was expecting one), but this one dragged his attention toward the kitchen. He trained his eyes on the walkthrough between the two rooms, tuning his ear to the conversation. Even before he heard his name his interest was piqued.

"Doug?" Gordon asked the caller. "Yeah, he's home… Sure. Hold on a sec." Gordon poked his head into the living room. "There's someone on the phone for you."

"Who is it? Grady? I told him not to call after eight. I'm sorry, Dad."

"Not Grady," his father said, covering the bottom half of the telephone with his hand. *"It's a girl."*

"A girl?"

His heart nearly smashed through his chest. He couldn't believe it. What girl would be calling him at home, after eight on a weekday? Furthermore, he couldn't remember giving his number out to anyone, let alone a girl. As he pushed himself off the couch, leaving Buffy behind and wishing there was some way to pause live television, his head swam in curious waters.

"A girl?" he asked again, as if the notion not only confused him but was somewhat repulsive.

His father nodded, a proud smile cracking his face. He handed his son the phone.

"Hel-Hello?" He knew he sounded like a fool, but he couldn't help it.

"Hey, you," a gentle, sweet voice said.

"Uh, who is this?"

Laughter on the other end. Soft giggles that—for some reason—hit his ears like torpedoes. *Oh, God. I've ruined it. Whatever this is, I've fucking ruined it.*

"It's Maddie, you nut."

"Ohhhhh, Maddie! Right. Of course. I knew that."

His dad watched him with eager anticipation. Doug waved him away, throwing a weak, playful kick in his direction. Dodging the lazy attack, Gordon scampered into the other room. A second later, Doug could see the crown of his head poking out from behind the wall separating the rooms. His father's eyes revealed themselves, blinking with anticipation.

Doug scooped up the grocery list off the table, crumpled it into a ball, and hurled it at his father's head. His dad used the wall to shield himself.

"How'd you get my number?" Doug asked, watching in case his father returned.

He let his guard down but listened for the subtle click of someone eavesdropping from the bedroom line. He doubted his dad would do that, but, then again, he hadn't expected Maddie Rice to call, so anything was possible.

Maddie giggled. "There is this new invention called *the phonebook*."

Sarcasm. He loved it. "Oh, yeah. Duh."

"Anyway, I was just calling to say hi. Missed you at my end-of-year party."

"Oh yeah. Well, I had stuff going on."

"Heard you were on some sort of scavenger hunt."

A heavy pang thumped him. Heartbeat pounding, he lowered his voice. "Who told you?" he asked, in a whisper.

"Eh, you know. Word gets around. Hope it was worth it."

He started to doubt the true identity of the caller. If the woman from the cemetery, the one Karen had so thoroughly detailed in her sketchbook, could infiltrate their dreams, who was to say her influence couldn't preside over the real world? Maybe this wasn't Maddie. Or maybe it was. Maybe she had been possessed by the dream woman like Randall and Alphie had.

Something told him to hang up. Right now. Hang up and remove the phone from the wall, rip the electric right out of the drywall. Both of them, the one in his father's bedroom included.

But he didn't. "I'm sorry?"

"Hope it was worth missing my party."

"Oh!" A cool rush of relief broke across his forehead. "Oh, yeah. I mean, no—no, it totally wasn't. I wish I was over your house…having…*fun*."

"Yeah. Well, listen. I know it's getting late. I don't know if you have phone rules at your house—but I'm only allowed an hour a night, and I only have five minutes left."

"Oh." Doug didn't have any phone rules. It was rare he talked to Grady and Jesse for longer than five minutes. "No, I don't have any."

"Lucky!"

She cleared her throat, as if she were about to drop a news bomb on him. The atom bomb of news bombs. He braced himself for whatever was coming, though he had no reason to suspect the news was anything bad.

"So…uh, I have a question for you," she said.

"Okay…"

"My folks and me—well, mostly I—I mean, *me*. Shit. Okay, here it goes— I was wondering if you wanted to have dinner with me on Friday. *Us*. My parents and me."

"Dinner? Like another party?"

She giggled again. He was glad he was keeping her entertained, even if he was acting dumb on purpose. "No, silly. *Dinner.* You. Me. My parents. And they said to bring your dad. It's cool if he wants to come."

"Really? Just us? I mean, just you, me, and our parents?"

"Yes. Is that a problem?"

He didn't answer right away, his head transforming into a highway of speeding thoughts.

"I mean…you don't have to say yes." She sounded defeated, somewhat rejected.

Doug slapped his own cheek to snap himself out of this embarrassing stupor. "No! I mean, yes. Yes, I'd love to. I just have to check with my dad."

"That's great."

Creeping into view from behind the wall, a hand emerged with its thumb pointed at the ceiling.

"And he approves," Doug said. "Apparently he has no concept of *privacy*, either." Doug hurled a pen at him.

"What was that?"

"Nothing. Friday night—we'll be there."

"Perfect! Six o'clock sharp."

"See you then."

He hung up the phone. His father entered the kitchen, folding his arms across his chest.

"So…" he said, his eyes narrowing. "A date."

"It's not a date. It's just dinner."

"It's a date, dude."

"Dad. It's *dinner.*"

"Judging from the goofy look plastered on your face…it's a date, dude."

Doug bit his lip. "Okay, it's a date. And can you stop saying *dude?* It's weird when you use it."

Gordon pretended like he was offended. "I can say *dude.* What's wrong with me saying *dude?*"

"I don't know. You're old. It's weird when old people say dude. It's like…unnatural."

"Is this actually happening?"

"What?"

"I'm old?"

"Um, yes." Doug's head nodded like a bobble doll.

"I'm only forty-two."

"That's old, dude."

"That's old? Forty-two is old?"

Doug snickered. "Well, it is to me."

"Eighty-five is old. Forty-two is young. I'm practically a baby."

"Then what am I?"

He walked over and ruffled Doug's hair. Doug didn't even fight it. "You haven't even been born yet. Practically."

Doug rolled his eyes. "Whatever."

"Hey," Gordon said, turning to the fridge. He opened the door and took out a shiny red apple. Biting into it, he said, "You know you'll always be my baby, right?"

Doug froze. He remembered his mother saying that once, in what seemed like another life. "Yeah. Yeah, I know, Dad."

"Good." He swallowed a mouthful of apple and closed the fridge. "Why don't you go wash up and get ready for bed. Tomorrow, we'll get you ready for your big date."

2

"A date?"

"I know, right?"

Grady cackled in his ear, inciting a buzz of static. "That's crazy, dude!"

"I know, right?"

"Your dad is gonna be there, though?"

Doug paced around the kitchen, as far as the telephone cord would stretch. He ate his microwavable pizza as he walked back and forth, killing time before his dad came home from work. "Yeah. Is that weird?"

"A little. But we're only fourteen. I guess it's normal. Her parents are probably worried you'll knock her up."

"Gross, dude. But who knows? Maybe they'll leave us alone for a little."

"You gonna make out with her? Touch her—"

"Dude."

"What? Just asking. Geez. That *is* what you do on dates, you know."

"You don't *know* anything," Doug said. "We're just hanging out. Nothing more."

"AKA tasting her tongue flesh."

"That's so fucking nasty, man. Why do you have to ruin everything?"

"If you get to second base I'll be so jealous."

"I don't even know what second base is. Is that a lot of tongue? More than the usual amount?"

"I think second's hand stuff. You know—like grabbing and groping. Or it might be oral. I'm not sure. I don't keep up on these things. Jesse's the sexpert. Ask that pervo."

"I guess we'll see what happens. Not sure I'm ready for this."

"Dude. Get ready for this. You're gonna be in high school next year. We're, like, gonna get laid all the time."

"You're an idiot if you think that."

Grady giggled, a high-pitched squeal that needled Doug's ears. "Just messing with you. We'll be virgins forever. Just wait 'til Jesse hears about you and Maddie, though. You'll never hear the end of it. Kid's got jokes for days."

"He thinks he's funny."

"He's a goof."

Doug sighed. "All right, man. I just wanted to tell you the news."

"Thanks for calling. My mom is taking me to the library. It's our weekly trip."

"Enjoy."

"I'll catch you later."

"Buh-byeeeee."

Doug hung up the phone and slipped on his shoes. One of his daily chores was to get the mail, and he'd heard the mail truck idling outside while he'd been on the phone. On the way to the mailbox, he noticed his world seemed sunnier. It was hot outside, the sun beating down on this summer afternoon, but it wasn't just the heat that warmed his flesh and filled his veins with liquid comfort. It was his mood, the feelings he had for Maddie Rice. With Friday night looming so close, his nerves were on high alert. Everything seemed slightly different, sharper, more focused.

When he woke that morning, he had felt more energetic than the last few weeks combined. Instead of waking with fractured images of terrible dreams, he had pictured the face of Maddie Rice, her radiant smile. The terrible shapeless shadows that accosted him and his friends in the empty, run-down version of Hooperstown Chemical didn't resurface until well after breakfast.

When he reached the mailbox, a cloud drifted in front of the sun, throwing a dark shadow over the lawn, the entire street. Doug barely noticed, his head still buzzing from the big news. He retrieved the mail, shut the box, and headed back up the driveway. Behind him, Mrs. Gallo jogged past with her golden retriever. She greeted him, but Doug was too busy digging into the mail to be bothered. Lazily, he waved at her over his shoulder.

The mail was mostly junk. A few bills and bank statements, but the rest was *actual* garbage, circulars for stores no one outside of Hooperstown had ever heard of. A few flyers from local lawyers asking "IS YOUR CHILD SICK? HAVE THEY BEEN TREATED FOR THE FOLLOWING CANCERS IN THE LAST SIX MONTHS?" The types of cancers were listed below these questions, starting with Leukemia, which was bold and underlined. He flipped the cold call advertisement—which later he'd surmise was in very poor taste—to the back, not thinking much of it. The stack was pretty thick, but he went through it quickly, finishing his run-through before he reached the stoop.

An envelope slipped out of the pile and landed on the welcome mat. He bent over and picked it up. The nondescript note was addressed to him. Simply, it read: Doug. The handwriting was awful, the letters bent awkwardly, lazily scribbled. It could have easily been written by someone who hadn't passed first grade.

Curiously, he flipped the envelope over.

Little smudges of dirt stained the paper wrapping in numerous spots—fingerprints, Doug noticed.

The envelope unnerved him. *Someone* had dropped by in broad daylight and delivered the note. Had it been the mailman? He didn't think so. There was no address. Just his name. He doubted the mailman knew who he was. No, it had to come from someone else. Mrs. Gallo? No, that was dumb and made zero sense.

A shiver jolted him.

All across the golden sky, storm clouds gathered.

How quickly things could change in a day.

How quickly the life of a fourteen-year-old kid changed in one night.

3

As rain droplets peppered the window, Doug sat at the kitchen table, chin resting on folded hands, his eyes glued to the envelope. He was hesitant to open it, and not because of the anthrax scare. There were other reasons to be scared. Mainly, everything that had happened during the night of the Hunt.

This is stupid, he thought, scooping up the envelope. *You're being dumb.*

The big hand on the clock above the sink went around twice before he made his move. Slipping his thumb underneath the fold, he broke the seal. The note dropped onto the table, face down. Flipping it over, Doug's heart raced.

Dumb, dumb, dumb. It's a note. A note can't hurt you. Ink and paper, that's all it is.

For a second, it felt like his heart had stopped moving altogether. Nothing inside him seemed to work properly, his blood hitting traffic in the veins. Sweat beaded on his forehead, ran down the sides of his body from underneath his arms.

Though the author was unknown, the note was simple.

SUFFER THE SEASON
A PLAGUE AMONGST US ALL
YOU ARE THE CHILDREN OF THE LAST SUMMER
DEATH FOR THE BETRAYERS COME FALL

He read the note twice, three times. By the fourth go-around his head began to ache. A sour taste burned in the back of his throat. He thought he might get sick.

Getting up from the table, he found it difficult to take his eyes off the inscription. Breaking eye contact with the mysterious message, Doug scurried across the kitchen and stuck his head in the sink. He retched. Once. Twice. Three times. Nothing came out, although he felt extremely sick, fatigued and nauseated, like he'd suddenly come down with a serious stomach bug.

When it was apparent he couldn't throw up, he made his way back to the table. He took a sip from the Pepsi he'd poured himself earlier. It settled his stomach almost immediately.

Think. Who could have delivered this?

Doug wracked his brain. The suspects were few. The note could have come from Jesse, he guessed, though it was highly unlikely. Di Falco was the prankster of their little group, and if this ended up being a joke, he would be high on the suspect list. However, the tone and voice didn't sound like Jesse at all. The kid was terrible at English, hated creative writing, and there was no way he could craft something so...*concise? Stylish?* It wasn't the poem of the century, but it surely hadn't been written by a kid who had barely passed eighth-grade English with Cs. Unless he was operating with a partner, and Doug didn't think that plausible. What happened that night in the cemetery had shaken Jesse to the core, and if there was ever such a topic that was off-limits to kid around about, the Hunt was it.

That left a few others. Karen.

Not her, Doug thought, solely on the way she had acted during their interview. She had been visibly upset, barely able to effectively tell her own story of what happened that night. There was no way she'd leave this as a cruel joke or otherwise.

Jimmy?

He'd been so withdrawn lately that Doug guessed it could have been him. But that didn't make sense either. There was no motive, no reason he could have had to send this creepy message.

That left Alphie Moffit and Randall Benoit. Both boys, according to what Doug had followed in the Sunday paper, had not been seen since the last day of school. The search for the boys wasn't completely over, but so far the police were unable to find them anywhere. According to reports, every inch of Hooperstown had been searched, the bordering woods and all. Doug didn't necessarily believe that, because they would have found them, wouldn't they? It wasn't like they had vanished into thin air, never to be heard from or seen again.

Yeah, and they shouldn't be walking through the cemetery like zombies and puking up black sewage, either, should they?

No.

Yet, he'd seen that with his very own eyes.

If it *was* one of them, Doug had to hand it to them. The last time he'd seen Alphie, he was in no shape to be walking around. He had looked more like a monster than a young man heading into the twelfth grade. According to Grady, Randall had looked even worse.

SUFFER THE SEASON.

What did that mean? What did any of it mean?

It's a clue, he thought. *We're supposed to solve it.*

It appeared the Hunt had not ended.

And who was doing the hunting, Doug wasn't sure, but he couldn't shake the feeling that he and the others were the prey.

4

Two devils on her doorstep.

She hadn't seen Brennan or Dakota in days, not since she had left them and gone to check out the youth center. But here they were, in the flesh, standing on the patio of her mother's apartment, grinning as they plotted mischief.

"Come with us," Brennan said, fixing the wool winter hat he wore three-hundred-and-sixty-five days a year, no matter what the weather and social norms dictated.

She looked back inside, down the hallway. Mother was sleeping, even though it was pushing one in the afternoon. It'd be another hour or two before her nightmares let go of her, before she woke up groggily and demanded breakfast. Eggs and bacon. Toast, lightly crisped. Not burnt. God help Jewel's sorry soul if the bread was burnt.

"I shouldn't."

Dakota made flatulence with his tongue and lips. "Come on, bitch. You never fucking hang out with us anymore."

Brennan opened his jacket, revealing a stash of fireworks he had taped to the inner lining. He looked like one of those suicide bombers who targeted busy marketplaces in the Middle East. "Pat Wolford's parents visited their folks in Alabama. Came back with a shitload of fireworks."

"We're gonna go out to Miller Park and shoot them off. Maybe put some M-80s in mailboxes."

As tempting as that was, she knew she'd catch shit if she wasn't home to make her mother breakfast. "I really shouldn't."

"What the hell is wrong with you, Jewel?" A ripple tore across Brennan's brow. "You've been so weird since school ended. You hardly ever hang out anymore. It's always 'I'm busy' or 'I'm not in the mood.'"

"Is there something wrong?" Dakota asked. "Something you're not telling us?"

"You got a boyfriend or something?"

Dakota tapped Brennan's shoulder, as if the question sparked a great epiphany. "I bet it's a boyfriend, dude!"

"Whose dick you suckin', girl?

"It's not a boyfriend," she said, speaking through her teeth. "And I'm not sucking any dicks. I just…need some time to myself."

"Okay, you're acting fucking weird."

"Hella-weird," added Brennan.

"Should we call a doctor? Are you sick? That cancer shit is going around. Do you have that?"

"What?" Jewel said. "No. Don't be idiots."

"Oh, so we're idiots now?"

"You were always idiots. I was an idiot, too."

The two heathens glanced at each other, their faces scrunching with utter confusion.

"So," Brennan said, "you're not an idiot anymore?"

"Too good for us, Conti?" asked Dakota.

"Conti? Sounds more like *Cunti* now."

The two clowns bellowed with laughter.

A bolt of rage surged through her in a flash. She lashed out, grabbed Brennan by his collar, and drove her knee into his crotch. A high-pitched yelp escaped him, and he crumpled forward. Dakota came up behind her, arms out, ready to subdue her. She sensed him there and drove her elbow into his chest, knocking him back a few steps.

"Listen to me, you little fuckwads," she snapped. "I want you to turn around and never, *ever* come back. Do not talk to me. Do not call me. Do not show your face around me ever again. If we pass each other in the halls in high school next year, pretend you don't know me. Because you do *not* know me. Understand?"

Brennan's face contorted and constricted, as if he was trying to hold in a public fart. His pallor deepened to pink tones. White spittle bubbled on his lips. Baring his teeth, he remained silent, despite Jewel waiting for his answer.

"I asked you a question, dick-for-brains," she said, gripping his collar even tighter.

"Fine," he said, teeth clenched so tight that thick cords stood out on his neck.

She whipped her head in Dakota's direction. "You?"

"You're such a bitch."

"I know."

Dakota studied her eyes, then nodded.

"Good," she said, letting go of Brennan's collar. "Now get out of here."

"Not wise to make enemies of old friends," Brennan said, fixing the collar of his denim jacket.

"What're you gonna do about it, huh?" Snarling, she took one step toward them. "What?"

Sadistic smiles crossed their faces as they backed down the stoop and then the little stone walkway that led to the shared driveway. She watched them pick up their bikes, hop on, and pedal off down the street.

After they were out of sight, Jewel sat down on the stoop and cried into her hands. Her whole body hitched as the tears came forth, pouring out of her. This transformation was a lot harder than she had expected. She was killing off pieces of her past and killing—she discovered—hurt.

It hurt a lot.

From behind her, down the hall, footsteps padded on the carpet.

"Jewel?" she heard her mother ask, sleep straining her vocal cords.

Jewel didn't answer. She wiped the stream of tears from her eyes and refused to face the hallway, the creature standing in it.

The Monster.

"Jewel, get your ass inside. Make me breakfast."

Jewel took her time getting to her feet, collecting herself. When she did, she noticed she'd been sitting on an envelope. Curiously, she picked it up.

JEWEL had been sloppily scribbled across its face.

Stealing a look back inside the apartment, she saw her mother had disappeared into the kitchen, probably to make some coffee. Using the precious moment of being alone, she tore into the envelope, removing the letter inside.

Four lines.

The note began with, SUFFER THE SEASON.

"What is that?" Now her mother was standing behind the screen door. She'd seemingly appeared out of nowhere. "I asked you what the hell is that? A bill? Another *goddamn* bill? Who gave you that?"

Jewel folded the note, readied to stuff it in her back pocket. "It's nothing, Mother."

"It's nothing, Mother," Ava squawked, a poor attempt at mocking her in a child's voice. "Give it."

"No."

"What do you mean, 'no?'"

"I mean, *no.* It was addressed to me."

"Girl, if you don't give me that right now…"

"What are you gonna do, Mother?" She stood defiantly, much like she had against the two goons who'd just left her doorstep. Straightening her spine, she puffed out her chest, attempting to cast the most intimidating shape she could. "You gonna hit me? Again. You want a replay from the other night?"

"Hitting you would be the kindest thing I do to you."

"You've never done a kind thing for me, Mother. Not once. Not ever."

"I let you live. That's kind enough. Now give me the note before I break your fucking jaw, you sassy-mouthed cunt."

"You use that word a lot, Mother. *Cunt.*"

"Well, that's what you are—an ungrateful, unappreciative, loudmouth cunt, in need of a good ass-beating to learn herself a lesson." She narrowed her eyes, and the faintest trace of a smile touched her lips. "Come in and get your lesson, girl. Don't make me come out there and drag your ass inside. You won't like what happens if that's the case."

"I think *you're* a cunt, Mother." She watched her mother's eyes bulge, becoming almost too large for her sockets to handle. Like corks ready to pop from cheap bottles of bubbly. "I think you're a callous, stupid cunt. And maybe it's not your fault you're that way."

"You better watch your tongue, girl," Ava said, venomously.

But she didn't. She let it all flow out freely, every single thought. "I think you've had a pretty shitty life, Mother. Maybe Grandmama and Grandpapa didn't love you enough, so you went out chasing booze and drugs, fell in love with the wrong kind of men. Men who treated you like shit. Men like Daddy, who beat you down and never picked you back up. So you just stayed there, down in the dirt, and now you want to drag me down there with you."

Her mother's face trembled, unbridled fury building within.

"I almost feel sorry for you, Mother. *Almost.* But you're weak. You allow your life to control you. See, people can choose who they want to be, and you've *chosen* to be a callous cunt. Not to mention a terrible mother."

"I'll fucking kill you," Ava growled. She pushed on the screen door without operating the handle, almost breaking it. The metal frame creaked as the entire thing shuddered, Ava's weight against it.

Behind Jewel, kids rode past on their bikes. A neighbor across the street shuffled down their driveway to get yesterday's mail. A few apartments down, a lawn service was cutting the grass and trimming the overgrown weeds near the sidewalk. There were far too many witnesses for Ava to do what Jewel knew she wanted to—slam open the door, grab Jewel by her hair, punch her nose until it was nothing but bits of bone and loose skin, and then drag her back inside where she could administer further punishment. Jewel felt safe outside, safer than she'd felt in a while.

"It's not too late to change, Mother."

Pure hatred burned in Ava's eyes. If this conversation had happened behind closed doors, Jewel's face would have been used as a punching bag. She would have woken up tomorrow with welts and bruises. Hell, she might not have woken up at all. This was bad. She'd never stood her ground before, not like this. She was heading into uncharted territory, a lonely place she could never return from.

"It's not too late," she said again.

"I'll give you five seconds," Ava Conti said, her voice low and raggedy, "to get your ass inside this house, to take your punishment like you deserve, or I swear to God, Jewel, you will not live to see the sunrise."

"No, Mother. I will not come inside."

Ava smashed the door frame with her fists. The entire apartment seemed to quake.

Jewel couldn't help it; she flinched.

"GET IN HERE NOW!"

Jewel stood her ground. "No. I won't."

Cables of flesh appeared on her mother's neck. Her lips quivered, bent inward as if her mouth were a vacuum, sucking them in.

"I'm leaving," Jewel said. "I don't know when I'm coming back."

"You come back, you're dead. You're a dead girl. You hear me? You leave and there's *no* coming back. I will… I will not accept you back into this home."

She smirked.

"You think this is funny?"

"Home," Jewel said. "This never felt like home." And it was true; it hadn't. It had always felt like a place she'd lived more than a home. Hell, Brennan and Dakota had *homes*, even if they weren't perfect. She knew what homes were supposed to feel like. Here, with mother, was just another stop along the way.

"You ungrateful cunt. After everything I've done for you. After the clothes, the food—"

"Goodbye, Mother."

Ava snarled. "You have nowhere to go. You'll come back."

"Not this time."

She turned and walked down the driveway, leaving home with nothing but the clothes on her back, the shoes on her feet, and the cryptic note in her pocket.

Friday night took forever to show its face. Doug drew an X through the date on the calendar next to the telephone, his cheeks split by the widest of smiles.

"You ready to go, killer?" Gordon asked his son, swinging his car keys around his finger.

He was wearing a nice button-down shirt and khakis. It was the nicest he'd dressed in years, since the days of dragging the family to Sunday Mass. But since Mom and her final episode, Dad had stopped going to church. Quit believing in things like God. Doug hadn't noticed, not until he had seen him so handsomely put together, but he suddenly realized their home was absent of all religious imagery. Every cross—not that there had been a ton to begin with—had been taken down, every Bible had been tucked away or donated to the local thrift shop, every little mention of the Good Lord erased. There had once been a laminated card with an illustration of Jesus propped on the fireplace mantle, a keepsake from his grandfather's funeral several years ago.

"Yeah," Doug said, tossing the pen on the counter. "How do I look?" He spun around, holding his arms out, allowing his old man a good look at the new pair of jeans and the silk button-down. He had wanted a bowtie to match, but his dad had talked him out of it.

"You look great, bud." Gordon shoved his hands in his pockets and leaned against the wall. "You know, you probably don't want to hear this, but I think your mother would be really proud of you." He sniffled, and Doug noticed a single droplet clinging to his eyelash. "She'd be happy for you, you know?"

The sting of raw tears burned the back of Doug's eyeballs. He swallowed what felt like a lemon. Somewhere into his stomach his heart dove. "Yeah..."

Gordon wiped his eyes. "Ah. All right. Let's head over there. It'd be a shame to keep the young lady waiting." He grabbed the bottle of wine off the counter and headed for the door.

Looking around the kitchen, Doug took a deep breath, collected his wayward thoughts, and followed his father out the front door and toward the car.

6

Maddie's greeting was exactly as he had pictured—her smile was wide, displaying two perfect rows of teeth. She stepped aside and happily waved them in.

"Hi," Doug said nervously, hustling inside.

"Hi," Maddie bubbled.

"Hey, Maddie," Dad said, following his son inside. "Pleasure to meet you." He extended his hand, and she took it. After a cordial shake, their hands returned to their respective sides.

"Pleasure to meet you too, Mr. Simms."

"Please. Call me Gordon."

"Okay," she said. A giggly outburst shook loose from her throat. She closed the door behind them.

Doug watched his father glance around the foyer, admiring the architecture, the spiraling staircase that led to the second floor. The vaulted ceilings seemed to rise higher than that, almost as if the McMansion harbored a third story. The stairs and the wooden-plank flooring were stained honey oak, the sheen of polyurethane so glossy that Doug could almost see his reflection.

Gordon whistled at the sight.

"You sound impressed," Maddie's father said, emerging from around the corner.

Dad nodded. "Yes. You have a beautiful home, Mr. Rice."

Maddie's father winced, as if he were a demon and hearing "Mr. Rice" was an effective phrase from an exorcist's passage. "Please, call me Charlie. Mr. Rice actually hurts my ears."

"Charlie," he replied, shaking the man's hand. "Gordon."

"Gordon," he repeated. "I like that name."

"Well, I can't take credit for the choice."

Mr. Rice flaunted a humorous grin. Then he turned to Doug. "You must be the young man my daughter is always talking about."

"Dad!" Maddie shouted through her teeth.

Snorting as his belly bounced along with the hearty chuckles, Mr. Rice put his arm around his daughter. "Just kidding around, darling. I need to have a little fun with this, you know." He cupped a hand around his mouth, as if he were about to whisper a secret, but then spoke in his regular tone for the whole room to hear. "It's called an *icebreaker*."

"Yeah, well, break ice some other way." Grinding her teeth, a tinge of embarrassment combing over her, Maddie faced Doug. "He's joking. I don't—"

Doug giggled, blushed. "It's okay. Honest."

Maddie's grimace morphed into a grin, her brow climbing her forehead with a sense of relief.

"Come in, everyone!" Maddie's mother shouted from the kitchen. "Dinner's almost ready! Get it while it's hot!"

"You guys hungry?" Mr. Rice asked.

"Starving," Dad said, rubbing his belly.

"How do you feel about roasted chicken, sweet potatoes, and creamy spinach? Apple pie and ice cream for dessert?"

"You're making my stomach grumble with joy, that's for sure."

"Me too," Doug added.

"Come on then," Mr. Rice said, waving them on. Quietly, he added, "Before the wife gets agitated."

His dark, bushy eyebrows twitched in comedic fashion, and Doug knew right then and there he was in the right place. This was a good home, he thought. Good energy. Exactly the way a home should feel. And that wasn't to say their own home generated bad energy and wasn't up to par—it was. But the Rice's residence felt different. There was a lot of love here, and he could sense it, could almost wrap the glowing aura around him like a blanket.

"I heard that!" she said, referencing her husband's little jab, and, in unison, everyone giggled their way into the kitchen.

7

After dinner was over, Doug covered his mouth and slowly released some gas, hoping the quiet burps weren't loud enough to alert Maddie. Or Mr. Rice. Or Mrs. Rice for that matter, even though Doug had always been told a good burp meant compliments to the chef. The meal had been as good as Mr. Rice had advertised. The apple pie and ice cream for dessert were to die for, and everything that had come before it had Doug drooling for seconds.

As Mrs. Rice cleaned the dishes in the sink, Maddie and Doug ventured outside onto the back deck. They sat down on the porch swing and looked up at the star-clustered sky, each of them gazing so intently yet trying to think of something meaningful to say. Doug managed to break away from the cosmos' strong pull and looked through the kitchen window, spotted Mrs. Rice eyeing them. When she noticed Doug watching, she cast her head down, went back to scrubbing the dishes with more vigor than before.

"I had a good dinner," Doug said.

"Yeah, it was fun. Sorry for my parents. They insisted they meet you first."

"Oh, no big deal. Honest. It was good they were here."

"Really?"

"Yeah. I mean, I guess."

"I don't want you to think it will always be like this."

"Always?"

"Yeah. I mean—the next time we hang out, it won't be with them breathing down our necks. I *hope*." Her face bunched together as if she weren't quite sure of this claim.

"Ah. Got it." He squinted. "So what you're saying is…there's gonna be a next time?"

She burst into laughter. "Yes. Yes, of course. Unless…you don't *want* there to be a next time?"

"No, no, no. Of course, I do."

Her face beamed with a wide smile, the brightest he'd ever seen. Staring into his eyes, she slipped her hand into his, lacing their fingers together.

He squeezed to let her know this was okay. More than okay. It was perfect.

"This is nice," he said, and she giggled again.

This is nice? This is nice!? What are you, a moron? The inner scolding sounded like it had come from Jesse, and he couldn't *not* picture his friend shaking a finger in his face, threatening him to sack up or else he would steal his super rare collector's edition of *Maximum Carnage*, the red SNES cartridge he so proudly displayed on his dresser, under his favorite Lawrence Taylor poster.

"It is," Maddie agreed. "It is nice."

"Is it me, or is it super hot out here? I feel like I'm about three seconds away from bursting into flames."

"Well, it is summer."

"It is summer, isn't it?"

She giggled once more, putting a hand over her mouth. Apparently, everything he said was funny. Which was…good? He couldn't tell, but he was beginning to sweat a lot. He could feel dribbles of nervous tension rolling down his sides. His armpits had become saunas. Moist, stinky saunas.

Maddie's mom was still watching them from the kitchen window.

He pretended like he didn't notice, spying on her from the corners of his eyes. "Your mom is watching us. Not gonna lie, it's kinda freaking me out."

"I know she is. I'm sorry. Is it weird?"

"Only a little. Okay, maybe more than just a little. But not mega-weird. Mega-weird would be her, like, popping out of one of these bushes with a platter of crackers and cheese. I mean, on a scale of one-to-ten, spying on us through the kitchen window might be like a seven?"

"Should I tell her to fuck off?"

This time, Doug giggled. "Nooooo. Don't do that. Are you trying to get me banned for life?"

"Why not? You wouldn't want some privacy?"

Her eyes beamed at him. In them he could see what she wanted—a kiss. They practically begged for it, and he wasn't dumb. If he'd been two, three years younger, he might have been blind to the signal, but not at fourteen. But, despite the knowing and the fact he very much wanted to grant her the wish, there was no way he could plant one on her now, in front of her mother.

Plus, if this was going to be a regular thing, if there *was* a future here, he wanted their first kiss to be a story. A memorable moment. Not, *hey, remember the first time you kissed me in front of my mother?* No. Eff that. Doug wanted their first kiss to be somewhere cool, somewhere romantic— the beach, the pier, maybe atop the Ferris wheel on the Seaside Heights Boardwalk, overlooking the ocean and the glittering trail of moonlight that led toward the dark horizon. But not here. Definitely not here, and definitely not now.

"I'd love some privacy, absolutely." He talked fast, too fast almost, so rapidly his tongue could barely keep up. "Just…I wouldn't want her to think I'm a bad influence on you."

"You're sweet." Her finger touched his chest, where his heart beat erratically, reaching dangerous tempos. "I was kidding, by the way. If I told my mother to fuck off right now, we'd never see each other again."

He nodded. Was his face sweaty? He couldn't be sure. He thought it might be. *Shit, do I smell?* A faint odor tickled his nostrils, but he supposed that could have been something other than his body's natural response to a flood of pheromones. Maybe the Rice's outdoor garbage can was nearby. Maybe a neighbor's. Taking in a lungful of this unknown malignant odor, he realized Maddie was staring at him. Confused. Creeped out? Probably both. Her look and the odd smell made him sweat more, and suddenly his legs were drenched.

"Are you okay?" Maddie asked.

"What? Fine. Yes. Why?"

"You're…"

Sweating? Shit. She can see it. That's gross. I need to bail. BAIL. BAIL.

He waited for her to respond, but she never completed the thought.

"Never mind. Hey, so tell me more about that scavenger hunt. Sounded cool. Wish I could have tagged along, but you know…the party."

"Scavenger hunt? Oh, right. That." He shrugged. "It was fun. Nothing memorable happened. No good stories or anything." A nervous laugh freed itself from within, and he felt his cheeks burn with further shame.

"Uh-huh." She could tell he was lying. He was sure of it. "You know, you don't have to be nervous around me."

She let go of his fingers.

"I'm sorry." He hung his head. There was only one way out of this—he needed to tell her the truth. Didn't someone wise once say *the truth will set you free?* Maybe that was his mother's saying or maybe that one belonged to Jesus. He couldn't be sure. "I just... I really like you, Maddie."

"I like you too, silly. I wouldn't have invited you to dinner with my folks if I didn't."

"I know. I guess...shit. I guess I'm just trying too hard."

She rubbed his knee. Squeezed. His groin suddenly swelled with traveling sensations, like the magnetic pull of ocean currents.

"It's okay. Just, you know... Relax."

"Okay." He wiped his forehead, removing a layer of greasy sweat. "So...how was your party? What'd I miss?"

"Ah. The usual. There were no major incidents." Now he could tell she was the one avoiding the truth. "Although Todd Roberts and Amanda Summers snuck off about halfway through the second movie to go make out in the downstairs broom closet."

"Oooooh. Juicy."

"Yeah. And then..." Her face went still. "Well, there was one incident, actually." She cleared her throat as if she was on the verge of choking. "With Bishop." Her eyes slowly fell away.

"Bishop?"

"Our poodle."

"Oh. What happened?"

"It was weird. Do you know Abby Allen?"

"Yeah. Of course."

"Well, she wasn't feeling well and decided to take a walk. She took Bishop with her and... I dunno. Something...*happened.*"

Doug's arms rippled with gooseflesh. "What happened?"

Her lips bunched together. "Don't know...not *exactly*. I couldn't get a straight answer from Abby, but when she returned from the walk...she was...different."

"Different how?"

"Distant, maybe? Like she'd seen something that haunted her. Like a ghost."

Flashes of that night in the cemetery flipped through his mind. Alphie in his reduced state—his tattered clothes and gray flesh, the malodorous ichor he vomited into Jesse's mouth. Everything about that night flooded his mind, leaving him temporarily dazed.

"Doug?" Maddie said, freeing him.

"Yeah?"

"Where'd you go?"

"Nowhere. I'm here. You were saying…about Abby."

"Yeah. She didn't say anything in front of Mom or Dad, but when we were alone…"

"What'd she say?"

"She said she was attacked."

"Attacked?"

Maddie nodded.

"Who attacked her?"

Her forehead shriveled like the skin of old fruit. "That's the thing. It's kind of impossible."

Doug gulped, waiting for her to divulge Abby's claim. He'd seen his fair share of the *unbelievable* lately, and he doubted anything Maddie was about to tell him would be too farfetched for him to buy. Insanity was all around him that summer, and he needed to stay tough. Strong. Emotionally impenetrable. Like he had for his father when his mother had turned on them, during the years that followed. "Trust me. I think a lot of impossible things have been happening around here lately."

Her eyes slimmed, expecting him to elaborate. Instead, he waited for her to continue. "Well, Abby said it was Lauren Sullivan."

"The cancer girl?"

Maddie bit her lip and nodded subtly. He could see the tension touching every muscle in her face. A part of her, maybe the majority of her, believed Abby had been telling the truth.

"Which sounds impossible, right?" A humorless laugh slipped between her lips. "Because Lauren is in the hospital and not doing well according to what my parents have said. They said… They said she might not make it."

"That's terrible."

"But Abby, she was shaken. She believes Lauren attacked her and Bishop. And Bishop…"

"What happened to Bishop?"

Her eyes filled with tears and Doug knew—the dog was dead or missing, or both.

"Jesus." Doug squeezed her hand, wishing they hadn't broached this topic. The night had been going so well. "Maybe Abby is telling the truth. Maybe it *was* Lauren."

"But how? She's sick, in the hospital. My mom made some calls. Lauren hasn't left her bed since she went in."

Doug wanted to tell her everything, every single moment that he and his friends had experienced since the start of summer. The Hunt, the impossible memories that night shared with them. But now wasn't the time. Maddie wasn't ready yet. If he told her, she might think he was nuts. She might kick him out. Tell her parents. Might never want to see him again.

He couldn't have that. Not with these feelings left to explore.

Doug found he couldn't answer the Lauren question. All he came up with was this: this was the summer where *the impossible* was now *possible*, and no one, not even the healthy, were safe.

8

From the mini fridge in the corner of the garage, Charlie Rice pulled two cold ones. He handed one to Gordon, who was absent-mindedly admiring Charlie's collection of tools and his workbench setup. In the center of the garage rested a '63 Impala, a long cloth tarp covering more than half of it. The revealed portion of the body was in rough shape, rust-eaten and heavily dimpled throughout, but Charlie seemed to be in the middle of restoring it. Tools were scattered near the front tires, and a car jack had been raised underneath it. Cars were never Gordon's thing, but he pretended to be impressed with the progress.

"She's a beaut," Charlie said, raising his Corona.

Gordon tapped necks. Then they each guzzled, half their beers gone in a few swigs.

"Not much of a car guy, myself," Gordon admitted, wiping his mouth with his wrist. "But I will agree—she's very pleasant to look at."

"I want to thank you for coming over," Charlie said, changing the subject.

"Thank you for having me."

The subtle cringe was noticeable, couldn't slip past Gordon's perceptive wit. Whatever Charlie was going to say next would likely cause a stir, and Gordon suddenly felt uncomfortable about the whole evening. "I want to admit something to you, and I hope you won't take offense."

Alerted, Gordon shuffled his feet. "What is it?"

"Our invitation was twofold."

"How so?"

"Well—first, yes, my daughter seems to have some…" His hand danced in the air, searching for the right word to grab. "…*infatuation* with your son."

Gordon grinned. "Yeah, I'd say the *infatuation* is mutual."

He sipped the Corona through a joyous, cherubic smile. A part of him was proud of Doug. Very much so. It was the first time he'd expressed interest in girls, and there was some fatherly instinct that had taken over, some primal emotion that lent itself to the nature of his son's budding hormones. It was weird when he broke it down that way, but since everything that had happened, especially the history with his mother—well, Gordon was surprised Doug pursued girls at all. A small part of him thought Doug would shun them, commit to a life of solitude. Never get married, never have kids—the everlasting effect of his childhood trauma.

"Agreed. And it's nice and we—my wife and I—support them one-hundred percent."

"As do I."

"But there was another reason for having you over, Gordon. And I hope this doesn't ruin what has been a wonderful evening." Charlie nibbled his thumbnail. "Gosh, I feel terrible for what about I'm about to say, but I didn't think you'd come any other way."

"I'm all ears, Charlie."

Charlie's cheeks deflated, causing a slow, slashed-tire noise to escape his lips. "It seems my law firm has gotten caught up in this Hooperstown Chemical fiasco."

"Oh?"

"Yes. And I've been assigned to investigate the case."

"Oh?"

"And I was wondering if you were willing to collaborate, maybe provide me with some details. Being a veteran worker, you might have some insights that could be of some use."

He nodded, finally seeing this for what it was. "You mean *cooperate*."

Tucking his lip between his teeth, Charlie shook his head. "No, I mean *collaborate*. Work *with* me on this."

Gordon nodded and set his beer down on a nearby rolling cart used to store hand tools, wrenches and socket sets. He folded his arms across his body and asked, "What exactly are you asking me?"

Charlie Rice sighed. "I know it might seem hard. I know you might feel like a traitor. After all, you've been working there for near as long as any other employee. But I assure you, if the stuff we're hearing is true, if Hooperstown Chemical *is* responsible for illegally dumping toxic waste and polluting the town's public water system—then anything you give me, anything we can prove, will be helping. You'd be helping the town and the families, both of which are going through some very difficult times right now. Six kids are sick, Gordon. Another half dozen have reported similar symptoms, and there are whispers that even more cases could be confirmed by the end of the week." He took a breath, as if the whole situation was weighing him down. "I think this is real. Now we have information—"

"Hooperstown Chemical has given me and my family a life. A pretty good one."

This information stunned Charlie Rice, stopped him dead.

Gordon swallowed the lump in his throat, then picked up the beer. Took a swig. Then another. The bottle was more or less empty before he blinked. "They were there for me through everything. I bought my first house because of them. I raised a son on my salary. Provided my family with everything they needed and then some. We live comfortably. More importantly, when we had fallen on tough times—when Sharon was going through her...her, uh, issues—they were there for me. Gave me as much time off as I needed. Not only that, but they never came down on me when I had to leave early or came in late because of doctor's appointments or tests. They stood by me when they could have easily fired me and gotten someone more reliable. I haven't forgotten that."

Charlie flashed a warm smile. "I understand that. I really do. But this... This is huge. Beyond us, really. Far beyond any debt you think you owe them. Far beyond superficial loyalties." He shook his head as if he didn't believe the truth himself. "Kids are sick. Dying. Your son drinks this town's water. Bathes in it. Plays in it. My daughters, as well. What if this happens to one of them? How loyal will you be then?"

Gordon looked away, unable to ignore Charlie's tonal shift. "We don't know that the plant's responsible. There's no proof. None I've heard of, anyway."

"Is that what they told you?" Charlie shook his head with disbelief. "I shouldn't be surprised. But... Look. Between me and you—there's proof, man. Plenty of it. We could really use some eyewitness accounts, maybe some documentation to put a nice little bow on things and..." He must have seen the look on Gordon's face, his demeanor shift, because Charlie's confidence took a hit. "Look, man. I hate to be the one to break it to you, but...my firm estimates the plant will be forced to shut down within two weeks, tops. The official investigation will start then, but I'm doing preliminary surveys, trying to get a jump on the specifics. Gather as much info as I can before the Hooperstown Chemical lawyers step in and shut me out."

Gordon looked up from the concrete floor, his tongue poking his cheek out. "Sounds like a war."

"It will be." Charlie's gaze took a cold turn. "And whose side do you want to be on?"

9

Taking her dishrag with her, Mrs. Rice disappeared from the window.

"Do you dream?" Doug asked Maddie, who'd taken a spell of silence while Doug had drifted off into his own mind. "I mean, regularly? Recently?"

She shrugged, seemingly indifferent. "Sure. I dream."

"What of?"

"What are my dreams about?" She eyed him dubiously. He could tell the topic weirded her out, and maybe it wasn't the topic itself but how he approached it. "I dunno. Nonsense stuff, really. I dream every night, but they're mostly fragments. I hardly remember them. Sometimes I'll see something in real life and it will remind me of a dream I've had. Has that happened to you?"

You wouldn't believe me if I told you, he thought, but did not say. He wasn't sure what he could and could not tell her yet, how she'd react to certain information, the happenings around Hooperstown. The stuff going on behind the scenes.

"Sometimes," he told her. "Though, I've been having these weird ones lately. And some of the others have too."

"Others?"

Damn it. There he went, opening his mouth, spilling his guts. There was no turning back now, no sense easing her into the chaos at hand. Jesse and Grady would probably be pissed, but who cared? She had to know. It was a dick move to keep things from her, especially since she lived in town, and had friends who were and could be affected. In some way, she was already a part of this. If Abby Allen's account was to be believed—and he did believe her, despite having no proof—then she had been touched by the Mother's influence.

Plus, Maddie was easy to talk to. Once his nerves cooled, once the perpetual sweating died down, talking became easy. Second nature. He could do this all night. She could too, judging from the way she laughed at his stupid jokes.

"Jesse and Grady. They've had the same dreams as me. Same *exact* dreams. It's like we're all linked."

"But...how?"

"Okay," he said, turning his whole body to face her. "What I'm about to tell you sounds impossible, more so than what Abby told you, but it's true. I swear on my life."

"Okay..."

He could see she already didn't believe him, but it was too late to stop now. The train of truth was off the rails, rolling down the mountainside, and no barricade could stop the momentum. "So, remember when I said nothing happened on the night of the scavenger hunt?"

"Yes?"

"Well...I kinda lied." A nervous swallow. Heat flushed his forehead. A bead of sweat dove from his armpit, down his side. "I lied a lot."

10

He'd gotten through most of the story, had to stop a few times because of the way her forehead had folded, creased with confusion. He was about to reveal what Karen had told them, her experience with the ghosts of Cedarborough, when his dad opened the patio door and strolled onto the deck, looking weary and ready to go. His face was long, void of his usual character, and he yawned, covered his mouth, and excused himself.

"Ready to go, bud?" he asked, holding onto his hips. The Rices filled in the open doorway behind him.

"Can I have five more minutes?" He hit his father with that hopeful stare, the one that sometimes allowed him to get what he wanted. Seldom did it work, but he figured it was worth a shot.

"The Rices have been more than kind to let us stay this long."

Maddie's parents shared a glance, and Doug didn't exactly know how to interpret the exchange. Surely he didn't do anything. But the strangeness of that subtle glance and the way his dad had spoken, his defeated tone, the lack of energy behind his request, clued him into the fact that something had happened. A fight? Maybe not. An argument? No, nothing that bad. It wasn't like his father had stormed out here, grabbed his hand, and barreled back through the house in a fit of rage. But there was an awkwardness between them, something palpable, something that strained the moment.

"Okay," Doug said, getting off the swing.

Maddie followed him.

Before he reached the back door, he turned. "I had an amazing time, Maddie."

"Me too. Call me tomorrow?"

"Absolutely."

They hugged each other, and it felt weird to display such affection in front of their parents, but he didn't care. It felt right, and he needed to prove that this—whatever the hell it was—was real.

"Come on, bud," Gordon told his son, holding out his arm to usher him back through the Rice's kitchen, to the front door. "Thank you for a lovely evening," he told no one in particular.

The Rices walked them to the front foyer and waved them goodbye.

Once inside his dad's car, Doug turned. "What happened?"

"What do you mean?" Gordon started the vehicle, put it in gear, and drove down the street.

"You know what I mean."

A curt laugh tumbled forth. "I have no idea, Doug. Tell me."

"You were acting weird. I saw it in your face... I see it now."

His face grew increasingly rigid, as if he knew he couldn't hide it. "Okay, okay, if I'm being honest—Maddie's father and I had a little talk. A discussion of sorts."

"Oh?"

"Do you know what he does for a living?"

"Lawyer or something?"

"Yeah. Well, his firm is investigating Hooperstown Chemical. My job."

"For what?"

"Remember those kids I was telling you about? The ones who were sick?"

"Sure. Of course. It's been in the papers."

"Well, it seems there's a rumor going around that the plant is responsible. They're claiming we've been dumping toxic waste—disposing of it improperly—and that it's getting into the town's water supply. Thus making the kids sick."

"Is it true?"

Gordon's throat moved, as if he'd swallowed a pebble. "No. Not to my knowledge. There are protocols for that stuff. We have a whole department responsible for the removal of hazardous waste."

"Where does it go?"

"The waste?"

Doug nodded. He was curious about this. He'd thought the kids getting sick—the "cancer cluster" as the papers had dubbed them—was a result of the Mother of Dead Dreams and whatever stranglehold she'd placed over the town. Now, he wasn't so sure. Toxic waste could have tremendous negative effects on the human body, knowledge he'd learned in Earth Science in great detail just this past year. Plus, he'd seen *The Toxic Avenger* more times than he could count on both hands.

"The waste gets loaded onto a truck and then transported out west. I don't know what happens after that—not for certain—but from what I gather, the bad stuff is dumped into the ground, hundreds of feet below the surface, in the middle of the desert where there are no people."

"Really?" Doug asked.

"That's what we're told."

"But what if it's not true? What if it's deception?"

Gordon shrugged as he pulled onto the main highway. "I can't imagine they've been lying to us this whole time."

"What if they said they were doing these things and really they were just dumping the stuff into the ground here, in Hooperstown?"

"Well..." his dad said, as if he were juggling the different ways to answer this, "anything is possible, I suppose. But I trust management. The plant manager, Dylan Walker—he's a good guy. Has two kids, always goes to church on Sundays."

"Just because someone goes to church and has kids doesn't make them a good person, Dad."

Cocking his head sideways, Gordon said, "No, I guess not. You know, you're getting pretty smart in your old age. A lot smarter than you look." He ruffled his son's hair, keeping one hand on the steering wheel, his eyes glued to the road.

"Don't change the subject."

"I'm not. I just think... it's bullshit, that's all."

"What about the pipeline?"

In the shadows, Doug saw his old man's cheeks flex. "How do you know about the pipeline? Been doing some research?"

"I guess so. Maybe I saw an article in the paper about it."

The dreams. You saw it in your dreams. The Mother showed you. The pipeline runs underneath her lair.

"It's true. There was a pipeline that led to the river, which led to the ocean, but that was for discarding safe materials. Nothing toxic was ever allowed. Basically water and other harmless liquids. The plant produces a lot of waste, so they figured it would be cost effective. Plus, they needed to intake water for cooling purposes. They started building it somewhere upriver, deep in the woods, so it would run from there, to the plant, through town, and back to the river again." He smiled. "I'm boring you."

"No, not at all. This is very informative."

"You never cared about the plant before."

"Well. That was before…" *The Hunt? The nightmares? The Mother of Dead Dreams and Moving Shadows, her haunted touch?* "That was before people were getting sick. Kids. My classmates and stuff."

Dad nodded. "I wouldn't give it much thought. I guarantee you, in a few weeks this will all blow over and everybody will blame the sick kids on something else. The food we eat. The air we breathe. Terrorists. Y2K." A humorless laugh rose in his throat, barely made it past his lips.

But Dad was wrong. It didn't blow over.

Instead, it got worse.

Much, much worse.

CHAPTER NINE

We Are The Dreamers of Dead Dreams

From the mouth of the cave, the dead woman who came from the land of dreams, somewhere beyond the stars, some black place of rot between the spaces of time and celestial vacuums, came stumbling forth, her naked body covered in ticks and other woodland parasites, caked with wet earth. Her flesh was loose and baggy, some of her pale surface sliced and hanging off in flaps, revealing the tender rawness of her muscle. Her eyes were glowing as she planted her shaky feet in the dirt, her knees wobbling, nearly knocking against one another. As she approached, her thin lips reared back like a vexed mutt expressing territorial dominance.

In the dream, Doug backed away, but his dream logic only allowed him to retreat so far. In real life, he would have run away, something even his dream-self was acutely aware of. He would turn and dash off into the woods as fast as his feet would carry him. He had run track and field this past spring, so he was fairly certain he could find the forest's exit in almost no time at all. Safety was not that far. But the dream had other plans, demanding his presence in front of the Mother of Dead Dreams, keeping him within her reach. So there he remained.

"I've been waiting for you," she said, her voice a growl and nothing more. Animalistic. Primal.

There was nothing sophisticated about her. She was more machine than human, simplistically designed for one thing and one thing only (whatever that was exactly, Doug didn't know).

A scar ran from between her breasts down to her coarse thatch of pubic hair, the healed incision looking like a pink snake, unfurled and stretched to show off its length. As she walked toward him, getting nearer and nearer, the skin fusing the scar together began to open. Whatever had been holding the seam together, time and the natural ability to heal one's self, was slowly decomposing. Crumbling apart. A gray undulating wave moved beneath her skin, too colossal for her body to contain.

Where the thing within found the room to exist, Doug hadn't a clue. But this was a dream. A place that existed far beyond the confines of reality. In the Lands of Sleep.

"We've all been waiting for you. All the children. Mine."

From behind her, in the mouth of the cave, faces appeared. Pale, dead faces. The faces of Hooperstown's children, the sick and malignant. Their eyes were crusted over, colorless little vacuums. Dirt powdered their clothes. Some of the children sported pajamas, nondescript and character-themed alike. Cracked lips. Vacant smiles. Grimy faces and hair washed in the filth of this place. Their ages varied. The young ones dragged blankets or teddy bears, items meant to provide comfort and warmth but now looked sinister in nature, companions of the damned. Skinned knees. Broken bones, arms hanging limp at their sides.

These were the ruined children of Hooperstown, and they were coming.

Their Mother led the charge.

Above, the sky swirled, clouds gathering in cones of chaos. Apocalyptic tornadoes crafted to bring about The End. More symbolism Doug would dissect later. But now, he focused on the Mother. Her stomach. The scar that was coming undone.

What looked like a finger wormed through a tiny opening just above her navel. As she continued to close the distance between them, another finger dug through. Two more. An entire hand.

Disgust turned Doug's stomach.

Two hands slid through the fleshy fissure. Like a magician parting stage curtains, the hands each grabbed a side and pulled. Her stomach tore open, spilling buckets of ruddy water. A face emerged, a glistening sheen of afterbirth coating their pasty veneer.

This was no child.

What came out of the Mother's stomach looked like an adult man. It could have been human, he supposed, but the skull was oddly shaped, oblong with knots across the top of its hairless dome. Its maw opened as if it meant to scream, exposing a dozen or so teeth, pointed like ten-penny nails bent at strange angles.

The dream allowed Doug to retreat a little more, but not much. He couldn't see behind himself, couldn't look over his shoulder; an unbreakable energy kept him from budging another inch. The invisible force held him there, forced him to watch this abomination free itself from its chamber of flesh and bone.

Once out of the womb and on patrol, the hideous being crouched on all fours, its appendages mimicking crab legs, the arachnid-like bend, though the angles were all off. The anatomy defied nature, and even his dream logic couldn't rightfully interpret the image.

But the thing crawled fast toward him, in a blur.

Its head spun like the hand on a boardwalk game's pinwheel. As it neared, everything became a series of slow-motion events. He noticed pincers sticking out of the thing's cheeks. They made awful clicking noises as they closed on each other.

The dream had run out of space, and Doug found his back nearing a dark void. Standing on the edge of the dream, Doug waited for the end. Above, the sky grumbled with rolling thunder.

The thing closed in.

"My child," the Mother spoke, her words filling his head, infecting him like a cancer growing on his soul, leaving behind its eternal touch. "You are mine."

The human-crab-thing closed in, jumped for the kill.

As the thing dug its pincers into the side of Doug's skull, he exited the dream like a rocket ascending the cosmos.

1

Randall Benoit felt like the embodiment of death. At first the world looked like a giant blur, a smear of pastels and early-morning shadows, shades of purple that bounced across his vision. Seconds passed. Minutes. Everything eventually sharpened, took focus. He began to make out outlines. A dresser. An alarm clock. The television. His Nintendo 64 next to it. Posters of bands he liked hanging on the wall. An acoustic guitar in the corner, the one that had gotten minimal attention despite his parents dropping a pretty penny on lessons. The window to his right with the blinds cracked, allowing just enough light inside to induce a killer headache.

He lifted his head an inch off his pillow and immediately rested back down, clearly not ready to start the day and unsure how he'd gotten here, in this room. The last thing he remembered was walking through the cemetery, feeling extremely faint and ill, in desperate need of medical assistance. How everything had hurt and ached, how he preferred death—*actual* death—over that torment. The rest of the night was a vague memory, a montage of various scenes he couldn't fully shape in his mind. He recalled the woods. His hands committing unspeakable horrors. But whether that had been him or something he had witnessed someone else doing was up for debate.

It could have been a dream. Yes, that was it. Just a dream. Nothing more. It was his dream-double that acted out those atrocities. That must have been it. There was no way he was capable of such nasty deeds.

When he looked down he saw his clothes were ripped and torn. Not only that, but they were filthy. Crumbles of dried mud were sprinkled across the bed sheets. Dark, chocolaty stains marred his comforter.

He peeled the layers off his body, noticing his arms were also dirty and scratched. Red lines covered almost every inch of his exposed flesh. His body burned with each movement, intense flames licking every available muscle. He noticed open sores on his skin—some on his arms, some on his stomach. He felt his face and touched some wet, swollen lumps there as well. The pain was sharp and stabbing and he wanted to cry. Not only from the agony that continued to sweep through him, but because he felt lost and alone, on the verge of witnessing his own extinction.

He felt ready to die.

It was a struggle, but he shoved off the covers completely, revealing more clues about that awful night. More dirt and blood. His legs were covered in bruises, lacerations that oozed creamy pus. He thought the dark circles on his calves were scabs, but they turned out to be ticks, swollen from several days' (or weeks') worth of feeding.

How long was I out?

The fact the parasitic arachnids had ballooned to the size of quarters was concerning. They had burrowed into the skin an inch, maybe more. There were egg-like bumps all across his arms and legs, and he wondered if those were ticks, too. Ones that had dug tunnels into skin that had scabbed over.

Holy fuck.

Everything ached. *Everything.* He didn't need a Lyme test to know that he had it. His bones felt like rusted metal, corroded to a stage of beyond brittle, infirm structures set to fail at any possible moment. Maximum effort was required to swing his legs off the bed, to plant his feet on the carpet.

It took him five minutes to exit his room, enter the hall, and find his way into the bathroom. He'd used the wall as a guide, holding onto the door moulding for support as he passed the rooms of his parents' house. He called out his parents' names, but he had no voice. His throat had dried up, along with everything else inside him. He needed water. Needed the ticks out of him.

Needed his body back.

Calling his parents' names again, getting the same results, he realized he was probably alone. They were most likely at work, and his sister, Tina, was probably at the beach with her friends. That was how she spent every summer—at the shore, soaking up the sun, swimming in the refreshing salty waters of the Atlantic, scoping out guys and determining which ones she'd date next. She went through them like toothbrushes; used them for a few months until they were soft and no longer effective, then discarded them and found a new one.

In the bathroom, in front of the mirror, Randall was shocked at what stared back at him. He hardly recognized himself. If he wasn't seeing it with his own two eyes, if someone had instead shown him a picture of how he currently looked, Randall would not have believed it was him. A purple circle was stamped over his right eye and the eyelids were nearly swollen shut. His face was gaunt, thinner than he'd ever seen himself. It seemed as if he'd lost thirty pounds since his last memory, the night in the cemetery. A skeleton with flesh. That's what he looked like now.

I can't... I couldn't have been out that long. What have I been doing all that time? Why hasn't anyone been looking for me? My parents? My friends? WHAT THE HELL WAS I DOING?

Bad things, answered a terrible, croaky voice.

Shadows crawled into his field of view, the bathroom darkening. The light bulbs above the vanity sizzled and dimmed. The window lost the light coming through it, as, outside, clouds gathered over the sun, blocking any sense of cheeriness the day held near. Soon, the bathroom was a cave, an endless cavern without light. The mirror continued to reveal his degenerative state. Behind him, in the shadows, obscured patterns formed and coalesced near the edges of what he could still see. Two arms draped over his shoulder, their touch comforting. The pale extensions probed his body, crawling like serpents, exploring fresh territories.

For a second, he went numb. He thanked whatever was responsible for this hallucination because the much-needed reprieve from reality was welcome. The pain had been too much to bear, and he had thought the only way to end the suffering was to hang himself from the oak tree in the backyard.

Hands felt him up. Every lump, every cut, every bruise. Slender fingers, dirt-encrusted and cracked from dehydration, toyed with the holes in his black T-shirt.

"*Hello, child,*" a voice said, and he already knew to whom it belonged. It was the woman, the one from his dreams, the woman he'd run into in the cemetery on the night before the Hunt. It was *her* who'd changed everything. *Altered* him. Made him rotten inside and out. "*You are most unwell.*"

"What have you done to me?" he asked the shadows.

He started to pray, to make deals with false deities. He promised to quit the bad things he'd grown fond of, smoking too much bud and engaging in premarital sex, things that would land him in the Pits of Hell, if he actually believed in such a thing. And he didn't. Not until recently. He believed in something now—but what exactly? Well, that was to be determined. But regardless, he prayed, he begged, to the gods, to anyone who would answer.

Behind him, everything was black. In the bathroom, it was just the woman's arms and his own reflection and the endless dark. After he spoke, two glowing circles burned like lanterns just behind him. Over him, floating in the air. He swore a grinning mouth materialized from the shadows below the two brilliant eyes, but things were still too bleary to confirm.

His neck hairs rose, a concerning chill sweeping through him. "What am I?"

"*You are my child,*" she whispered, her voice hoarse and lacking strength.

Whatever she was—whatever her true nature—she was weak. At full power, she could be something special, but there was a barrier limiting her potential. He could sense that here, in the bathroom. In the dark.

"*You are all my children, and you are all special. You will be with me now.*"

Tears trickled down Randall's face. "I don't want to... I don't."

The thing behind him came forth, the eyes attaching itself to a face. It was a hideous, semi-transparent thing. A nose, a mouth, all crooked and warped. A face that was hardly made of skin, more like old parchment, rough and weathered, peeling and cracked. Teeth. *God*, the teeth. He'd never seen teeth so sharp, not even in the mouths of apex predators, lions or wolves. Whetted to dangerous points. Designed to kill. Not just to terminate, but to *mutilate*. The thing's reflected image, which hardly revealed any particular sex, warped like wax against the touch of a hot flame. The contortions continued in psychedelic fashion, shredding Randall's conception of reality.

"*YOU ARE MINE NOW,*" the thing shouted, or tried to—its voice still lacking amplification. The face rose above him, continuing to flaunt its treacherous ivory daggers, floating toward the endless black ceiling like a balloon rushing toward the stars. "*YOU AND ALL THE CHILDREN OF THIS VILLAGE ARE MINE, AND YOU CAN DO NOTHING TO STOP IT. I AM FREE NOW. FREE FROM THE BAD PLACE.*"

From where the thing's stomach should have been, there was a slit in the fabric of space. A long slimy rope hung from it, dangling just over his head. It jumped around like a worm on a hook, squirming as it lowered itself from the void above. Randall looked up, tears blearing his vision. But he could see, even though he didn't want to.

The worm-like rope coiled itself around his neck, pulled, raised him off the tile floor, even though it wasn't tile anymore. Now it was black, a cosmic mouth that had consumed this material plane. Everything was black. Decayed. This world, the one he'd found himself in, was nothing but an ever-expanding cavern of nothingness, full of despair.

No, he said to it. *No, I will not go.*

The rope, the thing's umbilical cord, refused to release him. It hoisted him, pulling him higher into the darkened sky.

In a second, everything above him filled with teeth. He could smell rot, the stagnant nature of this place breaking down, decomposing in a fetid swamp of oblivion.

No. NO!

The mouth above him opened wide. It never gave him another opportunity to protest.

He disappeared into the Land of Teeth, choking on the cord that had once given him life.

2

Just before quitting time, Alan Sayers, a local handyman, peered into the Benoit's backyard. He wasn't sure why his eyes wandered that way. He'd been out on the Dickersons' back deck, fixing the railing for the last hour and had no desire to look in that direction. But, in one fateful moment, he peered over the white vinyl fence and stared directly into the backyard. Particularly because the giant oak tree that held solid, thick branches, sturdy and armlike, caught his attention. Even more so, the object swaying back and forth, tied to the end of a long rope.

It took about three seconds for Alan to realize what the world was showing him. His brain was slow to catch on, but once he did, his eyebrows nearly catapulted from his forehead.

"Oh, my sweet Lord Jesus," he said, dropping the impact driver onto the loose deck board and backing away as if the unsightly image could reach out and touch him.

The kid, no older than eighteen, swung back and forth like a candy-stuffed piñata after the participant's first whack. His body was covered in cuts and bruises and dark spots. His face was a mess, but the thing that really prickled the flesh on Alan's arms and legs was the boy's smile, stretched ear to ear as if his final seconds of life were the most pleasant ever.

As he backed up, preparing to run inside to call 9-1-1, the wind blew. With it, a carrion stench tainted the air, wet and putrid. That smell followed Alan Sayers all the way inside, all the way to the telephone, and all the way home.

It followed him into his dreams.

3

"I don't want to go to the stupid Pirate Parade in Lea Bay," Grady said for, like, the five-thousandth time.

His parents stood before him, dressed in full pirate regalia. His mother wore a tattered corset and his father was cloaked in a buccaneer's jacket, both capping off their ridiculous looks with matching red bandanas, tricorn hats, and black knee-high boots. Loose tokens jangled in their pockets with each step. His father toyed with the frills on his poet's shirt, rubbing the flashy fabric between his fingers.

"What are you going to do while we're gone?" his mother asked, her arms folded across her chest. She tapped her foot on the faux-wood linoleum floor.

"I told you guys," Grady said, rolling his eyes. This was getting absurd. But it was always like this—them asking a thousand questions, wanting to know every single detail about his life, no matter how minor. There was no way to escape the interrogation process, so it was easier to face it head on, to appease them and answer their endless barrage of inquiries. But he had to take his shots when he could—an eye roll there, a snarky comment here—to let them know he was displeased. "I'm going to the library with Doug and Jesse."

They exchanged looks of sincere disbelief.

"Oh, come on!" Grady practically shouted.

He was walking a fine line. On one hand, he wanted to voice his gripes and do so loudly, so he'd be heard. After all, the only way to instill change was to rebel. He'd learned that lesson in history class—well, maybe not that *exact* lesson, but he'd been paying attention and saw that any monumental movement throughout the course of history began with an act of rebellion. But there were consequences to consider. For example, he wanted freedoms, but he didn't want to get grounded, not in the heart of summer. The Popes' notorious groundings were known to last upwards of three weeks, and that—right now, with everything happening around town—would virtually kill any and all chances of helping Doug and Jesse solve the case of the mysterious local occurrences. And let's face it: Doug and Jesse *needed* his help. Plus, he had something to prove. For one, that he *wasn't* a coward, no matter what his past actions might infer.

Past is in the past. The only thing that matters is the future.

The only thing Grady currently saw in his future was the inside of his bedroom, for about three weeks straight.

"Don't take that tone with us, young man," said Mr. Pope, peering over his glasses. "You show us some respect."

Grady raised his hands. "Sorry, sorry, sorry. Just…look guys, I'm fourteen now. I'm going to high school next year. I need you to stop treating me like a baby."

Again, silently, the Popes conferred by gazing into each other's eyes. Smiles broke across their faces, the kind Grady didn't know how to interpret. A smile like this could go either way.

"Just the library?" his dad asked.

"Yes."

"And then straight back here?"

Grady dawdled over the answer. "If that's what you want."

"It is."

"Then...yeah, I guess."

His father scratched his chin with the hook he now wore for a hand. "Come to think of it, why would three teenage boys choose to spend their summer vacation at the library? Seems...*curious*."

Grady thought he'd gotten out of this with relative ease, but he should have known better. "Dad, for the last time, we have a summer report we're working on for English next year. It's a thing now. All the kids are doing it."

"How can they assign you homework when you haven't attended the school yet?"

"It's optional. It's suggested. To get us ready for the ninth grade. I'm telling you. Call Mrs. Ferrera if you don't believe me. She'll tell you."

It was a gamble. He didn't really think his old man would do it. If he did, well, then he had a pile of unread comic books sitting in the corner of his room to catch up on.

His pop's eyes slimmed with clear suspicion. "I don't know if I believe you."

"God," Grady whispered beneath his breath, hanging his head. "Call her then."

"Tell us the truth, Grady, and we won't judge. Are you three going to the library to look at porn on the Internet?"

Grady snapped his head back up, his eyes practically shooting out of their sockets. "*What?* No. What the— Why would you even think that?"

"Gary!" his mother said, almost at the same time. She smacked his arm.

"What?" His hands rose as if he expected her to swat him again. "I read in the paper that the librarians are finding pornographic materials on the library computers, just, you know, out there for anyone to see. Some sort of prank, I guess—and I just wanted to make sure—"

"Why would I go to the library to look at porn?" Grady asked, jerking his shoulders while facing his palms toward the ceiling. "We have the Internet here. I could just go into the living room and look at porn."

Gary Pope's eyes expanded. "So *that's* where all the porn on our computer is coming from, huh? How interesting. You know, there is such a thing as a 'history folder,' young man. Each web browser has one. Bet you didn't know that, huh, mister smarty-pants."

"I know how web browsers work, Dad. We use them at school!" He pointed an accusatory finger across the room. "And I don't look at porn. If there is any porn-looking going on in this house, it's from you!"

Gary Pope coughed into his hand. "That's ridiculous, I have no idea—"

"Okay, okay, gentlemen," said Mom, stepping between them. An odd look crossed her face, one of general unpleasantness. Her cheeks grew raspberry pink.

"He must be lying, Marcia. He must be—"

"We'll talk about this *later,*" she said in her scolding voice.

"But—"

She cut him off with a stern look. Those green eyes meant business. "I think…that…Grady is right. He's old enough to stay home alone. And he's old enough to meet his friends at the library."

Reluctantly, Mr. Pope nodded. "Oh-kay."

"Okay," she said, spinning toward her son. "We trust you, Grady. We do."

Staring at his father, Grady nodded. "Okay."

"The library and then home. No stopping anywhere else. Got it?"

"Yes, ma'am."

"Good boy. Now give your momma a hug." She opened her arms and waited for her son to drag himself over to her.

He did so, slowly. His shoes felt as if they were stuck in drying cement. Finally, he reached her, opened his arms, and accepted her embrace. She snuggled his cheek, kissed him. He wanted to barf.

If Jesse had been here, all bets would have been off. Endless jabs, all throughout the afternoon. A constant stream of overbearing mother jokes.

Hugging his mother, praying the moment would end in a blink, he went over the afternoon plans in his mind. Very little of it included a trip to the library.

Flicking on the youth center's lights, James Fritz placed his briefcase on the table next to the door. He scanned the room, his eyes sweeping across the opened folding tables with upside-down chairs stacked on top of them, the ping pong table in the left-center, and the small makeshift bar used for the nightly snacks and refreshments.

"Jewel?" He moved away from the entrance and over to the table, started removing the chairs and placing them on the floor, tucking them underneath so the backrests touched the table's edge. "You can come out now. It's me."

From behind the bar in the back, a bad case of bedhead rose above the slapped-together wooden structure. Her hair hung in knots and unruly curls. She looked grumpy or hungover—but there was no alcohol here. But he knew Jewel hadn't come in with any, so Fritz decided that a hard night's sleep on the hardwood floor was to blame for her disheveled appearance. And he couldn't blame her. Even with the blankets he had gathered from the storage closet, it was rough.

"Sleep well?" he asked.

"Like a baby," she said, and he knew she was lying.

He took a break from the chairs and walked back over to the table where he'd put his things. "Got you a coffee. Black?"

"Like my soul."

He smiled. "I say the same thing to my wife."

She took the coffee from him, sniffed the tiny opening on the plastic dome lid. "Except, your soul ain't black."

"And neither is yours."

She frowned at this. Took a sip. Recoiled when she burnt her mouth. "Jeez-us, goddamn!"

He winced. "You know this is technically a *Christian* youth center. You might want to refrain from using the Big Man's name in vain."

"Sorry. It's just really fuc—I mean, *freaking* hot."

"I think *freaking* still counts as a curse word…you know, in the eyes of the Lord, but I'll allow it since one—we're not technically open yet, and two—we're not in the classroom."

She smiled, blew on her coffee.

"They put a warning on there for a reason," Fritz told her, moving past her, back toward the table.

"Yeah, well, I'm dumb."

"Didn't mean it like that."

"I know."

He placed a chair on the floor and kicked it underneath the table. "You know," he said, rotating back to her, "we agreed that you could stay here for a night. One."

"Yeah…"

"It's been three."

"I know, just…" She shook her head. "I can't go back. Home, that is. I won't."

Fritz sighed. He'd seen her face that night, the night she showed up at his door crying, screaming, trapped in a state of perpetual agony. She had looked like she wanted to die. Olivia had been the one to answer the incessant knocking and had been rightfully confused. The sobbing girl couldn't even talk she'd been crying so hard. Despite not knowing her, Olivia had let her inside, settled her down on the couch.

They'd debated about what to do with her. Olivia, despite being a caring and benevolent individual who had organized food drives and volunteered at soup kitchens during the holidays, had refused to listen to her husband's plea to let the girl spend the night. "We can't help her," she had told him. "The cops can. Social services."

Fritz had argued that those options were the worst things they could do, *put her through the system*. She had already traveled that road and traveled it well and look where that had gotten her. *Here*. No, the system had failed her, continued to fail her, and if he didn't do *something* about it, then she was destined to live this life forever. Or worse—not live at all. Plus, Jewel had come to them because she trusted him, and to call anyone of authority would have betrayed that trust. But…his wife had none of it. In the end, Fritz had agreed to drive her to the Hooperstown Police Department, to let them decide Jewel's future. Of course, that had been a lie, as he had driven her to the youth center instead.

Olivia will kill me if she finds out, he thought. He felt so guilty about hiding it from her that he almost came clean earlier this morning.

Almost.

"I can't," Jewel reiterated. Tears stood on her eyes, her lashes growing visibly wet. "I can't go back into the system. It's... It'll kill me."

Fritz sighed, hung his head. Then he took a long swig from his coffee while his brain tried to work out the correct next approach. "Jewel. If anyone finds out about this, about you being here, I can get into some serious trouble. Like, 'lose my job and my wife divorces me' kind of trouble. You realize that, don't you?"

"She abuses me," she said, and not for the first time.

She'd detailed the abuse when Olivia had set her down on their couch. The drug use, the cigarette burns, the objects Ava Conti had chucked at her daughter's head. It was all disgusting and disgraceful and made Fritz want to open up his home to her even more.

If it's true, Olivia had said. *She could be making the whole thing up.*

"I know it's tough. I know it's the toughest thing in the world."

"Do you?" Jewel stood there defiantly, her nostrils flaring. "Did your parents abuse you when you were a kid? Did they hit you and call you names day-in and day-out?" She showed him the bruises that ran up her arms. "Did they?"

Fritz swallowed. He knew damn well he'd never experienced a fraction of the abuse Jewel had. "No, they didn't. But I've been in education long enough to *know* things. I've seen families go through what you've been through and much, much worse. Trust me."

She just stared at him, and he wasn't sure she did trust him. Not anymore.

"Jewel," he said, sitting down, taking off his glasses and wiping them on his shirt. "You can't stay here forever."

"Put me in a hotel room."

He scoffed. "First off—I'm not made of money. Secondly—even if I was, they would throw me in jail for kidnapping you, if I got caught. You have to understand this."

"No one will know. It'll be our secret. I promise."

He shook his head. "Can't happen. I'm sorry."

Her eyes watered, darted back and forth several times.

"I'll drive you to one of two places—I can take you to the police station, where I can place a phone call with child services and tell them everything I know. Or I can take you back home."

Her eyes burned at the idea. It was like he'd asked to drag her body over a bed of nails.

"I take it option one is more appealing."

"I hate you," she growled.

"Jewel…"

"I knew I shouldn't have trusted you."

"Jewel, you know—"

"Shut up. I don't want to hear it." She stormed over to the table in the far corner where she'd stashed her bag of clothes. Fritz had bought her a few clean outfits from the Rag Shop down the street. "All my life, people have disappointed me. Figures you would, too."

"That's not fair, and you know it."

She rushed for the front door, bag swinging over her shoulder. "Fuck you, asshole," she grunted, pushing her way through the door and out into the parking lot.

Fritz stayed where he was, debating whether to go after her. In the end, he decided to place a phone call.

"Yes," he said, less than five minutes later, speaking into the phone on his desk in the cramped office. "Yes, Officer Neville, you can help me. I'd like to file a report."

As he told the officer everything, Fritz couldn't shake the feeling that he'd just sent the girl off into a war she'd never win.

5

Jewel walked down the side of the highway with no clear destination in mind. She figured she'd walk until her feet gave out or she reached the ocean, whichever came first. If the former happened, she'd hurl herself in front of speeding traffic and hope the collision would break her neck on impact, just be done with this life, this suffering. If she somehow managed to reach the beach, she'd sink beneath the Atlantic and never resurface.

That was the plan, anyway.

A half hour later she came across a local ice cream shop (The Sprinkle Shack) and figured she'd pop inside to use the bathroom. Hopefully, they weren't one of those "restrooms are for PAYING customers only" joints. If so, she'd piss on their floor. Boy was her bladder full.

As she strolled up the ramp, she heard someone call her name.

"Jewel?" asked a boy, his tone chipper. Not a boy. A young man. Someone well past the awkward, voice-cracking stages of puberty. "Jewel!" he called again.

His voice was much too perky to deal with right now, and she almost ignored him, kept walking so she wouldn't have to subject herself to that kind of positivity. She looked up, confused, the sun shining brightly in her eyes, blinding her from uncovering the young man's identity.

"It's Adam."

She squinted, waiting for her eyes to adjust. Glancing at the parking lot, the scintillating hoods and tops of stationary vehicles, she saw his Lumina, never realizing she had strolled right past it.

"Adam…" she said, almost deliriously, as if trying to pluck a portion of a dream from her memory. She was out of it, starting to feel dizzy. Disoriented. The sun and the heat had clearly done a number on her brain, and all she wanted was to empty her bladder and bask in the glory of central cooling. Plus, she was hungry. Starving actually. Hadn't eaten a full meal in four days. Stomach rumbling like an earthquake, she tried concentrating on the conversation at hand.

"Yeah, from the youth center." He spoke as if *he* were the confused one. As if maybe *he* had mistaken her for someone else.

"I remember."

"I hope so." Adam gestured to the girl next to him, the one violating the unspoken rule of personal space. She had practically attached herself to his side. "This is Katie. She's a friend." Katie giggled as if *friend* had an entirely different meaning to her, and the true nature of their relationship was a secret between them. "Katie, this is Jewel. She's from that Youth Group I volunteer at."

"Oh cool." Katie flashed her an obligatory smile. "Nice to meet you."

Jewel wanted to respond cordially, but she couldn't find the energy for niceties. Not at a time like this. Not when her bladder weighed twenty pounds and all she wanted to do—what she really wanted to do—was punch someone's face into bite-sized pieces. She blamed those feelings on Fritz and his stupid turncoat measures. Actually, she blamed his wife. *She* had wanted Jewel out, not Fritz. *She* had suggested they call the cops, social services, and who knew who else. Yeah, Olivia Fritz was a huge bitch, all right. Jewel wanted to smash her cute, mousy face into putty.

"You okay?" Adam asked, a concerned look combing over his features. "Like, you look sunburnt. And exhausted."

She was both but didn't say. "I just have to use the bathroom."

"How long have you been walking? Where were you going?"

She looked around as if the answers were written somewhere in the parking lot. Of course they weren't, so she was left to her own devices. "I...dunno. I'll see you later."

She walked toward the front door, the day spinning around her. For a second she thought she might faint, lose her balance and smack her head on the ice cream shack's aluminum exterior, or worse, the wrought-iron railing that bordered the ramp. The latter would knock her the fuck out, that was for sure, and she couldn't think of a more embarrassing way to end this exchange, save for maybe pissing her pants.

Behind her, Adam whispered something to Katie that sounded like, "Here are the keys, go wait in the car," but she wasn't sure. Her guess was probably close enough because she heard the patter of footsteps following her toward the shop.

Once inside, the air-conditioning hit her like an unsuspecting tidal wave, but not in a bad way. It was refreshing, the frigid air immediately restoring some of those *holy-shit-I'm-gonna-pass-out-and-die* feelings. But she wasn't out of the woods yet. The cold air freshened her up, but it didn't heal every wound. A part of her was still open, still bleeding. Most of her still wanted to die.

Adam followed her to the bathroom. She turned to him before opening the door and heading inside.

"You're not following me inside, are you?" she asked, mustering a smile. It felt wrong to smile with so many negative emotions rumbling inside of her. Dirty. Something taboo.

"No," he said, as if it were obvious. "No, just wanted to see you here safely. You were...wobbling."

"Wobbling?"

"Yeah, you know." He gyrated his entire body to mimic her gait. "Sure you haven't been drinking?"

"No. Not drinking. Not today. Can you do me a huge favor? I hate to…ask, but…"

"What is it?"

"Would you buy me a water?" Directing her attention at the ground, she admitted, "I don't have any money, and I feel like I'm going to die."

"Don't worry about it." He turned and headed over to the counter, asked the girl manning the register for a Dasani.

She closed the door, did her business, and speculated about the future, the tiny note folded in her back pocket, an unsolvable riddle scratched on its surface: SUFFER THE SEASON.

She mused about the boy who wrote it, if it had been a boy at all.

6

Traveling in broad daylight was risky business when you looked like a corpse from *Return of the Living Dead,* but Alphie Moffit made it work. He was surprised no one had pulled over and asked him if he was okay, if he needed help or if he wanted them to call someone. Maybe the cuts in his face weren't that bad after all, maybe the tumors that had grown on his arms and legs weren't *that* noticeable.

He really lost his faith in humanity when he strolled past a jogger. The woman was facing him, coming from the opposite direction, and they shared approximately three seconds of eye contact. Even though her face twisted with absolute revulsion, he hoarsely whispered, *"Help me."*

She did nothing. Sped off as fast as her legs could carry her. And to be honest—he couldn't blame her. If *he* had been in *her* shoes, he probably would have skipped past, leaving him to fend for himself. It was a very human thing to do.

He was a freak. At the very least, he looked like one.

Alphie could feel the blisters and boils on his face. Each time he summoned the courage to test them, the slightest pressure sent spikes of agony throughout his skull.

Please, let me go, he pleaded with the Mother.

Not until you deliver the messages, she silently replied. *The chosen children of Hooperstown will know my name.*

He kept going, not entirely cooperating. It was weird, this feeling of being in control of his own body, but also—not. There were a few times on this pilgrimage when he'd rebelled, forcing himself to travel outside the path laid out before him, his route, so to speak. He'd gone to the Simms' household, deposited the clue as instructed, then headed across town to deliver the Conti girl's gift. The Mother had seen her through Randall's eyes on the night of the Hunt, and for some unbeknownst reason, she had taken a liking to her. Alphie hadn't the slightest idea what role she played in what was to come, but something about her made the Mother of Dead Dreams giddy.

Dreams, she said, reading his thoughts, every single notion that appeared in the space between his ears. *It's her dreams, and they are quite delicious.*

Alphie didn't understand the Mother, not entirely. What made her tick, how she existed, what she planned to do in the town he called home—none of it had been revealed. He did know one thing, though; whatever was coming, whatever she had in store—it was bad. Particularly for the children, but the parents would get theirs, too.

Oh yes, child. They will. Everyone will suffer the season.

He'd crossed the path between the two schools, the middle and high, and was now traveling farther along, passing copses of willows that flanked the pathway. The unpaved stretch of walk was typically a shortcut through town, mostly populated by bicyclists and dog-walkers. On this particular day, it was sans both. Alphie, fading in and out of the light, kept pace with his influencer and walked toward his next destination. He had a pocket full of riddles and this wouldn't end until they were delivered, every last one.

He walked for ten minutes, studying the trees, taking in their vibrant green foliage, admiring their life. If he were a tree, his leaves would be wilted and browning, starting to curl at the ends. Probably would have already shed some, sprinkling a circle of dead things at its base.

A circle of dead things.

That was how he felt. Part of that circle, lying at the feet of the Mother, the Tree of Which All Things Are Created. There were more dead things, plenty of them, and they were all tools used to build whatever she was crafting.

The bleary distance showed movement on the horizon, where the path took a bend. There were three objects, and they were gaining size. Alphie's heart took a hit, a spike that left him reeling.

People. On bicycles.

People who could save him.

He readied his voice to call for help. Dragging his foot, which had grown sore and had been hard to put weight on. He limped toward the objects, praying they'd be of some assistance. At the very least he hoped they had the good sense to put him out of his misery, euthanize him like the sick, mangy animal he had become. He knew that wasn't likely the case, but if they called the cops on him, he'd get *somewhere*. Being killed by a cop sounded interesting. He wondered if he had the mobility to pull off such a thing. If he acted like a lunatic, would they just shoot him?

Act like a zombie. They'll take you out for sure.

Reading his thoughts, the Mother of Dead Dreams prepared. She began to steer him off the path, toward a cluster of drooping willows.

No!

She was aiming to avoid interaction with these approaching riders. He tried pulling away from her, but, like a magnet, the collection of foliage hauled him in.

No!

He fought, digging deeper and summoning every speck of strength he could harness, and tore free from the connection. For about three seconds he was separated from his abuser. Using the time wisely, he turned and sprinted toward the riders, jumped in the air, waving his arms above him. Just before she took control of her host once again, he flopped on the trail's dusty surface, figuring that would buy him more precious seconds, allowing the riders to get closer before she sent him off into the trees again.

With luck, the riders spotted him. He heard their voices—kids, he noticed, *tweens*—call out to him. He couldn't hear exactly what they were saying, but it seemed positive. In his favor. Like they might *actually* help him. See him through this. Provide him with comfort and care. For the first time since this debacle began, he felt hopeful.

But he also felt something else. The Mother's rage as it burned through his veins. His disobedience would probably earn him a punishment of sorts, but he didn't care. If it meant an end to this suffering, her retaliation would be well worth it.

"Whoa!" said one of the bikers, the one who arrived first. The other two were in tow, not far behind. Stopping abruptly, the back tire skidded, kicking up dirt and dust. The kid grimaced like he'd just seen the grisly results of a nasty car accident. "What's up with your face, dude?"

Alphie was on his knees now, peering up, light filtered in through the trees. He shielded the bright slashes from his eyes, trying to behold his rescuer's face. He felt the Mother using her resources to restrict his voice, tightening his throat. Choking him. His lungs failed to fill with breathable air. The taste of acid was bold on his tongue.

"You okay?" a second boy asked.

"Guys," the third, a girl, said cautiously. "I think we should call 9-1-1."

"Closest pay phone is probably the 7-Eleven on New Main."

"There are houses literally on the other side of the path. We can cut through—"

"I'm not knocking on some stranger's door!"

"Grow a sack, Sam!"

"Shut up, Wendy! You grow a sack!"

"Both of you!" yelled the clear leader of his magical trio. Good things came in threes, so Alphie had always been told, and right now—these were the three best things that could have happened to him.

You will be punished, the Mother said, her anger splitting his nerves like a hot blade through a slice of tender meat.

He squinted and saw a shadow taking shape behind his three rescuers. It didn't take long for the outline to fill in, become a definite thing.

An actual being.

No...

Yes...

The Mother had split from him, took her naked form and approached the three tweens from behind, each step silent and unsuspecting. Alphie got the sense that even if her footfalls were as loud as a bulldozer driving into the side of a derelict building that the kids would not have heard her approach. No, only Alphie was privy to her visage, her haunted mold. Her sounds. Her labored movements and shallow breaths.

She eyed the three, individually at first, giving them each a cursory glance, as if picking the best apple out of the bushel. She settled on the leader of the pack and stalked him from behind, crouching low. The other two didn't take notice as she weaved between them, avoiding contact with the bikes, stepping past them with a certain amount of grace, a nimbleness she hadn't possessed back when Alphie first met her back at the caves. She had been a lot weaker then, but now…

She's getting stronger.

With each dream she eats, with each child she infects.

Standing directly at the leader's back, she lowered her lips to his ear, as if whispering a terrible secret. Her lips parted and a black slithering tongue rolled out, slimy and smooth. It moved irregularly, convulsive, not the calculated and fluid approach of—say—a sleek python. Viscous fluids, dark blue like denim ink, dripped steadily from the fleshy extension.

NO!

In response, her eyes shimmered like valuable tokens, golden globes of almost certain death.

Alphie knew what would happen. He didn't even need to look.

The black tongue entered the kid's earhole, worming its way inside. The leader pawed at his ear as if an annoying fly had buzzed nearby. In reality, he sensed something, maybe a tickle, maybe a touch as light as a feather, but in whatever plane of existence the Mother resided in, that phantom, gray world that existed between theirs and the spirit realm, she was shoving her tongue inside him, lapping at his brain, drinking from his thoughts, transferring a litany of diseases and deadly filth.

She's burrowing herself in him! he thought and remembered that was how it had begun for him. *Her sickness. Her cancer. She's going to occupy that space, wait until he falls asleep and then—*

BAM!

She will feast.

On his dreams.

Terrible dreams, he recalled, those first few days after the Hunt. Like he was continually falling from some celestial space, a utopia that existed above the sky, beyond whatever was above *that*, some unknown paradisaical territory where empyrean spirits endured. He would fall and fall and fall until he hit the dirt; he was a comet, a fallen star, an asteroid that had collided with the clay of the earth. Then he had become a prisoner of sorts, he had found himself in the presence of people who dressed like pilgrims, early settlers, white people who lived in a small community in the woods. He'd lived as their prisoner for some time. He remembered they kept examining his swollen belly, poking and prodding, whispering prayers over and over as if it were an object to be worshipped. A prize from the sky. Oh, look at what these people had won.

And then, with no warning at all, they had come for him, taken whatever was inside. Left him open and bleeding, a jagged wound that would never heal, not properly. A rushed incision that would undoubtedly grow to become infected, diseased, gangrenous.

It would kill him.

Her.

The bastards had left *her* to die.

And they had stolen something.

Something important.

Life.

Alphie watched as the black worm of a tongue exited the kid's other ear, stretching, testing its length. The kid looked confused by what was happening, continuing to scratch both ears, as if something had burrowed its way inside him. Something insignificant and harmless.

"Are you okay, Dan?" asked Sam.

"My ear," Dan said, unsure. He swatted again. "Feels weird." His pupils shrunk in the surrounding white space, and he dropped to his knees.

Alphie watched as the Mother withdrew her long black tongue, watched the slippery organ retreat through the kid's skull, back into the void of the Mother's mouth. She grinned as she took several steps back, wiping away the ichorous juices running down her chin. The act left behind indigo smears on her arm. She shook with laughter, revealing two rows of sharp teeth, maybe twelve in all. Little points perfectly designed for puncturing thick materials, mainly the flesh of her enemies. Her eyes shimmered like the summer sun reflecting off turbulent waters.

In a blink, she was gone.

Dan dropped to the chalky earth and began to convulse.

Alphie wanted to cry as the other two kids huddled over their fallen friend. But he had no tears to spare. He had no emotions to provide whatsoever.

Mother was in control now, and more victories awaited her infernal scourge.

7

"Do you really think Box-booger is going to tell us anything?" Jesse asked, walking down the sidewalk, avoiding the cracks that zig and zagged across the cement. It was an old superstition, *kid's shit,* he knew, but he couldn't help it. It wasn't like he *needed* to avoid the cracks. It was just something he did. Call it boredom, call it habitual, call it mini-OCD—Jesse didn't know if there was a proper name for it. He played the game anyway, stepping over each and every craggy line the sidewalk put before him. "I mean, the guy's a dick. Plus, he hates us."

"Correction," Grady said, raising his forefinger. "He hates *you.*"

"Well, he tried to bang your mom."

"So that means he likes me."

"No, dude. That means he likes your mom. You're just a cockblock. Whatever. Doesn't matter. Let's just say he isn't too fond of us. Kids in general, really. I've seen him yell at students in the hallway, like, really lay into them. That dude totally needs a new profession. Like, go make pornos or something, man. Teaching just isn't his thing."

Grady cackled. Doug joined in, shaking his head, a slight tremor of disapproval despite some laughter.

"I'm serious! You see that guy's mustache? Perfect for like a '70s-style porno. Looks like a furry blonde caterpillar. Bet he's got the pubes to match."

"Dude," Doug said, continuing to shake his head and wincing as if he'd eaten a candy that was much too tart for his tastes. "You've never even seen a porno. Not a real one, anyway."

"Have to. Jimmy has a whole closet full."

"Bullshit. Magazines, maybe."

Jesse's eyes lit up. "Nope! He's got a secret stash. I'm pretty sure Mom and Dad don't know about it. I mean, they freaked out last year when they discovered his *Playboy* collection. If they found the motherload, then I'd definitely know about it."

"Whatever. Speaking of Jimmy…" Doug said.

Jesse had been quiet on the subject, the topic somewhat embarrassing to talk about. He thought of his brother, locked away in his room for going on four weeks now, refusing to come out, only leaving his bed to eat or relieve bodily waste.

"Much of the same," Jesse said, coughing into his hand. "Wish he'd talk to me, you know." Jesse removed the water bottle from his book bag, took a sip of water, and cleared his throat. "I feel like he could help us. Especially with that riddle. He was always the best at solving them."

"Can we talk about that?" Doug asked. "I've been dying to talk about that."

"Ugh," Grady said. "Do we have to? I want to pretend it never happened."

"Dude. This is like the biggest breakthrough of this whole…*case.*"

"Case?" Jesse said, snickering. "What are we? Detectives now?"

"I mean, what else do we call it?" Jesse didn't have a better word, so *case* was what it became. "Look, whoever this *Mother* is, she clearly wrote this for us."

"I know. But it freaks me out. If she can send messages to your house and infiltrate our dreams—where does her power stop? And what the hell does she want with us, anyway?"

"I don't know, man. That's what we need to find out."

"From Box-booger?" Jesse asked, snorting with laughter. "Gee-zus. I can't believe the fate of our summer rests in the hands of fuckin' Box-booger."

They turned onto their old teacher's street and immediately spotted the moving truck parked in the driveway.

"That's it," Doug said, pointing.

"Shit. They coming or going?"

"Let's hope going."

They hustled down the sidewalk and Jesse no longer cared about stepping on the cracks. The concrete was uneven and choppy, in desperate need of repair, but the boys managed their way over to Boxberger's house without tripping, falling on their faces.

Outside, Boxberger himself was loading up the truck with cardboard boxes. Carrying one over, he stopped in mid-stride when he noticed the three faces at the end of his driveway.

He set down the box on the asphalt and arched his back.

"We come in peace, teacher-man," Jesse said, holding up two fingers. "We mean you no harm."

Boxberger licked his lips and folded his arms. "Harm? Di Falco, you couldn't fight your way out of a paper bag."

Jesse shrugged and turned to his buddies. "It's probably true. But it would totally depend on the thickness of the paper and the size of the bag."

Doug elbowed him in the ribs, gently. "Shut it," he whispered. "Sir, I know you're not a huge fan of us—in kids in particular—"

"I like kids just fine, Mr. Simms," he said, wearing a proud smile. Then he shrugged as if that statement weren't entirely true. "Most of them. Definitely not that one." He directed his finger at Jesse.

"I'm insulted!" Jesse said, feigning utter disappointment, slapping his cheeks like Macaulay Culkin on the poster for *Home Alone*.

Grady shoved him aside like a referee restraining a boxer from throwing a punch after the bell sounded.

Doug continued. "Look, we have some questions to ask. We know you're a history buff, especially local history—and well, there are some weird things happening around town, strange stuff, and we were wondering if you could help?"

Boxberger looked utterly perplexed. His face wrinkled, his forehead bunching around his eyes. Deep lines appeared that made him look decades older. "Weird things?"

From the front porch, Mrs. Boxberger emerged. "Lou? You almost done? I made sandwiches for lunch." Her gaze shifted to the three boys. "Oh? Who are your...friends?"

"Not my friends, Rita. Not my friends at all. Students. Well, *ex*-students." He made sure to emphasize *ex*, seeming very proud of that fact.

"Ah. What...um, what are they doing here?"

"Well, it seems I made some impression on them over the last two years, and they wanted to say goodbye. Isn't that right, boys?"

Jesse opened his mouth, but Grady covered it with his hand.

Doug spoke before Jesse could free his tongue. "Yes, that's right. Mr. Boxberger was our favorite teacher, ma'am. We just wanted to say goodbye. Er, properly."

A warm smile conquered Rita Boxberger's face. She almost blushed, clearly proud of her husband's effect on his students. Jesse knew this was the reaction they needed, and that Doug had done a better job with concocting a quick story, better than anything he could have come up with. If Grady had allowed him to speak, this trip probably would have ended with Rita Boxberger chucking the first available knick-knack at their heads. An exaggeration maybe, but also—let's face it—when Jesse talked, anything was possible and often nothing good came of it.

"Well, isn't that the sweetest thing. Why don't you boys come inside? I just made fresh lemonade."

Boxberger frowned. "Rita, that's not—"

"Love to!" Doug said.

"Excellent!" Rita said, waving them inside.

Boxberger glared at the three of them, his jaw tightening. His teeth threatened to break off at the gums.

As the three of them hiked up the stone trail to the porch, Jesse beamed at his ex-teacher and said, "Relax, Box-booger. We're just gonna have a nice chat. We'll be out of your hair before you know it."

Boxberger turned several shades of red. Jesse suspected if they were in some back alley and not in the center of some Central Jersey suburb, Boxberger might have reacted differently. Maybe he'd say something derogatory or threaten him with a little violence. Or maybe he'd say nothing at all. Instead, maybe he'd just kill him and leave his body in a dumpster. Either way, the message written on his teacher's face was clear; it read, *don't fuck with me, kid*. But Jesse had never been one to listen to the advice of teachers.

On his way inside the Boxbergers' home, he coughed again. He hoped he wasn't coming down with the summer cold that had been threatening him all week.

8

When Jewel opened the bathroom door, two cops were waiting for her. She had no place to go, no place to run. Behind them, Adam was chewing on his knuckles. She could see on his face that he hadn't been the one to buzz the bacon, but he might have been the one to rat on her location once they asked for it. She couldn't blame him, not one hundred percent. He didn't know the trouble she was in, couldn't possibly understand. And even if he knew, if he had known everything, what was he supposed to do? Lie to the police? He was a good kid. He wasn't like her, wasn't broken. He had a life to live.

She went willingly. The two officers escorted her to their squad car. Across the street, she spotted Fritz in a Dunkin' Donuts parking lot, observing the whole scene as it unfolded.

Bastard, she thought, her fists tightening. A flash of fire burned beneath her scalp, warming her entire face. She thought her head might pop off like the top of a volcano.

Once in the car, she curled her body into a ball.

"Please don't take me back," she pleaded, crying now.

The officers, now seated, looked to each other, each wearing tentative masks. About ten seconds later, the driver clicked the key in the ignition, turned over the engine, put the car in gear, and drove out of the parking lot.

Hopelessness settled in, resting on Jewel's shoulders like dead weight she would never shed. If the cops weren't going to help, if Fritz wasn't interested in keeping her safe, and if Adam refused to save her, then who would? Who would rescue her from the deepest depths of hell?

No one.

She was all on her own.

No one could save her.

No one from this world.

9

The three of them stood in the Boxbergers' vacant kitchen, each with a glass of lemonade set down before them. Mrs. Boxberger apologized for not having any chairs to seat them; mostly everything had been packed away in the rental. They resigned to standing, leaning against the naked counters for support. The boys were exhausted from their trek across several neighborhoods in the late-July heatwave.

"So what brings you delightful children to my now ex-house?" Boxberger asked, a faux smile etched across his face.

He was grinning like a mad fool, maintaining his best behavior in the presence of his wife, who was currently in the back room taping up boxes. What he had really meant to say, Doug suspected, was something along the lines of, *What the fuck are you shit-bricks doing in my goddamn house?*

"We need some information," Doug told him, narrowing his eyes. "About Hooperstown."

In the back room, Mrs. Boxberger shuffled around some boxes, the audible sound of heavy boxes being set on the hardwood floor echoing throughout the stripped house.

Boxberger eyed the opening between the kitchen and the hallway as if what he was about to ask were a secret he didn't want her to overhear. "What about it?"

"It's history."

Boxberger scoffed. "You want a history lesson? Now?"

Jesse rolled his eyes. "Oh, come off it, man. We might be in some serious shit here."

"Keep it down," he said through clenched teeth, his eyes hinting at the other room, his wife. "What kind of shit? If you're in trouble, why did you come here? Why haven't you gone to the police?"

Doug cleared his throat and tried to speak softly. "You know the kids who are getting sick? The cancer stuff?"

"Yeah, kinda hard to miss. It's all over the news."

"We think it might have to do with something... I don't know... Something *we* did. Maybe."

He jerked his head back as if Doug's claim were a backhanded slap. The skin around his eyes grew tight. "What? No. Kids, *children*, that is not how cancer works." He chuckled at Doug's theory, leaning back against the counter. "Those kids are getting sick because the local chemical plant has been dumping toxic waste into the ground near the water supply for almost three decades. That's one of the reasons we're moving, actually." A proud smile overtook his face, and Doug had never seen Boxberger radiate such positivity. It was weird watching the man's mustache curl up at the ends. "Rita—I mean, Mrs. Boxberger—is pregnant."

"What?" she called from the back of the house. "I heard my name. Do you need more lemonade?"

"No, baby!" he called back. "Just telling the boys that we're expecting!"

"Oh, okay!"

"Congrats, Mrs. Boxberger!" Jesse called out to her, a sarcastic smile plastered to his face. Whispering to Mr. Boxberger, he said, "I can't believe you found someone who'd let you knock them up."

Boxberger turned several shades of red. He flung a forefinger at Jesse's face. "You shut the fuck up, Di Falco, before I break your stupid face."

Jesse giggled, making a childish *oh-I-so-scared* face.

"Both of you," Doug said, stepping between them. "Knock it off." He turned and glared at Jesse. "Especially you."

But Boxberger wasn't done. "Looks like someone already beat you up pretty good, Di Falco." He gestured to Jesse's arms, which had several bruises running up them. They looked worse in the dim lighting of Boxberger's empty home. Doug had noticed them earlier but thought nothing of it. Thought maybe they were sports injuries or just Jesse being Jesse. He was always accidentally hurting himself. "Mouth off to the wrong person? Huh, you little shit?"

"No," Jesse said, almost defensively. He tucked his arms behind his back, as if embarrassed by the unsightly marks. "Summer league. Took some elbows grabbing rebounds."

"Mm-hm."

"Look," Grady said, finally stepping in. "Are you going to help us or not?"

"I don't know what you want, not exactly. You still haven't told me." Boxberger checked his watch. "I really must get going. Rita shouldn't be lifting heavy things, not this far along and— Rita! You're not lifting anything heavy, are you, hon?"

"Nope!" she called back. "Just labeling boxes!"

"Good!" He turned back to the boys. "We're moving tomorrow morning, and we have to get everything into the trailer."

"We'll help you," Doug blurted out.

"What?"

"If you give us twenty minutes of your time, tell us what you know about certain things, then we'll help you for an hour. We'll lug as many boxes onto the truck as we can."

Boxberger's grin stretched. "Got yourself a goddamn deal there, Douglas Simms."

"Good."

Grabbing his chin, his eyes glimmering with curiosity, Boxberger asked, "Now, tell me why you think you caused twelve local kids to catch the Big C."

Doug looked to his friends. Grady nodded. Jesse did the same.

"Okay," Doug said, turning back to his old teacher. "On the last day of school," he said, and proceeded to tell him everything.

CHAPTER TEN

Legends

1

"Aaaaaaand, I'm done," Boxberger said before Doug could finish. "Get out. All of you. Now."

He had begun with an abbreviated version of the Hunt, but once he got rolling there was no stopping him. Details were divulged, specifics that weren't easy to swallow, especially for a practical man like Louis Boxberger.

"This really happened, sir," Grady said. "I… I wasn't there for all of it, but I saw most of what Doug described."

"I don't care for practical jokes, especially when I'm busy and in the middle of, literally, the most important time of my adult life. I'm moving and I have a pregnant wife to look after. So kindly take yourselves and your goddamn jokes and get the hell out."

"Does the *Mother of Dead Dreams* mean anything to you?" Doug asked, abandoning the rest of the story. He'd gotten through most of it, the important bits, leaving off with Randall Benoit puking into Jesse's mouth.

Boxberger stiffened, noticeably. Creases formed in his forehead, three dark lines stacked on top of each other. "Dead dreams?" he asked, though it was hardly a question and more of a *Hell yeah, I've heard of HER*. "I've heard of certain local legends, sure. Is that why you wanted to know about the history of Hooperstown? The old Thomas Hooper legend?"

A pang of instant panic drummed inside of Doug's chest. "Yes. Yes, we want to know about it."

"I'm assuming Mr. Jacobs never taught you any of this in history class. Never mentioned anything about Thomas Hooper and how this town was founded?"

Jesse hooted. "Jacobs? That jobber sat at his desk and made us watch movies every day. I'm pretty sure he painted eyeballs on his eyelids so we couldn't tell he was sleeping when the lights were out."

Boxberger rolled his eyes and nodded as if this wasn't exactly news.

"Tell us about the Mother," Doug said, unable to strip the desperation from his voice. "The one we keep seeing when we dream."

Boxberger checked his watch. "It's getting late in the afternoon and I don't have—"

"Please." Doug's eyes pooled, a combination of frustration, sadness, and wanting—no, *needing*—to know what was happening, how the Mother of Dead Dreams fit into this mess. How his own mother knew about her nearly a decade before this mysterious force came to drop a plague over their town.

"We'll give you *two* hours of moving boxes," Grady added, sweetening the pot.

Boxberger sighed, folded his arms across his body, and hung his head. He was clearly exhausted, and Doug figured he knew there was only one way to get them to leave—tell them the goddamn story. "Okay. Okay, fine. I'll tell you the Hooperstown fable. What I know of it, anyway. But then we're done here. Got it? No more garbage about playing in the cemetery and zombie-like kids puking up black stuff—I don't want to hear about any of your fantasies, okay? Kids are getting sick for one reason and one reason only—that goddamn chemical plant. Got it?"

Doug and the others exchanged looks. He hadn't thought Boxberger would buy the story and suddenly felt stupid for mentioning certain parts. The main idea was whatever they had done on the night of the Hunt, they had released the Mother of Dead Dreams upon an unsuspecting town. *Their* town. The one they called home.

Or, come to think of it, maybe they hadn't. Maybe someone else had released her. Maybe there was more to the story they didn't know.

"Okay," Doug said, nodding. "We got it."

"Good." Boxberger sucked in a vapid breath and began the legend the way most fairy tales do: "Once upon a time…"

2

Through clouds of fog, several canoes traveled up the river from the bay where the ship—The Speurtocht—had docked a few hundred feet from the sandy shores. The English captain, Thomas Hooper, led the charge, with his crew of men and the Dutch sailors he had absorbed on his journey to the New World. Hooper and the settlers followed the river—what would later be dubbed the Red River due to the amount of blood spilled there over the years—until he deemed the current too strong, forcing them to make land. There, about twenty miles from the bay, they set up camp.

And they would never leave that place.

But they weren't the first settlers. No, there had been a small tribe of indigenous people, the Lenape, who had built a small community no more than a mile from where Hooper's explorers had made landfall. At first, the Lenape were very accepting of their new friends, giving them food and water and helping them hunt, farm the lands. As you can imagine, the Europeans wore out their welcome, and rather quickly. They began taking charge of things, setting up rules, acting like the Lenape were subservient, lesser people, pawns to do thy biddings, and so it goes. So, naturally, the good people who originally founded the area now known as Hooperstown rebelled. They told Hooper and his settlers to leave their place, their home, and reside elsewhere.

Hooper, as you can imagine, didn't take kindly to that, and ending up forcing the Lenape out of the area using tactics best described as "violent." The legend speaks of one death, a young Lenape who tried to murder Hooper as he bathed alone in the river, but things went sideways for him. Hooper ended up murdering the young man—a boy, really, sixteen years of age—by cutting his throat with a pocketknife, spilling his blood in the river, thus leading the Lenape to dub it Mhukòntëp Sipu, *which roughly translates to Blood River, which, over time, was eventually changed to Red River, as if changing "Blood" to "Red" was somehow better, less graphic, less of a reminder of the truth that happened all those centuries ago. Shit, they even named the town next door after that horrific sequence of events. Imagine? A town named after a murder? What a world we live in.*

Anyway, Hooper and the settlers stayed, and the Lenape were cast out. Rumor had it they moved westward, found another spot to lie low, until more white men sailed across the ocean and history repeated itself. But the Lenape, as peaceful and passive as they were, grew angry and upset—rightly so—and refused to give up their home. And who could blame them, really? This was their home! They had been there for decades, generations. It would be like if you and your family had lived in a house your entire life, your grandparents before you and their parents before that. Then one day the government comes in, knocks down your door, uses your amenities, sleeps in your beds, eats your foods, fucks your mothers (oh yes, Hooper's men were rumored to be quite the crude bunch). Next thing you know, you're kicked out. Tossed on your ass in the street. Left with nothing. Not very fair, is it? Of course not. But that's what happened.

Now, you might have rebelled against an act of eminent domain such as this, might have stood up for yourself. But it's an entire government. They have resources and weapons and numbers—but most of all, they have power. And when you don't have those other three things, you don't stand a chance against power. So, the Lenape moved on from their home, abandoning their own peaceful paradise in search of a new one. And they found one eventually, but it wasn't the same. Nothing, of course, is the same as home. Home is where the heart is and all that jazz; there's no place like it as Dorothy says.

In an act of desperation, the Lenape called upon the Spirit World to help guide them. Not sure of the details, no one really is because, of course, this is a legend, and a legend is only but a small truth stretched to the brink of absurdity. But whatever happened, whatever séance or ritual was performed, it brought forth a gaping hole between two worlds—the world we reside in, the reality we all accept and know to be true, and the dark world, the one we sometimes visit when we close our eyes at night, a mirror of reality, a place where evil things sometimes lurk. A black cavity opened somewhere near the Hooperstown settlement, and the two worlds merged. Some settlers saw a comet, a shooting star that had zipped across the sky, leaving a trail of cosmic dust in its wake, a bright glittery streak on the night's dark canvas. Others claim they saw a door in the woods, an invisible force turning the knob and opening it. What they saw come through wasn't human, though it tried to look mortal. So legend has it.

But that comes later. Let me tell you about Thomas Hooper and the day he went for a walk in the woods, the day he happened upon a young Lenape woman. Just a girl really. All alone. Wandering the forest.

Now, heeeeeere's where the story takes a turn. Some say she was already pregnant. Knocked up, as you kids like to say. But there's another version, a darker version, where Thomas Hooper took the girl—no older than sixteen—and had his way with her. I won't elaborate on such a horrible act, but you three... You can use your imaginations. You know what I'm talking about, right? I don't have to spell it out for you, do I? Huh? No? Good. All right. After the deed was done, Hooper took the girl captive.

Yes. You heard me right. Captive.

He abducted this young woman, brought her back to camp, and threw the girl in a cage. He swore there was something about her, something he didn't like. He told others that she was a spy sent to their camp in order to discover weaknesses in their newly formed community so she could go back, tell her people, and then they would come lay siege to their slice of paradise. But there was another reason he took her captive, the real reason for taking the girl.

He had knocked her up, and she was to have his love child.

So into this makeshift cage they had built from downed timbers she went, because, obviously, he couldn't allow her to roam the community. She *would escape! Back to her camp! Thomas Hooper couldn't have that, so he imprisoned her.*

Weeks passed, and she grew further along in her pregnancy, at a speed much faster than the camp's doctor deemed normal. Within three months she appeared almost eight months into her term. See, the women of camp were insanely jealous because, since their arrival in the New World, not one of them had been able to conceive. The ones that had miraculously gotten pregnant suffered terrible miscarriages during their first few months. Hooper was convinced the Lenape had cursed this land before they were forced from the area, and that was the reason the wives couldn't bear children. He'd written about his frustrations in great detail in a diary he kept. His wife had become sick from their infertility. Mentally, that is. She nearly went nuts because of it. It put a terrible strain on their relationship, along with the other hopeful and expecting husbands and wives. Some men blamed the women for not being able to give them a son or daughter. See, to give birth to a child is the greatest gift this world has to offer, and the people of Hooperstown had been denied such basic, yet paradisaical delights.

So, Thomas Hooper made a decision. His decision was to give his wife the child she couldn't have.

The community's doctor informed him the girl wasn't going to make it. The pregnancy was going badly, and the baby would die if they didn't take it out early. Without much of a choice, Thomas Hooper decided to cut open the young Lenape woman and take what he thought was rightfully his. So that's what he did. He sliced open the girl's bloated belly, brutally extracted the infant from the womb, and then revealed to the camp his only son's name—Thomas Hooper Jr.

The girl died, unable to survive the savage and unorthodox procedure. Or did she?

For the sake of brevity, I'll say—no. She wasn't dead. Not really. On the outside she appeared lifeless, a stiff reminder of our mortal chambers, how fragile one's life can be. But on the inside? Hooper had learned from the Lenape that a spirit never truly dies, it just moves on, though he could sense the girl's spirit never went anywhere, that it remained in that cage of a human body. And that frightened the living shit out of him. Her spirit was alive all right, as alive as the woods were at night, as alive as the trees and the crops and the wildlife that rustled in the branches while they slept.

Thomas Hooper knew she was dormant, not dead. So, they buried her lifeless corpse in a cave, deep in the woods. Had a woodworker make her a nice sarcophagus, a proper piece to appease certain gods who might be angry with him, a last-ditch effort to make amends with those he had wronged. A group of men from town cemented the sarcophagus in the earth so no one, not even an unsuspecting wanderer, an explorer of uncharted plantations, would find her, locate her, dig her up, and set her free, set her loose upon an ignorant world. He feared she might have powers beyond his understanding, claimed his strange and unsettling dreams were to blame for this reasoning, and suspected one day she might use these gifts to lure in prey, people she could use to set her free. That was why they took so many precautions laying her to rest, that was why it took nearly a month's worth of hard labor to carpenter the sarcophagus and make enough cement from mud to get the job done.

They also borrowed from many Pagan rituals, scribbling ancient symbols all over the inner walls of the cave, hoping that would keep her down there, bind her caged soul for all eternity. Much of what they performed was utter bullshit, supernatural rubbish they had learned across the pond. Even if the spells they had cast were genuine, they would be no match for what the Lenape had summoned to the lands, the Mother of Dead Dreams. Sure, her spirit may have fled this woman's mortal cage, but she still walked through the Land of Dreams.

And in the Dream World, the Mother grew stronger.

And stronger…

And stronger…

3

"What happened to the settlers?" Doug asked, failing to notice he had chewed through most of his thumbnail.

"Oh, funny you should ask," Boxberger said, the story clearly amusing him. "See, the kids who had grown up in the Hooperstown settlement grew very sick and most of them died. Yeah, about twenty or so, *legend* has it. Another curse placed upon the land by the indigenous people of the Jersey shore." Boxberger waved his right hand in the air, as if telling the boys to discount everything he had just told them. "But who knows what's true and what isn't. All of it could be bullshit."

Jesse raised his hand as if the kitchen were a classroom. "You said there was a diary. From Hooper himself."

"Yeah, a *diary*." He used air quotes around *diary*.

"What about the kid?" Grady asked, hungry for details. "The one Hooper stole from the Mother?"

"Oh, *him*." Boxberger pressed a finger against his chin. "Come to think of it, I'm not sure anyone knows what happened to him. Or *allegedly* happened to him. Like I said—this is a tall tale full of allegories and metaphors, you know—shit like that. Not meant to be taken literally. Sort of like the Bible. I mean, does anyone actually believe the entire world flooded, that some asshole built an ark and crammed every animal known to man on it. Nah, of course not. The Mother of Dead Dreams is a cautionary tale that people enjoyed telling each other, something that comes with an important lesson. And that lesson? Be a good neighbor. Don't overstay your welcome. You know, like, the settlers." He lowered his gaze. "Like you three muskrats."

The kids looked to each other, reading each other's minds.

"I think it's real," Doug said, nervous to be the one to put that conjecture out there. "All of it. The legend, everything. We…" An invisible touch pawed at his throat. "We think we saw her."

Confused, Boxberger narrowed his eyes. "Saw who?"

"The Mother of Dead Dreams," Grady answered. His haunted eyes twinkled, the memory of that terrible ordeal settling in.

"She was there that night," added Jesse. "In the cemetery."

Boxberger scoffed, leaned back. "Kids… No, just…no. None of that happened. It's just not possible. I'm sorry. It's just not. Whatever you all saw, you must have hallucinated. Were you given drugs? I mean, were any of you on drugs? The older kids—maybe they slipped something into your Pepsi-colas, I don't know."

Jesse rapped his knuckles on Doug's shoulder. "Forget it. Professor Pimply-Dick here won't believe us. We're wasting our breath. Besides, we got what we came for. Let's bounce."

Boxberger threw up his hands, almost celebratory. "Finally." He stepped aside and motioned them to the front door. "Out you go. Don't the let the door hit your asses on the way out. But I wish you all a great rest of the summer. Really. I do. Stay out of trouble. Don't do drugs. Especially the kind you snort or absorb rectally. Be safe and all that jazz."

They mumbled privately as they walked through the kitchen, into the living room, and toward the front door. Doug didn't feel like they had accomplished much, though, it was *something*. The origin story was a big piece of the puzzle, if in fact it held any truth. But it wasn't the whole thing. There were still more dots to connect, lines to draw, and mystery to unfold. Like how the Mother had been recently unleashed and how she was controlling the infected, like Alphie Moffit and Randall Benoit.

Halfway down the driveway, Boxberger called to them.

"Hey!" he said.

They turned, faced him, each with an arm over their eyes to block out the rude sun.

"Be careful out there. Have a safe summer."

His wife was behind him now. One of her arms was wrapped around his waist, hand over his belly, as if he were the pregnant one. Her other hand clutched a beautiful white flower.

4

Several hours later, they finally made it to the library. Grady felt good about being in the company of seemingly endless rows of books because then the pitch to his parents hadn't been complete bullshit. It was mostly, sure, but his parents would never know; they were too busy dressing up like pirates and using a nearby town's parade as an excuse to get absolutely shit-faced. If he came home with a book tucked under his arm, they'd be happy.

"What are we doing here?" Jesse asked, shoving his hands in his pockets while Doug utilized the search bar in the computer's "book lookup" system. The operating system was archaic as the library itself; a black screen displayed green letters in Courier and no other graphics. He typed in "Red River" just to see what would come up, and the combo triggered a few hits. The keywords needed to be precise because the system would only display whatever he typed in. "We should be at the park. Skateboarding. Playing basketball. Shit, *anything* but doing research. I mean, how many kids spend their summer vacation doing homework?"

Doug slimmed his eyes and furrowed his brow. "Come on, man. You said you were into this."

An exaggerated sigh escaped Jesse, one Grady had been expecting. He'd seen the face he'd put on back at Boxberger's and sensed Jesse was growing bored. He had never been the academic type, and a trip to the library was probably as exciting as watching fingernails grow. To him, anyway. Grady loved this stuff. Just being in the library, among the stinky cologne of old, well-read books, was a bit of an aphrodisiac. The surroundings were akin to wrapping himself in a warm blanket on a frosty winter night.

"I am," Jesse said, stiffening. "Just, not how I wanted to spend my *entire* summer."

"Dude, kids are getting sick," Grady said from behind them. He was flipping through a magazine, *Popular Mechanics*. In all honesty, he only understood a fragment of what had been written within its pages, but he wanted to impress the others by reading something a little highbrow. "Our friends. Classmates." He ditched the magazine on the closest rack, not where it belonged. That also, he thought, would earn him a couple of cool points. "They need us."

"I just didn't want it to be like this. Dedicating every waking moment to saving the town. Lately, I feel like that's all we do."

"You're not dedicating every waking moment. Quit being so dramatic." Doug looked away from the computer, turned, and faced him. "You're still in summer league, your parents put you in that lifeguard training class at the beach, and you have that New Jersey Nets basketball camp coming up in August. You're doing lots of stuff."

"Yeah, but not with you guys!"

Grady clapped a hand on his back. "How sentimental."

"Shut up, Grades. I'm just saying—all work and no play makes Jesse a dull boy."

Grady rolled his eyes. "Ugh, I hate that movie. It's soooooooo boring."

"That's because you're afraid of everything." He snapped his fingers, an idea bursting into his brain. "We should watch it tonight. Sleepover. We'll double it up with a werewolf movie. *Silver Bullet,* anyone?"

"Can't do a sleepover tonight," Grady said. "My parents already hate me for going on *this* little excursion. Then again, they might be obliterated enough to agree to anything."

"Man, when are you going to tell them to cram it up their crapholes? You're almost in high school, for Chrissake."

"Yeah, well, we can't all have the *cool* parents."

A passing librarian, mid-sixties, her hair done up in a gray bun, wearing blood-red glasses several sizes too big for her mousy face, shushed them, pressing a finger against her lips for effect. She let her eyes linger on them, and Grady couldn't tell why, but the stare chilled him. It was as if she were daydreaming about boiling and cooking their boy meats. He almost laughed at the notion, but her eyes—*damn*, her eyes were colder than a block of January ice. And they twinkled with this *knowing*, as if their heads were books that she could crack open and read every scrawled thought within. Those eyes, they were not lips, but they smiled anyway.

Then she left in a slow march around the corner.

"That was some creepy shit, right?" Grady whispered, once the librarian disappeared.

"Super creepy." Jesse shook his entire body as if a chill dove the length of his spine. "What were we talking about? Kubrick? Werewolves? Sleepover? Yeah?"

"I'm with Grady on this one," Doug said. "I...kinda want to spend the night with my dad."

Jesse shook his head, disappointed. "Why?"

"I've been thinking." He rested an elbow on the table, leaned on it, and bit down on his lip. "About my mother."

Grady perked up. "Oh?"

"Yeah. Before you get excited—the both of you—I want you to know I'm still not sold on the idea of a visit. But I've been thinking...it can't be coincidence. Can it? I mean, my mother warned me about this years ago, right? Or am I imagining that? I can't believe her crazy ramblings about dreams and a woman who might want to abduct me and the things that are happening around town are all unrelated. I just can't. There are too many similarities. Boxberger said they buried that woman in a cave, and I've dreamed about that cave. *We've* dreamed about it."

"That's kinda what I've been telling you, dude," Grady said.

"Okay, okay." Doug took a deep breath. "I'll ask him then. I'll ask him to take me."

Grady pumped his fist. Jesse gave a nod, a subtle *good for you*.

"Are you sure?" Grady asked, reeling in his excitement. "I mean, you don't have to yet. You can still think about it."

Shaking his head, Doug said, "No, I want to. But I have a request."

"What is it?" Jesse asked.

"I want you two to be there. In some capacity. Just there, even if you're standing outside. That is, if my dad allows it."

Grady and Jesse looked to each other, held a brief conference with their eyes, and then said in unison, "Sure."

"Great."

Seconds after that affair was settled, two girls appeared from around the corner. Grady's heart leaped the second his eyes fell on them. He almost blurted out, "Oh shit," but caught himself before that embarrassing moment came to pass. Instead, he elbowed Jesse and whispered out of the corner of his mouth, "Three o'clock, dudes."

The other two spun in the proposed direction, spotted the two girls making their way over to them.

"Oh sweet," Doug said, and Grady sensed a change in his mood. Doug waved to the girls, an awkward waggle of a limp wrist, but only one of them waved back.

Maddie Rice.

To her immediate left was Abby Allen, who wore a tight, apprehensive mask of a girl who didn't want to be there. She moved toward them like her feet were cemented to the bottom of five-gallon buckets.

Grady almost swallowed his own tongue when the girls stopped a few steps away from them and said *hi*. He managed to choke out a *hi* back.

"Are you okay?" Abby asked him. Her hair was done up in short pigtails. She wore a pink shirt, the front embroidered with sparkling silver jewels that formed a happy face.

Grady's eyes bounced around the aisle, pretending he didn't catch what she'd said. The titles and author names on the spines of the surrounding books read like word search puzzles. A dizzy spell came over him, and he gripped the computer desk for support.

"What's wrong with this one?" Abby asked Doug, who could only shake his head.

Jesse elbowed Grady in the ribs twice as hard as Grady had his.

"What? What's up? Oh, hey," he said, smiling, waving, grinning like a courtyard jester about to reveal the grand gag of the evening.

"Is he..." Abby said, addressing Doug again, "...drunk? On drugs? Heard snorting Adderall can really fuck you up. Did he do that?"

"No," Jesse said, stepping in. "He's just a brain-dead moron. Luckily, it's a condition that will pass. Now, can someone tell me exactly what Bonnie and Clyde are doing here?"

Abby glared at him, bouncing on her heels, a boxer's shuffle if Grady had ever seen one. He watched her face tighten, every muscle constricting with anger. He knew she wanted to rip Jesse's head off for no other reason than she didn't want to be here, and he was making this forced situation a lot harder.

Grady didn't know why, but he liked it, the way she conducted herself. Her snarky attitude and cresting anger made her look somewhat...

Pretty? Was that the word? He thought so.

She cleared her throat. "Speaking of brain-dead morons, Clyde was a dude, *dude*."

"Yeah," Jesse said, his eyes shifting back and forth. "Pssh. Yeah, duh. I knew that. Of course. I was just testing you. Making sure *you* knew that."

She rolled her eyes, clearly unimpressed. Then she turned to Maddie, spinning faster than a top. "Why did you bring me here? You're not *actually* friends with these losers, are you?"

Grady was a lot less insulted than he probably should have been. In her defense, this was the second time he'd acted like a complete idiot in front of her, the first being that day on the bus when he'd fumbled his way through that less than exhilarating conversation. Grady wasn't good at this sort of thing, talking to girls. But it was comforting to know that Jesse, undoubtedly considered the "coolest" of their trio, sucked hard at it as well.

While Maddie calmed down her friend, gripping her by the shoulders and dragging her behind a towering bookcase overstuffed with non-fiction hardbacks, Doug turned to them, formed a huddle as if he were about to call a game-winning play in the Super Bowl.

"Okay," he started, and Grady saw where this was going before it got there. "I'm sorry I didn't tell you guys, but I invited Maddie to tag along. Be...you know...part of this."

Jesse's mouth hung open. "What? Why?"

"Because she's cool, that's why."

"Oh, she's more than cool," Grady said teasingly. "Isn't that right? You sly pooch." Winking, he nudged him with his elbow.

"Shut up." Shaking his head, Doug continued. "Look. I told her everything, okay? Everything that happened that night in the cemetery, all the strange shit we saw before it."

Jesse's mouth cracked open. His tongue ran along the inside of his mouth. "Dude?"

"What? I trust her, okay?"

Grady spied on Maddie and Abby, and he watched Abby reluctantly go along with her friend's request. He couldn't blame her; nothing about their group was very alluring. Three losers who played too many video games and engaged in a whole lot of geeky traditions, held hour-long debates on such nerdy topics like *which mutant from X-Men would you rather be?* No one wanted to hang out with them. Well, maybe they'd consider Jesse because he was in shape and had the whole athletic thing going for him, but surely not the other two.

Inside of two minutes, Maddie was leading her friend back over to the computer terminal.

"Sorry," Maddie said, hinting at a smile. "All right. Abby." She placed a hand on her friend's back, gently pushing her forward. "Tell them. Tell them what happened the night of the party."

At first, Abby didn't speak. Only stared at the shelves behind them.

"Come on, Abby," Maddie said, bumping her with her shoulder.

"Okay. *Geez.*" Abby cleared her throat and threw a glance at the ceiling. Small delays. She even pretended to kick a rock, but there were no rocks on the thin library carpet. Breathing deeply, she nodded. "Okay. So, I was walking Bishop, Maddie's dog, the night of the party, when—"

5

When her story concluded, Doug just stared at her. His brain served him a buffet of questions and new riddles, so many that it was hard to concentrate on just one. His vision fuzzed a little, like an old television set having trouble with the reception. Stealing a glance at his friends, he saw they were reacting similarly, their minds buzzing with thoughts and revelations and more components to this complex puzzle.

This hunt, he thought. *It's not a puzzle. It's a scavenger hunt. Only, we're hunting her, and she's hunting us.*

Or me.

He couldn't help but feel at the center of this, more so than the others. He knew that was because of his mother, what she'd told him, her sickness and everything that followed after she had fallen ill. Her connection to the Mother of Dead Dreams, whatever it was exactly.

"You believe me?" asked Abby, incredulously. Doug witnessed tears building in her eyes, the kind you couldn't hold onto for forever. "You actually believe me?"

Doug was the first one to say he did. "Yeah. Yeah, of course we believe you."

"Oh, God," she said, lowering her chin, throwing a hand over her eyes. She shuddered as the leftover grief from that awful night swept through her. A comforting hand landed on her shoulder, and Maddie pulled her in for a best-friend hug. The two girls squeezed each other, hung on like the earth below was crumbling apart.

After her emotions were purged, she came up for air.

"Sorry," she said, brushing away the final tears that clung to her lashes. Once they were gone, she faced the three boys, seemingly ready for the barrage of questions that were sure to follow.

"So," Doug started, jumping in before others had a chance. "Lauren was...possessed?"

Abby swallowed. "I… I guess you could call it that. She wasn't her, that's all I know."

Grady stepped in. "How do you know?"

"Didn't you hear the story, numbnuts?" Jesse asked. "Lauren ate the friggin' dog."

"Yeah, but—" Grady stopped, thought about what to say next, knowing it would require a delicate delivery. "But couldn't it have been her? Just…a little different?"

"I don't understand the difference," Abby said. "It was her. I mean, her face, her body. But her eyes, they were different. Whatever makes her *her*. Whatever makes a person a person—a soul, if you will. Lauren's was gone. Replaced by whatever that thing was."

Doug motioned to the others, calling them back into the huddle. "One second," he told the girls, holding up his forefinger. Once the three had taken a few steps back and were out of earshot, Doug asked, "What do you think?"

"Clearly dealing with the same thing Randall and Alphie were," Grady said, sounding certain.

"I mean, yeah, clearly," Jesse added. "The question is, what do we do about it?"

Doug sighed. "We need to find this woman. The Mother."

Grady and Jesse winced simultaneously, not the plan they were hoping for.

"Was afraid you'd say that," Grady said.

Jesse, who looked no more excited about it, said, "Come on, Grades. Not up for a little adventure?" Looking aside, his snarky smile was interrupted when he coughed into his hand.

"You mean, up for a little suicide?" No one laughed at that joke.

"We need to find her weakness," Doug said, ignoring Grady's quip. "All villains—even the archenemies—have a weakness. Right, Jess?"

"Yeah, but this isn't a comic book, man." Standing up, wiping his mouth, he broke the huddle first. "This is real life. People are dying."

"Kids," Grady reminded him. "Kids are dying."

Doug nodded. "Yeah. Notice the adults haven't been catching cancer? Just kids."

"That is weird," Jesse admitted. "But we haven't ruled out that this could all be coincidence. I mean, the chemical plant *could* be causing the kids to get sick."

"You think the chemical plant made Lauren Sullivan eat Maddie's dog?"

Jesse snapped his fingers. "Fair point. So what's the play, hot shot? We gonna knock down this Mother's door? Bust in there like Ghostbusters and shit? Zap her with the proton packs we *don't* have? I mean, come on. What are we doing here, guys?"

Doug cracked his knuckles, a habit his father constantly tried to break him of. "We still haven't tracked down Jewel Conti. Or Alphie. Or Randall for that matter."

"Did I hear you guys say Randall?" Maddie asked, her brow furrowing. "As in, Randall Benoit?"

The three of them broke the huddle, formed a line, and faced her.

"What about him?" Doug asked.

"You didn't hear?"

The boys looked to each other as if one of them might have known something. Heard something. A whisper of news. Anything. But the confusion on their faces didn't fade.

Maddie gulped, the sound audible. And loud. "Randall...someone found him."

"What do you mean *found him*?" Jesse asked, tempering another series of coughs with the back of his hand.

"Guys... Randall is dead." Maddie nodded as if to let them know this wasn't just another rumor around town, another tall tale. It wasn't another legend or some version of the truth stretched beyond reasonable plausibility. It was the honest-to-God truth.

Randall Benoit is dead, Doug thought, and he wondered how long before someone would be saying the same thing about the five of them.

CHAPTER ELEVEN

Daddy's Home

1

When Jewel opened the door, the last person she expected to see reclined on the living room couch was *him*. In fact, she never truly expected to see *him* again. Ever. Her first instinct—like always—was to run. Turn around and bolt as fast as the confines of reality would allow.

But she couldn't run. Not today. Behind her were the two officers who'd brought her home and Ava Conti, both of which blocked her potential escape. Their shadows draped over her, dark reminders that no matter where she ran, how far she got, this would always be the result.

Home. With him.

Her father, John Conti, looked much worse than he had before getting himself locked up. Older, but not in a wise, charming way. More in a wilting-flower way. His hair was grayer, the whiskers that formed his beard almost completely white, stained yellow around the mouth from nicotine abuse. The Confederate flag tattooed on his bicep sagged a bit, the result of his deflated skin, the same with the iron cross on his forearm, the trail of skulls and crossbones on his other. Once a muscular man, he'd lost almost all of his body weight and definition. Years and years of shooting smack into his veins and eating unhealthily had taken its toll. He was now skinny as a pole, wearing fat-free skin that flaunted his ribcage. She wasn't surprised to find two beer cans accompanying him, the recliner's cupholders each holding one. This was the image by which she'd always remember him; too drunk to rise from the couch for her homecoming, a resting beer ready for each hand, and a deceptive smile spreading across his unshaven face.

She glanced back over her shoulder, her eyes pleading with the two officers. Their attention was suddenly turned elsewhere, anywhere but her eyes. Everywhere but the monster sitting on the living room couch pretending it was still human. Jewel wondered how the man made it this far in life, how no one had killed him yet. Surely, he'd pissed off some bad people in his day, the wrong kind of bad people, the killing kind.

Surely.

"All right," said one of the officers, completely turning his back. "Have a great day, folks."

She opened her mouth to say something, to protest this arrangement, but her mother shut the door before she could utter a single syllable.

Darkness now. No light save for what little filtered in through the paper-thin blinds. She felt trapped in a cave with two bears, both ready and waiting to tear her apart, limb from fucking limb.

"Hi Daddy," she said, her voice scratchy, barely audible. "This is a...ah-em, a surprise."

"A good surprise," he said, questioning her tone, "or a bad surprise?"

She didn't answer, didn't want to. She supposed she could lie, but at the same time, she wanted him to know the truth. It was a daring game to play, but oh so satisfying.

Then, something hard smacked the side of her head. *WAP!* Her vision softened, moved in squiggly lines. She knew what had hit her before she turned to see her mother's grin hovering a few inches from her face.

"When your father asks a question, you answer. Git it?" Ava's grin twitched, morphed into a heinous snarl.

It smelled like she hadn't showered in days, weeks. The BO was overwhelming even for Jewel, who didn't smell like a bar of Ivory soap herself. Her breath was rank too, stinking of a tuna and cheese sandwich that had been sitting out for a few days, collecting flies and a spread of bacteria. The collective aroma of the living room (mixed with the beer-belch odor) and she was ready to throw up what little remained in her stomach. She was surprised the two officers hadn't smelled the white-trash perfume from the stoop, not a single ingredient of the strange miasma. Or maybe they had but didn't want to be bothered with scoping the place out, didn't want the responsibility of deeming the apartment an unsuitable living situation for a fifteen-year-old girl. A discovery of such might include too much paperwork, might keep them past their scheduled shift.

She hated the cops for leaving her, allowing her to remain in this home with unfit, undeserving parents. But was it any worse than the alternative? A life of being shipped from foster home to foster home? She'd been down that road before and it wasn't smooth pavement. No, it was a rocky trek, one she didn't exactly prefer over...*this.*

"Good to see you, Daddy," she said, her teeth clenched. "I'm happy you're home."

Lips spreading, he gargled a laugh. "Sure you are, sweet pea." He glared at her like a wolf eyeing a delectable meal. "Why don't you prove it? Come over here and give your Daddy a kiss."

Her whole body tensed. When she didn't move right away, her mother nudged her, pushing her forward a few steps.

"Go on now," Ava said.

She talked like she had a mouthful of chew, her words barely decipherable. Jewel wondered how the cops didn't know she was loaded on heroin and cheap beer. Had she acted normal in front of them? Really? They really bought that act, that faux *Sweet Home Alabama* accent and the fluttery eyelashes? The "oh my God, thank the good Lord you found her" speech that had been recited and practiced more times than she could count? It didn't add up. It was like they wanted her to suffer.

They just don't care. No one does.

The whole situation made her sick, more so than the unpleasant quality of the living room's tainted air.

Ava nudged her again. "Give your Daddy a kiss. C'mon, girl."

The walk over to the couch seemed to last minutes. It was only ten paces, but still—with every step, her calves ached. Her temples pulsed with pain. Her heart-turned-jackhammer chipped away at the concrete walls of her chest. Once she was in range, she tasted bile. The acidic burn lined the back of her throat. A dizzy spell took over, and she grappled with a sudden bout of lightheadedness.

He presented her with his little-more-than-a-five-o'clock-shadowed cheek. Lips curling at the ends, a low, broken laugh slipped past his mouth. It was the worst sound in the world.

The bastard was enjoying this. He reveled in her repulsion.

She wanted to hit him. Punch him in the jaw. Scratch out his eyes, tear them loose from the sockets, watch the sinewy strands that connected them to his skull snap like overstretched taffy. This man was the source of her troubles, almost all of them. It was his fault her mother was a junkie. His fault Jewel had been held back in school, responsible for the nightly beatings that kept her out of class for days, weeks, until the bruises faded. His fault she'd grown up so hateful. He'd taught her to despise people who were different from her. People with different color skin, different cultures, different lifestyles, different preferences. He'd taught her to hate them all, and she was tired of it. The puddle of hate within had dried up, and she didn't want to be that person anymore. Too much energy had been spent on hate and she was exhausted.

But she didn't hit him. Didn't dislocate his jaw. Kept his eyes where they were, sunken in their sockets. She leaned in, pecked him on the coarse coating that covered his cheek, ensuring her lips didn't linger longer than necessary. In and out; she was done. Requirement fulfilled.

"That's nice," he said in that fraudulent voice. What he meant was, *You can do better, sweet pea. Much better, and I want to see it. Feel it. Do better, sweet pea. Do better.*

Before she could blink, she was across the room, inching toward the hallway. Her room was steps away. There, sanctuary waited for her, a temple of silence and inner reflection.

"Where you going, girl?" John Conti moved like he wanted off the couch but couldn't leave because of the beers. A drunken fog held him there, and for once Jewel was thankful for the invention of alcohol. "You don't want to catch up with your old man?" His eyelids fluttered, fending off a wave of drunken sleep.

"Do you really care?" she asked. "About me? About my life?"

The questions seemed to have some effect. His grin weakened, faded into the surrounding field of those grayish-white bristles. "Now, why would you say a thing like that, sweet pea?"

There was an opportunity here, she thought, to settle a few things. But one glance at Mother, the reddish hue that was beginning to color in her features, and she knew any more sass thrown her father's way would spark an argument. Or worse—a severe beating. Her father was capable of doing terrible things, things she had not forgotten about. Time may heal all wounds, but the mind is a catalogue of pain.

"Forget it," she said sheepishly. "May I be excused? I'm feeling…not good."

John looked to his wife. She glanced back, continuing to cook in the hatred for her own flesh and blood. Her face sizzled from all the nasty things circling her mind. Jewel could read her thoughts with perfect clarity. She didn't need psychic abilities; there was no hiding her thoughts, her intentions, not from her daughter. Her mother was as predictable as a Disney movie.

"Sure thing, sweet pea," John said. "You need time to process this, I understand. But when you're finished…searching your feelings or whatever the fuck it is you're gonna do in there…come on out. Talk to Daddy. It's been three years since I've seen you, and we have so much to say to each other."

Another cold grin. He sipped from his can of beer, let out some gas the loudest way possible, and then kicked back another sip.

"Yes, Daddy," she said, and turned, the two words leaving a poisonous aftertaste on her tongue.

"That's what I like to hear," he said, and although she couldn't see them, she knew his eyes were twinkling like the brightest stars in the night's summer sky.

2

In her room, she cried. She hugged the pillow against her face and screamed into it, a lung-clearing outburst that actually strained her esophagus. The cotton-stuffed fabric only suppressed so much, and she knew the harsh vocals had traveled down the hall, into the living room, where two monsters sat plotting more ways to ruin her life, keeping her from being the kid she was and the grownup she wanted to become.

They like this, she thought. *They enjoy seeing me like this. Down and out. They probably wish I would kill myself. It would be easier for them. Then they wouldn't go to jail for murder.*

Not for the first time, she thought about doing it. Not with a gun. She had never fired one and there were too many variables, too many ways she could fuck it up. The only thing worse than living with Ava and John Conti would be living with them as a disabled person. Or, worse yet, a semi-conscious vegetable, unable to leave when things got bad. Plus, breathing out of a tube for the rest of her life didn't sound all that attractive. She'd seen way too many news reports on botched suicide attempts via firearms.

There were other ways to do it, though. A razor blade down her wrist. *Down* being the operative word. Across wouldn't do much. It would open the right vein, sure, but it would take too long to empty, and the longer she bled, the more time she had to change her mind, get herself patched up. Cutting vertically was best. That ensured the vein would open and spill true. She would pass out long before she had the chance to second guess her terrible decision. There was always a good old-fashioned hanging. That was a sure-fire way to die, though she didn't like the idea of dangling from the end of a rope for thirty seconds. She could also overdose. Her parents had enough narcotics lying around the house to get the job done. But that didn't guarantee successful results, either. What if she didn't take enough? What if she survived? She was pretty sure her parents would be pissed; not because she tried to kill herself, but because she used up their stash.

As she wondered where she could snag a boxcutter from, a knock came at her window. Startled, she nearly fell off the bed. "Jesus Christ!" She gripped her pillow, ready to hurl it at whoever was playing peeping Tom.

It was Adam. One of his hands waved excitedly while the other combed his messy but perfect hair. A remnant of a smile touched his lips, a nervous greeting she was actually happy to see. Before she went to the window, she checked over her shoulder, listened for one of her neglectful parents to come barging in. Of course, that didn't happen. She could have screamed bloody murder, and they'd probably just wait it out and collect the body later.

She opened the window, just a crack at first, thinking he owed her an explanation.

"Hi," he said, his smile spreading.

"Hi," she said awkwardly. If her father caught a boy outside her window, there would be hell to pay. He'd have no reservations about beating the shit out of a minor. Small potatoes compared to his other offenses. "What are you doing here?" She kept her voice low, making sure she couldn't be heard over the living-room television, which continued to replay reruns of *M*A*S*H*, her father's favorite. It was a John Conti tradition whenever he came home from a jail stint—cheap beer and *M*A*S*H* marathons.

"I wanted to see you," he replied sweetly. "Make sure you were okay."

"I'm fine."

"You didn't look it."

"Well, I am now."

"Positive?"

She wanted to tell him the truth, but it was too heavy, too thick to lay on him. He was a nice boy, a sweet kid, and she didn't want to burden him any more than she already had. She especially didn't want to confide in him her thoughts of suicide.

"Yeah, why?"

He shrugged in a cute way. "I don't know. You look…off."

"My father just got out of prison."

"Oh." This was news he clearly wasn't expecting. She could tell by the way his brow arched, the way his eyes popped. "Well, that's… Is that good?"

"Not really."

"Interesting. Well… I'm sorry to hear that?"

The way he delivered that last line in the form of a question made her titter. "Are you?"

"Of course. I hate to see people in distress."

"You're a good person, you know that?"

He shrugged, news he already knew. "Yeah, I've been told."

"I'm not a good person, Adam. Not even close."

"Jewel…"

"What? I'm not."

"What happened to turning your life around?"

Her eyes flicked off elsewhere.

"Come on. You're not…" He looked around, waving his hand as if he were presenting everything around him as a gift. "You're not *this*. This doesn't define who you are."

"How do you know?"

"Because… I see the good in you. Fritz sees the good in you."

Fritz. She'd almost forgotten about him. He'd been the one who called the cops. She was pretty sure of it. After her anger simmered, she realized she'd treated him a bit too harshly. He'd been gracious enough to let her lay low for as long as he had.

"Shit."

"What is it?"

"Fritz. I was an asshole to him."

Adam nodded, smirked. "Yeah, he, uh, told me."

"He did?"

"Yeah. He actually wanted to come here himself but thought it would be a bad idea."

"I need to apologize."

Adam waved off the idea. "He knows you didn't mean it."

"Still…"

"Look. I have to go. Why don't you drop by the youth center later? We'll hang out. I'll kick your butt in ping pong again."

"Pssh. You wish you could beat me."

"Maybe I'll let you win again then?"

She found her smile once again, and for the first time she realized it had been Adam who'd brought it out—her happy. Happiness, for her, wasn't a place or a thing—it was a person.

It was Adam.

"Yeah, I'll see if I can escape."

"Jewel!" her father shouted.

"Shit." She rushed to shut the window, closed the blinds, and then hopped on the bed. Lying down, she pretended to be resting.

The door slammed open, and her father's wavering statue appeared in the doorway, his eyes scanning the room for uninvited guests. "Someone in here with you?"

"Jesus, Dad. No."

"You sure?" He sniffed as if there were foreign scents in the air. "Smells off in here."

That was funny coming from him.

"Dad, there's no one in here with me. You want to check under the bed?"

At first he didn't move. But after a few seconds, he moseyed over and got down on his hands and knees. He was slow to do so, the all-day drinking clearly having its effect.

"Jesus Christ," she muttered. "Are you serious?"

He rose from the floor, glaring at her angrily. "I don't like *liars*, Jewel." He'd spat his way through most of that sentence.

"I'm not lying to you."

"If I find out you been sneaking boys in here..." He flashed his puffy, diseased gums and rotting teeth.

"I haven't been sneaking boys in here."

"You better drop the attitude, missy." His finger migrated to his belt, and he began fingering the buckle loose. "You remember what happens when you give me attitude."

Her eyes fell to his waist. "Sorry, Daddy."

His finger lingered there, and she held her breath, waiting for the moment to pass.

"Yeah," he said, a smile taking over his lips. "Yeah, you remember all right."

His hands fell to his sides, and she could breathe again.

"Don't make me remind you double good, y'hear?"

She nodded.

He left without speaking another word. After he left, she buried her head in the pillow and cried some more, mentally going through the places she could snag that boxcutter from.

3

Alphie Moffit awoke on a sandy bank, cold water lapping at his ear. Every muscle felt aflame, and lifting his head was one of the hardest tasks he had ever accomplished. The picturesque nature before him was edging toward nightfall. The sun shot streaks of tangerine and strokes of lavender out among the knobby collections of clouds. Dark bruises and pale starlight invaded the sky from the east.

Alphie sat up, taking in his wooded surroundings. He had no idea where he was or how he'd gotten here. Here, being near the outskirts of town, somewhere along the infamous Red River, he guessed. The last thing he recalled was seeing those kids, seeing the Mother's bold attack, the spread of her deadly infection. Alphie stumbled to his feet, hoping it had been a terrible dream, a nightmare from which he'd soon awake. But the truth was, it wasn't a nightmare. He knew that deep down, though a part of him remained hopeful that these memories were false, that reality was not the terrible sequences his brain projected.

His feet failed him, and he tripped, staggered into a tree, but used the trunk to keep himself upright. The woods blurred before him, a hazy layer that refused to lift from his vision.

In the near distance he spotted a cave. Sage-green garland dangled out front, covering the entrance, but not enough to block anyone or anything from trespassing the threshold. For some reason, Alphie was drawn to the opening, compelled to continue toward the dark mouth, eager to discover what horrors lived inside. There was nothing he wanted more than to encroach on the inky egress, wrap the darkness around him like a jacket and snuggle the unknown. There was something comforting about the cave, something familiar, like an old home you could always come back to, time and time again. Something about this slice of darkness in the middle of nowhere recharged him, rejuvenated his aching bones, injected life into his tired and torn muscles. The closer he grew, the more energy he was awarded.

Come to me, something called. *Almost there. I can feel you. Can you feel me?*

He could. He could feel a tugging at his chest, an invisible rope coiling around his heart and towing him along.

In seconds he was pushing aside the dangling foliage, melting into the dark. It was like passing beneath a waterfall; the absence of light cleansing his soul, absolving his sins. Deeper into the dark he traveled, until the light behind him was all but gone. His eyes adjusted after a while, and he could make out portions of his new environment, the craggy nature of the cavern's walls, the uneven terrain beneath his feet.

A few more paces and he bumped his head on a low-hanging stalactite. He knocked his head pretty good, enough to summon a few black stars against the already-dark backdrop of the cave. It was nothing more than a brief delay. He followed the unknown path deeper and deeper, twisting and turning, using his hands to feel along the walls, until he reached a clearing.

There was light here; torches, seven of them. Where they'd come from and who'd put them there, Alphie did not know. For some reason, he seemed to recall putting the torches there himself, but he couldn't be sure, not one hundred percent. These days, nothing was certain, and there were enough false memories rattling around his head that it was hard to decipher what he'd done and what had been done by the Mother.

Welcome. The greeting had come from within his own head, but the voice did not belong to him.

He shuffled to the center of the clearing, scanning the high-arching walls of the sizable chamber. Over him, stalactites hung like deformed dog teeth. The musty smell of the room filled his nostrils and seeped into his lungs. Crumbles of bedrock had scattered across the ground, suggesting erosion of the ceiling above. He wondered about the safety of this place, about being here for an extended length of time. Sensing the ceiling could topple at any moment, he searched the area, trying to find the reason he'd been invited here, the purpose behind his journey into the center of this cavern on the outskirts of town.

That was when he noticed he wasn't alone. In the rock columns connecting the floor to the ceiling, he saw bodies, several of them, molded into the formations.

Bodies. Actual human forms.

It was odd to say the least. They had amalgamated with the natural material, becoming one with the rock like some grotesque 3D painting. Alphie marveled at what he saw, wondering how such macabre displays were even possible. Arms and legs protruding from beneath the rugged surfaces, moving languidly like primitive animatronics. He noticed there were five people total, all of them older.

Adults.

They were mostly faceless, their identities unknown, save for one of them. Alphie recognized the man from a photo in the local paper from a month back. One of the chemical plant workers who'd gone missing—Lenny Howell. His eyes were open, wide, staring—at what, Alphie hadn't the slightest clue. Something that wasn't inside the cave. Something that lived inside his mind.

Something he was dreaming.

The prisoners of this hellish institution were all making noises, sucking sounds, but with their lungs and not their mouths. Like they were breathing past some obstruction in their throat. *Wind,* Alphie thought. *They sound like wet gusts of wind.* Five separate blasts of air going off at once, the howling kind, almost wolf-like. The noise caused his spine to run cold with an awful shiver. He knew he shouldn't have come here, should have resisted the call—this was a bad place where bad things happened. He could feel it in his bones, a sick sensation that claimed his marrow.

You can't run, warned the voice within. *This is where you live now.*

He dropped to his knees, the weight of this place too much to carry. His vision fell upon the dirt, a metallic object that was surprisingly bright considering the frail light the torches provided. Fingers probing the hard surface, he began brushing the earthy dust away.

It was a pipe. A large one. As he uncovered more of the tubular shape, he noticed the pipe ran across the entire chamber, evenly dissecting the room. A little farther down the line, he saw something sticking up from the ground, another pipe, only smaller and thinner.

The abstract shape of a woman stood behind it, her arms and legs wrapped around the paint-chipped, rust-eaten metal extension, as if she were a firefighter sliding down the house pole. He hadn't noticed her before; the shadows hid their kind well and she was one with their dimness.

After dismounting the pipe, she planted her feet in the dirt and stepped away from the shadows, though a dark shape seemed to follow her, a loyal companion born of shade. Her golden eyes glimmered, sparkling like polished coins. A dark liquid had been slathered over her flesh, coating every inch of her. Like she'd taken a bath in the filth of whatever ran through those pipes, whatever disgusting concoction the plant pumped through, around, and into the town. As she got closer, a new smell conquered the air. This was a strong odor, one he could feel invading his nasal cavities, seeking passage into his brain.

Stepping into the flickering torchlight, he could see the liquid held a bluish quality to it, a dark denim color that was almost black. *Almost*. It dripped from her, and there was so much of it. A trail of dark blue followed her, every step a waterfall of indigo secretion.

She walked as if she'd broken both her ankles, each step as awkward as the one before it. Alphie thought she'd fall for sure. But miraculously, the gods of this place were on her side, and she kept her balance the entire way.

She stood before him, her hypnotic gaze forcing him to stand perfectly still. He watched helplessly as she gripped the sides of his face with both hands, smearing the dark-blue ink across his cheeks and ears. Staring into the Mother's eyes, he caught a glimpse of the future, a town in ruin. *Hooperstown*, that little slice of heaven a stone's throw away from the Jersey shore. Though, this was not some suburban paradise, not anymore. The skies had grayed over, sick with perpetual storms. In the streets, the gutters were lined with the dead—adults and kids alike, their bodies covered in open sores, oozing with decay, eyes stretched wide with their final look at the grim, world. Hordes of flies buzzed with delight as they colonized the departed. It looked like something had spilled across the lawns and sidewalks, slick puddles of oil that ran off and formed rivers, although Alphie knew it wasn't oil—it was the same dark ink that covered the Mother's body.

In a snap, the vision disappeared. He was back in the cave, the Mother of Dead Dreams leering at him, her lips twisting with endless hate. He felt threatened, as if she wanted to end his life, but also…he felt needed. She wasn't done with him. Not yet. There was still work to do, and perhaps there would come a day when she no longer required his services, when she would destroy him like any good god would a worthless abomination.

But that day was not today.

She stepped aside and his vision fell on the vertical pipe, specifically the opening at the top. He heard the rush of turbulent water and felt a rumble beneath his feet. He realized he was standing on the main pipe that led to the chemical plant and traveled underneath the town.

Do it, the Mother said without moving her lips. That magnetic pull tugged on him once again, summoning him toward the pipe. The world around him became dreamlike all at once, and he found himself floating on ahead, his stomach rumbling, the contents within threatening to rise up and make itself known. He watched his hands grip the pipe on both sides. His head hovered over the opening, looking down. The sounds of liquid tumbling through the pipeline were loud, too loud for him to concentrate on anything else, but he couldn't see anything inside. It was dark. It was hard to tell if there was really something happening down there or if this was a product of his imagination. The smell made things clearer; it was real. All of it. The chemicals within made his eyes tear, water, burn. The inside of his skull felt like someone had started a bonfire on his cerebral cortex.

Then, he felt it. The rush up his throat, the sudden wave of nausea, his stomach ascending. Out of his mouth, an ichorous substance exploded forth. His aim wasn't perfect, but the majority of the purge made it down the tube, into the main. Another wave broke on him and another round of vomiting commenced, the dark liquid sputtering past his lips. He heaved again and again, purging his body, filling the pipeline with his sickness.

Not his.

Hers.

He felt awful, and not from the vomiting or the intermittent bouts of nausea—he felt awful for being a contributor, for allowing the Mother to use him as a vessel for her disease. She'd passed the scourge onto him, and he onto the town.

Twice more he threw up. Then, the five people who'd been suspended above him, fixed to the columns of rock, began to break free from their confinements. The hard material that once restricted their movement immediately grew soft and jellylike. The rock stretched like chewed taffy, and it didn't take them long to free themselves from their temporary prisons. Alphie watched them slide down the columns, to the cave's floor. Like cattle headed to the house of slaughter, they ambled over to the pipe, each carrying a belly full of their own sickness. Like him, they released their disease upon the dying city, puking their inky guts into the main. One by one, after they were finished, they fell to the side. Rolling in the muddy, clay-like earth, they squirmed, holding their stomachs, continuing to make those awful noises, howling like tiny windstorms.

Alphie joined the howling, the noises involuntary. He hated every moment of it. He wished for death to come sweep him off his feet and carry him away, toward the light.

A light that didn't exist in this place.

Then the chamber began to spin.

He passed out before the Mother could hook her claws into him. Before she could send him on his next task.

4

Several days later, when Jessie Di Falco got home from basketball practice, he went immediately for the sink, filling his water bottle from the tap. Cocking back his head, he squirted a stream of cold water down his throat. The beverage was refreshing, just the perfect temperature. Not warm. But not cold enough to give him brain-freeze. Rehydrated, he went to the freezer to make himself some pizza rolls. Dinner wouldn't happen for a few hours and he couldn't wait. Plus, he'd earned that snack on the court, scoring twelve points during the scrimmage, nabbing six boards and compiling four assists. All of that in only twenty minutes of action.

Killed it today, he told himself, satisfied with the stat sheet's final results.

Mrs. Di Falco raided the fridge for vegetables and told him she was going to make a special dinner, a home-cooked feast, a rarity due to the Di Falco's consistently busy lives. They were hardly ever home together. Between Mrs. Di Falco's part-time job, Mr. Di Falco's full-time job, and the kids always off with their friends or participating in sports, quality time together had taken a hit.

Tonight would be different though. A call back to those family nights. Dinner, maybe even a movie. Mr. Di Falco was due home at five, Mrs. Di

Falco was off, Jimmy wasn't manning the candy stand on the boardwalk, and Jesse was home early from practice and didn't have any plans to hang out with friends. Tonight was perfect for a good ol' fashioned feast. Spaghetti and meatballs. Mussels and linguini. Penne Vodka. Stuffed eggplant. A real smorgasbord of their favorite meals.

Special.

Jesse rushed up to his room, stripped off his clothes—which had that odd, old-locker-room funk emanating from them—and hopped in the shower. It was while he stood in the tub, underneath the blast of hot, steamy water, that he began to feel a little lightheaded. More so than usual. It wasn't abnormal to feel sluggish after a practice or a game, especially when he hadn't eaten much throughout the day and gone hard on the court, but this— this was different. The tub surround literally shifted, spun in carousel-like fashion. His arms instinctively shot out, his hands gripping the shower doors' rail. Lowering himself to his knees, he braced against a shooting, stabbing abdominal pain. Like someone had taken sharp, serrated blades and repeatedly jabbed them into his stomach. The pain was so bad he shouted, barking as the agony tore through his midsection. The unwelcome sensation toured his body like a rampant rollercoaster coming off the tracks, heading in unpredictable directions.

He opened his mouth and a spray of dark blue ink shot forth, coating the shower doors. The sickness was immediately washed away by the water pressure, dissolving, becoming naturally lighter from the cleanse. But nothing washed away the anguish within.

Everything spun and Jesse turned, sliding down on his bottom with his back against the tub's ceramic wall. He ended up curling into a ball. Gripping his stomach, he hurled again, an explosion of midnight blue fanning out, splattering against the tub. He began to whimper softly, mostly from the pain, but also because of the unknown, the mystery surrounding this sudden sickness.

Also, because he felt like he was dying.

Another violent gush spewed out of his mouth, and he spent the next five minutes hunched over the drain, the water pouring off him, feeling like he would vomit again. When the spell was over, he sat up, wiped his mouth, and stared at the dark smear until the water washed it away.

He saw a shape in the funny, inky smears, the way some religious fanatics think they see the Virgin Mary in a coffee stain. But this wasn't the Virgin Mary, though. This was Mother.

And she was angry.

5

An hour before the youth center opened its doors to the troubled children of Hooperstown, James Fritz stepped inside the building and flipped on the lights. The place was just as he'd left it—pretty clean from the night before. Adam had stayed late to help clean up; they had thrown a massive pizza party, celebrating some of the members' birthdays, some of which had passed, some of which were forthcoming. The garbage bags were sitting in a pile next to the door, waiting to be taken out on trash day, which wasn't until tomorrow. He'd have some of the volunteers take it to the curb, just so the place didn't start to culminate that party-trash odor.

He set down his bag, coffee too, and started taking down the chairs from the tables, placing them on the ground. After he cleared a whole table, he heard something shift, scrape against the concrete floor.

Turning his ear to the corner of the room, he focused his gaze, keeping an eye out for movement of any kind. The haunting feeling that he was not alone alighted on his shoulders, causing a cold sensation to trickle down his arms.

"Hello?" His eyes slimmed. The anticipation of what he might find was killing him. An invisible wrench turned his heart like a screw.

Then, it happened. Movement. A quick blur. A ghost of a shape. Behind the stacks of unused chairs, a large shadow shuffled. A body. A person, living and breathing. Not once had he come to the center and found a squatter, though Ben Draper, another group leader, said he'd seen a homeless guy camping in the woods out back. Fritz had never seen anyone back there. Rumors of a whole community of homeless living in tents had circled the town's rumor mill over the years, but he had never seen the evidence himself. Which didn't mean it wasn't true, but Fritz had trouble believing in things he could not see.

Like God?

Yes, exactly like God. Even though the youth center, where he spent the majority of his summer, was Christian-based, James Fritz hadn't devoted a single second to prayer. Not since he was old enough to think for himself. With great pleasure he had shed the beliefs his parents tried to instill in him as a small child, stopped believing in the Almighty around the same time he discovered Santa Claus had been his parents playing make-believe once a year. That the whole charade of a fat man squeezing down the chimney was all just a clever ploy to get kids to walk the line year-long, and he had assumed the stories of God were no different.

Yes, James Fritz was not a believer in things he could not see, but today...today felt different.

"Hello?" he asked the visitor, who continued to shield itself behind the chairs. "I see you. You can come out now. Make this easy on both of us so I don't have to call the cops."

As he got closer, he saw the visitor had long hair. Curly. Falling at the shoulders. A girl. A teenager, he suspected. She had her head buried between her knees, her identity remaining a secret, but Fritz suspected he knew the intruder.

"Jewel?" he asked, straightening his posture, placing his hands on his hips. "Jewel, you can come out now."

She didn't move.

He shuffled his feet but kept his position. The last thing he wanted was to spook her. She already hated him, and—if he was being honest—for good reason. He had betrayed her, even if she hadn't left him with much of a choice. He couldn't let her disappear and walk the streets alone, allow her to become another runaway. At least at home she'd have a roof over her head and wouldn't go hungry. At least she wouldn't die. If Olivia ever found out he had let her go—or shit—*helped* her run away, then she'd divorce him in a second.

He took her feelings into consideration as he approached. In the event she was on drugs or some mind-altering substance, a sudden advance in her direction might put her on the defensive. Might cause her to act irrationally or violently. Or both. That was how people got hurt in these situations. Fear makes people violent. Fear gets people hurt.

He didn't want to get hurt.

"Jewel, come out from behind there. Whatever it is, we can talk about it. Are you okay? I know you probably hate me for—"

The figure rose but kept her head down, laser-focused at whatever was going on around her feet. Black tangles of hair dangled in front of her, continuing to conceal her identity. The girl's clothes were dirty; dusty-dark smears decorated her pale-yellow blouse. As he got a better look at her, Fritz realized the young girl, the intruder, wasn't Jewel Conti.

"Who are you?" he asked, a rush of adrenaline causing his legs to run numb. "How did you get in here?"

She lifted her gaze. Swollen back eyes containing golden circles beamed at him. Now his whole body went numb, the shock of seeing…well, whatever it was he was seeing. A ghost? This girl was so pale she looked like a corpse. Tilting her head sideways, her hair fell away, and for the first time Fritz got a clear look at her face.

He recognized her.

"Holy shit," he said, stumbling backward. It was Lauren Sullivan.

Lauren Sullivan who had *died*, passed on from her short battle with leukemia. He'd read about her death in the paper no more than two hours ago, had almost choked on his bagel with cream cheese as he did so. It highlighted some of the other children who had gotten sick over the last few weeks, shifting the focus away from them and toward the big question— who was responsible for this mess? The writer concentrated on making the claim that Hooperstown Chemical was the leading suspect, that they were solely responsible for the town's sudden rampant sickness. There were even whispers of a class-action lawsuit, that there was enough evidence to file one, and that the claim was beginning to garnish national attention. Apparently the cancer cluster had a page-two mention in *USA Today*.

But all of this didn't matter, not now. Because right now, James Fritz was staring at something that shouldn't be.

He was staring at a dead girl.

"I…" he managed, but nothing more.

She moved from behind the chairs, walking on wobbly knees, feet that were barely able to support her weight. Not that she had much. Her frail frame was mostly skin and bones, lacking definition. She hadn't been that bony during the school year, Fritz was sure of it.

The gold rings that made up Lauren's eyes fixed on Fritz's, and he found himself powerless to look away. He wanted to. God, he felt like he *needed to*. As if staring into those dark, inky pools and bright burning rings were like watching something forbidden unfold. There was something sinister about those eyes, and...*ancient*. Otherworldly. He was trespassing uncharted waters here, embarking on a journey from which there would be no return.

"Lau—"

He started to speak the girl's name, but she made a noise, a feral grunt, and he stopped. Watched her walk over. Watched her arms extend, her fingers touching the shirt buttons covering his chest. He immediately felt sick inside, like his organs had decayed and turned to rot. Like cancerous mold had taken root and grown within him, spread throughout his body. His veins felt stuffed with sickness, the lack of blood flow causing a spell of lightheadedness. A dizzying spin overtook him, and he stumbled sideways.

You are mine now...

The girl had spoken, but the words had not come from her mouth. The voice was in his head. He felt violated, as if some sacred line had been crossed. A line *she* had crossed, entering his head, accessing his thoughts without permission. She was inside him, probing around, sifting through his memories and everything he held there. Every secret. Every little piece of information that made him, every fiber of his being.

She went through it like a stack of mail.

You will find her...

Who? he asked.

You know her name. She will be mine. She hurts as I hurt. She is in pain, and I will free her.

He knew the name, knew it before he had to ask. *Jewel*.

She will be my daughter. She will be my truth. And she will be your disease. She will grow inside you all. As will I.

Fritz began to cry.

The last thing he saw before blacking out was a vision of Lauren Sullivan mounting him, opening her jaw impossibly wide, and a rush of some dark, sap-like substance exploding forth.

Then, impenetrable black.

Nothing else.

CHAPTER TWELVE

All of My Children

1

When Liam Rooker awoke that morning, he knew something was different about the world. He could sense it the same way he sensed classmates sneaking up behind him, kids who meant to tack a "kick me" sign to his backpack and enjoy a good laugh at his expense. The day ahead was much like those demoralizing occasions, only bigger, stronger, more foreboding.

He threw off the bedsheets, got dressed, went about his morning, feeding the cats and getting the daily newspaper for his parents (who were still asleep and probably would be 'til around noon). They were off today and usually took advantage of those precious days to catch up on their "beauty rest" (their term, not his). Not that Liam minded. He found good use for that *alone* time, watching cartoons or playing video games. In a little more than a month, he'd be back at school, dealing with the usual shit—loads of homework, dodging bullies, avoiding interaction with girls at any cost. Only, next year he'd be in high school and those problems would be magnified times a thousand.

Liam was dreading the ninth grade. Like most kids, he wished for an endless summer. Begged, actually. To whom? Well, whoever would listen. He often prayed for it, not that his family was a religious bunch. No, not even close. But he knew about God, the illusionary gifts He offered in exchange for good behavior and the occasional one-way conversation. He'd been known to reach out to the Big Man Upstairs from time to time, you know, to ask for the important things in life; good Christmas presents, birthday gifts, passing grades, and a clear path home from school sans the regular local bullies.

Important *kid* things.

Today he prayed that summer would never end and, lo and behold, someone answered. The prayer had been sent off in the morning while his parents were sleeping, and it was answered later when they were outside doing yard work, pulling weeds from the garden and watering the plants and flowers. He was indoors playing a video game, *Diddy Kong Racing*—his personal favorite. He was on a quest to beat the game for the third time. For some reason, he never got bored of that one.

A knock sounded on the front door. Liam paused the game on a boss level, a boat race against a giant, curmudgeonly octopus, and pushed himself off the couch. The door was right around the corner from the living room, and, before he could set eyes on it, another knock came, same cadence as before.

"Be there in a second!" he called out, and then added, "Geez" under his breath.

Liam went to the door and opened it. The man standing on the front porch inspired a pang of fear in Liam's chest, his appearance oddly off and unsettling. He recognized the guy from something his dad had shown him in last Sunday's paper, an article about the strange disappearances of a couple of chemical plant workers. Joe Frusco was his name, if memory and the photograph from the paper served correctly, and now he was standing before Liam, looking quite strange. Looking...

Alien?

He didn't want to say it, or hell—even think it—but Frusco looked like he'd just stepped off an alien spacecraft. A sickly green tone dominated his skin. A dark liquid leaked from almost every facial orifice, but in smears rather than streams. As if it were blood that had stopped bleeding some time ago and the evidence of the incident hadn't been cleaned up yet. The stained skin didn't seem to bother Frusco—in fact, nothing seemed to. His eyes wandered behind Liam, looking down the hall and into the kitchen.

"Where are your parents, little one?" he asked, his voice rough and almost inhuman. Liam squinted at his face, noticing something else that begged to be discussed. Fleshy knots had sprouted on his cheeks, little growths that had...*blossomed?*

No, that couldn't be right. But it was. He squinted, leaned forward and had himself a better, closer look.

Sure enough, Liam saw malignancies flowering on his cheek, something with petals and a solid center.

Impossible, he thought. *And disgusting.*

But at the same time...pretty neat. He scanned the man's face once again, noticed two more aberrations, one near his hairline, the other under his left ear. Little sprouts begging for water and sustenance, pleading for life and the chance to bloom into something magnificent.

"Where are they?" Frusco snapped. He bared his teeth and each whitish nugget was outlined in midnight green fluids. Liam couldn't help but think of chlorophyll, the pigment he had learned about in science class last year.

"Out back," he answered, jerking his finger toward the back door. "Gardening."

Joe Frusco snarled, his upper lip quivering with subdued rage.

A clear sense of danger brushed over Liam. He went to close the door in Frusco's face, but he was too late, his internal alarm a few seconds delayed. Frusco wedged his foot between the door and the jamb, stopping the momentum immediately. Liam turned to run, opened his mouth to call out to his parents, but Frusco, God damn him, was faster. One arm wrapped around Liam's waist, the other bringing a hand to his mouth, hiding his scream from the world.

Liam fought, kicked, punched, but to no avail. He found himself floating away from his house. Down the porch. Across the lawn. Into the patch of woods across the street. He screamed into Frusco's hand, but it did nothing to help him. There were no neighbors out and about, everyone staying inside, avoiding the oppressive July heat. There was nothing he could have done to stop the abduction.

As Frusco carried him off deeper into the woods, the world began to smell different. It reeked of earth and mold, the slow rot of a failing ecosystem, and almost certain death. The smell overtook him, causing a slight moment of overwhelming dizziness, forcing him to enter a foreign realm of infinite blackness.

He woke up sometime later in his bed, feeling like he'd come down with a severe case of the flu. Sweating profusely. Nausea. His bones aching as if he'd worked them into a state past utter exhaustion. Every muscle hurting to the touch. Under his fingernails, he noticed something growing, something green, something *alien*.

His mother and father were standing over him, talking to each other, arguing about what to do next. He couldn't hear them. The world was silent save for a distant ringing. An incessant beeping. He could read their lips though. Words like *hospital* and *doctors* and *cancer* were mentioned, almost within the same breath as each other.

Liam closed his eyes. It felt good, tremendously effective in staving off the bouts of nausea. As he slept, he dreamed he was a tree, growing in the center of a dying planet. Above him, a giant watering pot tipped, spilling freshets of clear water over him. The pot was handled by an enormous woman, a towering giant who walked among the stars, the cosmos, the distant planets. As she watered him, she smiled, a calming interaction which brought warmth to his wooden bones.

Her name was Mother and he called her such.

Brennan Scruggs sat on a lawn chair in his father's garage, cracking open one of the old man's beers, a Miller High Life. The son of a bitch was at work, pulling long hours at the hospital, doing whatever doctors do, and his mother was out at spin class, whipping her already-hot bod into better shape.

Fucking slut, and he knew it was wrong to think that way about her, but he couldn't help it. He knew why she was off working hard on sculpting her toned body—so she could flaunt her skin whenever the opportunity presented itself, which was every time she left the house. He wondered why his father allowed her to wear such skimpy outfits in public. He couldn't figure it out, why he would want his wife showing off her legs, bare shoulders, outfits that left very little to the imagination. Whenever they went to the supermarket, he could see every eye follow his mother—the men full of desire, the women, jealousy—every lingering stare. It enraged him. A part of him wanted to beat every motherfucker who mentally undressed his mom, but also, a part of him wanted to pistol-whip his father for allowing it to happen.

Why? Why did he do it?

Brennan was ninety-nine percent convinced she was cheating on the old man, anyway. She'd disappear for hours at a time, claiming she was just "going to the gym," and probably, sometimes, that was true. But twice? Three times in one day? Nah, that didn't add up. No one worked out that much, and as good as his mom looked (*barf*), there was no way she was hitting the weights that often. No one had that much energy.

Brennan crushed another empty can in his fist and tossed the aluminum carcass into a black plastic garbage bag. After he reached a nice buzz, he planned on taking the garbage deep into the woods to destroy the evidence. His father's mini fridge was always packed with beer, so he probably wouldn't notice if a few went missing, but he'd grow suspicious if there were suddenly a bunch of empties lying around.

Before he shuffled back over to his father's stash, he heard a knock on the door that led to the side of the house.

Shit! Did someone know he was in here? No, that was impossible. His mother had left only fifteen minutes ago and his father, due to the influx of sick kids, was pretty much living at the hospital. No one else would drop by, no one that mattered anyway. The only person he hung out with on a regular basis was Dakota, but that douche-stick was home, feeling "under the weather." His words. Brennan figured his best friend would be back on his feet in a couple of days, and then the two could plot some havoc. There was also Jewel, but since their little spat, she hadn't been seen or heard from.

Good riddance, he thought. Jewel was always dragging them down, anyway. She'd been cruel to other kids in their grade, sure, and that was pretty entertaining, some of the stuff she'd done to them. Like the one time she'd given Ben Treadway a wedgie so bad his tighty-whities ripped free, and she had paraded the shit-stained rags around the entire playground, showing off her accomplishment to the entire sixth grade. Ben's family moved away not long after that and Brennan couldn't help but think that little incident had something to do with it.

Fuck Jewel, though. She had changed so much since then. Hell, she'd changed so much over the last six months. It was after Christmas break, he supposed, that she'd gotten really weird. Less mean. Less abusive to the other students. She'd calmed down a lot, not wanting to take part in the usual hazing, tormenting kids on their way home from school. She used to revel in chasing kids through the woods, threatening to break their bones if they were ever caught. The fear she'd instilled in those little pukes used to excite her. Fill her with a sense of purpose.

But not anymore.

Cunt. Brennan thought. *Big fucking cuntlicker.*

He wouldn't have been so mad about her decision to turn over a new leaf if he didn't like her. But he did like her. Too much, he thought. In the *more-than-friends* way, something he promised himself he wouldn't do. He'd had feelings for her going back to the fifth grade. She was his first crush, and because of this, he lacked the ability to express himself properly. He didn't tell a single soul that he crushed hard on Jewel Conti, not even Dakota. Part of the reason he didn't tell his best friend was because he thought Dakota felt similarly, that he had a thing for her too, and he didn't want their dynamic to grow into some clichéd love triangle that would surely end with the two of them throwing down for the love of their lives. Fuck that soap opera bullshit.

Another knock sounded on the door. Brennan remained frozen in the lawn chair, unable to find the strength to get up.

"Hey," a voice said. A female. A girl.

Jewel.

"Can we talk?"

Was it Jewel? It sounded like her, sort of. But also not. Maybe because the door was between them.

"Jewel?" he asked, setting down his beer.

A brief pause. "Yeah, it's me," the girl said, sounding unsure.

Curious, Brennan rose from his chair. "What are you doing here?" He brushed off some potato chip crumbs that had landed on his shirt. "I thought you didn't want to talk to us anymore?"

Another pause, which raised some red flags, but Brennan ignored any and all warnings. This was Jewel here, and if there was a chance he could get back into her good graces, he was willing to throw caution to the wind. Whatever it took to make things right, he would do it.

"I... I just want to talk." The voice was small, lacking confidence. Very un-Jewel. She had always been a girl who knew what she wanted; whatever she desired, she went out and got. He'd expected her to answer, "Open the door, shithead." But what he got was a timid, apologetic response that—quite honestly—soured the moment.

"Why would I want to talk to you, *Cunti*?" He made sure to speak with venom.

"I want to...make things...right. Better."

Why was she talking like that?

"Don't *you*?" The innocence in her voice was starting to piss him off.

He marched over to the door, gripped the knob, twisted, and pulled hard.

A figure stood in the doorway, but not the one he had been led to believe would be there.

It wasn't Jewel.

It was Carol Bentley, a girl a year younger than him. He knew her because she lived on his street, and his father had mentioned her over a family dinner a little less than a week ago.

She was one of the sick kids.

He backed away, his first instinct to retreat. She didn't belong here. She belonged in the hospital, resting, trying to get better. Not here. And why *was* she here? They had absolutely no interaction over the years, except for the few times they made eye contact when Carol was in her driveway playing with her friends, chalking the blacktop or riding scooters. She had always been driven to school because the Bentleys were weird and didn't want their daughter being subjected to the stuff that happened on the school's public transportation system.

"What are you—"

Carol rushed into the room, her eyes blazing, two golden ovals that burned brighter than the sun. It was almost blinding. He forced himself to look away, but it wasn't easy.

"Look at me," Carol said, still trying to mimic Jewel's voice. "You want me, don't you?"

He couldn't avoid her gaze for long. Something within her eyes called to him, compelled him to face her. Giving into the temptation, his eyes locked onto hers. There was no breaking their gaze now; their connection was concrete. He felt strange, looking at her, peering into those glowing pools of radiant light. The golden shine took him by surprise, and he felt captivated by their brilliance. It infiltrated him, his body. Squirmed through him, like everything beneath his flesh was dirt and whatever she'd planted inside him was growing, the roots taking hold, spreading upward toward the surface.

And it felt good. Sort of. A tingling of peace that massaged its way into his muscles from his neck on down.

"You want to kiss me," Carol said, her Jewel-like voice suddenly unraveling, becoming very unlike Jewel's. "You want to sex with me?"

Sex with me? Brennan thought, the strange way of putting it snapping him out of the feel-good state, a reprieve he hoped was temporary. He thought those few seconds might be his only opportunity to escape. Whatever was happening here, it wasn't good. As if the glowing golden eyes weren't enough indication, then the strange growths that had populated on the girl's face were the determining factor—she was sick, all right. From what, exactly, Brennan hadn't the foggiest. He wondered if his old man had any clue, either.

He studied her face, the flowery extensions that had bloomed on her flesh. Little pink petals extended from her cheeks, four separate instances, placed evenly apart. One on her forehead, one on each cheek, and one on her chin. He couldn't help but think if he traced lines, connected the dots so to speak, that they would form a cross. He wondered if the peculiar growths held some religious implications. Probably not. Probably coincidence. Either way, the small pink petals freaked him out. He went to back away, refusing to allow himself to catch whatever this girl was infected with, when he tripped over the lawn chair.

He went down on his elbows. Pain shot through his arms, needles stabbing his fingertips.

The girl was on him. Straddling him. Holding him down, forcing his shoulders against the bare concrete. She was strong, a lot stronger than he was, which also seemed improbable. No, scratch that—*impossible*. She was a girl, a scrawny one, and he was a dude, one who wasn't particularly buff, but he should have been stronger than her. Yet she had the strength of not only an older boy, but an older man.

"*Sex with me,*" she said, her voice warbled and deep, sounding very unlike Jewel now, unlike Carol Bentley, and unlike any human Brennan had ever interacted with before. "*Sex with me now, Brennan. Don't you want to? Oh, Brennan, make me sex with you.*"

He struggled under the pressure she applied, kicking out his legs, seeking leverage of any kind. It was like being trapped underneath a car, the weight of her pressing down on him. Moving her proved to be an impossible feat, and within minutes he surrendered and lay still, waiting for her to do whatever she came here to do.

Sex?

For whatever reason, Brennan understood that sex to her did not mean what it meant to him.

She opened her mouth and stuck out her tongue, only the expected pink, muscular extension did not come forth. It was brown and wood-like, rough like tree bark. Not stiff, but fleshy. Slimy. Something viscous dripped from its thin tip. A tip that looked like a...

Holy fuck, he thought. *It's a...a...*

He couldn't ignore the phallic resemblance. It writhed its way out of Carol's mouth, squirming like a worm seeking refuge inside its earthy domain. The gummy syrup that dripped from its end landed inside Brennan's mouth, and he almost screamed from the disgusting nature of its taste. It was sour, but on some other *alien* level. It burned, too. It tasted like lemon-scented house cleaner, but somehow worse than that.

It tasted like a disease.

The roughly textured tongue lowered, searching for access to his mouth. He scrunched his lips tightly together and tilted his head to the side, still unable to break away from her gaze completely. Her eyes burned with the golden brilliance once more, brighter than before. The shine that entered his eyes split his brain in half, or so it felt. His ability to move was immediately squashed when she took her hands and gripped his head, forcing him to look straight. Her fingers wormed past his puckered lips and stretched them open, creating a passageway for her tongue. The bark-covered extension slithered its way into his oral cavity, and he felt an explosion of fluids coat the back of his throat, fill his mouth. The squirt was warm at first but cooled off within seconds. Then, like a good spice, the burn settled in. The bathroom-chemical-cleaner-like taste torched the roof of his mouth, his tongue, obliterating his taste buds and his inner cheeks, melting away the skin, turning his mouth to nothing but a goopy stew of flesh and muscle and melty teeth. Everything was beginning to burn and soften, and he wanted to open his jaw and speak, but he couldn't make it happen. He felt the lower half of his face dissolve, become replaced by something else.

Something that budded. Blossomed. Grew.

Later, when he found himself standing in front of the bathroom mirror, Brennan Scruggs saw what had replaced his face below his nose; it was green and flowery, strands of foliage and overgrowth peppered with little buds that had already begun opening, pollinating the air. Floral fragrances dominated the room. He could see little spores flitting through the air, filling the room like flurries of snowflakes from an ashen sky.

3

Kim Ortiz's parents pretty much hated her; that was a fact. She was fourteen and still wasn't allowed to date. What were they waiting for? College? They wouldn't even approve a supervised meet up at McDonald's. At this rate, she was aiming to be a senior in high school who still hadn't rounded first base.

They were lame, overbearing assholes who stalked her every move. The only reason they allowed her to have a cell phone was so they could keep better track of her, around the clock. If she wasn't home ten minutes after the school bell, they'd call her, ask why she hadn't come home yet. And if she didn't answer? Holy shit, what an escapade that was. They would threaten to lock her in her room for the entire summer, promise to keep her prisoner until September rolled around.

So, she obviously wasn't stupid and made sure to answer every call, no matter what.

Like today, for instance. She was out with friends at the skate park on Vaughn Avenue, watching the boy she crushed hard on for the entire eighth grade, Robbie Ramos, pull off a couple of kickflips and backslides. He even winked at her when he caught her staring. Embarrassed, she flashed him a smile, one that hopefully found sanctuary in his heart, and then she continued to gawk at him while he rode the railing down to the lower area where a towering halfpipe stood, waiting to be conquered.

She was just about to watch Robbie drop in when her phone went off, an annoying noise that sometimes echoed throughout her nightmares. On the small square screen, *HOME* appeared, and she bit her lip in disgust.

"Yes," she answered on the second ring.

"Come home," demanded her father's voice, though, it almost sounded nothing like him. The voice was too deep, dark. Not that her father was a cheerful man, but this was on another level of drab. She couldn't believe it was him.

"Who is this?"

The voice didn't answer immediately, almost as if the speaker on the other end was debating whether or not to lie or tell the truth.

"It's your father." The response was so slow that it almost seemed robotic. A machine answering in place of a human being. This reminded her of a certain scene in *T2: Judgment Day*. "Come home now."

"Dad?"

Another brief pause. "Yes, daughter."

Daughter? Daughter? He'd never called her daughter, not even in jest. This was beyond bizarre. Something very wrong was afoot, something she couldn't quite predict but knew to be true.

Her intuition went to work, and she debated hanging up.

But the call had come from HOME. Her caller ID didn't lie. Couldn't. Could it?

Cell phones were a relatively new thing, and she'd only had hers for a few months now. She supposed these things could be hacked like computers but wasn't confident in that assessment.

"Are you okay?"

"Yes."

No explanation.

Okay then.

"Put Mom on."

Another moment of contemplation, the silence palpable and heavy. "Okay."

Zero emotion, an empty shell of a human being. It wasn't like her father ran around the house like Robin Williams or anything, but he never acted like a log. She began to wonder if he'd been replaced by a pod person.

"Hello? Kim?"

"Mom?"

"Yes, sweetheart?" Finally, a morsel of normalcy. "You okay?"

"Yeah. Is *Dad* okay? He sounded weird."

"Oh, your father is just in a mood. You know how he gets."

Um, not really. Her mother was acting off too, but not as "Plan 9" as her father had, so she brushed it off. *Maybe they're drunk or something.* It was summertime and they'd been known to crack open a few bottles of wine before the socially acceptable five o'clock drinking hour, but they usually kept it casual. She'd never seen them shit-faced, fall-over-their-own-feet smashed this early in the afternoon.

"What do you guys want?" she asked, getting to the meat of his parental-summoning burrito.

"Oh, could you come home, Kim?" Mother's voice was sticky-sweet and much too unbelievable. Like some overacting stage actor desperate to show up their seasoned co-stars.

What the hell is wrong with them?

"Why? What's wrong?"

"Nothing, darling. Just...well, we miss you."

Miss me? They'd been overbearing in the past, sure, but never had they called her home because they missed her.

"Um, okay..."

"And we want to talk about your...freedoms."

"Freedoms?"

"Yes. We both think it's about time you…well, you've shown interest in dating, haven't you?"

Shocked was not quite how she felt. *Mind blown* was more like it. Her mother's words almost dizzied her. "Um, are you serious?"

"Yes, honey. Oh, please come home. Won't you?"

"I'll…" She watched Robbie Ramos totally wipe out on the halfpipe. The other skaters rushed over to peel him off the polished wooden incline. "I'll be right there."

It took her twenty minutes to walk home.

As she strolled up the stone walkway that led to the front porch, she felt uneasy, like she was about to walk into a situation that was beyond her comprehension.

The front door was cracked open, which was strange because Kim's father was always ranting about keeping the door closed, that leaving it open even a smidge would invite in mosquitoes and other unwanted insects. He'd been pretty meticulous about such things, so this was already a red flag that she should turn around and steer clear of *mi casa*.

Freedoms, though. Goddamn freedoms.

She pictured a world where she didn't have to check in with them five times a day, just to tell them she was still breathing and wasn't engaging in forbidden activities such as drugs and premarital sex. That was the semi-perfect world she wanted to live in.

And it was only one awkward conversation away.

She pushed open the door and the smell hit her like a slap in the face. Recoiling, hand hiding the lower half of her face, Kim's features twisted with a mixture of fear and confusion. The bold stench was wet and moldy, like a crawlspace that had taken on water and was never properly aired out.

After she got over the initial shock of the smell, she ducked inside, and closed the door behind her, sealing in the pungent odor. In hindsight, she probably should have left the door open so the foyer could air out, but she wasn't thinking clearly.

Heading upstairs, she removed her hand from her mouth. "Mom? Dad?"

No answer, and the smell worsened with each step. By the time she reached the top, she could barely breathe, the malodorous scent working its way into her lungs, coating them with—what felt like—a heavy layer of fog.

"Mom?" she said, nearly shouting. She had two steps before the upstairs landing, but she was hesitant to take them, suddenly fearing for her own health. "Mom, Dad—it smells *disgusting* in here. What happened?"

No answer again, and now she was starting to panic.

Should she call the cops? The thought was alluring. If anyone could help, they could. Her parents clearly weren't here, there was some awful smell that was jarring to her senses, and everything about this afternoon had been completely abnormal.

As soon as she decided that calling the cops was in her best interest, she heard her mother call from around the corner and down the hall.

"Kim, honey! We're in here!"

In here, meaning their bedroom. Or hers. She couldn't tell.

"Okay!" she called, torn between journeying on and phoning the police. Despite the latter being the obvious choice, she fought off her intuition and took those last two steps. Why? Because it was her mother and father, and she trusted them. If they were here, then it was probably safe. Whatever was happening, they could explain it.

Besides, if she reached them and the situation appeared beyond her capabilities, she could always turn around, run downstairs, and dial 9-1-1.

She set foot on the upstairs carpet and rounded the corner, froze when her eyes took in the condition of the walls.

They were covered in ivy, a dangling garland of leafy vines. Spots of lichen had grown in some areas, in the corners where the ceiling and walls met. Dirt smeared the carpet, boot prints that had been ground into the coarse threads.

What the hell?

She had no idea what this was, but it terrified her.

"Mom?"

"In here, darling," her mother said, the words coming from her parents' bedroom. The door was slightly ajar, and Kim could see the glow of the television, the only source of light in the room.

She started toward it, taking in her surroundings, examining the walls and the overgrowth, discovering details that were probably better left unseen. Black spots that could only be mold had claimed parts of the drywall, looking like blackholes settling in a misshapen universe. Kim wondered if she should still be breathing in this stuff and slipped her T-shirt up over her nose, just in case. As she got closer to the door, she thought she saw the dangling foliage move, curl as if it were responding to her movement.

She froze.

It didn't move, did it?

She thought it had. Eyeing the leafy extensions, she darted past them, ready to sprint in the opposite direction if need be.

"Mom! What is happening?"

"Come here, darling," her mother said, calm as ever. Her voice was all smiles, and she could picture her mother's pure-white teeth gleaming without using any imagination. "We have a surprise for you."

She almost changed her mind, opting for running downstairs and calling emergency services. The way her mother spoke, that last sentence sent a shiver down her spine, a bolt of panic through her chest.

But it was mother, so she endured.

Reaching the door, she noticed lichen had grown on the knob, nearly covering every inch of brass. She used her elbow and nudged open the door, allowing herself a peek inside.

Her mother was standing in the center of the room, facing the window, with her back to Kim.

"Mom?" she asked, hating how small her voice sounded. It was mousy, strained with terror. Panicked. Her chest felt like it was drowning. "Mom? Please? What is—"

Her mother turned and Kim screamed, hollering until her vocal cords surrendered and gave out.

Annabelle Ortiz's eyes had been torn out, replaced by two flowers. They were growing and shrinking, almost the way a set of lungs would inflate and deflate. Her smile was what terrified Kim the most, as if her mother was having one of the best days of her life. Kim never knew her mother's lips could stretch that wide.

"Hi, honey," she said with certain elation. "So glad you're home. To discuss your *freeeeeeedoms.*"

A vertical trench had been carved into her mother's chest. Greenish-blue fluids leaked from the open cavity. Behind the aroma of wet earth, she smelled chemicals. Like bleach, only much stronger. The bedroom was covered in vines and leaves and clusters of springy moss.

Dizzy with fear, Kim backed out of the room. Her mother never stopped smiling.

Kim spun, now ready to make that phone call to the local authorities. She ran.

Right into a solid object with a soft center.

Father.

Dad.

She looked up.

His eyes bloomed, budding with delicate violet petals.

"Hello, daughter," he said. "About your freedoms…"

4

Cilla Boston climbed off the Roadster Rollercoaster in Action Adventure Park—a small theme park on the border between Hooperstown and Red River—and immediately went searching for her mother, scanning the rows of faces belonging to the kids on the ride. She didn't see her right away, and even though this was no ordinary thing to panic over, her heart flittered like a butterfly caught in a net. Not quite as bad as the time that strange man in an old Chevy Caprice pulled over while she was walking home from Tiffany's house and tried to pull her into his backseat. That was extremely terrifying. Luckily Tom—her mother's boyfriend at the time—had taught her a few self-defense moves. Really, the only one she'd committed to memory was GO FOR THE BALLS. And she had, kicking that perv-o square in the ball bank.

But that was two years ago, when she was nine—now she was eleven and, if she was being honest, way too old for Action Adventure Park. But let's face it—tonight wasn't about her and the endless hours of kiddie rides and boardwalk-themed games. It was about Rodney, the guy her mother was seeing, and their little date. No one had been around to watch Cilla, not even grandma, who was currently enjoying a nice, week-long Caribbean cruise with grandpa.

Cilla didn't care much for Rodney. He wasn't as nice as Tom had been. Sure, Rodney said and did all the right things, but there was something off about him. Something she didn't quite trust, and even though she couldn't articulate what that was exactly, she knew one thing—they wouldn't last. Rodney was just a placeholder until someone better came along. Or until Tom came back, which Cilla would have placed good money on. It hadn't been the first time they'd split. Two times before. Tom always came back after a few weeks, apologizing for whatever they'd been quarreling about. He even brought Cilla her favorite donuts upon each return, a whole box of Boston Cremes.

Bostons for the Bostons, he had said, riffing off their last name. Clever. She liked Tom.

But not Rodney. Fuck that guy. That's right. *Fuck him.* She used words like that now, had since she started hanging around some of the eighth graders at school. They taught her all types of words, things worse than *fuck,* things she would never dare let slip in front of mother. Words like alternative names for the reproductive organs she'd learned about in health class, dirty terms that made her giggle and run and tell her seventh-grade friends (like Tiffany).

"Mom!" she called out to the small crowd of parents. Some turned their heads, looking temporarily concerned, but within seconds they went back to focusing on their own lives. A part of her wondered if they would help if she actually was lost and separated. She suspected not—people were mostly too involved with their own shit, too busy to lend a helping hand to a complete stranger, even if that stranger was an eleven-year-old girl who couldn't find her mother.

So cynical, a voice spoke in her ear, though she turned and there was no mouth to match the words. She also didn't know what *cynical* meant, not exactly, though she'd heard the word before. Using context clues, she suspected the word meant she was distrustful of most humans, and if so, that would be correct—she hardly trusted anyone. That was probably because her father had run off when she was little—Tom's theory, not hers. But those were daddy issues she could examine later in life. Now, she needed to find her mother and Rodney. Hopefully they were as done with Action Adventure Park as she was.

She looked around the crowd and couldn't find them. She even glanced over at the snack stand. She saw a couple of people buying a big tub of popcorn but didn't see Kristin Boston or Rodney Landis. Scanning the immediate area once again, her eyes came up empty.

Shit.

Fuck.

Cock-knocker. That was her new favorite cuss word and she used it for almost everything. As she recited the naughty word over and over in her head, she moved away from the Roadster Rollercoaster, toward the snack stand, thinking maybe her mother and latest love interest had taken a seat near the benches.

Upon closer inspection, they had not.

Panic really started to settle in now, her chest tightening like someone had snapped a rubber band around her. She breathed in through her nose and out through her mouth, an even cadence, and that seemed to help alleviate the tightness, but it was still there. This couldn't be happening. Not to her. It didn't make sense. They had been right there, watching her ride the Roadster Rollercoaster.

Sort of.

They had been smooching some.

Kissing each other's earlobes. Swapping spit. Things that probably should have been kept behind closed doors, but they were in that overly affectionate stage of their relationship, and they didn't care who saw what or where. Cilla had spied her mother fingering the button on Rodney's jeans the other night while they were in the kitchen doing the dishes. Like they couldn't wait 'til *after* she had gone to bed to do that?

Cock-knockers.

She moved away from the benches, toward the arcade where she'd been a few hours ago, where she'd won a handful of tickets playing Skee-Ball, tickets she could have cashed in for prizes, but didn't, because the prizes were cheap and for kids and totally not worth the five-minute wait to talk to the girl behind the counter.

Come here, Cilla, a voice called to her. *I have a prize for you.*

"Who said that?" she asked, turning, spinning in a three-sixty motion. Her brain tingled a little, felt funny. The voice had appeared out of nowhere, yet the speaker spoke as if he were inside her head. Or was it a "her?" She couldn't tell. The voice was deep and raspy, definitely belonging to someone older. Someone her grandmother or grandfather's age, perhaps. Maybe older.

"Hello?" she asked again, spinning once more. No one paid any attention to her.

Over here, Cilla! the voice said again. Changed now. Different. Smaller. Younger. Girl-ish. It was weird. Maybe there were two different people talking to her. One was impossible enough, but two? She was starting to feel reality slip away from her. The world went dreamy, foggy. *Behind the arcade!*

She turned and saw a girl waving to her. The building that contained the arcade hid most of her, but her torso on up was visible. She waved her hand as if she'd never done so before and was being coached. Robotic-like. Automatic. The smile plastered to her face was kinda freaky, wide and full of teeth. She didn't recognize the girl, not at first.

Your mother is over here!

"Where?" she said, suddenly feeling lightheaded, like the world could fade to black any second now. "I don't see…"

She yawned. So tired. Exhausted, actually. Barely able to stand on her own two feet.

She felt sick.

And she was walking. Toward the arcade, toward the girl. She hadn't meant to. A part of her wanted to run in the opposite direction, but this was a dream (so it felt) and she no longer felt in control of her own actions.

When she reached the girl, Cilla realized who it was. Donna Horner, one of the girls who'd taught her the word *cock-knocker*. Great. Donna was a good girl—well, not really, but she was a friend, a familiar face, and she'd help her out until her mother found her, or until she found her mother and Rodney.

Donna waved her on, then vanished behind the building.

Cilla took the corner, rounding the bend and avoiding a small cluster of park-goers, holding her stomach and trying to hold back a spray of vomit. She wanted nothing more than to unload those cheese fries and zeppoles. Everything about her felt awful. She felt she could lie down on the concrete and sleep for days.

A part of her wanted to.

The same part that wanted to turn back, run from this place screaming.

Again, she couldn't.

She walked, headed down the side of the building, and stopped when she set her eyes on what was waiting for her.

Her mother. Rodney. On their knees. Donna Horner was behind them, a hand on each of their shoulders. The girl's eyes glowed a magnificent gold color, radiant like the morning sun, how the shine spreads over the horizon. Bright. Blinding. Her smile never left her face; her lips were stretched that way, seemingly permanent. Her head was tilted sideways at an odd, confusing angle, like a dog perplexed by the commands of its master.

Still smiling.

Cilla bent over, retched, but nothing came out. "I feel so awful…"

You won't, Donna said, without moving her lips. *You and the other children will feel perfect soon enough. You'll never feel another bad thing again. I will take care of you. I will provide comfort.*

As the woman spoke—a woman now, no longer a girl—Cilla watched her mother's eyes pop. Explode outward in a spray of gunky crimson. They were replaced by blooming flowers that ballooned from her sockets. An orchid sprouted, extending out, the petals luscious, a cute pink color. Its labellum lapped the air like a tongue catching rainwater.

Next, it was Rodney's turn. His eyes swelled, much too big for his skull to handle, and like a firecracker, they erupted, shattering into globules of red, sticky matter. They were immediately replaced by orchids too, bluish petals germinating in the bloody caverns where his eyes used to be.

Both her mother and Rodney were expressionless, as if their loss of sight and the terrible things that replaced them were no big deal, just an everyday occurrence. She thought they were under some spell, and Donna had been the one to bewitch them.

A witch, she thought. *That's what she is.*

A part of her knew she wasn't Donna though, not anymore. That was the same part of her that wanted to run, wanted to purge the carnival snacks from her stomach. Parts of her that were now useless.

She looked on in horror as bluish-green tears leaked down her mother's face, and Rodney's.

I will take care of you, her new mother said, right before the world spun out of control, a carousal that didn't stop until it welcomed the darkness.

Cock-knocker was her last thought before she remembered nothing.

5

Hooperstown Medical was in an uproar.

Dr. Aaron Watson hustled down the pediatric ward where he was the chief physician, stopping and speaking to each one of the nurses. They were in a frantic state as well, unable to attend to a single patient for very long. There were too many patients, an overload, and some of the children coming in were being moved to other floors until transportation arrived. The plan was to transfer them to more functional facilities with greater capacity. Some of the older patients, the kids who'd been there since the beginning of summer, were being sent to Robert Wood Johnson in New Brunswick.

The ones who made it.

Watson couldn't help but think of Lauren Sullivan, how the cancer had taken her in less than two months. She hardly had a chance at beating the thing. Her body didn't seem like it wanted to fight and had responded negatively to the treatment. Like it had rejected any and all offers to rid itself of the disease. In fact, Watson thought the treatment accelerated the cancer, which was almost impossible.

Impossible was a word that had been thrown around a lot here lately.

"Where are we at?" Watson asked Nurse Higgins. She was refilling her station cart with supplies when he approached.

She twisted toward him, a long, worried look molding her features. "They're coming in droves now." She shook her head. "Some of them have reported…hallucinations."

"Hallucinations?"

Higgins nodded. "Yeah, it's weird. One girl's parents—she's in A-25 now, Pricilla Boston—said they were at Action Adventure Park when she started going into seizures, talking about their eyes…and *flowers* for eyes."

"Flowers for eyes?"

"It's strange to say the least. But she wasn't the only one. The Ortizes are in B-16, reporting similar things. Their daughter came home from a skate park, passed out on the living room floor, and started taking about vines growing out of the walls."

"Christ. Is their bloodwork back?"

Higgins moved some paperwork around on the counter next to her cart. She presented the results. "White cell count is off the charts for both. Like, really, really high."

"No leukemia cells present?" He scanned the sheet, the test results failing to meet his expectations.

"Nope. It's…"

"If you say impossible one more time…" He flashed a faint smile, a poor attempt to lighten the heavy mood. Watson had always excelled at keeping a positive attitude, especially in times of great stress and demoralizing events, but now, even he was having trouble keeping pace with the current situation.

"It's just…this is unheard of. Their symptoms are not matching up with anything I've learned about cancer."

"Well. What else can it be? The signs are all there. The Sullivan girl had heavy traces of leukemia cells."

"Yeah, but the others…" She shook her head, as if the words she was about to speak might be taboo. "It's like the cancer is mutating. Trying to hide itself from us."

Watson didn't want to say the word, but that was *impossible*. He cursed himself for even thinking it. "I know. Hey, how are we looking with transfers?"

"RWJ is doing everything they can to help. We've been telling the parents that they have the best childhood cancer department in the entire state."

"Which is true."

"Walker says New York Presbyterian and CHOP in Philly have reached out. They're willing to send doctors and extra staff if need be."

"That's gracious of them."

She shrugged. "People want to help."

Watson nodded.

Help. They would need as much as they could get.

POWER DOWN

(an interlude)

1

Dylan Walker threw the last knickknack—a family photo of his wife Lena and their two boys—into the cardboard box, closed the top and taped it shut. After, he breathed a sigh of relief and scanned his office one last time. So empty it looked foreign, a place he'd never been rather than a place he'd spent almost every day over the last ten years. Dylan would miss this place, this job, and the people he worked for.

A minute later, one of the maintenance workers poked his head in the open doorway.

"Any more boxes, boss?" asked Albert Wallace. He looked solemn, broken down, as did most of the remaining staff.

"Yes, Al. One more, if you don't mind."

He shuffled inside and grabbed the box off the desk. Before he left to throw it in the back of Walker's Lexus, he paused, stopped, and turned around. "Do you think this is it? The end of this place?"

Walker hung his head. "I don't know. The board seems to think so. Seems like the attorneys have enough evidence, and with the amount they're suing for, it will completely bankrupt the company. Not to mention, fixing the issues and getting this place back to regulation, back in the good graces of the state's environmental department..." He shook his head. "I think it's safe to say we should all be looking for new jobs."

Al nodded as if he understood, his eyes falling sideways. "I feel awful for everything."

Walker put up a hand. "Don't. None of this was our fault. We were doing as we were instructed. How were we supposed to know the effects it would have on the community?" Walker's eyebrows rose, expecting some sort of response.

"I guess you're right. We were only following orders. And we didn't know any better."

"Exactly," Walker said, strolling over and placing a comforting hand on the man's shoulder. "We are the innocent ones in all of this. We work for a company, and it's the company's fault for not properly educating us."

"I heard you were being dragged through the mud, Mr. Walker. That you were mentioned specifically in the lawsuit."

At this, Walker glared. "Well. Don't believe everything you read in the papers. Journalism has gotten very sloppy in this town. Very sloppy. When this is all over, you'll see the truth."

"Oh," he said, nodding, again, like he understood. But Walker could see the doubt registering in his eyes.

"Listen. It will all work out. You'll land on your feet again. Remember, any recommendations or references you need, don't hesitate to reach out."

Al nodded and began to turn. "Thanks, Mr. Walker. You always were my favorite plant manager."

"I appreciate that, Al. I really do."

"Are you leaving right away?"

Walker walked him out and shut the office door, sealing in the last decade of memories behind them. "I'm going to walk the plant one more time, do a lap, see if there's anyone else left before I lock the place up for good."

Al smiled at him, a goodbye smile that fronted more as a defeated grimace.

2

Once Al finished stocking the Lexus, Walker thanked him, tipped him a twenty for helping lug his effects, and then headed back inside to see if there were any other stragglers, people savoring the last bit of legacy that was Hooperstown Chemical. The parking lot was empty, except for one car: Gordon Simms's burgundy Honda Civic.

Walker knew where to find him.

He moseyed on past the "welcome" kiosk, down the hall, and past the rows of vacant offices, everything gone from them including the furniture. He headed out back, across the concrete walkways, down the path that led to the rear of the plant where the storage units sat bordering the Red River, which flowed past the plant and into the woods and, from there, to the bay where it emptied. Sure enough, he found Gordon standing in front of the now-empty storage containers.

"Knew I'd find you here," Walker said, approaching Simms, stopping about twenty feet from him. Simms always had an attachment to the storage containers. They had held some volatile substances in the past, and Simms always prided himself on keeping everyone in the plant safe.

As Walker approached, Simms didn't turn around. Instead, he applied his focus on the giant empty containers, the three of them towering over the two men, the entire plant.

"Remember when container three caught fire back in '92?"

"Of course. You thought we were all canned." He paused to pull a pack of smokes from his pocket, lighting one up as if he had all the time in the world. "Bad times back then. Bad times."

Simms lowered his head. "We all told the same story when the regulatory commission came down on us. They came down hard, but...we never faltered. Never deviated from the story. Told them we had no idea what caused it, that the reaction inside the container was unbeknownst to us. That it was an anomaly. That it shouldn't have combusted like it did."

"I remember, Gordon. What's your point?"

Gordon turned. "Point is, we knew exactly what caused that fire. That it was our mistake."

"And?"

He flinched, then shrugged.

Walker's neck grew hot beneath his collar.

"And...sometimes I wonder what would have happened if we had just admitted it. Just like if we admitted that we knew the pipeline was faulty and compromised, which is why we haven't been using it. Which is why we've resorted to driving the shit out into the woods and dumping it in the soil. Too close to the river."

Walker took off his glasses, began cleaning them, the smoke continuing to dangle from his lips. He needed to keep his hands busy, otherwise the urge to grab Simms by his throat and choke the life out of him might grow too strong. "No citizen goes out into the woods. We decided it was the safest place to dump. We decided that together."

"Did we?"

"Oh, you're going to claim innocence in all of this?"

"I never wanted to dump. Not once, not ever."

Walker put his glasses back on and threw up his hands. "You know we couldn't afford to transport those hazardous materials properly. It would have cost us millions. You of all people know what that would have done to our profitability."

"Our profitability?" Gordon spit at his feet. "Our children are dying out there, man. My son's best friend is in the hospital right now, probably..." He choked back the words. A tear rolled off his bottom eyelash, streaking down his face. "Probably dying because of this shit. Shit that *we* did." The man's voice was uneven.

Walker seethed. "We don't know that, and even if that's true, we couldn't predict the outcome. How were we supposed to know this stuff causes cancer? We're not scientists. We're business people."

"You're unbelievable, man." Shaking his head, Simms scoffed. His jaw flexed with anger, and Walker waited for the man to explode, combust much like the storage unit in '92. "You're so full of shit. We all knew the outcome. We knew dumping anywhere near the river would have some sort of effect. Hell, we talked about it."

"We were dumping in the woods, Gordon. Remember that. The woods. Not the river."

"The river runs through the woods, Einstein. You dump that stuff into the soil anywhere near it and you have no idea where it goes. Besides, you ever go on a run with the people you sent out there? Huh? Have you? How do you know they were doing what they were instructed to do? How do you know they *weren't* dumping in the river?"

Dylan only stared at him.

"You don't know. You don't know shit." He shook his head, beyond disgusted. Simms's color had drained from his cheeks, and now he looked like one of Hooperstown's sick. "And what is it—some coincidence that two of the knuckle-fuckers you sent out on these little missions just *happen* to disappear right before all this shit goes down? Huh? That a coincidence, Walker?"

"I don't like your tone, Gordon. I suggest you calm down."

Gordon did calm down. In fact, he even flashed his old boss a smile. It wasn't genuine, Walker knew, but it was better than having him rant and rave.

Walker was getting pissed. How dare he talk to him like that. After all he did. For the company, sure, but also for Gordon Simms personally. When the man was going through hard times at home, who had been there for him? Who'd given him countless sick days, fudging the numbers so he wouldn't run out of PTO, so he'd still have some after the whole ordeal with his wife was over?

I did, Walker thought, and he didn't realize he'd been biting into his lip. The taste of copper washed over his tongue. He cast aside what remained of his cigarette, flicking it as far as the wind blew.

"I know what you're thinking," Gordon said, nodding. So smug. So knowing. "And yes, I appreciate everything you've done for me, for my family. But that doesn't excuse what you've done, Dylan. Doesn't excuse it one bit."

"You wouldn't even be standing here today if it wasn't for me."

"Maybe that's true. Maybe." He shrugged, uncaring. "Or maybe I'd be somewhere else if it weren't for you. Somewhere better."

"You'd be on unemployment, probably living in the street with your faggot son."

Anger flashed over Gordon's features once again, and for a second Walker thought the man would lash out at him. Strike him. Try to knock off his head.

He wished for it.

That's right. Hit me. I'll sue the fuck out of you, you prick.

But he didn't. The anger bled, the rosiness faded almost as fast as it had arrived. The sickly complexion returned.

"We could trade hypotheticals all day," Gordon said, stuffing his hands in his pockets. "I assume you already know, but I figured I'd tell you anyway, man to man." He glared at him, teeth clenched. Then he exhaled, as if that one breath of fresh air let go of all the anger and hate with it. "Walker, I'm testifying."

Dylan had to restrain himself from committing cold-blooded murder. The ripple of pure rage that funneled through him actually distorted his vision. Everything moved in waves. *"What?"*

"Yeah. Against Hooperstown Chemical, against you. I'm going to tell them everything I know. The truth."

"You can't. You..." He realized he was shaking, trembling with indignation.

"I know you're angry, and hell—if I was in your position, I'd be pretty angry too. But what's right is right, and I plan to make things so. You know, maybe some of me *is* responsible. I should have spoken up. Or quit. But I allowed it to happen. Probably because you took such good care of me when my wife was dealing with her issues—"

"—Fucking psychopath should have killed you, stabbed you in your sleep!" His teeth were clenched so hard his jaw let off a painful pop. He ignored the rush of agony that followed.

"Nice," Gordon said, wincing. "What I was trying to say is...I don't owe you shit. I owe this town, those families who are suffering."

"Fuck them and fuck you."

"Goodbye, Walker."

Gordon hung his head and shoved past him, almost as if he wanted Dylan to lash out. Throw a punch. Trip him. Knock him to the ground, plant more evidence of his guilt in the form of a bruise. A cut. A laceration. A broken nose. It would all sell so perfectly in court.

Instead, Dylan watched him walk away, resisting the urge to bend Gordon Simms over his knee and spank the pants off him. "I'll fucking sue you, Simms. I'll fucking *counter*sue you! For spreading libelous bullshit! Slander! That's right! I'll sue you for defaming my good name! I have a good reputation in this town! I'm… I'm a…" His voice faded, grew quiet. "I'm a *good* person," he said in a whisper, which sounded a lot like a lie, even to himself.

Gordon ignored him, the whole spiel, and headed up the steep path. Once he disappeared beyond the horizon, making his way past the maintenance shed and into the distance, Walker got down on his knees, feeling out of breath and, oddly, a little dizzy.

"Fucking son of a bitch," he muttered as beads of sweat broke across his forehead. For a second, he thought he was having a heart attack.

His vision blurred, getting grainy, fuzzy near the edges. In the short distance, about where Simms had taken his last stroll over the horizon, a woman now stood. She was naked save for a few streaks of dirt that did nothing to cover her privates. Her long black hair looked like a nest of snakes, a hive of dark tangled curls, and if he didn't know any better, he'd say each clump was moving, slithering through the air, across her shoulders. She bit her lip, and Walker felt his pants bulge and tighten.

He looked down at his growing erection, then back to her.

She was gone.

Come, a voice said, entering his head. It tickled him with promise, a sense that maybe not all was lost, that maybe he could save himself; the only thing that truly mattered at this point, because this town was beyond redemption. Beyond saving, no matter what Gordon Simms believed.

This town was *fucked*.

So he listened to the voice and followed the peculiar fragrance of damp earth and dead, moldering things.

3

The woman led him back inside the plant, deep down, past the engine rooms and the turbine station, downstairs into the condenser room, near the intake where the plant drew water off the river to help cool the station. The basement-looking building was dark and damp and reeked of moldy earth. In fact, Walker could see black spores clinging to the walls in several spaces. Had it always been like this? It had been a long time since Walker actually left his office and came down into the plant. He was always too busy with meetings and paperwork to check out the daily operations and functions of the site, to scope out the condition of the place. Besides, that was what the other managers were for, people like that fuck, Gordon Simms. They were supposed to keep the place clean and safe, a healthy working environment for every employee.

But this place—he didn't feel safe down here.

"Who are you?" he asked the woman. She now stood near the intake pipe, running her finger along the metal cylinder as if it were a prized possession, a valuable antique that would one day be worth millions. "Answer me," he said, getting pissed that she wouldn't give him a shred of attention.

He sensed moving feet behind him. Whipping his head to the side, spinning around, he saw nothing but shadows. And there were many shadows, motionless and lingering.

"Listen," he said, turning back to the woman. "I don't—"

She was in his face now, her eyes glowing like long-lost treasure, gold and blinding. He squinted against the wealthy shine. The woman reached out, gripping the sides of his head. He tried to pull back, release himself from her touch, but it was no use. Whatever her eyes were doing, they were having some effect on him. He couldn't move, powerless to the laws her eyes had sanctioned. Her pull was magnetic, and he'd become ensnared in her influence.

He wanted to speak, ask so many questions, his mind teeming with possible explanations. But he had no voice, no words. Just the flow of the golden light his eyes continued to drink from. Pools of effulgent beauty in which he drowned.

Shapes slithered into his vision. He was able to separate himself from the light long enough to see her hair had come alive, those black ropes of messy tangles and knots unfurling before him. He blinked and saw the ropes were not ropes at all; they had evolved into snakes, black mambas, their jaws widening, their venomous fangs bared, ready to snap down on Walker's throat. An incredible sense of danger spiked his nerves, and Walker tried everything in his power to break the spell.

It was no use.

As more shapes filed into the condenser bay, he watched the woman's reptilian hair wrap around his neck, curling around his throat, squeezing his esophagus until it became difficult to breathe. They were kind, though, and allowed just enough airflow without completely cutting off his oxygen.

The shapes that had entered the area were finally revealed, and Walker could see several residents of Hooperstown ambling into view. He saw Peggy Long, the woman who worked in bookkeeping, stumble her way toward the condenser. Lucas Clarke, a kid he recognized as someone that "worked behind the counter" at the hardware store on Route 9, shuffled toward the condenser, holding his stomach like he had taken one too many shots of Rumple Minze and wanted to hurl all over himself. Trevor Cortez, a local police officer, wearing his full blue uniform, staggered forth, looking pale and sickly and in need of a good bodily purge.

Dozens of townsfolk entered the room, each looking full of sickness and disease and...*rot*.

The Woman allowed his eyes to wander, to enjoy the calamity unfolding before him. He wasn't sure, but he thought he saw stuff growing on their faces, greenish-blue slime that flowered from their pores. Some of them had growths sticking out of their scalps, little vines that mingled and twined with their hair. One woman had flowers for eyes.

What the hell is happening?

The Woman beamed. *This will be reality now. You will help us spread my disease, the very one you and your kind helped create.*

No. I...

The golden glow intensified, burning its way directly into his brain. There was a flash, a stark brightness that completely blinded him, and then everything went entirely dark.

When his view faded in, he was staring down at the open valve on the top of the condenser tank. Instead of taking in water off the river, the machine was pumping the water out. Into the river, through the town.

The water was dark, a bluish-green that bordered on black.

The townspeople had formed a line. One by one, they were taking turns vomiting into the open valve, like worshippers showing up to receive communion.

Turn after turn, they poisoned the town's water source, spreading their disease and rot, extending vines of decay and devastation.

The Woman smiled as she wrapped herself around Walker's body. The black mambas went to work on his neck, sinking their teeth deep into his flesh, filling him with their deadly poison as expert hands rubbed his swollen crotch.

PART THREE

The Growing
August 3rd, 1998 – September 2nd, 1998

CHAPTER THIRTEEN

In Dreams We Trust

1

Doug sat in the corner of the room while the nurse changed Jesse's IV. Grady stood next to him, gnawing the skin off his knuckles. Jesse's mom and dad lingered in the opposite corner of the room, watching their son as they hugged each other. After the nurse finished performing her routine tasks, recording data from the monitors and drawing blood, Jesse gave everyone in the room the thumbs up.

"How are you feeling, Jess?" his dad asked.

"A little tired."

It was hard to look at him, and Doug felt guilty every time his eyes fell away and settled on something else. *Anything* else. A bone-white complexion replaced his usual, lively pallor, lacking vitality. A band of sweat broke near his hairline, beads that dotted the pallid flesh. He was hooked up to all kinds of wires and computer monitors, and every fifteen minutes a nurse came in to check on him. Sometimes they fiddled with the equipment, sometimes they only popped in to ask how he was, if he was comfortable, and if he needed anything.

"We should leave," Mr. Di Falco said, breaking from his wife. He walked over to his son and planted a kiss on his forehead.

Doug could tell he'd been crying recently, the sadness clinging to his puffy and irritated eyes. Mrs. Di Falco looked much of the same, her eyes bloodshot and swollen. Doug figured the pair hadn't slept much over the last three days, and really, who could blame them. Their youngest was currently fighting for his life, engaged in an uphill battle that had already claimed at least one life, and if the whispers were any indication of the truth, more lives were likely to be lost at the hands of this terrible disease.

"Wait," Jesse said, shifting uncomfortably. The hospital bed looked as stiff as an ironing board, and he'd been fidgeting since company had arrived. "I want to talk to my friends."

The Di Falcos exchanged looks.

"All right," said his father. "Talk to them."

"Alone, I mean. A little privacy, please?"

Mr. Di Falco, normally pretty lax and fairly responsive to his kids' requests, sighed deeply and folded his arms. Doug wasn't sure why he was so hesitant to leave the three of them alone. "All right. Five minutes. We'll be outside. But then we have to leave. You need your rest."

Jesse opened his mouth, probably to make a joke along the lines of *I'll sleep when I'm dead,* but then closed it, probably thinking it wasn't such a good time to kid about such things, not while *death* was creeping in all around them. Doug could feel a grim presence in the room with them; *Death* itself, he figured, watching over the sick and making arrangements.

"Five minutes," Jesse agreed.

His mom and dad nodded, left the room, Mr. Di Falco's hand on his wife's back the entire way out. They closed the door behind them.

"Holy shit, I thought they'd never leave," Jesse said, tossing his head back on the stiff pillow. "Love them to death, but gosh—a guy needs a little breathing room."

"How are you?" Doug said, walking over to the bed. "I mean, *really*—how do you feel?"

Jesse scrunched his face together. "Really? Five minutes is all we have and that's what you want to talk about?"

"I'm worried for you, dude."

Grady stepped forward, separating himself from the wall. "We both are. I couldn't sleep last night. Not a wink."

Jesse brushed off this claim with an exaggerated eye roll. "Come on. Guys, I'll be fine. This is just a minor setback. Doctors seem really optimistic. Said they caught it early enough and blah blah blah, yada yada yada. I'll be tip-top in no time in at all. Docs say I may even be ready for the first week of school."

Grady looked to Doug, shadows of disbelief creeping across his features.

"What?" Jesse asked. "Guys. You believe me, don't you?"

"How do you feel?" Doug asked, adamant this time.

Jesse huffed, his shoulders slumping. "Fine. Tired, I guess. Like I could sleep for days. Do you remember when Teddy Tisdale got mono from Leslie Sommers? He said it felt like he could sleep for a week straight? Yeah, I guess it feels like that."

"This is my fault," Grady said, almost catatonic.

"How the hell is this your fault?"

"In the cemetery. If I didn't run."

Jesse shook his head. "Dude. No. Absolutely not. We've already been over this. That was no one's fault."

"It happened because Alphie Moffit spit that shit in your mouth," Grady said, his eyes growing wet with tears.

"Well, yeah, probably, that has something to do with it."

"Has anything weird happened?" Doug asked. "Like, remember Lauren Sullivan? What she did to Maddie's dog?"

"Are you asking me if I ate a dog, Dougie?"

"No." Doug folded his arms. "Have you...gone anywhere? Done anything? Woke up with dirty feet or anything weird?"

Jesse shook his head. "No, dude. Nothing. I've been here. They check on me every ten minutes or so. My parents only leave at night. There are doctors and nurses all over this place. Where the hell am I gonna go?"

"What about your dreams? Any stranger than before?"

Jesse went stiff. "Well, they've been a bit weird. Stranger than usual, I'd say. And not the same as the ones we've dreamed."

"Like what?" Grady asked, brushing away a tear, catching it off the eyelash before it rolled down his cheek.

"They're...darker. More disjointed. A lot of shadows and shapes. I...I can't help but think that the dreams...they belong to *her*."

"Her?"

"The Mother."

Doug nodded. "What are they about?"

"Can't make much sense of them." He stared past them, trying to place himself back in the dreamworld. "There are these shadows. They're dancing. Around a fire. Things are crawling through the night. The sky. There's a shape moving among the stars. Like a giant dragon or something. I don't know. I can't tell."

Grady shivered.

A cold nothing pressed against Doug's neck.

"It's..." Jesse bit his lip. "Actually terrifying."

"Sounds it. What do you think it means?"

Jesse shrugged. "Fucked if I know. I don't know what any of this means." He yawned. "When are you going to see your mother?"

"Soon. This week."

"Will you tell me what she says?"

"Of course."

Doug hated to feel this way, but he couldn't help it. He hoped his friend would last that long, long enough to tell him everything that happened. He clearly didn't look well, and he wasn't an idiot—he knew all that stuff the doctors were telling him about returning to school after Labor Day was largely fabricated or good bedside manner.

Mr. Di Falco popped his head into the room. "Time's up, guys."

They said their goodbyes and shuffled out of the room.

Doug couldn't ignore the notion that this might be the last time he would ever see his friend.

2

The diner was quiet and so was Jewel Conti. Swirling a small heap of mashed potatoes, mixing them with the soggy green beans and mushy carrots, she stared at her plate thinking about what she was going to do with the rest of her life, or shit—just the next couple of years. Her father coming home had changed things. Her mother was one thing. She could deal with her kind of crazy, knowing how to avoid her and how to toe the line before crossing it, keeping the woman in check, even though, lately, things had gone haywire. In any case, her father being thrown back into the mix was definitely too much. The two of them together was like a Category 5 hurricane merging with an F1 tornado—the results were always cataclysmic.

"Not like him," Adam said, swallowing a bite of his medium-cooked steak.

"Huh?" Jewel said, lifting her head from a cloud of thoughts. "Him?"

"Fritz. Not like him to miss a night."

"Oh. Yeah." She set down her fork and rubbed her eyes. Running on empty, Jewel needed nothing more than a good night's sleep. She debated grabbing a hotel room, one that would allow to her to check in without a credit card, one that would take the twenty bucks leftover from dinner. She doubted she'd find such a thing, even at the little love shacks on the wrong side of town. "That is…weird."

"You okay?" Adam leaned over his plate, giving her his full attention, something that unfortunately could not be reciprocated.

"Yeah, just…spacey."

"Home?"

"Yeah."

"Want to talk about it?"

She shrugged as if to say, *What good would that do?*

"Sometimes just talking helps."

"Okay," she said, scooping up a forkful of mashed potatoes. A sad-looking green bean came with it and she put both in her mouth, chewed, and swallowed. The small bite filled her stomach, and she set down her fork with no intention of picking it back up again. "What would you like to know?"

Adam pulled his lips to one side. "I've heard things—rumors, I guess. Your dad—he was in jail for murder?"

"*Was.*"

"He's out. Free? Just like that? For murder?"

"As of a few days ago, yeah. And it wasn't murder. Drugs, mostly. Lots of drugs. Also, he beat the shit out of a cop, which complicated things."

"Jesus. Guess having him home has been a little difficult then?"

"Ding-ding, ding-ding. Get the man a prize. Would you like the shiny red car or go for round two, where anything can happen?"

He smirked, ran his fingers through his hair, messing with the sloppy comb job. "Smart ass."

"Sorry. Diner food brings out the worst in me."

"I doubt that. So. Your father. He abusive?"

His question hit her like a gentle slap. "Wow. Really getting in there, all personal-like, huh?"

"You don't have to answer if you don't want to. I just want to clarify what I've heard."

"And what have you heard?"

"Just that you come from a rough family life. It's nothing to be ashamed of, really."

Despite his kind spin on the conversation, she couldn't help but feel *ashamed*. She was ashamed of it all, and no good-natured buddy talk would convince her otherwise.

"Yeah, no, I'm not," she lied. "Who told you that stuff? Was it Fritz?"

"No. Fritz doesn't talk about his students' personal affairs. Just some of the other kids at the youth center. Ones that go to your school."

She hadn't recognized anyone in her grade at the meet-ups, but with a graduating eighth-grade class of just over six-hundred kids, it wasn't much of a surprise. She didn't keep up with the who's-who gossip, and since she was notoriously feared, kids tended to keep away from her.

"I see," she said, nodding, trying not to let her embarrassment show. She had hoped the youth center would be a place to start over. Instead, it turned out to be much of the same old shit.

"Don't let it bother you. There's no judgement or anything like that. It's just...you know. Kids talk. Adults too, but kids are worse."

"Yeah, sure." A vigorous nod and she was ready to talk about something else. "So..."

"So, your dad..."

"Ah. Yeah." She bit her lip. "Abusive. More verbally than physical. He hit me with a beer bottle once."

"Jesus."

"Yeah." She leaned over the table, turning her head. Pointing just above her right eyebrow, she said, "See the scar?"

Adam leaned in for a better view. "Oh...oh yeah."

"Three stitches. No big deal. My parents told the hospital I hit my head on a table. Dicks, right?"

"Yeah..." He leaned back, furrowing his brow. "I...I had no idea it was that bad."

"Eh, that's probably the worst that's happened. I mean, he put cigarettes out on my leg once. Twice on my arm. But that was so long ago."

"Holy shit."

"Yeah." Her eyes downcast, she shifted in the booth. "Am I freaking you out?"

"No. No, not at all. I'm sorry—I don't mean to sound so..."

"Shocked?"

"Yeah."

"Well, my house ain't sunshine and rainbows."

"Yeah, I can see that."

"It wasn't so bad when he was away. My mom—she can be brutal—but she's so much worse when he's around. It's like...he comes home and winds her up, like one of those dumb toys we used to get inside Happy Meals. Crank the motor and watch it march across the floor."

"She feeds off his callousness?"

"Yes. *Exactly*. My mom, she's mostly talk—though, she did chuck an empty beer bottle at my head recently—but mostly, she just curses and says 'cunt' a lot."

In mid-sip, Adam choked on his milkshake.

Jewel tittered.

They both laughed.

"I guess it is kind of funny," she said, "when it isn't so sad. And terrifying."

"What do you do? When they're like that?"

"Lock myself in my room. Most of the time they won't break down the door. Too much of a pain in the ass to fix it. They learned after the first few times. If things are really bad, I just leave. Go places. Hang out with Brennan and Dakota."

"Friends?"

She paused, giving the thought time to sink in. "Used to be. We had a falling out."

"What happened?"

Her eyes lingered in his, a goofy grin finding a home on her face. "You did, sort of. Mostly Fritz, but you—you too."

He beamed at this. "Aw shucks."

"I changed, and they didn't like the new me."

"Well, I like the new you."

"You didn't know the old me."

"Well, I heard she was kind of a bitch."

She cackled at that. It was funny because it was true.

"I'll pay," he said, grabbing the check the waitress had dropped off at some point when Jewel had been talking about her father and the bottle that had cut her.

"No," she said, shaking her head. "No, that's ridiculous."

"Stop it. I insist."

He pulled the check away before she had a chance to snatch it from him. Putting the slip between his lips, he dug out the total amount of his wallet, slapped down the bills on the table, tip included.

"You're a gentleman," she said, fancy-like, with faux southern charm.

"That was a pretty good rich-person impression, if you don't mind me saying."

"I don't mind you saying and thank you. I've been practicing that one for a while."

"Can you do any other impressions?"

The waitress came by, scooped up the money. Adam told her to keep the change. They got up, and he walked Jewel to the exit.

"I can do a pretty good Bart Simpson," she said, pushing through the door.

Walking down the stairs behind her, Adam said, "Let me hear it."

"No way. It's too embarrassing."

"Come on."

She walked over to his car, turned and rested her back against it. "Nope."

"It's embarrassing?"

"Yes."

"You just told me your deepest, darkest secrets in there, and now you're too embarrassed to do an impression of a cartoon character."

"Listen, maybe on the second date I'll do impressions for you."

"Date?" His eyes wandered a bit, but she ignored this stop sign, every romantic movie she had ever seen blinding her from the truth. "Jewel, there's some—"

Instinct took over and she pushed herself off the car, wrapped her arms around his head, and pressed her lips against his. The kiss lasted all of two seconds, and then he backed away, arching his spine in the direction it wasn't meant to go, separating from her forward embrace.

She stepped back, wiping their saliva from her lips. "What's the matter?"

He spun in a circle, hands on his hips. "I'm sorry, Jewel. I'm so sorry, I…" He winced, grimaced as if he'd just gotten a paper cut under a fingernail.

Then it hit her. When she'd been wandering down the side of Route 37 and found that ice cream shop, The Sprinkle Shack, she had run into Adam. He had been with a girl. She couldn't recall her name, but she immediately remembered how the girl had looked at her. Her eyes. Watching. Warning.

Those were *girlfriend* eyes.

"Oh fuck," Jewel said, placing a hand over her forehead. "You have a girlfriend. I totally forgot."

"Girlfriend? No, what girlfriend?"

"That girl from the Sprinkle Shack."

"Katie?" He laughed, brushing back his parted curls. "Katie is just a friend."

Jewel felt out of breath. "Then what? If you don't have girlfriend, then what's the big deal?"

"Jewel," he said, grabbing her hands, holding them against his chest. He showed her the saddest puppy-dog eyes she'd ever seen. "Jewel, I'm gay."

3

That night, Grady lay on his bed, staring up at the ceiling. The window unit finally kicked on, pumping a cool flow into the bedroom after the temperature hit seventy-seven. His parents usually set the thing, and if he knew how to, he'd keep it a lot lower than that. Cooler was better, especially at night, which was one of the reasons he preferred winter over summer.

As he was lying there, he thought about Jesse, the tough exterior he'd put up. Grady knew it was a front, knew it the second he'd strolled into that room and took one hard look at his friend's eyes. Jesse was scared, obviously. Petrified. Not that he could blame him; if Grady had been in that position, the nurse would have to change his gown hourly. Jesse was terrified at what the future might bring, but he hid his apprehension well, masking his fear in a shroud of jokes and overall silly behavior. Exactly what Jesse did best.

Thinking about Jesse kept Grady up well past the hour he normally fell asleep. Last night he hadn't slept a wink, not a single second. He had tossed and turned and every time he closed his eyes, Jesse was there, sitting on his hospital bed, crying and feeling sorry as a team of doctors crowded around him and told him he was going to die. That the cancer was irreversible, and it was only a matter of time before the disease ate its way through him like the acid the monsters bled in *Aliens,* only slowly, from the inside out. It was a terrible thing to watch over and over again, but Grady couldn't shut it off. Like a broken television set with a missing power button and no remote, it was the only channel that played, and Grady wondered when the show would finally end.

Tonight was different, though. He'd snuck into his parents' medicine cabinet and grabbed himself a bottle of NyQuil, the cherry-flavored kind, which didn't taste like any cherry Grady had ever eaten, not even the artificial-flavored lollipops he used to get from his mother's trips to the bank. This tasted much like medicine, but that was okay. He wasn't drinking the stuff because he wanted a nighttime refreshment; he wanted to sleep like the dead.

About a half-hour after he ingested the recommended dosage, he started to feel its effects. His breathing slowed and his eyes grew heavy, and soon after he couldn't keep them open even if he wanted to. Closing them, a comforting warmth swept over him, a blanket of good feelings and familiar sensations. Everything around him felt heavy, weighed down by gravity and something else, something unexplainable. Something good.

Within seconds of shutting his eyes, he was out.

It took a few moments of wading in the darkness before the dreamworld materialized. Grady found himself looking at a grainy scene, unable to decipher where the gods of this phantasmic realm had planted him. With each step, more of this environment defined its view. There were pipes all around him, steam whistling and shooting off from unknown sources. The room smelled wet, like the bathroom after a hot shower. Underneath the odor, he detected the faint scent of moist earth. The farther he traveled into this room of industrial design, the bolder these strange fragrances grew.

There were whispers in the dark that sounded like scratching, fingernails against glass. Grady kept moving, not because he was curious, but because the dream drove him. He felt like a slot car, unable to travel outside of its designated track. He passed more piping and machinery, catching a view of various dials and knobs and levers. Smoke billowed out from a pipe on his left, filtering semi-transparent clouds into his path, shrouding the rest of the long, dark hall from his vision. Pushing into them, he broke through and came out on the other side. Here, the hall opened into a massive room, several stories high. People in white coats were working, hustling across the floor, most of them holding clipboards with important papers on them—important, he suspected, because the workers couldn't keep their eyes off them. As they bustled about, Grady noticed a large tree had grown in the center of the room, a towering oak whose leafy top was lost in the dark shadows above. Grady suspected the tree never ended, that in this world the trees extended into the farthest reaches of the galaxy and the places beyond.

He kept shuffling forward, the frenzied workers of this establishment scurrying past him, paying no attention to his presence. The dream brought him before the tree, close enough that his dream-nose could sniff out the bark, the wet-wood scent that suddenly dominated the Tall Room. The workers continued to hustle, spin their dials and adjust the settings on their machines, all while Grady watched the bark of the Tree begin to flake off. The hard skin came off in chips, popping like popcorn kernels. Something moved beneath the bark, pulsing like a worm wriggling beneath the softest soil. This seemed to grab the attention of everyone in the room. The workers stopped whatever they were doing, turned toward the oak tree, and focused on its softening belly.

Suddenly, the tree trunk split like a hatching egg, throwing more bark at the watchers' feet. No one moved. They continued to look on, fixed on the birth of this unknown entity, their feet rooted to the floor.

The floor, which was no longer a metal slab fastened down with thick anchor bolts—no, it was now an earthy surface, sparsely covered by a patchwork of grass. No longer were there towering pipes and machines, computers stacked on top of each other. The industrial stage had faded, lost within the evolving space of the dreamworld, and had now become a woodland backdrop. The smell of fresh morning dew filled the air, and Grady took the odor deep in his lungs, and, oddly enough, it soothed him despite witnessing the endless tree give birth to this unknown form.

An arm punched through the bark, sending bits of wood and squirts of embryonic fluid outward in a wide spray. No one moved. Grady glanced to his right, saw the workers were no longer workers, but people dressed in ordinary clothes, though their faces had changed, had devolved into something less…human. Growths had bloomed on their cheeks, bright green blotches that reminded Grady of the moss that would collect on the surface of shiny-wet rocks near a waterfall, thick and spongy. The crowd wore this vegetation like beards, some of the collections long enough to braid. Some had flowers for eyes. Some had lichen growing on their ears. Leafy stalks of varying thicknesses extended from their heads.

He turned back to the tree and watched the hatching.

Next, a leg kicked through the center, cracking more of the tree's sheathing, spreading the birth canal wider, preparing for the final push. This seemed to appease the audience, a feeling that gathered on Grady's shoulders. The Mother's subjects hummed in unison, a hymn-like melody that rose with the passing seconds, foreign sounds to Grady's ears, yet so familiar. The humming droned on, the three notes repeating over and over again.

They were helping the birth along. As they hummed louder and louder, the thing within the tree pushed furiously toward new life. Grady wanted to turn his head, look away from this monster's birth, but found he was powerless to do so. The dream reminded him it was still in control, forcing his eyes upon the grisly nativity.

A rush of bark and gelatinous fluid exploded outward, sprinkling the grassy pad before it with a filthy combination of wood and afterbirth. The miasma caused Grady to lurch forward with every intention of hurling, but the dream would not allow such a thing. He was forced to keep it all down, and there would be no release from this brand-new smell that now ruled the atmosphere. Grady watched in horror as the thing stepped out of the tree's cavity, a cadaverous, hairless being about the size of an average adult. Its milky complexion could be seen easily through the translucent slime that covered its body. Ears that came to a point reminded Grady of elves. When it opened its eyes, he saw the bright gold shine and instantly knew who had given birth to this demonic entity, *The Mother of Dead Dreams*. She was the mother of this dream and she was the mother of this foul beast, the thing that opened its mouth to reveal endless rows of carnivorous teeth. A tail, about the length of a guitar neck, wagged behind it.

It glared at Grady, and he shrunk back, ducking into the crowd. But he didn't get very far. The crowd, controlled by the dream's master, bunched together, making it impossible for him to pass. He looked around, seeking an egress, but there was nothing available.

Grady turned back to the hairless creature. He could hear it breathing as if the sounds were coming from his own body.

The Mother was standing behind its new kin, wrapping her filth-caked arms around its bone-white body, its hairless landscape of new flesh. Dirt mixed with the clear embryonic jelly, tarnishing the creature's clean form. It didn't mind. It only stared at Grady with a childlike curiosity, its head tilting slightly, waiting for permission to destroy.

The Mother growled in its ear.

Then, like a canine released from its owner's grasp, it charged at its perceived threat.

Grady turned, tried to run, forgetting about the blockade of The Mother's faithful followers, and not caring very much about them either. He tried to force himself between them, but the dream held its position.

The creature's shadow fell over him.

He stared in horror.

The beast crashed down on him. He felt pain, only for a second before—

4

Grady woke up. It wasn't late, not really. Just after midnight. His heart was racing and he could feel the throb pulsing in his temples. He'd never experienced a dream that lucid before. It had felt so real, like he'd actually been there. After a few minutes of sitting up in the dark and trying to breathe normally, he finally came down from that heightened state of pure terror.

He decided he needed to call Doug, right this second. He didn't care if the call woke up Mr. Simms or if he accidentally woke up his own parents in the process. He needed to talk to him, tell him what he'd just experienced. A part of him thought maybe Doug had dreamed the same thing.

Carefully, he crept his way downstairs, making sure to avoid the areas of the floor he knew were soft and apt to squeak. The slightest creak was like a crack of thunder in the silence of the night. The oak floors were old, in need of replacement, so unfortunately, they often betrayed him in times like this, times when he wanted to sneak downstairs for a midnight snack or to play video games because he couldn't sleep.

When he reached the bottom of the stairs, he paused, waiting to hear movement coming from their bedroom or to see the light in the hallway explode with a burst of blinding luminance. Neither happened, and he figured he was in the clear. He went immediately for the kitchen and grabbed the phone off the cradle. He punched in Doug's phone number, which he had committed to memory.

"Hello?" Doug answered, the call barely completing its first ring.

"Doug? You're up?"

"Was literally about to call you."

"The dream?"

"Yeah," Doug said, and Grady heard his throat click from a hard swallow. "Yeah, I had it too."

"This is bad, isn't it? That's what the dream means?"

"I think our town is in big trouble. Unless we stop it." He sighed. "I mean, unless *we* stop *her*."

"The Mother."

"Exactly."

"Tomorrow. We should do this tomorrow."

"Yeah, tomorrow. I think I have a plan."

"Okay."

"Oh shit," he said, whispering frightfully, and Grady's heart skipped a beat.

"Doug? You okay? What happened?"

No answer.

"Doug?"

Still no answer.

Oh shit, Grady thought. *She's come for him. She's sent that thing after him! He's as good as dead! He's—*

"It's nothing," Doug said, finally. "I thought I heard my dad."

"Jesus, man. You scared the hell out of me."

"Sorry."

"I guess I'm just a little jumpy. Probably the dream. It felt so…*so real.*"

"Do you think Jesse dreamed it too?"

Grady hadn't considered it, although it made perfect sense. He wouldn't be surprised if all the children of Hooperstown had dreamed it. Or some variation. She was in them all, her touch growing more powerful, gaining more abilities with each second her spirit was allowed to exist, breathe inside their dreams.

"I guess. We should call him. Tomorrow."

Doug concurred.

Grady hung up the phone, traveled back upstairs, climbed into bed, and tried to fall back to sleep.

But it wasn't possible.

Every time he closed his eyes, the hairless creature was waiting for him, those golden circles for eyes blooming wider and wider, until all he could see was that brilliant flash of sparkling light.

5

"You're gay?"

Adam nodded, a smile controlling his face. "Yes."

"But...that girl you were with...the look you were giving me... I..."

His smile dwindled. "I'm sorry, Jewel. I didn't think I was being anything but friendly. I'm sorry if you're confused. I didn't mean to..."

Her head swam, none of this making sense. She'd never met someone who was openly gay before. Sure, there had been some people in her class who'd been rumored to be, but never anyone who'd admitted it, come out, especially not to her. Probably in fear that she'd use it against them, get bullied for it. In truth, they were right. The old Jewel would have used their sexuality as a weapon against them, berated them every chance she could get.

The *old* Jewel, not the *new* one. The new Jewel didn't care about one's sexuality. It made no difference to her.

"Here's the thing, though," Adam said, placing his hands on his hips. "Not a lot of people know about it." He scratched his neck. His new smile looked more like a pained grimace. "Like, maybe three."

"Three?"

"Yeah, including you."

The weight of this information pushed down on her.

"Jewel, my own parents don't even know. Not yet. I haven't...well, I haven't come out yet."

"Oh Christ."

"It's scary. The whole thing is... I mean, you understand, don't you?"

She leaned against his car and closed her eyes. "Yeah, I understand."

"It's hard to trust people. Not everyone is very accepting, not in this town. I can't tell anyone at the youth center. Some of those kids, their families raised them as hardcore Christians, and they wouldn't understand. I've heard them use all sorts of derogatory words, in normal, casual, everyday conversation. You know the kind." His cheeks puffed out, and he released a gust of air.

"Yeah, I know the kind." She'd used some of them when she hung out with Brennan and Dakota, and she'd once called Brenda Mottenburg a "big dyke" to her face, which actually made the girl cry. Brenda had missed school the following day, and Jewel knew that couldn't be coincidental. At the time, Jewel had been proud of that accomplishment, but now—shit, now there was only a deep shame, a boulder of regret resting in the pit of her stomach.

A tear leaked from her left eye.

"Jesus, Jewel," Adam said, finding that smile again, even though it was a shell of its former arrangement. "Not worth shedding a tear over."

"It's not that," she said, dragging her wrist across her cheek. "I've just… I've done terrible things, Adam. I've said terrible things to people…"

"I get it."

"You do?"

"Yeah. I know the person you were. But your past doesn't define you, not really. It's what you do with what you've learned, how you approach your future—that's what makes you who you really are."

A burst of laughter, the corny kind. It felt good to erupt with that positive outburst. It lightened the load in her tummy. "So wise."

He shrugged. "I read a lot of philosophy. What can I say?"

For a minute, they talked. Small conversations that circled around each other. Then Jewel said, "You don't look gay."

He looked confused by this statement, but not exactly offended. "What does gay look like? Or, should I say, what do *you* think gay looks like?"

She opened her mouth, expecting to supply him with a decent answer, but then realized she didn't have one. "I…I don't know, I guess. I thought I did."

"You were expecting someone a little more…flamboyant? Elton John dancing around the parking lot with the rose-colored glasses and a sparkly, neon jacket?"

She couldn't help it—she tittered.

"We're not all like that, you know?" Though a small part of him was probably offended by her question, he masked his sting with a humorous grin.

"I'm sorry," she said. "I…shouldn't have."

He raised both hands. "It's okay. But now you know."

"Never trying to kiss another boy as long as I live."

Now he laughed. "Ha! Don't say that. That would make me feel horrible."

A brief silence passed between them, and she decided to shift the conversation in a different direction. Somewhere darker.

"Do you dream?" she asked, using her nervous energy by dragging her foot across the pavement.

"Dream?" He squinted. "Like, dream-dream? Or like, Martin Luther King, *I Have A Dream*?"

"Dream-dream." The twisted memories from previous nights came flooding back to her, myriad thoughts and images. "Nightmares, actually. I've been having them a lot lately. Actually, a lot of strange things have been happening lately."

"Like what?"

She told him about the last day of school, that night at the movies, what she'd seen in the woods.

"It really freaked me out. You know, usually I can hold my own, but I looked into that kid's eyes and I saw…" She recalled the golden circles that bordered the black holes. Dead planets for eyes. "It was… It was really terrifying. I think even at my parents' worst, I never felt that afraid."

Adam didn't seem like he was totally convinced that the story held some truth.

"Ever since I've had these weird dreams." She dug into her back pocket and produced the note that had been left on her doorstep. "Feel like I'm going a bit crazy."

Adam took the note and read it. *"The Children of the Last Summer?"*

"I know, right?"

"Gives *me* goosebumps."

She glanced down at his arm and saw he wasn't kidding. "I don't know what it means."

"Well, unless someone is having a laugh at your expense…" He folded up the note and handed it back to her. "I'd say someone is coming after you."

"Wow, thanks for making me feel better."

"What does this have to do with the dreams?"

"Funny you should ask. I don't know exactly, but there is this woman in them. She's looking for me. Calling to me. Telling me to come. Join her.

To become one of her children. I don't know—the dreams are very dark, shadowy. It's hard to see. And it's very disjointed."

"Non-linear?"

"I guess so. Things don't make a lot of sense."

He nodded. "Non-linear."

"Whatever. The whole thing freaks me out and I feel like something terrible is happening—not just to me, but this entire town. There's this sense of doom…"

Adam shrugged. "Maybe it's just because of those kids getting sick. One of them died, I heard. That girl. She was in your class, right?"

Jewel nodded, her eyes finding pavement.

"They even shut down the chemical plant. It is getting crazy around here, come to think of it. Maybe what you're feeling stems from that."

Stems, he said. She thought of the woman in her dreams, the one with vines growing out of her mouth, her nude body tangled up in a jungle-like overgrowth. Sitting missionary on a bed of thistles and thorns. A dark moon behind her, glowing dimly in a dying world. Those awful eyes burning with golden circles, much like the boy in the woods, the one who'd looked dead rather than alive, yet still had enough life to follow her.

"Jewel?" asked Adam, snapping his fingers in front of her face. "I lost you."

She recollected herself. "Sorry."

"Where'd you go?"

She shrugged. "Not so far away."

"Lying to me?"

Another shrug, lazier this time. "So, do you dream, Adam?"

"Not the way you do."

"You haven't had any nightmares lately?"

He shook his head. "No. Not a single one."

From the bushes, James Fritz spied on them, waiting to make his move. He coughed into his hand, felt wetness sputter past his lips. No surprise that he found the mucus dark, barely visible in the shadows that clothed him. With each breath his chest crackled like dry, crumpling newspapers. His body was frigid despite the temperature maintaining the upper eighties, the sweat pouring off his brow. A shiver wracked him, attacking his nerves, every limb quivering, under attack from phantom sensations. A case of the sniffles had come and never left, and he found himself constantly wiping his nose.

What the hell is wrong with me? he asked the darkness that had gotten inside him and refused to leave. Whenever he thought he was strong enough to fight off the sick, sour feeling, he pictured the dead girl, Lauren Sullivan, hunched over him, puking a tar-like substance into his mouth, forcing him to swallow every available drop.

She had passed whatever death sentence she had acquired onto him. It was only a matter of time before he suffered the same fate. Time was limited. So were his actions. He couldn't rebel against the voice that commanded him, instructed him to carry out these wicked errands.

Forgive me, baby, he said, thinking of his wife. Fritz knew he'd never see her face again, knew it the second the dead girl showed up at the youth center looking like a hideous shell of her former self. *I love you.*

This was what he got for doing the right thing, for volunteering his time and energy into making a difference in some kids' lives. He should have listened to Olivia, pulled back on the amount of time he spent away from her that summer. He'd volunteered every previous summer, dedicating a good chunk of his spare time to helping others.

Be a little selfish, she had told him, back when they spent an entire night organizing cans of pasta and green beans for a local food drive. *Take some time for yourself. And me.* She had looked at him with her eyebrows, the way she sometimes did when she wanted to get a point across, a little quirk that had always tapped the center of his heart. *You deserve it.*

He should have listened to her. In the end, it was the guilt that got him. If it weren't for people like him in *his* life, maybe his path would have turned out differently. Maybe he would have failed to grow up an educator, a principal in one of the biggest regional school districts in all of Central

Jersey. Maybe he would have ended up an addict instead. A criminal. Or shit, maybe he'd be dead.

There was no telling what path he would have taken, but he knew one thing—it wouldn't have been a good one.

No, those kids needed him, even if Olivia couldn't completely understand. Or maybe she did understand, but just didn't care. Either way, in the end, she had been right.

She was always right.

And now he was here.

Dead anyway.

Jewel leaned into Adam and tried to kiss him. He pulled back.

He watched the rest of the scene unfold, waiting to make his move. He clutched the tire iron in his right hand, and from out of the shadows, from behind the small collection of bushes near the fringe of the parking lot, Fritz stepped out with purpose and malicious intent.

7

By the time Jewel saw him, it was too late.

Fritz hobbled from the shadows, clutching the tire iron with both hands. He had the weapon raised behind him, ready to bring the iron down on his first victim. The slash down looked effortless and hit Adam across the back of his head. Jewel watched the kid's eyes bug with utter shock. His pupils sliding back coincided with his fall, and he hit the parking lot hard and without resistance.

"Adam!" she yelled, focusing her attention on his unconscious (and bleeding) body, rather than doing the smart thing and running for her life. Those precious seconds she spent concentrating on him doomed her, and when she peered up from him, Fritz was in her face, reaching, his fingers threatening to tighten around her throat.

She opened her mouth to beg for mercy, but again, her actions were too little too late. His fingers gripped the sides of her neck, his palms pressing firmly against the soft part of her throat. He pushed her up against Adam's car, allowing his body weight to smother her. She tried to move, shifting her vision from side to side, hoping to see the shadow of someone passing by, someone who could help or call the police or scream for someone else to come over and join the party—but there was no one and nothing but the dark, the trees that neighbored the parking lot and the other cars, the owners inside the diner and not coming out anytime soon.

She was alone.

Adam was probably dead, his head split open and bleeding onto the pavement.

She looked back to Fritz, pleading for her life with an innocent stare. Her eyes would have to speak for her, and she allowed tears to come forth. But when she saw what lived inside *his* eyes, her heart stopped, and her blood chilled her veins.

Golden circles. Bright. Burning like the fires of some fresh hell.

She was immediately reminded of the boy in the woods on the last day of school. His eyes were of the same make, and although he had seemed powerless against his own actions, there had been a part of him that rebelled against whatever had invaded his earthly body. He'd begged for help. Fritz, with his jaw clenched, the muscles in his face pronounced, seemed to be driven by the same force, yet he was not trying to rebel against it. Whatever had him had sunk its claws in deep, and he was helpless as the entity within took over, obliterating whatever remained of his soul, whatever made him *him*.

She tried to kick him in the nards, but his body was pressed against hers, allowing little movement. She couldn't even lift her knee into his genitals, which seemed like an easier, though less effective, maneuver. He'd pinned her good, and a dusky darkness had begun to slip its way into the corners of her vision. She felt faint. It was hard to breathe. Air fought its way in and out of her lungs, and the harder she tried to regulate what should have been an involuntary function, she found the darkness was accumulating, taking over.

She blinked, and Fritz's face had been replaced by another.

Suffer the Season.

It was a woman, her pale, sickly-green complexion taking up most of Jewel's vision.

A Plague Amongst Us All.

The woman caressed her cheek, the slime of her touch coating Jewel's flesh, sending a wave of chills throughout her stiff body.

You are the Children of the Last Summer.

A motherly smile warmed the woman's face. A deep-sea-blue fluid crawled out of her nose, bleeding over her curled lips.

Death for the Betrayers Come Fall.

Before the parking lot faded to black, the woman opened her mouth and spread her pestilence, the raw, malodorous scent of some malignant underworld annihilating the atmosphere.

It smelled like an endless summer spent in the deepest, darkest pit in hell.

CHAPTER FOURTEEN

Mom? Are You There?

1

His father's car idled in the parking lot of Benton Mental Health Facility. Doug glanced at the tall, square-shaped building, which looked no different from any ordinary office building. Its brick exterior could have belonged to some medical complex or rehabilitation center. Hell, it could have been any old mundane workplace, stuffed with cubicles and people dressed in shirts and ties, flower-patterned dresses, their hair done up with a touch of modern perfection. He wasn't sure what he had expected. Maybe a dark, foreboding castle-like mansion that sat atop a hill. Behind it, lightning streaking across forlorn skies. A building with its windows caged so the patients within could not escape. Heavily guarded, men in blue uniforms standing watch along the perimeter with AK-47s strapped to their hips.

Then he reminded himself this wasn't a prison, a place where people were sent to be punished. This was a place where people were sent to get better.

In the backseat, Grady shifted uncomfortably, and Doug knew the tension of this precise moment had hopped inside his skin.

Doug's father turned from the driver's seat. "You okay, Grades?"

"Yes, sir."

"You can stay outside if you like."

Doug faced his friend, putting on his best *it's-okay* face. "I understand how weird this might be."

Grady shook his head. "No. Nope. Don't worry about me. I can handle it."

Doug and his father exchanged looks, then they both returned their attention to the backseat.

"Okay. Let's go."

Gordon Simms got out first and then the boys. As they approached the front door, Grady and Doug hung back, Grady looking like he had something to get off his chest right then and there but didn't want Doug's dad hearing what he had to say.

"What is it?" Doug whispered, low enough so his father wouldn't hear.

"How are you so cool about this all of a sudden?"

Doug shrugged. "The game has changed."

"What does that mean?"

"It means," Doug said, stopping, "that our friend is in a hospital bed right now, dying. That's what it means."

Gordon Simms was already at the door, holding it open. "You ready, sport?"

Doug sucked in a deep breath. "Yeah."

He trailed his father through the front door, Grady following faithfully behind.

2

The inside of the hospital smelled like bleach and artificial lemons, a scent that Doug would recall with perfect clarity for the remainder of his life. A janitor mopped the hallway as the three of them headed past. A few doctors gathered outside an office, chatting away about the stability of one of their patients. Doug heard one of them use the phrase, "Progress is being made," but that was all he caught. He wondered if they had been his mother's doctors, but he doubted it, even though his father had told him she was doing much better of late. Most of the time he had tuned out his father's stories about visiting Mom, mainly because every time he spoke of her the nightmarish memory of that night came flooding back, a vivid and sensory-encapsulating impression that was just like being there. He hated recalling everything that happened that night, the way the flashback made him feel on the inside, sick and slimy. Like there was this permanent injury within him, a wound that bled from time to time, whenever his father opened it with tales of Mom and how "well" she was doing.

Now, as he stepped toward a small nurses' station, that wound was open and bleeding and hemorrhaging at a rate he'd never experienced. Every time he blinked, he saw his mother in his room, in the middle of the night, stalking the dark corners, pacing back and forth like a tiger in its cage, waiting for the right moment, whispering to the shadows that crawled over her, concealing her face. Moonlight gleamed off the kitchen knife in her hand. Her whispers bounced between the walls, gibberish, nonsense things his young, fragile mind could not handle. It was like she had spoken another language entirely, an ancient tongue that lacked vowels of any kind. A bunch of letters strung together at random.

He shook away these memories and proceeded to follow his father's lead.

"Good afternoon, Mr. Simms," said one of the nurses as they reached the counter. "Sharon's having a particularly good day." She turned her attention immediately to Doug. "And she's looking forward to seeing you, young man."

He knew it was meant to sound like a positive thing, but her words filled him with harrowing thoughts and a bug-crawling-under-the-collar sensation. Fighting off the shivers that coiled around his bones, he mustered up enough courage to smile at her. The nurse smiled back, though she didn't need to; this was not a place of smiles.

Doug turned to Grady, whose fish-out-of-water vibe was almost palpable, a thing he wore like a chain around his neck. He knew Grades was scared; his eyes told no lies. Doug was glad he had come along, happy he'd put the past behind him and was coming through for a friend. There was a period of doubt where Doug thought he'd bail at the last minute, that scene from the night of the Hunt, that image of Grady letting go of Jesse's arm and sprinting off into the dark, clearly responsible for that projection. But Grady had shown up. He was here. Which was good, because in the coming months, Grady would have to gather all the courage he could—to help in what was to come. What that was exactly, Doug hadn't the slightest clue, but the summer had taken them down a strange and terrible path, and sooner or later that path would end, because no path goes on forever, especially not when you're fourteen.

And there would be a fight waiting for them. Of that much, he was certain.

Doug was prepared to end this. He was prepared to give it his all. He wanted the Mother of Dead Dreams to dream her last dream, project her last nightmare.

But most of all he wanted his best friend back, out of the hospital and with a clean bill of health. He wanted every kid to recover, beat the disease that was plaguing their town. He wanted everyone to live happily ever after, even though that wasn't reality—reality was pain and death and disappointment, and the Mother of Dead Dreams was the bringer of those things.

"Are you excited to see her?" the nurse asked him, and he took a moment to clear these very adult cobwebs from his thoughts. He felt like he was daydreaming in the back of class, and of course that reminded him that summer was almost over, and it wouldn't be long before school started up again. It almost felt like there hadn't been any summer at all, though that wasn't accurate. Just, he'd spent a great deal of it trying to figure out who this mysterious Mother was and why she was causing Hooperstown's children to get cancer and had spent very little of it on fun things like trips to the beach and water parks and town fairs—the fun stuff kids lived for, the impressionable memories that stuck.

"Yes," he said finally, lying through his teeth. He wasn't excited. He was nervous as all hell. Terrified actually. Every part of him yearned to retreat, run out the front door without looking back. "Yes, I am."

The nurse closed her eyes and nodded, then walked around the counter to lead them down the hall. She took them to a door. A guard, a man with a soft belly and the charm of a mall Santa, blocked the entryway but stepped aside when he saw the four of them approaching. Before the nurse opened the door and led them inside, she turned to the boys and bent over, lowering her eyes to their level.

"Now," she said, keeping the pep in her voice even though Doug knew he was about to hear a warning. "You might see some things inside. *Unusual* things."

The second those words left her lips, he pictured inmates dangling from the light fixtures, slinging poo across the room while speaking in tongues. Lunatics in straitjackets rocking back and forth, muttering nonsense to each other, arching their heads back and laughing wildly while the nurses and doctors tried everything to calm them down, offering them sedatives which were knocked out of their hands, sent scattering across the dirty-white floor. A group of orderlies restraining some of the patients who were having episodes, strapping them to a table and forcing downers down their throats.

Of course, he knew this wasn't reality, that these were images inspired by the garbage he'd seen in movies, on television. He was sure it wasn't like that at all. It couldn't be…

"You might see some odd behavior," the nurse added. "But just know that none of the patients here are dangerous. Okay? Think of them as sick people who just want to get better."

"So…" Grady said, the gulping of his throat audible. "They'll be walking around?"

"Yeah, sort of. We're going to the meeting room where families come to visit and talk, but we'll have to walk through the main floor. It'll be fine. Just stick close to me, don't touch or even acknowledge any of the patients and you'll be A-OK. Okay?"

Grady looked terrified by this news, but he held it together. The nurse ignored his face, and Gordon put a reassuring hand on his shoulder and asked him if he would be okay. He even mentioned the car again, if he wanted to sit inside and listen to the classic rock station instead. Grady mumbled something in response that sounded like, "I'll be fine." Doug wasn't quite sure of it though, wasn't sure if he would be fine.

"Come on, Grades," Doug said, wrapping his arm around his friend's neck. "This will all be over soon."

3

They didn't see *some things*, not really. The wildest thing Doug saw while briefly strolling across the main floor was some guy talking to himself while playing checkers. The other patients were watching television or doing activities, reading and piecing together puzzles, but no one was out of line, pitching a fit, doing anything he'd seen in *One Flew Over the Cuckoo's Nest*. Doug was almost disappointed. A part of him wanted a cool story to tell Jesse during their next hospital visit.

"Right this way," the nurse said, opening a door in the back of the room.

Gordon led the kids on through. The next room looked like the school cafeteria, long table benches stationed in rows, placed evenly apart. There weren't a lot of people. Doug counted six groups visiting with family members, all of them far enough away so the family next to them couldn't eavesdrop on their discussion. There were a few guards stationed throughout the room, planted in each of the four corners. Doug's eyes immediately went to their belts to see if they were armed, but he saw no guns. Tasers, but no guns.

"You ready, bud?" Dad asked.

Doug didn't even realize he had stopped walking. "Yeah," he replied, taking baby steps, following the nurse to the end of the row. He could see where she was leading them, to an empty table save for one lonely body—his mother.

Sharon Simms.

Her back was to him. He couldn't see her face, only her long, curly hair, which fell on her shoulders, the same thick auburn ribbons he remembered her having, only some of the color had faded with age. His heartbeat quickened with each step. A part of him wanted to revolt, to abandon this half-brained idea. He looked to Grady, but his friend kept his eyes trained ahead, concentrating on where they were going, occasionally glancing around at the other families.

"Sharon," the nurse said, taking the lead. "Sharon, your son is here." Her voice was pleasant and soft, as if introducing the greatest thing in the world to a small child barely capable of understanding such things.

Mom turned, her face beaming with delight. Her smile was strong and radiant, and even though she looked a little older than he had remembered—a few more lines etched into her face, a few more shadows and wrinkles—she looked more or less the same. She wasn't handcuffed or confined to the floor, not that Doug expected them to have her chained like Hannibal Lecter, but also—he assumed she'd be restrained in *some* way, just in case. *Better safe than sorry* was an ideal he thought a place like this might adopt. Especially considering what had happened the last time *(KILL YOU SAVE YOU KILL YOU SAVE YOU)* they were together. But no. She was free. She could reach over the table and choke the life out of him, if that was her choice.

"Hey there, kiddo," she said, resting her chin on the palm of her hand. "You finally came."

Every footstep felt like he had bricks for shoes. His father's hand encouraged him to move forward. Grady hung back, almost hiding behind Gordon as if he were a child initially scared to see their favorite cartoon characters come to life in the form of a costumed actor.

"Hey, hon," Dad said, breaking the ice. "Good to see you."

"Good to see you too." She was all smiles now, and Doug thought if she smiled any harder or wider, her cheeks would split open. "Come, come. Have a seat."

Doug looked to his father, seeking permission.

"Go ahead," Dad said.

Doug climbed his way onto the bench. Grady reluctantly sat beside him. Dad didn't sit, opting to stand behind the two boys as if he were facilitating this meet and greet and not part of it.

"Well," the nurse said, "I'll be right over here in case you need anything. If you do, just holler."

"Thank you, Nurse Hammet," Dad said.

"Pleasure."

As promised the nurse retreated to the corner, lingering near one of the guards. She whispered something, probably a warning, and Doug felt a little more at ease. He guessed they would watch her closely, just in case something *did* happen, in case his mother decided to finish the job she had started all those years ago.

He didn't believe that would happen, but then again, there were a lot of things Doug Simms never thought would happen, things that had come to fruition lately.

"You brought a friend," she said, her eyes wandering to Grady, still smiling, always smiling. It was as if her lips were a mask for the things she was thinking.

(SAVE YOU KILL YOU SAVE YOU)

"Hi," Grady said, shifting, trying to find a comfortable position. His throat clicked when he swallowed. "I'm Grady."

"Pleasure to meet you, Grady."

An awkward silence drowned the moment, and Doug wasn't sure if their arrangement would ever recover.

"So," Dad said, putting a hand on Doug's shoulder. "Doug got almost all As and Bs last year. His teachers said he's more prepared for high school than ninety percent of his class. Isn't that amazing?"

Sharon's eyes grew wide, a proud smirk nesting on her face. "That's great, honey. That's really amazing—I'm so proud of you." Her response was over the top, as if speaking so jubilantly would erase the horrors of back then. She was probably drugged too, mildly sedated, and that might have contributed to her behavior.

"I got mostly As and Bs, but a couple of Cs, though," Grady added. "Pretty good, considering, you know, I didn't do a ton of homework. I slept through homeroom most of the time and..." He trailed off when he realized everyone had turned their eyes on him. Sometimes his nerves got the best of him, and the result was him babbling about whatever came to mind first.

"Sorry," he said, shaking his head. "I'll...I'll shut up now."

"Grady," Dad said, "why don't you and I take a little walk."

"Are you sure that's okay?" Doug asked his old man, surprised Dad was willing to leave him alone with her.

"Yeah," he said, "It'll be okay. Sharon, is that okay with you?"

"Yes," she said, nodding vigorously. "Yes, that's...that's very fine."

"Okay, good." He leaned into Doug's ear and whispered, "I'll be right over there if you need me."

Grady got up from the table, staring at him with those *good-luck-dude* eyes, and followed Dad to the closest corner of the room, which looked just out of earshot.

"Hi," his mother said when he returned his attention to her.

"Hi."

"This must be weird for you," she said, a breath of humorless laughter escaping her. "I know how you must feel."

He wanted to tell her that she had no idea how he felt, no possible clue. But he refrained. The clock on the wall ticked down, and he wondered how much time they were allowed. He'd come here for answers and now he wasn't sure he'd get them.

"I want to apologize," she said, her tone changing, no longer jovial and upbeat. She sniffled, the onset of tears closing in. "For what happened all those years ago. For what...what happened. What *I* did."

"You don't have to," he said, nodding. "I get it."

Suspicious eyes. She bit her lip. "Do you?"

"You just...had an episode. It wasn't your fault."

Her bottom lip quivered. "Why did you wait so long to see me?"

Her question lanced his heart. Floodgates opened and a tidal wave of guilt rolled over him. "I dunno. Scared, I guess."

"Yeah. Yeah, that makes sense. I'd be scared too. But you don't have to be scared of me anymore. I'm...I'm doing a lot better. I have help now. I know I have a few demons, but now I know how to defeat them."

"I'm happy for you."

She nodded, understanding. "You don't seem happy. You seem...lost."

He shrugged. "I guess I am. A little."

Her eyes slid from side to side, as if the walls were narrowing. Moving. Collapsing on one another. "I get the feeling you didn't come here to visit me. I mean, *really* visit me. To talk about banal shit like schoolwork, to introduce me to your friend." Her eyes narrowed and she leaned in, dropping her voice in a whisper, hiding her words from listening ears. "Did you?"

He swallowed. He didn't feel like he was in danger, but he didn't feel safe either. Still, those memories of her on top of him, angling the knife down at him, the tip of the blade coming within inches of penetrating his throat, were replaying themselves, over and over again. He couldn't shake them no matter how hard he tried and staring into the eyes of the same woman who'd caused those memories wasn't helping.

"No," he said plainly, keeping his voice hushed to match hers. He wasn't sure if anyone could hear them, but at this point, he didn't care. He'd come for answers, had gotten this far, and he needed to finish this thing. "I came to ask you stuff. Because I think you can help me. Help *us*, I mean. Help the town."

She leaned back in her seat. "It's happening, isn't it?"

He didn't know exactly what *it* was, but he had a pretty good idea they were talking about the same thing.

"The kids," she said. "They're getting sick?"

He felt his heart sink, land somewhere beneath his bowels.

"I've heard whispers of it," she clarified. "In the halls. Small things. But whenever I ask about the rumors of sick kids, no one tells me."

"Yes. Kids are getting sick."

"They'll blame the plant, you know." She grimaced. "And with good reason—that place is death." A faint snicker now, most unsettling. "I always told your father that, but he never believed me. Said everything was fine there, that they knew what they were doing. That the town was safe." She shook her head. "They're not innocent in this, but they aren't the only cause behind the disease."

"It's her," Doug said. "The Mother."

Sharon didn't react. It was as if he'd said nothing. "You've seen her?"

He shook his head.

"In dreams?"

He nodded.

"That's where she hides. In the dreamworld. Existing. Waiting. Scheming. Trying to draw people in. Innocent, feeble minds that are easily manipulated, easily accessed."

"What do you mean?"

She leaned forward some, making sure no one in the room could hear, especially her husband. "Have you ever had a thought, a notion so...*impure?* Something so terrible and horrible and savage on every level, that you would never, *ever,* in any way, consider acting on it? Something so awful you wondered why and how you even thought of it in the first place?"

He couldn't recall anything specific, but he nodded anyway. Playing along, he thought, was probably the best way to gain more information.

"That's her. *Them,* actually, these things that exist in the worlds between. We see them as shadows in dreams but make no mistake—they are trying to access us, worm and slither their way into our thoughts, wage war on the battlefields within our minds. They live in this place, but we can keep them from planting seeds in our mental soil, prevent their ideas and sinister intentions from taking root. Sprouting. Blooming. Spreading like weeds through cracks on a sidewalk."

She paused to catch her breath. Before she continued, she glanced at the corners of the room, making sure the coast was clear. Dad and Grady were talking amongst themselves, watching, but from a safe distance. The guards took turns watching everyone in the room, and Nurse Hammet had the ear of one of them, hardly paying attention to the meeting, but looking over at them from time to time.

"In our case," she continued. "In *Hooperstown's* case, it's just her. The Mother of All Eternal Things. She's been here since the beginning. Watching. Waiting. Biding her time, looking for the precise moment to strike."

"I heard her story. Well, a part of it. I heard about the group that settled here. Thomas Hooper. His wife. And what they did to..." He swallowed. "That girl."

"Who told you such things?" she asked, her eyes narrowing to slits.

"A teacher. Mr. Boxberger."

She glanced upward, staring at the ceiling as if further information were scrawled there. "Don't know that name, but I'd very much like to meet your teacher. He sounds...interesting."

"That's not possible."

Sharon Simms seemed distracted by this, her eyes wandering off. As if someone were trying to talk to her, as if words Doug couldn't hear were eating her attention. Then, suddenly realizing where she was, where she'd been, she nodded sheepishly. "That's a shame. I feel like I could get along with this...Boxberger."

Doug shrugged, as if this were inconsequential. "They moved."

"Ah. I see. A shame indeed. It's just that...I've never met someone who knew the old tales. Not in a very long time."

"How do you know them? The tales, I mean."

She froze, her eyes widening. "I told you. Dreams. She used to come to me. Show me things that happened to her, how those men took her, abducted her. Not *her*. But the one who'd eventually become the Mother's vessel, her pathway to this world, this plane, the real one of which we live and breathe. I'd see her slither out of the shadows, out of the dreamworld, and merge with the body of the innocent pregnant girl. The one Hooper murdered in cold blood to fill a void, to give his wife the child she always wanted. *Ohhhh*...what mothers do for their children."

Doug hated the way she spoke those last few words. A chill came crawling up his neck, fingers of ice running along the back of his skull.

"Did your *teacher*," she used air quotes around the title, "tell you everything about the Mother? How much did he know?"

Doug was at a loss, confused as to why she cared so much about Boxberger and his final lesson. "A little bit. Not much."

She nodded as if this were a good thing. "This all started when I was little. Younger than you. I was playing with my friends, out near the woods. My one friend, a girl my age, suggested we head into the woods. That she had something to show me."

"I know this story," Doug said with confidence. "You used to tell it to me sometimes. Before bed."

"You remember."

Doug nodded. "I dreamed it too. Once. On the last day before summer vacation. On the day this whole thing began."

She smiled. "I was hoping you would. That dream was meant to be a warning. That you should run far, far away from the Mother and her scourge. But...it would seem...you've become very much a part of it..." She shook her head. "I tried to save you all those years ago. I was trying to save you from what is to come."

He ignored this part, not wanting to revisit his mother's idea of *saving* someone. "None of that matters now. She's here. And she's winning. The real question is how do we stop her?"

Her face went dark, the shadows of the room spilling across her features. "Oh, my little traveler—there is no stopping her. She is death. And death is inevitable."

"I don't understand—there...there has to be some way to kill her. To end this."

"She is a plague, a disease upon mankind. And now that she has been freed, there is no stopping her."

"Diseases have cures."

"Not this one." His mother glared at him, sharpening her gaze. "She will spread and grow and conquer and eat and grow some more, until there is nothing left of this town. The country. The entire world. This is the end, my little traveler. Welcome to the apocalypse."

"You're wrong."

"I am not. I have seen the future, the street gutters lined with the dead. Our bodies piled higher than the streetlights and powerlines. Entire neighborhoods made up of houses of dead bodies. Black blood making rivers of our streets. The Mother wading through it, towers of the dead stacked on overgrown lawns. She spreads pestilence wherever she walks, and she will walk until the end of time. In the Land of Dreams, she lives forever." She leaned in, closer than before. "This is why I tried to save you, kiddo. To excuse you from this terrible end. To hide you from her all-seeing eye."

"Save me?"

(KILL YOU SAVE YOU KILL YOU SAVE YOU)

"Yes. I tried to save you. Because that's what mothers do. They save their children. Protect them, whatever the cost."

"You tried to kill me. You didn't try to save shit."

She shook her head adamantly. "No, I tried to save you. Prevent you from suffering at the hands of her deadly touch."

"No, you tried to *kill* me. Both of us. Dad and me. You...you didn't save anybody. You weren't doing us any favors."

She winced with suspicion. "Oh, you will understand soon enough. Her plague has begun and by the time you reach your end, you will wish I had saved you. You will beg for the knife I tried to put in your heart."

Doug hung his head. He had heard enough. It had been a mistake coming here, and not only had he learned nothing of how to save the town—and themselves—he had learned the truth about his mother, a truth he had known all along, though he wanted to believe in something different.

She was fucking bonkers.

"Goodbye, Mother," he said, pushing himself up.

She rose with him, reached out and grabbed his wrist. Pulled him close. "Kill yourself. It's the only way. It's the only way to avoid what's coming. She will plant her seeds inside your eyes and you will live forever in her fields of bloom, and trust me—child, *trust me,* that is *not* the place you want to spend your eternity, so help you God."

As she finished her pitch, Hammet and the guard peeled her away from him, undoing her grip finger by finger. She didn't let go easily. Her eyes cast an icy, haunted stare at her only son. There was no regret in them, not a speck. If they had been left completely alone, Doug thought she would have killed him the first chance she got.

"Listen to me," she said, shuddering with a deep sadness that had been building for the last seven years. "Listen to me, goddammit." Then she turned to Dad, who'd come hustling over as soon as he saw things taking a southern turn. "Gordy, do it. Do what we talked about. You take care of him. Of yourself. YOU DO IT, YOU HEAR ME? YOU FUCKING SAVE HIM!"

Doug turned and his father pulled him close, hiding him away from her. She continued to shout and scream, which brought more guards and nurses, all of whom worked hard on dragging her away from the scene. Doug hugged his father close and his father hugged him back, and together they watched as an orderly administered a shot, pumping his mother full of sedatives. The drugs seemed to work rather quickly, and within a few seconds she'd stopped screaming and carrying on about "saving" Doug, his friends, and anyone else in Hooperstown that Gordon Simms felt close to.

In under a minute she was gone, and Doug realized this would be the last memory he would ever have of his own mother.

In the car, Gordon broke down and started sobbing, pounding his fist against the steering wheel because, well, he had to hit *some*thing, and he figured the wheel could take it. A few breaths later and he was composing himself, allowing the anger to bleed out and doing everything he could to alleviate the simmering rage. Next, he turned to the boys. Doug slouched in the front seat, watching his father, sadness sparkling in his eyes. Grady sat in the back, looking down at the floor, the awkwardness of the moment weighing down on him.

"I'm really sorry about that," he said to them, wiping the last remaining tears from his eyes and face. He ran a wet hand across his shirt, ridding his purged emotions once and for all. Silently, he promised himself he'd never spill another tear over this mess, but he also knew that was a lie he'd told himself many times before—and yet, here he was.

"It's okay, Dad," Doug said, reaching out, grabbing his arm. His son's touch was not only comforting, but it was *everything* to him. It meant more than words could express.

"I love you so much, bud. I'm sorry that happened. I thought... I thought she was doing better. They told me she was making progress." A flare of anger flashed across his face at the mention of Benton and the people who worked there.

"It's fine," Doug said.

His boy looked fine, perfectly normal, which inspired uneasiness. Doug reacted as if they had pulled up to his favorite store and found it had closed early for the day, rather than getting attacked by his dangerously delusional mother. That well-there's-always-tomorrow outlook dug its way into Gordon's heart, and that hurt almost as much as if Doug had gotten pissed and told his father off, blaming him, telling him the whole situation was his fault, that he was responsible for the hollowness of the last seven years.

"It's not fine," Gordon said, leaning his head back against the rest. "I thought she was better. She was fine last week. And the week before that. Completely normal. I just...don't understand. She hasn't had an episode in...*years*."

Doug offered a cheery smile. "We'll be okay, Dad."

Who's the adult here? Gordon wondered.

He turned from Doug and focused on the backseat, craning his neck so he could face their guest. "How are you holding up, Grades? Good?"

"Me? Oh, yeah. I'm just...dandy."

"I'm sorry if that scared you."

"Me? Scared?" Grady waved him off, even though he looked like he'd unexpectedly bitten into something spicy. "Nah. I walked in on my mom taking a shit once. *That* was scary. Nightmares for weeks. This?" He jerked his thumb toward the mental health facility. "That was a walk in the park."

Gordon smiled, but the recent chain of events only allowed his lips to stretch so far. "That's...disgusting and I'm not necessarily sure I needed to know that, but...thank you."

He turned back to the wheel. Cranked engine. The mechanical roar was a gift for his ears as it snuffed out the silence. He wondered if he'd ever come back after today. If he should. He had to remind himself that he and Sharon were still officially married, that he hadn't pursued legal options despite his work buddies and neighbors suggesting it should be done. Every time the conversation had come up, every time he thought he had the courage to go through with it, there was a little voice in the back of his head that told him she wasn't evil or a bad person. That she was fine and had just gone through something traumatic. That her brain—whatever was wrong with it—could be fixed, re-wired like any old electrical problem.

But after today, he knew he'd been wrong about that. There was no fixing her. Whatever was internally broken could not be pieced back together.

He decided he'd pursue a divorce as soon as he got home, make some calls to some lawyers, get the ball rolling on what should have happened years ago. It was time to move on. To start a new life.

He looked to Doug, wondered if he'd be okay with it. Figured he would be considering this was the first time he'd seen his mom in seven years and that she picked up right where she left off. He could see in his eyes that he was done with her. Whatever reason he had decided to come for, it no longer mattered. This chapter of his life was now closed.

"Ice cream?" Gordon suggested, his hand lingering on the gearshift.

Doug and Grady glanced at each other, their faces breaking into wide smiles, and suddenly it didn't seem so bad. He reached over and mussed up his son's hair, realizing he hadn't taken him for a haircut all summer. Quickly, he wondered what other chores he'd shirked due to the amount of stress the plant's closing had placed on him. Had he forgotten to pay bills? To send out the last car payment? It was possible. At the moment he couldn't remember doing either for months.

But right now, none of that mattered. Right now, Doug was smiling. Watching his only child's mood lighten in contrast to the darkness they'd just experienced—that filled Gordon Simms with a warm touch, a sense of everlasting solace, an impression he wished would last forever.

CHAPTER FIFTEEN

The Root of All Evil

1

When Jesse dreamed there was mostly darkness. Shadows, really. Flitting flickers of dim shapes trespassing areas of light, a whirlwind of obscurities. He crawled through these imaginary places, feeling the sandy grit of the wet shore on his fingertips, his knees. Beyond the beach, an abandoned carnival took form, a vague silhouette at first, but as the dream matured the details were penciled in. And as things sharpened, he noticed there wasn't only a carnival, but a boardwalk along the Atlantic Ocean, located over the bridge connecting Red River to the small seaside towns that made up the Jersey shore. The strip of attractions, arcades and carousels and ice cream parlors and boardwalk games, had been touched by the Mother's apocalypse, resting under disastrous, gloom-ridden skies. Armies of vines and overgrowth of varying distances had conquered what was once considered a small sliver of paradise. As Jesse pulled himself from the dark ocean waters, he could make out the smiling clown face that rested atop the funhouse entrance, its unintentional malicious grin hidden behind nests of ivy and sheets of creepers, vegetation that had grown from the sickness of this dying world.

Kneeling on the beach, he felt like *The Last Man on Earth*, knowing everyone he had ever loved and cared for had gone the way of the malignant scourge. He was the lone survivor of this place, this alternative reality where the Mother had gotten what she'd come for, and seemingly much more. She'd taken the world in her grasp, crushed reality between her all-powerful fingers.

But *he* was alive. And how could that be when he felt so dead inside? So hollow. So alone. A shell of the kid he once was, reduced to a lethargic lump that only left his bed to rid himself of bodily waste. He used to have so much energy, ready to take on the entire world with the snap of two fingers. Now, he could barely lift his head from the pillow without the assistance of a nurse. He felt dead inside, yes, but he also felt dead on the outside too. A part of him knew he'd never leave this hospital bed. He'd never see his friends again.

He was eternally stuck.

Was this it? This dream? Was this how it truly ended? Was this his personal apocalypse?

He walked the beach, toward the dead world, toward the derelict strip of a place he once loved, a place his parents used to take him and Jimmy to have fun, a little reprieve from the insipid days of playing video games and reading comic books, things that *rot* the brain according to every overly-concerned parent. His shoes felt heavy, sodden with ocean water. The world smelled of death and decay and earthy spoils around every bend. Within seconds, he found himself traveling along the boards, a light wind bringing forth new smells. He pushed past them, his brain recognizing that this was a dream and that none of it was real. A possible future, maybe, but for now the world was intact and his friends were safe. Family, too. He needed to survive this dream, needed to get back to reality so he could warn the others of what was to come.

The old adage "if you die in your dream, you die in real life" never felt more truthful than it was right now.

He scurried past a closed candy stand, the signs on the front shouting out THE BEST SALTWATER TAFFY ON THE JERSEY SHORE. To his left was an arcade, next to it a bar made popular for its live music and two-dollar jumbo pizza slices. He moved his way down the boardwalk, entering a patch of mist that hid the distance. Now, everywhere he went was on the edge of the dream, and each step could mean his last. Eternity waited for him. A long fall to certain death. He carefully maneuvered his way through, touching the boards with his toes first before fully committing an entire foot.

Ahead, the mist began to clear, swirls of ghost-like material stretching and curling away. The boards before him led to the carousel encased in a stout, cone-shaped building. Jesse ambled on, feeling separated from his own consciousness. The dream was taking him further and further without consent. A slave to what came next, Jesse blinked and found himself inside the building.

The walls were thick with ivy and lichen, spores of mold that bloomed into fuzzy black flowers of perpetual decay. Vines thick as dock line covered the floor, looking like an unruly nest of snakes. They even squirmed like snakes, unfurling in slow motion, crawling across the base of the carousel. Jesse followed their path of travel, saw the vines run up the exterior of the circular attraction, coiling around the bars that lined the pad's outskirts. The plastic horses and elephants and tigers were covered in the filth of this dead world, black spots of ruin and greenish-blue growths that had begun to collect petals and flowery shapes.

When Jesse got closer, he saw these growths had eyes. In fact, there were eyes all over the carousel, golden circles planted in the leafy tangles of deadly vegetation. They blinked, and his dream-self shivered at the thought of getting near them. In a second, figures appeared on the saddles atop the plastic animals. They were the townspeople of Hooperstown, though he didn't recognize their faces. They wore the clothes of early settlers; the women in white blouses stained with dirt and smears of grass; the men sporting navy-blue cloaks over their white-linen shirts, ruffled at the wrists, and wide-brimmed hats of varying heights.

They were the lost settlers of Hooperstown.

Jesse paid particular attention to the woman closest to him, because that was what the dream demanded he focus on. Her blouse was cut open in the front from her breastplate down to her privates. Sausage-like innards poked through the opening, and, surprisingly, there was little blood. Jesse felt sickened by the sight, but he could not look away. He followed the red vine that had grown out of her, the bodily extension that snaked around the animal seats.

Then he heard a baby cry.

The next moment positioned him on the carousel. Every settler on the ride was looking at him, staring the way the dead stare into nothing—except they weren't staring into *nothing*, they were staring into *him*, and he immediately felt haunted, touched by the ghosts this town had done such a good job concealing from the public. It was *their* fault this was happening. They had wronged what was right, done a terrible deed and slaughtered an innocent, and summoned forth a dark soul from an alternate realm. They had brought this plight down on Hooperstown. Upon Jesse. His family. The other sick kids and their loved ones.

They started this.

Jesse followed the red vine of an umbilical cord around the corner. He continued until a hand fell on his shoulder, immediately stopping him.

"Do not," a man said in an accent that was unplaceable. He reminded Jesse of the Shakespearean play Mrs. Hebert tried to get her English class to read last year. *Tried* because the language was practically unreadable, boring as all hell. They had read *The Giver* instead. "Thou shall not stop her. She is Mother."

The woman with her red stuffing exposed turned to him next, her eyes wet and sparkling. "She shall take what is hers. From the land. From the town. She is pestilence, and she is ever-hungry." Tears streamed down the new mother's face, her cheeks glistening like crystalline rivers limned by a bright and buoyant sun.

Jesse pulled away from their penetrating stares, stepped around an elephant with a man seated on its back. He avoided the man's gaze, and the dream allowed such, concentrating on the cord that led to new life. Jesse was frightened by what he might see dangling from its end, if the dream lasted that long. His dream-sense told him things were starting to break down, come apart at the seams. In the distance, the walls began to fuzz and fade, the black designs made up entirely of mold and filth beginning to crumble.

He turned another corner, saw the red vine stretching beyond the carousel, somewhere into the next level of the dream. Before he stepped off the rotating floor, he turned back and faced the riders.

They were different now, no longer the early settlers of Hooperstown. They were his friends. Grady and Doug were there, sitting atop two horses. Behind Doug, Maddie Rice sat on a tiger while Abby Allen perched on an elephant's back. Jewel Conti was seated next to her, and he wondered why she was there; she wasn't his friend. His entire basketball team was seated behind her, and he thought that was weird, the order of things. To the right, he saw his brother, Jimmy, and Karen Howard. Pale figures, all of them. Sick past the point of a healthy return. Black rings had been stamped around their eyes. Frail lips, flaky and eternally dry.

The dream morphed again, supplying the kids with machines that monitored their vitals, like the one attached to Jesse right now in the real world. Breathing tubes in their noses, IVs in their veins, transferring everything they needed to survive. Except that wasn't true. The fluids being pumped into their veins weren't the healthy clear color Jesse was accustomed to; the liquid was dark and inky, a deep-denim blue.

Dye.

From the plant.

The stuff was flooding their systems, poisoning their dream-selves. As the seconds ticked off the dream's clock, Jesse saw their bodies swell, their veins bloat and change color, matching the hue of what was left in the drip bag. Doug opened his mouth, hiccupped, and a gush of indigo spilled out like projectile baby vomit.

Jesse turned away from the damned children of Hooperstown and faced the final act of this terrifying sequence. He was in the basement of the chemical plant now, the Mother's lair.

New lair.

The walls were caked with earthy grime, a spread of hazardous fungus, foliaceous layers abloom. Trees had grown upward, busting through the ceiling and stretching beyond the roof. The oak trunks were as thick as sewer pipes, the bark rugged and chipping away. People crowded the room, though they hardly looked like people. Things were growing out of their heads, flowers budding from their skulls, canes of vegetation projecting from their skin.

One man dressed in a business suit had an onion for a head, the top split open, exposing a collection of twigs and jellied brains. A woman had branches for arms, unformed fruits blossoming where her hands should be. She licked the infantile ends of her wooden extensions, moaning with pleasure with each lap. A man in the corner had orchids for eyes, and he began to pluck each petal, only to realize they just kept growing back. None of that stopped his personal assault. He cried after each removal, whimpering like a scolded child. Another woman was plucking strawberries from her daughter's face, greedily shoving them into her own mouth, the sanguine juices running down her chin, pooling on the floor below. It looked like blood. The girl, whose face was an all-you-can-eat vegan buffet, laughed playfully as her mother ate from her facial offering.

Most of the others were in ruin, facing extinction, their faces scarred with mold spores, soiled with abnormal herbage. Leafy protrusions. Vines that twisted around their bodies, strangling them. Some hung from the ceilings like party decorations, green ropes tied around their ankles. Their throats had been slashed and they bled bluish-black substances onto the bed of soil that was layered over the metal floor. Growing things had begun to sprout, none of it looking like any plant Jesse had ever seen, dreamworld or not.

This was a garden of death and decay.

This was cancer.

He finally faced the woman of the hour, *Mother*. Her naked body had merged with the far wall, and she was spread across it like Jesus on a cross, ready to die for His sins. The Mother wasn't dying on her cross, though. Quite the opposite. The red vine that had led him to this stage snaked through the center of the chemical plant's basement, curled around the gargantuan oak, and ran up the wall, attaching itself to the Mother's stomach, pumping her full of nutrients and eternal life. She writhed in place, moaning as the juices of this dreamworld funneled into her. Her eyes flicked open and found Jesse. He couldn't turn away from those burning circles of pure gold. He couldn't do anything but watch her nude frame gyrate with the ultimate pleasure.

She ran her tongue along her lips, then pinched the pink muscle between her teeth. Jesse was reminded of the magazine stack Jimmy kept hidden in his closet, and then he began to grow hard, his belt tightening around his waist. This embarrassing public moment seemed to please the Mother, and she moaned some more, louder, her orgasmic throes intensifying. Her stomach swelled as the red vine transferred life into her. It grew like a balloon, inflating until Jesse was pretty sure her flesh was about to pop.

Then it did.

Sort of.

Ripped was more accurate. Her belly split open like a poorly-stitched seam and an explosion of red stuffing came out, a viscous slop that splattered the soil below. Wet clumps hit the floor, a gelatinous collection of malformed afterbirth. The chemical plant's new inhabitants came rushing over to what had fallen, began shoveling the putrid food into their mouths, smearing their lips with handfuls of crimson clots. The woman who'd been feasting on her daughter's facial fruit scooped up a handful of the scarlet slop and smashed her daughter's face with it. They both laughed like children playing a funny game, and the mother continued to assault her child with the red filth, rubbing the spatter across her flowery mask of a face.

Jesse looked up in time to see a hairless creature burst forth from the Mother's gaping stomach. Its frame was milky-white and more bone than muscle. Bat-like ears decorated the sides of its head, and it lowered its jaw to reveal massive, canine-like teeth. It growled, striking fear into Jesse's bones. He felt himself shiver, back away.

"*I am coming,*" the Mother told him, the wall of vines and patchy overgrowth beginning to absorb her, take her into its green, leafy folds. The creature hung out of her open cavity of a stomach, ready to pounce on the world below. "*I am coming for you and your friends and all of my children. I will grow you. You will be mine. You can live with me in the Green World. I will be your Mother for eternity.*"

Jesse flinched as the dog-like beast launched itself from the Mother's busted womb.

Then he woke up to the smell of coffee, his parents talking in the corner of the room, a nurse taking note of his vitals. There was hint of wet mud in the air, and he wondered why his toes, peeking out from under the bedsheets, were smeared with dirt.

2

"Karen, it's me," Jimmy said, fighting back tears. Each moment cut like a knife. "I *really* need to talk to you. I... I have things I want to say. About *it*, about that night. About everything that happened this summer. So if you could call me back, that would be...that would be great."

He'd been trying Karen all morning. Well, all summer really. Ever since they broke up, she had stopped returning his calls. In the beginning, he guessed that was okay. She needed her space. He needed his. They needed a period for everything to settle, for their emotions to simmer. Things had gotten heated. She was adamant they couldn't see each other anymore, and he was less inclined to believe that was true. In the end, he had no choice in the matter. What she said was final, and that was that.

He'd holed up in his room all summer. Didn't come out unless it was to go to work, occasionally to eat and hit the head. He didn't enjoy life as a recluse; he wasn't an introvert, never had been. He liked people, being around them, going to parties and hanging out with friends. The nights spent with large groups were some of the best nights.

But since that night in the cemetery, Jimmy hadn't felt like doing anything with anyone.

Fear had gotten to him. Gotten *inside* of him. And it was driving him to the brink of insanity. At work, if a customer strolled over to whatever game he was manning, he'd flinch the second they opened their mouths. At home, he couldn't even walk inside the house without ducking from shadows that weren't there. He slept with nightlights, something he hadn't done since he was about five. Everything was scary and haunted, and Jimmy felt like he belonged in a mental health facility, Benton perhaps, not allowed to mingle with productive members of society. He wondered what his parents thought of him, wondered how concerned they were. If they were, they didn't show it, and that was because their hands were full with Jesse.

The cancer.

Though it wasn't true, Jimmy blamed himself for his brother catching the Big C. It was after the Hunt that he'd started acting strange. Coughing. Getting tired after a simple basketball practice. He hadn't recognized the signs, mostly because he'd spent a good portion of his time in his room, but he'd heard his parents talking. Heard Jesse and his friends in his room, outside in the backyard, swimming in the pool. He could have just looked out the window, seen his brother shooting hoops, and noticed that he wasn't moving the same. He didn't have the stamina he once had. Normally, Jesse would chase down every rebound, but after the Hunt, he'd dogged every loose ball. It wasn't like his brother to get lazy on the court, even during a simple shootaround.

And then there were the coughing fits. At night, Jimmy had heard every single hack, mostly because he was too scared to close his eyes, fearing he'd dream. Dream of her. Instead, he listened to his brother's coughing and that kept him from voyaging out into those dark waters that flooded his sleep. Some nights weren't so bad, though. A couple spells here and there. But some nights...well, it was a wonder his parents hadn't suspected something sooner.

Jimmy had. And he hadn't said anything. He knew something was wrong, but he couldn't bring himself to get involved. He was dealing with his own problems. Like the fact every time he crossed the threshold to his room into the hallway, his chest felt like it would explode. His heart would start pumping like the needle on a sewing machine. Full-blown panic attacks a few times, room-spinning experiences that made him want to vomit.

And the best part was, he couldn't even remember what actually terrified him. Sure, he saw things in the cemetery that night, but what? A woman? Yes, he thought so, though her image had faded with time, had devolved into a shadowy shape that haunted his nights. In his dreams—his nightmares—he always returned to the scene, Cedarborough Cemetery, and he was always there with Karen Howard, her puffing away on her cigs while he stepped in front of her, his knees bent and hands raised, ready to protect her from the evil that had laid claim to that place. Even though that wasn't how it had gone down in real life. In reality, he had run as fast as his feet could carry him, leaving Karen behind, even though he was confident she could take care of herself, despite her pack-and-a-half-a-day habit. Stamina would get her eventually, but the sprint from where they had been to the car wasn't that far, not really, and she would have been fine. *Was* fine.

So he thought.

In the nightmares, the shapeless wonder attacked them both, and even though he gave it his best shot, he had failed to protect her. Himself. In real life, he had run like a frightened kid from a barking mutt, never looking back. A part of him remembered telling her to run first, to get out of there, that he could handle the intruder, but he couldn't remember, not fully. And he couldn't verify what had happened because she wouldn't return his fucking phone calls.

He picked up the phone again, tapped her digits, and listened to the dial tone. He curled the phone's cord around his finger, an exercise of nervousness. This time, a voice answered on the third ring.

"Hello?" It was Karen. Her voice sounded groggy, and for a second he doubted it was truly her. But he'd called her cell phone, the Nokia she'd gotten for her birthday several months ago.

"Karen?"

"No, this is Sheila," the woman spoke. Sounded like she'd been crying, her voice strained, her words cracking. "This is Karen's mother. Is this…is this…Jimmy?"

"Yeah," he said, his voice low. Whatever news he was about to receive, he wasn't ready for it. "Where's Karen? Is she okay?"

The woman answered with a snivel. Some staticky sounds of sadness followed and Jimmy felt everything inside him fall to the floor.

No.

It can't be.

The first thing he thought was the C word. Ever since Jesse's diagnosis, along with the two-dozen other reported cases, he thought it was only a matter of time before the whole town caught it. At the very least, it was only a matter of time before someone else he knew caught it. A friend. A *lover.*

Fuck.

"She's sick, Jimmy. Real sick." Sheila Howard's strained voice sliced through Jimmy's nerves, and he found himself on the brink of a complete breakdown. He wept silently, keeping the phone away from his lips so he wouldn't have to subject the already-broken woman to his outbursts. "But she's growing. Oh yes, she's growing big and strong, my girl."

"Growing?" Jimmy asked, confused. The woman's voice was slowly morphing. Deeper. Darker. It was hard to tell if her tears were responsible for this sudden change in inflection, or if she were doing it intentionally.

"Growing. Growing big. Strong. She'll need to be for what's to come."

"Oh, right."

Still didn't sound like the woman he'd been talking to only seconds ago, but he figured he'd cut her some slack. She was in mourning. If the reports, the combination of local investigative journalism and the town's rumor mill, were true and the cancer cells were as aggressive as they were saying it was, then the kids of this town were screwed. If Karen Howard had it, then her mother had every right to mourn.

"You're growing strong, too, Jimmy. Biiiiiiig annnnnd strong." Her voice was completely different now, her tone. She practically sung the words, sounding much like a child herself. Whomever this was on the other end, it wasn't Sheila Howard. Someone posing as her, but *not* her.

"Who is this?"

Heavy breaths. Rhythmic laughter, the way a witch would proudly cackle before tossing a boy into her tasty stew. *"You will know my name. I am Mother."*

Jimmy slammed down the phone on the cradle, his heart hammering wildly out of control, so hard his chest hurt. He wondered if it was possible to have a heart attack at his age, even though he worked out four, five times a week. Energy drinks probably didn't help his heart health, so he suspected. He leaned back in his chair, trying to catch his breath, but it was getting away from him. He needed something to drink. Water. Something to calm him before he went into cardiac arrest.

As he left his room and tore down the stairs, he coached himself to breathe. Slowly. In through the nose, out through the mouth. Consistently. This was how panic attacks were fought—breathing steadily until the mind was calm and clean of triggering thoughts. Once the mind was at rest, the body could continue to go about its existence, undisturbed.

To a degree, it worked. He reached the fridge, ignoring the note that told him his parents would be staying at the hospital until late, and that there was pizza money on the island. Opening the door, his focus immediately fell on the Brita pitcher and saw that it was empty. Whoever had been last to use it never filled it back up, and as he shut the door, he realized it had probably been him.

Cursing himself, he lugged his tired, stressed body over to the kitchen sink, grabbed a glass, and poured himself a few mouthfuls from the tap.

Despite the floaty stuff, he drank it anyway. Three quick gulps and it was gone.

He wanted more, so this time he filled the glass to the brim. Or intended to. About halfway up, the water began to change. Darken. He didn't stop the flow, allowing the muddy liquid to reach the top. Examining the water, bringing it to his eyes, he inspected the bluish-green tinge, clearly noticeable. As he was looking, the water from the faucet changed. Darkened even more. It became a sludgy blue-black color, thick like tar. The plumbing began to make an unwelcome noise; the pipes shuddered, and Jimmy's feet buzzed as the floor trembled. Something underneath the sink clunked, and murky water began to trickle out from between the cabinet doors. A small pool formed around his Air Jordans. A step back from the sink didn't make him feel easier about what might come next.

The inky substance came out of the faucet in gobs, pumping the sink full of the sick stuff. It began leaking over the sides, running along the false drawers and cabinet doors. He backed up, reaching blindly for the phone on the wall. Removing the phone from the mount, he prepared to punch the proper digits, but then his thought process collapsed, and he forgot who it was he was supposed to call. A plumber? The water company? 9-1-1? He didn't know who to call but guessed he should start with his parents. As he dialed their number, someone knocked on the front door. He turned and saw a shadow moving behind the obscured, decorative square glass.

His mother's phone went to voicemail and he left her a brief message: "Mom, it's Jim. Please, come home. Something's…something's happening. Something bad."

He hung up and then drifted toward the door, the entire scene unfolding like another fragment from one of his dreams. He actually pinched his arm to make sure his feet were rooted in reality, and he found himself awake and perfectly alive.

He opened the door.

Karen was there, staring at him, two shoots of smoke steaming from her nostrils. She cast the extinguished butt in the nearby bushes.

"Hey…"

"Hey, stranger," she said, a little smirk tracing her lips. It quickly faded once she inspected his face, the haunted nature of his features.

Collapsing into her arms, he began to weep.

3

Light faded in. The scene was foggy, unclear, a blur of abstract colors, undulations of fractured lights. The first wave of agony collapsed over her, her entire body ablaze with overly-swollen muscles and deep bruises that reached her bones. After a few seconds, Jewel could see more of herself, but not beyond her own hands. Head swimming with thoughts that made little to no sense, she leaned back, allowing the top of her skull to rest on some rough, pitted surface. She stayed there for a while, her consciousness slipping, threatening to pull her under again, to welcome her back to the spaces of broken dream sequences and hallucinatory memories. She tried to fight them off, the black bleeding corners of her vision. She tried to hold onto something, memories of what happened last—she focused on the diner parking lot, talking to Adam, and seeing Principal Fritz creep in on them. Very clearly she could see the tire iron connecting with the back of Adam's skull. The pool of blood that seeped out from under him had also taken root in her mind. She would continue to see it for years to come if she managed to make it out of here alive.

Wherever *here* was.

Her focus gripped the waking world and reality began to sharpen. The area was dark. She saw a lot of green vegetation, vines crawling up the walls, overgrowth clinging to every corner. The massive room smelled wet, like the forest after a fresh rain. A slimy earthworm wiggled near her hand, slinking its way under her palm, seeking refuge in the pad of dirt below.

Soon, everything was visible. Wherever she was—she couldn't tell where exactly, not right away—was indoors. Tall, gunmetal walls, streaked with rust stains, extended up, towering over her, covered in a decade's worth of unruly vegetation, vines as thick as tree branches, dense patches of ivy. Stairs led from the ground floor up, access points to several levels, catwalks that bordered the industrial structure. Scaffolding had been erected in multiple spots, each stage blanketed with the same amount of evergreen overgrowth. A cylinder-shaped storage tank sat in the center of the room, a small tree growing through its middle, its branches untamed by reality and extending out in several directions.

Then she saw people moving about, pacing the room, slowly, a confused parade with no clear destination. As her focus honed in, the blurry conditions fading, she saw the people were mostly children. She also noticed several people lying in the layer of dirt that covered the floor. Among the weeds and unnatural greenery birthed from the peculiar terrain, she saw *bodies*. Dead ones. Adults. Some of their throats were slashed, slits so wide and deep that even in the distance she could see the whites of their vertebrae. Puddles of blood soaked into the displaced earth. She couldn't help but think their demise watered the wild plant-life, somehow aided this makeshift greenhouse of death and disease, accelerated the unnatural growth that ruled over this facility, which had only closed down a week ago.

She felt uneasy. Trying to move, she realized she couldn't. Not more than a few inches. She shifted her weight and saw that several vines had grown around her belly and legs. The more she fought to free herself, the tighter her constraints became. The exposed flesh on her legs bulged as the ropey, woody-stemmed plant constricted.

"*No!*" shouted a fearful voice. Panicked. Begging.

Jewel turned her head in the direction of the plea and saw Fritz on his knees, a ninth-grader behind him. The kid, Morris Delaney, held a knife to the principal's throat, the tip digging into his flesh below his beard stubble, drawing a dribble of scarlet down his neck. Morris's face was riddled with nasty growths, pine-green scabs and dead-gray knots commonly found on the bark of malformed oaks. Most of his flesh was lumpy and scaly, symptoms of some disease far beyond Jewel's comprehension, far beyond anyone's. She couldn't look away from what was about to happen, even if she had wanted to.

"*I did what she asked. I did everything she demanded of me!*"

Morris leaned into Fritz's ear. "*Death for the Betrayers Come Fall,*" he recited, then ran the tool across Fritz's throat, opening his tissue like a bagged lunch.

Jewel flinched. Her principal grabbed at his throat, attempting to dam the flood that burst from the wound, but all the hands in the room would not—could not—slow the flow. Scarlet squirted between his fingers. The amount of red really surprised Jewel; she did not know that much blood existed in a human body, let alone a man's throat. The artery continued to pump, shooting continuous red squirts between his fingers. Fritz choked on his own life, and Jewel got the sense he wanted to say something, something meaningful that would make sense of all this insanity, this world that had so quickly gone to hell. She watched his eyes, saw them roll up behind his eyelids, and then center themselves again. He was fighting off the inevitable, the creeping dark that was coming to claim him once and for all.

He looked at her, tears pouring from the source, rolling down his face in crystalline rivulets. Jewel caught herself whimpering and felt tears of her own tickling her flesh as they sluiced down the contours of her nose.

I'm sorry, his wet eyes said, loud and clear. *I failed you.*

She wanted to tell him that he hadn't, that he'd done quite the opposite, gave her an opportunity to turn her life around in a way no one else had before. But that message was lost in the daze this place pressed down on her, smothering her emotions like a wet blanket over a midnight campfire. She felt dull on the inside, hollow. Her eyes continued to produce tears, the perfunctory kind. She wanted to feel more but couldn't.

Her body was a hostage to this place, wherever, whatever it truly was.

Once more, Fritz's eyes rolled up under his lids and, this time, never returned. Still gripping his throat, he fell to the side, and his head smacked against the steel floor. His hands let go of his throat, but the blood continued to pump, the spurts shorter now, reminding Jewel of the cheap, dollar-store water guns she used to get as a kid, how they hardly produced any stream at all. In minutes, the bleeding stopped altogether, and Fritz's neck became a red, glistening trench she couldn't tear her eyes from. Fritz's complexion had already started to blanch, every muscle in his body tightening with death's eternal grip. Lifeless eyes looked out into worlds far beyond this material one, and from that dark palace there was no return.

Morris dragged Fritz across the room by his feet, toward a pile of other bodies. There were at least two dozen other dead adults, a small heap of wasted parents, killed by their own kin. Cassie Simmons and Jeannie Hanson were tipping watering cans, showering the dead with a clear liquid. At first, Jewel thought the stuff was gasoline and that they were prepping to burn the dead, the best way to dispose of the evidence, she figured, but she didn't smell gas. When things began to sprout from the pile, thin, stretching green wires, she realized it wasn't gas at all—it was water, the most basic ingredient for all life.

The weeds grew at an unnatural rate, rising from the bottom of the pile, twisting and coiling through the air. In seconds, the stems were sprouting buds, and seconds after that the buds were blooming, opening, the petals unfurling like the wings of a baby bird taking flight for the first time, stretching, exploring the air around its feathery release.

Something gripped Jewel's face. Not something—*someone*. She found herself staring into the eyes of Brennan Scruggs, though his eyes were not his own. Golden circles had replaced what used to be an autumn-brownish color, immediately distancing Jewel from the boy she used to know. She knew this was not Brennan, and even though the kid she used to hang with was possibly alive somewhere inside that casket of a body, she knew he was no longer in control of what came next.

Or was he?

She recalled the day on the porch, how angry he'd been. In another location, a more private setting, things might have gone down differently. He might have taken things too far. She'd gotten the sense that Brennan wanted to hurt her, *do* things to her, nasty things only a kid like Brennan was capable of. There was an animalistic quality to him, an untapped part of him that—given the right urge—could make itself known to the world.

She could smell the hate on him.

"*Everything must grow,*" he said. Disgusting, leaky knots had manifested on his face, tuberous tumors, open and sweating dark fluids. "*Don't you see? Everything must grow?*"

"Scruggs," she croaked, hardly sounding like herself. "Help me."

He looked scared now, nervous. Like his current actions had been forbidden and he suddenly realized he was under the eye of a vengeful god. "*Grow. We all must grow. We take root and grow and grow and grow—*"

"Scruggs. We need help. *You* need help. You're sick. Please..." She found some control over her limbs and began tugging at the root around her abdomen. "Get this shit off of me."

"*AND GROW AND GROW AND GROW—*"

She lost him. He stood up and started spinning in circles, reciting the same two words over and over again. No one else in the room paid any attention to him. Cassie and Jeannie continued to water the dead, and their efforts had proven worthwhile—the weeds had grown about the size of an average adult, the ends had bloomed, creating beautiful explosions of bright orange and pink, petals that injected color into a cold and dark green-gray world.

She wrestled with the vines, wondering how long before one of two things happened—either she became like Brennan Scruggs, a mindless slave to the Mother, or until she ended up like Fritz, dead and bleeding, a seed that would eventually develop, become destructors of everything; this place, this town, this godforsaken world she—until recently—never wanted any part of.

4

"I hate your dreams," Grady said, shaking his head. "I hate them, they're stupid and they don't make any goddamn sense."

Jesse's parents had left the room at his request, and the three boys and two girls had crowded around his bed, listening to the dream of an apocalyptic pier and the sinister carousel that had suddenly transitioned into the base-level beneath Hooperstown Chemical.

"Dreams never make sense," Jesse said. "Until they do."

He was in worse shape than their last visit. His skin was noticeably paler, his lips less pink. The circles around the boy's eyes had darkened. The sickness within was breaking him down, bit by bit, and the longer Doug stared at his friend, the more he realized their enemy was invisible—and how does one fight something they cannot see? He thought similarly about his mother, her mental health. *Invisible monsters. All around us. We are constantly fighting invisible monsters.*

"I think that chemo has gone to your brain," Abby said, folding her arms.

"It is going to my brain," he quipped. "Like, literally."

Maddie placed a hand on his shoulder and said, "What do you mean, 'until they do?'"

Jesse bit his lip and winced like it hurt. "I think... I think I know where she is. The Mother."

"Where?" Doug said, perking up. His eyes wandered to where Maddie had put her hand, a tinge of jealousy sweeping through him. "Where is she?"

"I think she's...she's at Hooperstown Chemical."

"Dude," Grady said. "How could you possibly know that? I mean, dreams are bullshit, dude. They're just images of stuff we think about while we're dreaming."

Jesse shook his head. "No, this is different. It's not like a regular dream. It's a... It feels so fucking real."

Grady looked to his friends. "I can't believe it. Guys." When they didn't answer him, he stomped his foot. "*Guys*. We're not buying into this, are we?"

Doug glanced up at him. "Do we have any other option? Any other clues?"

"Other than the love letter that mysteriously showed up in your mailbox?" Abby sighed as she shivered. "No, we don't."

"I think you should go there," Jesse said. "To stop her."

"That's insane," Grady said, tossing his hands in the air, waving the whole idea off before it could gain traction with the others. "I'm not going anywhere near that place."

"You said you'd help us," Doug told him. "What's gotten into you?"

Grady backed away. "I don't know, man. I feel like... I feel like this is all wrong, you know?"

"That's *her*. The Mother, she wants you to feel that way. She wants us *all* to feel that way. So we're easier to control."

"No," he said, shaking his head. "This is all...bullshit. All of it. We're making it all up. People are getting sick because they drink the shitty water in this town, and that's it."

"We've all drank the shitty water in this town," Abby said. "I know I have and I'm fine."

"Grady," Doug said, drilling into his friend with his eyes. "You know it's real. You *saw* what happened in the cemetery. You *know* what happened to Jesse."

Grady's lips quivered. Doug wouldn't blame him if he collapsed into tears. A part of him wanted to cry too. Purge the negative emotions. Rid himself of the sadness.

"You should scope it out," Jesse said. "Ride by, see if you spot anything unusual."

"Unusual how?" asked Abby. "The place should be a ghost town."

"Then it should be easy to spot something unordinary. Duh." Jesse coughed and covered his mouth. The blip on the vitals monitor spiked, and Doug expected a parade of nurses and doctors to come rushing into the room, but nothing happened. Jesse closed his eyes like something hurt, and then opened them, squinting against the fluorescent lighting. "It feels right. I...I don't know how else to explain it. I feel a connection to that place. Like...I should be there."

"All right," Doug said. "We'll check out the plant."

Grady turned, squinting. "We will?"

Doug nodded. "This is it, man. This might be our only chance to solve this thing."

Grady hung his head, knowing he had been defeated.

"All right," Maddie said, "so what's the plan?"

For the first time that night, Jesse's eyes sparkled with life.

CHAPTER SIXTEEN

All Things Must Grow

1

The night that injected itself over Hooperstown in late August brought with it a sense of everlasting dark. From almost every street corner, you could smell something rotten in the air, a fetid stink of a town gone wrong. Stick out your tongue and you could taste death, the earthy-wooden flavor of bodies rotting beneath the soil. Every road looked haunted, every parking lot vacant. The days weren't much better; fossil-gray clouds stole the sun from the skies, cool and airy afternoons laying waste to the last granules of summer. But the nights were still much worse. Empty and soulless, a town lost on the edge of total destruction.

It was like Hooperstown had forgotten how to live.

And everyone knew why. It wasn't a secret. The kids were sick, a great many of them—over forty cases now and not a single one of them was getting any better. Some of them had died, that total up to eight now. Funerals had been held, speeches given, and press releases promoting positivity in the community had been handed out to the public, who collectively gobbled that shit up, said their prayers, and relied on hope and the good grace of God to get them through these harsh and cheerless times. Some government officials showed their faces, promising to test the water and ensure everything was safe and on the up and up, but everyone knew that was too little too late. They couldn't change the past, thirty-plus years of illegal dumping and turning their cheeks on certain indiscretions, a system that was morally bankrupt but rich in the pockets, an original design so flawed from day one that it never should have been allowed to continue in the first place.

The ladies and men who had come from the Capitol left satisfied with their results, felt good enough to deem the water drinkable and useable. Which was funny because they had never stepped foot inside the closed-down chemical plant, never once tested the water from the source.

Doug Simms thought it was weird, but he'd seen a great many weird things this summer. Whether it was adults acting stupid or the Mother's hold over this place, he didn't know. One thing *was* certain—he and his friends knew the truth, what was really happening in this town, and they were the only ones that could stop it.

Why?

Well, no adult would believe them, of course. They'd debated that in the weeks after visiting Jesse in the hospital. Maddie had wanted to get on the horn, call a town meeting, and tell everyone that there was an ancient, evil spirit—a god, if you will—who was poisoning the kids, and parents too, using their bodies to carry out her intimate desires. Grady told her she was nuts for thinking anyone would believe her, that he hardly believed her himself.

Even Abby was there to talk her friend off that ledge.

2

"No one will believe us," Abby said. She popped a smoke in her mouth, one she'd stolen from her mother's purse earlier that day and offered the other kids a drag. Every single one of them refused. *More for me,* she had thought, taking in a deep lungful. She thought it was ironic (that Alanis Morissette chorus playing in her head) that she'd taken up smoking when her best friend had been taken by cancer, even had a gray laugh about it. "We should keep this shit to ourselves."

Maddie rolled her eyes. "Then we should let the other kids know. We could use all the hands we can get. You've seen the *missing persons* posters in this town? There's ten on every streetlight. We know she's taking them."

Grady held up a finger. "We don't know that for sure, though. Do we?"

"We know enough, Grades."

Doug swung on the swing. Maddie had planted herself on the swing next to him, moved her knees back and forth but kept her feet rooted in the sand below. The playground behind the North Hooper Elementary School was completely empty, not that they had expected a big crowd. The park over on Johnson Avenue was more popular, but they had wanted to come to a place that would be less populated, despite Maddie's plea to assemble and conquer. Plus, their old school playground brought a sense of familiarity, took them back to a time when things were a little less complicated. Back to a place when the most important things were who was fighting who underneath the monkey bars or who was swapping spit behind the maintenance shed.

"I really don't want to go to that place," Grady whined. "Why can't we just…convince our parents to move?"

This wasn't such a bad idea, but it wasn't like the average family could pack up and leave whenever they wanted. Doug had tried to explain this, several times.

"You know why," he said, shooting Grady that *stop-denying-the-inevitable* look he'd perfected over the last week and a half. "We can't move. Besides. She'll find us. Wherever we go, so does she. We can't outrun our dreams." He wiped the sweat from his brow. Despite the pre-autumn winds, it was still hotter than a house fire. "And even if we *could* move—why would you want to? This is our home. Our town." He jumped off the swing, stood in the center of them. "There's no running from this thing, Grady. Not this time."

"Fuuuuuuck," Grady said, covering his ears with his palms. "Fine. Fuck it. I'll do it. I'll go to the stupid fucking chemical plant and probably die and ruin my parents lives when they have to bury me early and…" He shook his head. "Fuck, I'll do it."

"You say 'fuck' a lot," Maddie said.

"Only when I'm nervous."

Abby smiled behind the fog her cigarette created. "So, what's the plan then? Break into the plant like we're the Ninja Turtles busting into the Technodrome?"

Grady leaned into Doug's ear, created a divide with a flat hand, and practically yelled, "Dude, she watches Ninja Turtles."

"I can hear you," Abby said, holding out her palms. "And yeah, I watch Ninja Turtles, okay? My brothers raised me on that shit."

"Oh shit, you have brothers? How old?"

"Older than you." She shot him a daring look, and her smile broadened when Grady swallowed hard. "They play football. Juniors and seniors."

"Great."

"Can we get back on track, please?" Maddie asked. "Focus." Everyone turned to Maddie, expecting her to take the lead. "My dad says everything's locked up. His firm finished their investigation, but the whole area is still taped off, and they put an unbreakable padlock on the front gate. There's barbed wire on top of the fence, so we can't climb it."

"If Jesse's dream is right, then how are the other kids getting in?" Grady asked, the first sensible thing he added all day.

Maddie bit her lip. "You guys aren't going to like this."

"Jesus, what?"

She brought out her Powerpuff Girls spiraled notebook and flipped to a page depicting a basic sketch of the chemical plant. In red pen, she circled the back portion of the property, where the condenser bay met the Red River. "Here."

"Here, what?" Grady asked, not understanding. Or not wanting to. Abby wasn't sure which, but despite his attitude toward this whole situation, Grady Pope was really growing on her. She felt it, that subtle knot in the center of her stomach, how it tightened whenever he spoke. "I don't see anything."

"It's the river. The Red River. Where the plant takes in water, where I circled. It cools the machinery down during the manufacturing process. It's why they built it there, so close to the river. The natural water formation was more profitable than having to constantly shut down production and cool off everything the old-fashioned way. Instead, they built an intake and voila! They have an efficient, financially-viable method to keep up with production costs."

Doug stared at her as if she were a hambone and he was hungry. "You're so smart."

Grady elbowed him directly in the ribs, and when he had his attention, he mocked his friend's previous statement and made pouty lips and googly eyes. Doug elbowed him back, twice as hard. Abby watched the whole thing go down, chuckling under her breath, while Maddie continued to glance over her map.

"What's so funny?" she asked, taking her eyes off the doodle and directing her attention toward her friend.

"What?" Abby asked, tightening her lips around her smoke. "Nothing. Nothing at all."

She glared at Abby. "Well, what do you guys think?"

"What do I think?" asked Grady. "I think it's nuts. That's what I think."

Doug tagged Grady's shoulder. "Grades..."

"No, seriously. You want us to swim in that sewage water, into the intake? Is that the plan? Holy shitballs, no. Just, *no*. All sorts of *no*."

"Those government people said the water was safe."

"And you believe those assholes?" Grady huffed incredulously. "Come on, man. You're not stupid. You can't possibly believe that garbage."

Doug hung his head like he knew Grady was right. And he was. No one believed that was true, even if the adults didn't want to speak out against it. Not all of them went along with the lies, however; Allison Greco's parents had formed a little alliance—consisting of twelve members—to investigate the truth. Rallies, fundraisers, and backdoor meetings, a noble attempt to rally the community and fight back against the powers that be, all while people like Maddie's father took the legal approach and battled through the court system. Last Abby had heard, the coalition wasn't going too smoothly. No one really wanted to join the cause, lend their verbal support, and even the local newspaper refused to give them a spotlight.

"All right," Doug said. "Fine. It's dirty water. But we've been exposed to it our entire lives."

"Well, we only moved here last year," Maddie said, holding up her pen.

"Yeah, but Grady, Abby, and I—we've swam in this water, drank from the tap. Even after we found out it was bad, our parents still made us brush our teeth with it. If we haven't gotten sick yet, we're not going to."

"That's a fool's statement," Grady said. "Tell that to Jesse."

"You know why Jesse's sick."

It was Grady's turn to avert his eyes. "Fuck. *That* again."

"That night," Doug confirmed. "It's all about that night. Everything that has happened, it happened because of the Hunt."

"Well, that's simply not true," Maddie interjected. "This town was screwed way before that. It began when Hooperstown was first settled. Whatever happened, wherever this Mother came from, she was born then, with the first settlers."

"Boxberger told us the story," Grady said. "Said Hooper's perverted ass knocked up a sixteen-year-old. Sick-o."

Abby's stomach soured, and she cast her cigarette in the sand. "What the fuck, man?"

"Yeah, I know." Grady wrinkled his nose. "I mean, what kind of douche-saddle knocks up someone old enough to be their daughter. Or fuck, *grand*daughter."

"It's disturbing for sure," Doug added.

"And probably not that uncommon during that period," Maddie added further. "Anyway, Mr. Boxberger is correct, according to the research I've done."

"You've done research?" Doug folded his arms, clearly impressed. "On this? Awesome."

"After you told me what happened that night, the Hunt, and then what Abby told me…what happened to Bishop." Eyes downcast, she sniffled and wiped away a drop of sadness. Shook her head. "Anyway, I've been spending two days a week researching Hooperstown, the stuff that went on here."

Perky, Doug beamed as she spoke. "Cool."

Grady rolled his eyes.

Abby smiled, though he didn't see it. Better that way. The last thing she wanted—needed—was a boy following her around like a dumb puppy wagging his tail. That boy being Grady Pope, least of all. She promised herself she'd do a better job hiding her interest going forward.

"Then there was the chemical company that came along in '68. They built the pipeline and those workers mysteriously died."

Doug knocked Grady on the chest with his knuckles. "We dreamed about that. Didn't we?"

Grady rubbed his temples. "I think so. This is all very confusing."

"Things have been pretty quiet since then, though," Maddie said, closing her notebook. "Except the kids getting sick, which didn't start until recently." She nodded. "When those two men who were working at the plant went missing."

Doug and Grady exchanged looks.

"What two men?" asked Abby, toying with the idea of lighting another cigarette. "I never heard about two men."

Maddie held up a finger and went back through her notes. "Let's see... Yep, we have a Leonard Howell and Joe Frusco. Went missing two weeks before the last day of school. Approximately. Their truck was found out near the woods at the end of Bittern Lane. It was suspected they were dumping chemicals into the river. The police found a couple of empty barrels near the Red River. Practically kickstarted this whole thing. It also ended up being what Daddy called 'a real coffin-nailer,' in terms of the case." She grinned proudly at this.

"So, she got to them?" Grady asked. "The Mother?"

"Or they got to her. There's a disconnect somewhere. It doesn't add up."

"A lot of this doesn't make sense." Grady blinked several times, as if he were trying to wake up his brain. "If they let her out, why did it take two weeks before she revealed herself? And what's with the tree in the dream? That thing, that monster growing out of it?"

"That's why we need to get inside the chemical plant," Doug said. "There's something growing in there."

"There was also the woman in the cemetery," Grady said. "In white. Remember?"

Doug nodded. "Yeah. We never did figure out who it was."

"Great job, Scooby and the Gang," Abby said, placing a cigarette between her teeth, biting down. "You let the scary man in the mask get away."

Grady blew her a raspberry. "Listen, it was scary as shit that night, okay? I nearly shit myself. Twice."

"Heard you ran away," she said, pushing him now. She wanted to see what he was made of. A cruel game, but it was how she played it with boys. "For all we know, maybe you did shit yourself."

He stood there, frozen, his face twisting and his cheeks darkening with cherry blush.

"This is getting us nowhere, Abby," Maddie said. She tossed her notebook on the steps leading up to the platform in front of the slide. "We need to put our heads together and think. No adult is going to help us, you're right. So...we have to do this ourselves. Or..."

Grady stared at her. "Or... what?"

Maddie thought carefully before she spoke. "Or she's going to poison us all..."

3

The crew walked their bikes up the Rice's driveway, Maddie leading the way. The paint job on her turquoise and pink Huffy sparkled, still shiny and new-looking. The white tread on the tires barely had any dirt on them, save for the few puffs they picked up today. He smiled. A kid's bike told a lot about them. Either the ride was brand new or she didn't bike much. Doug wagered on the latter. He pegged her more of a stay-inside-and-read-books-all-summer girl, and that was okay. Doug liked books, air-conditioning too.

He fought off the urge to walk up to her, plant a big kiss on her lips. Something he might try later if the two of them got the chance to sneak off alone.

"What the fuck are we doing?" Grady said from behind them.

Abby, who had just finished spraying herself with a pint-size bottle of Victoria's Secret Pear in order to conceal her smoky scent, laid her bike on the blacktop. Then she shrugged. "Kid's got a point."

"We need to plan this out," Doug said, though planning was the last thing on his mind.

"Why don't we consult Doctor Dream-Boy?" Grady offered. "Maybe Jesse can dream us up a solution."

"You know that's not how it works."

"No, I don't know anything. You said so yourself."

"Well, that is true."

"Guys," Maddie said, putting up her hands. "Enough. Geez. Are you guys always like this?"

Both boys shrugged.

"More or less, yeah," Grady said, lowering his kickstand. "Seriously, though, we talked about getting into the plant through the intake—a crazy-ass idea I'm totally *not* on board with for the record. But we never talked about what we're going to do when—if—we get inside."

The other three looked to each other, knowing Grady was correct. They hadn't discussed that at all. Getting inside was half the battle, sure. But the other half was figuring out what to do once they were face to face with the Mother. No one had seen her in real life. For all they knew, she wasn't even a material thing. She could be a ghost, an illusion. A giant smoke monster. Or...just a *feeling*, an undefined force they sensed sneaking up behind them. She could be nothing at all. Just an idea. A legend that never died.

Doug's eyes wandered beyond the Rice's property, scanning the street and stopping on a boy (their age, maybe a little older) mowing his parents' lawn. He was a scrawny kid and Doug could see his ribs, even from several houses away and across the street. Struggling to push the mower along, he fought through the ankle-high grass. The mower launched mulched clumps of greenery as it went, sprinkling the lawn with fresh clippings. Doug knew the struggles all too well, having the same problem with his dad's archaic model. Gordon Simms had refused to pony up for a new mower, one of those self-propelling jobs he'd seen advertised during Monday Night Football all last season. Nope, Gordon had stuck with the older model, probably because he didn't have to cut the grass anymore now that Doug was capable. Plus, the old man probably assumed it would teach him some valuable lesson, feed him some sense of accomplishment. Earn that extra twenty bucks a week, work hard for it and all of that.

Doug's eyes wandered from the lawn mower, to the pile of tools resting in the kid's driveway. Behind the weed trimmer was bottle of weed killer, the brand-name type. The jug sat there, and Doug swore he saw a golden glow around it. Alarms went off in his head, and his eyes exploded open. A rush of adrenaline coursed through him, so much he thought he might pass out from the thrill.

She's a weed, he thought. *She's a goddamn weed.*

Abby tittered. "Who's got weed?"

Shit, he thought. *Did I speak that aloud?*

"You okay, dude?" Grady asked, waving his hand before Doug's eyes. "Are you having a stroke?"

"No," he said at once, bouncing on his heels. "No. Guys—I think I got it."

"The weed?" Abby grinned.

"Shut up, Abby." Maddie shook her head. "You've never even smoked weed before."

"No, but I would. Give it up, Simms. You know someone?"

Doug ignored her. His attention fixated on the bottle, ideas running through his mind a million miles a minute. "*She* is a weed. The Mother."

"I don't get it," Grady said. He leaned in closer, peering into Doug's eyes, examining his whole face. Close as he could get without kissing him. "Are you sure you're okay? Jesus, you're not losing it on us, are you?"

"No," he said, pushing him away. "The dreams. What did they all have in common, the ones we shared and the one Jesse had?"

Grady shrugged. "I don't know, man. It's hard to remember."

"There were weeds, flowers and plants of all kinds. They were growing, remember? All over the place. Wherever her lair was."

"I sort of remember."

"She's like cancer, right? She takes root and grows, and it's not a good thing. Like a weed, she's unwanted and hard to kill. Like cancer."

"Okay…" Grady said, sounding confused.

"How do we get rid of weeds?" Doug asked them, surveying their puzzled expressions.

Grady was the only one to venture a guess. "My mom and dad usually spend a whole day yanking those fuckers up. Some of them are big. Hard to pull out, especially when they've been there a while. They say, anyway."

"There's an easier way to kill a weed, and it's been in front of us the entire time."

The three looked to each other, no one offering any solutions.

"Chemicals," Doug said, his smile growing much like the sinister ecosystem beneath the ground floor of Hooperstown Chemical.

4

Reggie's Hardware opened at precisely 8:00 a.m., and Grady, Doug, and the girls pulled up exactly three minutes later. Each of the teenagers had their pockets stuffed with cash, some they had culled from their allowance, some they had gotten on an advance, some known and some unbeknownst to their 'rents. It was desperate times, and desperate times called for calculated risks—or, if Jesse had been there, the situation would have called for "a big dangly pear sack." That, to the best of Grady's knowledge, meant "balls."

Doug and Grady carelessly tossed their bikes on the curb while the girls stood theirs behind one of the strip mall's many columns. The boys rushed toward the entrance. Doug opened the door and held it for Grady and the girls. Once inside, they immediately searched the aisles for weed killer, wondering if this stuff was kept by the paint solvents or down by the gardening area. Grady, who was no stranger to trips to the hardware store having been dragged there every weekend since birth, suggested they shoot over to the garden department.

Sure enough, the weed killer was on a big endcap right before the doors leading out back, where the store kept its outdoor decorations, pavers and plants. They went through the products, reading the ingredients and sales copy, looking for the most destructive mix, but also keeping their pockets in mind. They only had about a hundred between them, and they didn't know how much they would need to fight whatever they would run into.

"This one," Grady said, pointing to the white jug. It was an off-brand product, not one of the household names he was used to. But it clearly stated on the front, in big red letters, that it "DESTROYS EVERYTHING!" And that was exactly what they needed.

Maddie took a small bottle off the shelf and began reading the label, her eyebrows raised with intrigue. "Looks pretty good." She flipped the bottle over, showing the label to the rest of the group. Her finger tapped something she wanted them to see.

Grady leaned in and read the words, "MADE IN HOOPERSTOWN, NEW JERSEY. Ah, a local company," he said, as if the town would be better for it if they went this way.

"It's made by Hooperstown Chemical, dweeb."

"Yeah, I knew that."

"Ew," Abby said, disgusted. "I can't believe they're still allowed to sell that shit."

"They're probably not," Maddie said, shaking her head. "Definitely telling my father about this." She must have realized how *goody-two-shoes* that sounded, and then waved her hand as if it were no big deal. "You know, just to help him with the case."

"Whatever," Abby said, shrugging. "It's cheaper, anyway. We'll probably be able to buy an extra jug at that price."

"Yeah," Doug said, hating to be the bearer of bad news. His eyes narrowed a bit, looking at the bottle with reservations. "But is cheaper better?"

The other three looked at him, stared at each other, and then back to him. "Yes," they said, practically at the same time.

"In our case, anyway," Grady said, the self-nominated expert on such things. "We need all the extra fire power we can get. Because we're also going to need these."

He picked up a box off the shelf, held it out for the group. It was a backpack sprayer that came with a tank and an attached wand. Grady thought they would look like *Real Ghostbusters* breaking into the empty chemical plant that was, for a lack of a better term, "haunted." He pictured them spraying down the Mother's infected hosts, melting them into puddles of bone and skin. Then focusing their attention on the Mother, her true form. He didn't know what that was yet, so he imagined a giant face with cancerous growths marring her flesh, bulbous tumors swollen with pus and infectious disease, ripe and ready to pop under the slightest pressure.

The thought actually made him nauseous, and the strawberry Pop-Tart he'd eaten for breakfast began to make its ascent.

He pushed the grotesque image from his mind, concentrating on the now, the tangible, the things he could see before him.

"'Lightweight for easy use,'" Maddie read from the back of the box. "Swell."

"You put the chemicals in the tank and the stuff sprays from the wand when you press the button," Grady told her.

"Yeah, I see that." She flipped the box around. "There's literally a diagram on the back."

"Literally," Abby added.

Grady put his hands up, surrendering. "Okay, geez."

Doug pointed to another box. "What about this one? It's ten dollars cheaper per box."

"That's a pump sprayer." Grady pointed to the picture. "They're a pain because you have to manually pump that handle to build up enough pressure so it can spray. Totally time consuming and not the best bang for our buck."

"Okay," Doug said, putting the box back on the shelf. "Didn't know you worked here."

"I probably *could* work here," Grady said, looking around the place, feeling confident. "All right, let's grab this shit and get out of here."

Across the counter, the man—"GREG" his name tag read—glowered at them. He looked to be in his mid-forties, but Grady assumed he was a lot younger and only looked older because of shitty genetics. There were only a few whiskers left atop his shiny head, and they were a perfect blend of the color they once were (brown) and the color they'd eventually become (gray).

"What is this?" Greg asked, looking at the four bottles of weed killer and the four chemical sprayers.

"We'd like to buy them," Doug said. "You know...obviously...since we, like, put them on your counter."

Greg continued to stare as if they'd been sent from another galaxy to procure human specimens. "You're all like...twelve."

"Fourteen, buddy," Abby responded with an icy glare. "Ring it and bag it, pronto."

Greg snorted and narrowed his eyes. Leaning back, he folded his arms across his chest. "I don't think so, little lady. These are very dangerous chemicals, known to cause cancer in the state of California, and we have a very strict policy about selling dangerous items to minors." He seemed proud of this practiced speech, even gave them a quick shake of his head in a *well, take that!* sort of way.

"Well, we're not in California, ass-breath," Abby said.

Grady snickered, thinking this girl was the perfect replacement for Jesse, not that anyone could replace their best friend, but still—she was almost his twin. This sudden thought also brought on waves of sadness because their best friend wasn't here to hurl the hilarious zingers himself. He tried his best not to think about it and shook the comparisons from his thoughts.

"So," she continued, "I'll say it again—ring it and bag it. Pronto."

"I don't like your attitude, Missy."

Grady watched Abby's eyes enlarge and instinctively stepped in front of her, blocking her from tearing off the man's head. "I think what my friend here is trying to say is that we've been sent for this stuff. By her grandmother."

"That's not what I'm trying to—"

Grady shot her a wide-eyed glare, the kind that told her to *zip it, don't lip it*.

She followed along, keeping her next remark to herself.

"Sorry about that," Grady told Greg. "Her grandmother is very ill. Lives by herself. Grandfather passed on years ago. Cancer got him. His balls, mostly. Did you know a guy can get ball cancer?" His palms greased with sweat, and his heart was firing off like the cannons of a galleon engaged in battle. "Did you?"

"Yeah," Greg said, his brow curling like a worm. "Yeah, I did."

"Good. Now, like I said—her grandmother's all alone. The yard is practically overrun with weeds and other unwanted veggies. And she's paying us a pretty penny to take care of it." Grady clapped his hands together in prayer. "So, please. Pretty please? Don't disappoint her grandmother. Helping her means the world. To her. And...to us." Inspired by those soul-crushing television commercials, the ones showing footage of once-abused animals needing a loving home, he hit Greg with those sad-puppy eyes. He even made them sparkle with potential tears.

"Oh…" Greg said, shifting like he had pebbles in his sneakers. "Oh, I see. Um. Well, I guess in that case…"

"Thanks, Greg." Grady beamed at him. "You're a true hero."

5

"Um, that was fucking awesome," Doug said, the second the door to Reggie's Hardware closed behind them, the bell on the door chiming briefly. "I can't believe that worked!"

"The power of improv," Grady said, all smiles. "I think I might try out for the school play next year. Think I can hack it in the theatre game?"

"Dude," Doug said, clapping a hand on his friend's back. "Definitely. That was early-Tom Cruise screen magic." He corralled the box containing the sprayer and one of the jugs in one hand while he picked up his bike and hopped on.

"I'm impressed," Abby said to Grady, throwing a leg over the seat of her Huffy. She opened her pack of cigs, toying with the idea of sparking one up.

"Thanks," he said, his cheeks blossoming with a touch of red. He nodded at the pack of cigarettes in her hand. "You shouldn't smoke, you know. It's bad for you."

"Thanks, dad." She smiled, winked.

"I'm serious." Scraping his toe on the sidewalk, he added, "It'd be nice to have you around for a while."

She nodded, not quite sure how to process that.

"Are you two coming?" Doug asked, pedaling around the parking lot, steering with his large purchase on his lap.

Maddie was following him, also trying to nail down the awkward steering situation. They managed, but it looked as if one hard jerk of the handlebars would spill them on the pavement.

"Yeah," Grady said, picking up his bike.

As Grady pedaled away, Abby looked down at the pack of smokes, deliberated, and then tossed them into the trash can resting against the column.

She felt healthier already.

6

"I think I can fight her," Jesse told them. He was sitting up in bed, the first time he'd felt well enough to do so all week. "I mean, not out there obviously." He looked out the window, wondering what the fresh air would feel like in his lungs, then turned back to Doug and tapped his left temple. "But in here."

"You're going to mind-fight her?" Grady asked, his face crossed with confusion. "How the hell does that work?"

"No, you moron." Jesse coughed into his hand. "Look, the last time I went into a dream with her, I came out with dirt on my toes."

"So what?"

"So, in the dream, I was walking barefoot through a bed of dirt." He gaped at them, wondering how they weren't putting this together.

Doug squinted. "What are you saying? You're going to fight her... in the dream?"

"Exactly!"

"She's not Freddy fucking Krueger, dude," Grady said.

"I know that!" Jesse shook his head. "Dudes. Take the dicks out of your earholes and listen to me. She exists in the dream-world. That's where she lives. It's a real world that we can only get to when we fall asleep. For us, it feels unreal, like a fantasy, something make-believe. But for her...it's an actual place she lives in. She hasn't crossed over into our world yet."

"And how do you know that?" Grady placed his hands on his hips, waiting for his response.

"Because otherwise she wouldn't be trying to reach us like this."

"'Reach us?'" Doug asked. "What do you mean 'reach us?'"

Jesse glanced sideways, trying to nail down his thoughts. "It's like...this is how she gets inside us. The tainted water from the chemical plant... I think she's poisoned it. Or someone has. I think the chemicals get inside us and it makes us...susceptible. The water makes us dream very specifically. It acts as a...a...*transport* to her realm."

Doug and Grady glared at each other.

"You know how nuts that sounds?" Grady paced back and forth, shaking his head. "You're saying that our entire lives, we've been drugged? Dream drugged?"

Jesse held up his forefinger. "Do you remember those white flowers Boxberger had on his desk the last few weeks of school?"

Again, Doug and Grady exchanged casual glances.

"Yeah," Doug said, shrugging. "Sure."

"I've seen the same flowers in the dreams. Every dream, I see that white flower. That fucking flower."

"So what?" Grady said.

His immediate dismissal didn't sit well with Jesse, and Jesse let him know by gritting his teeth and smacking his own head against the pillow.

Grady said, "Doesn't mean anything, does it?"

"Of course it means something!" Jesse pointed at the door, the one his parents were just outside of, probably listening to every single bat-shit crazy thing that came out of their mouths. "I asked Nurse Penny about it."

"Nurse Penny?" Doug asked.

"Yeah, she's my nurse. Lovely woman. She makes a great chicken noodle soup."

"Really?"

"No! Not really. Soup comes from the kitchen. She doesn't make shit. Now are you listening to me or what?"

Silence from the other end of the room. Stillness too. Both boys handed their bedridden friend their undivided attention.

"I asked Nurse Penny about it, and she looked it up. Found it in a book one of the other nurses had, some gardening nut. Anyway...*Datura*. Showed me a picture and everything."

"What the fuck is...*Datura?*" Grady asked.

"I'll tell you, Grades. Keep your pants on and your flapper shut, all right? *Datura* is a species of flower that induces dreams. Lucid dreams. Dreams that are so real it feels like you're awake."

Grady looked like he wanted to open his mouth but opted to keep it shut.

"I think...that's what's been put in the water. Or a large dose of it." Becoming lost mid-thought, his face wrinkled. "I don't know, maybe she's been at it since the beginning. Since they built the pipeline."

Doug scratched his nose. "But if she's still...*dwelling* in the dream-world, then how did she get this flower in the first place? How did she pump the town full of this stuff if she's not even, technically, alive?"

Jesse shrugged. "She has minions. Somebody helping her." He snapped his fingers. Eyes bugging, he said, "That shape in the cemetery."

"I thought that was just Alphie," Doug said. "Wasn't it, Alphie?"

"Too tall." Jesse squinted, trying to remember. "Shit. That night is such a haze. I feel like the chemical bath I got really scrambled my brains."

"Nah," Grady said. "Your brains were already scrambled way before that."

"Eh, fuck you, Grades. When did you grow a pair and get wise?"

"Look," Doug said, stepping to the foot of Jesse's bed. "Boxberger—" It hit him. An idea. A huge one. His eyes stared off into the corner of the room.

"Doug?" Jesse asked.

"Boxberger. White flower. That day we went to his house. Do you remember?"

"Of course. What about the white flower?"

"Mrs. Boxberger...she was holding one. One of your...*Daturas?*"

Jesse nodded. Then his face soured. "She was?"

"When we left, I saw her. I thought I'd seen the flower before. In a dream."

"What if it wasn't real?" Grady asked. "What if the Mother made you imagine that Mrs. Boxberger was holding a flower, you know, to fuck with you?"

"I know what I saw, Grades."

"But how can you be sure? How do we know we're not dreaming right now?"

"We know the difference between dreams and reality." Doug nodded, sure of this. "Though there might come a time when we don't. And that time might be coming soon. I don't know how Boxberger and the white flower fits together, but he's gone anyway. They moved out a few days after our visit. And about the flower—we don't exactly have enough time to research this thing. The town is getting a little sparse, if you know what I mean."

Jesse cocked his head. "No, what?"

Doug turned to Grady. "I don't even know how to explain it. Can you?"

Grady nodded. "People are going missing, essentially. At a crazy rate. I feel like half the Sunday paper is a bunch of *Have You Seen Me*."

Jesse didn't seem all that surprised. "Are the police doing anything?"

"As much as they can, I guess. Get this, we had some government jackasses come test the water. Said it was *fine*." Grady cackled. "Can you believe that shit?"

"I can, actually." Jesse shook his head. "Which makes me wonder even more about this Datura business. Maybe it's not detectable."

"Whatever the case is," Doug said, "we have a plan. We're going into the plant. The girls are coming." He told him the rest of their plans, including the jugs of weed killer they had purchased and were now storing in Doug's dad's garage.

"Wicked plan," Jesse told him.

"You think it will work?"

"Fuck if I know." Jesse rested his head on the pillow, threw one leg over the other. Cracking his best smile, he said, "I'm going to stick with the dreams."

"I don't like this," Grady said. His worry was evident, the way his voice hiccupped while he spoke. "I mean...we're not together. It's not the three of us. Remember when we promised we'd spend all summer together? Just the three of us?" A huff of air blew past his teeth, whistling as it went. "Now it's just us..."

"You have the girls," Jesse told him, happy for him but simultaneously glum. He wriggled his eyebrows for effect, to hide the pain from his face.

"Not the same."

"Boo on that. You guys will do great. I promise. And I'll be there in spirit."

Grady sighed, gave him that *well, if that's the best you can do* smirk. He ambled over to the side of the bed as if he were sleepwalking, trespassing through collected dream sequences himself. When he reached Jesse's side, he bent over and wrapped his arms around his friend squeezed him tight. Jesse hugged him back, not as desperate.

"Jay-sus, Grades," he said, coughing over his bud's shoulder. "Don't kill me."

Grady pulled back. "Dude. Not cool."

Doug walked over to the other side of the bed and hugged the two of them, holding them like he never wanted to let go, as if he wanted to prolong the moment forever.

Jesse didn't let them know it, but he wished it had lasted. Because he knew what waited for him at the end of the road of dreams, and that it might ultimately destroy him.

CHAPTER SEVENTEEN

In The Garden of Dead Dreamers

1

On the morning of August 27th, a week before Labor Day, a week and two days before the new school year was scheduled to start, Doug Simms hooked his old Red Flyer Wagon to the back of his bike using the manila rope from his dad's hardware cabinet. His father had tried to sell the wagon at the last neighborhood garage sale but couldn't because he wasn't willing to budge on the asking price, and for that Doug was thankful. He then stocked the Red Flyer with the jugs of chemicals and pump sprayers purchased a few days earlier and set off down the driveway, down the street, and toward

Maddie Rice's house, where the other three members of his gang were expected to meet.

He pedaled carefully, taking the street corners delicately, making sure not to tip the wagon. Sharp turns would spill the contents and possibly flip the Red Flyer, both of which were counterproductive. He couldn't risk cracking open one of the jugs. There was no time (and no funds) to buy more.

Down Jacolby Avenue, he passed a kid mowing his parents' lawn. Like the other day, at a quick glance, nothing looked unusual, but Doug found himself drawn to the mundane task, the details. The kid had chosen to mow sans a shirt, and there were marks all over his bare back. Black marks. A closer look showed the black marks weren't just marks, but growths about the size of baseballs, and they had flowered in several places—across his shoulder blades, down his spine, up his neck. Doug got close enough to make out the petal-like folds in the growth's texture, and when the kid cocked his head in Doug's direction, Doug could see the golden circles that had conquered his eyes, those yellow rings of hellish infernos. The kid opened his mouth like he wanted to shout a warning perhaps, but a dark substance filled his oral cavity and leaked down his chin, splashing his chest and cut-torn jean shorts.

Doug pedaled faster. He rounded the next street and almost stopped dead, slowed to a crawl instead. The gutters were flooded with the same dark substance that had been leaking from the kid's mouth. The storm drains had filled and overflowed and were pumping the sickness-coated slime back into the road. There was a giant crack in the pavement that zigzagged across the way, and that too had filled with the mysterious substance. The stuff began to bubble and rise, frothing as if it were sentient and growing angrier with each passing second.

Despite everything in Doug's mind telling him to take an alternate route to Maddie's place, he pumped his legs, dragging the wagon behind him. He avoided contact with the dark substance, but it wasn't easy. The entire area reeked of harsh chemicals. The stench bit Doug's nostrils, stung the muscle behind his eyes. A slight burn in his retinas produced tears, blurring his vision. He dealt with the symptoms, doing his best to ignore them like the entire town had ignored their symptoms for thirty-plus years, and rode faster, directing himself around the dark spills that threatened his good health.

Up ahead, he saw a man kneeling on the curb, sticking his face in the gutter. As he got nearer, Doug saw what the man was doing—he was drinking from the teeming sewers like a horse at a stream, his tongue lapping up every mouthful of carcinogen-heavy drink it could handle. When Doug passed, the man looked up, his lips stained to match the blacktop, a cosmic darkness that penetrated more than just his flesh. His smile, his gums matched his dark lips. His eyes glowed ablaze, planetary globes of golden light glimmering amongst a blackened skyscape. The man hissed, reached out for him, a feral attempt to destroy something good and pure, something on the heavenly end of the spectrum. But the attack was lazy, hardly an attack at all, and the man went back to drinking the dirty water that plagued this town with ravenous hunger.

Doug cycled on, leaving the street overrun with hazardous materials, and took the turn onto Bayberry Way a little sharper than he had wanted. Two of the wagon's four feet left the ground, only for a second before settling back down. The sprayers and jugs shifted, and Doug glanced over his shoulder, seeing one of the jugs had tipped over. The plastic didn't look cracked and he didn't see any spillage, and he didn't want to stop (not here) to inspect them. Not after what he'd seen.

He drove past a woman sitting in a car. She had cried dirty-blue tears, the evidence sticking to her cheeks, and her expression was wiped clean. Staring, gazing at the road, as if waiting for something to happen.

A group of kids hung out on their front lawn. Their clothes were filthy, stained with the same moldy muck that had taken this town by storm, that had left it poisoned and fragile and full of fear. They watched Doug as he pedaled by, and Doug was beginning to wonder if there was anyone left in town that *wasn't* sick.

Where the hell are the cops?

He expected to see the boys in blue doing something about it, but then realized the opportunity to do something about it had passed a long time ago, well before Doug was born. Before Doug's parents were born. This went back to a time before time. Perhaps before that. Somewhere, someplace, someone had an opportunity to squash this evil entity, this presence that Jesse had claimed was born in the Palace of Dreams, and they hadn't. They had let it go, let it exist, left it to wander the dark regions of the worlds between, and sooner or later, evil, when left alone, would find the light. Light is a necessary component for all living things, and under the powerful combination of darkness and light, evil spreads. Like a cancer. Growing and eating, eating and growing, until there is nothing left but the end.

And like cancer, evil can be defeated if discovered early enough.

The Mother hadn't been discovered. Or maybe she had, and the founders of this cosmic problem hadn't the stones to deal with it in the first place; they'd allowed it to exist, gave it permission to fester and sore until it seeped into the bloodstream of this town—the goddamn water supply—and now they were all dealing with it.

Too little, too late, Doug thought, turning another corner.

He crossed the main drag of Route 37 and knew Maddie's house was just a few streets down. He passed more houses, their lawns beautifully maintained and decorated with vibrant gardens, full of life and cheery hope. Maddie's street looked pretty safe from the spreading sickness, in fact— there was no evidence of the Mother's touch anywhere near these parts. He sped by a jogger whose face was normal, smiling, full of good health. She bounced to the tunes in her ears and waved to him as she passed. He waved back but found it hard to smile considering the madness he'd just witnessed.

We have to finish this. Today.

There was no other option. The Mother could not be allowed to continue spreading her disease, not a day longer. It was already too late— probably—and this mission was a death trap. He knew that. No amount of weed killer on planet Earth could stop her. She had already built her dominion, her toxic paradise, and had taken her seat on the throne of this new world, full of such life.

Full of such death.

No, he fought with himself. *No, it's not true. If we stop her, we can stop it, and then we will all be saved.*

He prayed that was true, but deep down…he knew otherwise.

Knew that no one would ever be saved.

Knew that this was the summer of death.

2

Doug pulled up to Maddie's house two minutes before the designated meeting time. Maddie and Abby were already outside, sitting on their bikes and snacking on breakfast bars. Doug pulled up to the bottom of the driveway, not wanting to lug the wagon up the incline. He squinted through the burst of bright morning sun that flashed over the Rice's roof.

"Where is he?" Doug asked, looking for Grady, any evidence of him.

Maddie shook her head while Abby just stared on as if she had called it, had known he'd chicken out at the last second.

Doug hung his head, then checked his digital New York Giants wristwatch. There was one minute left and he was confident his friend would show. He'd wait it out, give him an extra five minutes if need be, but he didn't want to leave without him. Doug had a feeling they'd be outnumbered at Hooperstown Chemical, that the Mother had her children all lined up and ready to fight at her command.

After two minutes of waiting, Abby shot Doug a *you-know-he's-not-coming* look and a pang of disappointment rifled through Doug's chest.

"Give him another two minutes," Doug said, leaning his bike on its kickstand.

"What's the point?" Abby asked. "You know he's gonna puss out."

"You don't know that."

"Wanna bet on it?"

"He'll be here." He tried to convince himself of that, but the past wouldn't let him forget that fateful moment in the graveyard. "Maybe he needs a few extra minutes to convince his parents. They're kinda weird like that."

Abby continued to chew her bubblegum, blowing bubbles the size of her face. She didn't look convinced that that was the case, and the longer they stood there waiting, the farther her smile stretched on her face.

After ten minutes of waiting, Doug thought maybe he shouldn't be standing on the sidewalk with a wagon full of lawn chemicals. That if one of the Mother's eyes were to see him, she'd send the dogs after them. Even though he felt safe in Maddie's neighborhood, he didn't want to risk it.

"Give up yet?" Abby asked.

Maddie hung her head, looking just as disappointed as Doug felt.

Doug swallowed his pride. "Maybe he got stuck at home."

"Yeah," Abby said, rolling to the bottom of the driveway. Before she took off down the street in the direction of the chemical plant, she said, "Keep telling yourself that."

3

Grady had awoken with enough time to shower and do his chores (straighten his room and take out the garbage), even had a few extra moments to eat a big bowl of Captain Crunch Berries. The second he was about to make for the garage to get his bike, his father stepped in the throughway leading into the living room, blocking his path to the mudroom.

"Where do you think you're going at this hour, mister?" he asked, hands on his hips, peering down at him over his glasses. "It's only eight. Shouldn't you be sleeping in? School starts next week. Might as well get your rest in while you can."

There was something different about his old man, but he couldn't put his finger on it. It was how he spoke. The way he winked at him.

Grady felt invisible spiders dancing across his neck. "I was…was…meeting some friends, sir."

"Were you?" His father's smile was crooked and all wrong. He cocked his head sideways, expecting further explanation. "That's interesting, sport. Veeeeery interesting."

Grady stepped back. "Are you okay, Dad?"

"Fine. Why do you ask?" Before Grady could say, *You're acting like a fucking psychopath, that's why,* his father said, "It's you who's acting different, Grades. Up at the crack of dawn during summer vacation. Tsk, tsk."

Grady took another gigantic step away, and his father matched him stride for stride. "Dad, I'd really like to go now." He could hear the tremble in his own voice. Knees shaking, Grady looked around the room, saw the morning sun beaming through the front storm door. A box of light shone on the foyer, meaning the front door was open, meaning he could make it outside, down the steps, around to the garage. Only problem was he needed to open the garage door from the outside, and the only way he could do that was by punching in the four-digit code on the electronic keypad. Which wasn't a problem in theory; he had the code, had used it every afternoon since his father installed it two years ago. But there was the issue of time. If he took off and his father chased him, there would be no way he could punch in the numbers before his old man caught him.

"Thinking about running," his father said, still smiling. It was the smiling that really got to him, wrenched every nerve in Grady's body. That damned widening of the lips, how they curled at the ends. He hated it because that meant his father was one of them. One of the Mother's children. "Running like you did that night in the cemetery? Oh yes. Daddy knows all about that. Mother knows too. You're a coward, son, ain't no shame in it. Natural response to fear. Every human experiences the same thing. You just did what everyone else would have."

"Not a coward..."

His father threw his head back and laughed. "Yeah...yeah, you keep convincing yourself of that, pal. Yoooooou keep on convincing!"

Run, he told himself. *Run. Get to the garage. It's your only hope.*

He grabbed a kitchen chair and slid it in front of him, creating an obstacle for his old man. A small obstacle, but maybe enough to earn him a few precious seconds.

Grady turned and sprinted for the opening between the kitchen and foyer, didn't even bother looking back to see how much time he had before his dad wrapped his hands around his neck and yanked him in reverse. Still running, he concentrated on the storm door, the square of natural light that almost blinded him. When he got to the door, he took out his key, hoping the plan he formulated on the fly would actually work. Once he was through the storm door, he turned, shoved the door shut, and slipped his key into the lock below the handle. Locking the door, he twisted the key with all his might. With luck, the key snapped off inside, and when his father reached the door, he could pull down on the lever, but the door wouldn't open.

His father put his weight on the door, driving his shoulder into the storm glass. The door flexed against the frame, but it wouldn't budge any further. Anger fixed his face, and he began to snarl, foam leaking from his lips like the big scary Saint Bernard in that Stephen King movie. His father's eyes were wild with contempt, and Grady backed up on the porch, his heels dangling over the first step.

"I'll kill you, you little runt! I'll kill you!" His father grunted some more, continuing to try the door, jiggling the broken lock. He drove his head into the glass this time, but the barrier held. Grady thought it was only a matter of time before it broke.

"You're sick, Dad!" Grady yelled. "But I'll help you!"

He was crying as he yelled this, not caring if the neighbors could hear him. For all he knew, they were one of Mother's children too. Shit, maybe the whole town was. Maybe he and his friends were the only ones left.

He checked his watch, saw he was already ten minutes behind schedule, and he still hadn't reached his bike yet.

"You're not going to do a damn thing, young man! Not a damn thing!" Bellowing with rage, Mr. Pope slammed his fists against the door, smearing greenish sap on the glass. It reminded Grady of the gel-like substances found inside an aloe stalk. "You and your friends will rot, you hear me! YOU WILL ROT FROM THE INSIDE OUT!"

His father's mouth filled with a dark, watery substance, like pen ink. The stuff leaked down his chin, staining his white robe a lovely midnight blue. Then, he backed away, disappearing into the early-morning shadows the house had to offer.

Grady didn't have time to breathe. He wasn't sure how smart his father was under the Mother's touch, but if he held any rational intelligence whatsoever, then he'd know where Grady was heading, and he'd know the garage was still accessible through the mudroom.

Grady sprinted down the walkway, around the front of the house, and over to the garage. He punched in the digits—his birth month and day—and listened as the opener pulled up the door, more noisily than he would have preferred. He kept checking over his shoulders, expecting someone else to come waltzing up the street, the dark blue sickness draining out of their eyes and ears, soiling their clothes.

But there was no one in the streets. The road was empty like most Sunday mornings in late August. People were likely on vacation, spending time with their kids before shipping them back to school. Or they were inside, reading the morning the paper and having their first cup of coffee. Dads and Moms were at the stove in their bathrobes, cooking their kids breakfast, sausage and pancakes shaped like their favorite cartoon characters. They were going about their Sunday, ordinary routines for ordinary times.

But Grady didn't actually believe that. Couldn't. Not after *this* morning.

The garage door opened enough for him to duck under without getting on his knees, and his bike, which he'd stashed near the door, was still there, prepped and ready to ride. Just as he hopped on the seat, the door between the garage and the mudroom slammed open, rattling the tools on his father's workbench, the jars of nails and screws and other fasteners along the shelf above.

His father roared with anger and hopped from the top step to the floor. Rivulets of dark dye streamed from his eyes. He'd clearly smeared the stuff across his cheeks and forehead. It looked like a pen had exploded in his pocket, except the pocket was his face.

Grady gave his father one last look before turning his attention on the empty street.

"COME BACK HERE, GRADY! YOU ARE NOT PERMITTED TO LEAVE THIS HOUSE! YOU'RE A COWARD! COME BACK HERE, PUSSY-BOY!"

There was a mad cackle that followed those demands, but they were already in the distance. Grady pedaled down the driveway, into the street. Halfway down the block he looked over his shoulder, saw his father standing in the middle of the street, shouting, the front flap of his robe open, exposing his genitals to the entire neighborhood.

But no one came out.

No one came to see the big fuss.

Grady wondered if the whole town wasn't dead already.

4

DO NOT ENTER signs were posted on the chain-link exterior every ten feet or so, and just in case that message wasn't clear enough, VIOLATERS WILL BE PROSECUTED warnings were posted between *them*. Doug led the girls past the main gate, which had been double-wrapped with heavy, break-resistant chains. The locks—there were several of them—were as thick as Doug's wrist, impossible to cut through even with a superior set of electric bolt cutters.

Doug had read in the paper that the local police patrolled the area periodically, every two hours or so, to make sure no one was trespassing. He and the girls had waited for the last patrol to pass, maximizing their time to sneak in.

"Are we really climbing through the intake?" Abby asked, pedaling behind Doug and Maddie. "Are we really doing that?"

"What other option do we have?" Doug asked.

"I don't know." She gazed up at the fence. "Fence isn't that high."

"You want to tangle with that barbed wire?"

The look on her face suggested she didn't.

"That's what I thought. Let's go around back and see how impossible climbing up the intake is."

They pedaled around the outskirts of the property, Doug carefully watching the woods for movement. He wasn't sure what he expected. Half of him thought a greeting party would be there to meet them, some of Mother's influenced flock. But there was no one, save for the police car, and the cop had scrammed rather quickly. Not a single person could be seen from the outside of the plant. The territory behind the fence consisted of several buildings, some industrial looking, some full of offices and executive suites. Abandoned, all of it. Even though the plant had been shut down, exhaust puffed from the giant smokestack, swirls of white that merged with the ashen sky.

Doug had taken a tour of the place during one of those bring-your-child-to-work days a few years back. Trying to recall the layout from his memory, he studied the back half of the plant, where the intake met the river. The river hurtled past the opening, which looked like a giant pipe, half submerged in the white, turbulent stream.

"It's still our best option," Doug said, slowing down as he approached the river. As he did, he noticed the fence extended into the river and around, joining with the fence on the other side of the plant, making access to the intake almost impossible.

Shit.

Variables.

"Good going, fearless leader," Abby said. "What now?"

The trio arrived at the river, slowing to a stop. Maddie climbed off her bike, set it down where the grass ended and a sandy bank began.

"I didn't think the back half would be fenced off," Doug said, extracting more memories of the past. During his tour, that fence hadn't been there. He was sure of it. It must have been a new addition, something the plant implemented recently. Had to be.

Doug turned to the girls. "I'm sorry." He propped up his bike. "I... This wasn't supposed to be here."

Abby shrugged. "Well, we tried. Might as well go home now. Guess I'll go to sleep and wait for this queen bitch to come get me in my dreams or whatever the fuck."

Maddie offered him a comforting smile. "You tried," she said, but the words hardly registered.

Doug shook his head. "There has to be another way inside."

"We could always knock on the front door," Abby said.

Maddie shot her a *you're-not-helping* look.

"What?"

Up near the tree line, a shadow flickered into view, and Doug knew they'd been caught. Done for. Whatever surveillance the Mother had installed around this place—it had worked. Their plan had failed. Fell flat on its face.

"You guys!" the figure shouted from the hilltop. The boy waved his arms over his head, and then pushed his bike toward the edge of the decline, started pedaling down it. "Whoa!"

The trip down was a rocky one, but the boy managed to keep his balance. Once he reached the bottom of the hill, he began to speed toward the trio, who still didn't know what to make of their new guest.

And then Doug saw the bike, recognized the orange handlebars and black frame at once.

"Grady?" Doug's face broke into a wide smile, and he actually giggled. His friend hadn't abandoned them after all.

"You guys won't believe what happened this morning!" He ditched his bike while the wheels were still spinning. Shedding his JanSport backpack, he ran up to them, his eyes wide with fear and excitement. "My Dad, he's... *Fuck*, he's one of them."

Doug gripped Grady's shoulders, shook him a little, hoping to settle him down. "Calm down, Grades. What happened?"

Grady stuttered through the whole ordeal, how his father had tried to stop him, how he'd been acting so unusual. How he'd *turned*.

"Jesus," Abby said, seeming genuinely concerned.

"I'm glad you got out of there." Doug clapped his friend on the back. "But I have some bad news."

"Oh, God. What happened?"

"There's no way in." Doug pointed to the intake, the fence surrounding it. "Someone blocked the intake since the last time I was here."

"Mother?"

Doug shrugged. "Don't know. It's possible, I guess. Or maybe it was always here and I just remembered it wrong."

"Well," Grady said, not sounding the least bit crushed. "Good thing I brought a backup plan."

"Backup plan?"

Grady scrambled over to his bike and picked up the JanSport. Unzipping the bag, Grady revealed a long tool. "Took it from my Dad's stash. He has all types of useful shit. Figured it might come in handy, you know, just in case."

Doug watched his friend work the bolt cutters, the teeth gnashing in the air. "That's great, Grades, but the locks on the gate look pretty substantial. I don't think we could cut through—"

"Forget the locks," Abby said, taking the bolt cutters from Grady, swiping them like a snatch-and-run thief. He gave them up without a fight. She ambled over to the chain-link fence, put the mouth of the cutters to one of the galvanized wires and snipped. The teeth snapped the wire with ease, and Abby turned to the group, spreading her arms like Vanna White showing off a potential prize. "Ta-da!"

"Holy shit," Doug said, "I didn't even think of that."

"Well, that's why you need me. To break into things."

"Didn't realize you were such a criminal," Grady said, sounding impressed.

"I'm not, twerp," she said, handing him back the bolt cutters. "I just know a few things."

"All right," Doug said, nodding. "Let's do this."

5

It was morning but Jesse wanted to sleep. Deep sleep. Sleep like a corpse, though he didn't want to think about that, not at a time like this, not when death was so...*near*. He could almost sense it, that icy eternal touch tapping the sides of his pillow, making him comfortable, waiting for his guard to come down. Waiting for the right moment to nab him. He didn't want to admit the time had come, but he couldn't deny its presence either. The hospital reeked of it, the way a carnival always smells like fried dough and buttery popcorn—this place reeked like decomposing carcasses and antiseptics.

He wanted to close his eyes, drift off into that dream-world, but more importantly—he wanted to help his friends. Knowing he couldn't do so any other way, he turned to his mom who sat next to him, a paperback copy of Richard Bachman's *The Regulators* on her lap and holding a steaming cup of coffee in both hands.

"Mom?" he asked, sounding desperate. He'd need to amp up the intensity if this was going to work.

"Yes, dear?"

"I can't sleep." His eyes fluttered, tears in them.

"Close your eyes."

"I tried. All night. I'm so tired, but I can't sleep."

"Aw," she said as if she saw a cute puppy. "Well, the doctor said this might happen. A side effect of the treatments. But if you close your eyes, I bet you'll pass right out."

"Do you think they can give me something? Just this one time? I'm really tired and not feeling well. I think I just need some rest."

She looked at him for a second, then closed her book. Rising, she put the novel and her coffee cup aside. She left to go find the nurse, and when she came back, she wasn't smiling.

"Can't sleep, kiddo?" asked Nurse Penny, immediately checking his fluids. She fussed with the clear drip bag and moved around some tubing.

"No." Jesse commanded those puppy dog eyes to perfection, knowing they'd work on the hardest of souls, and luckily Nurse Penny's was made of Jell-O. "No, and I'm so tired."

"Well, I got permission from the doc to administer a little aid." Scrunching her face, she wiggled her nose, and then held up a syringe. The tube was clear and for all Jesse knew it was a placebo. But he hoped not. He hoped whatever it was would knock him out for a good long time.

You die in your dreams, he thought, *you die in real life.*

It was theory he would put to the test tonight.

"Will it work?" he asked.

Penny unloaded the syringe into his IV. "Oh yeah. Like a charm."

Before he could open his mouth to thank her, he was out like a lighthouse come sunrise.

6

The river smelled bad. Worse than anything Doug could have imagined. The stench bit his nose, the chutes behind his eyes that led into his brain. His whole face stung from the filth that traveled the river. It got so bad he had to turn from it.

"What's the matter?" asked Abby. "Not so sure of your genius plan now?"

"Leave him alone, Abs," warned Maddie. "He's doing the best he can. We all are. This isn't easy on any of us."

Abby nodded, rolling her eyes. "Well, if we're gonna die, might as well die trying to save the world, right?"

"No one is forcing you to be here." Maddie bore into her friend, although *friend* was becoming less and less accurate. This wasn't the first tiff they'd had that morning, and Doug hated to see their relationship crumble before him. *Because* of him. "You're free to leave whenever you want."

Abby raised her palms in the air, surrendering the argument. "Relax. I'm just trying to be the voice of reason, that's all. I mean, we could always hop on our bikes and ride to Canada. Nothing bad ever happens in Canada."

"Bad stuff happens in Canada all the time!" Grady shouted.

"Name *one* bad thing that's happened in Canada."

Unprepared to answer that, Grady stumbled over a response. "I... I-I don't know. Like stuff. Moose. They have moose there, don't they? They, like, destroy stuff?"

"That's what you came up with? Moose? That's your answer?"

"Guys," Doug said. "Stop. Concentrate." He pointed upriver, toward the intake pipe. The opening was roughly the size of one of those rotating tunnels you'd find at a funhouse entry. Plenty of room, but Doug's only concern was how steep the climb would be. And wet. "It's not that far of a swim to the intake. Everybody ready?"

"Not looking forward to getting wet," Abby said, unable to keep her comments to herself. "Should have brought a bathing suit."

Doug ignored her. So did everyone else.

"All right," Doug said. "Everyone put your sprayers on."

They did as he said, putting their arms through the straps, the plastic containers holding the weed-killer resting comfortably against their spines. The sprayers were fairly light and easy to move around in, so Doug felt confident that swimming would be no different. The river's current seemed to move pretty quickly, and the only problem he could foresee was the pack getting damaged near the straps, maybe breaking off. But there wasn't any way to predict that. The fabric straps seemed sturdy enough, and they'd have to make do.

"On the count of three…" Doug said. "One…"

"Three," Abby said, and jumped into the water.

The other three followed her. Doug held his nose as the current swept him under. The water was cold, freezing in fact, but the smell trumped the temperature. The harsh chemical odor traveled up his nose, down his throat, into his stomach, and he felt everything he'd eaten in the last twenty-four hours bubble and froth, threaten to rise to the surface. He fought off the urge to puke and pumped his arms, grabbing at the water and propelling himself toward the intake. The rush of water, the bubbling current, sounded like he was inside a tornado, a constant whir that sounded incredibly dangerous, *was* dangerous if he didn't respect its power. However, three years of swimming lessons, spending nearly entire summers at the Di Falcos, swimming in their beautiful pool, and the whole days he used to spend in the Atlantic Ocean, bodyboarding and surf lessons, had prepared him for this. He swam better than the others, making it to the front of the pack. The intake tunnel was in sight, just ten feet away.

"Help!" he heard someone shout from behind him. "Help!"

He looked over his shoulder, still paddling against the current, and saw Grady was losing traction. Not only that, but he was taking a series of short, white waves to the face, the hazardous flow breaking in his mouth.

Maddie swam back for him, grabbing him, keeping his head above water. Abby helped.

"Come on!" Doug shouted. "Not much farther!"

Doug, feeling comfortable the girls could bring in Grady, kept reaching for the edge of the intake, the metal cylinder's lip. A few more strokes and he was there, gripping onto the corrugated metal shell, pulling himself out of the river. He immediately turned and reached out, hoping the girls had been able to lug Grady along. They were kicking their legs in unison, Grady helping, the three of them moving as one unit. When in range, Doug extended himself as far as he could go without sacrificing his footing and gripped onto Grady's fingers. Using his weight, he yanked Grady out of the water, onto the metal footing. Next, he helped the girls out of the river.

The four of them sat down, each collecting their breath. The river had tested their endurance and strength, but it had also tested their resolve. Doug thought they passed with flying colors.

"Jesus, dude," Abby said, glancing over at Grady as she pushed a clomp of wet hair away from her eyes. "Who the hell taught you to swim?"

Grady took in short breaths and held his chest. "I don't know what happened. I got caught in the current."

"I'll say."

"We made it," Doug reminded them between sucks of air. "That's all that matters."

After their breath returned and their nerves were relatively settled, they checked the sprayers to make sure none of them were damaged. Doug inspected his and couldn't find anything wrong; the plastic container was in good shape, the straps held, and the chemicals within were still present.

"All right," Doug said. "Let's climb."

The four faced the tunnel, the incline, and began to move their way up it.

7

A smoky horizon, the fading sun a blur of magentas and tangerines. Jesse rises from the sandy shore, turns to see a sprawling forest, thick with vines and trees and exotic greens. No entry from what he can see, but as he looks down the shore, he spots an opening into the forest, can see it because there's a big sign alerting him to the location. ENTRY HERE, it says in big red letters, lit like a NO VACANCY sign in front of a '70s motel.

He doesn't trust the sign or the forest, but he has no choice because the only other option is meandering down the endless sandy shore. The path winds, twists and careens, and eventually offers him a small clearing. Firelight glows, igniting the area and peeling back the creeping shadows. Jesse stumbles over to a log, a spot where the dream wants him to sit.

He does.

In a blink, a man appears on the other side of the campfire. He's wearing a red rag like a bandana, and Jesse cannot tell if the bandana is blood-stained or dyed that way. He can't make out a lot of the man through the crackling flames and the blur of smoke, but he knows the man is Native American. From his right earring hangs three feathers. From his left dangles a tiny bone, three of them, each hinged together, bent awkwardly at different angles. Small white fibers extend from the bone, and, instinctively, Jesse knows this is a bird's wing.

The man's eyes are hard to see through the flames, and Jesse only catches glimpses. At first the man doesn't say anything, only stares, as if he is the one who has come to this conclave for information, not the other way around.

Jesse is patient. Sits. Waits. Grows increasingly nervous, half-expecting Bird-Wing's eyes to ignite with golden circles, letting him know that the dream is a death trap.

But he doesn't think that will happen. Something within his dream-self's soul eases him off the ledge.

"You are weak," Bird-Wing says unceremoniously.

Jesse, a little offended, chews his lip. "I am not."

"You don't know what you are. You are just a boy."

"I can fight."

Bird-Wing chuckles. His chuckle quickly turns into a good, old-fashioned knee-slapping hee-haw. "Good one. That's a good joke, white boy."

"I'm not joking." His cheeks burn with embarrassment. "I'm ready to fight her. The Mother."

"You are always joking. Always laughing. I shall call you, White Boy Who Always Laughs."

The insult burns, but he keeps his comeback to himself.

"You are not ready," Bird-Wing says again, his appearance shifting in the firelight. Warping like any good dreamlike vision would. "You are weak, sick, and unable to continue. You should turn around right this instant. Go back to where you came from. Live out the rest of your life. There is still hope for you in the Land of the Living. Here..." Bird-Wing looks over his shoulder as if he's being watched and knows it, and wants—needs—to keep tabs on the bustling shadows. The trees move like mechanical arms, the wind streaking through them, rustling their loose leafy greens. Jesse swears he sees movement, a giant beast amongst the dark backdrop, but he can't be sure. It fills his dream-self with a shot of fear, and he begins to shiver in spite of the healthy campfire. "Here," he says, turning back and facing the flickering flames. "Here, in her world, you are as good as dead."

"I am not."

"We only exist because of our dreams. That's all a person has. Dreams make us. They inspire. Drive us. They tell us who we are in ways the real world simply cannot."

"I don't understand," Jesse says, and he doesn't. Typical dream, taking the nonsensical turn.

"Of course you don't. Because you are not ready."

Jesse launches himself to his feet, swinging his arms, ready to throw down against anything and anyone. "I am! I am ready!" He beats his chest with heavy fists. "I'm ready to do this."

A shadow falls over Bird-Wing's face, and his features darken as the flames shrink, an invisible blanket pressing down on them. The skin around the Native American's eyes wrinkle, bunching together like a wet towel. He suddenly looks older, by a hundred years. Rearing his lips, he flaunts acicular bones that line his gums.

Jesse cowers, plants himself back on the log, stays there, frozen.

"It would be unwise to raise your voice again," Bird-Wing says, keeping his own voice level. Very little emotion when he speaks, and that actually brings Jesse a sense of safety. Comfort. "You never know what you might spook out here, along the edges of the dream. It's a dangerous place we're in, wouldn't you agree?"

Jesse nods, though he has no idea.

"You're not ready..." Bird-Wing brings his cupped hands to his face. Through the strengthening fire, Jesse can see a small mound of some white, powdery substance that looks like cocaine resting on the vision's palms. Jesse has only seen cocaine in Scarface and Goodfellas, required watching in the Di Falco household, but never in real life. He is sure Bird-Wing is presenting him with enough cocaína to kill an average adult. Before he can refuse a bump (that's what they call it, right?), Bird-Wing's mouth forms an O and blows a gust of air strong enough to move weighty branches. The powder leaves his hands in a cloud and merges with the fire. The flames dance, sizzle and change color, converting into a dark, deep-pine green combustion. Splashes of emerald wash the trees, the sky, the old man's face (what Jesse can make of it), in a glow of flickering light. "...but you will be. Strong. Follow me."

Jesse has no choice whether to follow or stay behind, and in a blink, Jesse discovers he's still in the forest, only it isn't dark and there is no campfire. He is standing on a path in broad daylight, the sun throwing streaks of light through leafy branches. He can still smell the woodsmoke somewhere in the near distance. He doesn't see Bird-Wing.

Jesse walks along the designated path, his dream-sense pointing him in the direction he is destined to travel. Surrounded by nature, Jesse feels a warmth overtake him, filling his bones with comfort, enough to where he actually believes everything is going to be okay, just fine, that maybe he'll survive this after all. It's weird what being surrounded by light and towering greens can do for the soul, how much healing power Mother Nature can provide, even if the effect is merely temporary, and possibly, exclusively psychological. But it is enough to cure him of the notion that death is the only way out of this realm.

He presses on, following the sequence the way the dream has built it. He comes to another clearing, this one stocked with fallen pine needles sans a welcoming fire. Two bodies stand in the center of the clearing. One woman. One man. Both are naked, not a stitch among them. The woman, her bronze skin glimmering in the sunlight, is a little older than Jesse, but not by much, so Jesse thinks. The man is much older, old enough to be the girl's father. His white-man face is thick with a white-man beard, also white, like a snowfall. There is a smile inside that beard, his lips shaking like two pink snakes doing the nasty inside a thicket. The girl is not smiling. Her brow is creased with worry, and if Jesse stares hard and long enough, he can see her fingers shaking. Trembling. Her knees quivering as whips of fear lash her nerves.

Jesse's eyes fall to her belly, a bulge of new life. Jesse thinks she is ready to pop right then and there, just like the health class video once showed him. He was disgusted then during his first viewing, and the thought of it now disgusts him further. The baby's head crowning between the mother's legs, the retrieval, and the flood of afterbirth that pours out of the mother's womb. These images conjure up a false stink and he wants to puke. Hoping the dream will not show him these things again, he watches on.

The girl stares into the naked man's eyes, tears rolling out of hers. The man holds a knife, a makeshift piece constructed from rock and clay, and holds it tightly, his knuckles blanching. He runs the sharp tip across her belly, not slicing it open but pretending to do so.

No, Jesse thought, not pretending. Practicing.

As the man bites his lip while stretching that sick smile, Jesse's eyes focus on the woods behind them, what the dream decides to show him. In the trees, he sees it.

It.

A creature with shimmering golden rings for eyes, a jaw that hangs down revealing long, sharp vampiric teeth. Dark hair that floats with the wind. Its white body, whiter than the bearded man's nude buttocks, is bony and frail, looking like it has not eaten a good meal in years. Maybe decades. Centuries. It watches the scene unfold much like Jesse is watching, only the frail organism looks on like the two bodies are an elegant feast, turkey legs the size of a giant's fists and frothy smashed potatoes loaded with melty cheese and bits of chewy bacon.

The skeletal creature licks its cracked, peeling lips.

The Mother.

The girl sees the creature in the woods, locks eyes with it. A silent pact is made, and the Mother climbs down from the branches with the grace of a chimpanzee. Crawling on all fours like some primitive primate, she inches her way into the arena. The white man has no idea what is taking shape behind him, pays no attention to the danger that is sneaking in the shadows. He's too busy running the blade across the pregnant woman's belly, ready to conduct his profane delivery. The next swipe actually draws a scarlet line across her midsection, and the girl shrieks, takes several steps away from her abuser.

That is when the Mother takes her.

The girl's mouth unhinges, her jaw opening impossibly wide. Eyes rolling back into her head, she tilts her chin back, her neck cracking from the force. The creature mounts her arched form, putting its feet on her knees, its hands on her shoulders, shifting its golden circles for eyes down the girl's throat. Cones of sparkling yellow shoot from its eyes, filling the girl's mouth with a brilliant shine, almost blinding Jesse and the dream-world's vision. Then, the creature fades like a ghost leaving actuality, takes a vaporous shape, a tornado of fog and smoke, and curls in the air above the girl's mouth, hovering just past her lips. Then, all at once, the fog goes billowing down into the tunnel of the girl's throat, disappearing inside. Her throat contorts as the thing passes through, flexing unnaturally, as if it fights all the way down, punching and kicking and trying to tear its way to the bottom.

Once the thing disappears inside her, the girl snaps her head straight ahead, her eyes beaming like headlights in the dead of night. Her stomach distends, losing the round, circular shape it once had. Instead, lumpy protrusions, hard sacs of tumorous design replace the once beautiful circumference. The belly flesh sags, stretches, leaving behind marks that will never fade. Her color withers like autumn leaves.

The sickness takes holds.

The white man's smile shrinks like a snapped rubber band. Fear pulses within him, and Jesse can smell it. It smells like piss or the boy's locker room after eighth period gym.

The girl lunges. Two hands break free of her stomach, punching through the flesh, spilling all sorts of fetid fluids. A new smell hits the air, and Jesse covers his nose, but that does nothing to lessen the malodorous quality. Hands reach out, grab the white man's belly fat like it's a curtain and pulls the flesh apart. The man's howling screams lift birds from their nests in the trees. He looks down and sees the Mother removing fistfuls of innards, tossing them aside like garments she no longer wants.

Jesse tries to back up, but his back is against the wall of the dream. He's forced to watch the Mother tear this man apart, her aggressor, her attacker, her captor. She rips and tears her way to new freedoms. When she's finished, there's more of the man spread around the clearing than there is standing on two feet. The white man falls in a pile of his own red ruin, and the squish of his face landing on a slab of what looks like raw beef is enough to make Jesse squeal.

At the noise, the Mother turns.

She stares directly at him, the golden circles of her eyes alive and burning with pure hatred.

"You..." she coughs, hardly sounding human. There is a lisp, and Jesse immediately thinks this is how snakes must sound, if snakes could speak the human tongue. "YOU ARE NEXT," she bellows. Then, she rushes him, the arms in her stomach reaching out, the baby within her belly falling to the ground, dragged by the umbilical cord.

Jesse shrieks, puts up his hands in defense.

Blinks.

Nighttime again. Stars overhead. An orange blur growing over a kindling fire, the crackling of breathing flames.

"Not ready," Bird-Wing says, a knowing smile touching his lips. "Not ready at all."

8

Waiting for the others to finish their climb, Maddie ran her fingers along the intake's metal structure. She couldn't help but think of enclosed water slides, their tubular nature bringing back memories of last summer when her folks took her to Bugwater Beach, the indoor water park in Eastern Pennsylvania. Inside, the air was thin, hardly breathable but definitely better than Chemical River. Someone had engraved symbols and quotes into the metal constructs. Her fingers slid across them, feeling for a sense of their age. The markings were still sharp, so they hadn't been chiseled that long ago. A week at most.

She backed away, taking in the dreadful décor. The symbols looked like ancient hieroglyphics, generic drawings of birds and triangular-shaped eyes and three squiggly lines stacked on top of each other, things that held no meaning to her, but maybe meant something to the person who had carved them. There were quotes etched into the metal too, and judging from the styles and fonts, they had been scratched by different authors. One read, ALL HAIL THE MOTHER. Another read, ALL THINGS MUST GROW. Another, written with less grace, claimed, I'M SICK HELP ME. She felt bad for that particular author, as they clearly still had some control over their actions, and their last plea for help had been engraved on a sewer tunnel no one would see until it was too late. *A shame*, she thought, as she read another quote, this one a popular song lyric warning a certain mother not to let her offspring travel in a certain direction. The lyric had been misquoted, the author clearly knowing the song but not all the words, but that was okay because Maddie *did* know the song and knew all the words, and she understood the message behind them.

This was *hell*.

Looking ahead, she saw mostly shadows but sensed there was a way in up ahead. The water was ankle high and easy to navigate, especially in comparison to the swim. That ordeal had tested her athletic abilities, so much so she was now convinced to give the swim team a shot next year. She would implore Abby to tryout as well, given how she'd assisted Grady through the turbulent whitewater. Maddie surprised herself with her own strength, and the fact that she still had some to spare, had beaten the others up the intake, seemed almost impossible. Yet here she was.

Doug was the second one up the pipe. Sucking wind, he clambered over the ledge, onto flatter ground. Maddie, letting the shadows of the tunnel magnetically draw her deeper in, neglected to help him up. Next, Abby reached the top. She, along with Doug, helped Grady over the ledge. Once the three of them were safely up, Doug called out to Maddie, who'd wandered a considerable distance away from them.

"Mads?" he said.

Her flesh prickled when he called her by that nickname. Only close friends and family called her Mads, and the way it sounded from his lips exhilarated her. She was crushing on him *hard*, and she forced herself to remain alert, focused on the task at hand. But it was difficult. Ever since their first date, not a day went by she didn't think of him.

"Yes?" she responded, turning back. They were silhouettes against the tunnel's oval light. She could hear the rumbling of the river in the distance, fading to whispers. "What is it?"

"This is bullshit," Grady said, hands on his knees and trying to regain his breath. "Bull. Shit." A strand of saliva dangled from his lips and he spat onto the tunnel's floor. "Gross. I think I'm sick now. I can feel it inside me. Throughout my entire body."

"Relax, Grades," Doug said. "We're not sick yet. And even if we are, all we need to do is stop *her* and it will all be over."

"How do you know?" He stood himself upright and glared at his friend. "I mean, how do you actually know that?"

Doug squinted. "I don't, man. I just...it has to. She's causing the sicknesses. It's all her."

"Is it?" Grady stomped his foot in the long puddle. Water splashed over Doug's shoes, Abby's too. "Is it *all* her fault? Or is it this godforsaken chemical plant?"

"I'm sure the plant has something to do with it, but—"

"We're fucked!" Grady shouted, grabbing his hair with both hands. "We're absolutely fucked here!"

"Calm down, dude," Doug said, coming to his friend's side, trying to hold him still. Maddie thought the kid might slide back down the chute, into the chemical-infested river just to end it all right here and now, saving himself from the months of suffering that might lie ahead. "You're freaking out for no reason!"

"It's a good goddamn reason to freak out over!" Tears welled in his eyes. "I don't want to end up like Jesse! I don't want to end up like him!" He threw his hands over his eyes, concealing his sadness, the entire summer's worth of fear and frustration and sorrow coming out all at once. His body quaked with measured sobs, hitching with each outburst.

Doug threw his arms around him. Grady collapsed to the floor, and Doug went with him.

"Cut the stem," Abby said, looking up at the ceiling, "and the flower dies."

"What?" Doug said, continuing to console his friend.

Abby pointed at the ceiling, the words scrawled across the vaulted curvature of the dome. "Cut the stem," she read, "and the flower dies."

Grady peeled back his face from Doug's chest and followed Abby's finger.

Maddie stepped forth from the shadows, clicking on the mini flashlight she'd clipped to the elastic band of her pants. Somehow it had survived the swim and still worked. Surprising, since she'd picked it up from the dollar store the day before yesterday. She shone the light on the advice written by some anonymous author. The group took a minute, their eyes running over the words again and again, making sure they didn't misconstrue the message.

"You think it's true?" Abby asked the group.

No one had an answer, but there was only one way to find out.

Grady separated from Doug, rose, and dried his eyes on the back of his hand.

With both hands, Doug gripped the wand attached to the tank on his back. "It feels like it should be. The Mother is responsible for a lot of the bad that's happened here. She was here when they built the tunnel through Hooperstown. She killed those workers back in the sixties. She's been here a long time. Waiting. Waiting for someone dumb enough to get sucked into her pull. To free her."

"Well," Abby said, turning her eyes on him as a devious smile sprawled across her face. "Let's clip this bitch then."

9

She took the woman's hand and her touch was soft, gentle, the way a mother's should be; welcoming and warm, a lift for dampened spirits. Jewel gazed into her blue eyes, fully expecting to see a different color, one of rich tokens and long-lost treasure. But they were not gold, far from it, and the presence of this white-robed woman brought her instant comfort. Her belly was huge, bloated with the late stages of creation, ready to release her spawn at any moment, or so Jewel thought. She also thought a woman this ready to pop shouldn't be walking around a dingy, mold-infested cabin of filth. Not to mention, the industrial surroundings offered many hazards, too many things to trip and fall over. No, the woman should be at home on bedrest or, ideally, at the hospital gripping the hands of nurses and trying to push that thing out of her. Sweating. Straining. Feeling like she was being split apart. All the lovely things that accompanied childbirth.

But not here. *Definitely* not here.

"You're probably confused," the blonde woman said, smiling a perfect smile. Her teeth were cleaner than any Jewel had ever seen. They almost sparkled. "It's okay. I'm not here to harm you."

Jewel's attention migrated from the woman over to the shadows of the plant's condenser bay. The chamber that had been so full of nature and greenery had now disappeared, changed back to an ordinary industrial warehouse-looking room about as big as her school's gymnasium. There was still evidence of overgrowth. Ivy dangled down the walls, not as thick as it had been. The ground wasn't lush with leafy plants; there were no flowers with colorful petals to speak of. Hardly the impressive garden it had been. A few weeds had risen through the cracks in the rusty-metal covering of a floor, but that was it. A pile of dead bodies lay in the corner, adults mostly, and some moss-like substance was flourishing on their cold skin, but that was the extent of the alien landscape's peculiar touch. Where it had all gone, Jewel didn't have a clue, but she figured the pregnant woman might.

She bent over, a necklace of white flowers dangling before her. "You saw it, didn't you? The paradise?"

Jewel opened her mouth to speak, but her throat was too dry for words. She needed water badly, just a sip.

"You don't need to answer," she said, her smile most unsettling. Jewel began to wonder if her face was permanently fixed like that. "I know you've seen it. A lot of the children have. That's the Mother's vision for this world. The paradise she hopes to bring with her. Her divinity."

There had been nothing *divine* about it, Jewel thought. If anything, it had been a terrifying vision. Plants that moved, that looked at her hungrily. And the smell—God, she had smelled that awful stench, an earthy rot permeating the air that had somehow followed her from the vision to the real world, still present, however faint.

She didn't speak her misgivings to the lady, didn't see the benefit of telling her otherwise. Instead, she nodded and hugged herself, hoping the lady would release her, free her from this place, even though Jewel knew that wasn't why she was here.

She had become her *prisoner*.

"The flowers make it possible," the lady said, showing off the necklace of white flowers, yellow pollen sacks extending from their centers. "Daturas aid the process, allow you to dream while being awake."

Hallucinations? Was that what she had experienced?

"Moonflowers, I like to call them." The lady looked down on them fondly, her face cherubic and full of pride. "They help with Mother's influence. They're quite magical."

Jewel wanted to reach up, rip the string of flowers from her neck, and pluck every petal. Then, pregnant or not, she wanted to punch the lady in the face.

"Enough about that," she said, letting go of the necklace and facing Jewel. "We need to talk about you, Jewel Conti."

She was surprised the woman knew her name, but at the same time, she wasn't.

"I have a baby inside me that needs to come out." She rubbed her balloon of a belly in a circular motion, slowly, calming the beast inside.

Jewel had already decided, at this young age, that babies weren't for her. She wanted no part of being a parent; her own had helped her arrive at that conclusion. Even though she was confident she could parent circles around them, having a kid was something she wanted no part of. "And it needs a mother."

Jewel tilted her head.

"Me?" the lady said, her smile falling a bit. "Oh, I'm afraid I won't live past the birth. It's going to be a painful, complicated delivery, and…well, it might be a little messy as well."

Jewel pictured the delivery they had shown in health class last year. She had thought it was pretty cool, the way the newborn slipped out of the womb, and she hadn't looked away from the messiness that followed. Jewel figured all births were slimy and couldn't wrap her head around what the lady was talking about. Of course she would survive it. It was rare for a woman to die in childbirth nowadays, modern medicine and all.

"I'm afraid," she said, as if she could read Jewel's concerns, "this is no ordinary child. He is Mother's. He is strong. And his life will mean my death. You understand, don't you?"

She didn't but nodded along anyway.

"It's okay," the lady said, seeing through her. It was scary how easily the woman could read Jewel's expressions, see through her lies. "You'll see soon enough. You have been chosen, Jewel. Chosen by the Mother. She's seen you while you sleep. She sees what you dream about. About the life you wanted, about the life you've always desired and deserved. You don't deserve the way your parents treat you. You don't deserve your shithead friends."

She bent her neck, referencing an object to Jewel's right. Jewel glanced over and saw Brennan Scruggs facing a wall, taking steps toward it, but not going anywhere. Emerald spittle dangled from his lips. He looked braindead.

"He's in stasis, yes. But he'll come alive soon, just in time for the ceremony," the woman said. "He has a thing for you…"

Jewel turned back to the lady, so many questions populating her thoughts, all of them crowding the passageways to her mouth. She couldn't decide on just one and instead asked nothing. It didn't matter though; the lady could read her as easily as a children's book with pictures and big letters.

"He's okay. Just dreaming. Seeing the future, what the Mother has in store for him." The lady looked around, her eyes examining the walls, the tree that had grown in the center of the room, the branches that stuck out of the metal container. "This place is for dreamers."

Jewel's eyes found a familiar face, only the face had shut his eyes and wasn't opening them. Adam lay on the floor, about thirty feet from where Jewel couldn't move from. "Adam…" she said, her voice rough, uneven. She barely recognized it as her own.

"Oh yes!" the lady said, perking up at Jewel's discovery. "He's no good for you. Doesn't take interest in the ladies from what I gather. He won't do at all, Jewel. You should let him go. But don't worry—our Mother has other uses for him. He will carry out meaningful tasks in the Long Garden."

A hint of confusion draped over Jewel's face, and the lady smirked, closed her eyes as if she knew she had made a silly mistake, as if she had expected Jewel to know what the Long Garden meant. She had assumed incorrectly.

"Her paradise, hon, what she intends to make out of this shit-hole town. And eventually…the entire world. *Our* realm."

Jewel still didn't grasp the concept; in fact, she thought the lady was nuttier than a squirrel's turd. She continued to nod along with it, knowing well how to handle unstable people. After all, she lived with two of them. *Don't argue with their logic,* she thought, *that will only make it worse.* That was good advice that had kept her from taking too much abuse over the years. Sometimes it was hard. Sometimes it felt good to rebel. But you had to pick your battles. Know when you could get away with shit and when you'd catch a good beating. You had to know when you could take it.

This was not one of those opportune times.

This was a beating she didn't want to catch.

She glanced over at Adam's unconscious form, feeling sorry he'd been dragged into this. If she hadn't taken Fritz's advice and gone to that stupid clubhouse, then none of this would be happening. Adam would be safe, probably hanging out with his girlfriends, going on dates with guys who looked like they could model for the underwear section of the Sears catalogue. It was *her* fault he'd been knocked out, dragged here to die.

This place is for dreamers, the lady had said, and Adam was dreaming all right. But for how long, Jewel didn't know.

"You can't escape," the lady said, smiling again, and Jewel wanted to break the bitch's nose against her knobby knuckles. She could deliver a good punch, and she didn't think the lady could handle it. "You wish to harm me," she said, as if she found the notion adorable.

Her smile broadened. This woman was full of confidence, and if Jewel had learned anything from her two idiot friends, Brennan and Dakota, she had learned overconfidence was a weakness to be exploited. Arrogance was the devil's game and it had always gotten them in the end.

"You can't harm me, Jewel. I know what I'm doing. I've been preparing for this moment my whole life. It took a lot to get me this far. I've...fought...*hard* for this." She grew emotional. Her smile was there still (of course it was), but it had taken a hit. Her eyes had grown wet, and she was looking down at her stomach, gripping the future with both hands. "It wasn't easy getting pregnant like it is for most girls. It wasn't easy finding someone willing to take this journey with me. It wasn't easy spreading Mother's touch, either. It took years. Three goddamn decades, but finally..." Tears of joy poured down the woman's face. "Finally, we have arrived. And no, Jewel." She clenched her jaw, gritted her teeth. "No, you will not stop it. You will rise to the occasion and perform your duty. You will bow down to your Mother."

Jewel wanted to tell her that she was tired of mothers, being a slave under the rule of parental law. Instead, she squeaked out one question and one question only: "What is she?"

At this, the lady's grin beamed. "It's simple, hon. Our Mother...She is God."

CHAPTER EIGHTEEN

The Miracle of Life

1

Gordon Simms was having his morning cup of joe when the doorbell rang. It was just after nine and he wasn't due to meet with Charlie Rice and the other investigative team until ten-thirty. Already dressed in his shirt, tie and black slacks, Gordon sipped his hot coffee slowly, looked up from the newspaper, and then lowered the mug to the table.

When he didn't come running right away, the bell sounded again, this time getting Gordon to rise. "Coming!" he shouted, a little perturbed that his morning routine had been interrupted. And for what? He hoped it wasn't some trio of old ladies come to preach about the Miracles of Jesus, the Gift of God. He had no time for that, and even though he'd usually act politely and send them away with a "no, thank you" or a "no, really, I'm not interested," today was not that day. He wouldn't think twice about slamming the door in their faces and might even enjoy doing so.

It was stressful times for Gordon Simms. The investigation was nearing its close, and Charles had told him the lawsuits would soon be filed. The civil suits alone would bankrupt Hooperstown Chemical, effectively terminating Gordon and the hundreds of employees who were all—at this point—still receiving a paycheck, temporary severance money. After the suit went through, the checks would stop, and Gordon hadn't the slightest what to do, how to keep the roof over his and Doug's head. He knew a few people in the nuclear industry, and there was a nuclear power plant about forty miles south of Hooperstown. He figured that would be the most logical next step if someone could get him in. But he wasn't too worried about that— with his skillset, he could work anywhere—but at the same time he was. The unknown, the future ahead, was scarier than it ever had been. Worse than those dark times, the years spent watching his wife's brain slip, degrade, spiral toward an eventual collapse. At least he had seen the regression, watched it unfold—now, he couldn't picture the future or what it would hold for him and his son.

"Yes?" Gordon said, opening the door, seeing that it wasn't three women thumping bibles, holding rosaries out like they were performing an exorcism. "Hey, Ted."

Ted Burrows, a neighbor from down the block, stood on his porch, looking a tad confused. Like he'd forgotten exactly why he'd come here. Gordon didn't know the man that well, other than a few short exchanges here and there, whenever he happened to be outside when the man was walking his dog. He seemed all right. Normal. And that was more than he could say about a few of his neighbors. "Hey, Gordon. You have a minute?"

"Yeah," Gordon said, checking his watch, making sure, even though he knew exactly how much time he had before leaving to meet the lawyers. "Yeah, I've got a few. Want to come in?"

"No," he said, a small smile curling the ends of his lips. "No, this won't take up too much of your time. Just...have you seen Doug?"

Folding his arms, Gordon straightened his pose. "Today? No. Last night he told me he was getting up early to meet some friends. They were riding their bikes to the Di Falcos. He said he was helping them with some chores around the house, you know, on account of Jesse and all."

Ted nodded. "Yes, yes. Shame what's happened to him. Shame what's happening around this community, of course."

"Of course."

"Just..." He winced as if Gordon's story were a simple math equation that looked wrong upon initial inspection. "Are you sure that's where they were headed?"

Gordon narrowed his gaze, shifting uncomfortably, eventually leaning a shoulder on the doorjamb, hoping that would relax him. "That's what he said, Ted. Did he do something? Something I should know about?"

"No, no. I mean, no, I don't think so. Doug's a good kid. Friends, too. Just...I saw the weirdest thing on my way home from the grocery store this morning."

"Well, what was it?"

"Well...I saw Doug and two of his friends, the black girl whose father's that big shot lawyer—you know her?"

"Maddie Rice."

"Yeah, her. The other girl I didn't recognize, but I guess that's not important."

"What is important, Ted?" He was growing impatient. He also didn't appreciate the way he spoke about Maddie and her father. As if the color of their skin mattered, as if it defined them. Obviously, it didn't, but to Ted Burrows, the color of one's skin seemed worth a mention. The bitter aftertaste of his morning brew was replaced by a sour flavor. "You gonna spit it out?"

"Yeah, sorry. Just been a weird morning, that's all. Look, I saw Doug and his friends riding their bikes, and in the back of the wagon Doug was towing...there were all these chemicals."

"Chemicals?" Gordon's entire face wrinkled with confusion. "What chemicals?"

"The kind used for killing unwanted vegetation, I gather. They were lugging garden sprayers too; I think the pump-action kind. Can't be too sure. I didn't get a good look as I drove by."

Gordon ran the information through his cognitive process and couldn't come up with a reasonable explanation. Then it dawned on him. He actually started chuckling. "Oh, well, obviously he and the others were going to the

Di Falcos. Like I said, to help with chores. Maybe they needed help with a little garden control. I'm sure everything is all right, Ted. Thanks for your concern but—"

Ted shook his head adamantly. "They weren't headed to the Di Falcos."

"How do you know—"

"The Di Falco family lives over near West Shire Road, if I remember correctly." Gordon's non-response meant *yes, that is absolutely correct and how the hell did you know that?* "Good people those Di Falcos. Used to go to my church. Now I don't think they go at all. Kids are older now. I get it. Anyway, I remember where they lived. Dropped some pamphlets off to their place once—you know, church stuff—but that was, gosh, ten years ago? Maybe longer?"

"Where do you think the kids were headed, Ted?"

At this, Ted swallowed. "They were headed north on Old Crow Road."

"Old Crow? That's…"

Ted nodded. "In the direction of Hooperstown Chemical. Yep. My thoughts exactly." He shrugged. "Thought it was odd they were lugging that stuff toward the plant, that's all. And the stuff they were using was that generic crap, you know, the stuff they actually made there. I only know because I used the stuff myself recently, last week in fact. Damn weeds are cropping up everywhere lately. You notice that?"

Gordon, still trying to compute everything he'd just been told, shrugged and said, "Well, it's rained a lot." But that wasn't true. It hadn't, in fact, it hadn't rained much at all. It had been a dry August. "Ted, I really must get going. Thanks for stopping by."

"No problem! And hey, if you ever want to—"

Gordon slammed the door in his face, not feeling the least bit bad about doing so. He headed straight for the kitchen, the phone specifically, knowing he had to make a bunch of phone calls, knowing he had to make sense of the information he'd just received. If it was true, why was Doug heading to Hooperstown Chemical? The place was off limits to the public, obviously, and there was no way inside, but he also knew kids were resourceful, and even if they couldn't get inside, hell, they might try. And trying to get inside the place was apt to get one of them hurt. Seriously injured. Between the barbed wire fence and the uneven terrain, not to mention the Red River being so close—Gordon didn't like anything about them being there.

His first call was to Charlie Rice, telling him he would have to reschedule.

2

"Not enough time to get you ready, little bird. Not enough time to help you fly."

Bird-Wing sits on his log, and the fire crackles before him. His shape is undefined, the scope of the dream unable to settle down. Jesse's heart thumps. The beat of his pulse sounds off for all the dream-world to hear. His whole body feels off. He feels distant. Disembodied almost.

"Not strong enough either," Bird-Wing tells him.

Anger creeps in, filling Jesse's veins with hot lava. He burns all over, but his cheeks and forehead flare the most. He wants to stand up to Bird-Wing, tell him he's wrong. Mistaken. That he is strong enough. That he might not be ready for what lies ahead, but he will be soon. Under the right guidance. Under the right mentor.

Bird-Wing laughs. "I am not here to train you, little bird. I am not here to help you, either. I am no guide. I simply…am."

"Shut the fuck up," Jesse says, surprising himself. He didn't think he had the power to speak, let alone so aggressively. Letting the anger out soothes him, if only temporarily. Still, it feels good. "I am going to fight her. I am going after the Mother and there is nothing you can do to stop me." He looks at his palms, and he isn't sure why. He thinks the dream wants to show him something, and the dream does. Two symbols, none he's ever seen before, have been carved into his wrists. One is a triangle with an eye in the center of it; the other is three squiggly lines stacked on top of each other. The markings are fresh and bleeding. "What is this?"

Bird-Wing glares at him, seemingly unhappy with how he was spoken to. "Those are her words. Her language. Ancient symbols from ancient times. *She is marking you, little bird. You've gotten too close to her, seen things that are not meant to be seen.*"

"The cemetery?" He remembers that night, what was supposed to have been a memorable adventure with amazing friends, buddies he'd keep for life, but it had quickly turned into a terrible nightmare. He remembers having that inky substance vomited into his mouth. How awful that had tasted. He should have known then that he was sick, infected by the town and their evil deeds, their corruption that dated back to when his parents were kids. Earlier. From its inception. Since Thomas Hooper and his unforgivable act. Jesse should have known he was fucked—and deep down, he did. And that was why he wanted to make the most of this summer. Why he didn't want to spend every waking second on solving the mysteries of the Mother and everything that had unfolded during the Hunt. Because next summer wasn't guaranteed.

Can't think like that, he tells himself, his parents' words rubbing off on him. *Think positive. Positive thoughts breed positive results.*

That's shit, he corrected himself. *Whatever is gonna happen will happen, doesn't matter how many good vibes or prayers his friends and their families send. What will be done, will be done. Fate has a path for us all.*

Bird-Wing's eyes slim to slits. "Maybe the cemetery. Maybe something else. You are one of her children. One of the sick. One of the dying. Death is a close place to the dream-world. Consider them cousins."

"I..." He shakes his head, trying to wrap his mind around this. It seems like too much for a fourteen-year-old to take, and he wants to give up. Maybe Bird-Wing is right. Maybe he's too weak. Powerless. Just an insignificant speck of dust in the great cosmic storm. The Mother is a titan in comparison. She rules over this dream-world. She owns it. It is her realm, and he is a guest, and guests do not get to decide what's for dinner.

"I am not worthy," Jesse says, realizing the words are true.

"Now you understand," Bird-Wing says. A nod to illustrate just how true it is. Jesse is nothing here. And now he knows it.

"But I can still fight."

At this, Bird-Wing looks quite surprised. There is a sudden change in the boy's voice, and it does not sit well with him. He begins to rise from his log, looking awfully tired of this conversation.

"Sit the fuck down," Jesse tells him.

The apparition stops mid-motion. He stays crouched, shooting his laser-like eyes into Jesse's.

"*I understand what this is," Jesse says, nodding, surveying the surroundings, the layout of this particular sequence. Suddenly the woods around him, the dark gaps between the trees, grow eyes, glowing golden circles that blink off and on, like passing aircrafts in a twilight expanse. "You're trying to get me to quit. To give up. To fail." He shakes his head, stands his ground. Puffs his chest like the one time he got into a locker room brawl with Joey Fontaine after basketball practice last year. He's ready for a brawl now. Oh boy, is he. Adrenaline floods his system, and he feels like he can take on the moon. "But I won't. I'll never give up. Even if it kills me."*

Bird-Wing, still half-crouched, drills holes with his eyes. Jesse doesn't waver, doesn't look away. He stands. Stares. Never backs down. Doesn't matter what comes next, he won't budge.

Bird-Wing's eyes burn with rings of golden fire. His jaw lowers, showing off long, serrated teeth, canine-like, designed to tear through the toughest meats. Saggy skin crowds his face, and suddenly the Native American hardly looks human. The thing underneath his skin isn't ready to reveal its true self, but it comes very close to undressing its human form. Bird-Wing's face looks more like a cheap Halloween mask now. It practically falls off his face.

"*She will get you," Bird-Wing tells him, his voice rough and angry like a nest of hornets. "She will make you suffer, and all the children like you. Your physical form will perish slowly. Your soul will agonize eternally."*

"*We'll see about that."*

Bird-Wing rises above the flames, his face melting, giving way to the creature beneath. Its flesh is rugged, riddled with deep pockmarks, burrows that seem to run through his skull. Dark fluids leak from his mouth and he drools into the fire, which crackles, becomes agitated by the touch. Bird-Wing grunts, growls, directing his anger and fury at the only soul before him. Jesse doesn't shrink from the unsightly beast. Instead, he stands his ground.

It's not real.

It's just a dream.

You cannot die here.

"*OH, BUT YOU CAN!" the creature shouts, and lunges after Jesse.*

He doesn't move. Doesn't retreat. He plants his feet firmly in the soil and lifts his chin, ready to take on the beast and whatever else this Mother throws at him.

He's willing to die for this. His friends. The town he grew up in, the pleasant life he's lived for fourteen strong years.

He doesn't flinch. Not even a blink.

The monster elongates, stretching to the top of the trees. It roars, an attempt to strike fear in its game, but it does nothing of the sort.

"Attack me!" Jesse begs. "Stop being a coward and attack me!"

The thing rushes down at him, zeroing in like a hawk after a field mouse, and just before its teeth can close on Jesse's throat, the dream transitions. He's somewhere else now, the forest and the towering monstrosity absent. Bird-Wing is gone, no trace of him remains.

He's in a room. A hospital room. His hospital room.

He sees himself in bed, eyes closed, the monitor beeping steadily at his side. His parents are there. His friends, Doug and Grady. Everyone is weeping.

Blood.

Crimson streams from their eyes. When they simultaneously turn, he sees their eyes have been hollowed out. Dark cavities, endless in their design, have replaced their visual components. They don't even look all that sad, their mouths still, faces blank sheets of pale skin.

Doug's mouth moves first. "You'll never get out alive, Jesse."

"Just give up now," Grady says.

"Your Mother demands it," his mother says, though her voice is off, waaaay off, not even close to how she sounds in the real world. She sounds like a cloud of wasps ready to attack with their stingers out.

"Come on, son!" his father says happily. He waves. It's creepy seeing him wave without eyes, and the two streams of blood leaking down his cheeks doesn't help. "Kill yourself! The faster you die, the faster we can alllllllll move on!"

"You won't get me," Jesse says. "I won't die. Not until the Mother dies. I won't."

"Yes, you will," they all say in unison. "YES, YOU WILL. YES, YOU WILL." Together, their voices sound like a choir of demonic angels.

Suddenly they're in his face, crowding his vision. From their eye-less caverns, blood pours into his vision, syrupy streams of dark ichor filling his mouth. *He can taste it, and it tastes like death. The end of his short life, a life stunted by the growth of another, a Mother, whose roots has taken firm hold, whose essence has flourished. The final leg of his dream journey has come to a close, a trip to the dark regions of his mind wasted, gone forever.*

"YES, YOU WILL. YES, YOU WILL," they scream into his face, but he doesn't close his eyes.

He doesn't dare.

Fall asleep in a dream, die in a dream.

Die in a dream, croak in real life.

Jesse decides he isn't gonna croak, isn't going to kick the bucket. No way. No, he's gonna live.

Fuck, he's gonna dance.

All the way to hell.

All across the Mother's Long Garden.

3

Grady went over how to use the sprayers again. Abby needed the most instruction; she'd forgotten how to operate the wand, which Grady thought was fairly simple. If it had been Jesse or Doug who had forgotten, he would have been more than happy to lay into them. But not Abby. He let her slide.

"Your hand is shaking," she said, pointing to his wand.

Sure enough, she was right. He didn't need to look to know it was vibrating like Frankenstein's monster after an electric jolt. "Yeah, well, what can I say? I'm amped."

"Scared?" Her hazel eyes were big, expanding like a fresh universe.

"Well, no. Not really." He wasn't sure how the lie would take, but figured it was worth a try.

"I am," she admitted. "I'm terrified."

He couldn't tell if she was serious or not. With Abby, that seemed like it would always be the case.

"Seriously?" he asked, playing along, anyway.

"No," she said, rolling her eyes. "Let's go. Let's get this Mother." She turned the corner, entering another dark tunnel. The circle of light coming from the intake disappeared behind her.

Grady followed, as did the rest of their quartet.

"What do you think she is?" Maddie asked from behind them.

"Ask Doug," said Grady. "His mother has seen her?"

Abby spun. "Is that true? Your crazy mother has seen *the* Mother?"

Doug stopped in his tracks. "Yeah, I guess. But don't call her my *crazy* mother. She's not crazy. She's just...not *well*."

"Whoa," Abby said, holding out her palm like a traffic cop. "Didn't mean to offend you, just...she *is* crazy, right?"

"Yeah, but you don't have to call her crazy." He shrugged. "I just don't like it."

"Fair enough." Abby clicked her tongue. "So, what's the deal then? How does she fit into all of this?"

"My mother was young when she saw her. Or should I say—got *near* her. I don't know if she ever saw her. She claims she didn't go into the cave." *(There are some places the light won't travel in here.)* "She said she stood outside and waited. But that she felt something."

"Well, spill it," Abby said, waggling her wrist, asking for more. "What did she feel?"

"Just...just feelings. I guess that's when the dreams started for her. She was plagued by them, all throughout her life. They came and went. She had a breakdown in high school, tried to kill herself. But doctors and her parents—my grandparents—thought it was typical teenage drama. They didn't take her seriously, the part about her dreams. Not until later..."

"When she tried to kill you?"

Every eye was on him. Grady felt bad for Doug, for him having to relive the past. But it seemed necessary. They were heading into battle, and it was best if they knew everything about their enemy.

"Yeah, I guess," Doug said, directing his attention to the ground.

Grady's eyes drifted, fixating on the spot where the glow of Maddie's flashlight illuminated the tunnel's wall. There were more symbols carved here, much of what they'd seen back at the intake. Simple carvings, fishes and triangles with eyes, were chiseled into the metal enclosure. Almost every available inch. He couldn't believe this much work had taken place over the last month. It was easily two years' worth of vandalism. It made him wonder what they would find up ahead.

Who they would find.

It would explain the disappearances. Dozens of kids had gone missing, grownups too. Were they here? Residing in this abandoned facility? It seemed to make sense, but he didn't want to throw that theory out into the wild. He didn't want to alarm the others unless it was necessary.

"OH MY GOD!" Abby screamed the second she turned the corner, heading into the second tunnel. She threw her hands over her face and stumbled back.

"Relax!" a voice said from around the corner.

Grady readied his wand, prepared to spray whoever came around the bend. But once he saw who it was, he stopped.

"It's me, it's me!" said Jimmy Di Falco, turning the corner, hands raised toward the ceiling. Karen Howard shadowed him, hiding behind his shoulder. "Jesus!" Jimmy bent over to catch his breath and then glanced up at the four figures he almost stabbed with the lawn tool he was carrying. He used the hoe to hold himself up, keep his balance. When he saw Grady and Doug, his eyes widened. "Shit. Grady? Doug? What the hell are you two doing here?"

Doug bit his lip. "From the looks of it…the same thing you are."

Jimmy stood up straight. "This is too dangerous, Doug. You need to leave. Right now. All of you. This place…it's… It feels rotten."

Grady knew that, probably more than Jimmy did. Although…he didn't know what Jimmy had seen that night in the cemetery. After the Hunt, Jimmy hadn't been the same. Karen, either. He recalled the sketch Karen had shown them during their interrogation behind the mall.

The Mother had gotten to them, too.

He wondered what their dreams were made of these days.

"We're not leaving," Doug told him, his voice firm.

Jimmy studied him. Grady. The girls. After a minute, he nodded. "Okay. Fine. But if you're coming with, you better stick close. Stay together. Don't stray from the pack. Got it?"

Doug looked to the rest of the group. "Okay," he said, shrugging. "More the merrier."

"Exactly." Jimmy's eyes fell on each of their packs. "What is this? Some *Real Ghostbusters* shit?"

"Dude, that's what I thought," Grady said, half-excited. It was his favorite cartoon after all. Seven years after its last air date and he still couldn't get enough of the reruns. He didn't tell anyone that, of course. Heading into high school, he wasn't supposed to watch cartoons anymore. That was kid's stuff.

"It's chemicals," Doug told him. "Weed killer."

Jimmy nodded, as if no further explanation was needed. "That's...that's actually genius."

"Isn't it?" Grady grinned. "I thought so, too."

"All right," Jimmy said, shining his own flashlight in the direction he and Karen had been heading. "I think there's a way in up ahead. We heard voices coming from that way before but got turned around and ended up here, somehow."

"How'd you get in?" Abby asked.

"We climbed the fence," Karen said, pulling up her torn shirt. Dark red lines stretched across her ribs. They were still dripping. "Barbed wire really tore us up. It was worth it, though. Especially if we end this bitch."

"The Mother of Dead Dreams?" asked Maddie.

"Yeah. *Mother.*" Karen looked on dreamily, as if everything she'd experienced over the last three months was suddenly replaying in her mind's personal theatre.

"All right," Jimmy said, grabbing her hand, weaving his fingers between hers. "Let's go. If anyone wants out, now's the time to say so."

The kids looked at each other, the apprehension over what was to come apparent, drawn on their faces. But no one backed out. No one quit. Even Grady, who was hot beneath his shirt and sweating like a roasted hog, said nothing. He let the moment pass. The opportunity to escape slipped away. He would see this through to the very end. Fate might have other plans, but he couldn't choose where the road ended.

Grady gripped his wand. He felt powerful doing so. Righteous. Like Karen said, he was ready to end this bitch.

"Let's move," Jimmy said, and headed up the group, leading the kids deeper into the dark, dank tunnels of the plant's intake.

4

She followed the lady in white over to the tree. The branches were beginning to bloom. Flowers had exploded open, spreading wild colors—Egyptian blues, grape purples, and pineapple yellows. Fruits had grown from the stems as well, garish growths big enough to sit comfortably in her palm. She reached for them, never considering if the fruits were poison or not. If they were, and the Mother truly *wanted* her, then she figured the lady in white would stop her.

But she didn't.

Jewel plucked the fruit from the tree, brought it to her nose, inhaled its exotic scent. Smelled like fresh peaches except the fragrance was bolder. More alluring. She wanted to bite into it, flood her mouth with juices never tasted by any other human on this planet. Or so she thought.

"Is this real?" Jewel asked.

"It's as real as you want it to be," the lady responded. "What is reality? Is reality something you can feel, touch, taste? If so, then lots of things are real. Your dreams are real. In a dream you take your five senses with you. You feel emotion. You react to what's happening around you. If that's not reality then I don't know what is."

Jewel was confused by this, but she didn't spend too much time thinking about it. The fruit was weighing down her hand. Bringing it to her mouth, she closed her eyes.

"That's right. Eat. Eat from the Tree of Dreams. Become one with the other side. You will need to take the essence of the dream-world with you if you are going to parent this child. You will need its power."

She didn't like that. Anything this woman told her to do was immediately suspect. Jewel's teeth rested on the fruits soft, juicy skin, and stayed there. A few seconds ticked by. She looked to the lady in white, hoping to see her good-natured smile falter. Leave her face. Fade into a snarl. But it didn't. She was fine with it.

Jewel removed the fruit from her mouth and tossed it on the ground. "Never mind. Not that hungry, actually."

She could tell, on some level, the act of rebellion reached her. The lady in white didn't throw a fit—in fact, she kept smiling, even after the fruit trundled away from them—but Jewel noticed a subtle change in her face. Her complexion ruddied some.

"That's okay," she said, blinking. "There will be plenty of time to build strength later. We have a ceremony to prepare." She rubbed her stomach, calming the beast inside. "It's almost time to deliver the child to the new world. Ohhhh," she said, beholding Jewel's tepid expression. "It's okay, Jewel. Being a new mom *is* scary. I have to admit, I've never been one myself. Too many problems getting pregnant. You wouldn't believe the lengths I've gone through to grow this thing." A wince cocooned in a smile. "It's a shame I won't live to see its birth. But it's the sacrifice that must be made. I'll still live on in the Land of Dreams. My spirit will never die—spirits never do. Remember that, Jewel. There is no such thing as death, only transference."

She would never remember that because she was barely listening. The surroundings were taking her in, and she suddenly grew terrified of this place. Fear nestled against her skin. The future was grim, and even if she did survive whatever horror was to come, the world would change and certainly not for the better. The vines hanging down the walls began to move, curl and slither like waking snakes. The branches of the tree before her began to sway, as if the wind were alive in this place. The sparse patches of grass beneath her feet began to grow.

She was hallucinating again. She had to be.

A layer of mold blanketed the piled bodies where Fritz lay with his throat slashed. She wanted to run. All the way home. Even if hell was waiting for her, her junkie parents in the middle of an awful rage, it was better than whatever this lady in white was offering. She'd rather exist under the rule of her awful mother and father than deal with whatever waited for her on the other side of this vague ceremony.

"I know what you're thinking," the lady in white said. "It's okay to be scared. New worlds are often scary. The unknown is terrifying for us all. But you will be fine, I promise. We all have a role to play in what's to come. You may not be ready for it, but you will be."

Jewel tried to run but found her feet as heavy as cinderblocks. She was glued to the floor, the powerful drug she'd inhaled, the airborne hallucinogen released from those pretty white flowers around the lady's neck, keeping her controlled. She realized she'd never leave this place, not alive.

Not of her own free will.

"Let's just get this over with," Jewel said, succumbing to fate. There was no use fighting it. The harder she fought, the tighter the hold.

"Now we're talking," the lady said, her smile growing even wider now. "Come. The ceremony will begin when my husband returns."

"Your husband?"

She nodded, her grin spreading so wide it forced her to close her eyes. "Yes, my husband. He will ensure the ceremony goes according to plan."

Jesus, Jewel thought, *there is another one of them?*

"He will be back momentarily. He needed to deal with a few…unforeseen interferences."

"Interferences?"

A curt nod. Her eyes were cold now. She showed her teeth, her lips curling inward. "Yes. Interferences."

Whatever they were, they clearly annoyed her. *Good,* Jewel thought. *I can use that. Whatever it is.* Then she wondered if her thoughts were hidden, wondered if she should be thinking at all.

"There seems to be a group of kids who think they know what's happening here, and they want to stop it. Little do they know, what's happening here is a good thing. For the town. For the world. The Mother only wants to replant the seeds of this planet. Sometimes a garden gets overrun with weeds and damaging insects take over, consume every viable nutrient, drain life from the succulent greens. Sometimes, to keep a healthy garden, you have to rip up everything and start anew. You understand this concept, right, Jewel?"

Jewel nodded.

"Good girl." Her eyes bounced over to the door, to her knowledge the only entrance in and out of the hangar. "Your doubts will calm in time. Once my husband returns, all will be shown to you. I promise."

Jewel wondered who the kids were, *where* they were. Was it too late for them? She hoped not. If burning this place to the ground was the plan, she'd need all the help she could get.

"In the meantime," the lady in white said, grabbing her hand, squeezing. Her touch was cold and corpselike. "Let me introduce you to her. *Mother.* She's right over there."

5

Two right turns guided them farther into the plant, and Doug's nerves started to get the better of him. Had they gotten lost? Twisted, turned around? Were they heading in circles? He assumed the condenser bay was just ahead, around the bend. According to the map he'd sneaked a look at, the one he'd borrowed (stolen) from his father's desk, they were close. It hadn't seemed like such a long walk, but then again, that had been a piece of paper he was looking at. How it scaled, he had no idea. Either way, he got the sense they had taken a wrong turn. They had been traveling for a solid five minutes, trekking through the polluted puddles and slipping in the greasy filth the intake canals had to offer.

Disgusting down here. The smell added to his misery, and he felt the grossness of the tunnels seep into every porous opening his body offered. He wondered how long his immune system would take to recover from the damage this place would cause.

Can't think about that right now. Need to concentrate. Focus.

Jimmy led the charge, gripping his garden hoe with both hands, ready to swing at the first sign of trouble. Karen followed, carrying a kitchen knife. It looked dull, unable to slice through a peach, but she was ready and commanded the tool with authority, ready to stab invading shadows should the situation call for it—and Doug assumed the situation would call for it. Doug and the other three teenagers brought up the rear, surveying the tunnel walls, the strange symbols engraved there.

The current tunnel led them deeper, and each step away from the river was one step closer to never returning to open air. Maddie's flashlight did its best to show them the way, but it was starting to fail. The light flickered but stayed on, dim and lacking the power to clear the shadows. It was a miracle the thing worked at all considering how much water it had taken.

"Did you bring extra batteries?" Doug asked.

"Don't think it's the batteries," she said, tapping and shaking the device, temporarily prolonging its effectiveness. Her effort worked, but after a few seconds the light started to shudder, threatening them with total darkness.

"Come on," Maddie pleaded, gripping the flashlight like a loved one seeing the light at the end of death's mortal tunnel. "Stay on. Please."

Her request was denied, and the beam fluttered, three quick flashes, before shutting off and drowning them in darkness. No amount of tapping and shaking brought back the light, and she tried, quite vigorously, but to no avail.

"Great," Abby said. She scoffed. "Now what?"

Jimmy said, "There's a door up ahead. I saw it before the lights went out. Maybe it leads us into the condenser bay. You know, where…"

Doug knew what he wanted to say. *Where the Mother lives.*

"Just up ahead," Jimmy promised. "Watch your step."

Doug shuffled ahead. He stepped on the back of someone's shoes, and when that person cried out—he'd caught her heel with his toe—he realized it had been Maddie. "Sorry!"

"It's okay," she whispered, as if there were ears in the dark, ears she didn't want hearing.

He couldn't help but think about kissing her. The thought grabbed him, took hold, and he couldn't shed the notion no matter how hard he tried. With perfect clarity his mind's theatre showed him how it should be done: a hand on her shoulder, spinning her around, him leaning in and planting a big one right on her lips. No one would see. No one would know. Even though they were together, everyone present and accounted for, in the dark they were alone.

Don't do it, begged the angel to his devil. *Now is NOT the right time.*

But would there ever be a right time? For him—for her—would there be *any* time at all? Not when each moment could be their last. He knew what waited, knew what dwelled beyond the dark hurdle before them. Not exactly, no, but *something*. Something big. Dangerous. Something that would probably kill each and every one of them.

They weren't ready. They were kids. Kids were not meant to deal with such things, things like death and murder, tasks meant for more capable hands, undertakings geared toward those who were trained and prepared. The kids were neither. They were...*kids.*

I'm not a kid, he thought. *I'm...*

But he was a kid. He knew it. There was no sense ignoring the facts.

Oh yeah? If I'm such a kid, then what about this?

He went for it, seizing the moment. A gentle touch on her shoulder, light as a feather, but enough to capture her attention, forcing her to turn. In the dark he felt her body rotate. Face him. He gripped the tops of her shoulders just like he imagined. Even though there was only darkness, he closed his eyes anyway; it felt right to start a kiss, especially a meaningful one, by closing his eyes. Then he leaned in, visualizing where her mouth *should* be, hoping he wouldn't miss, hoping he wouldn't plant his lips on her eye or nose, or somewhere more embarrassing. He went in, trying not to overthink it or psyche himself out, his lips separating, waiting for that warm meeting with hers. There was a brief moment of regret, a second where he thought she might not accept the gesture, that she might scream out in horror and recoil, but that notion quickly faded.

Her lips were soft. Still wet from her swim in the river. Not only did she accept the kiss, but she kissed back, passionately. Forcefully. The pressure was intense; he felt it in his gums. Their friction produced sucking sounds, but no one seemed to notice, no one seemed to care. The noise was hidden beneath footsteps in the puddles, and their canoodling went undetected. After the initial moment of fear passed, Doug was able to enjoy the kiss for what it was. Their embrace lingered, the kids stealing every second they could get away with. Once they parted, Doug imagined her smiling, wiping his saliva off her bottom lip. Glowing. Her eyes fluttering with glee.

Her hands squeezed his arms, migrated upward, gripping his collar. She dragged him back, asking for seconds. The next kiss was shorter but just as impactful. When finished, their foreheads touched, and then they spent the next few minutes holding each other, savoring every brittle moment. Doug wished it could last forever, these precious seconds. But it wouldn't. Like every moment in time, it had to end.

Without warning, a beam of light flooded his eyes, blinding him. A painful pressure stamped invisible thumbs into his eye sockets, deep. He threw his hands up, shielding himself from the bright burst. Maddie fiddled with the flashlight, cursing the damned thing's inconsistent performance, its inopportune timing. The rest of the group spun on their heels, facing them.

Doug backed away from her, breaking from their sweet embrace, looking guilty. Maddie shone the light on their friends, her eyes darting back and forth, trying to appear as innocent as possible to their curious eyes.

Play it cool, play it cool, play it cool.

Abby, Grady, Jimmy, and Karen were already staring with varying degrees of surprise and general amusement. Grady hid a smirk behind his hand, while Abby only stared at Maddie, her eyebrows making the climb up her forehead. Faint grins spread across Jimmy's and Karen's faces, as if they were looking at their own past.

"Ummmm....*what* was *that*?" asked Abby, and Doug knew she did not approve of what she had just caught the tail end of. "What did I just see? What is happening?"

"Nothing," Doug said dismissively. "Nothing at all."

"Didn't look like *nothing*, Boy Wonder."

"It wasn't...wasn't what it looked like."

"It was nothing," Maddie assured her. "It was..." Her pupils continued to dart around the whites of her eyes. "You saw nothing."

"I don't believe you," Abby said, her finger toggling between them. "Not one bit. Fess up."

"All right, children," Jimmy said, stepping between them, into the glow coming from the temperamental flashlight. "Let's get a move on. We shouldn't be wasting—"

Metal hinges groaned as the rusty metal door swung open. A shadowy figure stepped through the opening, a foot landing in a small pool of water, making a wide splash. The figure held up a lantern, illuminating his face, the Mother's scratched symbols on the wall behind him.

Doug saw the man's face, and his stomach plummeted.

It was Boxberger. He donned a white robe with gold frills, a crown of white flowers. The floral scents were overpowering, which was actually a nice break from the harsh chemicals that patrolled the air, hindering their supply of oxygen. Boxberger's beard had grown since the last time Doug saw him, that day they showed up at his house looking for answers.

"Hey," Jimmy said, turning, "what the hell—"

The thing that happened next happened all too quickly and there was no stopping it, even *if* Doug had the foresight. A gleaming flash streaked through the air and a wet sound followed. Before anyone could react, Jimmy was holding his throat, his fingers desperately searching for the damage, the new opening he needed to plug up before things got too bad. But it was already too bad. Red poured through the cracks between his fingers, so much it didn't seem possible. Everything became skewed, the world now off balance, as if some galactic giant had kicked the planet off its axis. As he sank to his knees, Jimmy continued to hemorrhage. Boxberger stood before him, the knife in his hand no longer shiny and glinting but drenched in a concerning amount of Jimmy's blood.

Karen screamed, "NO!" and reached out, trying to grab Boxberger's hands, attempting to wrench the weapon free. He reacted by striking her jaw with his elbow. Her head snapped sideways, and Boxberger booted her lower back, sending her stumbling headfirst into the tunnel's wall. She went down hard, the impact leaving her stunned, floundering lazily in the puddles below.

Doug took one hard step, meaning to rush forward, wanting to take a shot at Boxberger, but the evil aspect of the man's eyes flickered like a warning in the dim glow of Maddie's flashlight. Getting close would mean death, a violent, horrible end, and Doug valued his life. It was apparent Boxberger had come here for one thing only: *blood. His* blood. The blood of the children. *Fucking kill them all*, his face screamed. *Every last one of them!*

Without hesitation, Boxberger plunged the knife into Jimmy's chest. A hard thud, a wet slap, and a wheezy scream fired off all at once. As if the violence of the stabbing was not enough, Boxberger twisted the blade, skewing and wrenching whatever vital organ he had already pierced.

Jimmy's mouth opened as if he meant to cry out, but nothing came out save a bright scarlet sputter.

Grady, shaking like a wet dog, backed away. Maddie directed the beam at Boxberger's face, lighting up his sick smile.

"Now, kids," he said, stepping closer to them. "There's no need to run. The Mother wants to see you." He pointed the blood-slicked knife directly at Doug, the man's grin spreading like a spill. "Especially *you*."

6

"Back again so soon?" Bird-Wing asks. The campfire flares, cycles through several shades of orange, crackling as it breathes. "I missed you."

"Stop this," Jesse says. He's clenching his fists. His jaw. Everything in his body feels tight, constricted. Like he's trapped in a pit of snakes that coils around him, squeezing every bone his body offers. "I want to fight you. Right here, right now. Winner controls Hooperstown. I win, everyone goes free. Every single one of my friends. You turn them back. The sick get healthy and the dead come back to life. If I lose...then it's yours. All of it."

His smile wriggles like a dying earthworm stuck in a languid crawl. Jesse can make out his pointed, curved teeth sticking out between his lips, the top and bottom overlapping, reminding Jesse of a Venus flytrap when its outer lobes come together, trapping whatever unfortunate insect happens to land on its trigger hairs. Jesse knows he's dead meat if Bird-Wing accepts his offer, but he has no other option. There is no escape from this place. The sedative will hold him here until the world devours him, and he's powerless against that hold.

"The dead never come back," Bird-Wing says with finality, his voice rough and smoky. The laugh that follows sounds like the choke of a busted car exhaust. "Never. You will learn this. You will become one of the dead and you will wander the dream-world forever." Bird-Wing sprinkles dust over the fire and the hot logs spit mountainous flames. "You are no match for this place. You are no match for me. Your Mother."

Jesse paces back and forth, plotting his next move. He doesn't take his eyes off the entity wearing Bird-Wing like a cheap costume.

Think, he coaches himself. Think.

Jesse thinks. That's all he does. But there's nothing he can think of, nothing he can do to physically overpower this creature, not on its own turf. In the lair of the enemy, he knows he's at a disadvantage. Like being on a rival's home court, the power of the crowd influencing the flow of the game.

Those long afternoons in the gym won't help him here. But he doesn't have to use his strength. He has other options.

He has his mouth.

"All right, fuck-stick," Jesse says, folding his arms. "This is how things are going down. I'm gonna go over there and shove my foot up your brown eye so far you won't be able to shit for a month."

Bird-Wing cocks his head like he doesn't understand. And maybe he doesn't. Hard to tell if the term "brown eye" registers in the creature's personal lexicon.

Good.

"That's right. You think you're tough sitting on that fucking log? Let me tell you something, you old bitch—you're nothing. You're nothing but a fake piece of shit. This place?" Jesse scans the trees, acting unimpressed by its haunted ambience. "This place is just a fake. A phony. A fuckin' fugazi. You think you can intimidate us? Scare us into believing that we're sick? You're nothing, you know that? You don't scare me. If you were truly so powerful, you wouldn't have been hiding in that fucking cave all these years. You would have gotten out. What kind of asshole lets some circle-jerkin' pilgrims bury them? Huh?" Jesse gathers his confidence, shooting a wide smile in the apparition's direction.

The thing only glares in response, its eyes glowing, the golden circles intensifying.

"That's right," Jesse says, nodding. "You're *that* asshole. I'm gonna jam my foot all up in your ass crack. Hope there's enough room up there for these Jordans because my size eight is coming for you, bitch!"

Bird-Wing stands, the length of him of stretching like taffy. His skull is deformed, melting and warping like plastic meeting a blowtorch. Its forehead implodes, caves in on itself. Its jaw unhinges, twisting, its teeth becoming hooks, ivory arches with sharp tips ready to pierce Jesse's flesh if given the opportunity. Its flesh undulates; its entire appearance moves like a flame in the wind. Bird-Wing is as tall as the trees now, though he doesn't look much like the Native American whose form this beast had taken. Looks more like the troll from some horror movie Jimmy had shown him a few years back. Maybe the thing that clung to the shadows in Greenwood Village, the thing that looked and sounded like a little girl but obviously wasn't. Maybe that was Mother all along.

Whatever the case, the Mother was using that image of the troll against him. The thing had taken on the form of a diseased woodland miscreant, its face filling up with pockets of pus and festering boils, swollen and red, ready to burst at the slightest touch. It drooled, long strings of saliva dangling from its lips. Its teeth were bigger, sharper than ever, and one bite would rip Jesse in half, he was sure of it.

Jesse did the only thing he could think of.

He turned.

And ran.

7

Jewel followed the lady in white past the Tree of Life, navigating around piles of unconscious bodies. She couldn't look away from the latter, wondering if they were dead or just sleeping. Their chests rose and fell, some of them wheezing as if they had a severe case of asthma. The signs of life answered her questions but didn't make her feel any better about her situation. What was happening to them? Were they sick? Was she next? And what was that stuff growing on their flesh, the green mold-like fuzz that populated their arms and necks and some faces. She didn't want to become like them, didn't want to partake in anything the lady in white had informed her of, especially raising the unborn child in her belly.

She was too young for that shit, a kid herself. Motherhood was not an option, and Jewel decided right then and there that she would fight to keep herself child-free. Whatever she could do to keep herself from growing up too fast—she would do it.

"Just over here," said the lady in white, her smile radiating. She beckoned Jewel forth with a curled finger.

Stumbling forward in a daze, still hungover from the effects of the white flowers, Jewel found it hard to concentrate on any one thing. Her mind swam through her options, what she should do and when she should do it.

Obviously, *running* seemed like the best course of action. After all, the lady was pregnant and she wouldn't give chase unless she wanted to risk a miscarriage, and something told Jewel she didn't. There were minions mulling about, a few townsfolk who were pacing the bay, heading in unspecified directions. They looked lost. Wanderers without purpose. Waiting for the lady to give the word, waiting for clear direction.

The delivery, Jewel thought. It would be all hands on deck once that baby was ready to pop out.

She followed the lady over to the far corner. Propped against the wall and sitting on a bed of floral arrangements was a wooden box—a coffin. It was open and angled so Jewel could see what had been hidden inside.

A body.

The Mother.

She'd been wrapped in cloth, her image hidden beneath dirt-stained bandages. The first thing that came to Jewel's mind was those old mummy movies, the ones in black and white, the ones her father used to watch whenever he was home from a night of thievery and hard drug use, six beers deep and ready to pass out. He would fall asleep and she would always stay up, lying on the floor and watching the cheesy classics while her mother tied one off in the bedroom.

"She's been preserved," the lady said with delight. "See, Hooper and his men, after the Mother had served her purpose, didn't know what to do with her. They feared if they killed her the dark god inside would transfer to another body, attach itself to another host. They had sought out ways to rid themselves of this *demon*—their word, not mine—by seeking out the natives, but of course the local tribe wanted nothing to do with them. They had warned Hooper about the thing that lived in the forest, had warned them about the nature of the woods and the ways of the old, the gods who had come there before them, but of course Hooper and company disregarded their claims, and now they would have to pay. So, Hooper and his men took to older customs, thinking if they mummified the corpse then they would keep the spirit trapped inside the host. The Egyptians believed keeping the bodies of the dead intact would ensure spiritual transference to the other side. A safe passage to the worlds beyond this physical realm. What we like to call—the dream-world."

Jewel's head began to hurt as she absorbed this information. It was a nice story and all, but what she gathered was Hooper and his men had royally fucked up, and that beneath the carapace and layers of filth, an evil woodland god lived and breathed, and worse—had access to their minds, in some fashion, and soon—very, in fact—that subdued spirit would be allowed out of its human box, free to create and reshape the world as it saw fit.

That was about the size of it.

"It was over thirty years ago, a bright summer day in 1972, that three kids wandered into the woods, as some kids are wont to do. They didn't think much of the cave they had stumbled upon, but what one boy and one girl found inside there...well, it shook them to the core. It got inside their minds, caused them years of suffering. Night terrors. They couldn't sleep at night for fear the Mother would reach them. She showed them things no nine-year-old should ever see. Terrible visions of the past, the history of the town they lived in, the things that Hooper did to the poor innocent woman he had found wandering through the forest that one afternoon. The thing he had put in her belly in order to preserve his lineage." At this, she rubbed her own belly. "Those kids moved far away from Hooperstown a few years after that incident in the forest. Their dreams faded some, but unfortunately you can't outrun your dreams forever. They still dreamed. Of each other. Of that day. Of Mother. As adults, two of those kids sought each other out, reconnected even though they had moved to opposite ends of the country. Technology made this possible. The invention of something called the Internet. They had met in an AOL chatroom the boy had created called—THE MOTHER OF ALL THINGS THAT GROW. Can you believe it?" She tittered, seemingly impressed with how things had played out. Surprise had crept into her voice as well.

"Over the years," she continued, "they plotted. They moved back into Hooperstown, got married. Legally changed their names because they wanted to stay hidden from the other one, the girl that joined them in the woods that day, the one who never left. They were surprised—although, not really—to find she had gone nuts, tried to kill her son and husband while they slept. See, she was too close to the Mother, and the Mother had infected her. It wouldn't have been so bad if she went along with it, embraced her nightmares and followed the Mother's design—but she resisted. It scrambled her up. She's currently sitting in a mental health facility forty-five minutes north of here."

"Why are you telling me all of this?" Jewel asked, unable to peel her eyes away from the mummified corpse.

"Because it's important you know the history..." The lady put a hand on her shoulder, gave her bones a comforting squeeze. "...because when the ceremony commences, when you offer yourself to Mother, you—"

Jewel snapped out of it, shoving the lady's hand aside. "Wait, what?"

"Yes. You will become one with her. The Mother. What did you think, Jewel?"

"No... I can't."

"It's okay..." The lady continued to hold her smile, acting like nothing affected her. Jewel thought a punch in her pooch might change that, but she didn't have the strength. Everything was still hazy, her thoughts included. Standing upright took an exorbitant amount of energy. She felt her shoulders lax, ache. She wanted to rest her eyes. Curl up into a ball like a cat napping on a porch rocker. "It's okay, Jewel. It's all okay."

"It's not okay." She backed away, two steps. It was all she could manage.

"Jewel, let me explain something to you. I know you. The Mother has showed me who you are, what your home is like. Hell, my husband—the boy from the story I just told you—has been inside your home."

"He has..."

"Yes." Still smiling. Damn that smile. "Louis Boxberger stopped by last year. You were out playing with friends or something. He told your mother he was concerned about your grades, that you were slipping, more than usual. That wasn't the case, though. I mean, you were slipping. Your grades are shit, Jewel, some of the worst he's ever seen in his career as an educator. But that wasn't why he dropped by your parents' apartment."

"W-why?"

"Because Mother asked him to. She needed a host, Jewel. For when it was time for me to give birth, she would need someone to carry on. Someone low, someone who needs her, someone who doesn't have much of a Mother at all. There were a lot options in Hooperstown—you'd be surprised how many broken homes there are in a single town, even one as perfect looking on the surface as Hooperstown. Oh yes. Many kids have terrible parents, many terrible mothers. Neglectful, selfish, impatient caregivers who would gladly trade their kin for a breath of freedom. But yours was worse than the rest, Jewel. Ava Conti is a terrible person, something I'm sure you are well aware of. I mean, how many parades of men did she blow while your father was in the can? I've lost count myself."

Jewel didn't speak. The thought of defending her mother made her stomach turn.

"Whatever you have to do for a buck, I guess," the lady said, her confidence riding high. "You are the perfect specimen for Mother's reincarnation. She has selected you above everyone else. *Everyone*. Goes without saying, but this is an honor you cannot—will not—refuse. Do you understand what I mean, Jewel? This is very important. A transference is easier when both parties are willing."

Too stunned to speak, Jewel's eyes avoided contact with the lady's. A hopelessness settled inside her, resting in her bones. There was no escaping this place. That was becoming very clear now. The bodies on the pile were beginning to move, shaking. Waking. She saw Adam come to life, his head lifting off the soft soil that layered the ground.

"It's almost time," the lady said. "Our little dreamers have dreamed their last dream."

8

Boxberger waggled his knife.

Doug stood in front of Maddie, ready to catch the blade with his heart if need be. He was ready to die for her. He could still taste her kiss, a flavor he wished to savor forever, as long as he lived. One glance around his surroundings and it appeared his existence was about to be cut short.

"Your mother has created a world of shit for me," Boxberger snapped. Spittle sputtered off his lips as he spoke. Some clung to his teeth. There was venom in his voice, trapped aggression that had finally been released.

"What are you talking about, psycho?" Doug felt his knees shake. For a second he thought they were going to buckle, send him to the puddles of filth below. What did his mother and Boxberger have to do with one another? Boxberger had only moved to Hooperstown a few years ago. His mother had been in Benton for much longer than that. It didn't add up. "My mother is in a mental health facility up in Benton. You don't even know her!"

A twisted grin pulled at the man's lips. He advanced, a calculated step landing softly in a puddle, a mixture of Jimmy's blood and chemical waste. "She never told you? The story about the boy and the girl and the cave in the woods. She had to. A bedtime story for Dougie Simms. Yes, that almost has a poetic ring to it, don't you think?"

The thing was, she had told him that story. Before bedtime, just like Boxberger said.

And he dreamed it. In the beginning of summer.

"She never went deep into the cave with us. All the way in. If she had just gone *all the way* with us, it would have been so much easier."

"That was...*you?*" Doug's mouth dropped open. "You're the boy?"

Boxberger nodded, his smile a white beacon in the tunnel's fragile light.

"What the hell is going on here?" Abby asked. She had jumped behind Grady, who looked just as terrified as Doug felt.

"I'll explain later," Doug told them.

Boxberger pretended to launch himself at the kids, causing them to jump. Maddie screamed in Doug's ear, which brought on a quiet, continuous ring of tinnitus.

"No...you won't." Boxberger seemed pleased with having the upper hand, enjoying this little cat-and-mouse game. There were no holes in the wall for them to scurry into, and it was only a matter of time before they ran out of real estate. He continued to push forward, forcing the kids back, deeper into the tunnel. "'Cause I'm gonna gut all four of you like a school of lost fishes. Oh yeah. I've been waiting all summer for this. You really have no idea. I've dreamed of this moment a thousand times. It took everything I had not to cut open the three of you when you came knocking on my door that day, asking questions you shouldn't have been asking. I begged my wife to let me do it—BEGGED HER. But she was insistent. To wait. To have patience. She insisted the Mother would have a use for you, Doug Simms. Because of who you are. Because of what your mother did on that day in '72."

"Can we spray this fucker already?" Grady asked, his voice wavering.

Doug debated what kind of effect dousing the man in chemicals would have. Maybe none. *Probably* none. But what choice did they have? They were backing themselves into a corner, and Boxberger was eager to see what their intestines looked like.

"Let's do it," Doug said, and positioned his wand.

The four of them held up their weapons and took aim.

"What the hell is this?" Boxberger asked, continuing to act like the situation amused him. "This is cute, I'll give you runts that."

"Ready..." Doug concentrated on Boxberger's face. "One... Two..."

"THREE!" Grady yelled, and fired first.

Four streams of chemicals shot out, splashing Boxberger from the chest on up. He reacted by throwing his hands over his face, protecting his mouth and eyes from the blasts. Then he dropped to his knees, rubbing his irritated skin vigorously, attempting to wipe off the dangerous mixture. Next, he started screaming. Bloodcurdling howls that echoed in the oval chamber. The outburst caused the four of them to shrink back, to look on in horror as the chemicals worked their magic, seeping into the man's pores and inflicting pain.

"IT BURNS!" he shouted. "IT BURNS! IT BURNS!"

"Holy shit," Grady said. "It's working!" He primed the wand for another spray.

Then, Boxberger stopped moving.

The four removed their fingers from the triggers, each believing their plan had worked, that Boxberger had accepted his defeat.

Slowly, Boxberger removed his hands from his face.

Doug expected to see the man's flesh in ruin, scraps of skin dangling, revealing the raw redness beneath. Blisters of devastation. Craters of instant decay. But his face was fine, untouched, looking like he'd just splashed a handful of water over his face to freshen his mood.

"Gotcha," Boxberger said, his smile creeping back across his face.

"Oh fuck," Grady said, backing away.

The chemicals had done absolutely nothing.

Doug readied his wand, telling himself that maybe they hadn't used enough, that maybe they needed to unload more.

Boxberger licked the spray off his lips. "I think I taste water. Lots of water. Say, did you buy the cheap stuff?" He clicked his tongue several times and waved a condescending finger back and forth. "Something your parents should have taught you brats—you always get what you pay for. Never skimp on the important things."

He slashed the knife in the air between them.

The girls yelped. Grady made a noise that sounded like a ghost haunting a gothic castle. Doug swallowed what felt like an egg.

"There's no use fighting the inevitable. Tell you what? The three of you," Boxberger said, pointing to Maddie, Abby, and Grady, "come here and I'll end you quick. A fast throat-slash and that's it. You'll bleed out in seconds. No torment, no suffering. Nice and easy. How's that sound?"

No one volunteered.

"If you struggle...I'm gonna make you hurt. Bad. *Real* bad." This brought him joy. "I know which death I'd choose."

"Fuck you, Box-booger!" Doug said. It was the only thing he could articulate.

He chuckled softly. "That's not even my name. Changed it to Boxberger when the wife and I moved back here. You can still call me that, though. I like it. It's creative."

"I hate you."

"I know you do. But I hate you more. So much more. I hate that little runt Di Falco even more than that. A part of me is sad he isn't here so I could cut his belly open and remove every little piece of him—but, then again, I know he's suffering in that hospital bed. Living each day, wondering if it'll be his last. Wish I could see his pale face, his body lying on that hard slab of death." He squirmed as if all the joy in his body were too much to hold inside. "Ahhhh...it just warms my heart knowing that one day—and one day soon—he'll close his eyes and never open them again."

"You're wrong," Doug told him. "Jesse will pull through. The doctors are confident."

A burst of laughter. "Oh, sweet child. So innocent. So dumb. Really Dougie, you should be more grown up by now. You're going into high school for Christ's sake. Quit acting like a fucking child."

Even though Boxberger had a point, Doug didn't let his words affect him.

"Your friend will die. His spirit will travel to the other side, and he will rest with the Mother forever." He flashed his cold smile once again, and Doug shivered in its presence. "As will all of you once I escort you to the land of eternal sleep."

The kids took another step back, and Boxberger proceeded to gain on them. The distance was closing. Doug knew it was only a matter of time before his ex-teacher ran out of things to say. The time to use that knife was coming soon.

Doug had no intention of watching him butcher his friends.

But there was nowhere to run. Nowhere to hide. He looked around and saw only darkness, the shadows the tunnels provided. There were no doors, no way out. The way back to the river was now ahead of them and Boxberger was blocking the path. They were being pushed further into the dark, further into the unknown. And there was nothing more terrifying than the unknown.

"Okay, kiddies," Boxberger said. He wiped Jimmy's blood on his white robe, cleaning the blade, making room for more red. "Enough talkie, more bloody."

As he moved in, bringing the knife to his ear, a figure dashed behind him, moving in a blur. It crashed into him, knocking him against the tunnel wall. The impact sounded off with a hard clang, Boxberger's skull hitting the metal structure with force. It was enough to knock his glasses off his face.

Karen, using the power of her legs, forced her weight (all one-hundred-and-twenty pounds) against Boxberger's body, pinning him against the wall.

"Go!" she shouted. Red trickled from her nostrils. She gritted her teeth, pushing against Boxberger, keeping him—for the moment—still. Boxberger was in a daze, but who knew how long it would last. His head had hit the metal pretty hard, but it wasn't enough to put him out. His eyes rolled, and Doug could tell he was on the verge of losing consciousness but was managing to stay lucid. "I said GO!" Karen screamed, louder this time. "Go! Find a way out!"

Doug turned to the others. "Let's move!"

"We can't leave her," Abby said, panicking.

"She's fine. She can handle it." He didn't believe that himself, but he sounded convincing enough.

The four scrambled down the tunnel, their footsteps splashing along, drowning out the scuffle behind them. Doug didn't look back. He followed the direction of Maddie's light, how it bounced off the walls, trying to find them a way out.

Twenty feet later and the tunnel guided them to the right. When Maddie's light fell upon an alcove that housed a ladder, a series of metal rungs bolted to a flat wall, Doug felt his hope return. It wasn't much, but it was something.

"We should go back," Abby said, her eyes darting in the direction they had come. "We shouldn't have left her."

Doug couldn't disagree with the last part of that statement. "She told us to go."

"Well, we shouldn't have listened."

"It's too late now," Grady said, and he was right. Doug knew it. Backtracking would be a waste of time. If Karen managed to overpower Boxberger—or better yet, kill the bastard—then she would catch up eventually. If not...well, it made no sense for a lamb to return to the slaughterhouse he had just escaped. "Let's see where this takes us," Grady said. "See where it leads."

No one audibly agreed with him. Doug mounted the ladder first. When he was about ten feet up, a third of the way to the top, he looked down and saw his friends reluctantly take to the rungs and begin their ascension.

That's when they heard the scream tear through the intake system, echoing throughout the tunnels.

9

Karen watched the kids bound off into the dark. Relief washed over her. She didn't think they'd listen, thought they'd stick around and get themselves killed. Boxberger had been temporarily restrained, but she knew her efforts would only go so far. She could feel his energy bouncing back, his strength restoring, and she had only ten seconds, maybe twelve, before he was back at full strength.

It happened quicker than that.

He shoved her off of him, pushing her back a few feet.

She lost her footing, her left sneaker slipping in the puddle. She went to the ground hard, landing on her elbows. Pain shot into her shoulders, down her arms. She wondered if her bones had cracked. Rolling over, a numb, tingly sensation crawled over her, guiding the hurt away.

Boxberger rose to his feet. With one hand, he fixed his glasses, placing them back on his face. The other hand gripped the knife, his knuckles growing white. In the shadows of the tunnel, she saw his smile return.

"You little cunt." He marched toward her, grabbed her by her hair, and lifted her to her feet. She screamed. "You almost ruined me. Had you been quicker, you could have taken the knife from me. You had a genuine opportunity to win, but you were too slow. I guess youth doesn't always triumph." He sniffed her neck like a dog getting the sense of the human before it. "Youth has its disadvantages. You always think you're protected, that nothing bad will ever happen to you. That the world, as scary as it seems, cannot reach out and touch you. That you're infallible and perfect. You take risks, like the one you just made. Most of the time they pay off, because you have no fear. You have nothing to fear when you're young because you don't know any better. You know nothing of the world, the horrors we face on a daily basis. How fragile our lives are. You know nothing about pain and torment, of lives lost."

Karen tried tuning him out, but he spoke directly in her ear.

"You know nothing of loss and grief, but today you will learn." He pointed with his knife, directing her attention to the dead body of Jimmy Di Falco, his crumpled, bleeding form. "He is your lesson." Then he nibbled at her ear, placing her lobe between his teeth and biting down.

She squirmed, tried to break free from his grasp, but she couldn't. His strength was back, full-force, and there was no escaping his clutches.

A roar of laughter echoed. She screamed, cried out for help. Maybe the kids would come back, realize she had made a grave mistake in letting them go on ahead without her. But the seconds passed and the darkened area they had trotted off down remained a black void of no movement.

She was alone.

She would die alone.

"He is your lesson," Boxberger repeated, "and I will teach you another."

As he ran the blade gracefully across her throat, she tried to scream once more, but there was nothing left inside of her save for the flow of red that poured from the new wound.

Infinite darkness chased her away from the world.

10

Jesse runs and the landscape changes behind him. The forest falls away, breaking apart like buildings in some apocalyptic earthquake. The crumbling world collapses upon itself and is renewed in another image, this one familiar but also not.

Another hospital room.

The same one he is currently in, maybe, but it looks older. Fourteen years older to be exact. Fourteen years, six months, and two days.

The day he was born.

His mother is cradling him. Jimmy, three years old, just a toddler, is tugging at his mother's gown, wanting to take a look at his baby bro. Mrs. Di Falco bends on one knee, allowing big brother a look at the preciousness bundled in so many blankets.

Jesse can't see himself from his position in the room, and the dream does not allow him a closer look.

Jimmy's face lights up at first glance, a cherubic joy that touches Jesse in the center of his chest. The boy's mouth forms a thrilled O. His eyes twinkle with wonder and amazement. He is happy. Happier than happy. He throws his arms up in celebration.

"Brother!" young Jimmy shouts. It's the best day he's had in three years.

"That's right, Jimmy," Mother says. She looks over at Jesse—older Jesse—as if she can see him. As if he is not a ghost in this new dream but a participant. "That's right. Your brother is here. He has arrived." His mother's eyes glow a radiant gold, and Jesse realizes this dream is not a mirror of the real world, no replay of past events.

Jimmy turns. His eyes are also glowing, ablaze with eternal hatred.

Jesse backs away. Can't. A wall behind him. The edge of the dream.

"You want to see him?" Mother asks. "My son? My beautiful baby boy?"

Jesse wants to tell her no, HELL NO, but he cannot speak. His voice is dry. A sound escapes his throat, but it means nothing to this cold, dead world he's found himself trapped in.

Mother cradles the infant. It begins to cry as she moves away from the nursery, and toward him. Young Jimmy follows, holding onto Mother's gown. She trails him across the hospital room.

Jesse does not want to look, but the dream forces his eyes on the baby. The infant. The thing bundled in Mother's arms.

He looks upon it and screams.

There's no baby inside. Just a nest of black widows, crawling about, their spidery limbs stretching, finding purchase on the fabric. Eggs begin to hatch, spawning more tiny horrors, more black widows. They crawl up the Mother's arms, underneath the sleeve of her gown. Up her neck. Over her smile, between her drawn lips. Up her nose. They cover her face now. Jimmy's too.

The kid is grinning as the black widows make their way past his teeth, into his mouth, spinning threads of webbing as they scurry about. The entire room is alive with them. The walls pulsate as thousands, hundreds of thousands, slink along the drywall's surface. Their thin, wiry legs scraping against the walls and each other, sounding like a thousand whispers at once.

Jesse feels webs cling to his neck. He smacks them, thankful the dream has allowed such an act. He spins around, trying to rid his flesh of the sticky sensation as cold lightning rides his spine.

Flailing around now, knocking the crawling creatures from his shoulders and brushing them out of his hair, Jesse runs for the hospital door, the dream's only egress. There is the window, but he isn't sure what floor the dream has placed him on—a high fall could lead to a broken neck, and a broken neck in the dream means—

He spares himself the repetition. He knows the rules.

Rushing through the doorway, he hears the Mother laughing. Little Jimmy too.

"You can't run forever," the dream god says. "I've already got your brother."

Now in the hallway, Jesse turns back, watching his mother's face melt into a hideous mask, a far cry away from anything human. Her flesh liquefies, streams down her face like runny egg yolks. Her eyes intensify, burn brighter than any light he's ever seen.

"You lie," he says, unable to imagine how the Mother has obtained Jimmy. Jimmy who last Jesse saw was locked in his room, counting down the days until the summer ended and school began. There is no way she could touch him there...in his room.

Mother shakes her malformed skull. Pinkish-purple growths the size of tennis balls break out across her face, swelling with pus and other rotten substances. "He came to me," she says. "He came to save you, and in return, he caught the eternal sleep. He is with me now, walking the dream-world. His soul is eternally mine. Just like all the children of your camp. This town will soon be mine, and there is no hope for you and your friends." She snarls. "Now give yourself to me! STOP FIGHTING IT."

He runs, unwilling to believe that Jimmy is gone.

He runs into another scene.

A tunnel.

At the end of it, Jimmy lies face down in a puddle.

The puddle is red, and he is not moving.

11

Doug popped the top of the hatch and climbed through the cylinder-shaped opening just wide enough to squeeze through.

He pulled himself up and swung his feet to the side, placing them on the catwalk suspended over the main intake room. A quick survey of the area revealed much of what he'd caught glimpses of in his dreams. Several people ambled about, looking like zombies from old Romero flicks. They stumbled without purpose, no destination in mind. They'd get to one spot, turn around, and return to their previous position. Farther across the room, he spotted a woman in a white gown, dressed similarly to Boxberger. She wore a crown of thistle and thorns, a necklace that held a string of white flowers. She was waving her hands the same way Mrs. Di Falco sometimes did when telling a story, and the lady's voice echoed throughout the tall room. He couldn't make out what she was saying—the distance was too far, the echo too great—but it sounded like she was explaining something to the girl standing next to her.

Even from behind, even though he couldn't see her face, Doug recognized the listener.

It was Jewel Conti.

Figures she's a part of this, he thought, helping the others through the hole.

Once they all found their footing on the catwalk, they crouched down, keeping out of sight from the servants below. Doug watched as they studied each other's faces, taking good long stares, as if expecting someone to formulate a plan, speak it aloud. When no one offered any ideas, they turned their attention to the lady and Jewel. Doug turned his ear to the scene, trying to eavesdrop on their conversation. But the distance was still too great, and he couldn't hear a single coherent word, only the carrying echoes of their voices.

Starting to make his way down the catwalk, Doug waved them along.

Maddie stopped him. "What if they see us? Hear us?"

Doug shrugged. This was their only option. Their only play. They couldn't return to the tunnels. He hoped Karen had fared well against Boxberger, but his gut told him otherwise.

"We don't have a choice," he told her. "Let's get closer. See if we can hear anything useful."

Grady pointed at the lady and the girl next to her. "That's Jewel Conti."

"Ugh," Abby grunted. "I hate that bitch."

"Do you guys think she's a part of this? Like, maybe she's helping the Mother out?"

"I don't know, Grades," Doug said. "But let's find out. We should grab as much info as we can before making a decision on what to do next. Just like before. Just like all summer."

Grady nodded, agreeing with everything.

Doug was impressed. Grady was clearly frightened, but he'd let the girls go ahead, putting him first in line in the event Boxberger followed them here. The kid had found his courage and Doug couldn't have been prouder. His actions were commendable, and if the pair lived to see tomorrow, he'd give Grady all the praise in the world.

Doug led the parade down the catwalk, closer to the lady in white and Jewel Conti. They continued to discuss the matters at hand, keeping their voices low, and the kids were unable to piece together any of the conversation. Their words continued to echo in the vast chamber, the acoustics of this place great for carrying and tossing around sound, but not so great for eavesdropping on faraway conversations.

Once they were closer, a few feet from sitting parallel to the lady in white's position, Doug saw what the duo were facing. It was a coffin of sorts, and although Doug couldn't clearly see inside, he knew there was a body inside. The coffin looked old, wrapped in some sort of sheeting, and it smelled just as ancient. Even though the bay was moldy, and the earthy aromas dominated the air, Doug could smell something rotten beginning to make itself known. As he neared, his stomach began to churn. A heavy pressure sat at the base of his throat, warning him of the consequences should he inhale too much—like being reacquainted with breakfast.

In position now, Doug could hear *some* of what was being said. The lady in white was talking to Jewel, telling her a story. Jewel was doing a whole lot of nodding and looking, not a whole lot of participating.

"Do you understand what I mean, Jewel?" the lady asked. "This is very important. A transference is easier when both parties are willing."

Transference?

Even though he'd come into the conversation late, he knew what the word *transference* meant. She was going to transfer the Mother to Jewel? She was going to…*possess* her? Judging from her reaction, Jewel didn't sound like she was one hundred percent on-board with that. It was as if the lady in white—whom he could now see was Mrs. Boxberger—a *very* pregnant Mrs. Boxberger She was still trying to convince Jewel to submit.

Below, the bodies strewn across the floor suddenly began to rise. They were sluggish to their feet, like late sleepers not accustomed to such ungodly early hours. Once up, they paced around the immediate area, as if having no clear direction in mind. Some circled the tree that had grown in the center of the bay. Some tried to pick the fruit hanging from the branches. Some just stared at the magnificent aberration in awe.

"It's almost time," Rita Boxberger said. "Our little dreamers have dreamed their last dream."

Doug studied the faces of the sick, the malignant ones. They were people he recognized, most of them, people from town. They were his classmates, future high schoolers. Well, *future* was tentative right now—the kids below looked pale and sickly with bruises circling the skin around their eyes. Some of them were coughing into their hands. Some picking at open sores on their cheeks. Stroking the green patches of growth that had sprouted on their arms and necks.

There were other members of the Mother's congregation too, besides kids from school, people Doug knew. He saw his father's ex-boss, Mr. Walker. The man was kneeling, his hands clasped together in prayer. He faced the Mother's open sarcophagus, which rested a good distance from him. His lips moved rapidly, reciting some unknown hymn. Others were acting similarly. Doug noticed most of the adults used to be workers at Hooperstown Chemical. Some were parents of the children that were present. Everyone had the Mother in their eyes. Some glowed brighter than others. Some didn't glow at all.

The kids outnumbered the adults four to one.

"Jesus," Grady said under his breath. "All the sick kids…the cancer cluster patients… They're here."

"Not all of them," Doug said, referencing their friend. He wondered how Jesse was holding up, how he was faring in the Land of Dreams. Wondered if he was still alive. "But yeah, most of them. Adults too."

"What are they doing?" Maddie asked.

The gathered were dressed in white robes just like the Boxbergers. Even Jewel had cloaked herself in the snow-white attire.

"Some sort of ceremony," Grady guessed. "She said *transference*."

Doug nodded. "I think… I think Mrs. Boxberger is going to have that baby."

"Oh yeah," Abby chimed in. "That broad is ready to burst. Big time."

"Then, someone needs to carry the Mother."

"I thought the Mother was already a thing?" Grady shook his head, trying to unstick his thoughts. "I mean, wasn't she a thing? Didn't we see her in the cemetery?"

Doug bit his lip. "We saw something, but not her. She probably wasn't powerful enough yet. She needed to…feed on more souls."

"She's like a vampire? Instead of blood, she needs dreams. And souls."

"*Exactly*. She latches onto people through their dreams. A spirit that wanders in and out of our dream lives. When she gets powerful enough, she becomes this god-like entity, and her dreams start to cross over into reality. It causes people to hallucinate."

"I don't get it," Abby whispered. "Where does the cancer come in?"

Maddie pointed to the corner of the bay. There were wheelbarrows overflowing with white flowers, the same ones that rested around the Boxberger's necks. "Those are Daturas."

"The dreaming petals?" Grady asked. "The ones Jesse told us about?"

"Exactly. They must have been dumping them in with the chemical waste. The Boxbergers must have known the plant was dumping into the river. Somehow they added their own ingredient."

"Shit." Grady swallowed. "The flowers must have been what made us susceptible to her."

"Makes sense," Doug said. "The Boxbergers must have been at this for years, supplying the plant with the flowers."

"Some flowers are infused with certain chemicals to help make pigments and dyes," Maddie told them. "They could have easily slipped the Daturas into their shipments. Who knows how far they went to infect the town?"

"So the Mother gets stronger," Doug said, "by easily slipping into our dreams. In return, some of us get sick. Because of the chemicals, sure, but also because she's eating us. Literally feeding off us."

"To grow," Grady said. "She wants to grow, remember?"

Doug noticed the weeds that had grown on the ground below, the greenery sticking out of the thin layer of dirt that covered the floor. The Tree of Life standing tall in the center of the bay. The patches of mold that had sprouted on the infected's exposed skin. So much growing. So much life. She was taking something from them (their lives, their souls), and giving them something back.

Whatever it was, Doug needed to end it.

They all did.

Or there would be nothing left of their town.

And soon after, there would be nothing left of the world.

It would probably take a long time. Years. Decades. But all things grow—sicknesses, ideas, children—and all growing things could be stunted with the proper measures.

Doug grabbed his wand, held it tight. He was ready to begin the stunting.

"Ready?" Doug asked the others.

Their silence was confirmation enough.

"You little fucks," said a snarling voice from behind them. Their heads snapped in the direction of the growling intruder. It was Boxberger. He was holding onto the knife—the blood-slicked blade dripping—and he looked really, *really* pissed. His glasses were cracked, both lenses. A long gash ran along the skin beneath his eye. Flowery explosions of blood flecked his robe, dirtying up the pureness of its appearance. Without needing to be told what had taken place back in the tunnel, Doug knew whose blood it was. "I ought to gut each and every one of you *right now.*"

Doug backed away and stole a look below. The room had turned its eyes on them. The lady in white. Jewel.

His skin crawled with instant dread.

So much for the element of surprise.

"Husband!" Rita Boxberger called up. "Do not touch a hair on their heads."

Grimacing, Boxberger abandoned his pursuit. "Of...of course, dear."

Doug could tell it took every fiber in his body to obey his wife. A murderous rage crossed his eyes. Doug could feel the hatred emanating through the man's pores, could almost smell his loathing like a bad cologne.

"Good." Rita's smile leaked across her face. "Now...bring them down. We have a ceremony to get on with."

12

Jesse blinks, finds himself standing in the circle of center court. High school gymnasium. He's only played here once, an AAU game last year. It was the worst game he's ever played. Two points on twelve shots. One assist. The coach pulled him after nine minutes, never put him back in. He quit AAU after that game, mostly to focus on school ball, but also because he was embarrassed of that one dismal performance. Embarrassed and disgusted.

The bleachers are populated with Hooperstown's dead. His brother is among him, courtside seats. Jimmy's got more holes in him than a piece of Swiss cheese. He leaks puddles of scarlet blood onto the floor below him. His mouth, slicked with shiny crimson streaks, is agape. Flies buzz around his head. His eyes, open and gazing, just stare—at what, Jesse can't tell, but it's nothing alive.

There are others like Jimmy. Dead. Bleeding. Slashed open. The ones that haven't been stabbed or sliced have died from the disease, the plague of Hooperstown. Sickly corpses. Bruised flesh. Fully-grown tumors, the size of baseballs. Even though this is a dream, the collective smell of the dead, their expired flesh and rotting meat, fills the air, and Jesse thinks he might be sick. He keeps himself from hurling on the school's insignia—the hammerhead shark. The school mascot, Hammie, is also sitting in the bleachers. A giant fishhook has been inserted through his head, and there is blood, so much blood, that it has spilled onto the court, trespassing the inbounds line, running like the Red River that borders the town Jesse has called home his entire life.

The digital scoreboard on wall behind the basketball hoop flips to 0-0. There's a clock counting down. The numbers don't make sense and clearly time doesn't matter in the game that's about to begin. Jesse is suddenly holding a ball.

He looks up, across the court, and sees her.

The Mother.

She is naked, leaving nothing to Jesse's imagination. He feels things move within him he's never felt before. A rush of excitement, particularly behind his jockstrap, and he doesn't know why. It's not like she's attractive. She's grimy as hell; dirt smears soil her flesh, grass clippings are sprinkled throughout her hair, and she has bruises—black welts—that cover almost every inch of her. Her black bush of pubic hair is the size of a small animal, and there are things crawling through the coarse thicket, ticks and spiders and other thin-legged insects. Disgusted as he is, he cannot look away from her. This is the first time he's seen a woman in the nude before, live and in person, and even though it is a dream and not real—not in any usual sense of the word—it feels real enough, more real than reality itself. He stares at her nipples, their hardened state, and feels himself growing below his waist.

"You like what you see?" asks the Mother.

Her eyes are glowing, and he finds them hard to look at. Her lips are fixed in a terrible grin, another negative selling point, another reason to look away—but alas, he still can't. Jesse feels overstimulated by this sequence of the dream and wishes he could shed his own skin. Detach from his own soul and flee. His anxiety builds and it feels like his heart might explode.

"You can touch me, Jesse. I won't mind."

He doesn't want to touch her, not at all. He wants to run, turn and bolt. Get far away. To where, he doesn't give a shit, so long as it's away from her.

The Mother.

She approaches, each footstep in sync with the hammering of his heart.

"It'll be our secret. You like secrets?"

He wants to tell her "no," that he hates secrets. Fuck secrets and fuck her. But still, she moves on him and his mouth stays closed. She's close enough to where her smell overpowers the dead's. She smells like the forest on a cool morning before the sun rises, the damp-earth aroma stuffing his nostrils. It's intoxicating and he tries to ignore its power, its influential effect. But he has no power, not here, not in the presence of this formidable being, this creature of infinite authority. She rules these dream-lands. She is the architect of nightmares, shaper of derelict worlds, and mother of all living and dead things.

Here.

In this realm.

But outside, she is shit.

And Jesse knows that.

The world flickers like a light bulb signaling the end of its run. Another world appears when this one darkens. The gym gives way to a tall industrial unit, a warehouse-looking room that mirrors the gymnasium in size. Quick flashes reveal a tree in the center of the intake bay, growing out of the ground. It's full of life, this tree. Flowers pop. Fruit, alien-looking growths in myriad colors and shapes, swell from the ends of its branches. There are people in white robes gathered before a makeshift stage constructed of collapsed building materials, metal beams and wooden columns and sheets of plywood. On the far end of the room, the white-robed men and women of Hooperstown, some of whom Jesse recognizes, are kneeling before the ceremony. Jesse sees the Boxbergers leading the charge, sees the Mother—the real Mother—in her fragile, reduced form sitting in a box of death, cocooned in old cloth, awaiting her resurrection. Jewel Conti is there, *holding an enormous book as a very pregnant, about-to-pop-any-second Rita Boxberger reads from it.*

As Rita recites the incantations aloud, words and phrases Jesse cannot decipher from the next world over, Mr. Boxberger runs a knife along his friend's throat. Arterial spray fans out from Doug's neck, raining blood on the gathered.

"NOOOOOOOO!" Jesse shouts, as he watches his friend slump forward, dead before his face meets the ground.

Grady's next. His throat opens like an envelope. A wet, red gush. Grady is gone.

Then Abby.

Maddie is last.

The four of them bleed out, twitching as they are released from this world.

The gym again.

Mother stands before him. Her hand cups his genitals as his flaccid member moves up her wrist. She squeezes. It feels good and bad at the same time.

He wishes all of it away, but here, like in the real world, some wishes don't come true. Most don't, in fact.

He opens his eyes and she is there, staring into his with those burning halos of gold fury.

"It's too late for them, Jesse Di Falco. Your friends are already dead."

"No," Jesse says, whimpering. His face is slick with tears. "No, it's not true."

"It is true. They are dead. Gone. Their souls now belong to me, just as all the good children of Hooperstown will soon be mine. I WILL FEAST ON THEIR DREAMS FOREVER."

Her teeth are exposed, sharp like pencil points. There are so many crowding her mouth that Jesse cannot count. Hundreds line her gums. Her face contorts, as if she's aged a thousand years within mere seconds. Wrinkles fill in her once-smooth flesh, dark lines of epochs come and gone. She stands before him, holding his privates, her ancient mask running like mascara in a heatwave.

"THEY ARE DEAD AND I WILL EAT THIS TOWN'S DREAMS JUST LIKE I WILL DEVOUR YOURS FOREVER FOREVER FOREVER."

Jesse tears himself away, stumbles and falls. He lands on his back. The Mother crouches like a predator ready to pounce on injured quarry.

Like a crab, Jesse crawls on all fours away from the drooling woman, her eyes wide and feral and seeking to tear him open.

He shakes his head.

"It's not true! None of it! They're still alive!"

The Mother only grins. Begins to crawl toward him like some primitive primate, supporting her weight with her knuckles and feet.

"This isn't real. NONE OF IT IS REAL."

But it is real, he thinks. Some of it, at least. If not now, it's the future. It's what will happen to his friends.

Unless he does something to stop her.

But what?

How can you stop something that cannot die?

And then, as the Mother closes the distance between them, he knows what he must do.

CHAPTER NINETEEN

Forever in Her Fields of Bloom

1

"No sign of forced entry," the cop said, and Gordon Simms wanted to throw his hands up in surrender. It had taken a good hour to convince the police to send someone out here, and now that an officer had shown up—two actually—getting them to check the perimeter of Hooperstown Chemical had been a major chore. It was true what they had said about the cops in this town—lazy as anything.

"I know that," Gordon said, signaling to the stretch of fence that wrapped around the entire circumference of the plant's property. "But look how much fence there is. They could have gotten in another way. Here, let me—"

"Are you telling us how to do our job, sir?" one of them said, Jacobs according to what he'd told Gordon.

"No." Gordon feigned innocence. "No, not at all. Sorry. Look. I just want to find my kid. He hasn't checked in with me like he was supposed to, and I'm...worried about him. A neighbor saw him heading in this direction, and I just have good reason to believe he's here. Okay?"

The cops eyed each other, and Gordon could see they weren't buying the story. Still, they shrugged their shoulders as if they had nothing better to do and were going to help him regardless.

"All right," said the officer who'd introduced himself as Baum. "Lead the way, cowboy."

Gordon followed the fence around to the side of the plant, instinct taking hold. He shielded his eyes from the bright sun that streaked through the gray clouds, the late-summer sun pressing its heat down on him. Sweat poured from his hairline, and he dragged his forearm across it, clearing away layers of perspiration.

Then he stopped.

He spotted the small cluster of bikes. The red wagon, just like Ted Burrows had mentioned.

"There!"

He took off racing down the bumpy terrain, not paying attention to the dips and divots in the footing. The cops called out, telling him to wait up, but he ignored them. Burrows had been right—they *had* come to Hooperstown Chemical. But for what?

None of it made sense, but Gordon couldn't rationalize the thoughts of children, what ran through their heads. Maybe that was part of the problem. Maybe if he could think like Doug, connect with him on a deeper level, then maybe they wouldn't be in this mess to begin with. He knew he hadn't been the best father he could have been these last three months. He'd promised Doug he would do things, take him places, but the only father/son time they had was that disastrous trip to visit his mother, and they hadn't even gone alone. Grady had been there. Hardly the one-on-one time he and the boy needed.

You sure fucked up, Gordy, his own father's voice echoed in his thoughts. His own father who hadn't been there for him, either.

Ever since Sharon had tried to kill them in their sleep, tried to "save them from their dreams," he knew he had to step up as a parent. Be there more. Take on both roles. And he felt like he had, but he also felt like he'd done the bare minimum, enough to keep things afloat, and that wasn't "being there," not really. It was what any ordinary parent might do, but Gordon didn't want to be like any ordinary parent. He wanted to be better. The best.

Please, God, if he's okay, if he's alive and comes home safely, I'll do better. I promise. Swear on my life.

Gordon reached the bikes, began inspecting them immediately, not waiting for the cops and their donut-filled bellies to come bouncing over. There were no clues revealing the kids' purpose of coming here. Just four abandoned bikes and one empty red wagon.

Gordon's eyes followed their probable path to the fence, saw the cut in the chain-link, the slit just tall and wide enough to fit the average teenager.

Son of a bitch, Gordon thought. *They're inside.*

Breathless, both cops eventually caught up.

"Holy shit," Baum said, bending over, placing his hands on his knees. "Guess I need to hit the gym more often, huh?"

Gordon didn't have a response for that. He turned to the cops. "I think one of you should call these kids' parents and one of you should come inside with me." He gave them the names of the kids, all except Abby's because he didn't recognize the bike. "Call their folks. Tell them what happened."

"Now wait just a minute," Jacobs said, "I don't like you shoutin' orders at us, hoss. Why don't you—"

"Why don't you just do your job?" Gordon snapped, and he wondered if he'd take that tone with a seasoned officer, not some kid who looked like he'd just graduated high school.

Jacobs backed down, stared at him. "Sir, I'm going to do just that. But you need to watch your tongue with me. All right?"

Amped, Gordon realized how he'd spoken and backtracked. "You're right. I'm sorry. Just...my kid's inside there and I just...want him back. It's dangerous. So much that can hurt him in there, and I... I just want him back." He was almost crying. Almost.

"I understand," Jacobs told him. "Have a little one myself." He squinted against the sun, scoping out the layout of the plant. "Listen, I'm gonna head back to the car and radio for backup. I'll tell the station to reach out to the kids' parents. Baum—you take Mr. Simms and scope out the perimeter, see if there's a way inside. But if you find one, you wait for me. Okay?"

Gordon nodded. It was as good a deal as he was gonna get.

Jacobs left to head back to the car like he promised, and Baum held open the slit in the fence, wide enough for Gordon to crouch down and squeeze through. Once on the other side, Gordon did the same for Baum. Together, they walked down the small hill and entered the paved pathway that reached around the entire property. It wasn't that long ago Gordon held a very important conversation with Dylan Walker on this path and had basically told him to go fuck himself. He'd felt good then.

He didn't feel so good now.

Gordon lightly jogged down the path despite Baum telling him to hold up, that his legs weren't meant to do this much running. Which was an odd thing for a cop to tell him, but Gordon didn't say so. He continued searching for a way inside the plant. It was conceivable they hadn't locked the place up completely, that one of the doors inside the operating station had been left open.

What are you doing here, Doug? Why would you come here? What the hell were you thinking?

Gordon tried the first door he came across and found it locked. He rushed ahead to another one. Baum's voice was getting farther and farther behind. He told him to hold up again, but Gordon wasn't going to listen.

Damn right. I need to find my son.

Gordon tried the next door and found that Walker had left it unlocked. The hinges groaned in protest, but the door swung open regardless. A wall of impenetrable black faced Gordon, an inky barrier that brought forth promises of no return. Without second-guessing himself or the potentially dangerous scenario ahead, he darted inside, ignoring the protests of the cop behind him, ignoring the warning the dark void was trying to silently convey.

A small sea of white robes knelt before the makeshift altar, a collection of building supplies the Mother's faithful had pulled together last minute. Rita Boxberger—not her real name, but one she'd chosen to adopt and embrace—stood atop it, holding Jewel Conti's hand as if she were her mother. Jewel looked like she was out of it. Even Grady could tell she was not herself, further untethered from her typical degenerate swagger. More distant than she had been on the last day of school. He had expected her to be full of piss and vinegar, hurling insults at them the first chance she got— but she had been relatively calm that last day. Now she looked even more at ease.

Maybe it's drugs, Grady thought. Or maybe she was just tired of acting like a complete asshole all the time. Whatever the case, he was glad she wasn't a part of this thing. Rita seemed to be holding her against her will, the effects of this unique ecosystem placing her in some sort of subservient trance. The same way his Dad had been.

Grady whispered to Doug, "How the hell are we getting out of this?"

Boxberger must have heard him because he tilted his head and shushed him. He gripped the knife and angled the sharp metal, ready to slash them across their throats if they disobeyed. Grady figured there was no reason to rebel, not yet. Not when Boxberger looked so eager to end their young lives.

As Rita addressed her audience, starting with, "Mother's Most Faithful," and continuing with how things would play out, Doug turned his head, just slightly, and whispered to Grady, "We're gonna have to get crazy."

"How crazy?"

"I don't know." He glanced around nervously, seeing if Mr. Boxberger had heard him. If he had, the knife-wielding maniac gave no inclination. "But we're running out of time."

"I know that." Grady nodded at the open casket, the dried-out corpse within. It was crazy to think a dead body had caused so much chaos, had been the source of so much evil. Every single bad thing that had happened in this town derived from it. But—no. That wasn't right. It was men who had caused this. Thomas Hooper and what he'd done to that corpse back when it was full of flesh and blood, when it had been most alive. The infamous explorer had started a chain of events that would plague locals for centuries.

And it was people, human beings—the Boxbergers, specifically—who kept Hooper's tradition of encouraging dread and horror, promoting terror and sickness, draining the townspeople, stripping the community of its ambitions and taking away the one thing that inspired hope—their children. Their future. The town's sunshine on dark days ahead.

All in the name of *Mother*.

All for the sake of some nameless demon. A disease. An ancient evil that had rooted itself in the soil of this planet, perhaps from the dawn of time, when the universe was just a speck of dust floating across a dark expanse of infinite nothingness. Like all things that grow, eventually that evil rose to the surface.

It had blossomed.

It was here.

Grady knew how screwed they were. If whatever lay dormant in that withered corpse was allowed to live once more, there would be no stopping it.

It had to stay where it was.

Dreaming.

In the Land of Sleep.

Grady's eyes wandered across the bay, over to the tree.

The Tree.

It was alive, its fruits growing noticeably larger as Rita delivered her speech.

Grady elbowed Doug. "Look," he said. A frail whisper. Hardly a breath.

Doug followed his eyes.

The Tree sat there, unprotected. No one stood guard save for one person, and he was stationed a good fifteen feet from the area. It was Mr. Simms's old boss, Dylan Walker, the plant manager. He hung back, the last line of defense if someone were to attack the sacred sapling.

"We need to kill that tree," Grady said.

"How do you know?"

"Because..." Grady shook his head. He didn't know—not for certain. It was a theory. And there was only one way to prove it. *Try to kill it. Bring it down.* "Because nothing should grow here. I mean *nothing*." He looked down and dug his toe into the layer of soil beneath his feet. He rubbed away the dirt until his toe revealed the metal flooring beneath.

"There's no room for roots to take hold."

Doug glanced down and nodded. "The Tree."

"But they took our chemicals," Maddie reminded them.

Abby nodded to the corner of the room where their sprayers were lazily piled on top of each other. No one was guarding them either. "They're only right there. We just need to break away."

She was too loud. Boxberger stepped in front them, bent down, and waved the knife in their faces. "If you maggots don't shut the fuck up, I will cut out each of your tongues."

"Husband!" Rita snapped. "Do not interrupt our ceremony."

Boxberger rose, turning to his wife. "Sorry, hon," he said through gritted teeth. "But our guests were being quite rude."

"Never mind them. Prepare to light the torches."

Boxberger did as Rita requested, leaving the four prisoners and walking over to the row of unlit torches. He removed a lighter from his pocket and began igniting the wicks one by one. After six were lit, the front row of white-robed citizens each took one and rejoined the gathered.

Rita clutched her stomach and cried out. "Oh God!" she screamed.

"What is it?" Boxberger asked. "Honey?"

"Ohhh," she said, hurting but also seeming to enjoy the agony. Grady saw traces of a smile tug her lips to one side. "Oh, baby, it's time. The child is ready to come forth."

Grady felt sick just thinking about watching the woman give birth. He hoped he wouldn't be forced to watch. He remembered the health class video, how it disgusted and amazed him all at once. He knew the temptation of having her anywhere near him would be too great to ignore. Even if closing his eyes were an option, he knew he wouldn't be able to look away.

"Grady!" Doug said, nudging him. "Let's go! Now!"

Abby and Maddie were already on the move, skulking back into the shadows while Boxberger's attention had shifted to his wife.

Doug headed for the chemicals.

Grady held his breath.

This was it. Their last chance.

Then the floor began to rumble, and a smattering of screams peppered the audience.

3

"Wake up, Jimmy!" he shouts in his dead brother's face. Jimmy is on the ground, in the corner of the intake bay. He's next to others, the ones that had populated in the bleachers. "Wake the fuck up!"

Jimmy's catatonic stare does not change.

"Awww, how cute," the Mother says from behind him. "But enough of this uselessness. Come. Join the others. You cannot escape your fate."

Jesse turns to her. Her naked form has not changed. She's as hideous as ever, the tumors on her flesh expanding, filling with polluted fluids. Tar-like substances drip from her teeth. Spiders spin webs throughout her hair.

She is the filth of the world.

She is Mother.

"I am not afraid of you," Jesse tells her, and she doesn't seem to care. She keeps approaching him, reaching out. Her fingernails have lifted back and there are things wiggling in the fleshy beds beneath them. Thin, stringy extensions, like insect legs. It takes him a second to realize they are stems, weeds rising for the apocalyptic occasion. They're growing out of her ears. Her mouth. Small vines of life, seeking to enter a new host. "I'm not afraid to die."

"Die, you shall."

A betrayer's smile fixed her lips. More things grew out of her, her pores, every opening her body offered, those stems of hate stretching out for him. So much hatred flowed from her, an abhorrence for something she wasn't, something she never was and never would be—human.

"This isn't about revenge," Jesse said, shaking his head. "This isn't about getting revenge for that girl in the forest, what that man did to her." He is crying now, but his thoughts won't stop, won't leave him alone. He's piecing together the final sections of the puzzle, everything falling into place. It's the hate he sees in her eyes, and it's aimed at him. "This is about us. Human beings. You...you want to destroy us."

A radiant glow seizes her eyes, like a light bulb exploding with light before it floods with darkness. After the flash, they whiten, grow cloudy. Her wide smile remains where it is, a staple of her grotesque display. "This realm was so much better without your kind. The Old Gods controlled everything. We were life. We were existence. For eons we wandered this realm, made it how we wanted. So green and vibrant and full of intoxicating scents and peaceful sounds and everlasting harmony. And then one day...it was all over. We were banished from this paradise, sent to exist inside another realm. Most of us died there. Shriveled and withered away to dust. It is what happens when one is no longer allowed to create. As gods, we were made for it. To create, to give life, to watch the worlds we grow breathe and prosper. It is our purpose. But take that purpose away and what do we have? Nothing. Zero. Everything was stolen from us. It was unfair! Banishment from our own creation had taken its toll, and we paid for it with our lives. I watched them all die, every one of my brothers and sisters. We grew sick and old and our bones shriveled up until the darkness came and, one by one, took us away.

"I was sent to the dark place, a territory parallel to the one I helped spawn. I was able to look in on my creation, to see what had become of it. I was able to watch it grow. Evolve. It was my hell, you understand. That is hell, to have a mother watch her child grow up and not be a part of it. You understand, don't you? Don't you? DON'T YOU?"

Jesse does understand, but he does not say so. As the Mother stalks the ruins around them, Jesse taps the dead flesh of Jimmy's cheeks. "Wake up, big bro. Wake up."

"For eons I wandered this Land of Dreams. I returned to the forest where I came to do my thinking, my creating back when I had purpose. And I found her...the girl. Lost. A lost wanderer like myself. I was able to talk to her. Through her dreams I showed her things, who I was and what had become of me. And when the white men came for her, when they stole her innocence and claimed her body, ripped the newborn from her womb like plucking a fresh berry, I was able to help. She let me in. I crawled into her and she carried me, and together we were destined to take back what was hers and mine—she would take back her body and execute those who had stolen her innocence, capture their souls and make them suffer like she had suffered, forever—and I would have my creation. The world I carried in my womb, the one I had given birth to."

"You can't," Jesse says, shaking his head. "You can't. We have lives to live. Don't you *understand*? Your time is over. For whatever reason, you are a god no longer."

Her appearance doubles in size. Her eyes glow hot once again, blazing circles of eternal wrath. "AND WHAT RIGHT DO YOU HAVE?"

Jesse shrinks.

"WHAT MAKES YOU SO SPECIAL? WHO DECIDES WHO LIVES AND DIES?"

For this, he has no answer. He thinks he might but does not want to say. When he sees he must answer, that the Mother expects one, he squeaks out one word: "God?"

"GOD?"

"Yes. You know." He points toward the sky. "That God."

She growls. "THERE IS NO GOD. THERE IS ONLY THE FORCE OF ALL LIVING THINGS. THE ONLY GODS WERE US. MY KIND. MY BROTHERS AND SISTERS, AND NOW WE ARE NO MORE. THERE IS NO RULER, THERE IS NO ONE CHAMPION OF CREATION, ONLY CHAOS."

"Well..." Jesse says, and his voice feels like it will break any second now. "Well...someone decided on us. Us, meaning people. Someone gave us a chance."

She snarls. The weeds that have grown out of her swim through the air, looking for stuff to latch onto, to grow around.

She looks to grow.

"You are the weeds of my garden."

"Ah, shit."

The stems hook around Jesse, coiling around his arms and legs, tightening like a snug belt. The tree behind her glows like the sun. The light is almost blinding.

He shuts his eyes, feels a delicate warmth wash over him, and then he prays.

If there is a God, he hopes He can hear him.

4

Jewel's muscles felt like concrete. Her eyes weighed down her face. So exhausted and malnourished that her skin felt as if it were sagging off her bones. She wanted to crawl into a ball on the floor and fall asleep, a *dreamless* sleep, void of any influence from the one they called Mother.

The woman next to her rubbed her belly, told her husband that the time had come to give birth, and Jewel barely heard the words fall from her mouth—everything around her sounded off like soft echoes in an empty room. She saw Adam in the crowd of white-robed folk, his eyes holding onto golden rings, burning circles of indignation. He'd become one of them, one of the Mother's disciples, a pawn in whatever game she was playing. Jewel wanted to cry, her heart breaking for him. He'd been a good soul, a beacon of light in her darkest hour. He'd been a great friend, perhaps the best she ever had. More than she ever deserved, of that she was certain.

And now he was a slave to the Mother.

She wanted to save him. Swoop in and rescue him from fate's cruel hand.

Her eyes drifted away from the gathered and over to the four kids who weren't under the Mother's thumb—Doug Simms, Grady Pope, Abby Allen, and Maddie Rice. She'd tangled with all four during her bullying days, had probably gone after Grady the worst of it. Maddie was newer to school, so she hadn't had the time to properly welcome her to Hooperstown, but she had been on her radar. She recalled the last day of school, that brief altercation near the school's entrance, the one Principal Fritz had broken up. If it weren't for that moment, would Fritz have pulled her aside? Brought her into his office? Given her that stupid flyer? That had been the moment that really changed things for her, set her on this journey of self-discovery, this summer of personal development. It was funny to look back on the past, the moments that shaped her, the precise influences that sent her tumbling down paths she never thought possible. Some were easier to locate than others, and for Jewel Conti the moment was as clear as the bright summer sky. That scene, her looking down at the literature Fritz had given her, and the thoughts that bloomed in the back of her mind—*why not? Why not me? Why can't I change?*

She looked away from the kids and saw Fritz stumbling about. He'd had his throat slit and the blood had stained his neck and chest area, a bright red bib of death. But that didn't stop him from moseying around the intake bay. A lot of the dead had risen, were walking around like marionettes controlled by heavily-intoxicated puppeteers. Their limbs were mottled with lichen and other fungal growths.

Jewel hated seeing Fritz like that. Her anger began to rise. A flash of heat boiled beneath her cheeks, and she could feel the warm burn come on slowly and then start to blaze. She wanted to turn and punch the lady in white right in her pregnant stomach. Throw her down the little throne she'd made for herself—well, commanded the others to make *for* her, out of scraps of building materials pilfered from around the plant. She wanted to see this woman hurt. Everything that was happening here, everything that had happened, was orchestrated by this blonde-haired, blue-eyed twat, and Jewel wanted to make sure she paid for her sins.

Oh, and she also wanted to set fire to that dead, rotting carcass of the Mother. Those dry bones would go up like a thirsty Christmas tree. In her mind's eye she could see the old skin-bag covered in flames, her silent screams hidden from the world. It was a glorious sight Jewel wished would come to fruition.

Before Jewel could bend down and pick up the rusty metal strap she'd been eying up, the one that looked just sharp enough to slice through soft, delicate flesh, the ground began to move. Shift. Rumble.

An earthquake, she thought.

The goddamn earth was splitting apart.

Jesse knows he's a goner. Good as dead. Might as well take him now rather than drag the whole thing out. Even if he does survive this little stroll down nightmare alley, what waits for him on the other side? A longer, more agonizing death? Not only does he have to watch himself wither away, watch his cell-growth abnormally accelerate and take over his body, but he has to watch his parents watch him go through this degenerative process, and that's almost as heartbreaking as knowing you're gonna die. He doesn't want that. He wants to live long or die quickly—no sense fighting only to die in the end.

Fight to live, *someone tells him. Maybe it's a parent or a doctor or a teacher, someone with some authority. Someone who's been through some shit. Someone qualified to make such a statement. An adult.*

But it's not an adult, certainly no doctor or teacher or parent.

It's Jimmy. His big bro.

He's standing next to him, several open knife wounds sparkling with fresh scarlet across his chest. Bleeding. Sluicing down his body. Life running out of him in tiny red rivers. He's already dead, Jesse thinks. He's already gone in the real world, the one he left behind—but not here, not in this place. This is a world where the dead can still walk because the dead dream too.

Fight to live, little bro, *Jimmy says again without moving his lips. He claps a hand on Jesse's shoulder, gives him a wink. There are tears pouring down his face, tears of sadness, tears of joy. A mix of emotions. This is the end of one journey, the beginning of another, and the Di Falco brothers know wherever they are headed, they are headed there alone.*

Jimmy takes a fistful of the thin vines that have started to constrict around Jesse's arms, and rips them away.

The Mother shrieks, a hideous sound that makes Jesse cringe. Fistful after fistful, Jimmy tears away the extensions coming from the Mother's flesh.

"YOU WILL NOT DEFEAT ME," she thunders. "I AM ETERNAL. I AM GOD. I AM THE ONE WHO CREATES. YOU SHALL NOT DISOBEY YOUR MOTHER. I AM EARTH. I AM THE SUN AND THE STARS AND THE ENTIRE UNIVERSE. I AM THE DARK WANDERER OF DREAMS, RAVAGER OF REVERIES. I AM FOREVER AND I WILL LIVE INSIDE YOU UNTIL EVERYTHING IS UNDONE AND YOU ARE ALONE AND I AM YOUR PITILESS MESSIAH."

Jimmy finishes ridding his brother of the stems that tried to take him. They lie in a pile on the floor, curling and browning. Dead.

Jimmy grabs his brother by the shoulders. Looks him in the eye. "Team Watchmen," he says, as if it's a question.

"Team Watchmen," Jesse says through the tears, the needling of his eyes. The world is blurry, and he rubs the tears away, as much as he can before a new wave comes forth.

Then they turn to Mother.

Jesse looks at the shadow that appears to his left—it's Karen. She's dead too, her throat cut up pretty good, deep and clean enough to where a look inside turns Jesse's stomach.

The three of them face the Mother of Dead Dreams.

She is not happy, snarling and baring her teeth, those sharp, demonic points gnashing together, threatening to shear apart their flesh. Jesse, alone, was scared, but now, with his brother and Karen beside him, he is motivated. He feels powerful. In the shadows of the intake bay, he feels most alive.

Then there are others.

More of the children of Hooperstown.

More of the sick. Lauren Sullivan. Vanessa Peters. Kim Ortiz. Brennan Scruggs.

The Mother's children, though, they don't seem to be hers at the moment. They seem to be free. Free to move about the dream-world as they please. Controlling their own actions.

"WHAT IS THIS?" she snaps, backing away, her feet shuffling quickly, bouncing to the right and left, as if an attack is imminent, but from where she does not know. "YOU ARE ALL DEAD. YOU ARE DREAMING AND YOU ARE DEAD AND IN HERE I AM GOD AND YOU WILL NOT DISOBEY YOUR ONE TRUE MASTER, I WILL GROW ON YOU AND EAT FROM YOUR DELICIOUS FRUITS, YOUR MINDS AND YOUR DREAMS AND THE WORLDS WITHIN YOUR HEAD. I AM THE COLLECTOR OF YOUR BROKEN SOULS."

Jesse is the first to step forward. "I think it's time to wake you up, you moldy-ass shit-stained bee-yotch."

At this, she howls, furious and animalistic.

The sick kids of Hooperstown gather, get ready, and charge.

The battle to live rages on, and the bones of the dream-world begin to quiver.

6

"Holy shit!" Grady shouted as the ground jolted. He lost his footing and went down to one knee and looked up, saw the lady in white trying to hold her balance atop the wreckage. Miraculously, she kept both feet rooted, supporting her weight despite having a watermelon for a stomach. Her graceful maneuver saw her through to the end of the tremor.

Debris fell from the roof and managed to hit nothing but the ground. Grady wanted to see a scrap of metal land on top Rita Boxberger's head, crush her skull, effectively ending whatever malformed creature she was carrying around inside of her. He kept referring to the dream he had, the birth of that strange hairless being, how it had crawled out of the Mother's stomach looking for bloodshed and mayhem. How he wanted to be somewhere else when the moment arrived.

You can't run out on them again, he said, tempted to bolt right then and there. With Boxberger preoccupied with the ceremony, there was nothing stopping Grady from getting the hell out of there. The white-robed folk were too busy with what was taking place around them and the people of Hooperstown, the ones covered in unsightly growths and tumors, were hardly any threat at all. They looked braindead, incapable of doing him any harm.

Grady actually moved to run, turning his entire body to sprint off.

Then he saw something. Just a flash. It looked like a hologram, something projected, like Princess Leia in *Star Wars* when R2-D2 plays back the message for Obi-Wan. A flicker of light in the shape of a human being.

It was Jesse.

Or shit, it *looked* like Jesse. His mouth was open and he was screaming at someone. Probably telling him not to puss-out again. That he couldn't abandon his friends, not like this, not in this moment. This was *his* moment, his last chance to prove himself. To show them he wasn't a coward, that he wasn't the spineless twerp they secretly thought he was, despite their best efforts to tell him otherwise.

Grady turned, facing the casket that held the Mother in place. Her body had shifted somewhat during the quake and was now poking out more than she had been.

What had Rita Boxberger said? What had Grady overheard her telling Jewel? They preserved the body so the demon within wouldn't escape? The preservation of flesh kept the spirit alive within, a prison of skin and bones. Well, what if he destroyed the body? Obliterated it? Wouldn't it stand to reason the spirit within would die as well?

He didn't know, not for sure, but it made sense.

Spotting the chemicals they had brought with them resting in a pile in the corner of the bay, an idea sparked. He'd read the labels countless times before, feared using the stuff when his parents asked him to help with the landscaping. It was a baseless fear because the odds of the stuff combusting were next to nothing, but still—WARNING: CONTENTS FLAMMABLE inspired bouts of dread every time his eyes had run across it.

Grady looked over his shoulder to the same spot where Jesse had appeared. His friend flickered again, mouth moving, trying to say speak.

Grady read his lips.

Too late.

He flickered out of existence once again.

Come on, Jess, he thought. *Come back. What are you saying?*

Jesse did come back. Mouth moving, fast, too fast, but Grady caught a word. *DESTROY.*

It was enough.

He blinked out, then returned a few seconds later.

HER.

DESTROY.

HER.

Destroy her.

Then he looked toward the center of the intake bay, his finger focusing on one thing and one thing only: *the Tree.*

The confirmation Grady needed.

Before fading out for the last time, the image of Jesse winked, blew Grady a kiss.

He was pretty sure that was the last he'd see of his friend, and that crushing thought brought a kaleidoscopic blur of tears to his eyes.

7

"What the hell was that?" Baum asked, holding onto the maze of pipes that covered the wall. If the plant had been operational, then those pipes would have burned the skin off the cop's hand. Gordon didn't bother mentioning that to him. He had opted to take hold of the scaffolding to his right during the tremor.

"Felt like an earthquake."

"In Jersey?" Baum was practically beside himself. "Mr. Simms—I must beg you to reconsider. I won't force you to back out on account of your son, but I will strongly suggest that you come back with me."

Gordon held his tongue. For a second. "You'd have to drag me out. And I'd have to be dead." He let go of the tubular scaffold and proceeded to march toward the intake bay.

"It's not safe."

"Then stay here!" he said to the cop. "The intake bay is just up ahead! Through there I can head out back, get a better look at the rest of the grounds!"

He heard the cop mutter, "Damn it," under his breath, and then listened as the patter of footsteps followed him.

Gordon was glad he wasn't alone. He was glad there would be a witness to whatever horrible thing was waiting for him just around the corner.

8

Doug grabbed Maddie's hand and escorted her away from the stage Rita Boxberger had climbed to address her audience. Abby followed closely behind, the three of them sneaking out of view from the lady in white and Jewel Conti—and of course, the dead, non-existent stare of Mother. Doug had expected the mummified corpse to fall out of the sarcophagus, but it had somehow remained tucked inside.

When the ground stopped shaking, Doug turned to them. "We need to reach the chemicals."

Abby shook her head. "They're not going to do shit," she said adamantly. "You saw how it affected Boxberger."

"Yeah, but Boxberger isn't one of *them*."

Grady popped his head between them. "I have a plan. Guys, I have a plan!"

Abby rolled her eyes. "This oughta be good."

"What is it, Grades?" Doug asked.

"You're not gonna believe this, but I saw Jesse. Right here. Right in the room. He was like a...like a hologram or something." Excitement lit up his face. "It was fucking awesome!"

Doug cocked his head. It couldn't be true, but Grady had never been one to lie, much less stretch the truth. Even if Grady hadn't seen Jesse, or an image that represented their sick friend, he *believed* he had, and that was good enough for Doug.

Doug went with it. "And?"

"The chemicals will work," Grady said. He was almost out of breath, gasping for every available huff of air. "We just need fire."

Abby reached into her pocket. "I got you covered." She produced a lighter, a silver square with a pull-back top. ZIPPO was printed in big letters across its body.

"Perfect," said Grady, rubbing his hands together. "All right. We get to the chemicals, and then we split up. Two of us concentrate on the rotting bag of shit in the coffin, and the other two concentrate on that tree over there." He pointed to the tree, which Doug noticed had grown more colorful. Bright blue and purple leaves had blossomed on its branches. "We spray the shit out of both, then light these fuckers on fire. The flames will take care of the rest. Easy peasy."

Everyone nodded in agreement.

Doug didn't want to throw out hypotheticals, ask questions like "What happens if we're caught?" or "What's Plan B?" Questions like that would only bring them down, make them reconsider the whole scheme. They didn't need that. They needed positivity. Even if none of them truly believed it would work.

Doug clapped a hand on Grady's back. "Good plan, Grades. This might actually be crazy enough to work."

"What might be crazy enough to work?" a voice asked from behind them, and Doug knew who had spoken those words even before he turned himself around.

Boxberger was standing there, his eyebrows arched just as if he were approaching two kids in the hallway, overhearing some naughty gossip. He even folded his arms across his chest, his tongue probing his inner cheek.

"Nuh-nothing," Grady squeaked out. "Nothing...at all."

"Didn't sound like nothing, you little shit-ass." He fixed his eyes on Doug. "Now, *you*, I can't touch. You are to be a part of this ceremony by my wife's request. Something about having the only son of Sharon Parks present fills her with comfort. Look, I can't explain it either, but it's her body and her ceremony and despite what recent events might convey—I'm actually a good guy, and a better husband. I just want the best for her, okay? But you three..." He took the knife and pointed it at Maddie, then dragged it across the air, making sure each one of them got a head-on look at the weapon that would exact their murders. "...are expendable. I can gut you like the worthless, insignificant bags of trash you are, and everything will go off without a hitch.

"But... That might make Mr. Simms here very difficult. He might not cooperate the same if you're alive." His lips toyed with a confident, wily smile. "So I'll keep the three of you alive, for now—no need to thank me, though—you'll all be dead by nightfall, along with mostly everyone else in this pathetic town. Though, *dead* is a loose term nowadays, isn't it? More like...*re-seeded*."

A few intermittent barks of laughter let Doug know Boxberger had truly lost his mind, as if stabbings and murders weren't enough. The sick bastard was enjoying every minute of this. Doug knew he had to make a play, that the doomsday clock was winding down. He couldn't wait for the birthing, the ceremony, whatever the fuck they wanted to call it.

The Miracle of Life.

He needed to act. And now.

"Mr. Boxberger," Doug said, sounding innocent. Somewhat scared. It was an act, an attempt to lower the son of a bitch's guard. He saw the knife fall to his side. "You don't have to do this. Please, I'm begging you. You can let us go. We won't tell anyone what happened here." He'd heard this very line recited in almost every serial killer movie out there, and even though it never worked, he was running out of options.

The man's face changed. He looked worn. Run down. Beaten by the long days and longer nights, the midnight hours spent in the realm of dreams. The dark lines in his face corroborated as much. His eyes lost some of the vigor he'd recently displayed. Teeth pinching his lower lip, Boxberger stared at the boy absently, as if his train of thought suddenly left the station.

Now!

Doug took one step and aimed his right foot at the bag of jewels between Boxberger's legs. He'd only played soccer for one year (the year before his mom tried to kill him) and he'd been a decent player, had only quit because the majority of his teammates were assholes and took the game too seriously. But he'd been good. Had a strong leg, his coach had told him. And now, he pretended Boxberger's man-fruit was a free kick at an open net.

But Boxberger was quicker. More prepared. He reached out, grabbed Doug by the throat and hoisted him into the air.

"You little fuck!" Boxberger bellowed, spittle flying into the air. "You think I'm that weak? You think I'd fall for such an amateur move?" He laughed in Doug's face, howling like a coyote before a big yellow moon. "You can't trick me. You aren't smart enough. I am an adult and you are a child, and you need to know your place in the world. And you will learn, boy. Oh yessssss. This will be a lesson like no other, I guarantee it."

"Forgot to tell you, Box-booger," Doug said, his feet kicking the air between them. "I never really paid much attention in your class."

Out of the corner of his eye, he saw Grady and the girls slink off.

"Bullshit," Boxberger sneered. "You practically aced every test."

"Eh, I just read the books. Couldn't stand your lectures. They were boring as shit." Doug cackled, enjoying this. This was how Jesse would have handled the situation. Get inside the enemy's head. Piss him off. Make him do something irrational. That was the play here. That was *his* Plan B. "God, you were so fucking boring. Everyone hated you. I mean, *every*one."

"You think I give a shit? I don't give a goddamn turd what you or anyone else in that school thought of me. I was only there as a cover. It was just a job so I could get here. All that time, my wife and I spent planting the seeds, using this place to poison the town. To spread the Mother's influence by using the moonflowers and the Red River. Nothing else mattered. Least of all that fucking school."

"Still, man. Everyone made fun of you behind your back. You know what Jesse told me once?"

"What? I'm dying to hear?" He looked as if he were starved and the forthcoming information was a savory steak.

"He said..." Doug had to stop because a series of giggles crowded his throat. "He said your wife was so hot, he didn't know how you pulled her." More giggling. He watched delightfully as Boxberger's confidence faded some. "He said there was no way a schmuck like you could get a girl like that...unless she was blind!" Doug erupted with uproarious laughter, and he couldn't help himself.

Boxberger shook him. "That's right. Get the chuckles in now, you little prick. Because in about ten minutes you won't be laughing."

"Husband!" Rita shouted. She was sitting now, holding her stomach with both hands, wincing as if someone had shoved a knife into her belly. "It's time!"

"Coming, dear!" he called back, then faced Doug again. "Anything else?"

"Yeah," Doug said, corralling his outburst, gaining control of his giggles. "Yeah, there is." Instead of laying into him some more, he nodded beyond him, beyond the stage built by the Mother's minions, and over to the corner of the bay where Grady and the girls were strapping on their sprayers, suiting up for the final showdown. Boxberger followed his suggestion, having himself a good look at what he'd missed by fucking around with Doug. "You guys are fucked."

"Aw, son of a bi—"

As Boxberger turned back toward him, Doug rammed his head forward, forehead first. He smashed the crown of his head against Boxberger's nose. An abbreviated crunch, like a potato chip bite, filled the brief silence. Doug felt a squirt of warm fluids splash against his forehead and trickle down the contour of his nose. When he brought his head back, he saw the damage he had done and was quite shocked by the results.

Boxberger let go of him. Doug fell to the ground, his feet unable to prepare for the sudden drop.

Boxberger took a blind swipe at him, the knife cutting through the air, missing Doug's throat by mere inches. Blood poured from man's busted nose, slicking the lower half of his face in scarlet ruin. The collision must have knocked some sense out of him too, because he had trouble walking. He staggered laterally and almost fell to his knees.

Doug picked himself up.

"I'll kill you," Boxberger said, his speech slurred. "I'll fucking kill you in the most violent, bloody way possible. I'll make sure your casket is closed at your funeral, you little—"

"Fuck," Doug finished the insult for him. "Yeah, I know. You keep saying that."

"BABY!" Rita roared.

Doug and Boxberger both turned toward the sound of her panicked voice. She was holding two fists of dripping scarlet. Red bloomed on the white cloth that covered her crotch.

"It's time…"

Dazed, Boxberger focused on his wife, leaving Doug to wander the bay. Free. Unmolested.

Then, Doug noticed the gathered were staring at him, rising to their feet. He knew exactly what they were doing. Protecting their Mother.

"NOW!" Rita's voice boomed, and that was when it all fell apart.

When Gordon opened the door and stepped onto the catwalk suspended over the intake bay floor, he almost gagged. There were a lot of smells choking the air, but the moldy wetness was chief among them, and he felt like he'd catch two black lungs with a single breath. The next thing that caused alarm was the amount of people in the room, the gathering below. His heart rate spiked as his eyes surveyed the bottom floor. There were so many people—more than fifty, less than a hundred—and the intake bay looked very different than it had only weeks ago, when Gordon had helped oversee the removal of certain items and materials. The place looked like it had aged a decade, overrun with weeds, vines and ivy growing down the walls. Not to mention the giant tree in the center of the room, a tree that had already began to sprout flowers and fruits.

None of this made sense.

"What the hell?" Baum said from behind him, stepping onto the catwalk.

Gordon turned around and shushed him. Whatever was taking place below, he didn't know, but Gordon didn't think it was in their best interest to be seen. He took a few steps along the catwalk, his feet landing softly on the metal footing, being careful not to make too much noise. He hoped Baum would follow his lead, but the clumsy oaf's footfalls shook the entire walkway, making way too much noise. Luckily, no one below looked up.

Gordon stopped him by raising a palm.

He took a closer look below, scanning the faces of the gathered. And that was when he saw them. His son and his friends. He saw Doug first. He was on the ground, holding his neck, in the process of kicking himself back to his feet. The other three were in the corner throwing the straps of some chemical sprayers over their shoulders, suiting up like firefighters about to step into a blazing house fire.

What the hell are they doing?

Gordon tried to wrap his mind around what was happening. Then he heard someone shout, "NOW!"—the single word echoing throughout the vast chamber. He focused on the speaker, a very pregnant woman wearing a white robe and a crown of twigs and small white flowers, a necklace to match. She was holding her stomach, her face strained as if she were trying to push out the baby on her own, no support from any of her friends, who were also dressed in white robes.

"What in the fuck?" Baum said from behind him, and Gordon wanted to hit him. Probably would have had he not been wearing that blue uniform.

Instead, he turned and whispered, "Shut the fuck up."

Baum was taken aback, looked down at him with a bent brow as if to ask him, *Did you really just talk to a police officer that way?*

Yes, I fucking did, he would have said back.

Moving down the walk, he saw a man who also wore a thorny crown of flowers strung together by twigs and brush, watched him hastily move to the woman's side. He held her hand and breathed with her. Some of the gathered in white robes began walking toward them, forming a circle around the pile of debris. And the...coffin.

Jesus, he thought. *Is that a body inside?*

From his position, he could just barely make out the thing resting inside, an old gray corpse that was wrapped in skin-tight cloth.

It was a fucking mummy.

His veins flooded with winter ice. He wanted to turn back, head toward the exit, wanted no part of whatever was afoot, but he wasn't going anywhere without Doug. Or his friends. He needed to reach the bottom, and the only way down was the stairs to his right, a little farther down the walk.

He began to push ahead.

Baum whispered, "What are you doing?"

"My son is down there." He pointed to the kid who had just risen to his feet. "I'm getting him, his friends, and I'm getting the fuck out of here."

"But...but what do I do?"

Gordon examined the young cop's features, the fear filling him. So innocent, so naive. They clearly didn't teach this sort of thing at the academy, one of those things you just couldn't prepare for. Emergency situations were like that. No books were ever written on how to think rationally during times of ultimate stress and worry, because there were too many variables involved, too many layers of unpredictability. This was one of those times, and Gordon thought the best way to handle such a situation was to just react, let the chips fall where they may.

"Just do what feels right," he told him, and for a second he thought the young cop was going to bolt. Turn. Run. As fast as those long legs of his would carry. But he stayed put. Instead, he removed the gun from his hip-holster. "Just be careful with that thing, cowboy."

Baum nodded.

The two men headed for the stairs, toward the unknown, toward the situation with way too many variables.

Toward almost certain tragedy.

10

Boxberger came to his wife's side and took a knee, immediately grabbing for her hands. He told her to push. Push. Harder. Harder. She told him the baby was coming any second now and that he needed to "get things in order."

Jewel didn't know what that meant, but as if the entire audience heard her, they began to close around them, forming a circle. Jewel didn't want the circle to close around her, so she took one collective step back.

You are a part of this, Jewel, a voice said, coming from seemingly nowhere.

Jewel spun around, expecting to see one of the white-robed freaks standing next to her, but there was no one. Then her eyes fell on the sarcophagus, the preserved body within. The hollow eye sockets of the dusty corpse. The fossilized teeth. She wondered if the thing was truly alive underneath the frayed bandages, wondered if the body would come alive any moment now, start walking around the arena, looking for brains to eat or blood to drink, whatever three-hundred-plus-year-old bodies do when they suddenly find themselves alive again.

Come be with me, the voice called to her.

Jewel knew it was coming from the Mother. She was too close to her. What had Rita said? *She's chosen you.*

Jewel backed away.

Don't be frightened. Together we will do great things. We will take this world back, return the lands to its rightful owners. We will rebuild the landscape, bring back the lush forests and dense jungles from the days of old. We will grow exotic gardens, eat fruits that could never exist in this current climate. We can reshape everything as it was—we can bring paradise back and you can enjoy it, all of it, by yourself. If you just give yourself to me...

She took another step back.

Now, Jewel—I am Mother and you will obey my command. I can take you, become part of you, but it would be so much easier if you were willing. Do not fight me, child. Do not reject me. You are chosen. You are the one who will carry me across the blue skies and green lands, through the realm of dreams and into the land of the living.

Invite me in.

No, she thought instinctually. *No, I will not.*

She felt a burn on the back of her neck, her arms and legs, the Mother's fury making nests of her bones. A strong hatred emanated from the cadaver, and it shot across the room like hot lasers.

You will. You have no choice, young one. You are mine now. I am Mother.

Jewel thought of her own mother, how much she hated the woman, how much she never wanted to grow up to be like her. How she hated her father and even though the apartment was emptier without him and his presence meant seeing less of Ava Conti, she still wished he was rotting away in a prison cell. She couldn't help it. They were terrible people, terrible parents, and she wanted nothing to do with them. Counting down the days until she turned eighteen, Jewel prayed for a freedom sought by most kids her age. Though most kids her age wanted to run from good homes, parents who gave a shit about them, maybe too much.

There was no way she was leaving one hell to enter another; letting the Mother out of the sarcophagus, letting her spirit take control of her body—that was a hell she'd avoid at all costs. Even if it killed her.

Jewel watched a hot jet of blood squirt from the slit between Rita's legs. The woman moaned as her knees quaked, and the moans quickly turned to screams. Boxberger was consoling her, wrapping his arms around her shoulders, but the look on his face, his wide eyes and jaw hanging agape, proved he was at a loss and terrified beyond rational thought.

This wasn't going as planned, that was the message his face conveyed.

Last chance, child, the Mother said. *Before I take you.*

She shook her head. Then her eyes fell to the knife Boxberger had abandoned next to the makeshift stage, the one a river of blood was currently flowing down. Scarlet showered the stage once more, and Jewel wondered how much blood was supposed to come out during the process, if any at all. She couldn't recall from the *Miracle of Life* video but thought she would remember if it had been as violent as what she was seeing now.

"You will never take me," she said, bending down and picking up the blade.

What are you doing?

"Ending this, you fucking cunt."

She walked forward with purpose, the knife in hand, watching tears sparkle across the lady in white's face as she arched back and bellowed for the whole town to hear.

11

Maddie was frightened, more so for how fast everything was unfolding than the perilous nature of their current task. Grady had told Abby and her to head over to the tree and start spraying. The movement among the white-robed folk concerned her, but not as much as the man guarding the tree. She knew his face from her father's computer—he was the one in charge of Hooperstown Chemical, the asshole who called the shots, the alleged monster who authorized the illegal dumping along the Red River. Basically, he was the guy Charlie Rice was after, and now he was the one standing between her and her final task.

I can do this. I can do this. Don't back down. Don't give up.

A sideways look in Doug's direction and she saw him squatting on the ground, getting ready to rise. She could still feel the pressure of his lips against hers, and it filled her with a peculiar comfort, one she'd never felt before. Just thinking about that single moment brought a rush of emotions, a spark that ignited in the center of her chest and ran a sizzling feeling to each extremity. Her bones warmed over. The concept of boyfriend/girlfriend was not foreign to her; she had a "boyfriend" at her last school, but it didn't last very long, and it didn't feel like this. No, *this* was special. This *summer* was special, even if plagued by sickness and the mysterious happenings brought on by a supernatural being known as the Mother of Dead Dreams.

"Let's go," Abby said, taking her arm and leading her over to the tree.

They bypassed the white-robed folk, who hardly paid them any attention. Their sole focus was on the birthing, the woman bleeding profusely from between her legs. Maddie didn't know all that much about giving birth, but she knew that amount of blood wasn't normal, not by any stretch. But also—she wasn't surprised. Since they'd arrived and she was able to get a clean look at Rita Boxberger's somewhat rotund belly, she knew there was something off about it, the amorphous shape that spasmed, the flesh that undulated.

The current scene, the amount of red spilling from the womb, made her want to vomit.

"Don't look at it," Abby suggested. Before Maddie could comply, she found herself standing in front of the tree, looking up. Its gnarled branches twisted and corkscrewed. Leaves and exotic fruits shaped like pears and mangos had budded and bloomed and were ripe for the picking, though Maddie doubted their nutritious value. In all honestly, they looked like candy, and the last time Maddie Rice checked, candy did not grow on trees. Still, a part of her wanted to pick a pear-sized fruit and bite into it. There was something appealing about the fruits, the potential exotic tastes that would wash over her tongue, the unique nectar they contained.

Yes, a voice beckoned her. *Have one. Just a bite. That's all you need, little one.*

She did not like that voice, the intrusiveness of it. Glancing over her shoulder, she spotted the Mother's fragile form and wondered if that was where the voice had come from, despite how impossible that seemed.

Then again, a lot of impossible things had happened this summer, and the fact this dormant creature was telepathically communicating didn't surprise her as much as it should have.

No, Maddie thought back. *No, I don't think so.*

EAT! something shrieked, filling her head with static, causing her whole body to hitch. The sharp pain nearly brought her to her knees. Hands clapped over her ears, she tried to block out what followed but it was no use. *EAT FROM ME. I AM THE CREATOR. I AM THE FRUIT OF THIS WORLD. YOU WILL EAT FROM ME AND I WILL GIVE YOU LIFE, AND I WILL WATCH YOU GROW. I AM THE MOTHER OF ALL THINGS THAT GROW.*

Frightened, Maddie turned to Abby, whose face was a mask of pure fear.

"I can hear her too," Abby said, lips trembling. "Block it out. She's trying to fuck with us."

"It's working."

Abby nodded. Indeed, it was.

Maddie eyed the ladder that led up to the catwalk and immediately thought about making a run for it. Leaving her friends behind, her *potential* boyfriend, first *real* boyfriend, and getting the hell out of there. Heading back home where it was safe and where she was most protected. With her mom and her dad and her sisters. Where the memory of her dog Bishop still lived.

But she couldn't. She didn't have it in her. Home didn't matter right now because if they didn't stop this, bring a close to the saga that had attempted to ruin the best summer of her young life, then there would be no home to return to. There would only be weeds and plants and flowers, poisonous petals that made them dream, dream, and dream some more. A world of falsities, mirages that tarnished everything the real world had given them.

A fake, pitiful existence.

That life wasn't for her.

She had a chance to stop the Mother's fantasy from becoming a reality, and that chance was happening right now.

She aimed the wand.

"Let's bring this bitch down," she said.

Abby cracked a smile. "Yeah. Let's."

As they pulled the trigger on their magic wands, two men climbed down the access ladder, and one man stepped in front of their spray patterns, taking the weed killer in his face, smiling as he did so. His name was Dylan Walker, and he had things growing out of his forehead. Little thorny knobs of perpetual devastation.

12

When Gordon's feet hit the floor, the first thing he saw was Dylan Walker facing Maddie Rice and the girl whose name he did not know. Outside a few of Doug's regular friends, he was terrible with names and faces. Regardless, Dylan Walker was approaching them, his posture threatening. His arms were stretched as if attempting to hug a tree, a thick oak you couldn't see around. His lips were pulled back, revealing teeth that had yellowed and turned almost green since their last exchange. The man's forehead was bunched, strained and displaying a thick wormy vein that snaked down the center. Gordon sensed the girls were in trouble. They were dousing the man in chemicals, pumping a misty stream directly into his face, but it seemed to have little effect. It only seemed to make Walker wet and more pissed off.

"Gut you!" Walker said, slobbering like an animal with rabies. Foam sputtered from his lips, and he didn't even bother to wipe away the mess. Instead, he focused on the two girls, backing them toward the stage. "I'm gonna cut you up and plant you in my garden." A heinous giggle escaped his lips, and the girls retreated, backing themselves even farther. He matched their steps foot for foot. "Watch you grow and grow and GROW."

"Walker!" Gordon shouted, cupping his hands over his mouth. It was too late to worry about drawing attention to himself. Plus, he had a cop with him—an armed officer of the law—and the people who were a part of this (*cult?*) gathering were starting to get restless, especially near the front of the bay where the woman in white went down screaming and grabbing the bun in her oven. "Walker, you stay the fuck away from them!"

"What are you doing?" Baum asked nervously.

"Breaking up this party—what the hell do you think?"

Gordon could tell the young officer wasn't ready for primetime, but he'd have to be sooner or later—so why not now? People were in trouble. They needed help. The *kids* were in danger.

Walker craned his neck like an owl on high alert. There was a feral look in his eyes, animalistic and predatory, and very hungry. He got the sense Walker wanted to feed off these girls, tear them to shreds and feast on their young flesh. Maybe Gordon was exaggerating but not by much. The man looked pissed and ravenous, and worse—unpredictable.

"I said stay the fuck away from them," Gordon repeated, stomping over to the tree, ready to put himself between the girls and the monster that Walker had become, not that he wasn't a monster before. Now his visage fit the bill. "Girls, get behind me. Get behind Officer Baum."

"But, Mr. Simms," Maddie said, her voice pleading, "the tree. We have to kill it. It's..." The girl squinted like a bright light shot off into her eyes, and she grabbed at her temples. The wand fell to the ground, dangling from the cord attached to the backpack. "It's...important. Only...way... *Uh!*"

She dropped to her knees. Her friend did the same, each of them grabbing the sides of their heads, writhing in pain, trying to shake off whatever was attacking them, but clearly failing.

Gordon didn't know what to do, how to help them. He panicked, feeling the same helplessness he felt with Sharon when she was going through her bad episodes. He hadn't known what to do then and he didn't know what to do now.

You're a failure. You're always gonna be a failure. You failed your wife, now you're gonna fail these kids.

"Dad?" a small voice said from behind him. "Dad, is that you? Is that really you?"

With tears in his eyes, Gordon spun around. "Doug?"

"Dad!" Doug said excitedly. He ran over and wrapped his arms around his father's waist and hugged him harder than he ever had.

"Awwwww," Walker said, a goofy grin settling on his face. The rims around his eyes were bright red, as if he'd been rubbing away an allergy-induced itch. His skin was so pale the veins beneath were visible. He looked sick, terminally ill, so close to death's door even Gordon heard the knocking. "Look at the happy family," he said, the same way a bully might mock an easy target on the playground. "Hate to break it up."

"Walker," Gordon said, moving so Doug was behind him. "I don't know what the fuck is wrong with you, but I want you to know that I can help. You're clearly...clearly *unwell*. I think you should come with me and Officer Baum here and let us get you to a hospital."

Walker cackled, a wheezy outburst that caused Gordon's neck hairs to rise. More foam bubbled on his lips, and Gordon didn't know how much more the man could take. He was in bad shape. Yet, here he was, standing before him, inviting a physical altercation.

"I'm going to kill you, Gordon Simms. I'm going to kill you in the name of the Mother. She will help me recreate this place. This town may have tried to cut us down, but we are strong, Gordy. We will rise. Like all life, we will grow. We will rise and grow above everyone and everything, and we will build a brand-new planet, one of lives worth living."

Gordon swallowed. "Walker, I don't know what drugs you're on, but you really need some help."

"*You need help!*" he hissed, pursing his lips. In a blink, that sinister smile returned. "And I'm going to give it to you."

Walker charged.

Gordon turned to Baum. "Now might be a good time to use that thing."

Baum looked terrified of the gun in his hands. He refused to raise it. "Mister! Now, I'm warning you."

He couldn't elevate the weapon in time. Gordon knew this. He also knew the young cop wouldn't have the guts to pull the trigger, even if he was able to take aim. So Gordon decided to meet Walker halfway and rushed toward him, fists out, knuckles eager to land on what he hoped was a glass chin. Gordon hadn't been in a fight since high school but fighting—it seemed—was like riding a bike; you never forget the motions and the exhilarating effect of the adrenaline flood.

"Dad!" Doug called after him, but he ignored his son.

He was already taking his first swing.

And that was when he saw the man was holding a butterfly knife. That it was out and coming for the soft flesh under his ribs.

Doug watched the blade slam into his father's side about the same time his father's knuckles connected with Dylan Walker's jaw. A shriek of surprise left him, and the sound was so shrill Doug didn't think his dad was the one to utter it.

"Dad!" he called again, watching his father stumble, holding the fresh, bleeding wound on his right side. Doug turned to Baum, the tears in his eyes flowing steadily now. "Please, you have to do something."

The cop raised his gun, ready to take the shot. "I don't have a clear shot."

Doug noticed Walker wasn't their only concern. Some of the gathered in white robes had turned their attention on what was happening behind them, had taken a keen interest in the girls. They were still on the ground, holding their ears, screaming out in pain, and the Mother's loyal supporters were starting to wander toward them.

We're so screwed, Doug thought, feeling all hope abandon him. What had been a simple plan was now so messed up he didn't see any clear path to victory.

Just then, something flickered near the tree. He was immediately reminded of what Grady had told him only minutes ago: *Jesse! I saw Jesse!*

It turned out Grady wasn't lying. A small flicker, like a candle in a breeze, showed the vague outline of his best friend. Next to the tree, the Jesse hologram pointed toward the trunk, screaming a message Doug couldn't hear. He tried to make it out, attempted to read his lips, but Jesse didn't last that long. He was gone before he could decipher the code.

"What? What is it?" Doug said aloud, his words soft like a muted breath. "Help me understand."

One last time, Jesse flickered into view. He was throwing punches at the tree, windmill-style. Then he faced Doug, winked, and blinked out of existence for what felt like the last time.

Attack the tree was the only sense he could make of it.

Bring it down.

Kill it.

Just when Doug started to formulate a plan, he saw a new figure appear in front of the earthly formation.

It was mother.

Not *the* Mother, not the Mother of All Things That Must Grow. *His.*

Sharon Simms.

14

He tries to warn them, tries everything to get their attention, and he hopes it works. He feels his energy fading, exhaustion settling in, every morsel of power evaporating. The Children are behind him, gathered, ready to take charge. The Mother is furious with their revolt. She crouches, ready to leap, ready to tear her own kin to shreds.

We are not your kin, *Jesse says without moving his lips.*

At this, she grunts. Then runs.

Like a horde of Vikings charging into battle, the Children rush to meet her.

What happens next is hazy, in pure, dream-like fashion. Which makes sense, because this is in fact a dream. An inescapable alternate reality where the rules of the real world have been thrown out the window and are now dying on the front lawn.

The Mother's form shifts, her hands transmogrified into crab-like claws, giant pinchers with corrugated teeth. She snaps at one of the Children, aiming for the neck, and her claw clips the kid's head right off, leaving it to roll across the floor of the intake bay.

Another comes at her from behind and hops on her back, trying to choke her out. Thrusting her upper half forward, the Mother flips the girl over her head. Before the girl can recover and scramble to her feet, the Mother pins her to the ground with her left claw. The right claw is busy snapping at more Children, fending them off. The girl tries to wriggle her way out from under the claw, but the pinchers close around her stomach, shearing her in half.

There's so much blood Jesse can barely stand the sight of it, and when the Mother tosses the upper torso aside like an empty food wrapper, the girl's guts come tumbling out. Jesse pukes, the stink of his vomit burning his nostrils.

One by one, the Children attack.

One by one, the Children fall.

After several minutes, the Mother stands over her victory, a smorgasbord of limbs and torsos and heads and innards. All the king's horses and all the king's men will never put these Children back together again, Jesse thinks, as he stands before the Mother alone.

Not alone.

Jimmy is next to him. So is Karen.

They are here and they are ready to fight.

"Let's finish this," Jimmy says.

"Yes," Jesse agrees. "Team Watchmen. Let's fight. One last time."

He reaches out, stretches his fingers, and they each take a hand. The three of them walk on ahead to face the Mother.

To end her.

To wake up from this terrible nightmare.

15

Before Boxberger saw her coming, Jewel had angled the knife down at the pregnant woman's belly. She ignored the gouts of blood shooting out of her vagina, focusing only on the thing that was trying to tear its way out of her. Jewel was convinced whatever was inside of that woman, it wasn't human. Who knew what abomination the Mother planned to bring into this world, what creature she had plotted to unleash upon them? The woman's belly contorted unnaturally, the flesh rippling, as if the beast inside glided around the womb like a shark hunting within its territory.

Jewel didn't hesitate, not this time. She refused to let the high-pitched screams that filled her ears bother her. Ignoring the static, she zoned in on her only task, the one she'd given herself.

Fucking end this, she coached herself.

The blade came down, the tip entering the woman's stomach, slipping smoothly inside, buried to the handle.

"NOOOOOO!" Boxberger shouted in her face as he went for the knife with both hands.

Jewel swung a fist that connected with his chin, although it did nothing to slow him down. He wrestled with her, attempting to pull the dagger out. She tried to fend him off, but ultimately, he was stronger. She knew she could do more damage if she twisted the blade around, cut at different angles. With all her might, she wrenched the blade around, digging a little deeper, rotating the blade from side to side, slicing through meat and muscle and vital organs. She put her body into it, collapsing her weight down on the handle, pushing until the tip of blade was *through* the lady, stabbing the debris beneath her.

Rita hiccupped globs of scarlet as she tried to scream.

"NO!" Boxberger cried out. His eyes were glassy, full of hate and panic. The expression he couldn't hide brought a jolt of joy to Jewel's heart. The damage to his wife's unborn child would be extensive, and so was the devastation to her own vitality. If Jewel had her way, both would not live. She intended to make it so.

"YOU LITTLE CUNT!" Boxberger bellowed into her face. "I'LL KILL YOU!"

She'd done enough. Backing off, she watched Boxberger rip the blade out of his wife's stomach, an arc of blood following its path through the air. Boxberger looked from his wife to Jewel, back to his wife again. Rita was swimming in and out of consciousness, nodding and blinking, her head lolling like her neck was made of jelly.

Close your eyes, you bitch, Jewel thought. *Close your eyes and go to sleep. Dream for me.*

Boxberger stayed with his wife and began patching her together, pressing his hands over the wound, covering up the blood that welled from the mortal puncture. The flow was too much, and crimson rose through the cracks in his fingers. Louis Boxberger whimpered. He rested his head on her legs, which were also sticky with red, and when he brought his head up there was a bloody mark staining his forehead.

"No, no, no," he said as Rita's eyes rolled back and disappeared, the whites of her scleras taking over. "This can't be happening, can't be happening, can't be—"

Rita's body convulsed, spastic jerks that drove more panic into her husband's face. His complexion was almost as colorless as his dying wife's. He tried to stop her seizures, draping his body over hers, but that did nothing to help the situation.

Jewel saw something peeking out from the bottom of her robe, a long and slender extension, like a weak twig lying among a pile of brush. It snaked out from under the fabric, a timid approach to entering the new world it had found itself. Jewel was hesitant to react, unsure of what she was seeing exactly. Then an arm came out, a normal baby arm, though it was covered in bluish fluids, an indigo dye that reminded her of new denim. The dye turned the spilled blood purple. Jewel gagged as an alien odor stormed her nostrils. She remembered dissecting a pig fetus in science class last year, the stink that wafted out of its guts when the swine's stomach was splayed open. The putrid smell of the room reminded her of the pig. She turned her head and coughed, fully expecting a stream of vomit to follow. Somehow, she kept from puking.

The creature dragged itself out of the womb, gripping an exposed metal beam and pulling itself toward freedom. The baby's arm was thinner than it should have been, gangly yet more coordinated than that of a newborn child.

This was no ordinary being. Nothing human anyway.

Jewel backed away. She thought she'd gotten to it, stabbed it right through its head, but she'd been wrong.

Another arm came out, extending, reaching for something to grab onto. Boxberger watched in horror as more of the thing revealed itself, gripping onto the metal beam and sliding out of the slippery chute of Rita's birth canal. He held his dead wife and cried out, asking for forgiveness, begging for the Mother to help his family through this tough, impossible time.

"Please…" he said, hitching with each sob. "Please bring her back. She carried your kind. She did everything you asked of us. We brought you here to be reborn, and this…" He looked upon Rita's face, her still features smeared with gentle strokes of red. Her eyes did not open. She was dead, her chest a flat canvas where no movement was detected. No breath. Not a single shred of evidence that she was alive.

For a second everything seemed still. The air became stagnant. No noise, not even the shuffling of feet. It was like everyone stopped what they were doing to watch the woman die. But that wasn't the case. From her periphery, Jewel watched Grady Pope charge up the makeshift throne, the wand from his chemical sprayer in hand, as if it were a fire hose and the Mother's sarcophagus was a blazing inferno.

"Hey, Boxberger!" Grady shouted, ending the silence.

Boxberger slowly looked up from his deceased partner, the flub in his cheeks jiggling, his jaw trembling. Tears streamed out of his eyes in clear rivulets. If Jewel listened close enough, she would hear the man whimpering softly.

Once he had Boxberger's undivided attention, Grady said, "If Jesse were here, you know what he'd say?"

Boxberger only trembled with the rage of a thousand angry gods.

"He'd say, 'suck on these big fat nuts, Box-booger!'"

And then the boy proceeded to unload the flammable chemicals on the Mother's eroded corpse.

CHAPTER TWENTY

We Dream of Endless Summers

1

She was radiant, her frame encapsulated in a magnificent golden glow. Like an angel sent from Heaven, her hair was long and flowing, shimmering with flecks of brilliant yellow, but not like he remembered. Not like he remembered at all. His memory of her was of unwashed hair, greasy and wiry, always unkempt, a woman who never bothered to keep appearances. A worn, tired face that always looked ten years older than she actually was. Someone who needed someone else to remind her to brush her teeth, comb her hair, wear clothes suitable for public display and human interaction, ones sans ketchup and mustard stains near the collar, ones without rips and tears. But all of that was gone now. The woman standing before him at the base of the tree was not the true image of Sharon Simms; she was a perfect replica.

A fake.

"You're not her," was the first thing he said, disregarding the smile and tender appearance.

This was another trick from Mother, the effects of her flowers on the human brain. He was imagining this, because deep in the back of his mind, he wanted this moment. He had wished for it so many times before, for his mother to return home, looking normal, looking healthy, looking sane. He would have given up all the Christmas presents in the world to open up the door one morning and see that very image—the one standing in front of him now—on the porch, smiling that motherly smile, cheeks rising up the sides of her face. He had wished it, dreamed it, made deals with gods he didn't quite believe in, and none of these things had brought her home.

"You're not her," he said again, softer but with more certainty.

Her lips curled like a Dr. Seuss villain, a mischievous grin spreading. It made Doug feel dead and cold inside, a hollow shell of a human being.

"I can be," she said with a titter. An innocent shrug. This was the Mother's last chance to trick him, to turn him into one of her own, into one of the brainless souls that wandered this room searching for a way to restore the old ways. *Her* ways. Doug saw what Jewel Conti had done to Rita Boxberger, and what had crawled out of the dead woman's womb. He tried not to look at it, but it was hard.

Because it was inhuman, monstrous, like nothing he'd seen in his wildest dreams.

"It's okay, son," the Sharon-Thing said pleasantly.

She even sounded like her, exactly the way he remembered.

"Come here," she said, "and take my hand. I will show you things. Places beyond this one, imaginariums where creativity has no limit. You can live there with me, forever. I can build a world for you, help you design your own. You will have the family you've always wanted. The mother and father you've always dreamed of. Everything just as you wished and hoped for."

A tear stung his eye, rolled down his cheek. "But it will be just that—a dream."

"Oh," she said, her reaction warm and sunny, as if this weren't such a terrible thing. "Oh, son—no. Dreams are not bad things. Dreams inspire us. They shape us. Sometimes more than the things we perceive in the ostensible real world. Dreams are our mind's reaction to the events of the physical realm. Mind you, some cultures have argued that the dream-world *is* the real world, and the physical world is just a prison, a place we're trapped in until we fall asleep, travel to when we are at peace."

"They don't feel real. They feel fake." He glared at her, his nostrils flaring. "*This* feels fake."

"That's because this world has tricked you into believing the opposite. Trust me. I know. I come from the dream-world and look at me—am I not real?"

Doug wasn't so sure what was and wasn't, but he dared not counter, push the Mother's buttons. Triggering the wrong one might earn him and everyone else a premature ending. He was hoping to buy some time, buy his *friends* some time. As he was talking to the Mother, he noticed Maddie and Abby had risen from the ground, recovering from the Mother's vicious assault. They toyed with their ears, and Doug could see little channels of blood leaking out from them, running down their necks. He hoped they were okay, that their hearing hadn't sustained permanent damage.

They gripped their wands, looked at each other, and then nodded. Behind them, the white-robed party united.

The Mother was at ease though, not concerned with what was taking place behind her.

"Come with me," she said again, extending her hand. "I can use you and children like you—the creative ones. You will help me bring back the world I once created, help germinate the Lands of Old, spread my seeds across the lands, restore order to all this…chaos. Bring back the lush green forests and vibrant flowers. In return, you can have your perfect life, the one you have always wanted, and it will be just as you imagine it, just as real, and it will last forever."

It was tempting. He watched his father fight with Dylan Walker, struggle against the man's power. He wasn't winning, but he wasn't losing either. The bleeding wound on his side hindered his ability to overtake Walker. If the struggle went on, Doug was sure Walker would outlast him. For now, it was a stalemate, and he hoped his old man could hold on just a tad longer.

"Forever, an eternity," Mother said, her final pitch.

Doug thought about it, the life he wanted. The life he truly dreamed of. Big breakfasts on Sunday mornings, his mom and dad sitting beside him. Telling them stories about his week, stuff that happened during school, the adventures after school with Jesse and Grady. He could almost smell the pancakes cooking on the stove, the batter browning. He could almost feel the morning sunshine breaking through the cracks in the blinds, warming his skin. Could almost feel the love between the three of them, the triangular bond that could never be broken.

It was a moment he would probably never have.

Only in his dreams.

"No," he said, raising his head, looking Mother straight in her eyes, which had now lost its human appearance, reverted to those golden halos. "No, I won't go with you. I won't be a part of your...*disease.*" He gritted his teeth, anger flashing through him, the uncontested fury coursing through his veins. His entire body burned like a phoenix rising from the ashes. "That's all you are. A disease. You're a cancer. You grow and grow until there's no room for anything else, and that's all you do—grow and conquer. You call yourself a god?" He sneered. "You're no god. You're just a...a bully. A piece of shit that kills and takes, that eats and kills. You give promises of false hope. You're the worst kind of mother there is."

"YOU ARE THE CANCER OF THIS WORLD," she bellowed as her features darkened. The mask of Sharon Simms started to bleed away, melt and burn like a marshmallow over a campfire. Her malformed head followed suite, caving in under the stress of the invisible flames that ate away at her flesh, the muscle beneath. "YOU WILL NEVER WIN. I AM HERE AND NOW, AND I AM FOREVER. THIS IS MY WORLD, MY REALITY, AND YOU WILL ALL LIVE INSIDE OF MY DREAMS UNTIL THE END WHICH IS NEVER, NEVER, NEVER..."

"Hey, bitch!" Abby called out. As she'd been ranting, spreading her lies, Abby and Maddie had sprayed the tree, emptied their tanks onto the trunk and what they could of the branches they could reach. Almost every leaf was dripping wet, drenched with the weed killer. The chemicals.

That flammable substance.

Abby raised her Zippo. She sparked the wick. She grinned at Mother, a grin that grew and grew. "Get lit."

The flame licked the air and the Mother barked at her, her face bleeding away, revealing the hideous nature of her true self. The flesh-colored exterior of Sharon Simms's face was streaky, a white and black zebra-like pattern showing through the runny human pigment. Her hair was no longer that of a woman's, but almost like the mane of a horse, coarse and wild and wet. She crouched, baring her sharp teeth. Her fingers stretched to the length of a healthy root, gnarled and arthritic-like, twisted at odd angles. Nails three inches long extended from bulbous fingertips. A feral growl emanated from her throat as she prepared to launch herself like an apex predator onto the trail of a great hunt. Her eyes glowed with the fury of a thousand suns.

But she was too late.

Abby had tossed the lighter at the base of the tree. The chemicals went up fast, quicker than Doug assumed was possible. There was a small pile of brush that had collected at the base of the tree, and that had clearly contributed to the quick start. Within seconds, the trunk was engulfed, the flames making their way to the branches, spreading like an army of ants marching up the sides of a neglected picnic basket. A trail of fire spread down the branches, setting the fruits and leaves ablaze.

Doug heard something mewl like a lonely cat on a fence post, and then realized it had come from the tree, the fruits themselves. The cringe-worthy sounds grew louder as the fire blazed brighter, more furiously. He watched the Mother stand before her creation, holding her fists in the air, screaming out as the tree of life became one big orange ball of destruction.

She dropped to her knees.

Her silhouette began to shrink. Much like her face, her body began to melt.

We're doing it, he thought. *We're killing her.*

The fight lasts minutes, over ten, and Jesse is out of breath. So are Jimmy and Karen. The three of them form a triangle around the Mother, and she shifts her focus, unsure where the next attack is coming from. She barks. Growls. She is an animal trapped in a corner, nowhere else to go but through them.

In the center of the intake bay, the tree is on fire. Blazing.

Good, Jesse thinks. It's over. They won.

"Do you see that?" he asks The Mother. "We won. It's over!"

The Mother shakes her head. Her features twist, contort, become something inhuman, a monster with yellow eyes and wrinkled, sagging flesh. A demonic force wrapped in human skin. She hisses with the anger of a thousand serpents. She slashes with her claws, swinging for their heads.

Jesse dodges the swipe, but one claw catches Karen across the face, knocking her to the ground. Within seconds, the Mother pounces on her chest. The lobster-like claws open around her throat, then snap together. Karen's head pops like a cork shooting out of a celebratory bottle of champagne. A trail of blood splatters the floor.

"No!" Jimmy shouts, watching the execution of the girl he loves, but there was nothing he could do to stop it. The Mother is too fast.

Jimmy turns to Jesse. "Finish her!"

"But—the tree," he responds, pointing over his shoulder.

"It's not enough," Jimmy explains. "She will still live here." He points to the ground, where the Mother's roots have taken hold. Jesse looks down and sees those roots. They are anchored to the bay's floor, loops of vascular extensions looking to drink from the world. They absorb Karen's blood, suck it like a vampire desperate for nourishment.

"Okay," Jesse says.

"I'll hold her off. You finish her."

Jimmy runs ahead, ready to launch himself at the Mother, ready to pummel her ancient bones. She stands from Karen's corpse and turns. Her face is painted with Karen's blood, and she does not bother to wipe herself clean. She smiles as if she loves the way the red clings to her lips and chin.

He turns, tries to find something he can use to end this. He thinks about his friends, what they would do in this situation, how they would help him. He wishes he could talk to Doug; he was always the smartest of the three.

Not book-smart; that award went to Grady. But overall smart. He was the one who would always get them out of bad situations, the one who would always solve their problems. Jesse thinks he should flicker back to the real world, like before, just to see Doug one last time, ask him what he should do, but when he closes his eyes, he discovers he can't. He's too weak. The failed attempt brings him to his knees. There is no more magic left in him; whatever power he had gained from this world, it has left. Maybe because it was the tree that had given him this ability. He was a part of Mother, and she is the tree of life, and because it is burning, dying, leaving this world and all the others, then he no longer has access to its generous gifts.

Behind him, Jimmy wrestles with the demonic form. He dodges her claws as they come for his head, attempting to deliver him a similar fate as the others. Jimmy is athletic and the Mother is weakened, so Jimmy continues to fair well against her lazy strikes.

Think. Think.

There is nothing around him save for the burning tree, the outline of ghosts, those shapes materialized from the real-world.

The tree.

Burning.

He can be a match.

Jesse walks over to the tree, hands out, ready to greet the flames. He feels the burn infiltrate his flesh. Soon, his body is an inferno. It hurts, but he knows the pain is only temporary. The results will live on forever.

As he walks over to Mother, he watches one of her claws clamp down on Jimmy's face. The teeth come together around his skull, squeeze, crack open his cranium like a walnut. The force of the crunch catapults an explosion of pink matter into the air. A chunky trail of Jimmy's brains decorates the floor.

When she isn't watching him, too busy focusing on the ruined skull of Jimmy Di Falco, Jesse sneaks up behind her, wraps his arms around her, hugs her close. He rests his head against her back. She struggles, tries to wriggle free, but it's no use. Jesse has her, has her good.

She bites at his burning flesh, drags her teeth along his charring skin. The pain hardly registers.

He feels himself fading out, the burning all too much. The blaze consumes his vision. The last thing he sees before checking out is the

Mother's face, burning, blackening, becoming everything and nothing all at once.

Die in a dream…

3

A shot of pain spiked across Gordon's midsection, setting his intestines on fire. He fended off another knife attack, sidestepping the swipe, and the blade ripped through his shirt but nothing more. Driving his fist upward, he connected with Walker's chin once again and sent the man reeling. Gordon used the few feet of separation to his advantage and got a running start. Dipping his shoulder, he tackled Walker and drove him to the ground. The man must have been too stunned by the uppercut because he had a clear shot at a fatal stab and failed to capitalize. Gordon landed on top of him, positioning himself on Walker's chest, pinning his arms to the ground with his knees. The first thing Gordon did was pry the knife from his fingers, which he did so with relative ease.

Walker's eyes rolled around, trying to find stability. Gordon didn't want to kill the man—he was clearly out of his mind and his actions were not of a sane person's. Still, he was dangerous, and if Gordon didn't put him down, then he might come back, try and hurt him once again. Or worse— Doug and the other children.

"I don't want to do this, Walker," he told him. Pain spiked where the knife had penetrated his side, a reminder of what Walker was capable of. "Don't make me do this."

Walker caught a glimmer of consciousness. He gritted his teeth, tried to move out from under the pressure sitting on his chest. Gordon kept his hold, pinning the man to the ground, not allowing him to squirm free.

"Don't. Stay still."

Walker grunted with frustration. "Kill you! Kill of you!" His eyes began to glow again, that bright yellow that was so very far from human. "KILL

KILL KILL," he shouted, spitting, his mouth unleashing flecks of white of foam. "KILL KILL KILL. KILL KILL KILL."

He reached up for Gordon's throat, somehow got his hands around his neck. It was the sudden surge of power that had caught Gordon by surprise, and he was too slow to get his hands up to block him. With surprising strength, Walker choked the life out of him. Or tried to. Came close enough. Gordon's vision dimmed near the edges.

He was left with no choice.

Gordon raised the knife, then slammed it down on Walker's chest. A puddle of blood pooled where the blade sunk in and disappeared. Gordon pulled the knife free, then brought it down once more, this time on the man's throat.

Walker let go of Gordon's neck, immediately clamping his hands on his own, trying to plug up the new hole in his body, the one that spurted long ropes of blood. Scarlet gushed through his fingers, flooding his neck.

Gordon jumped off, allowing the man to drown in peace. Within a few seconds, his languid movements stopped, and his body stiffened with the onset of death.

Gordon threw up.

He'd taken another man's life. Not just anyone's, either. A man he'd known for a good long time now, a man who'd been pretty kind to him in year's past, even if he had been a wicked son of a bitch in the end, responsible for tainting the town's water. He would rather see Walker in an orange jumpsuit for the rest of his life than watch him bleed out through a hole in his throat—but it didn't play out that way, and he had been left with no choice.

"No choice," Gordon said, dragging his sleeve across his lips, wiping away the vomit.

"Wasn't your fault, Dad," Doug said, putting a hand on his shoulder.

Together, they watched the tree burn, the fire raging out of control. The intake bay was filling with smoke...and quickly. It wouldn't be long before breathing compromised air would become an issue.

One by one, the white-robed clan stumbled toward the fire, seeking refuge amongst the flames.

"What are they doing?" Gordon asked, as if his son would know the answer.

"I think they're trying to save it," Doug said, seeming somewhat saddened by the gathered's collective decision to immolate themselves in the name of Mother.

The flames swallowed them. They were silent as the fire chewed them apart, reducing their clothes to rags, their flesh to hard, blackened crisps.

Kids and adults, gone within minutes. They walked to their deaths without hesitation. Without fear.

Gordon began to cry as the inferno crackled, its belly full of flesh and bone.

4

Doug looked past his father, saw the sarcophagus aflame, the corpse within hidden behind the flickering glow of the hungry fire. After a minute, the sarcophagus toppled over, crashing to the ground. It continued to burn, and with each passing second, Doug felt better.

It was over.

They had won.

The Mother was gone, defeated, sent back to wherever she had come from. There was no jumping from the old form to the new one—the only chance she had at doing so was in Jewel Conti, and Jewel was... Well...

She was in trouble.

Boxberger was backing her into a corner, knife in his hand, ready to slash, ready to end her life. He was yelling something Doug couldn't hear because his back was to him. Something nasty he suspected. Vile. After all, she'd killed his wife, the bearer of Mother's kin.

Doug didn't know how to react, so he tapped his father on the shoulder incessantly, and screamed out, "Dad! Look!"

His father rose from his knees, turned to where his son's ex-teacher was closing the distance between him and Jewel. Doug knew that even if his father sprinted over there, he wouldn't get there in time to stop what was about to happen.

"Baum," Gordon said, turning to the cop. "Stop that man. He's got a knife."

Baum followed Gordon's finger. He aimed his weapon.

"Stop!" Baum shouted. "You! With the knife! Stop! Or I will be forced to shoot!"

Boxberger did stop. He turned in slow motion until his face was revealed. His face was a mask of wet clay, deformed and misshapen, hardly the face of a human being. His snarl was fixed with sharp teeth, ivory daggers that hung out of his mouth. Whatever Boxberger had become, whatever horror had found refuge in his soul, it had come here for one thing and one thing only—to avenge its Mother.

Boxberger opened his mouth and hissed. Something long and green rolled out, something that slithered through the smoky atmosphere like a snake in a briar patch.

It was whatever had come out Rita's womb, that awful monstrosity that somehow lived through Jewel's attempted abortion. It had taken shelter in Boxberger's body, assumed control of his actions.

"Holy fucking shitballs," Baum muttered.

Doug watched the gun jump in his hands. The cop's nerves were on fire, and he was shaking like a wet dog. Then, to Doug's surprise, Baum took the shot. The loud pop jolted him. The bullet zoomed past its target, hit the metal wall behind it.

"Fuck," the cop said, shutting one eye, concentrating on the next attempt. He squeezed the trigger and again, the bullet sailed over Boxberger's head.

The seedling that had taken root in Boxberger's brain grinned with arrogance, a knowing, a realization that it was safe from the cop's poor aim. It turned its attention back to Jewel, who cowered in the corner.

"Come on," Gordon told him. "You can do this."

Doug held his breath.

The cop fired again.

This time the bullet tore through Boxberger's skull. A greenish white fluid ruptured into the air, splattering the wall behind him. It looked like someone had flung a kale smoothie in anger.

Boxberger dropped to his knees, the creature inside trying to escape through its mouth, slithering onto the floor. As soon as the snake-like creature reached the dirt covering, Jewel was there. She brought her foot down on what Doug perceived to be its head. A wet crunch echoed throughout the bay, and Jewel made sure the deed was done by grinding the splintered fragments into the ground with her heel. She stomped twice more just to be sure. Then she took a breath, looking to Doug, nodding, telling him it was over, that the thing was dead.

Doug nodded back, then scanned the room. The fire was still blazing, filling the air with dangerous fumes and black smoke. The good majority of the white robes had finished sacrificing themselves for a god who no longer lived, their bodies hidden within the inferno, burnt beyond recognition. Grady was helping the girls away from the fire, closer to the stairs that led up to the catwalk, toward a secure exit. The hellfire had yet to scale the walls, and their path of travel was safe from its trajectory.

"Are you okay, son?" his dad asked him.

Doug nodded. He wasn't okay though, not really, wouldn't be for a long time.

But at least he was safe.

At least he was alive.

And that was better than some.

5

Jewel walked over to the boy lying face down in the dirt, about thirty feet from the blazing conflagration. The survivors, the ones who had resisted the urge to bathe themselves in flames, were itching to get out of there, away from the smoke and fiery tower, but not Jewel. She wasn't leaving without her friend.

She bent down, lifted Adam's right arm, and draped it around her neck. She patted his cheek, hoping to wake him up, hoping to inject life back into him, but the effort failed.

"Is he alive?" someone asked, and she looked up to see Grady Pope standing there, his timid face hopeful and somewhat terrified.

Jewel wasn't sure if Adam was or not, but she nodded anyway. Grady lowered himself and took the kid's other arm, throwing it over his shoulder.

"One, two, three," Grady said, and helped lift the kid.

"Thank you," she said, suddenly regretting all those times on the bus, the times she had tormented him, embarrassed him in front of his peers. She didn't deserve his help. She didn't deserve any attention whatsoever.

"It's okay," Grady said, nodding.

Together, they hauled Adam away from the flames, over to where the others stood, ready and waiting to get the hell out of there, far away from the plant, the fire, and back to where clean air awaited them. The cop and the other adult took the unconscious boy from them.

"You kids go first," Baum said, directing them up the ladder with his finger. "We'll be right behind you."

Jewel climbed. When she reached the top, the sudden urge to jump into the spreading inferno pelted her thoughts. She could almost feel the tongues of fire licking her skin, the touch turning her flesh to hot ash. The painful demise was probably better than what awaited her at home, a long life of misery and daily torture. A fresh hell in an alternate form.

"Are you coming?" Grady asked as he passed her on the catwalk.

"Yeah," she said, but she wasn't so sure.

Home, a voice said in her head.

Mommy's waiting for you.

Daddy too.

Outside of Hooperstown Chemical, across the property, the streets were covered in blue and red flashing lights. A news van was already stationed outside the chain-link fence, a harbinger of more to come. A fire truck honked its horn, its siren blaring loudly as it found an empty space near the curb. Uniformed men and women were jogging up the hill that led to the main gate, and Officer Baum had left Adam's unconscious body in Gordon's care as he rushed down to meet them.

What story he'd tell them, Gordon wasn't so sure. But there was no way he could tell them the truth, the terrifying things they'd seen down there. Gordon had witnessed everything firsthand and still believed everything had been a vivid nightmare, an awful hallucination. There was no way everything he'd experienced was real, those images seeming too otherworldly, too transcendent.

But it had been real. All of it.

There had been a monster, a tree with strange fruits, the apparition of an ancient spirit. And men, women, and children who had lost their minds, walked into a towering blaze and remained there until the flesh melted off their bones. Gordon's head swum, the recent history breaking down his thoughts, collapsing his sense of what had been real.

Whatever tale Baum would spin, Gordon would back him up one hundred percent. Even if it was the truth, no matter how crazy it sounded out loud.

"We're okay, Dad," Doug said. He kept repeating that ever since they left the plant. He was pretty sure their roles were now reversed; Gordon was supposed to be the one reassuring his son. But no. Doug was fine—more than fine. The kid looked relieved. Tired, spacing out, on the verge of falling asleep standing upright—but relieved. Happy to be away from there.

"What happened in there, son?" Gordon asked, knowing he shouldn't have, immediately regretting it. "Help me understand what I...what I saw." He gulped. "Will you?"

The cops were approaching the plant now. Baum led the charge.

"Maybe," he said. "Maybe one day, yeah."

Gordon nodded and braced himself for the chaos that would follow, the barrage of questions he did not have answers for.

He squeezed his son's shoulder with his free hand and kissed the top of his head, wondering if *one day* would ever come.

NO FIRES BURN FOREVER,
NO SUMMER LASTS AN ETERNITY

1

Shades of autumn were felt and seen throughout the town, the slight and cool change in temperature, the first scattering of leaves sweeping the gutters. Three weeks after the incident at Hooperstown Chemical and the town still hadn't even begun to recover, and some thought their beloved home might not ever recover from such a terrible tragedy. Forty-three dead, most of them children, caught in one of the biggest disasters to ever strike the Garden State.

Stories had flown around town like a bird on an April hunt for nesting materials. Rumors of cults, kidnapped children, and a ritualistic sacrifice to an ancient legend filled the ears of the townspeople who loved to listen to such nonsense. Though the official police report, the one covered extensively in every local paper within a thousand miles and mentioned in every major news outlet across the country, was not far off—that a cult indeed *had* trespassed the recently shut-down and emptied chemical plant, that they *had* brought abducted children with them and sacrificed themselves along with their hostages, all of whom were known to be victims of Hooperstown's infamous cancer-cluster catastrophe. The Boxbergers were painted as modern-day Jim Joneses and Charlie Mansons, and not a single town resident mourned their demise.

The school year had been delayed out of respect for the victims, but also because the big court case, the lawsuit against Hooperstown Chemical, was scheduled to kick off, and that had held the anxious town's attention. Everybody was on edge, and everybody had their reasons. Mostly everyone was still freaked out about the incident, most residents taking *a-thing-like-that-couldn't-possibly-happen-in-my-town* approach, that stage of denial that never really worked out for anyone. Because it had happened and it had been bad, probably one of the worst things to happen on American soil in quite some time, mostly because of the nature of the violence, and that most of the victims were children.

Innocent children.

What had been left off reports—every single one, including the official paperwork filed away at the precinct—was the evidence of a strange tree that looked many years old (decades actually) that had seemingly grown quite tall in the matters of a few weeks. And of course the discovery of a small, snake-like creature whose brains were squashed in, smeared across the ground like the guts of a busted pumpkin. Officer Baum had to explain why he discharged his weapon and shot Boxberger in the head, and no one questioned his claim.

Gordon Simms, the only other adult witness, corroborated everything, explaining to Internal Affairs that the man simply had no choice, that Boxberger was beyond "deescalating." His word was enough for IA to drop the whole investigation, and enough for the state police to take them both at their word, despite certain "inconsistencies," small holes in their stories that didn't add up. That was okay because the two men were under great duress and it was more than possible for them to mix up a few things, have certain details muddled. Gordon had ascertained that the police, like the town, wanted to move past the tragedy rather than understand it.

That was the way of towns, and of people, after all; ignorance of wrongdoings was better than recognizing the internal blame. After all, it was *that* mindset that brought them this fiasco to begin with, all those years ago when a faulty pipeline had been installed beneath the town. It was that mindset that would change gradually over the next few years, well into the new millennium. After all, Hooperstown had skin, and like all skin, the cuts and wounds would heal over the course of time, leaving behind scars that were sometimes not so easy to cover up.

2

On September 6th, 1998, about a week after the tragic events at Hooperstown Chemical, the Di Falcos buried their two sons, Jesse and Jimmy, at St. Henry's on Portsmouth Avenue, opting for the church's cemetery over Cedarborough's. They had chosen two plots next to each other and had told the pastor leading the ceremony to make it short and sweet, not to drag out the sermon longer than necessary. "The bare bones," Mr. Di Falco had phrased it, though there were probably better expressions he could have used, something that didn't conjure imagery so closely related to death. Mrs. Di Falco had shuddered at the utterance.

To the shock of no one, the day was rainy with cool gusts blowing in off the ocean, just your typical funeral weather. A hot, dry summer and the weather people were calling for a wet and gloomy autumn, and although fall had not officially begun, the symptoms were in the air. It seemed like the whole town was in attendance. Grady and his parents. Maddie and hers. Abby had hitched a ride with them, *her* parents having no interest in going, not after attending Lauren Sullivan's funeral a month back. That had been emotionally exhausting for them, and they just weren't up for reliving the experience.

Jewel showed up, late, and she had come with that boy she had saved from the fire. *Adam*, Doug recalled, the kid who had spent three whole days in the hospital being evaluated for a concussion and broken bones. Somehow, he was okay despite looking like he'd taken a few licks from Mike Tyson. The right side of his face was purple and black, a swollen mask of pain. His parents were not present. His father had been one of the forty-three who walked into the fire and never returned. Other members of the community were in attendance, most of whom Doug had never met before.

The pastor gave a good sermon but didn't exactly stick to Mr. Di Falco's request. About halfway through, Mrs. Di Falco lost it and fell to her knees, trying to wrap both arms around Jimmy's casket. Mr. Di Falco had to pry her off like a wad of gum from the bottom of a shoe. It took several hands, close family members assisting him, to complete the task. The pastor had paused his speech, allowing the grieving mother to collect herself. It took about ten minutes for her to calm down, and Doug thought that was a miracle in and of itself.

When it came time to put Jesse and Jimmy in the ground, Doug felt a wave of sadness collapse over him. It would be the last time he'd see Jesse, his best friend since the third grade. There would be no more days filled of leisurely swimming, diving competitions, no more games of water basketball. There would be no more video games, no more *Primal Rage* tournaments, no more *Diddy Kong Racing* challenges, no more seeing who could blitz through *Super Mario Bros* the fastest without warping competitions. No more all-nighters, no more scavenger hunts. There would just be this empty hole in his heart, one he could never fill.

He wondered if any of those things would ever be fun again. As Jesse was laid to rest, he thought, *No, probably not.*

Two weeks later.

It was a Monday afternoon and the last class just let out. Jewel strolled through the halls, thinking high school wasn't the shit-show she thought it would be. It had its moments of uncertainty, its daunting tasks and considerable workload, but all in all—it wasn't terrible.

She met Adam near his locker. His face looked a lot better; the bruising had faded some and the swelling had gone down significantly. He was starting to look like his old self.

"You know," he said, walking down the hall, slinging his backpack over his shoulder. "You're looking awfully good today, Jewel."

"Gee, uh, thanks, guy. You're looking awfully dreamy yourself."

"Please, don't ever mention *dreams* to me again." He was kidding, of course, and nudged her with his elbow just to make sure she understood that.

Dreams, she thought. She hadn't had any since the debacle at Hooperstown Chemical, since she had stabbed and killed Rita Boxberger and boot-stomped her hideous creation. If she *had* dreamed, she didn't remember a single sequence, not a single iota. Not that she expected to. After all, the Mother was dead. Gone. Never coming back.

So she hoped.

She couldn't explain it, but she sensed it was over, the same way she sensed she'd no longer be friends with Brennan Scruggs and Dakota Chaffin once upon a time ago. That evil she had sensed lurking in the town's shadows was no longer there. Gone. Forgotten. Along with the dead—Principal Fritz, who'd given her that spark of hope, who'd helped send her down this path of personal victory. Who'd helped her in so many ways, really, more than he probably ever understood. Brendan Scruggs, the bag of shit he was, she still mourned his loss even after their falling out. Even after she realized what scum he was, that he'd probably end up living a life filled with heroin and booze, arrests and jail sentences. Still, he had been her friend once and she wasn't a cold, heartless person, surely never wished death upon anyone. The only ones she was glad to see go were the Boxbergers. She didn't shed a single tear for those fuckbags.

"Are you ready to do this?" Jewel asked. "For real this time?"

Adam sighed. "Yeah, definitely. I was ready before. But, you know, my Dad…"

She shook her head. "Sorry. Didn't mean to—"

He waved her off. "Stop. I literally just joked about the whole dream thing, so forget it. Besides. My Dad would have hated what I'm about to tell Mom, anyway."

"You think your brother will be home? Kill two birds with one stone?"

He shrugged. "Not worried about him. He won't care that I'm gay. It's Mom—she's the one I worry about. You know how mothers can be."

Oh boy, she thought, *don't I.*

She held his hand as they walked out the school's front door, allowing the crisp sunshine to rain down on them, the autumnal breeze refreshing on their cheeks.

"You'll be there for me, right?" he asked. "Through the whole thing?"

"Of course." She squeezed his fingers. "You were there for me."

"This is *different.*"

"This is *easier.*"

"Not for me."

She laughed. "Best friends forever?"

"Of course." Adam took a deep breath. "Okay. Let's do this. Let's come out to my mother. Let's tackle this thing."

She rested her head on his shoulder. In this moment, she felt she could tackle anything. Her own home, her own parents, the entire world.

Jewel Conti was forever invincible.

4

Grady slammed his locker shut and was met up with Doug and Maddie while they were locking lips. This was the fourth time this week and it was equally disgusting each time.

"Dudes," he said, not trying to conceal his revulsion. "What have I told you about swallowing each other's tongues in my presence?"

They separated, a string of saliva continuing to connect them like the spaghetti in that iconic *Lady and the Tramp* scene.

Grady retched.

"Sorry, Grades," Doug said, his face glowing. He was always glowing around Maddie. "Can't help it if Mads's locker is three down from yours."

"It's just gross, that's all."

Maddie wrinkled her nose, as if she found his aversion amusing.

"When are you going to hook him up with one of your friends?" Doug asked Maddie.

"We tried that already." She gave him those eyes.

Grady hated those eyes. It meant they were ready to trade spit again. Not now, not this second—but soon.

"Yeah, with *Abby*. And she's...you know."

Grady knew, all right. Of the four of them, Abby had dealt with what she'd seen by alienating herself, closing herself off from the rest of them, school in general. She had gone to class during the first week, but she'd yet to show her face in week two. It was okay. Grady's psychiatrist, Dr. Menlo, had told him people deal with grief and trauma differently, and that was probably Abby's way of compartmentalizing everything that had happened to her. Grady accepted that answer, mostly because that meant she was skipping school and acting weird for some other reason than him. He was off the hook.

Grady had his bad days. Good ones too. He found being around Doug made him feel better. Maddie as well, even when they were snacking on each other's lips. He felt normal around them. Like everything was the way it was supposed to be. Sometimes, the three of them talked. About what happened. About Jesse. About how much they missed him. It was normal and they didn't allow their feelings to overtake them, never letting the conversations regarding those dark circumstances drum on for too long. When one of them needed to talk, the others listened. When someone needed to cry, the others lent a dry shoulder. When someone needed to release the rage and punch something, the others handed them a Socker Bopper so they wouldn't break their knuckles.

It was a good system. It would get them through. Things would get better.

Every session with the psychiatrist helped, and after a while, Grady stopped blaming himself for Jesse's sickness, his eventual death.

It wasn't your fault. There was nothing you could have done.

He hadn't dreamed much over those last two weeks, but sometimes when he closed his eyes and peered into the darkness, he saw Jesse vomiting that dark fluid on the night of the Hunt.

"What are you losers doing later?" Grady asked.

Doug rolled his eyes. "My dad wants to have dinner with me. Alone. Has something he wants to tell me." He let out a deep sigh. "Can't wait," he said dully.

"Hope it's good," Grady said, "like you're getting a Dreamcast for Christmas or something."

Doug scoffed. "Dude, no one's getting a Dreamcast for Christmas."

"Yeah, I'm sure *some*one will. Rich kids, probably."

"Speaking of rich kids," Doug said, pinching Maddie's arm.

"Hey! Jerk…"

"What's up with the lawsuit, Mads?" Doug stole a quick kiss before she could punish him for the "rich kid" dig.

"Dad says they're reaching a settlement. Says it's going to be huge. The number I heard was a hundred-and-twenty-seven million."

Doug whistled. "That enough to put those bastards out of business?" Doug was hopeful. "For good?"

"Oh yeah," she said with no hesitation. "That's not even including the fines Environmental Protection will throw at them. Plus, I'm sure there will be more lawsuits over the fire. Like, why wasn't there a better method for keeping people off the premises? Even though they were shut down and the plant wasn't operational, they still owned the property. It should have been closed, and they were supposed to hire security to keep people out twenty-four-seven. That never happened obviously. Shit, we made it inside with relative ease."

"Well, it wasn't that easy," Grady said, remembering how he almost drowned in the river's white water.

He looked down at his watch, realized he'd be late catching the bus if he didn't start to make his way outside. "Gotta go, guys. See you tomorrow?"

"Of course," Doug said, throwing his arms around his friend. "You want a kiss goodbye, too?"

"No, you pervert." Grady pushed himself free. "Just don't knock her up, all right?"

"Grady!" Maddie yelled, taking a weak, half-hearted swing at his shoulder.

He dodged the fist with ease, even though the knuckles were never meant to land.

Doug threw a lazy kick at his rear, his toe connecting with the bottom of his JanSport. "Kissing isn't how babies are made, Grades. Thought we learned that in health class last year."

Grady made his way down the hall, toward the long line of buses. He waved over his shoulder. "See you boners tomorrow!"

He grinned the whole way there, thanking God—or whatever deity truly existed, if one did at all—that he had the best-est friends a guy could have. He hoped it would stay that way forever.

5

After dinner—a premium roast beef, the right amount of pink in the middle and sliced tenderly to perfection—Gordon Simms lowered his fork, rested the silverware on the edge of his plate. Next, he folded his hands in front of him, stared at his son with a faint smile. A smile that wasn't much of a smile if Doug was being honest. He wasn't sure if his father was going to tell him they hit the lottery or someone else they knew had died.

"Son," Gordon started, and by the tone in his voice he knew whatever it was, it was bad. "I got a job offer today," he told him, sounding positive, chipper, as much as he could be.

"That's..." Doug was skeptical. He was waiting for the bad news. A face like the one his father was wearing always spoke of bad news. "That's great, Dad."

"The only thing is, it's at a nuclear power plant..."

"Nuclear power plant?"

"...in Maryland."

"Maryland?"

"Yeah. Near Baltimore. South of the city."

"Well…you said *no,* right?"

Gordon stared at him.

"Dad?"

"Bud, I can't keep us afloat on our savings forever. I've got about another month's worth in the bank and that's it. Unemployment is barely helping." He toyed with his crumpled napkin nervously. "We need money. I need a job. And this…" He nodded toward the door, as if the job were just outside. Down the block. Around the corner. "It's a good one. Pay is twenty-five percent better than what I was making at Hooperstown Chem. Plus, I'll be doing less work, working less hours, which means we can spend more time together as a family. Cost of living is cheaper down—"

He had tuned him out. The only thing he had heard was that he was moving. No more Hooperstown, no more friends, no more *girlfriend.* All of it gone. Just like that. It was going to be as if *he* died, not Jesse.

Don't say that! he heard Grady scold. *Don't you dare even think it.*

"You understand, don't you, kiddo?" Gordon offered his son a smile.

"No," he said, a burn stinging his eyes. "No, I don't understand. I…I don't want to go."

"It'll be good for you. For *us.* Especially after…" He swallowed the rock in his throat. "…you know."

"What about my friends? My girlfriend? Maddie?"

"I know it's going to be hard, but—"

"No," he said, hating the whine in his own voice. He couldn't help it. The situation called for it. "No, *you* don't understand."

"Doug, bud—I get it. It'll be a big adjustment for the two of us."

He glared at him. "What about Mom? You're just going to what—pick up and leave her? Forget she ever existed?"

"No." He shook his head adamantly, as if Doug were missing the entire point of their conversation. "No, bud, not at all. I talked to your mother's doctors, just earlier in fact, and the last two weeks have been like some sort of miracle, they said. She's really turned things around."

"She has?"

"Yes. And I think you know why."

He nodded.

"Still hoping one day I get the whole story, but if you're not ready to talk about it, then…then so be it. But I'm ready when you are."

"Okay…"

"But…I have a feeling that your mother, the things she used to say, the things she used to do…" He shook his head again, this time clearing out the cobwebs. "I can't help but think her health and the…the *incident,* are related to each other."

Doug would tell him. One day. Maybe with his mother present, so they could fill in each other's gaps, complete the story together.

"Am I right?" Gordon asked.

Doug nodded.

"I thought so." He sat back in his chair, combed his fingers through his hair. "I need a beer. You want a soda?"

Doug told him he'd love one.

Gordon got up, walked over to the fridge to fetch their beverages of choice. As soon as he opened the door, Doug pushed himself up from the table, ran across the kitchen, and hugged his father.

Gordon turned and hugged him back.

Crying, Doug said, "I'm scared! I don't want to leave! I don't want to leave my friends! My home!"

Gordon, shedding tears of his own, sniffled. "Yeah, kiddo. I don't either. But…but sometimes…life sucks and we do what we have to."

After a moment where the two of them embraced, cried on, Gordon separated from his son, looking him in the eyes. "We come back on weekends. We'll get a hotel, or maybe Grady's parents or Maddie's can put us up for a night or two. That way we stay in touch with them, this town, everything that's going to unfold. You can still be there for them…" His words were lost in his tears. "Sorry," he said, drying his eyelashes on his sleeve. "You be there for them, and I will be there for *her.* And when your mother is ready…there will be a room waiting for her in Maryland."

Doug took a moment to process this. "Every weekend?"

"Every…damn…one."

His eyes continued to leak; there was no stopping the fall.

"Okay," Doug said, finally. "Okay, let's do it."

Gordon wrapped his hands around his son one more time, pulled him closer than ever before. "Thank you. Thank you, son."

He didn't know how long they remained in that pose, but Doug wished it would last forever.

Forever.

I am forever, the Mother of Dead Dreams had said.

But nothing lasts forever. He'd learned a lot of things in the summer of
'98, but that lesson was chief among them. Nothing lasts; not summers, not
friendships, not romances.

Not life.

Especially not that.

6

That night, he had one last dream.

It took place in the future, twenty, thirty years ahead. There was a party
at his house, a house he owned. Maybe it was in Hooperstown, but he
couldn't tell. The dream didn't tell him these things. For once the dream kept
secrets, and for that he was thankful. It wasn't good to know too much about
a dream, another lesson he'd take with him from that unforgettable summer.

Doug watched his house from the street. Everything he saw, he saw
from there, peeking through the windows. There were a dozen people
present, maybe more. His future self was holding the hand of his wife, and
she looked exactly like Maddie Rice, although her name was Madison
Simms now. Grady was there, a beer in hand, laughing at a joke someone
had just told. He was married too and his wife was standing next to him, her
arm wrapped around his, hanging on, drunk from the glass of wine in her
left hand. She swayed with laughter. Doug didn't recognize her.

Also present was a tall girl with lots of tattoos. At first, he thought it
was Abby, but no, the dream allowed him to know that she was absent.
Where she was, he didn't know. It didn't matter. She had gone her own way,
and for whatever reason—that felt like the right thing. No, the girl wasn't
Abby; it was Jewel Conti. She wasn't with a guy, not that Doug could see.
But she was standing somewhat close to two other guys—one of them being,
Adam, her best friend. The guy next to him laughed at the same joke, then
rested his head on Adam's shoulder.

Doug scanned the other windows. In the library, the room where bookcases took up all four walls from the floor to the ceiling, he saw his parents. They were having a quiet conversation. Smiling. Laughing at each other's corny, old jokes. His mother sipped from a glass of wine, his father from a small pitcher of beer. They stared at each other silently, lust in their eyes. It was a good moment, the best Doug could hope for.

Then Future Doug entered the room. The 'rents perked up. Stood. Came over to him. The three of them hugged.

From the street, Young Doug felt their comforting embrace. It was perfect.

Then the dream began to bleed away, swirling into a vacuum of black nothingness, the void where dreams usually go to die. No good dream lasts forever. But the best part of watching it all fade away—the sights and sounds and smells of that one malignant summer died along with it, were buried where the past also goes to die.

A place abandoned, but never so far forgotten.

ACKNOWLEDGEMENTS

Special shout-outs to the following people who've helped in one way or another while writing this book, whether they knew it or not: My wife, Ashley, who continues to allow me to torture her by pitching her bad ideas and inundating her with writing stuff. Ken McKinley for taking a chance. Kenneth W. Cain for his keen eye and endless wisdom. Sadie Hartmann, Janine Pipe and David Walters for having an early look and sharing their thoughts. Chuck Buda, Armand Rosamilia, Frank Edler, Hunter Shea, Jack Campisi, Jason Brant, Chad Lutzke, Todd Keisling, Ronald Malfi, and dozens of others for being there along the way.

ABOUT THE AUTHOR

Tim Meyer dwells in a dark cave near the Jersey Shore. He's an author, husband, father, podcast host, blogger, coffee connoisseur, beer enthusiast, and explorer of worlds. He writes horror, mysteries, science fiction, and thrillers, although he prefers to blur genres and let the stories fall where they may.

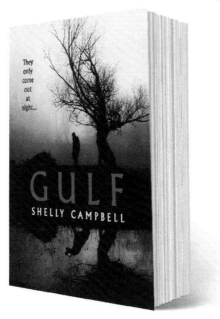

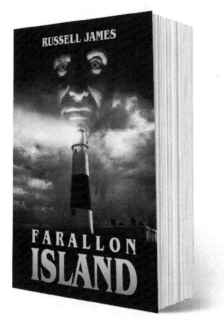

Nate Thalmann wants to escape his life as a Prohibition Era bootlegger. He moves with his pregnant wife Alice to the Farallon Island lighthouse, situated on a rocky islet twenty-seven miles off the California coast. Joining three other keepers and their families, he hopes for peace and a deep reconnection with his wife.

But one of the keeper's children finds a secret cave, and releases a malicious entity imprisoned within. It possesses a former keeper and soon the islanders are being stalked and slaughtered. The demon within the keeper plans to only leave Alice alive, at least until she's given birth to her child, who will become the demon's permanent vessel.

With no radio, no resupply, and no weapons, it is up to Nate to keep his wife and unborn child safe. But the body-hopping fiend seems to always be one step, and one corpse, ahead of him. Will anyone survive wrath of the demon of Farallon Island?

Made in the USA
Middletown, DE
05 July 2021